Stormdance

THE DRAGON SINGER CHRONICLES | BOOK 2

MICHELLE M. BRUHN

SONGWEAVER
MEDIA

Cover by Kirk DouPonce, www.DogEaredDesign.com
Map by Soraya Corcoran, www.SorayaCorcoran.com
Edited by Katie Phillips, www.KatiePhillipsCreative.com

ISBN 978-1-7349925-3-3 (paperback)
ISBN 978-1-7349925-4-0 (e-book)

For anyone who faces a storm
And worries that it defines them.

It does not.

TABLE OF CONTENTS

PRONUNCIATIONS & DEFINITIONS

A'dem (ah-DEHM) — *the planet*

Alísa (ah-LEE-suh) — *slayer, wayfarer, daughter of Karn & Hanah*

Allara (ah-LAH-ruh) — *(deceased) slayer, the second known Dragon Singer*

An'reik (AHN-rayk) — *"sold-soul", mortals who have given their souls to the Nameless in exchange for power*

Anam (AH-nahm) — *"soul"*

Aree (ah-REE) — *dragoness, hunter, mate of Saynan*

Aresia (ah-REE-shah) — *normal, fiddler from Me'ran, sister of Lethín*

Ari (AHR-ee) — *slayer, daughter of Namor & Tenza*

Arran (eh-RAN) — *the continent*

Belinor (BEHL-ih-nohr) — *a human figure of legend, who led humans, dragons, and fairy-folk to Arran*

Bodhrán (BOW-rahn) — *a wide, flat drum played by mallet or hand*

Branni (BRAH-nee) — *the Eldra of warriors and slayers*

Bria (BREE-uh) — *(deceased) slayer, warrior, the first known Dragon Singer*

Briek (breek) — *slayer, second-in-command of Segenn's eastern wayfarers*

Céilí (KAY-lee) — *a dance for two or more partners where steps are called; also a social gathering with music, dancing, and story-telling*

Chrí[1] (chree) — *(deceased) drek, name gives impression of lavender, Alísa's friend, mate of Rann, mother of Rís & Chrí*

Chrí[2] (chree) — *drek, name gives impression of bluebells, daughter of Chrí & Rann, sister of Rís*

D'tohm (dih-TOHM) — *the Eldra of wind & spirit, carries souls to the Maker's Halls*

Draemen (DRAY-mehn) — *normal, dairy farmer from Me'ran*

Drek (drehk) — *small, dragon-shaped creature that lives in the forests; plural form: dreki (DREH-kee)*

Elani (eh-LAH-nee) — *slayer, wayfarer, Alísa's aunt, wife of L'non, mother of Levan & Taer*

Eldra (EHL-druh) — *an angelic being given stewardship over specific aspects of A'dem; plural form: Eldír (EHL-deer)*

Faern (fayrn) — *dragon, scout, father of Komi*

Falier (fah-LEER) — *holder, slayer, son of Parsen & Kat, brother of Selene*

Farren (FAYR-ehn) — *songweaver, wayfarer with Karn's clan*

Galerra (gal-EHR-ah) — *dragon, flight-leader, daughter of Tsamen & Paili*

Garrick (GEHR-ihk) — *normal, elder of Me'ran, husband of Meira*

Graydonn (GRAY-don) — *dragon, son of Koriana*

Hanah (HA-nuh) — *weaver, wayfarer, wife of Karn, mother of Alísa*

Harenn (HEHR-ehn) — *dragon, scout, son of Tsamen & Paili*

Iila (EE-luh) — *dragon, hatchling, born to Rorenth's clan*

Iompróir Anam (YOHM-proh-ihr AH-nahm) — *"soul-bearer"*

Kallar (ka-LAHR) — *slayer, wayfarer, apprentice of Karn*

Karn (kahrn) — *slayer, wayfarer, chief, husband of Hanah, father of Alísa*

Katessara "Kat" (ka-teh-SAR-uh) — *holder, wife of Parsen, mother of Selene & Falier*

Kerrik (KEHR-ihk) — *(deceased) slayer, wayfarer, training master who left Falier in Me'ran, husband of Serra*

Komi (KOH-mee) — *dragoness, scout, daughter of Faern*

Koriana (kohr-ee-AN-uh) — *dragoness, scout, mother of Graydonn*

Korin (KOHR-ihn) — *dragon, warrior, mate of Rayna*

L'non (luh-NON) — *slayer, wayfarer, brother of Karn, husband of Elani, father of Levan & Taer*

Laen (layn) — *drek, name gives impression of rain dripping off leaves*

Lethín (leh-THEEN) — *normal, percussionist from Me'ran, brother of Aresia*

Levan (LEH-vehn) — *slayer, wayfarer, trainee, son of L'non & Elani, twin brother of Taer*

The Maker — *creator deity*

Me'ran (meh-RAN) — *Falier's home village*

Meira (MAY-rah) — *normal, elder of Me'ran, wife of Garrick*

Nahne (NAH-nee) — *the Eldra of those whose work cares for people*

Nameless Ones — *Eldír who turned against the Maker and were stripped of their names and stewardships*

Namor (NAY-mohr) — *slayer, retired, elder of Me'ran, husband of Tenza*

Níla (NEE-lah) — *the Eldra of healing*

Nissen (NEE-sihn) — *river dividing the hill country from the forests*

Paili (PAY-lee) — *dragoness, alpha in the Prilunes, mate of Tsamen, mother of Harenn*

Parrin (PAYR-ihn) — *a village in the center of Karn's wayfaring territory*

Parsen (PAR-sehn) — *holder, husband of Kat, father of Selene & Falier*

Prilunes (PRIH-loons) — *mountains dividing Arran's north and south lands*

Q'rill (kuh-RIHL) — *dragon, nurse, son of Tora*

Radharc Anam (RAD-ahrk AH-nahm) — *"soul-seer"*

Rann (ran) — *drek, name gives impression of a red-feathered bird, mate of Chrí (deceased), father of Rís & Chrí*

Rassím (rah-SEEM) — *messenger/scout, initially from the Southlands*

Rayna (RAY-nuh) — *dragoness, warrior, mate of Korin*

Rís (rees) — *drek, name gives impression of a red dawn, son of Rann & Chrí (deceased), brother of Chrí*

Rorenth (ROHR-enth) — *(deceased) dragon, an'reik, alpha west of the Nissen river*

Sareth (SEHR-eth) — *(deceased) dragon, scout in Rorenth's clan who turned to Alísa's side*

Saynan (SAY-nehn) — *ice dragon, combat trainer, mate of Aree*

Segenn (SAY-gehn) — *slayer, chief of the largest clan of eastern wayfarers*

Selene (seh-LEEN) — *holder, daughter of Parsen & Kat, sister of Falier*

Sesína (seh-SEE-nuh) — *dragoness, Illuminated by Alísa*

Serra (SEH-rah) — *slayer, bound to Me'ran, wife of Kerrik (deceased)*

Ska — *drek, name gives impression of light through water, Falier's friend*

Soren (SOHR-ehn) — *a village just south of Me'ran*

Taer (tayr) — *slayer, wayfarer, trainee, son of L'non & Elani, twin brother of Levan*

Taz — *slayer, wayfarer, from Me'ran, best friend of Falier & Selene*

Tella (TEH-luh) — *slayer, chief of a western wayfaring clan*

Tenza (TEHN-zuh) — *slayer, retired, elder of Me'ran, wife of Namor*

Tora (TOHR-uh) — *dragoness, warrior, mother of Q'rill*

Toronn (TOHR-ahn) — *slayer, chief, village-bound to Azron (Alísa's home village)*

Trísse (treeS) — *slayer, wayfarer, best friend of Alísa*

Tsamen (TSAH-mehn) — *dragon, alpha in the Prilunes, mate of Paili, father of Harenn*

Twi-Peak (TWIE-peek) — *double-peaked mountain just north of Me'ran*

Yarlan (YAR-len) — *slayer, village-bound to Me'ran*

FARREN'S SONG

I will tell you a tale
Of our tragic Bria fair.
Of empathy she never chose
That filled her mind with dragons' woes,
And how it did ensnare.

I will tell you a tale
Of her stubbornness and pride.
For none she told of hurt and pain.
Alone she fought the dragons' reign
Her heart against her mind.

I will tell you a tale
Of our stolen Bria fair.
For dragons took her for her song,
A broken mind to make theirs strong,
Death now her only prayer.

I will tell you a tale.
Will you heed my tale?

I will tell you a tale
Of a second Singer's plight.
Though taught to fear and taught to hide
Her dragon empathy inside,
Allara's flame grew bright.

I will tell you a tale
Of how dragons stole her still.
But though they sought her lyrics' aid,
With lullaby she took her blade
And proved her greater will.

I will tell you a tale
Of Allara's fearful flight.
For slayers feared her power too strong
And sought to end her dragon song
And douse her family's light.

I will tell you a tale.
Will you heed my tale?

I will tell you a tale
Of your daughter, sister, wife.
For Maker knows who else will find
The dragons' pain inside her mind
And songs that come to life.

I will tell you a tale,
But you decide its end.
For Bria stood and fell alone,
Allara driven from her home.
On you they now depend.

I will tell you a tale.
Will you heed my tale?

PROLOGUE

Farren didn't breathe as the final notes from his lute faded, leaving only the crackling percussion of the campfire. No applause came from the clan tonight, no acknowledgement of the words and melody he had woven tirelessly for the past three days. They knew what he had done and whose wrath it would incur.

His eyes met his chief's. Throughout the song, Karn's expression had betrayed all his emotions. First the bitter sadness that had lingered since his last battle. Since Alísa had been stolen again before his eyes.

Next came shock, the kind Farren himself would have felt if, upon entering his tent, he found that someone had used his lute and then left it lying on the ground outside its case.

Then anger, walking the line between indignation and outrage. Karn's face turned the color of his copper hair and his clenched fists pressed against his kilt's red and brown plaid. A younger man might cower, but Farren had earned too many gray hairs at Karn's side to fear him anymore. Only Karn's own clan, people to whom the secret of the Dragon Singers had already been revealed, had heard this song. Farren had revealed nothing new, but by presenting the tales in song he declared his intentions to bring such secrets into the light for many, many others.

Karn stood and spoke in a quiet growl. "Leave us."

Threat of dragon-fire could not have made the clan move more quickly.

Hanah stayed at Karn's side, sadness lingering in her silvery-blue eyes. The Lady of the clan stood tall with her auburn hair falling in loose waves over her shoulders, unbraided since the day she learned her daughter's fate. Her quiet way of mourning for her stolen daughter while remaining strong before the clan. Farren's heart ached at the thought of Alísa caught in the talons of the dragons, falling subject to evil's will.

Maker, save her.

Only one other person dared to stay in the chief's presence. Karn's apprentice, Alísa's intended, and Farren's co-conspirator, Kallar sat unmoving as the stone mountains surrounding this valley. Farren knew better. He had seen the fire in the young man's heart, and he silently prayed Kallar's fervor would help and not hinder as they convinced Karn of their plan.

"What was that?" Karn's voice was hot water just before boiling.

"That is Alísa's only chance."

Karn's arm sliced through the air as he stalked toward Farren. "Don't you dare claim you know how to save her—as though sharing these stories will do anything more than paint a target on her back!"

Farren kept his voice low and calm. "Ignorance and fear are the first steps toward hatred. By—"

"And what of Allara's first clan, when they were brought out of the dark? They tried to kill her! The only way to save Alísa is for *us* to find her. Spreading the secrets of the chiefs will only accomplish mass panic."

"How do you intend to find her first?" Farren spread his hands, indicating the surrounding mountains. "Will you search every mountain in a month? Storm every cave? Would even a year be enough time?"

"Don't presume to know what I can and cannot do—"

"Karn." Hanah, ever the reasonable one, placed a hand on the chief's arm. "My love, Farren's counsel has never led you astray. Let him speak."

Karn's chest heaved with every breath. One. Two. Three.

"Go on."

Farren nodded to chief and lady. "I do not wish to cause you pain, but I've lived among slayers long enough to understand the evil Alísa faces. How much time does she have? You need every person in Arran to be our eyes if we are to find her."

Karn shook his head, defeat in his voice. "Generations of chiefs have kept the secret of the Dragon Singers. I cannot go against their wisdom."

"Yes. You can." Kallar accused as he stood. His ice-blue eyes gleamed in the firelight, and his half-long, half-shorn hair proclaimed the warrior he never ceased to be. "You just won't. I knew you wouldn't, which is why I went to Farren first."

Karn's eyes widened. "You? You're behind this treachery?"

"If contradicting the 'wisdom' of men long dead is treachery—yes. What wisdom is there in keeping people in the dark?"

"To protect the innocent and keep order. There are others whose empathy is broken, who feel dragon emotions against their wills, yet are not Singers. If everyone knew dragon empathy was a warning sign, these innocent slayers would be in danger, as would the children of Allara and any other Singer who might fight for our side in the future. Would you risk so many for one?" Karn's voice barely whispered past his throat. "Even one so dearly loved?"

"Yes."

"Then I have taught you nothing! A chief cannot risk so much, even for their child. I—"

Karn's broad shoulders shuddered as emotion cut off his words. He bowed his head and covered his face with a hand, sitting back down on the log. Hanah went with him, taking his hand as the great chief wept.

Maker above. In all their years together, Farren had never seen Karn weep. Not even when Alísa was first stolen, nor when he came down the mountain after failing to save her. Even Kallar seemed stunned.

"Generations—" Karn breathed out, his voice slow and halting. "Generations of chiefs have decided how best to protect those under their care. Who am I to say otherwise? My heart yearns to do what you say, as though it is the rightest thing in the world. But the heart so easily deceives. Among so many who say it must be one way, how could I possibly be the one who is right?"

Hanah's arm slid from Karn's back as she faced him. "Fear, too, deceives. Perhaps it deceived all the chiefs who decided Bria's fate and which secrets they would keep."

She looked to Farren and Kallar, her chin lifted with command. "It is rare that wise counsel and brash action walk hand-in-hand. Surely you do not come simply with a heart's desire, but with truth and logic to sway the mind of a chief?"

Farren stepped closer to Karn, taking control before Kallar jumped in with blunt words.

"Karn, I believe the chiefs of Bria's day were wrong. This should never have been a secret. If I had known Dragon Singers existed, I could have told you long ago that Alísa was one."

Wide eyes turned on Farren, and he nodded. "Alísa's voice has always been especially moving. Once I even thought I saw an image in my head as she sang. I pushed it away as my overactive imagination rather than recognizing it as a sign. If people like me knew, we could help them at an earlier age. Train them to use or suppress their power so they aren't left to the mercy of the dragons."

Karn opened his mouth, and Farren rushed to answer his unspoken protest. "Yes, this knowledge could put them in danger from humankind as well, but that is why the song is so important. The words I've woven encourage understanding and support. Not all will listen, but many will."

"I agree," Hanah said. "Your tale gave even Bria grace. Though I fail to see how this helps Alísa now."

Kallar huffed and looked at Farren. "I told you to use the full song."

Farren inclined his head to chief and lady. "There are indeed two more stanzas. I thought it best that you hear it privately first, rather than cause you sorrow before the clan."

Farren raised his lute and lifted his voice once more.

I will tell you a tale
Of a final captured soul.
By tooth and claw, by scaled wing,
The dragons bid Alísa sing
To bring about their goal.

I will tell you a tale
But you decide its end.
To bring her home and save her soul
Her father's clan must play their role,
To Karn your hand extend.

Karn studied the ground as Farren lowered his instrument. As he had suspected, hearing Alísa's name and plight in song form affected the chief greatly. Now to convince him of the necessity of these stanzas.

"Such words may bring you shame among the clans, but they will make your plea clear. If others heed the song and learn of Alísa's whereabouts, messengers will be sent to you."

Karn met Farren's eyes, determination rising. "Shame does not concern me—only Alísa's rescue and the good of our world." He looked to Kallar. "You understand the consequences?"

Kallar nodded firmly, his jaw set. Something passed between chief and apprentice that Farren couldn't begin to guess, but the steadiness in Kallar's eyes made him understand how the young man could call his elders to follow him into caves rank with dragons' breath.

Karn stood and placed a heavy hand on Farren's shoulder. "You have convinced me. We will stop at every village on the way to Parrin, and you will tell the tales. Parrin is a major trading post—there will be many messengers and bards passing through who will carry the song on their way." His eyes hardened. "And every slayer chief who objects will answer to me."

The great chief released Farren's shoulder and marched back into camp. Hanah watched him go before rising herself, the grace of her movements betraying none of her sorrow. Striding to Farren, she wrapped her arms around him briefly, whispering her thanks.

Then she turned to Kallar. A moment of silent regard passed between them before she grabbed the apprentice and pulled him into a tight embrace. Kallar looked supremely uncomfortable, like he half-expected her to pull a knife from her skirts and stab him in the back. Just as suddenly, Hanah released him and walked after her husband into the cluster of worn leather tents.

Kallar watched her leave, his brow smoothing as though a great burden had been lifted from him. It lasted only a moment before Kallar's eyes hardened again and settled on Farren.

"The last line of the second stanza still doesn't rhyme."

Farren raised an eyebrow. "Do I tell you how to wield your sword?"

Kallar grunted. "I expected more from a professional songweaver."

"Art is never perfected, young slayer, merely set free."

Farren aimed for his tent, the chill of evening beginning to settle in his bones. Kallar took long strides to match his pace.

"You also focused only on women," the slayer said. "I told you, we don't know that men can't be Dragon Singers, too."

Farren inclined his head. "Granted. But so far, the pattern holds true, and something within a man of honor feels especially called to protect the women in his life. We want them moved to action, so that is where I laid my focus."

"That's" —Kallar paused, his eyebrows lifting as though impressed— "kind of manipulative."

Farren tsked and shook a rebuking finger. "I prefer 'perceptive'. 'Perspicacious', even."

"Whatever."

"Words have power, Kallar. You would do well to remember that and choose yours more wisely."

Kallar snorted, angling toward his tent. "Good night, Songweaver."

Farren chuckled through his own goodbye, wondering at the odd partnership that had grown between them. He glanced up as a sprinkling of stars shimmered through a break in the cloud-cover, and shivered under their gaze.

He had found Alísa bundled up on an evening much like this, pack over her shoulder and determination in her eyes. There had been a sense of peace in his heart about her leaving—a peace he had always associated with the Maker's will. But now Alísa was left alone in the talons of the enemy. How could he have been so wrong?

But the plan to convince Karn had worked. Now Farren begged the Maker and any Eldra who might listen that the song would bring them word of Alísa before her mind was too turned by the dragons to save— and before slayers came upon her and ended her misery with violence rather than care.

1

REMEMBRANCE

The bright emerald green of Laen's mane did little to mark her place among the trees of the forest. Already, Alísa and her companions had lost the little drek thrice. Graydonn's telepathic tracking skills helped them keep up, but the dragon had his own troubles weaving through the trunks. His taloned paws crunched ferns and fallen leaves and sent up scents of long-dried earth. Alísa rested a hand on his grass-green scales and kept her eyes in the boughs.

Selene's cloud-like voice lifted from behind them. "Laen, you're still going too fast."

"Maybe if she stayed solid while she led us," Sesína grumbled in all their minds, *"instead of taunting us with her dreki phasing short-cuts."*

Alísa smirked, looking back at the ebony dragoness. Sesína's emerald eyes met Alísa's, then rolled in a very human fashion. *"I'm just saying."*

Falier and Selene walked on either side of Sesína—the brother and sister duo from the Hold in Me'ran, and the first human friends Alísa had made in her new life in the eastern forests. Falier caught Alísa's eye and smiled at her. Alísa smiled back, trying not to grin like a fool. It had only been three days since he had asked to pursue her—she had to keep some dignity.

Falier had taken a day back at the Hold with his family to clean up from their adventure into dragons' caves, his jerkin fresh and crisp and his short brown curls and sun-tanned skin free of the mud and blood of battle. He had also shaved, much to Alísa's dismay. Maybe he would let his facial hair grow if she asked him, but that seemed an inappropriate request this early in their relationship.

7

On the other side of Sesína, Selene cupped her hands to her mouth and called for Laen again, effortlessly winding her blue-plaid skirt through the brush and brambles. Unlike Alísa, who had to pull her own skirt close. Everything about the short, blonde woman radiated grace and confidence.

Maybe one day I'll have that too. Knowing me, it will take much longer than Selene's twenty-one years.

Sesína snorted, hearing Alísa's thoughts through their mother-daughter Illumination bond—though, truly, it had become more a sisterly bond as the young dragoness grew.

"You're a leader of dragons now, Alísa," Sesína whispered through the bond. *"You can't be without* some *confidence."*

Alísa's boot caught on the forest floor and she stumbled, steadying herself on Graydonn's back.

Sesína cough-laughed. *"Grace, on the other hand..."*

Alísa didn't dare look back as her cheeks flushed red. Falier had to have noticed. So much for dignity.

"There." Graydonn pointed his snout to the right.

Sure enough, Laen sat on an oak branch a few trees away, watching them. The drek's silvery body shimmered even in the shade of the trees, the emerald-green mane running the length of her spine waving in the morning breeze like the grasses of the hill country.

"Slow!" Laen barked her annoyance.

Sesína growled. *"Take to the skies and I'll show you slow!"*

Laen unfurled her wings and growled back, telepathically sending the group a picture instead of a word—a much smaller Sesína with a piece of ebony eggshell stuck on top of her head, as though she had just hatched. Alísa laughed at the admonishment.

Sesína hummed with annoyance. *"Whose side are you on?"*

"Laen," Selene chided, hands on her hips. "We're counting on you to show us to your home. You can't keep leaving us behind."

The little drek's wings drooped as she let out a loud breath. Then she straightened and hopped to a pine branch, making an obvious show of looking back to make sure they followed.

"Bit of a firebrand, isn't she?" Falier said. Alísa looked just in time to see him give Sesína a light shove. "Don't have any of those in our little group yet."

Sesína flicked her tail in annoyance. *"That little twerp and I are nothing alike. I miss Chrí."*

A lump settled in Alísa's throat. *Chrí.*

Sesína's eyes dimmed and she hurried forward to nose Alísa's arm. *"I'm sorry."*

"We all miss her," Graydonn said solemnly. *"It will be good to remember her with her family today."*

Alísa sniffed and nodded, lifting her eyes to latch onto Laen again. None of them had visited the home of the dreki before. Possibly, no human had ever seen it, and the strained relationship between dragons and dreki made Alísa certain no dragon had either. At least, no dragon who lived to tell the tale. The dreki were a secretive people, supremely loyal to their friends and even more dangerous to their enemies.

Now, though, certain members of each race had united under a common purpose—the ending of the dragon-human war. A lofty goal, to be sure, yet they had made great strides already. Alísa and her dragon clan's victory over Rorenth had proven their willingness to lay their lives on the line for humans. Now she needed to find slayers willing to do the same for dragons.

Memories of her father rose in her mind. His desire to free her, and his refusal to listen when she told him her dragon clan was good. She'd had to fight him to get her dragons to safety. Her greatest failure.

"I was so proud of your flow of thoughts until you let that moment cloud it," Sesína said. *"You've accomplished much—remember that and let it be."*

"Let it be? He's my father!"

Guilt painted Sesína's emotions. *"Poor choice of words. I only meant that you shouldn't let someone's unwillingness to listen mark you a failure."*

Alísa shook her head. *"His clan is my family, and their lives are built on a lie that has them killing you, my other family. And I couldn't get them to stop."*

"Namor stopped."

The old slayer rose in Alísa's mind—watchful, battle-scarred, and stubborn. He had fought dragons all his life, whether as a mountain-storming wayfarer or as village-bound protector. He had nearly mind-choked Graydonn from the sky the first time he saw the dragon, but after seeing Alísa and her dragons defend the village, Namor had listened.

Still, he was only one slayer, and the other slayer of the village, Yarlan, had seen it all and remained antagonistic. She needed to convince many more slayers to have any chance of ending the war. Tonight's presentation to Me'ran would be the first big step—gain the confidence of normals, then use their testimony to bring her peacefully before slayers. There had been enough bloodshed already.

Laen chirped and trilled excitedly ahead of them, tickling the surrounding leaves with her outstretched wings.

"Here!"

A wall of trees rose up before them, the undergrowth between them thick with brush and bramble. Laen gave another trill and dove between two of the trees, leaving them to find their own path through. None stood out—unwelcoming, to say the least.

"Allow me," Graydonn said, padding forward. He studied the blockage, then plunged a wing into the tangled mess. With a small grunt of effort, he pulled back the brush and gave Alísa a respectful slow blink.

Alísa smiled at the dragon, ducking through the makeshift entrance, and gasped with delight. Lush green surrounded her, deep with life. Flowers of every color graced the forest floor, the tree trunk wall, and the branches above her head, some drooping to kiss the ground on delicate vines. A small creek ran through the space, sparkling where the morning sunlight peeked through the boughs. And amidst the splendor, dreki—at least sixty of them, jewel-tone manes bright against silvery bodies.

"Oh, wow." Falier stood beside her, their shoulders almost touching. "It's..."

His voice trailed off as awe rippled from him, echoed by the others as they entered the glade. The emotion felt like another kind of flower, opening up to bask in sunlight it could never hope to take in fully.

"Beautiful," Alísa whispered, finishing his sentence.

Falier looked down at her, his eyes softening as he reached for her hand. Alísa gave it, expecting him to use the skin-contact to aid his telepathy, as he typically did. This time, however, he merely slipped his fingers between hers and looked back out at the wonders of the dreki's home. A rush ran through Alísa, warmth rising in her chest.

A flash of emerald whisked past and settled on Selene's shoulder. *"Home,"* Laen chirped.

Out of the group, Selene looked the most overcome. She stayed completely still, only her eyes moving slowly over the scene.

Falier studied his sister. "You all right?"

Selene reached up to stroke Laen's mane. "It's a lot, but I'll be okay. The dreki are talking to each other."

Memory stirred within Alísa. Not only did Selene see what everyone else did, she also saw sound-lights and telepathy lines. While the space brought warmth and peace to Alísa, it must be over-stimulating for Selene.

Selene caught her staring and met Alísa's eyes. She gave a half-smile, her gaze flitting to Alísa and Falier's clasped hands before returning to the dreki and their home. Selene seemed happy enough with Alísa and Falier's relationship. Falier's parents, on the other hand... Both were amiable and outwardly supportive of Falier's choice, but Kat seemed to have reservations and Parsen was, as always, hard for Alísa to read. Hopefully, she could prove herself worthy in their eyes.

"Singer!"

Alísa whipped her head around to see five dreki in front of her. They turned flips and spun around each other, much like they did at Me'ran's céilí dances.

"Singer!" "Singer!" "Singer!"

Alísa smiled, letting go of Falier's hand to clasp her hands in front of her. "Thank you f—for your welcome. Your home is b—beautiful."

An image of the center of the glade slipped into Alísa's mind. *"Come."*

With a glance that called the others to follow, Alísa heeded their invitation. A few more joyful dreki joined them as they walked, while others stopped to stare at them with eerily-glowing eyes.

A drek with a blue mane swooped past Alísa and landed on Falier's shoulder.

"Drum?"

Falier gave an apologetic smile. "Sorry, Ska, I didn't think to bring it."

Ska's head and wings drooped as he let out a little sigh, then he leapt into the air to rejoin the rest of the dreki.

"You know," Falier called after him, smirking, "it's times like this I think you just tolerate me because you like the bodhrán."

Another image wafted into the minds of the group, one of them sitting on the ground. Alísa lowered to her knees, careful not to sit on too many flowers, though it was impossible not to crush a few. Falier sat beside her with Selene on his other side, while Sesína and Graydonn lowered to their bellies behind them.

As they settled, the dreki began congregating near them, hovering a few feet above the ground. Now that they were closer, Alísa noticed a few very small dreki, perhaps small enough to land on the palm of her hand. Adolescents. Their flight was less stable than the adults, more of a flutter than a hover, and their manes were a dusting of color along their spines rather than the flowing locks of the older dreki.

"In front of you, Alísa," Sesína said.

Alísa pulled her eyes from the curiosity of the adolescents and gave a little gasp. Laen hovered before her, accompanied by a drek with a ruby mane and wing-baubles. Chrí had shown Alísa a picture of her mate before she died, and a pull deep inside her recognized this as him.

Her heart pounded. She didn't know what to say. She didn't even know his name.

"Singer," the little male voice came, accompanied by a picture of bright red bird feathers and his name.

"Rann," she whispered. "I am so sorry for your loss."

Rann gave her a picture of Chrí nestled amidst Alísa's mahogany curls and nuzzling her cheek. The image was so real—the light pull on Alísa's hair, the smoothness of Chrí's muzzle, the soft sound of her breathing, and a deep love that filled Alísa's empathic senses. It was all so life-like it would live forever in her memories of her friend. The beauty of this gift from Rann sent a tear sliding down her cheek.

"Thank you."

The tiniest squeak drew Alísa's eyes from Rann's face to a little silver lump clinging to his mane. Her heart squeezed.

"Is that—"

Pride emanated from the drek. He looked to Laen, drawing Alísa's attention to a second silvery lump on her back, this one with shining purple eyes. The image Chrí had given her just before she died had two tiny eggs, one red like the father, one a lavender purple like the mother.

Rann sent an image of the two babies snuggled in Alísa's hands, accompanied by the feeling of a question.

Alísa grinned, lifting cupped hands. "Yes! Of course."

Rann landed on Alísa's lap—a gentle weight, perhaps only eight pounds—and nosed his passenger into her open hand. The little one squeaked and opened eyes a shade lighter than Rann's. Rann hopped onto Alísa's shoulder, giving Laen room to deposit the purple-eyed baby beside its sibling.

In Alísa's hands, the babies seemed even smaller, the two of them fitting perfectly in her palms. They curled together, tiny wings stretching and noses pressing into the warmth of each other. Neither had any hint of a mane, and the baubles that graced the ends of adult dreki wings were nowhere to be found either. The only color either drek had was its bright eyes.

Her human and dragon friends leaned in close, taking in the little lives with her.

"They're beautiful, Rann," Selene said, reaching a single finger to stroke the one with red eyes. "Have you named them?"

Rann gave a low, cooing trill. *"Rís."* An image of a red dawn accompanied the name—presumably the baby with red eyes. Then Rann pointed his muzzle at the purple one. *"Chrí."*

Alísa's heart caught at the name, but instead of the impression of lavender that came with the mother's name, a picture of bluebells rose in her mind.

"They're perfect."

Multiple dreki trilled above Alísa's head, drawing everyone's attention. Rann joined with his own trill. With one last glance at his children, he took to the air with the rest of his kind. It was time to honor the dreki who had given their lives.

The dreki hovered in a circle multiple dreki high, all facing the center. They stared into the empty space, their faces solemn and their emotions a mixture of the thickened air of grief and the deep green of peace. Then the dreki's eyes and wing-baubles began to glow—the sign their minds were joining in the deep, unfathomable way of their kind.

Squeaking trills brought Alísa's eyes back down as the baby dreki called to their kin. They fixed their eyes on the others, eye-lights fading in and out of the clan's glow as though they didn't know how to join yet.

Then the emotions hit.

Grief's thunderclouds darkened Alísa's mind, accented by strikes of anger, presumably for lives snuffed out too soon. As the dreki's minds became one, their power grew, as did their shared feelings. Alísa's heartbeat quickened as she remembered the last time dreki emotions had overwhelmed her. Her body tensed as her mind automatically began fighting against her empathy.

A nudge at her shoulder called Alísa from her thoughts. Graydonn's head came into view, and sorrow salted his voice as it entered her mind.

"It's okay, Alísa. Remember, you are stronger when you embrace your gift."

Alísa breathed. She had already learned this, and she chided herself for returning to old habits. With each inhale she took in the dreki's grief, and with each exhale she breathed out her own. Her heartbeat slowed, and though a sob wrenched through her, her pain and fear eased.

"There," the dragon soothed, returning his gaze to the dreki.

As the dreki's wing-baubles glowed, sparkles of color separated from them, little fairy lights coalescing in the center of the circle. The lights swirled around each other, dancing in and out like the dreki often did, until the shape of a drek with an orange mane appeared in their midst.

As one voice, the dreki said a name Alísa didn't recognize. Then the image faded away, only to be replaced by one of the same drek dancing in the air with another. The image faded again while another faded in, the new one of the drek as a youngster, snuggled between its parents.

Curious, Alísa shut her eyes and focused until the astral plane appeared. All the beings in the grove appeared as lights against blackness, each outlined in the color of their eyes. Beams of light shown from the dreki, almost a blinding white flowing into the center where the images appeared in the physical realm. A subtle change occurred as the image shifted again, a single drek's strand becoming brighter amidst the rays.

Alísa opened her eyes. Memories. The images were memories, each one streaming from an individual drek and materializing in the strange sparkles as the clan remembered their fallen kin.

Soon images of another fallen drek replaced the first, the clan cycling through memories of those they so dearly missed. Their grief renewed with each new honored drek, yet the dark closeness loosened its hold as memories unfolded, giving glimpses of joy and peace.

Then came Chrí's turn, her likeness shining with bright lavender hues and bringing fresh tears to Alísa's eyes. First came images of a mischievous youngster, then the passionate defender that Alísa had known. Rann shared a memory of bringing her some of the sweet lavenders that were part of her name, then one of her bringing him a dead bird with red feathers like in his name. Alísa fought not to giggle at the gift that was obviously supposed to be romantic.

Finally, Rann sent an image of Chrí curled around their eggs. The baby dreki chirped at the picture, bringing a silent sob to Alísa's chest. They never got to know their mother, yet they recognized her. Their grief was quiet, as if they knew they should be sad but didn't quite know how.

Alísa blew out a tremulous breath. Could she have done anything differently, something that could have kept these brave dreki alive? Perhaps not go into battle at all, but that would have been wrong, too. Then other lives would be at stake. She had known that going into battle meant facing death to keep others safe, and so had the dreki.

The images of Chrí vanished and another drek took her place, then another and another, until the remembrance came to a close. The dreki ended their mindshare, their eye- and wing-lights fading. Alísa sighed as the combined emotions faded into individuals. Though crowds could overwhelm her empathy, too, there was relief here.

The dreki began to disperse, sorrow, joy, and remnants of anger diminishing as individuals flew into boughs and other spaces in the grove. About a third of the dreki stayed nearby, many tiny glowing eyes fixing on Alísa and her group.

Rann flew back to Alísa's lap and nuzzled his children. The babies trilled at him, the sounds low and soft, and he answered with trilled coos before looking up at Alísa.

"Sing?"

She met Rann's steady gaze for a moment, then looked up to the few dreki remaining. All watched her with anticipation.

Only one song came to mind—one she had sung many times as her father's clan honored their fallen warriors. All growing up, she had known by that song that death wasn't the end, and that those who gave their lives willingly to protect others were honored above all. That was Chrí. Though her children may not yet understand the words, Alísa would make sure they knew this truth.

She exhaled, then pulled in a deep new breath, her tears renewing as she released it in song.

> Why must the good die before their time,
> And flames devour their prey?
> When will our mourning be made right
> And smoke break for the day?
>
> But in this world of suffering
> The Maker holds us all.
> His blessings follow those who stand,
> Though some to home He calls.

In her mind, the voices of her father's clan echoed the final two lines. Though terribly wrong in their thinking about dragons, they, too, stood for those weaker than they. So many slayers did. If she could only reach them with the truth about dragonkind, they would surely stand for both races and not just their own.

Alísa smiled as the remaining dreki chirped their gratitude before fluttering away, Laen and Rann the last to leave as they coaxed Rann's little ones onto their backs. Though anxiety still fluttered within Alísa as she thought of tonight's presentation, resolve became the foundation beneath it.

Tonight, the next phase in her quest to end the war would begin.

2

PRESENTATION

Excitement and nerves clashed within Alísa like the heat of the great bonfire against the coming chill of night. Everyone had come, just as she'd hoped, but with the eyes of every villager in Me'ran about to be fixed on her, strikes of lightning shot from her heart to her fingertips. The very same feeling she had before facing the teeth and talons of violent dragons. It seemed battlefields came in many forms.

She forced her eyes away from the people and to Falier, who stood only a few feet away. With his bodhrán drum strapped to his back, his fingers moving in warm-up patterns, and a light in his eyes, her pursuer exuded the eagerness she should have.

"Why did I let Falier talk me into this?"

Across the distance to the cave, Alísa felt Sesína's eye-roll through their bond. *"Love apparently makes one crazy. Remind me never to fall."*

Alísa blew out her breath, then stopped as Falier noticed her stare. She gave a smile she didn't feel, and he grinned back, the care in his twilight eyes sending a flip of a different kind through her stomach.

"You're going to do great." He spoke just loud enough for her to hear over the buzzing chatter of the crowd. "Just like we practiced."

Sesína sent a mental agreement as Alísa forced a nod. They had practiced. They had spent all day yesterday crafting their tale into a form Me'ran knew and would respond well to. A tale of heroism to convey the happenings of the last week. A tale of dragons willing to rise up to end the war between the races. A tale to inspire humanity to do the same.

Alísa loosened the reins of her empathy, letting it spread beyond her to Falier and holding it there before it could catch the crowd. She latched onto his eager excitement, letting it call her own from the depths of her mind. This wasn't just a nerve-wracking performance—this was the next step in her quest to unite the races and end the war.

That thought brought a true smile to her lips. Me'ran had already accepted her and the first dragons of her clan after they had proven their care for humankind by defending the village. Now Me'ran would learn of the other dragons who had risked their lives to keep violent dragons out of the eastern forests. As everything unfolded for the people through her songs and Falier's storytelling, they would accept the new dragons, accept her mission, and be the bridge between her and the slayers of nearby villages. With their support, the slayers would have to hear the truth.

Movement drew Alísa's eyes to the crest of the hill where a man and woman walked together, the evening sunlight gently gracing their backs as they joined the crowd. The people—so many people—gathered on either side of the great bonfire on the dancing grounds. Some stood, while most sat on chairs pulled from the Hold or on the log benches that normally surrounded the fire. A few children sat on the ground in front.

Falier's father, Parsen, stood with them before the crowd, his gaze fixed on the people. Parsen stood tall and confident before them, a holder respected by his village. He must have been taking roll in his head, for as the couple joined at the back of the group he raised his arms for attention. The crowd stilled at his call.

"A little over a week ago," Parsen began, "our village suffered its first dragon attack in many years. Through it, our world was turned upside down, not merely by the loss of property, but also by the revelation of our rescuers—the good dragons led by Alísa."

As Parsen spoke, Alísa scanned the crowd, searching for familiar faces. The rest of Falier's family stood on the far left side, the ladies easy to spot by their blond hair catching the firelight. Kat's eyes rested on Falier even as her husband spoke, the corners turned down in either sadness or worry. The story of the battle and Falier's part in it had been hard on her yesterday. Would a second telling be any easier?

Laen sat on Selene's shoulder and about fifteen other dreki perched on the roof of the Hold beyond the crowd. The rest of the dreki clan might be watching from the forest, but no eye-lights gave them away.

Namor and Tenza, a slayer couple in perhaps their mid-fifties, sat on a log at the front of the crowd. Namor leaned against his staff, his salt-and-pepper hair pulled back in a low ponytail, revealing eyes that were kinder now than when he and Alísa had first met. Vigilance still lived there, but now it made Alísa feel safe rather than guarded against.

Tenza's graying black hair swept from her temples in a crown of two braids, the rest cascading over her shoulders. She had a strong and quiet grace about her, like the swordswomen of Karn's clan. Like her husband, her almond-shaped eyes seemed to see all.

"But their fight to protect Me'ran was not the end of the story," Parsen brought Alísa's attention back to him. He neared the end of the introduction now—time to focus. "With Falier as their ally, they left to continue the work. Now they have returned with a tale to tell."

With a slight nod to Falier, Parsen took his place beside Kat in the audience. Falier stepped forward and pulled out his bodhrán, letting it sit at his side, held up by the shoulder straps. Head held high, he seemed completely in his element.

Alísa sent up a quick prayer to Eldra Nahne—the spiritual shepherd of holders and songweavers—asking for help to match him, to not let him down with the anxiety tying knots in her stomach. She breathed, focusing on the moment, and fixed her eyes on Falier.

The young holder began a quiet, rapid roll on his bodhrán. "Friends and family, tonight we tell you a tale of heroism. Of dastardly deeds of beasts lusting for blood, and of dragons who rose up and said, 'No more!'"

BUM, ba, ba, bum!

Falier hit a four-beat transition on his drum. Alísa's cue. Picturing Songweaver Farren—his confidence and love of storytelling—Alísa lifted her arms. She breathed as she moved, loosening her throat muscles to allow her words to flow. Just as they had practiced.

"Of a slayer who became dragon-friend, and the d—dragons who rose t-t-t-to t-train him" —*breathe, keep going*— "though normally the b— bitterest of foes."

bum, bum, BA, bum!

"And of a Dragon Singer" —Falier sent Alísa a look of admiration— "who inspired them all."

ba, ba, BUM!

Falier backed toward the fire, drumming the beat of the song she planned to sing. She smiled lightly, thinking once more of Farren. She had written this song in a style he created, changing the rhyming scheme a little to add her own flair. Perhaps, one day, she would get to sing it for him, too.

> I will tell you a tale
> Of a journey through the night.
> Of peaceful ones who rose to fight,
> Of battle looming, testing might,
> And how they might prevail.
>
> I will tell you a tale.
> Will you hear my tale?

As though part of the drama themselves, the dreki rose from their perches and flew to Alísa. Their wing-baubles caught the firelight, flashing color around her as their joy flashed over her mind. She latched onto their happiness, letting it chase away the last vestiges of her nerves and relax her stiff muscles. Farren would swell with pride if he could see her now.

> I will tell you a tale
> Of a dragoness so strong,
> Who waited all her life for song,
> Of hope through others proving wrong,
> And now she would not fail.
>
> I will tell you a tale
> Of a dragon young, but wise,
> Who saw through more than amber eyes,
> Rose up and bid a slayer rise,
> Whose heart has pierced the veil.

I will tell you a tale
Of a dragoness so brave,
Whose eyes are toward the weak to save,
Of heart and soul and flesh she gave
Unto a Singer frail.

I will tell you a tale.
Will you hear my tale?

I will tell you a tale
Of a fallen enemy.
A clan has risen, setting free
Man from fear's captivity
So peace can now prevail.

I will tell you a tale.
Will you hear my tale?

Falier rolled on the bodhrán as her song ended, bridging the music to the storytelling. Dreki whisked back to their spots as Alísa allowed Falier to take the foreground. He told the tale in much the same style as a traveling bard, embellishing the story with hyperbole, dynamic contrasts, and beats and rolls on his drum.

He told of the bloodlust of Rorenth, the alpha dragon strengthened by a dark bond to the Nameless Ones. Of how Rorenth had sent scouts to raze villages in the eastern forests to the ground, and that to defeat him and protect the people, the Dragon Singer needed the aid of more dragons. He facetiously told of his great fear riding a dragon for the first time, then spoke of the mighty Graydonn who would not let him fall. He told of Sesína's aerial acrobatics and hunting prowess that kept her human companions alive on the journey. And he told of the unwavering belief of Koriana, who led them through dangerous territories and became their emissary to Tsamen's dragon clan, where they all hoped for more dragons to join the fight.

The sun dipped below the trees as the story entered Tsamen's cave, adding an eerie ambiance to the tale. As Alísa waited for her next singing cue, she let her empathy flow out a little further and tasted the feelings of the crowd. Fear came first, though its strength was what one might expect from those hearing a scary story. Awe and wonder followed behind fear—a good sign.

When Falier's voice rose like the din of the dragons debating in Tsamen's cave, Alísa pulled her focus from her empathy back to his story. Her next cue was fast approaching.

"The dragons argued with voice and mind, some for the Dragon Singer, some against. The surly alpha female, Paili, rose above them all, ready to make an end of the Singer and her clan. But then, like sun breaking through the clouds, the Maker granted a new song—a song of warning that froze every dragon in their spot."

Pulling from her memories, Alísa sang the admonition she had received. She prayed it would stir the people here as well. The slayers of the other villages and the eastern wayfarers would never listen to a seventeen-year-old girl who claimed she knew the hearts of dragons. Warriors would need the testimony of these people, who had witnessed her dragons' bravery both firsthand and through this tale, if they were going to hear her.

> Who will seek wisdom in an age of violence?
> Only the quiet, who stand by nothing else.
> Who will listen to the quiet in a time of chaos?
> Only the ones who tire of the noise.
> Who will stand with the weak through the storms?
> Only the ones who too are affected.
>
> None will listen. None will stand. None will seek the truth,
> Until fire meets fire, and sword meets sword,
> Until man gives life for dragon,
> And dragon gives life for man.
> Woe to the ones who will not stand!

At the end of the song, Falier took over again. He told of the dragons who left Tsamen and Paili's clan to follow the Dragon Singer. Then came the message of the dreki, who told of Karn's march on Rorenth's mountain, and Alísa's desperate decision to join the fight in hopes of splitting Rorenth's attention in two. Falier told of daring feats by each of the dragons in the battle, painting each as a hero in their own right. Tears sprang to Alísa's eyes as he spoke of Sareth's sacrifice to shield her from Rorenth's wrath, and of the dreki who, with Falier and Graydonn, dealt the final blow at great cost.

"And so we stand before you today, with the very same dragons watching over us from Twi-Peak, recovering from their wounds so they can continue the fight for peace. But peace cannot be won by only a small clan of dragons and a couple of young slayers, no matter how incredible one of them might be." Falier shot Alísa a smile that made her blush. "And so we appeal to you. Take inspiration from the self-sacrifice of the dragons and their Dragon Singer and help us pave the path to peace."

Alísa breathed low and deep. She had been able to avoid speaking for most of this presentation, but as the leader of this movement, it fell to her to make the appeal.

"It has always been m—my hope to bring slayers into this c-c-clan as well. To p-p-present a united front and p-prove humans and dragons can live and work together in p-peace. I do not ask those who are not w—warriors to become so, but you, the p-p-p-p" —breathe— "the people they protect, have great influence."

The image of her father rose in Alísa's mind, of the shock on his face when he found her among dragons at the end of the battle. The pain of that encounter, when she had appealed to him and failed to gain his ear, was still too raw to expose to Me'ran—but the one thing she could convey from it was her need for others to stand with her. She needed the people. No slayer would hear her otherwise.

"I ask you to help us make ourselves known to the slayers of your neighboring v—villages. T-tell them what you know to be t-true so we can give them a chance t-t-to turn and join us in seeking p-p-peace between our kinds. The fighting will end, and the races will live in harmony, as they did in the time of Belinor and the founding of our c-c-country. And songs will be sung of the brave people of Me'ran, with whom it all started."

A silent pause, the end of the presentation, and relief swept over

Alísa. It was over—she had done it!

A cheer came up from a few in the crowd, as did a smattering of applause, but the sounds were awkward and silenced quickly when the rest in the crowd did not join in. Anxiety swam in Alísa's belly. She had stopped reading the crowd as she sang and spoke. She reached out with her empathy again.

Fear.

Shock.

Wonder.

Anger.

"'Give the slayers a chance to turn'?"

Alísa tensed at the venom-laced tone, her heart skipping a beat as the crowd parted for Yarlan to step to the front, warrior braids in his sandy hair and a sword at his hip. A slayer through and through, and one who had been antagonistic even after witnessing Sesína and the others save the village from Rorenth's scouts. His hate-filled eyes fixed on her, and it was all Alísa could do to not shrink back.

3

COMPROMISE

"By my people's stunned silence," Yarlan growled, "I can only hope they, too, know what this means. If the slayers—our protectors—do not turn, this dragon in human skin intends to destroy them! Just as she did the dragons who wouldn't follow her."

Alísa's heart raced as the silence of the crowd turned to angry mutterings and fearful murmurs. A few parents pulled their children from the front row. Falier came to her side, bodhrán slung against his back and brow creased in a mixture of confusion and anger.

No, no, no! This isn't what's supposed to happen!

Sesína's alarm shot through their bond. *"Are you in danger? I'm coming!"*

"No! Stay away. Seeing a dragon might antagonize Yarlan more."

"Singer." Laen's voice entered Alísa's mind as the drek flew from Selene's shoulder to hers. The drek stared down Yarlan as the rest of the dreki flew to the trees behind Alísa. Their agitated chittering clashed against the crowd's fear. Alísa pulled her empathy back, holding it as close to herself as she could to avoid being overwhelmed by the negative emotions.

"Silence!" Namor's voice carried over the crowd, quieting them. He leaned on his wife as they made their way up front, the missing lower half of his leg painfully obvious. "Yarlan has made his accusation. We must allow Alísa the chance to respond."

Namor's eyes softened as he nodded her forward.

Alísa breathed out, the respectful silence of the crowd relaxing the tension inside her. She steeled herself, bringing a picture of her father to the forefront of her mind. His strength, his courage, his words—all things she needed now.

Unbidden, she found Kallar in the image too, standing beside Karn in her stead.

She swallowed and shook the thought away. *Eldra Branni, give me strength.*

"I and my clan desire p-p-peace, not violence. We wish to bring the t-t-truth to the slayers in a way they'll understand. We will give them every chance to turn, just as we did the d—dragons. But if they w—will not stop k-k-k-killing innocent dragons, we must s—s—stop them."

"'Kill'," Yarlan growled, looming over her. "The word she won't say is 'kill'."

Alísa fought not to step back, taking strength from Falier tensing up tall and Laen hissing from her shoulder. Fear and fire rose within her, battling for control. Yarlan's words spewed poison over the people, taking the need for justice she presented and turning it to malice.

"Now she has dragons—many dragons—waiting in Twi-Peak for her command, and she asks us to march her to the homes of our friends and allies. Can we allow her to murder them?"

Many eyes fixed on Alísa, some waiting, some condemning. She lifted a hand to her chest, where her dragon-scale necklace hid underneath her shirt, and stared past the eyes to the wall of the Hold.

"I'm not t-t-t-t-talking about m—m—m—"

"She never said anything about murder, Yarlan," a male voice in the crowd interrupted.

Though the man spoke in her favor, Alísa's cheeks heated with shame. What kind of leader couldn't finish a sentence?

"Surely if our friends in Soren hear of this they'll understand."

"And if they don't," a woman near him said, "it's all right to just kill them? Because they disagree?"

The man was silent for a moment, and when his voice returned it held less confidence. "If what she and Falier say is true, the killing of innocent dragons is just as bad as them burning down a village."

"And what about *this* village?" Yarlan said, wresting back control. "Whether this girl is held in their thrall or actually on their side—"

"There is no thrall," Namor said, his voice once again bringing the others to silence. What Alísa wouldn't give for that ability. "Above all else, I am sure of that. Her mind is free and her heart is pure."

"Be that as it may" —Yarlan turned back to the crowd— "can we trust that dragons—humanity's enemy for hundreds of blood-filled years—have similarly pure hearts? They are mere minutes' flight from our homes, our livelihoods, our children. Would you risk these?"

Alísa had to say something—to insist on her dragons' goodness, to remind the people of the lives lost and the wounds taken on behalf of Me'ran and many other human lives. But the eyes of the people crowded in on her. She could feel her stammer rising up, ready to claim her words again like a highwayman preying on the weak.

No voice.

Falier must have recognized her struggle, because he stepped up, swiping his hand through the air. "Yarlan, enough of this! I've lived among these dragons, seen them risk everything for humankind—for us. Everything Alísa said is true!"

Yarlan tilted his head condescendingly. "Oh, it's your turn, is it? I wonder what the people have to say about your testimony, secret-keeper."

"You knew about the dragons long before we did and never warned us of the dangers," a woman said. "We might have been able to call for Chief Segenn and his wayfarers and had help when we were attacked."

Cold rushed through Alísa at the mention of the eastern wayfarers. If they had been here, she wouldn't have been able to stop them from killing Koriana, Graydonn, and Sesína right alongside the attacking dragons.

"Not to mention the secret of your telepathy," a man said. "How can we trust you when you wouldn't trust us?"

Falier looked as though he had been slapped. Where fear and indecision had kept them silent about Alísa and the dragons, they were far quicker to speak against him.

"I—"

"He kept the secret at our command," Parsen growled. "If you have something to say about it—"

"It doesn't matter who kept the secret." Yarlan pointed a finger at

Falier. "There's a reason slayers take young telepaths away from villages. An untrained telepath is dangerous—unable to control himself. How many times has he unwittingly seen your thoughts?"

Anger coursed through Alísa. These people had known Falier his whole life—how could they so easily forget the goodness she knew from only a few months? She wanted to take his hand in support, but held back for fear of sending the empathic feelings into him.

"I was trained," Falier said, desperation in his eyes as he looked over the murmuring people. "I was taught how to put up a wall to protect others from just such accidents."

Yarlan's eyes widened and shot to Namor. "You? You knew about this?"

"I certainly did not. Though it makes sense he had a wall, since you and I never sensed him." Namor raised a brow. "Who taught you, Falier?"

Falier glanced over the crowd, then cast his eyes down. "I can't tell you."

This made the crowd fidgety. Voices raised again as they speculated about another hidden telepath in their midst.

Yarlan rounded on Falier. "Once again you hide information your people need to be safe! Who trained you?"

"Do not blame the boy." A female voice rose strong above the crowd. Serra stepped out from among them, her olive skin glowing in the firelight. "He was, after all, only a boy at the time."

Falier tensed, apparently unsure what to think of her coming forward. Alísa had only met her once. Serra had met Koriana, Graydonn, and Sesína with great caution after they had defended the village, but though she cast her vote in favor of letting the dragons visit Me'ran, she had warned that she would keep her children far from them.

"He remains silent to retain my late husband's honor." Serra faced Yarlan and Namor. "But Kerrik would be ashamed of how you, his fellow slayers, treat Falier now."

"K-Kerrik?" Yarlan stuttered, then regained his composure. "Kerrik was wise and good. Why would he keep such a secret?"

"To save the life of a boy with powers too weak to protect him on the front lines." Serra gave Falier a look of apology. "The life of wayfarers is dangerous and grueling, often with little time for training before drawing the line at the Nissen River. Unlike Segenn, Kerrik did not believe in taking sons from their families only to have them fall in their first battle, so first-generation telepaths who just barely manifested the gift were given training to hold back their powers and respect the privacy of others. Falier and his family only did as they were told to save his life."

Alísa glanced at Falier as both relief and shame flowed from him—his secrets now revealed to all. He shifted under the emotions but somehow kept them from his face. But Serra wasn't finished.

"I stand by Kerrik's decision in this matter, though I am pleased to see he was wrong in one instance. Falier has proven himself capable in battle and brave in heart. My husband would be proud."

Falier's tension melted away with her words. "Thank you."

She nodded once, then strode back into the crowd with a purposeful grace that declared the matter over.

If only all matters were over. Yarlan recovered quickly, turning back to the crowd with a loud voice.

"None of this forgives the fact that—"

"I believe we've heard enough of your arguments, Yarlan." Namor lifted a hand to the crowd. "Surely there are others with opinions to voice? Let the elders hear them, and let the Dragon Singer defend her position."

Nerves shot down Alísa's arms. Me'ran's elders coming to the front meant the discussion would be grave. Yarlan glared at Namor for the dismissal, but as the elders came forward he retreated into the crowd. He'd proved himself a great foe, yet he held a certain degree of respect for his superiors.

Seven elders came to stand alongside Namor and Tenza, Parsen and Kat the youngest among them. Meira, one of the elders who had voted for the dragons a week ago, raised a cacao-skinned palm to the crowd, as though asking them to place their woes in her hand.

"What questions need answered?" she asked. "Come, don't be shy. Better to be up front than leave your doubts stopped up."

"What proof do we have that this stranger and her dragons won't turn on us?" a man said, his five-year-old daughter on his hip. "How do we know we're safe?"

"Safe!" one of the dreki barked. The rest took up the call as well, their baubled wings flapping with emphasis. Instead of convincing the people, however, the dreki's echoing answer seemed to spook some of them even more.

Alísa swallowed, willing her throat to relax so she could speak again. Though she hated how they had attacked Falier, having the attention off her for a short while had let her catch her breath. At a sharp bark from Laen, the rest of the dreki silenced for Alísa.

"Two weeks ago, you w—welcomed three dragons into your c-c-c" —*breathe*— "community because they saved your lives. These n—new dragons are no d—different. Despite the distance separating you from the second b—battle, their actions p-p-p-protected Me'ran from future violence. If this doesn't p-p-prove them, what can?"

"Dragons fight over territory all the time. How can we know this is any different?" The man dipped his head. "I don't doubt you, dear maiden, but dragons are crafty beasts, able to hide their intent."

She shook her head. "Not from me."

"May I?" Falier whispered, and at her assent he spoke. "If this were a battle over territory, they could have easily stayed at Rorenth's mountain. Why come here, where there are few mountains to hide from slayers or dwell in should the clan grow bigger? They follow the Dragon Singer."

"How many dragons are there now?" The female voice held a slight tremble. "And how many can she control?"

Alísa took a breath. This answer would only add to the fear, but she wouldn't lie to them.

"T-t-twelve." Gasps rose all around, many eyes widening with horror. She closed her eyes to complete her answer. "Plus one hatchling and three eggs."

Multiple voices rose from the crowd. "So many in such a short time!"

"Three or twelve, what does it matter if they fight for us?"

"We have two slayers to protect us. Two! Against sixteen?"

"Can the original three plus Alísa keep them in check?"

"They'll eat our game and livestock, burn our wood—"

Alísa forced a breath in and out, fighting back the fear pressing in on her. Though a part of her was angered by the peoples' refusal to see her dragons' great sacrifice for them, another part remembered her own fear when she was just a daughter of slayers. The trepidation as she faced Graydonn even after he had already proved himself safe. The way she had jerked back from Koriana's large, inhuman face.

Yes, the slayers' daughter remembered. How could she have thought this would be easy for them? How could she salvage this?

"Silence!" Namor raised his hands and the village settled into a respectful, yet uneasy quiet. He turned back to Alísa, but she kept her eyes on the bonfire. "Answer the rest of the question. How many can you keep under your control?"

Alísa shook her head, brushing against Laen's nose as the drek tried to nuzzle her cheek. It wasn't that simple. Namor knew that. Why didn't he speak for her—tell them what he already understood?

"It's not about c-c-c-c" —breathe— "control. They c-c-control themselves, and they f—f—f" —stop it! Breathe!— "f—follow me b— because they believe."

"There could have been more dragons," Falier said earnestly, "had Alísa been shrewd and appealed to the dragons' desires for territory or battle. Harenn told her of his other clanmates who would have come had that been the call. Instead, she appealed only to those who desired justice and peace. Her song gained the right dragons. Those are the dragons living in Twi-Peak. We have nothing to fear from them."

"What say you to that, Me'ran?" Namor said. "To dragons bound not through a woman's telepathic hold, but to their individual beliefs in the cause of peace?"

Alísa caught the slayer's eyes as he gave her the slightest of smiles. As the crowd murmured about his question, understanding filled her heart with relief. Though Namor's position as elder and slayer settled the responsibility of questioning her on his shoulders, he did still believe her.

The rest of the people, however, were clutched in a fog of confusion and uncertainty. One woman—the tanner, Alísa recognized—lifted a respectful hand and spoke.

"I'm willing to believe what Alísa and Falier have told us, even happy to take them to Soren to speak with other slayers, but I do worry about food. I assume that many of your dragons are adults—how much will a clan of dragons eat? Will the hunters in our area still be able to find food and sell their wares here? At the risk of sounding self-centered, our business relies on such things, and many of you rely on our work."

Alísa opened her mouth to speak, but another woman spoke over her. "Can we ask that the dragons only hunt on the north side of the mountain? Protect our area from over-hunting?"

Alísa shook her head. "D—d—dragons don't eat m—much, and it's d—difficult to hunt in the forest. They need—"

"And what about what we need?" Yarlan said from the crowd. "Surely if your dragons are as good and noble as you say, they can make some sacrifices. A show of good faith, if you will. You wouldn't want to cause a problem only the wayfarers can solve, would you?"

Fear seized Alísa, closing her throat again. She had the answers, and they wouldn't affect Me'ran nearly as much as they thought. Adult dragons only needed a good meal once every few days. They didn't need much, but they did need opportunity—open spaces where they could spot prey from the sky. Confined to the north side of the mountain, they would have a hard time finding what they needed. With wounded dragons, and dragonets soon to hatch, keeping up on meals was vital.

But as the people latched onto this 'show of good faith' and Alísa's fear clogged her throat, Yarlan's eyes lit with triumph.

In the midst of the murmurings, another elder spoke. "Yes, I propose a compromise—an opportunity for Alísa and Falier to prove their words, while giving our people safety. If these dragons can prove themselves good in real life—not in a battle far removed from us—we will support you before our neighboring villages."

Alísa fought back a tremble of anger, though she didn't know who she was more angry at—the people who demanded more proof of her dragons than even shed blood could provide, or herself, who couldn't do anything more than watch.

The elder continued. "Allow Koriana, Graydonn, and Sesína to visit our village, as we already agreed. Let any other dragon who comes near, whether landing or merely flying over, be escorted by one of these three dragons. The new dragons must never outnumber the originals, and Alísa will always accompany them. I don't think anyone can doubt her intentions toward us—if one or more of these dragons attacked, she would be the first to fight for us."

"I can attest to that," Namor added.

"Secondly, to address the issue of game—the dragons should confine their hunting grounds to the northeast of Twi-Peak. What say you, Me'ran? Would you agree to these terms?"

The elders took a vote, hands raised and lowered, voices agreed and dissented. All of it washed over Alísa like a winter storm her little tent couldn't stand against. She had failed to make the people feel safe, failed to present her clan to them in a good light, failed to speak when words needed to be spoken.

'You've taken an apprentice, of course.'

The words shot through her like lightning—a memory long-repressed. A woman, a fellow daughter of a chief, who should have given Alísa support and hope but instead gave disdain. Tears prickled at Alísa's eyes. Humankind had never accepted her.

"Alísa?" Her name snapped her from her numbness. The elders were looking at her now. "Will you agree to this?"

Alísa pulled in a breath. Despite the hardship this would put her clan through, this wasn't the worst of outcomes. The people hadn't reacted as she and Falier had wanted, had expected, but they were giving her another chance. Yet as she stared into the fire, unable to meet the eyes of the elders, that chance seemed so small. They were afraid of dragons who had faced death to protect them—what more could be done to convince them? And what hope did she have of gaining their trust if all she felt standing before them now was fear?

She rubbed the fabric of her skirt between her fingers. She had no other option. She couldn't just march into a slayer camp, declare who she and her dragons were, and expect anything besides bloodshed. She needed Me'ran just as much as she feared them.

Not trusting her voice, Alísa nodded and sealed her fate.

4

SPECTERS OF THE PAST

Three Years Prior

"A chief and his family should honor fallen warriors whenever the chance is given." Alísa's father looked down at her. His steady brown eyes gave her assurance as they approached a gathering of strange slayers. "Each one has given not only their blood for others, but their entire life as they came out of their families to serve with their whole being."

He gestured to the mountains behind them, one of them Alísa would later come to know as Rorenth's mountain. "It is rare that we have the opportunity to do so for a clan outside our territory, but Tella's father and I worked together to clear this pass of dragons two years ago, and she was among our warriors. This is why we cross from our territory into hers, to show our respect to the new chief and her dead."

Alísa's mother walked just behind them, her fingers once again adjusting Alísa's hair after the high winds of the mountain pass. She had braided a tight crown from Alísa's curls before leaving camp and had chosen a sky-blue dress that matched the thread of blue in the red and brown tartan sashes of the chief.

A man and a woman separated from the group of slayers, the woman drawing all of Alísa's attention. She walked with the swagger of a warrior. A quiver of short javelins lay against her back and a sword rested at her hip like she had been born with it. Scarred red dragon scale bracers, honey-blond braids tight against her scalp, and a rim of kohl around her eyes lent a sense of ferocity to the new chief.

Karn rested a hand on Alísa's shoulder, halting her alongside him. He brought his other hand over his heart, not fisted as a subordinate, but open in a sign of equality. Alísa fisted her own hand as she followed his lead.

"Chief Tella," Karn said. "It grieved me to hear of your father's passing. He was a good man and a valiant warrior."

Tella's eyes betrayed no emotion at the mention of her father, but her sorrow and that of her clan flowed through the astral plane like the breeze tugging at Alísa's hair.

"I know. Thank you." Tella's eyes lowered to meet Alísa's. "And who is this?"

Karn squeezed her shoulder—a signal to speak. Alísa swallowed down Tella's grief settling in her throat—a grief she herself would one day face as she, too, rose up to take her father's place. What should she say? Just her name? A condolence as her father had given?

"Alísa," she finally said. "I'm s—s—so sorry for your l—loss. B—B—Branni strengthen your hands."

A small laugh lifted Tella's lips. "There's no need to be afraid, girl. I don't bite."

Alísa swallowed. "I'm n—n—not—"

"She has a condition, Tella," her mother said, stepping forward to meet the new chief as well.

Heat rose into Alísa's cheeks, and she looked down. Her mother hadn't meant to shame her—Alísa's empathy made that very clear—yet it hurt all the same. Tella's gaze lingered on Alísa, the scrutinizing attention making her stomach churn until it moved on to Hanah.

Karn leaned in close and whispered. "Confidence..."

Memory filled in the rest of her father's phrase. '...covers weakness. Lift your eyes.'

Alísa clenched her skirts in her fingers, then forced her hands down and her eyes up. She wasn't afraid. She wouldn't be weak before Tella, a great warrior who had proven herself on the battlefield, fighting dragons even without the aid of telepathy. Alísa would never have such battle prowess, nor did she want it, but one day she would need the same confidence as she took Karn's place as chief.

Tella's gaze returned to Karn, a question in her eyes. "This is your whole family, then?"

"Immediate, yes. My brother and his family are back at camp."

She nodded absentmindedly, her gaze moving past Karn and over Alísa's head in the direction of their camp. "You've taken an apprentice, of course."

It was part question, part statement, as though the only correct answer was yes. Shame roiled in Alísa's belly, but no one seemed to notice her discomfort as her father told Tella of Kallar's recent injury that kept him from this meeting. Of his bravery in battle when his shield-partner pulled back from a dragon's flames and left his left side unprotected. Of how he had tamed the wild pain of the burns, turning it into a telepathic weapon that speared dragons from the sky as he waited for rescue.

A true slayer, and someone Tella would surely see as a worthy successor. Not like Alísa, who couldn't tame her stammer long enough to bring her father honor before his fellow chief.

Or soften slayers to the truth.

Or calm the fears of normals.

Sesína nuzzled Alísa's cheek, calling her back from the pain-filled memory. *"What Tella thought of you does not define you."*

Alísa sniffed back her tears, kneeling on the dancing grounds in the darkness of Sesína's winged embrace. *"But she was right. They all were. Tella, Toronn, my father. It all happened just as they predicted."*

A soft growl emanated from Sesína, bathed in the scent of clean, hot dragon-fire. *"Did they see you commanding dragons? Leading them in a battle that saved hundreds, perhaps thousands, of lives? You proved them wrong, and you will do it again."*

Alísa shook her head. *"I don't know if I can. I have the power of a Dragon Singer, but when it comes to leading humankind... I can't pull their attention like Yarlan, and I can't gain the respect Namor or the other elders have earned."*

Sesína opened her eyes, the green light of her gaze illuminating the dark space. *"You will gain their respect. What just happened sorely favored the others, but you have strengths of your own. You will show them."*

"It's all so wrong."

"Yes, it is. But we'll push through." Sesína bumped Alísa's shoulder with her snout. *"You always do, and the clan will follow your lead."*

Alísa breathed deeply, the air trembling in her chest. The thought should have been a comfort, but what if she failed them further? What if staying here and pushing through wasn't the correct choice? What if she couldn't make the villagers change their minds and it lost her the chance to reach slayers?

"What can I do?"

Falier's voice came from beyond Alísa's dragon-wing shield, low and contrite as though he had caused this. Now that the people had dispersed and their fear and anger were gone, Alísa released her hold on her empathy and felt the fog of his emotions seeping through the cracks in the wing shield. Many emotions twisted inside him, sorrow the greatest of all. What had happened hurt him too, perhaps just as much as it had hurt her, though in a different way.

"Let him see me," Alísa whispered through the bond.

Sesína pulled her wings away, allowing the cooling night air to hit Alísa's tear-streaked cheeks. Falier knelt just outside, hands fisted on his thighs and eyes full of concern. Alísa swiped at her tears and looked down.

"Oh Líse." Falier scooted forward. "I'm so sorry. I didn't—I never thought they'd react this badly."

"M—m—m—" The stammer rendered her silent again, bringing more tears. Why couldn't she get ahold of herself?

The buzz of Falier's telepathy came to life in her mind. *"Is this okay?"*

His voice was so quiet, borne by his ability alone rather than by Graydonn or another dragon. Though it indicated the lack of power that made him feel ashamed, in this moment it felt so very safe.

"Yes."

"What were you trying to say?"

"I never thought it would go this way, either. I knew people would be afraid, but—I thought the dragons' sacrifice and seeing what happened through our eyes would make them understand. The dragons aren't here to hurt anyone, to kill slayers, to take resources. They're heroes, and they're being treated like

villains. The people even treated you that way."

Alísa forced her eyes up. What mess had she gotten him into? *"I'm so sorry. Most new telepaths are treated poorly by normals when they're first revealed, but this—this was wrong. Me'ran knows you. They shouldn't have said the things they did. Especially Yarlan."*

Yarlan should have been the first to defend Falier, being perhaps only ten years Falier's senior and the father of two young boys who were sure to prove slayers themselves. The only reason he hadn't was because Falier sided with Alísa. Falier's people had turned on him because he stood with her.

Falier rubbed a soothing hand over her arm. *"That isn't your fault. I'm the one who kept my telepathy a secret, and I have no regrets about revealing it now. If anything, I should be thanking you for showing me I could use it."*

His gentle touch made her crave more. She reached for him, wrapping her arms around his waist. Falier returned the embrace, allowing her to bury her face in his shoulder.

"It will be all right," he whispered. "It's not what we wanted, but it only adds time before we reach our goal. We'll show them that the new dragons are just like Graydonn, Sesína, and Koriana. We'll prove we're working for peace, and Me'ran will help us win the slayers over. I'm sure of it."

Alísa wasn't sure. Falier's belief in her made her want to shrivel up and hide. She would disappoint him.

"You've beaten worse odds," Sesína whispered through their bond. *"Don't give up on yourself that easily. Neither of us will. Nor will the rest of the dragons—ack!—or these pesky dreki."*

Those last words made Alísa look back at Sesína. Ten or so dreki still watched from the trees behind her, but five of them clung to Sesína's head- and neck-spines. Laen sat on top of Sesína's head and chirped.

"Help."

The other dreki echoed Laen's declaration with chirps, barks, and telepathic words. If nothing else, Alísa had supporters among the other races.

A throat cleared behind Falier, and Alísa pulled away from him to look. Kat stood there, one of the final few humans on the dancing grounds. Her hands wrung her apron, and her eyes drooped with fatigue.

She jerked her head back toward the fire. "Namor would like to speak with you."

Trepidation swept through Alísa as she glanced at Namor and Tenza, the couple sitting on one of the logs at the fire. It seemed to be a running theme now for Namor to support her but always be held back by something. What did he have to say? How far could she trust him for aid?

Alísa swiped away the remnants of her tears and looked back to Falier and Sesína. "Stay with me?"

Sesína took a step forward, startling a couple of the dreki. *"As if you could keep me away."*

Falier reached up to pet Ska as the blue drek chose his shoulder as a replacement perch. "Of course."

Alísa led the way, exhaustion weighing down every step. A flicker of light drew her eyes to the Hold door, where Parsen and Selene reemerged. As the door closed behind them, figures moved inside the Hold. Falier had mentioned that a few families were living there while rebuilding their homes. Rorenth's scouts had destroyed multiple homes in their attack.

A strange mixture of guilt and fear prickled inside of her—guilt that she hadn't been able to stop the loss of property, and fear that the displaced families blamed her for that, too. She hadn't burned down the homes, and she had been part of the reason the rest of the village still stood, yet the feelings ached.

Alísa blew out her breath. She needed to be stronger. She wasn't a whimpering waif. She was Alísa-Dragon-Singer. Leader of dragons. Defender of the innocent.

Terrifier of the innocent.

Terrified.

Swallowing back the thought, Alísa sat on the log beside Namor's bench. Falier sat beside her, Sesína behind them, while the rest of the holders took the log on the other side of Falier. Laen hopped off Sesína as soon as Selene sat down, fluttering to the young holder's shoulder. The fire had died down but still illuminated each face clearly.

Namor looked at Alísa and breathed out his first word. "Twelve."

Alísa didn't know whether to smile with pride or duck her head in shame. Her empathy didn't even help—the only people she could feel were the holders. Even Tenza had her empathy bound so tightly that Alísa would have to stand right beside her to feel anything.

"Plus four little ones." Namor leaned on his knee. "You understand why the people reacted the way they did?"

Alísa swallowed. "How c-c-could I not? The remnants of their feelings c-crush me even now."

"Then you understand how careful you'll have to be in the coming weeks. One false step will send them into panic. They'll send messengers to the wayfarers, and the story will end here. We cannot repeat Bria's tragedy."

Scenes of fire and blood ran through Alísa's mind, and she shivered as the faces of the dead became the faces of Me'ran. Of Falier and his family.

"'Bria's tragedy'?" Parsen looked to Namor and Alísa in turn. "What am I missing?"

"A great deal," Tenza said. "This mess would be easier to clean if you and the rest of the world knew the tale."

She looked pointedly at Namor, something passing between them. Whether psychic words or the silent communication of couples who have spent decades together, Alísa couldn't tell. Namor gave a nearly imperceptible sigh as he looked back to the holders.

"What I am about to disclose is one of the Silent Stories—histories kept and passed on by chiefs and their seconds alone. They are the histories we wish to forget, yet duty compels us to remember. Secrets kept to protect the hearts and minds of our people."

"Secrets," Tenza said, her distaste palpable, "that hide past mistakes and leave us open to repeating them."

Namor closed his eyes as though they'd had this argument before. "One of these is the tale of Bria. The true tale of the first Dragon Singer, not the romanticized version of a stolen girl that the bards tell. Alísa has heard the story from the dragons' perspective already, but the slayers remember it differently."

Alísa leaned in. The visions she'd seen from Koriana were

memories passed on through Illumination and probably as close to the truth as possible, but the dragons wouldn't have known the slayers' side of the story.

The firelight played at the shadows of Namor's face as they did many a storyteller, but his face was graver and his voice lower than any storyteller Alísa could remember.

"Among the chiefs, the story is of a warrior woman who was kidnapped by dragons and then joined them. It was assumed the dragons bent her to their will after learning of the power in her songs. It was also assumed that when she and her dragons carved out a territory for themselves, they enslaved entire villages under them."

Namor looked to Alísa. "This, I think, is what Yarlan fears, though he has never heard the tale to the best of my knowledge."

Alísa nodded. Many slayers feared that a dragon might possess someone and bend them to their will. There had even been talk of it happening to her because of her dragon empathy—that she had a dragon inside her. Now that she knew dragons weren't spawns of the Nameless, she didn't know if draconic possession was actually possible—though their ability to compel a person through telepathy had been proven.

"The slayers who learned of Bria," Namor continued, "believed death was better than living under the control of dragons. When they faced Bria's army, they first tried desperately to free the villagers by killing only the dragons. In the end, however, they massacred both in the name of freeing human souls."

Falier tensed beside her, and the eyes of the holders went wide with horror. A chill passed over Alísa. Already knowing the story did nothing to settle her, and Namor's inflection said there was more to it.

"When the battle ended, Bria stood alone. A few dragons had escaped, and the slayers knew they had to free her soul before the beasts came back for her. They worked for days, telepathically trying to pull out the dragon inside of her, ignoring her protests that she had turned by her own free will. In their minds, no warrior such as her could ever have changed her mind so drastically—it had to have been possession."

Namor's eyes met Alísa's. "They couldn't believe it was true, not until they finally separated what they saw as the dragon from the woman." He looked down. "They ripped her *anam* from her body, killing her."

Alísa's heart skipped a beat. Ripped her soul from her body?

Talons scraped over packed earth as Sesína stood, her wings lifted as though to protect Alísa from the past. Falier's face paled, his fear matching Alísa's own.

"That's p-p-possible?"

"I do not tell this tale to frighten you," Namor said, his tone somber. "Only so you know the full cost should someone fear enough to call the wayfarers. Chief Segenn knows the tale and hopefully would avoid any rash decisions like attacking Me'ran, but it is a possibility."

Silence took the group, but Alísa's thoughts whirled. Things had seemed so simple before today. The people had accepted her and the three dragons, so coming back to Me'ran had made the most sense. Twi-Peak was a safe place for the wounded dragons and the dragonets soon to hatch, and Me'ran was the only place she had a chance to gain human aid before going to the slayers.

But now? Had she doomed this village to the same fate as Bria's?

Parsen looked to Namor. "I assume you have ideas of how to avoid this outcome?"

The slayer rubbed his chin. "It is a delicate balance we must find if Alísa is to win the people over and bring slayers to her side. On one hand, we must be cautious. Making the people more afraid will result in the wayfarers coming to investigate."

"On the other hand" —Tenza lifted a cautionary finger— "the fear already in the people will not alleviate itself. We must work to help them overcome it. That will require opportunities to see the dragons in a non-threatening light. Humanity will always fear what they do not understand, so keeping to yourselves in your caves is not the answer either."

Alísa pushed out a silent breath. Simply staying away from the village would be far easier, but it would merely prolong the problem and do nothing to help her find slayers willing to join the fight. But if she had just failed miserably in presenting her cause to normals, how could she possibly hope to win over battle-hardened slayers?

Alísa closed her eyes, forcing the thought back. There was no other way. She just had to make it work.

"I can have the dragons visit regularly. K-k-keeping to the rules of the c-compromise, the people can slowly g—get to know the new dragons. See that they want p-p-peace too and aren't a threat."

Falier grinned. "That's a great idea! They can come to the village square. There's plenty of room, and—"

"No."

All eyes turned to Alísa. She put her focus squarely on the fire. The word had leapt from her mouth without thought.

Sesína nosed her arm and whispered through the bond. *"I know you're afraid, but you can't avoid them forever."*

Alísa didn't respond. It wasn't just that, was it? There were logical reasons not to go to the square. She spoke carefully, keeping her stammer back as best she could.

"Not the square, near peoples' homes. Those most afraid of the dragons will feel threatened by that. And the square is w—where the main roads enter the village. We're more likely to be seen by p-p-p-people who don't know what's going on and might c—call the wayfarers."

Sesína's mind felt prickly as she accepted Alísa's answers. Unsatisfied, but apparently choosing not to argue at this time.

"What about here?" Selene offered. "The dancing grounds are big enough, and the Hold should block the dragons from sight of the paths entering the village."

"What about those coming in from the forests?" Parsen pointed an inquiring finger. "Hunters, like Alísa's imaginary family?"

"I did often wonder why they never came with you," Kat said quietly.

Alísa felt herself shrink under Kat's gaze. "I'm sorry. It was a n— necessary falsehood."

Silence took the group for a moment, then Falier looked to Alísa. "Graydonn has incredible empathic range. He would probably catch the mental signature of anyone coming in from the forest."

Alísa smiled. "Yes. I've seen him d—do it. He can even sense direction. He can k-k-keep a lookout."

The others seemed satisfied, and Namor straightened. "Then we have a plan. Maker help us all."

A glowing log in the fire pit popped, sending sparks into the air. Alísa watched as they all died out. Maker help them, indeed. Wasn't bringing humans and dragons together His mission for her? Then why had He allowed tonight to go so wrong? Why had He picked her for this task? Or, if it had to be her, why did He give her the speech impediment that kept humans from hearing her?

Silence covered the space for a moment before Kat finally spoke. "Namor, Tenza, thank you. I feel better about this with you at our backs. Can we offer you a room tonight, so you don't have to go home in the dark?"

Tenza looked to Namor, who nodded to the holder. "I believe we'll take you up on that. Thank you."

"What about you, Alísa?" Parsen said. "Or will you go back to the cave?"

Alísa shook her head. "Thank you, b—but I'm going to go home. The c-c-c-clan needs to know what happened." And as much as she didn't want to recount everything, the thought of facing the dragons seemed infinitely better than facing those staying at the Hold.

A quiet groan turned Alísa's eyes to Namor, where Tenza supported him as he stood. It was so easy to forget his missing leg—he was so strong and sure in everything. Why couldn't she be like him?

Alísa looked down as he caught her staring, then forced her eyes up again. "Thank you, for your help today."

Namor leaned on his staff, his smile tired but genuine. "The path you've chosen is a difficult one. Perhaps in helping you tread it, I will begin to atone for our peoples' many mistakes. For my many mistakes."

Alísa blinked. What could she say to that? Were there even any words?

"Good night," Tenza said softly, as though she knew Alísa didn't know how to respond.

"Good night," Alísa said as the two slayers followed Kat to the Hold.

What should she make of those two? Fear and anger filled her first memories of them, and even though they sided with her now, the feelings hadn't fully gone away. It was like what she had felt toward Koriana before the bond to Sesína changed everything—a fear of something that could crush her, even though she believed it wouldn't.

It seemed so surreal, the happenings of today. She longed to wake up to a world where people weren't afraid, one where they accepted her.

While she was dreaming, perhaps also a world where Rayna's wing wasn't shredded, Iila's parents had turned and come with them, the eggs had already bonded to dragons in her clan, and Sareth and Chrí were still alive. Perhaps the whole week had just been a bad dream.

An arm slid around her shoulders and pulled her in. "I know that look. I wish I could make it better."

Alísa leaned into Falier's embrace, soaking in his affection. "You help."

A wave of happiness came off him, and he planted a tender kiss in her hair. Butterflies flitted in her stomach, and she grasped onto the positive emotions like a drowning woman. Not all of the past week had been bad.

'Cling to joy,' her father had once told her when training to control her empathy. When it was too much for her to handle, she just needed to find joy and refuse to let it go. Sesína's growth, the dragons' respect, Namor and Tenza's support, Falier's arms. She couldn't let it all get lost in the noise, not now and not tomorrow when she once again would face the people's fear. And her own.

5

A HOLDER'S RETURN

An eerie quiet hung over the Hold as Falier and his family served their people, the tension of last night still palpable. The sounds of utensils clanking against wooden plates and of tea pouring from his mother's kettle overpowered the hushed conversations.

There had been far more chatter yesterday. Aside from Namor and Tenza, this group were all neighbors—three families affected by the attack by Rorenth's scouts a little over a week ago. Their lives had been changed by the introduction of the dragons, so last night must have been particularly grueling for them. But while a few here understood that the damage to the village would have been worse—perhaps even total—if not for Graydonn and the others, over half of them seemed to only get a bad taste in their mouths at the word "dragon."

"Holder Falier?" Serra's seven-year-old son held his empty plate over his head. "I'm done!"

The boy's eagerness, stark against the silence, drew a smile from Falier. "That was fast."

His ten-year-old brother rolled his eyes. Or attempted to—his whole head moving instead, swinging the warrior braids that reminded Falier of Kerrik. "I tried to tell him he still has to wait before playing. Ma says he'll puke if he runs too hard after eating."

Serra grimaced, putting a hand out toward him. "The whole Hold doesn't need to know that."

Falier did his best not to laugh. "No building for you boys today?"

The younger boy rested his head on his fist. "No. Mamá says everything's too heavy."

Serra ruffled his hair. "Maker willing, you'll get to help us seal the gaps in the boards in a few days."

The boy pushed his mother's hand away and Falier let out his pent-up chuckle, taking the empty plate back to the kitchen. They were good kids, and Serra a good woman. That Kerrik had been taken from them so early in their family's life was a terrible wrong. The war had to end. Why did so many people oppose his and Alísa's efforts to make it so? Did they not see it every day in the eyes of Serra and her children? In Namor's injury and his daughter's flight? In Taz's absence?

After many more returned dishes, Falier went out to the well by the stables and filled a bucket of water for washing. He looked up at Twi-Peak, squinting to see if any dragons were out yet. The visit would be nearer the lunch hour, but most of them had been cooped up for a couple days now. After two days of rest from the battle, they were probably ready to stretch their wings and hunt.

Falier passed his mother going down to the cellar as he brought the water to Selene and his father. Kat barely glanced his way, focused on the next task. The flat, round baskets she carried on her hip needed to be filled with food for those of the village who couldn't support themselves.

He poured the water into the dish-washing basin, then hurried to fill another bucket for rinsing. Delivery day. Typically a favorite of his, but now a tension settled in his stomach. The people he and his mother would deliver food to today were more likely to voice their opinions than the subdued crowd in the Hold. Normally, he enjoyed long conversations with them, but today likely wouldn't be a day filled with stories and banter.

Still, as his first delivery day since returning, it would be good to see them one-on-one again.

Grabbing a few more baskets and desperately wishing for some of the bread just coming out of the oven, Falier headed for the cellar. A chill tickled at his skin as he descended into the dark, his eyes adjusting slowly. Kat stood in the back corner, picking out potatoes and root vegetables for her baskets. She looked up at his entrance, then went back to her selection.

"I'm a little surprised to see you here," she said. "No dragon waiting to whisk you away?"

Falier chuckled, stopping at the fruit boxes to grab peaches and pears. "Maybe after the visit, but I told them I've got chores. Can't miss the deliveries."

"Didn't stop you last week."

Falier stopped, setting a pear back in the box. "Ma, I had to go. Alísa and the dragons needed a slayer with them. We had to stop Rorenth before he attacked Me'ran again."

"And what about now? Namor seems to think we're in even more danger now."

Falier swallowed, Bria's story filling his head. "That's why we have to make this work—why I'm going to tell everyone I can about the dragons visiting today. We all have a role to play."

His mother looked down. Her inhalation became audible, as though she wanted to say something but kept thinking better of it. What had gotten into her? She was usually so calm, so patient, so ready with words of wisdom and encouragement.

"Ma? What's going on?"

"It shouldn't have been you," she whispered. She gripped the side of the vegetable box harder and looked up at him, her voice rising. "You did the right thing, but it shouldn't have been you. Alísa needed a slayer—it should have been Yarlan who went with her, not you. Not my son, who was told that if he ever stepped onto the battlefield, he—"

Her voice cracked and she looked away, her arms shaking as she leaned against the wooden box. Falier's own heart shook. What should he say? How could he help her? He took another step, then felt a hand on his shoulder.

"Take Selene today," his father said. In this moment, Parsen seemed to have taken on Kat's unwavering calm, his gaze steady rather than constantly seeking the next thing. He walked past Falier to where Kat stood with her face in her hands. Parsen whispered something to her, his words too low for Falier to make out, and escorted her out of the cellar with a comforting hand around her waist. Kat's skirt brushed Falier's pant leg as she passed, the contact strangely unsettling, as though coming up against a barrier between them that neither could cross. Could he do anything to make it right?

Selene came down into the darkness of the cellar. She still wore her apron, her hair up in the bun she used when working the kitchen, and she carried a deeper basket than the others, with loaves individually wrapped in white linens. She tilted her head in question.

Falier nodded at the door. "Has she been like this since I left?"

Selene went to the baskets their mother had left behind. "Not outwardly, but her voice has carried the weight." She picked up a potato, checking for signs of rot. "We were all worried, you know."

Falier sighed and turned back to the fruit boxes. "I didn't mean to cause such strife."

"I know. But they'll need more than a song and dance and a confession of love to a girl who lied to them before they're ready to let you go. Especially Mamá. You're her baby."

Falier moved to the next section, where the grains and spices were stored. "Any advice?"

"Just gradual exposure. The visits with Alísa and the dragons should help, but she also needs to see you safe and competent in their world. Prove Kerrik's warnings wrong. It's not just that you want to be in that world—you belong there."

Selene looked at him with those eyes that saw everything. "And you do belong there, right? It's not just your infatuation with Alísa?"

Falier closed his eyes for a moment, feeling the air that rushed past him while flying, the spot at the back of his mind where his bond to Graydonn sat, the wonder of giants like Koriana and Saynan considering him a friend.

"Yes."

Selene nodded once and turned back to her work. "I'll take the west side."

Falier smiled gratefully. Yarlan lived on that side of the village, and since his trade was slaying, his family needed a delivery.

"Thank you." He hesitated. "Be sure to tell Yarlan too, about the visit today. As much as I'd like to keep him away, if he finds out some other way—"

"Already planned to." Selene carried her baskets to the cellar steps. "I'll see you at the visit."

Falier grabbed a loaf from the pile she had left. "See you then."

Me'ran wasn't the village Falier remembered. A tense silence hung over it as he entered. Though shops opened and the people went about their daily lives, the colors, voices, and moods all seemed subdued. Even the children playing kickball in the street seemed to play less for fun and more for necessity, focusing hard on the ball and forgetting to laugh.

Of course, it was hard to laugh when playing near three houses now reduced to piles of ash. Serra and other adults worked on the new skeleton of one of them.

Falier stopped briefly to tell the workers about the dragons' visit in the next couple of hours. One of the workers seemed interested, others—including Serra—nodded noncommittally, and two turned away as soon as "dragon" left Falier's mouth. He should have expected it after last night, but disappointment flooded him all the same.

Shifting his hold on the pile of three baskets, Falier headed for a small home with patches of flowers and vegetables. A few bees picked their way through the garden, showing more life than anyone else Falier had seen today.

Setting the baskets beside the door, he picked up the top one and looked it over, ensuring it was the correct delivery. Two women lived here—sisters, one widowed and one never married—and the elder had struggled with a persistent cough the last few days. Selene had given him a pouch with the tea their mother made to help.

Assured he had the right basket, Falier knocked the rhythmic pattern he always used.

Footsteps shuffled inside and soon the door opened to reveal Sendi. Her white hair pulled back in a bun, though a few stray curls made it look as though she had just thrown it together before answering the door. Her hazel eyes brightened as they landed on Falier, sending cool relief through him.

"Well, Falier, this is a pleasant surprise! I didn't think you would be making these deliveries anymore."

He grinned. "And miss seeing my favorite troublemakers? How is

Marris—has her cough gotten any better?"

"Much."

"Good. Ma sends her love—"

"Love isn't what did it, dear." Sendi bent down to grab an empty basket from inside the door. "I certainly hope Kat sent more tea."

Falier chuckled, exchanging baskets with her. "It's in a pouch under the potatoes."

"Very good. I would invite you in, but it might still be catching." She leaned against the doorframe. "Oh, but it is so good to see you back to your normal duties. The way you left without warning and then stood at the dragon girl's side all last night had us worried."

A warning pinched in Falier's stomach. "Worried?"

"That you were leaving us. Would stay up there" —Sendi pointed to Twi-Peak— "away from your people."

Falier drummed his fingers on the underside of the basket. He *was* leaving Me'ran, just not yet. Sendi was chatting amiably, like normal. After Ma's reaction and the builders', was there harm in letting her continue with this train of thought until emotions calmed down and Me'ran was on their side again?

Coward. That course of action wouldn't serve anyone but himself.

Falier cleared his throat. "Not yet, no. When Alísa and her clan leave, I'll be going with them, but that won't be for a while."

Sendi straightened, brow furrowing with concern. "Then, you are leaving us. All for a girl you barely know. There are plenty of nice girls here and in Soren."

Falier fought not to sigh. "Sendi, that isn't why—"

"I saw the way you looked at her last night. That girl—"

"Alísa." The correction came more sharply than intended.

"—has you wrapped around her finger. I never thought I'd see the day you, of all people, would choose a pretty face over your village."

Falier shook his head, searching for words. "I'm not. It's not her versus you."

Sendi gave him a severely patient look. "Just because you don't want it to be doesn't stop it from being so. You were there, dear—you heard the arguments. She and her dragons are disrupting the peace."

Falier set the empty basket down and held out his hands in entreaty. "Peace is what we're working for. Peace between the races ultimately affects Me'ran too. You remember the dragon attack last week, and how Taz and other slayers have been taken away from their families to fight in the war. She's working to stop all of it, and for the first time in my life I've been told I can help. I want to help."

"You help here." Sendi pointed at the ground. "Used to be that was enough for you. Now, when your people are wounded and frightened, you plan to abandon us?"

"I might be leaving, but I'm not abandoning you. I'm not doing this for Alísa." *Not solely for her, anyway.* Falier reached for Sendi. "I want to help protect you. It's what I should have been doing all along as a slayer, but better, because I'm working to end the fight."

She shook her head, pulling back behind the door as a shine filled her eyes. "Holder or slayer, you have a duty to this village. Not to the world, not to strangers—Me'ran. Seeing you outside my door today, I thought you knew that."

"Sendi—"

"Thank your mother for the tea."

The thud of the door shutting knifed a hole in Falier's heart. He stared at the wooden panels, unable to move or breathe.

How—

Why—

What had just happened?

If even Sendi was angry with him, what hope did he have for facing the rest of the village? Did everyone think he was abandoning them?

Falier forced a breath and bent to retrieve the baskets. Was she right? Was he turning his back on Me'ran? Was all his reasoning just an excuse?

No! No, of course not. He was a slayer and mind-kin to a dragon—he belonged in Alísa's clan now, fighting to show the world that human and dragon-kind could live together in peace.

He clutched the rough wicker. He was also a son of holders, unused to war and death. Flashes from battles past had plagued his dreams. Thoughts of his own death, or another's because he wasn't strong enough.

Thoughts of his people burning in another dragon attack.

Holder.

Slayer.

Me'ran.

Alísa and the dragons.

It wasn't an either-or question, and yet, it was. He told Selene earlier that he belonged with the dragons, but now? Now strained and broken relationships weighed like stones in his lungs, pulling at his breaths. This village, these people, were also where he belonged.

Falier stepped off the porch and back onto the road. His pulse pounded in his temples like a percussionist untrained in dynamics. He needed it to settle before he made his next delivery.

"Eldra Nahne," he prayed at a whisper as he walked, far more comfortable with the Eldra who shepherded holders than with Branni who guided warriors. Maybe one day he would reach out to Branni with the confidence of a slayer, but not today. "Help me serve my people today. If you've any strength of the Maker's to spare, I ask for it now. Help me calm their fears and build a bridge between my two worlds."

A change in sunlight lifted his eyes to the sky. Clear and blue, not a cloud in sight, yet with colorful shapes spearing through it. Six dragons raced over the village, drawing gasps of both delight and fear from the villagers. The dragons flew from Twi-Peak in a westerly direction, either about to train or just stretching their wings over the uninhabited parts of the forest.

Falier stopped walking and focused, reaching out to the green dragon near the rear. *"Good morning, Graydonn."*

The dragon's steady calm turned to a light happiness. *"Falier, shall I come for you? Saynan's going to have us spar before the visit."*

Graydonn banked back toward the village as his emotions turned to something else. It felt negative, but Falier couldn't yet recognize the exact emotion, even with Graydonn's next words.

"You are distressed, my friend?"

Falier breathed, trying to steady his emotions. *"I'll be all right. It's been a long day already. I need to finish my chores before the visit. If you have time afterward, though, I think a fly would do me good. Maybe after lunch?"*

Graydonn circled overhead, his glowing amber eyes now distinguishable amid the grass green scales. As Graydonn looked down, Falier felt a shifting in his own mind, as though the part connected to Graydonn were moving about.

Graydonn's tone softened. *"I am sorry. One day, they will understand."*

Falier looked back at Sendi's house, then to the people who had stopped to watch the dragon circle. *"Maybe some. I don't think they all will."*

Silence took the mind-link for a moment, then a flow of warmth from Graydonn began filling it. Peace. It was gentle enough that even a weak telepath could reject it if he wanted, but as it soothed over the ache in his heart and quieted the pounding of his pulse, Falier just breathed it in.

"I will do all I can to help you reach them," Graydonn said. *"I know how much you care for them."*

Falier blew out a breath. *"Thank you."* He looked back up at his mind-kin. *"Go on, train hard. I'll see you soon."*

Graydonn changed his course, flying back toward the other dragons with a light trumpet. The watching villagers looked from Graydonn to Falier, questions in their eyes. With breath filling his lungs a little more easily, Falier put on the carefree holder mask he had used so many times.

"The dragons are going out for some flight-training, and they plan to visit a little later at the Hold. Graydonn was just saying how much he hoped people would come say hello."

Again, a mixture of reactions came from the people. Some looked back up after Graydonn, brows furrowed. A couple of children pulled on their mother's arms and begged to go see the dragons. A few adults whispered to each other in tones Falier couldn't make out. It would be a while before the village settled again.

Falier adjusted his grip on the baskets and set his pace to match his calming pulse. He had two more deliveries to make—two more opportunities for either joy or heartache. He would press on, as he had learned to all his life.

Do his duty.

Serve the people.

MICHELLE M. BRUHN

And smile for them, even when it was just a mask.

6

THE FIRST VISIT

The hot summer air turned cool as it whipped past Alísa and Sesína, invigorating and breath-stealing. Sesína banked, joy filling both dragon and rider as ebony wings caught a new air current. Together in the sky, minds open and uninhibited, only the flight existed. Gravity their enemy, the whipping winds their uneasy ally, and the sky a reward reserved only for those with the courage to continually face and defy gravity's hold.

Underneath them, the great forest looked like mere blades of grass. With no large clearings in sight, they were safe from view of unsuspecting villagers. Alísa couldn't even see Me'ran. Strange how something so terrifying and all-consuming last night now appeared so small. It shouldn't have affected her so badly. At today's visit, she would need to keep panic at bay.

Alísa tightened the tie holding back her mahogany curls and focused on the Illumination bond. *"Think we have time for one more dive?"*

Sesína scoffed. *"There's always time for one more!"*

"I mean before Saynan starts the next round—"

Sesína dove. The sudden motion nearly threw Alísa, but she clamped her legs to the dragoness' withers and latched her fingers to the spine in front of her. Gravity had them now, pulling them faster and faster toward the forest below. The wind whisked away perspiration as quickly as it came and stole Alísa's breath as they passed their training partners.

Alísa braced herself as she felt Sesína's mental countdown. With a satisfying snap, Sesína spread her wings. Gravity's death grip turned to forward momentum, shooting them over the forest.

A happy rumble ran through Sesína's chest as she pumped her

wings, once again lifting them into the sky. They passed Koriana, Graydonn, and Komi as they headed back, aiming for a higher level of sky where two other dragons waited. Saynan, the ice dragon, instructed them today, pairing the clan's four adolescent dragons in sparring matches. Harenn, a red-scaled adolescent, hovered alongside him. Two years Sesína's senior, Harenn was bulkier and a foot taller at the withers, bringing Sesína's competitive nature to life.

The buzz of a new telepathic connection entered Alísa's mind. Saynan.

"Begin!"

Alísa and Sesína jolted to attention. Saynan typically waited for the dragons to be level with each other before starting a match, but they were still a few hundred feet below Harenn. The young red dove at them, gravity completely on his side.

Sesína yelped and swerved into her own dive, Alísa gripping her spine in panic.

"Remember, you don't always get to choose when the battle begins." The ice dragon's teaching voice was irritatingly calm. *"Rorenth was distracted when we came to him—most of the time the enemy won't wait for you to say 'Go.'"*

They had almost reached the trees again, gaining speed but putting little distance between them and Harenn. Sesína flapped hard to pull parallel with the ground, then swerved left, Harenn directly behind them. Alísa clung hard, knuckles white on Sesína's spine as the small dragoness snapped and spun from side to side to avoid their attacker.

"Harenn," Saynan said, his telepathy reaching all combatants. *"They haven't used their greatest weapon yet—now is your time to strike!"*

Alísa sucked in a breath. His instruction for Harenn subtly instructed her too—she should be singing. She reached for her strength song, but a light pain in Sesína's tail shocked her voice to a stop.

"That slap of Harenn's paw counts as a bite, Sesína." Saynan said as Sesína swerved away again. *"In a true battle, your balance would be off, and your turns would become slower. One more hit and you're dead."*

A sliver of panic rose in Sesína—they couldn't lose, not yet! *"Sing! Help me put distance between us!"*

Alísa sang, latching onto the strength song she had used many times before. She focused on their bond, pushing power into Sesína, while ignoring Saynan and Harenn's mental signatures. As the song melted into Sesína, the dragoness' fatigue began to lift. Next time, Alísa would remember to sing right away.

"Hang on tight." Sesína flashed an idea into Alísa's mind.

Alísa's stomach fell into her throat as Sesína pulled up sharply and back-flipped over Harenn. They moved so fast that Harenn had only just started swerving away by the time they were upright again.

"Nicely done," Saynan said.

Sesína gave chase as Harenn swept into an updraft, rising high above the forests. Alísa's strength coursed into Sesína and they gained altitude quickly. Sesína focused on Harenn's tail, ready to return the blow he had dealt her.

"Almost..."

Harenn twisted and dropped. Sesína flapped backward as they nearly collided. A light pain echoed through Alísa as Harenn slapped Sesína's tail again.

"And that's the round!" Saynan declared. *"Well won, Harenn."*

Alísa leaned over to see Harenn gliding out of his fall and turning a couple of victory circles.

"Combatants, to me," Saynan ordered.

Sesína pointed her nose at their instructor, her mood darkening.

Alísa patted Sesína's neck. *"Next time. You're still getting used to having a rider, and I should have sung for you sooner."*

Sesína snorted. *"You make it sound like it's all your fault. I'm the one making the wrong flight decisions."*

Sesína breathed heavily as she and Harenn pulled up on either side of Saynan. The three dragons began a long, loose circle as Saynan's light, sincere tone replaced his disconnected instructor voice.

"Your flip was well-executed, Sesína. You were quick enough not to lose your rider, and you turned Harenn's advantage around. Your agility impresses me."

Alísa smiled as Sesína's self-criticism lifted slightly, though she still harbored irritation at Saynan's surprise start. Alísa rubbed Sesína's hot scales, whispering through the Illumination bond.

"He's our teacher. It's his job to catch us off-guard like that. Better now than in an actual battle."

"I know. Doesn't mean I have to like it."

Saynan turned sapphire eyes on Harenn. *"Your tight follow of Sesína's twists and turns was astounding. As you grow, however, it will become less and less an option. When following an opponent, try to stay above them rather than directly behind. It will allow you more options even when you cannot keep up."*

Harenn's deep brown eyes brightened with understanding.

"Good. Well done, all of you. That was the final match, I believe. Singer?"

Alísa glanced at the sun, comparing its position in the sky to Twi-Peak. She tried to hold back her trepidation. *"It is indeed."*

The dragons angled into a lazy descent, aiming for the others, who flew a few hundred feet above the trees. Saynan widened the mind-link to bring Koriana, Graydonn, and Komi into the conversation.

"By the Singer's word, it's time for our visit."

Three pairs of eyes brightened at Saynan's words, and happiness pulsed from Graydonn.

"Falier says he is almost finished with his chores," Graydonn said. *"He'll be at the Hold shortly."*

A wave of relief ran through Alísa. The presence of the dragons would help her feel comfortable in front of the people, but the more friendly faces there the better.

Sesína pulled up alongside Koriana, the storm-gray dragoness dwarfing Sesína. Alísa reached out specifically to her, though knowing the others in the mind-link would all hear her too.

"Thank you for coming with me. I know it's not going the be the most comfortable thing for some of you." She glanced at Harenn behind them. *"But this is very important."*

Koriana sent back an affirmative, while Harenn barely brightened his eyes in acknowledgement. Alísa was dragging him into this—there might have been a better dragon to choose in his stead, but the dancing grounds would be cramped as it was. Bringing another large adult dragon instead of an adolescent would be too much.

Sesína banked and made a lazy circle over the Hold. Twelve people gathered already—Parsen, Selene, Namor, and Tenza among them. Alísa didn't see Falier or Kat.

Alísa braced herself as Sesína flapped to slow her momentum, ready for the inevitable jarring of the landing. Instead, she felt Sesína's sharp focus as the dragoness set down with as much grace as possible before the spectators.

Alísa smirked to herself. *Seems we all feel the need to perform.*

Dismounting, Alísa kept a hand on Sesína's withers, while the ground trembled with the other dragons' landings. Koriana and Harenn settled behind the others, their tails in the trees at the edge of the dancing grounds. The rest landed near Sesína, their bright eyes on the people.

Alísa focused on the clan's mind-link. *"Lower to your bellies. You'll look less threatening."*

Alísa placed a gentle hand on Komi's brown-scaled wither to lend the people a sense of safety. Komi was the oldest of the adolescents, practically an adult and close to Koriana's size, but her bright green eyes retained the wide-open curiosity of a younger dragon. Saynan was the largest dragon here today, his head seven feet off the ground despite lying on his belly.

Alísa stared at him, taking in the creature she once thought only a beast. The sharpness of his spines and talons, the angular shape of his face, and the glow of his eyes would terrify her if she didn't know him. How far she had come. How far these villagers still had to go.

"Hello, everyone. Meet Saynan, K-K-K-Komi, and Harenn." She gestured to each dragon in turn. "Please, c-c-come and introduce yourselves. And remember, d—dragons speak t-t-t-t-t-telepathically, but they aren't d—delving into your thoughts. I trust them with my mind and my life."

Cautiously, the people approached. Eyes flitted between the dragons and Namor, looking to the slayer for his reaction. Namor leaned on his staff with the watchful eyes of a shepherd, perhaps trying to discern whether the dragons before him were wolves, sheep, or fellow shepherds.

"Welcome, dragons of the Singer's clan," he said, his voice low and authoritative. "I am Namor, son of Lamik, the chief slayer of this village."

Saynan lowered his head closer to the humans' level. *"Thank you for the invitation into your village, Slayer. I've flown over many human villages, but never seen one this close."*

Alísa smiled. Subtle way to tell them he had never attacked a human village.

Saynan indicated the Hold with his muzzle. *"The way you construct caves for yourselves is impressive."*

Parsen cleared his throat. "Thank you. We call them houses."

Saynan tried the word. *"Houses. Thank you. What is your name?"*

"Parsen. I'm Falier's father."

Saynan's eyes brightened. *"Falier-kin! Your son brings you great honor. He is quick to listen and has proven himself in battle in a way perhaps no human ever has, utilizing a mind-kin bond to strengthen his own psychic abilities. You should be proud."*

Sadness tilted Parsen's eyes as he dipped his head in thanks. "I am."

"I've never heard of a white dragon before," a bald man said, caution in his tone.

Alísa smiled. Growing up, she had seen rare white dragon scales in a few pieces of jewelry, but had always assumed they were like an albino animal. In truth, white dragons were their own separate race, one that lived in the highest caves of the Prilune mountain range, far south of her father's wayfaring territory.

Saynan huffed a breath into the air, sending ice crystals swirling like snowflakes over his audience and garnering murmurs of delight. The bald man launched into questions about ice dragons, which Saynan answered with grace. Taking courage from their conversation, Komi sent her own flurry of questions about each person's hair, or lack thereof.

On the other side of Alísa, Sesína and Graydonn entertained their own small group of adults and one young teenage boy. No children, even though many of them had been allowed to meet Sesína a week ago. Perhaps last night had frightened off all of the parents, maybe even the children themselves.

"Hail, Falier!" Saynan's words drew Alísa's eyes toward the village. Falier and two other elders emerged over the top of the hill near the Hold. *"I wondered when you would show."*

Falier grinned, slipping into the dragon's telepathic conversation. *"Some of us have to work for a living."*

Emotions shifted in the gathered humans, moving closer to unease. Parsen silently tapped a finger to his temple, looking pointedly at his son.

Falier cleared his throat, switching to vocal speech. "Good to see you all here."

Alísa let out a quiet sigh. If only Parsen knew how far his son had come—what it meant for him to be able to automatically respond with telepathy.

"How long since you learned how to speak that way, Falier?" The elder Meira gave an encouraging smile. Her husband, Garrick, gave her a look, as though he thought speaking of telepathy a faux pas, but she ignored it. "If Kerrik only taught you a basic shield, it must have been fairly recently?"

Falier glanced at his father, answering with measured words. "Graydonn started teaching me about a month ago."

"What else have you learned?" Meira scoffed at Garrick's elbow in her side. "Don't you start. I've always been curious about the slayers' gift."

Tenza crossed her arms. "You could have asked us any time, Meira."

"Oh please, with that grump husband of yours?" Meira winked at Namor, who seemed to take the title with pride.

Alísa's smile faded as movement caught her eye. Yarlan crested the hill to the Hold, a scowl already on his face. Like last night, he wore his sword and warrior's braids. His sharp eyes caught hers and she looked away, lightning flooding her senses.

Stop it, she told herself. *There's no way he's coming for a fight—no slayer can take on six dragons.*

Yet a greater fear swirled—one far more likely to come true and too raw to assuage.

"He's probably here to keep an eye on us." Sesína stood behind her now, having sensed Alísa's growing anxiety. She growled quietly in her throat. *"Most of the people here are our allies. It won't be a repeat of last night."*

Alísa breathed, glad that the Illumination bond didn't force her to put words to her inner turmoil. She should have been able to keep the crowd pacified last night, even as they voiced their fears and concerns.

Her father could have done it.

"Is that the slayer, Alísa?" The buzz of Koriana's telepathy ignited in their minds. *"The one who caused all the trouble?"*

Alísa looked back at the dragoness rising to her feet. Anger simmered in Koriana, though not yet a boil.

Alísa considered her response. While Koriana's ire in her favor was a comfort, she didn't need the dragoness making things worse. *"He's the one who spoke first, but the others' fears weren't fully based in him. He merely gave them the courage to speak out, and scared me into silence."*

She cringed as the last thought slipped through. What kind of leader was she if one man could steal her ability to speak?

A rumble resonated from Koriana's throat. *"Then you should face him, Singer. Do not let fear in his presence become habit."*

Anxiety clenched in her stomach again. Koriana was probably right. She chanced a glance at Yarlan, who had settled back against the Hold wall, arms crossed.

The sounds of Koriana lying back down turned Alísa's gaze. At her questioning glance, Koriana blinked slowly.

"If I physically stand behind you, it will eliminate your power. You must go to him on your own. But" —a growl rumbled in her throat— *"I will be watching."*

Sesína lashed her tail, disagreeing with Koriana. *"I'll go with you."*

Alísa shook her head. *"I don't want you anywhere near him. The same goes for the other dragons. That will only antagonize him more."*

Sesína snorted her annoyance, then prodded Alísa's shoulder. *"He's just a loudmouthed bully, like that nasty Paili."* She pushed memories into Alísa's mind of the great red alpha dragoness who had tried to silence her, then of the dragons who had followed her despite Paili's attacks. *"You've faced that and won before."*

Alísa blew out her breath. Yes, she had faced something similar before. But Paili was a dragon, and Alísa's song silenced her arguments. The same trick wouldn't work for Yarlan. A Dragon Singer's songs were tuned to a dragon's heart, and they could see her own heart through them. They could still reject her, but they could not deny the truth in her words.

64

Humans, on the other hand, could feel the power in her lyrics and see the images she sent, but they could not know her through the songs in the same way as dragons.

Yarlan's gaze fell on her as she approached, and Alísa forced herself to keep moving. *Head high, lift your eyes, you are a chief.*

Pretender. Her own mind argued back.

Komi thrummed behind her, and Yarlan's eyes darted to the dragon, becoming daggers. She had seen that look on slayers before, just before they attacked with psychic spears.

"Wait!" Heart pounding, Alísa raised her hand. "It's laughter, d—don't—"

Many gazes shifted to her, including Yarlan's. He raised a condescending eyebrow.

"Do you truly think I would break the compromise?" He looked her up and down. "I am no fool who lets panic reign in me."

Alísa's cheeks heated, his tone making the subtext perfectly clear. She had let panic win, just like last night. She didn't dare turn her eyes from Yarlan, for fear the people would see shame written all over her face.

Quiet speech began again as Parsen attempted to restart conversation. Maker bless the holders. Alísa swallowed, trying to loosen her throat muscles as Yarlan's gaze still held her. Her voice came barely above a whisper.

"W—what are you d—doing here? I thought you were against the dragons c-c-coming."

"I am." He looked back out over the dancing grounds. "But I am for Me'ran. If any threat is near, I will be there."

Love flowed with those words. Its psychic scent was deceptively light, but the fact that she could feel it despite his telepathic shield spoke to its strength. If only she could make him see that his people weren't in danger, he could be a great ally, like Namor.

"Run and play with your little monsters," Yarlan said, watching Saynan with unblinking eyes. "The truth always comes out, and eventually this dream will reveal itself as the nightmare it is."

Alísa fought not to shudder with the weight of his words. If she walked away now, it would be on his terms, but she desperately wanted to leave. Needed to leave. She had no chance with Yarlan as it currently stood, but there were people here who perhaps could be swayed by her presence.

Without another word, Alísa returned to Sesína and Graydonn's group.

"Where are you going?" Koriana's hard voice entered her mind. *"You are an alpha—you do not bow to the likes of him."*

Alísa swallowed, trying to keep tears from forming at the dragoness' disapproval. *"Leaving might lower my standing in his eyes, but staying won't raise it."*

"If you back down now, you will always back down."

Alísa winced, unable to refute the statement.

"He's not worth her time," Sesína hissed. *"Let her focus on the people actually giving her a chance."*

Sesína opened a wing to Alísa, letting her stand in the comforting warmth of her inner fire. The people in the circle, oblivious to their psychic words, chatted amiably with Graydonn. A little wariness wafted around the circle, but no true fear or anger.

Alísa relaxed. Good things were happening here.

She glanced back at Koriana, noting that Harenn watched as well. *"Yarlan loves his people. If there's any chance to get to him, it's through them."*

The visit lasted until lunchtime, with a few people coming and going as time passed. Alísa kept watchful eyes on each group, switching between them now and again, but mostly allowing conversation to flow without her. Warmth filled her heart each time laughter sprang up, the dragons and holders all doing their part to make the small crowd comfortable. Only Yarlan never relaxed, his eyes sending cold through Alísa's heart each time they landed on her. Koriana spoke rightly—Alísa was on a path that led only to fear when she encountered Yarlan. And yet, what more could she do?

Alísa watched as the people dispersed, some to the Hold, some to their homes. Falier came up beside her, his emotions a mixture of happiness and tension as he looked out at the emptying dancing grounds.

"A good first day, I think."

Alísa hummed in agreement. "Everyone handled themselves well." Her eyes landed on Yarlan still in his spot, glaring at the dragons. She swallowed. "Except for me."

Falier looked at her, an eyebrow raised. "You were great. You helped the people feel comfortable around creatures twice their size."

"I m—meant with Yarlan. I shouldn't have—" Alísa shook her head, choosing a different path. "I wish he hadn't c-c-come. He would find out anyway, with you and Selene spreading the w—word during deliveries, but if we had just one day without him..."

She stopped as guilt wafted from Falier. He rubbed the back of his neck, avoiding her eyes. "That might have been my fault. I kind of told Selene to make sure he knew about the visit."

"What?" Alísa turned to him. "W—why? You know he's antagonistic. That he would c-c-come j—just to make it harder on us. Why would you make sure he was here t-t-today?"

Falier shook his head. "I thought it would be better than him finding out when he came to the Hold and unexpectedly saw dragons, or finding out second-hand. I figured it would be better to be up-front about it, as a show of good faith. How long could we have hidden this from him anyway? A day, maybe?"

"It would have been a good day."

Alísa looked down. She had to find a way to take her fear of Yarlan by the reins before she lost control. But how?

"It still is a good day." Falier's emotions wavered, as though he tried to convince himself as well. He touched her arm, making her realize she clutched at her skirts. "I know it's hard, but the alternative would have been worse. But I'm sorry it hurt you."

Alísa shook her head. "You were right. I need t-t-t—to get over it. I've faced antagonistic dragons before—antagonistic humans are just a gust c—compared to the hurricane."

If only her heart would believe her words.

The dancing grounds were almost empty—only the dragons, Namor and Tenza, Yarlan, and Selene remained. Selene waved goodbye to the dragons and approached Alísa and Falier, a bright smile on her face.

"Are you staying for lunch, Alísa?"

Alísa sent a questioning look to Falier, then looked back at Selene as she smirked at her brother.

"You mean he hasn't invited you yet?" Selene elbowed Falier playfully. "Some pursuer you are."

"I was getting there."

Alísa smiled, enjoying their banter. How different her life might have been if the Maker had blessed her parents with another child.

"I'd love to stay. Let me t-t-tell the dragons they can g—go home."

Alísa aimed for Namor and Tenza first. She jogged to catch up as they walked the path to the village proper, calling their names to get their attention.

Stopping before them, Alísa dipped her head in respect. "Thank you for being here t-today. I know it helped the p-people, and it was good for the dragons to m—meet you."

"It's a strange world you live in," Namor said, a light smile on his lips. "But worthwhile. Are you coming back tomorrow?"

"As often as we can."

"Good. Bring the same dragons as today. Let the people get used to these before adding others."

Tenza nodded. "You did well today."

Alísa's gaze lowered, her reaction to Yarlan forefront in her mind. She pulled it back to Tenza, whose eyes had never left her. The woman seemed to see right through her, regarding her with gentle scrutiny.

"Even so." Tenza looked toward Yarlan. "He isn't going to leave until the dragons do."

Alísa didn't follow her gaze, rubbing at her skirt. "Thank you again."

She turned back to the dragons. Falier stood to the side with Graydonn, speaking telepathically. The rest of the dragons looked to her, and at the first notion of Alísa's request, Sesína connected her to them.

"You were so good with the people." Alísa looked to each of the dragons in turn, including even Harenn. He had been civil, even if he hadn't jumped in like the others. *"Thank you all."*

"They were a delight. Though that slayer" —Saynan pointed his muzzle at Yarlan— *"I don't know what to do with him. I tried to engage him, but his psychic shield is up. He can't hear a word from any of us."*

Alísa sighed. *"I know. I don't think that will change anytime soon."*

"It's offensive," growled Harenn. *"Even though we have the ability, dragons rarely, if ever, block out telepathy entirely. If we don't want to be part of a conversation, we leave."*

"He's really scared of us, isn't he?" Komi cocked her head. *"Was there something we could have done better?"*

Harenn huffed. *"He's a typical slayer, full of hatred and literally closed-minded. The one holding the branch was fine, though I wonder how many dragons' blood is on his hands. At least Slayer's steam in the mouth shows he hasn't killed any of us."*

Defensiveness rose in Alísa. 'Slayer,' the way Harenn's mind conveyed it, meant Falier.

"What does that mean? Steam in his mouth?"

"An idiom," Saynan said, far less troubled by Harenn's words. *"It refers to young dragons who cannot breathe fire yet. I would argue, though, that taking part in killing Rorenth certainly counts as fire."*

Harenn dipped his head in a move reminiscent of a shrug. *"Is he planning to stare at us until we leave?"*

Alísa kept herself from looking back at Yarlan. *"Yes. I think it's time for you to go home."*

Komi cocked her head. *"You're staying?"*

"For a little while. I'm going to have lunch with the holders."

"Oo, the holders, huh?" Sesína bumped her shoulder. *"Sounds serious."*

Alísa rolled her eyes. *"I'll let you know when I'm ready to come home."*

As she spoke, a change in the clan-link indicated Falier and Graydonn joining the conversation.

"When you're ready? I guess I'll see you at midnight, then." Sesína looked up at the sky. *"Wait no, it's a Hold—you can sleep here if you stay that late. Don't wake me up."*

"I feel so loved."

"Actually," Falier said, *"Graydonn and I are planning to go flying later. I know you just trained, but after the long day it's been already, I thought it would*

be nice to just fly. Clear our heads, you know?"

The dragons agreed with Falier's assessment. As they prepared to take off for the mountain, Alísa tried to assess Falier's emotions. When they had spoken earlier, he had seemed fine, but now she felt pain in him. A feeling of betrayal.

Sesína pranced up to her, drawing her attention back to the present. *"I guess you won't have to wait till tomorrow to see me after all. Let me know when you're ready."*

Alísa smiled. *"I will."*

Sesína gave a grunt, then bounded after the others, launching into the air with the spike of joy she always had with wind under her wings. Alísa breathed it in, savoring its lightness before breathing it back out and turning to Falier. She searched him with her eyes as he plastered on an easy smile.

"Lunch?"

"In a minute. How was your m—morning?"

"Fine."

Alísa raised an eyebrow.

He sighed. "Sometimes I hate that you're an empath. It's like with Selene and her sound-lights—you both always know when I'm lying."

Alísa looked down. "I'm s—sorry. You don't have t-t-to—"

"No, don't be sorry. You ask because you care—I know that, and I'm glad of it. If anything, I'm kind of jealous I can't read emotions as well as you."

Falier scuffed his foot against the ground. "This morning was hard. People have never been so distant from me. Even Ma—Marris" —he stumbled in speech, as though he had started saying the name incorrectly— "and Sendi, two ladies who have been like grandmothers to me. They think I'm abandoning Me'ran, choosing the dragons over them. I can't get them to see that part of why I'm choosing the dragons is to protect them. It's because I love them, not because you're replacing them."

Alísa pressed her lips together. He was experiencing this because of her. If she had handled last night better—refuted Yarlan's words, not freaked out and let her stammer get the better of her—his people would see him as a hero. He killed the dragon threatening their lives. He stood in Yarlan and Namor's place. He had the bravery to befriend dragons.

"I'm sorry. That sounds awful."

Falier blew out a tense breath. "I pushed through it. That's all we can do right now, right? Keep moving and prove ourselves by our actions."

"That sounds exhausting." She smiled through her sadness and stepped into him, wrapping her arms around his waist. "But I'm with you."

Falier returned the embrace, a small space of happiness growing in the midst of his heartache. He had helped in her struggles so many times. It made her heart full to give back to him.

"Thanks, Líse."

She squeezed tighter and released him, smiling up as she pulled away. He held on a little longer, a brow quirking.

"Well, look at that. I think I caught you."

Alísa snorted, pulling back. "P-please. That was a f—f—friendly embrace, n—n—nothing more."

Heat filled her cheeks. She was bad enough at flirting. Did her stammer have to get worse every time too?

Falier let her go. "Careful—Graydonn said he'd start teaching me empathic sensing soon. Then I'll have proof when you lie like that."

Alísa laughed, her eyes wandering. They landed on Yarlan, stopping her laughter cold. He still stood beside the Hold, watching them, arms folded, scrutinizing their every move from the shadows.

Falier followed her gaze. Mirth fell from him, replaced by ire. When he turned back to her, a calm mask covered any outward signs of his true feelings. He offered her an arm, positioned so that he would stand between her and Yarlan as they walked, and switched to telepathy.

"Come on, let's get lunch and go flying."

The comfort of his presence made her thoughts flow easily. *"Above the worries and cares of the world. Until it's time to come back."*

"Until it's time to come back."

7

PAILI'S WRATH

"Can dragons drink tea?"

Alísa startled at the question, turning to look at Sesína. *"What?"*

Sesína laid on her belly with her head eye-level to a girl of about seven years. The girl bounced on her toes, black hair swaying over her tan skin and green dress. Behind her, a man with similar features chuckled and shook his head.

Sesína raised an eye-ridge at Alísa. *"You heard me. Can dragons drink tea?"*

Alísa excused herself from the group with Saynan and Koriana and approached Sesína. She passed Graydonn and Falier, who were trying to include Harenn in a conversation with a couple of Falier's musician friends.

Only five dragons had come to the village today, since Komi had bruised her wing in combat-training earlier. Saynan said the bruising would be gone in a couple of days, but it was far easier for her to fly straight to the cave than to ascend from the visit, so she had gone home.

The little girl's eyes widened at Alísa. She stopped bouncing and clasped her hands in front of her, attempting to appear well-behaved.

"Dragon Singer Alísa, can Sesína come to my house for my next tea party? Please?"

Her brother, about ten years old, ran up. "If Marri gets to have a dragon at her stupid tea party, I want a dragon to come play kickball on my team!"

The father cocked an eyebrow at his son. "Marri's request was full of respect. The dragons, Alísa, and your sister all deserve it. Try again."

The boy's shoulders slumped, and he gave a loud sigh. Then he straightened and looked at Alísa.

"Can a dragon come play with me, too? My friends will be so jealous if there's a dragon on my team."

Alísa's smile grew. After a few days of dragon visits, only Marri and her brother had been allowed to come thus far. Maybe what the other parents needed in order to feel comfortable would be a smaller, activity-based visit like a tea party or a ball game. Taking a dragon to the village square still sent anxiety through Alísa, but perhaps they could do this at the dancing grounds too.

"I think we can arrange a play-date here." She looked up. "If it's all right with your f—father?"

Sesína's eyes brightened and she crawled forward on her belly like an excited puppy. *Yes! Please?*

"I don't know," he said, rubbing his chin and looking at Marri. "We might need a bigger teacup."

Marri looked at Sesína as though just now realizing how big the dragoness was. "She could use a bucket?"

"I've seen buckets at the Hold's stables. I'll steal—err, 'borrow' one." Sesína looked at Alísa. *"Can dragons drink tea?"*

Alísa giggled. "How should I know? I'm n—not—"

A sound like thunder rattled through the sky. Sesína jerked her head high and stood, looking west as more sounds echoed the first.

Dragons. And they weren't hers.

Villagers gasped, falling back as the other dragons stood, every eye turning to the sky. The dragons growled, and fear rose in the people. Yarlan's sword slid from its sheath in the shadow of the Hold. Marri's father grabbed his children's hands, pulling them back as Sesína moved.

"What's happening?"

"I d—don't know." She looked to the dragons. "Graydonn?"

"I wasn't searching for draconic presences." Graydonn lifted his wings. *"I sense at least six, coming fast."*

"Singer!" Harenn trotted up, his brown eyes dimmed with worry. *"I recognize that voice. It's my sister Galerra, one of my parents' flight-leaders. If she's coming, it can only mean trouble."*

Alísa's heart raced. Paili and Tsamen, invading her territory? She looked between Harenn and Saynan, two of the five dragons who had come to her from Paili and Tsamen's clan.

"Why would they come here? Our border is far-removed from theirs."

Saynan rumbled in his throat. *"Knowing Paili, this is an attempt to remind you and her deserters of her strength. A power-play."*

Alísa clenched her fists, remembering how the alpha female had taunted and fought for every scrap of control when last they met. She didn't need this, one more fight to face, one more thing to scare the villagers. Falier stood among them now, working to calm them after the startling movements of the dragons. She needed to do that too—let them know the situation, then get her dragons into the air.

Eldra Branni, give me strength.

Alísa moved closer to the people, Sesína coming up behind her. Multiple people spoke at once, some to each other, a couple to her or Falier, terror in their eyes as they stared at the dragons.

Please don't let this undo all we've done!

Alísa raised her hands above her head in a silent call for attention. A few, including Falier, looked at her. When others didn't, Namor quieted them, barking their names.

"There's another d—d—d—" *Great Maker, not now! Please!*

"I've got you," Sesína said, connecting her telepathically to the humans.

Alísa pushed gratitude to the dragoness. *"There are other dragons coming. We will try to cut them off before they arrive. Get to the dragon shelter, just in case."*

Alísa ran to Koriana, pulling herself up by two spines as Parsen gave further instructions to the people. Sesína cut off the humans, leaving only the clan's mind-link in the astral plane. Alísa reached for it, feeling each of the dragons and Falier, all a mixture of worry, courage, and determination. She latched onto the latter two.

"Launch!"

Koriana took off so quickly Alísa barely felt the coiling of her muscles. After a few powerful wing-strokes, she caught an updraft and spiraled toward the clouds. In the west, seven shapes stood out black against the clear blue sky.

"Koriana, is there any way we can avoid a conflict?"

Koriana hummed. *"None carry a truce boulder, and they have not asked permission to fly in our territory even though they can see us now. They are here for a fight."*

Alísa gritted her teeth. This was supposed to be her clan's place of respite. No dragon coveted the forest. Me'ran was supposed to be safe.

"Singer," Harenn said, a tremor of fear in his voice that felt out of place. *"Let me go back to the cave and alert the others. I'm the fastest dragon here."*

Alísa pushed away Sesína's indignation at the claim. She would rather send Sesína—get her far from the fight—but Sesína would argue and Harenn was apparently willing. It would mean her numbers would dwindle to four, but if they could stay on the defensive until the clan got here, they should be okay. They had faced worse odds.

"Be quick."

Relief coursed through Harenn as he turned toward the mountain. It clarified something about his request, but she couldn't dwell on that now.

"Form up and roar a challenge," Alísa ordered the rest of the dragons. *"Show them our might."*

Koriana roared before Alísa finished speaking, surging to take the lead. More voices joined her battle cry, a song of different tones united in purpose. Alísa's heart thumped in her chest, their courage building up inside of her.

"Evade as much as you can until the others get here, but if they press toward the village, stop them."

Affirmatives came through, each dragon declaring their obedience with feelings rather than words. When the incoming dragons were close enough she could see their colors, Alísa reached out to Sesína.

"Connect me to their head dragon."

"Done."

Sesína's tone was low, nearly a growl, all play gone as she prepared to fight. Motherly instinct rose in Alísa—a fierce need to protect the hatchling she had Illuminated. She pushed it away and focused on the task at hand. Sesína had battled before.

Channeling Sesína's confidence and Koriana's deep strength, Alísa challenged the intruder. *"Galerra! What does Tsamen want here? The lands past the Nissen are under my protection."*

"As if you could hold them with your pathetic clan," the red dragoness sneered. *"Tsamen and Paili don't care for your forests, but my alphas do not take kindly to traitors and clan-stealers!"*

Anger pulsed through Alísa. She grabbed hold of it, letting her need to protect her clan fuel her. She would fight for them and Me'ran to her final breath.

"Attack!"

With a roar sparking flames, Koriana charged at Galerra. Alísa gripped hard as Koriana dove to avoid a grapple at the last second. Sesína continued her attack behind them, raking talons over the back of Galerra's wing. Graydonn and Falier circled in the opposite direction, taking them out of view. Above them all, Saynan shot a volley of burning cold at the dragon closest to him.

Alísa sang her strength song, her voice wobbling in pitch as Koriana dipped and banked. Power flowed from her, first in astral mists, then a swirling river that flooded the mind-link. Each of her dragons' essence pulsed at the edges of her power, and as her strength flowed into them, their courage flowed back into her.

Wind pummeled Alísa as Koriana banked hard and shot for an enemy blue dragon. It pulled up, talons extended to grapple. Tightening her legs against the shifting scales, Alísa braced for a collision. Once again, Koriana didn't take the challenge, twisting from the gleaming talons and aiming for the blue's wing. Her tail struck the outer edge, tail-spine ripping a bloody gash. The dragon faltered, but its roar held more fury than pain.

"Koriana, above you!"

The dragoness dove at Sesína's warning, and the wind yanked at Alísa's hair and clothes. Pain lanced through Alísa's mind as talons latched into Koriana's tail. The dragoness roared in outrage, but as she tried to pull away, the other dragon tightened its grip.

Alísa twisted, shouting to create a mind-choke. Her power pulled from the clan-link and shot for the dragon's mind. The psychic collision jarred her like a physical punch would jar her arm. She didn't pull back, continuing her call and spreading her power over the surface of the dragon's mind. The dragon slowed as its mind grappled with hers, but it didn't let go of Koriana, instead slowing her down with it.

The attacker roared as another's psychic power speared into it. Falier! The pain he shot into the dragon's mind made it loosen its grip on Koriana's tail, and Alísa completed the choke. Their attacker fell toward the treetops. Alísa didn't let go until it had disappeared in the boughs.

Alísa laid a hand on Koriana's hot scales, wincing as pain raked over her own mind. *"Will you be okay?"*

Koriana's voice was tired but steady. *"I will not be able to make sharp turns. Watch my back. I'll get us through this."*

Galerra roared in fury and speared for Koriana, two other dragons disengaging to converge on them. Alísa's dragons followed behind. Sesína zipped past one and screamed a battle cry as she flung herself at its head, knocking it off course. Another took its place.

Alísa switched to a binding song again, reaching for the dragon closest behind them. It squirmed against her hold, slipping from her like oil and shooting an arrow of psychic pain back at Alísa. It seared her mind like flames and she screamed, turning the cry of pain into another arrow. The dragon slowed as it focused on the psychic realm over the physical, Galerra coming up fast to take its place.

Alísa faltered. Should she finish binding the lagging dragon? Or switch to Galerra?

Another mind entered the space as tiny, ferocious barks filled Alísa's ears.

"Singer!"

Dreki! Relief swept through Alísa as they attacked the mind of the dragon she had been binding, using their combined mental strength to close over it. Alísa released her hold and switched her focus to Galerra. With a battle cry, she sent a psychic arrow at her. Galerra shielded herself just in time, raising and lowering her defense so quickly that she barely slowed.

"Hang on!"

Koriana's shrill warning made Alísa face front again, just in time for

Koriana to dive under the talons of another dragon. She made for the treetops, Galerra still on her tail. Her pain throbbed through Alísa's mind, but no fear accompanied it. It settled Alísa enough to sing again and offer up whatever strength Koriana lacked as her blood spilled over the forest.

The black dragon Koriana had just evaded followed with Galerra, dropping low to the trees with Koriana, while Galerra flew above and behind. Alísa attempted again to bind Galerra in a mind-choke. The dragoness shook her head as though physical motion could free her of a psychic attack. Galerra formed her own psychic powers into a spear, cutting through Alísa's choke. Alísa moaned in pain and pushed harder. She had to stop her, before—

"We are here, Singer!" Faern, Komi's father. Alísa looked east and saw the rest of the clan quickly closing the distance, Faern—the largest of them—at the front. Praise the Maker.

With white-hot talons, Galerra's mind latched onto Alísa's attack. Alísa cried out as pain and anger flooded over her, Galerra's voice ringing loud in her mind.

"Do not think this is over, Dragon Singer. Had you left our clan alone, you would have been safe. Now you will have to fight to hold onto even this pathetic existence of yours. We can spare fighters—can you?"

Alísa growled against the pain. *"Your mother is petty and cannot abide that her dragons have their own free will. Is this what you want, Galerra? To be a spare fighter?"*

Pain pulsed into Alísa's mind once more, then a stretching sensation she had never experienced before. Cold panic swept through her as she strove against Galerra, but she couldn't sever the connection before the dragoness forced herself into Alísa's clan-link.

"We will return. When you tire of playing at peace alongside this false Bria and carrying vermin on your backs, there is a clan of true dragons ready to accept you." Her tone turned mocking. *"Even wayward princes may be forgiven."*

Galerra pulled her presence back and veered west. She trumpeted, the call low and commanding, and her dragons disengaged, following their leader.

"Shall we pursue, Singer?" Saynan said, circling above them.

"Pursue!" The dreki barked, the sound rattling in Alísa's mind.

Alísa set a hand to her head and slowed her breathing. *"No. They are done for today—I caught that just before Galerra broke off the connection. We'll need to set a watch for when they come back."*

"With your leave," Koriana said, fatigue quieting her tone, *"I can assign scouts so there is always someone in the air."*

Alísa rubbed a hand over Koriana's scales. Ever a dragoness of action, even with her tail dripping blood from multiple deep gashes. *"Let's get you back so we can tend to your wound."*

Koriana made a clicking sound in her throat as she banked for the cave. *"I've had worse. Fire will be sufficient to cleanse and cauterize."*

Alísa nodded, then sought the dreki in both the mind-link and the sky. *"Thank you for coming to our aid. We might not have lasted without you."*

She found their forms as they came closer, their wing-lights dimming as their minds separated into individuals. She blinked a few times, wondering if she missed any in the brightness of the summer sky. There seemed to be only perhaps fifteen of them, not the thirty or forty she normally saw in battle.

"Laen, did you all just happen to be in the area? Or did you fly from home?"

The sensation of rain dripping off trees that accompanied Laen's essence cooled Alísa's throbbing mental pain. *"Home."*

Odd. Perhaps the rest of the dreki had been out hunting and didn't hear the sounds of battle. Dreki were fiercely protective of their homeland against invading dragons. Yet another reason why dragons never came to the forests. Another reason Alísa thought the clan would be safe here.

Alísa looked back to the retreating enemy. They flew in a more westerly direction than she expected. The Prilune mountains lay far to the south. Perhaps Tsamen and Paili had taken some of Rorenth's old territory.

Graydonn flew alongside Koriana, touching the tip of his wing to hers. Falier looked back at Koriana's tail, then up to Alísa.

"You all right?"

She fought not to wince at Koriana's pain. *"Relatively."*

Falier looked down and around them. *"There are a couple villages near here that might have heard the battle. Maybe the forest deadened the sounds, but if not..."*

He didn't need to finish the sentence. The wayfarers mostly patrolled the border of the forests at the Nissen river, many miles from here, but frightened villagers could send messengers to them, bringing a clan of forty-plus warriors against the supposed dragon threat.

Alísa must have made a face, because Falier slapped on an optimistic smile. *"I'm sure it will be fine. Even if someone sent a message to them today, it would take weeks of stopping to check on other villages before they made it to Me'ran. By then, we'll be ready."*

Alísa blew out a breath, far less sure. At the current rate of people coming to meet the dragons, it would be months before Me'ran would be ready to support her before the wayfarers. She needed to gain more trust. Maybe the dragons could do more for Me'ran—hunting for them, perhaps? No. Even if it weren't difficult for the dragons to hunt in the forests, such an act would harm the livelihood of any hunters or meat farmers—not the best way to make friends. Something else, then.

"We did just keep a clan of dragons from attacking them," Sesína offered, whispering through the Illumination bond. *"Maybe this attack by Galerra was actually a good thing for us—the villagers saw our new clanmates in action."*

"Maybe." Alísa hugged herself as Koriana's pain throbbed in her again. *"Koriana needs to get back to the cave. Why don't you take Graydonn and Falier and let the people know they're safe now. Be my eyes."*

Sesína sent a pleased affirmative and turned her attention to Graydonn, the two of them veering toward the village.

One of Koriana's spines pressed into Alísa's back as she and the rest of the clan angled upward, heading for the new cave. A week ago, when it was just Alísa and three dragons, a little cave closer to the forest floor had been home. Now, however, the clan required a more spacious cavern.

Alísa shivered as the wind whipped over her, tugging at her hair and skirt until Koriana swept through the craggy hole where the two peaks split off. Darkness surrounded them, the bit of light at the entrance too small and too high off the floor of the cave to do much good. Dragons could see in the darkness of the cave, but with a human alpha they had to make a few adjustments. With a flash of flames from Komi's maw, a small pile of wood ignited and the shadows of landing dragons flickered on the ruffled cave walls.

Alísa sucked in a breath as Koriana stopped on the upper landing, the dragoness' injured tail smacking against the stone floor. She slid down the scaly shoulder as Koriana lowered to her belly, getting out of the way so Koriana could curl her neck to begin cauterizing her wound.

"I'm sorry, Singer!" Komi connected to her, guilt coursing through her mind. *"If I had been more careful in training today, I could have called my father through our Illumination bond and there wouldn't have been a fight."*

Alísa shook her head. *"No one could have predicted this, and any of us might have gotten hurt in training. It's not your fault."*

"I know, I just—" Komi scratched the ground and growled. *"It was a hatchling-level mistake, rolling when Graydonn was that close to me."*

"And if he were here, he would be taking the blame for your injury. Rest easy, Komi. It's no one's fault except Paili and the dragons who follow her."

Komi's feelings of guilt didn't recede, but she slapped her tail on the ground in the draconic sign of agreement. That would have to be good enough. There were other dragons who needed their alpha's attention right now. Tremors of fear guided Alísa's eyes to the first. Many draconic emotions crowded her in this space, but hatchling emotions had always been more potent.

Alísa picked her way over the uneven cave floor, following Saynan to his mate, Aree, and their young charge. Aree nestled against a curve in the cave walls, her and Saynan's opalescent egg settled between her forelegs. Rather than folding in a rested position, one of her sapphire wings draped over her side to shelter a hatchling from the eyes of the other dragons.

Iila was perhaps only two weeks old. Her Illumination bond to her mother had been ripped from her in the course of the battle against Rorenth's clan. Whether her mother had been killed by one of Alísa's clan or Karn's, Alísa didn't know. She hoped the latter and that Iila's mother's killer wasn't one of the dragons in the cave with them now, but Iila's reluctance to interact with the other dragons in the clan seemed to indicate the former. They had done as they must to save the lives of innocents, but between Iila and the two eggs now left without parents, the aftermath was heartbreaking. Iila had barely eaten since they had taken her in, and with the way her fear coated the air, today's attack had very likely resurfaced terrible memories.

Alísa slowed her breathing as she neared, taking in the hatchling's distress and allowing it space. It only became more wild if she fought it, and, unlike with humans, she couldn't escape it by pulling her powers in close.

Aree's eyes dimmed. *"She spoke with me briefly this morning, her first time initiating with me. But when Harenn brought news of the attackers, she panicked. I had to force calm over her so she wouldn't hurt herself. I fear any progress we've made has been lost."*

Saynan nuzzled Aree's cheek. *"Do not despair. If anyone can make her feel safe, it is you."*

Alísa made eye-contact with Aree and spoke aloud for Iila's benefit. "M—may I see her?"

Aree made a light clicking sound in her throat, then pulled her wing back just enough that Alísa could see Iila's shining cobalt eyes in the darkness. Alísa knelt.

"Iila," she whispered, "precious one, you are safe. We fought them off and are setting up scouts. They won't get this close to our cave again."

Iila snorted steam, a draconic negative, and curled up in a tighter ball, hiding her face under a silver wing. Up close, Alísa could feel fluctuations in Iila's emotions. Fear dominated, but within it churned sorrow, anger, and determination—a dizzying combination.

Alísa stayed with Iila a little longer—silent, as were Saynan and Aree. No words could help Iila right now, and she needed to process her sorrow. All they could do was give her some form of stability and be there when she was ready.

With a few words of assurance, Alísa took her leave of Iila and Saynan's family. One other dragon needed his alpha's attention. This one would take balance—a careful reprimand and a harsh truth spoken in love. Part of her wished another might speak it for her, but she was the alpha.

Her eyes found Harenn resting in one of the crevices in the cave's walls, only his head, chest, and forelegs visible. He lifted his head as she approached, his eye-lights wavering.

"Singer, is there something you need?"

Alísa slumped back against the wall beside him. *"Thank you for going to get the others. Your sister's troop were far more coordinated than Rorenth's; I didn't know if we would win before the others arrived."*

Harenn blinked slowly, the draconic sign of acknowledgement. *"Those in the cave hadn't even heard the roar of threat, but they responded without hesitation."*

Alísa nodded. *"I have a good clan. Though they may not be the best of friends, they trust each other already."*

"We have you to thank for that." Harenn straightened his neck to look out at the rest of the cave. *"We follow the Singer, so our purposes are aligned."*

"Yes, I suppose so." Alísa looked at Harenn. *"But trust also takes honesty, and you weren't entirely honest with me, were you?"*

His eyes dimmed and he didn't look at her.

"You didn't leave because you were the fastest of us," she prompted. *"I felt your fear and assumed it was a fear that we would lose the fight if we didn't get help. But that wasn't what you feared at all, was it?"*

Harenn hummed in his throat, agitation rising. *"Trust doesn't mean I reveal my shame to the whole clan."*

Alísa kept her tone steady. This would be tricky. *"No, it does not. But when it affects the clan, I cannot just let it be. You are indeed one of my fastest flyers. Faern isn't. So when the reinforcements arrived, why was he at the front instead of you?"*

Talons scraped against stone. *"You wouldn't understand."*

"No?" Alísa straightened. *"Look at me, Harenn."*

He didn't move, muscles taut underneath his scales. Alísa fought not to fidget or wipe her hands on her skirts. Though the memory of him pained her, she imagined her father standing in command over his warriors. Then, slowly, Harenn curved his neck around. Guilt flickered in his dimmed eyes.

"I know what it is to go up against your family," she said. *"To save Iila and the others, I faced my father, uncle, and former betrothed."*

83

The scene rose in her mind, painful and visceral enough that Harenn likely saw it too. Her father at the mouth of a cave, L'non and Kallar behind him. His fear for her. The determination in his eyes as he moved to protect her, and then the betrayal that replaced it as she mind-choked him.

Alísa swallowed. *"Our situations are different, but not so much as you might suppose. I was terrified when I saw them, but my clan was in danger, and I did what I must."* She looked out at the dragons scattered throughout the cave. *"Galerra said this was only the first attack, so I need to know—can this clan count on you to protect them?"*

Harenn's eyes dimmed further as he followed her gaze, shame coming off him in waves. *"Yes, Singer. I'm sorry. I will not fail them again."*

The truth of his words settled in Alísa's mind. *"Good."* She paused a moment, his emotions resonating with her own. *"I know it isn't easy, leaving your family. If you ever need to talk, I'm here."*

Harenn's eyes brightened ever so slightly in acknowledgement, then faded again. Sensing his desire to be alone, Alísa pressed back out into the cave. The clan gathered in small groups, the largest gathering situated at the fire. Sesína, Falier, and Graydonn were there as well.

At the fire, Alísa sat between Sesína and Rayna, an emerald dragoness nursing a wing ripped through in the battle with Rorenth. Rayna's pain had lessened significantly in the last week, making it easier for Alísa to be near her, but full healing was still a month away.

Between her forelegs, Rayna held the two orphaned eggs, one blue and one a tawny brown. Alísa reached out and stroked each of their shells, feeling their timid sadness seep through her fingers. Without their biological parents, they needed to bond to another dragon before they hatched. A hatchling without an Illumination bond would not survive more than a few hours. Each day a different dragon held them in hopes that one of them might choose a surrogate parent, but so far no bonds had formed.

Alísa swallowed against her emotions. There was so much hurt all mixed up together in this space. Wounded dragons, eggs that needed new parent-bonds, a traumatized hatchling, terrified villagers—they didn't need border skirmishes to further complicate matters.

"It might not be as bad as you think." Sesína nudged Alísa with her muzzle as she whispered through the bond. *"When we gave Me'ran the all-clear, a bunch of them thanked us for fighting. Yarlan was awful, as usual, and there were others who stayed far away from us, but they can't deny what we did today."*

Alísa kept her eyes on the eggs. *"I wish I had your and Falier's optimism."*

Sesína gave a light purr. *"That's why we're here. How did it go with Harenn?"*

Alísa briefly relayed the conversation. *"I hope I handled it well."*

"I'm sure you did," Sesína said. *"You're good at things like that."*

"If only I were good at handling things like Yarlan, too."

"Some people can't be convinced. You can't change everyone's minds."

"No." Alísa sighed. *"But when the minds I can't change are better at influencing others than I am? What am I supposed to do then?"*

Sesína shrugged a shoulder, an awkward motion for a dragon. *"Let your actions prove you, just like us protecting the village. They'll see you—see us—for who we really are."* Her eyes brightened. *"And by that I, of course, mean the best dragon-human clan ever, with the most amazing alpha and—frankly—a rather fabulous beta."*

Alísa allowed a chuckle. *"And which beta would that be?"*

"Koriana. She's rather fabulous. I'm fabulousness incarnate."

"Of course." Alísa bumped shoulders with her affectionately.

She turned her attention to the others around the fire, Sesína connecting her into the conversation. Dragons thrummed and Falier laughed at something she had missed, but she smiled nonetheless. Troubles surrounded her—that much was certain—but so did life. Tomorrow she would press onward into the mess once more, for the sake of children who wanted tea parties and kickball, and for dragonets yet unhatched. She was made to bring humans and dragons together. She just had to cling to that knowledge, cling to that hope, and keep moving.

8

CÉILÍ CONFRONTATION

Alísa's heart pounded as the tempo of the céilí music increased for the third time this song. Parsen spun her to the right, and she grinned as her skirt flared. Kat's words became barely intelligible as she called the quick steps. The fiddler's melody flew higher and somehow the drummers kept up the complex rhythmic pattern.

Parsen spun her again before they separated. Alísa chanted the next steps in her head, hoping she could recall them well enough to not crash into the other dancers.

Advance past Parsen. Retreat around the other side. Side-sevens. Swing with the next lead. Side-sevens. Spin with Parsen. Five claps, which means...

The caller and fiddler dropped out as the tempo of the final chorus sped as quickly as the percussionists could go. Squeals and laughter echoed all around as dancers stumbled through the steps. Alísa nearly missed hooking elbows with the next lead, but he caught her and swung her back toward Parsen for the final spin.

Laughter and applause erupted from the dancers, most turning to acknowledge the skill of the musicians. Alísa sought Falier, seated with the other drummer beside the bonfire. Their eyes locked and she lifted her hands higher, giving her applause directly to him. His grin widened, and he gave her an exaggerated bow, flourishing with his hand.

"Nicely done." Parsen clapped Alísa on the shoulder. A teasing smile lifted his lips. "You only tripped twice that dance. Though it wouldn't hurt if you smiled more."

Alísa smirked, sure that she'd tripped more than that. "You'll have to p-p-pick one or the other. C-concentration, or smiles and missteps."

"What, you can't smile while you concentrate?"

"That skill seems to elude me." Alísa dipped her head graciously. "Thank you for the d—dance."

Parsen returned the gesture. "I'll try and give you another before the night is out."

Alísa smiled, then searched for faces she recognized as the crowd swirled around her. Perhaps someone who had danced with her before or who had come to visit with the dragons in the last week.

Her eyes caught on the man she had swung with in the last dance. His skimmed past in apathy. She found a butcher she had danced with weeks ago, but he turned away. Others she recognized as friends, but they already had partners. An elbow brushed her arm, and she turned to see a man who shook his head as though she had been the one to bump into him. Behind him, a woman glared at her, the couple's negative emotions souring the excitement in the air.

Pulling her empathy in more tightly, Alísa walked out of the mass of people for the third time this céilí. At all the other céilís, it had been difficult to get a break from dancing. Now it seemed she was a less desirable partner—no more an exciting visitor from the west, but a pariah. Even amidst the smiles and laughter, the astral plane held tension.

"You sure you don't want me to come keep you company?" Sesína's sleepy presence trickled into her mind. *"I'm allowed in the village without an escort."*

"I would love your company, but no. This is their night. I want them to have it."

"I'm not threatening. I'm—"

"—a dragon with glowing eyes, many pointy things, and an inability to sit still?"

Sesína hesitated. *"Can I come if I promise to sit still?"*

Alísa shook her head, though the dragoness couldn't see it. *"Not this time. Get some rest—Saynan trained you hard today."*

A flash of light caught her eye. A smile lighted on Alísa's lips as she gazed at pairs of tiny glowing eyes hiding in the trees.

Jealousy briefly ran through Sesína, followed by resignation. *"Okay. Tell the dreki I said to keep you company, and if they don't I'll... I'll... Make up a good threat for me. I'm going to sleep now."*

Alísa giggled, pointing her boots to the dreki. *"Good night, dear one."*

Stopping at the edge of the dancing grounds, Alísa looked up into the colorful eyes. Like with the battle against Galerra, there seemed to be only about fifteen dreki in attendance.

"Fancy meeting you here."

A trilling chirp, and a drek with red eyes flew from the branches toward Alísa. The evening sun revealed Rann, his ruby-eyed baby clinging to his back. Rann twisted around Alísa in two graceful circles before stopping in front of her, Laen with the purple-eyed baby coming out to join him.

"You brought the little ones!"

Rann came closer, establishing a telepathic link to Alísa.

"Pet?"

Alísa grinned and reached out, brushing a finger first over Rann's mane, then the baby drek's bare neck. The little drek purred, his wings stretched out over his father's. Alísa looked to Laen and saw the little purple female similarly mimicking Laen's wing movements.

Flight-training already? They were still bald and tiny, but their wings moved nearly in time with the older dreki. Their eye-lights faded in and out as they had during the remembrance, as though trying to join minds with their flight-trainers but not quite able to synchronize yet.

Alísa faced Rann again. "Remind me his name?"

"Rís," he replied, the name accompanied by the image of a red dawn. Then Rann looked to the baby on Laen's back. *"Chrí."* With bluebells.

"Yes, I remember." Alísa fought back surprise tears and tried to cover them, looking up to the other dreki. "Are you all here for the d— dancing?"

A mixture of excitement and wariness washed over her, along with scattered trills apparently meant to answer her question. She gave a questioning look to Rann.

"Watch," he said, sending a picture of dreki in the trees.

"You w—won't join this t-t-time?"

Rann arched his neck and nuzzled his son. *"Safe."*

Alísa looked back at the people. They loved the dreki, and, based on what little she knew of this clan, the dreki loved the people. Then again, they had been skittish the first time she saw them. At that céilí, a few of them came out to dance at Selene and Falier's musical call, the rest staying in the trees until Alísa herself sang. Perhaps it wasn't as normal as she thought for the dreki to dance with the people.

Alísa turned back to the creatures. "Just here for the music, then? It is lovely."

In response, melodic chirps and trills sounded in the trees, most of them flitting along the flute's melody, while a couple harmonized with the fiddle. The vocalizations had a slightly disjointed feel to them, each note seeming to come from a different drek in turn rather than any one drek singing a full phrase of music. The occasional tones coming from Rann and Laen made it sound like each drek had their own assigned pitch.

Alísa spun to the dreki's music, slowly at first, to not scare the dreki closest to her. Rann trilled out of turn and dipped to fly a circle around her, moving in the opposite direction. Laen joined him, the two dreki dancing around Alísa, while their little charges pumped their wings and tried to keep up with their father and auntie.

More dreki joined the aerial dance, and Alísa giggled with delight. She stopped and turned the other way, and the dreki twisted to fly in the opposite direction. Their joy spun through the air with them, and Alísa released her hold on her empathy to drink it all in. Joy tickled inside her like feathers rising on the wind.

All too soon, it ended. The song slowed and Selene's flute sounded a long ending note. The few dancing dreki arced higher, ending their choreography with a tight spin around each other over Alísa's head.

Alísa grinned as she looked up at them. "Thank you. I needed that."

The dreki trilled in response, flying back to the cover of the trees as sounds of the milling crowd came over the dancing grounds. Parsen's voice rose over the rest, but Alísa couldn't hear what he announced. Should she go back to them and try again, or stay here with the dreki? Dreki and dragons were far more comfortable company. Yet the point in being here was to help the people see her as a person again, not just the strife-bringing Dragon Singer.

Alísa waved to the dreki. "I'm g—going to go back now. See you later."

Bracing herself inwardly, Alísa walked the trampled grasses toward the people. The crowd had stopped moving, but they didn't seem to be in pairs. All faced the fire-pit as a male voice she didn't recognize rose into the evening sky.

Movement at the Hold drew her eyes. Falier and Selene, along with the other musicians.

Relief in her heart, Alísa headed for them. The voice in the crowd must be a storyteller giving the musicians a quick reprieve. Falier shook his hands at the wrists, loosening them up. Selene and the other woman each held an instrument in hand—a flute and a fiddle, respectively— while the two men besides Falier were unladen.

Selene spotted her first and waved her over. The others followed Selene's gaze to Alísa, Falier's face lighting up as he saw her approach. He stopped shaking out his hands and reached an arm to her, which she allowed to pull her into a side-hug.

"Having fun?"

Alísa smiled in response and pulled away before the hug became awkward for the others.

Falier resumed his loosening exercise. "You remember Aresia—"

The brunette woman with the fiddle, perhaps in her early forties.

"—Lethín—"

Aresia's younger brother, another percussionist.

"—and G'renn."

Low-fifer, a quiet giant of a man. To her relief, none of the musicians gave her dirty looks like some of the other villagers. Aresia had even attended yesterday's dragon visit.

"Nice t-t—to see you all again. Your music has been w—wonderful."

"Thank you," Aresia said. She looked to G'renn. "'Bear In The Brier' next? I think Selene and I need a little more time to recover after the last two songs."

Lethín chuckled. "Old age making you soft, sis?"

Aresia raised her fists in mock aggression, fiddle still in hand. "Still young enough to teach you a lesson."

Lethín lifted his hands in defense. "Okay, okay, I give."

G'renn rolled his eyes and looked back to Aresia. "We did 'Bear' last week. How about—"

"You need a break too?"

Alísa turned her attention from the song-selection conversation to Lethín and Falier. Lethín looked pointedly at Falier's shaking wrists and quirked a grin.

"Please." Falier affected a yawn and stretched. "I could do that last song in my sleep."

Lethín shook his head. "You're working too hard, especially for someone who's leaving soon."

"If you call that work, maybe you're the one who—" Falier stilled, his jovial smile slipping. "What do you mean?"

"You have a higher calling now, right?" Lethín nodded, not unkindly, at Alísa. "Yet you're still about your holder tasks every day before flying away to do who knows what with the dragons. I expected you to take it easy down here."

Falier's smile returned, though tighter than before. "I'm still a holder. I'm not just going to abandon my duties."

Lethín's smile held pity now. "Nobody would blame you. After all, you finally get to have the adventurous life you've always wanted, instead of being stuck here. Fame, glory—you'll have it all."

Falier tried to shrug nonchalantly, though it didn't quite work. "Well, adventure certainly, but—"

Lethín grinned with another shake of his head. "Always so noble. Oh, sounds like the story's winding down. You coming?"

Lethín turned to the crowd, tapping G'renn's shoulder to bring the others out of their conversation. The other musicians headed to the fire along with Lethín, but Falier didn't move. Selene quirked an eyebrow at him as she passed.

"Coming?"

"In a minute."

Selene cocked her head, her brow furrowing. She looked to Alísa, a question in her eyes, then followed the rest of the musicians.

"Was" —Falier started, first staring at nothing, then looking to

Alísa— "was that odd to you?"

Alísa nodded. "Are you okay?"

Falier shook his head. "I don't know. He didn't seem mad like others who have talked to me about my leaving, but it was..." He sighed. "I don't know. I should go, else I prove him right about 'taking it easy.'"

Alísa took his hand. "You don't have to."

"Yeah, I do. I'll be fine." He gave her hand a squeeze, as though that would convince her, but his eyes spoke pain. Still, she let him go when he pulled away, unsure what else to do besides watch him jog back to his spot.

The villagers applauded the storyteller just as Falier took his seat. Alísa leaned back against the Hold, not quite ready to try dancing again with Falier's hurt and confusion wadded up inside of her. It raised another ache within her. She knew the pain of leaving one's old life behind. While she hadn't been adored the way Me'ran loved Falier, leaving her father's clan had been difficult. Which was worse? The sudden break away that she had experienced, never saying goodbye to her cousins or Trísse? Or this drawn-out period Falier was going through? She hadn't had time to prepare herself, but she also hadn't had to watch those she cared for struggle to let her go.

The storyteller raised his hands in a call for silence. "I see we have visitors in the trees."

Alísa looked at the dreki. An excited murmur ran through the crowd and a couple of children near the edge of the group bounced on their toes.

"Perhaps a song to invite them over?" The storyteller looked back at the musicians, specifically Selene, who had charmed the dreki with her flute before.

"Oh! Miss Alísa!" Marri's voice rose before she ran to Alísa. The seven-year-old's shiny black hair spilled from her hair-tie from hard play and dancing. "Sing 'Maiden Fair'! The dreki love it! Can you sing 'Maiden Fair' again?"

The people's attention fell on Alísa. She had to stop herself from shrinking back against the Hold in embarrassment as other children latched onto the idea and begged her to sing and make the dreki dance again. Their excited pleas overcame her discomfort and brought a smile to her lips.

"All right," she said, stepping from the Hold's walls. "I'll sing—"

She looked up from the children into many eyes—some cold, some fearful. A few stared up at the mountain, as though her acquiescence alone might call monsters from it.

Cold flooded Alísa. "I w—won't call for the dragons. The words don't even c-c-call for d—dreki. It's just a folk song."

The adults' silence was louder than the children's giggles, reminiscent of the moment after she and Falier had completed their presentation. Alísa pulled her empathy tight around her—her only hope to escape the tide of fear and anger.

She searched the crowd for allies, someone who might speak up for her. Parsen looked at a loss, as did Selene. Kat's eyes seemed to land everywhere but Alísa. Namor and Tenza were nowhere to be found.

Falier set his bodhrán down, eyes full of concern. "It's just a folk song. It's not—"

"Forgive us if we don't quite believe you." Yarlan came to the front, the ice in his eyes colder than Saynan's breath. "She has, after all, brought monsters to invade the grounds of our Hold every day this week, then led them in attack patterns overhead, also by her songs."

Alísa fought back a shudder. Just like the presentation. She had to be better this time. Keep him from overpowering her.

"W—we're t-t-training to protect you. There's another c-c-c-c—"

"They fought off an attack for us just yesterday," a woman said. "If her dragons were going to harm us, they would have done so by now, or else they would have let the other dragons have free reign over Me'ran."

"Isn't this her dragons' territory now?" A man rubbed the scruff of his beard. "It might not matter whether we're here or not, they would defend this area."

Another man. "Still, they haven't harmed us."

"But there hasn't been a dragon attack here in seven years," another woman said, her voice trembling. "Nothing until she showed up."

That stung more than Yarlan's accusations, and with it more fear rose from the people. Alísa breathed out, pushing against it, then froze as

Yarlan turned on her.

"An excellent point. Her very presence is a threat."

Falier pushed from the crowd. "That's not true!"

Rage rippled from Falier, joining Yarlan's malice in colliding against Alísa's empathy. She took a step back. Breathed. She could hold it together. Her father had trained her for this. Just tighten the hold.

"Look at these people!" Yarlan threw his arm out toward the crowd. "This girl you so staunchly defend frightens them, and they can't say anything because her dragon enforcers are on standby in the mountain."

She should say something. Prove him wrong with a few calm words, yet she had none. Even if she did, all her energy was going toward keeping the anger, fear, and rage from overwhelming her. Where was Namor with his quiet strength?

"So, forgive us if we fear your little folk tunes." Yarlan sneered, victory already in his eyes as he set them on Alísa. "Perhaps if you want to prove your sincerity, you should keep your mouth shut."

Memory flashed. Words that destroyed her once. They cut through her empathy, a perfectly-aimed dagger slashing through her control. Someone in the crowd—Parsen, maybe—spoke argument, but she couldn't hear the words as all the fear and anger and anxiety of the people rushed into her gaps.

Yarlan was right. She was causing all of this. She couldn't keep them safe. Couldn't assuage their fears.

She should never have come back.

Alísa moved, twisting from the emotions and bolting for the Hold. She passed by the door closest to her, not wanting the people to see her enter, and went to a door on the dark side away from the fire.

She entered through the kitchen, still warm from dinner, and passed into the main room where she could breathe. The space was dark, lit only by two oil lamps on separate tables. Quiet. Safe. Where she could sort out the voices in her head.

She searched for the memory that would bring her to herself. Papá leading her through the steps. His gentle eyes as he soothed her fears.

And then the eyes of betrayal as she had mind-choked him.

No. Focus. Which emotion did she feel the most right now?

More anger polluted the space and her mind, making her wince. Concern came with it—soothing, but not enough.

"Líse?"

Falier. Not anger at her, anger *for* her.

It didn't help.

"Oh Líse, I'm so sorry. This is all Yarlan's doing. Everything we say he twists!"

'Speak clearly or keep your mouth shut!'

'You've taken an apprentice, of course.'

Falier reached out to pull Alísa into a hug, but she backed away, arms crossed over her stomach. She couldn't let him touch her. This wasn't like feeling a dragon's pain, where he had helped her before. This was a knotted web, a nest of serpents, where the sudden deluge of negative emotions tangled up with her own until she could no longer tell what was Alísa and what was not. If Falier touched her skin now, her volatile empathy would pull him in as well. Already his anger pounded in her head.

She reached for memories of walking through this before. She could work through it. Which emotion was most overwhelming?

"Alísa?"

Fear joined Falier's anger. She closed her eyes and pressed her hands to her ears. Falier didn't understand, and she didn't have words to make him understand. Fear and rage and confusion and pain rose as she tried to push against it all. She just needed to gather her thoughts and feel her own emotions, instead of everyone else's.

"What can I do? Tell me what to do."

How could she when everything inside of her was gibberish?

"Shield your mind, Falier. Now!"

The new male voice shocked Alísa's eyes open. Papá?

No. He couldn't be here, and he didn't know Falier's name.

Walking stick. Salt-and-pepper hair. Hard eyes that still carried kindness. Namor. And, bless him, he carried no new emotions into the room.

Surprise shocked through the astral plane. Then the air became a little less thick as Falier did as Namor said, but the relief was small as the

95

pounding emotions of the crowd echoed incessantly through her mind.

So much. Why had she let so few words cut through her?

Namor stopped before her. "Do you want me to talk you through it?"

Her first instinct should have been to recoil from him—she wasn't a little girl just learning her powers anymore. Yet, as she looked into Namor's eyes, she saw her father. The gentleness in his voice stirred memories from long ago, where thirteen-year-old Alísa huddled under her furs, trying to block out the noise. Her father would come in, telepathic shield in place, and in his soothing baritone would instruct her how to feel at home in her own mind again.

"Yes."

Namor set a hand on the table beside them, lowering himself into a chair. "Falier will need to learn this someday too, but it does not have to be now. Do you want him to stay, or leave?"

Alísa sank into a chair, exhausted. "He c—can stay."

"What do I do?" Falier whispered, kneeling beside Namor's chair.

"Watch and commit this to memory. Nothing more. Don't even touch her until we're through." Namor's voice lowered in both volume and tone. "Now, Alísa, what is the biggest emotion you feel?"

Alísa leaned her elbows on her knees, pressing her hands to her eyes. Flames lapped at her mind, blazing into and out of a gaping hole that needed filling, but greater than both was a great gray shudder pulsing through the other emotions and settling in her heart and stomach.

"Fear."

"Does any of it belong to you?"

"Y—y—yes." Alísa choked back a sob as she admitted it. So much of it was hers—it shouldn't be so.

"And what is it you fear, Alísa?"

"Their eyes." She stopped. The words had come so swiftly, yet she didn't know where they had come from. Their eyes?

"Details," Namor prodded gently. "What about their eyes?"

Alísa breathed, focusing, pushing aside the other emotions and pressing deep within the fear. Her heart raced and her arms trembled with the weight of her head.

Images rose in her mind—faces, some she knew and others she barely recognized. Each filled with anger, fear, betrayal, or disgust. In their midst came one face she knew all too well. Chief Toronn, with his unblinking hawk eyes that she only ever remembered filled with a loathing that made her feel so small.

'Speak clearly or keep your mouth shut!'

Alísa pulled back, opening her eyes.

"No," Namor said, "stay there. It can't hurt you right now, only set you free from everything else. What is it about their eyes that you fear?"

Alísa closed her eyes again, concentrating, willing the eyes back into view, Chief Toronn's in the center. He grew to overshadow the others, as though everything else she saw poured out of this one face. It haunted her memories and dreams with glares that told her she was worthless. The only child of her father, a stammerer, and a dragon-lover.

"T-T-Toronn," she gasped out. "They look like T-Toronn, my first chief from my home v—village. They look through me, telling me I'm something that I'm not. Or, s—something that isn't the whole of me."

Namor's eyes softened. "Good. The rest of the fear does not belong to you. Close your eyes, fill your lungs, and give back what isn't yours to keep."

Alísa kept pace with his instructions, allowing the peoples' fear to flow out and away from her. Her mind cleared considerably, and even the fear she kept had somehow weakened now that she understood it. Not everyone in the crowd was like Toronn, no matter how much their eyes reminded her of his.

"Good," Namor said. "What else do you feel?"

"Anger."

"Is any of it yours?"

"Yes." Her fists clenched. "I'm angry at Yarlan for t-t-twisting everything I s—say. I'm angry at m—myself for n—n—not being able to stop him. And I'm angry at those who didn't speak—"

She stopped, her eyes snapping open to look at the man sitting in front of her.

He met her gaze. He knew.

"Those who didn't what?"

A sob caught in her chest. "Who didn't s—speak up for me."

He nodded and gave her instructions to breathe the rest of the anger out, as though she hadn't just declared her rage against him.

"Is there anything else inside you?"

She went through the motions with him again. Confusion, most of which had belonged to the children. The piece belonging to her was merely a questioning of herself—whether she did the right thing in trying to bring peace between Me'ran and the dragons. And, if it was the right thing, why was it so difficult?

She took a deep breath and let the extra emotion flow away from her on the exhale.

"Is there anything else?"

Alísa paused for a moment, testing and tasting every emotion left inside of her. They still pushed and pulled against each other like tents fighting the winds, but everything that remained belonged to her.

"No," she whispered, opening her eyes. "Thank you."

"My daughter Ari has strong empathy like yours," Namor said, his eyes distant. "There was many a day I helped her find her way back to her own mind."

The world was silent for a moment, even the astral plane with both Namor and Falier holding back. Alísa pressed her lips together, a question on her tongue she wasn't sure she wanted to ask.

"I am on your side," Namor assured her. "But if I speak for you every time there is trouble, the people will look to me. They must look to you. You are the one who must refute their arguments. You are the one they must trust more than their own fear."

He reached for one of her hands, allowing her a moment to pull away if she needed before grasping it.

"And you have your own fear to work through, dear girl. A woman with a dragon inside her needn't fear what others think about her. I seem to recall a woman fearless enough to let a grumpy old slayer see all of her, and how it led to three dragons being accepted by this village. Perhaps it will take another show of fearlessness to bring the people to trust you."

Alísa trembled. Fearless was the last thing she felt before these people, especially since the last two times she faced the entirety of the village had ended in disaster. All she wanted right now was to wake Sesína, fly back to the cave, and stay there with the dragons forever.

Namor squeezed her hand and let go, beginning to stand. "When you know what you want to do, I will be there."

From seemingly nowhere, Tenza appeared at Namor's side. Had she been there the whole time too? Had she heard everything?

"You can go to her now, lad," Tenza said gently, taking her place at Namor's side.

Falier blinked, shaking his head as though the words had woken him. Alísa regretted asking him to stay, now knowing what had come out into the open. He was trustworthy, but to reveal such deep wounds now... What must he think of her?

His eyes held deep sorrow, perhaps some pity, though he held his shield in place, so she couldn't test his emotions to know for sure.

"Do you want to talk about it?"

Alísa shook her head. She had said enough.

"What do you need?"

She shivered under the weight of her revelations and Falier's sincerity. "I d—d—don't know. Hold me?"

At the tiniest beginning of his nod, Alísa dropped out of her chair and clung to him. He returned the fierceness of her grasp, pulling her close and resting his head against hers. She tried to restrain her sobs, but they came anyway.

Namor's final words were meant to be encouraging, but they haunted her. She needed to be fearless. Didn't he see that she was trying? She was trying, but she just couldn't compete with Yarlan. And the people's minds, they were foreign to her, full of emotions that invaded her and left her unable to speak. Unable to do more than run away.

Great Maker, what more can I do?

9

SLAYERS & HOLDERS

Falier had barely slept. Between Alísa's condition last night and his anger at Me'ran for causing it, he couldn't shut his mind down until hours later, when everyone else slept tucked in their beds.

He stayed in the kitchen this morning, baking bread and chopping vegetables. He couldn't be around the people just now, not after they had hurt Alísa so. He understood their fear, at least in part, but for them to accuse her—or stay silent as Yarlan got in her face—was wrong. And the way she had reacted to it all had woken a beast inside of him he had never known existed, one ready to protect her from everything.

Except his anger had made it even worse. At least he now knew how to handle this situation in the future.

The sizzle of stoked flames brought Falier back to the present. His father, too, occupied the kitchen, working the fire for tea and hash. Neither said anything as they worked, but Falier felt his father's eyes on him. He heard multiple soft inhales, as though his father planned to speak, then thought better of it.

Odd. His father rarely held back.

A crescendo of laughter came just as Selene opened the door, running in to get two more plates of hash. Falier peeked out.

"She's not out yet, lover boy," Selene said, a knowing smile on her face.

Falier rolled his eyes, giving his sister a mildly annoyed look, and returned to the oven. Deep heat rippled over his face and arms as he paused at the door. He focused on the sensation, letting something other than his fatigue and anger linger in his thoughts. The nutty scent of the fresh bread. The feeling of the wooden pallet in his hands.

"You know, bread bakes better when you don't let all the heat out of the oven."

Falier looked back at his father. "It's the last loaves of the day."

Parsen's eyebrows raised as he turned back to the fire. The moment gone, Falier pushed the pallet under the loaves, pulling golden brown perfection from the heat. He set it on the countertop beside the other loaves and re-latched the iron door.

Parsen cleared his throat. "How is Alísa?"

Falier leaned back against the counter. How much could he say without violating Alísa's privacy?

"Shaken. It was bad. Yarlan set off her empathy and it took Namor's help to fix it."

Parsen's eyes narrowed. "Yarlan attacked her psychically?"

"No, nothing like that." Except, now that he thought of it, kind of like that. "He flustered her. No, worse than that. I can't go into it, but he didn't psychically attack her."

Parsen relaxed a bit. "And how are you?"

Falier gripped the edge of the counter. "Angry. Frustrated. I get that people are scared, I do. But for them to accuse her like they did last night? To claim that the dragons are only acting for their own gain when their lives would actually be easier anywhere else? And then for Yarlan to shout at her and hurt her so badly? I don't understand it, Pa. We haven't done anything wrong!"

Parsen gave an almost grim smile. "It's a strange new world you've entered. Telepaths, dragons, war. Your mother and I have wondered if you've thought through what it will cost you to continue."

Falier looked at his father. "What do you mean?"

"Your relationships here, for one. This is the second time you've stood with Alísa against the village. Some people might not forgive that."

"Forgive?" Falier straightened, incredulous. "Are you saying I shouldn't have gone to her aid? Whether she's the girl I'm pursuing or not, Yarlan was practically screaming in her face after the presentation, and last night he demeaned her! I couldn't just watch it like everyone else was—"

Falier stopped himself, realizing too late that his parents had been among those to remain still and silent.

"No," Parsen said, stoic in the face of Falier's accusation. "We've always wanted you to be the kind of person who would stand up for others. But as one of the peoples' holders, they expect you to be on their side. It's a holder's duty to serve the people, to comfort them and assuage their fears—"

"Even when they're wrong? When they're hurting someone?"

Parsen paused a moment. "It's also our duty to walk them gently from wrong to right. It's why we've offered up the dancing grounds to the dragons' visits. Why we've been there every day—"

"You and Selene have." Falier shook his head. "Ma's been there once, and only briefly."

Parsen's eyes hardened, and Falier knew instantly he had made a mistake. "You don't know what she's going through, watching the son she adores chase the very thing she was told would kill him! You will respect her and the time she needs to walk through that."

Falier cast his eyes down. "Yes, sir."

Parsen heaved a sigh. "It's up to you how you live your life. If you believe the Maker has called you to become a slayer and fight the world at Alísa's side, we will support you. I just want to make sure you know what you're doing, before you cross a line and can't go back."

Shame cooled Falier's anger, turning it to a tepid brew he wanted to expel. His family was trying, in their own way. Though he didn't fully agree with it, he understood it. They were holders, their duty first and foremost to the people of Me'ran.

But he...

A thought ached through him, grating against his heart. He loved his people, wanted to please them if he could, would die for them if it came to that. But duty? That lay elsewhere now, and until this moment he hadn't quite realized the implications. And suddenly the air of the kitchen felt thick.

"If Alísa comes looking for me, would you tell her I'm going to the lake?"

Parsen studied him for a moment, then nodded and turned back to the flames.

Falier slipped through the outside door, catching a light breeze. The shadow of the Hold was long in the morning sun, and right now he needed warmth. Something to stave the ache in his bones.

He headed north, toward the forest path to the lake. As he rounded the corner to the dancing grounds, he saw people there, apparently having come out to enjoy the sun after breakfast. Multiple adults spoke in a semi-circle, while Serra's boys ran after each other wielding sticks as swords.

In no mood to talk with anyone besides Alísa or possibly Graydonn, Falier fixed his eyes on the path to the lake. If he made for it with purpose, hopefully he wouldn't be—

"Falier!" Selene called.

—interrupted. So much for that. He waved and kept walking, hoping she'd take the hint, but she excused herself from the people and jogged to his side.

"Where are you headed?"

"The lake." He jerked his head in that direction.

"Uh-oh." Her smile faded and she stopped in front of him. "What did Papá say?"

Falier slumped. "The sound-lights gave that away with only two words?"

Selene shook her head. "You only go to the lake by yourself when you're agitated."

Oh. That made a bit more sense.

"Pa just" —Falier sighed— "made me realize something I need to process."

"Do you want company?"

Falier paused. He did want company. But not Selene. Not this time. Right now, he needed someone who wasn't family. If only the mind-kin bond worked through mountain stone, he could call for Graydonn. He could also knock at Alísa's door and ask her to join him, but after last night he didn't want to risk waking her up if she still slept.

"No. I'll be all right."

Selene studied him. "Okay. Before you go—will you be seeing the dragons today?"

He shrugged. "I don't know. Maybe."

"Do you think they would be up for a visitor?"

Falier cocked his head. "You?"

"I figure it's time. I know there are more than I've met here, and..." She stopped, her eyes lifting as she searched for words. "They're your clan now. I should meet them all, before..."

Her eyes fell and set his heart aching again. Before everything got crazy again. Before his life was completely in the hands—talons—of strangers. Before he left Me'ran for good.

"Holder Falier!" the younger of Serra's sons called.

"I would like that," he told Selene while waving to the boy. "Maybe tomorrow, after the visit?"

"Holder Falier, I have a question!"

Selene chuckled, gesturing for the boy to wait a second. "Sounds good to me. Let me know once you've checked with Alísa."

"Of course. I think she'll be happy to have you come to the cave."

"And you?"

"Ecstatic."

Selene smiled, then nodded at the boy. He bounced on his toes as he waited for Falier's attention, his brother a couple feet behind him. Both boys were red-faced, the older with his stick-sword "sheathed" in his belt.

"Thank you for your patience. It's your turn now."

Falier leaned toward the boy as Selene walked away. "What is it?"

"If I become a slayer, will I have to choose whether to fight dragons or be friends?"

Falier hesitated. The thought of these children becoming warriors formed a pit in his stomach. He, Taz, and other village children had imagined fighting dragons at the same age, but these seven- and ten-year-olds covered in the dust of the dancing grounds seemed so much younger than they had been.

"I hope not," Falier finally said. "I hope by that time the war will be over, and there won't be any need to fight dragons anymore."

The older boy stared at him, a question burning in eyes too serious for a ten-year-old. "Do you think Papá was a bad man because he fought dragons?"

The question sent an ache through Falier's heart. The thought had never once occurred to him, nor had the question of how a fight for peace might affect the children of those the war had taken.

The back of his neck prickled, and he glanced back to see Serra watching them. Her eyes were like a panther's, one waiting to spring if he made the wrong move. Falier swallowed. He couldn't just ignore the question for fear of answering incorrectly.

Falier knelt to look the boys in the eyes. *Nahne and Branni help me.*

"No. Your father was a good man. He saved people. Protected them. There are bad dragons out there, and we need slayers who will stop them." His answer to the younger brother seemed inadequate now. Simplistic.

"I suppose," he started, acutely aware that more than just Serra and the boys listened now, "there will always be bad dragons out there, and we'll always need slayers willing to fight them. The important thing is we now know some dragons are good, and we should work to find peace with them. We need warriors willing to listen and learn before they decide to swing their swords."

Falier smiled to himself, remembering Kerrik. Though his gruff declaration that Falier would be killed on his first battlefield had cut through him, the man had probably saved his life. Whether Kerrik saw Falier as a slayer with zero potential or one who just needed time before stepping onto the battlefield, Falier would never know. But Kerrik had seen Falier's life as one worth saving.

"Your Pa saw more than many other slayers choose to. I think he would want that for you too."

Falier glanced up at Serra, searching for some sign that she wouldn't kill him. The panther in her eyes had left, in its place a simple contemplation. His answer must have been acceptable.

The youngest had already lost interest, running back to the spot where they had been dueling and calling for his brother to follow. The older boy waited, meeting Falier's eyes with determination.

"I will be just like him."

Falier nodded solemnly. "I'm sure you will."

The younger boy called again, and this time his brother answered, drawing his stick-sword from his belt and charging with a battle cry. Falier smiled, wiping the dust from his pants as he stood.

"You handled that well."

Falier spun at the female voice that was far closer than he expected. Relief flooded him as he saw Alísa.

Her eyes held laughter. "Sorry. Typically, I'm the j—jumpy one."

Hope rose in his chest. Though the circles under her eyes spoke to her night of sorrow, she wasn't distraught. It lifted his spirits to see her able to smile.

"You snuck up on me." He lifted an arm to her. "Are you in the mood for a stroll?"

Alísa tucked her hand into his elbow. "P-Parsen said you were going to the lake?"

He hummed an affirmative. "We can go somewhere else, if you want. But the lake is peaceful."

"That sounds wonderful."

Falier led Alísa to the path into the forest, fallen twigs cracking under their boots and ferns rustling with their steps. A gentle humidity hung in the shade of the trees, one that would turn uncomfortable later, but for now refreshed him. Squirrels chittered and birds sang in the boughs, all reveling in the beauty of summer. Alísa's eyes lifted to the branches, her gaze grazing from creature to creature in contemplation.

She noticed his attention, and as her eyes met his, a strange understanding moved through them.

"Are you okay, Falier? You focused on helping me last night, b— b—b" —she swallowed, looking in front of them now— "but I know you were hurt t-t-too."

Falier gave a wry smile. Right to the heart of it. Alísa wasn't really one for small talk. He stayed silent, sifting through the swirling thoughts and feelings. How could he put them to words when he didn't fully understand them?

"Pa and I talked this morning, about the villagers and the duty holders have to their people and—" He swallowed as his throat tightened. He would not choke, he would not let his voice crack. "And I realized something I should have figured out weeks ago. When I joined you on your mission to find more dragons, when I asked to pursue you, when I thought through the fact that joining your clan meant I would face battle for the rest of my life—somewhere in there I should have realized it."

Silence took him again. His mind whirled as he tried to form the words he needed to say. Alísa waited patiently. He loved that about her.

"I'm not a holder anymore, Líse. I'm a slayer. Or, at least, I'm walking the path through that transition. And that means my duty is no longer to Me'ran. But for so long they've been my world. Even when I was a boy playing slayers and dragons, serving Me'ran was the only thing in my mind. Not the slayers who would be my new clan. Not the whole of the eastern forests. Not the world. Me'ran. But now—"

A particularly loud bird cawed above them, and he stopped to watch it puff out its bright red feathers as it argued with a squirrel. The cacophony rose, swirling around like the jumbled thoughts in his head.

Alísa moved her hand from his arm, slipping her fingers between his. The sensation drew Falier back to the present, back to her eyes that somehow held both understanding and questions. She pulled gently and they continued on their path, the lake now in view.

"But now?" she prompted.

"Now I know I belong with you and the dragons. But how do I sever myself from what once was my world? Was Lethín right last night? Should I just—stop?"

Alísa shook her head. "That isn't you. I think that's why Lethín's words b—bothered you so. He spoke as though you've always wanted to leave and d—d—d—don't c-care about Me'ran now that you have the chance to go."

"Yes!" Falier turned to her, gesturing to the forest around them. "I'm not 'stuck here.' I've never felt that way. I care about my people. Does he really not know that? Do *they* really not know? Hasn't everything I've ever done shown them? Why can't they trust and support me now?"

Falier stopped, realizing as his words echoed over the water that he was very nearly shouting. And flailing both of his hands as Alísa watched him. Dropping his hands, he breathed out a sigh.

"I'm sorry. I just—"

Alísa wrapped her arms around his waist, the motion jerking his words to a stop. She whispered to him, her tone firm, as though this were the most important thing she had ever said.

"Don't. Don't apologize. It's not right or fair—they should know you better. No matter how they feel about me or the dragons, they shouldn't accuse you or throw sarcastic remarks."

Falier returned the embrace, his anger deflating as she spoke. "I don't regret anything. I know I'm supposed to go with you, and I want to. I just don't know how to let go yet."

"It's a difficult balance you're having to find." She squeezed him harder. "But the clan has your back. We've all left something behind. You are not alone."

Falier breathed in her words, pressing them into his wavering mind. They were true, not just words to ease his pain. Though not all of the dragons could be called friends yet, the trust and camaraderie was there, won in battle together.

He rested his head on Alísa's, pulling her tighter, hoping to physically convey that message back to her. Instead, she giggled. He pulled back to look her in the eyes.

"What?"

Another laugh tried to escape her. "It's nothing, really. It's just—this would p-p-probably be more c-comforting to you if I were taller."

A smile played at his lips. "What?"

"I'm sorry," she giggled again. "I didn't get much sleep last night. I j—just mean the angle is all wrong. Your head should be resting on my shoulder, and I shouldn't be on t-t-t-t-tip-toes."

Falier shook his head, a grin spreading. It was ridiculous, but her laughter was adorable. He looked further down their path and pulled out of her embrace, taking her hands.

"Come with me."

He pulled her after him, half-running until they reached a stump. He kicked it, looking to make sure it wasn't rotten. Satisfied, he looked back at her. Her confusion was adorable too.

"Up you go. Let's test your theory."

Alísa laughed and stepped up onto the stump, pressing down on his hand to steady herself. He had to look up a couple of inches now.

Alísa wrapped her arms around him again, squeezing his shoulders. He slipped his arms around her waist, laid his head on her shoulder, and closed his eyes. He practically melted into her warmth, her tenderness, her strength.

"Wow. I think you're right."

"Of c-c-c-course I am. I've been the one comforted so many t-t-t-times—I know what I'm t-talking about."

"You sure do." He rested there for a moment, letting her closeness melt away the chill of unknowns that had clamped around his heart.

Falier pulled back to look into her eyes. "Thank you, Alísa."

Her cheeks turned pink and she looked at his shoulder. "You're welcome."

Why was everything she did today especially beautiful? Would she let him kiss her? Or was it too soon? Oh, how he wanted to kiss her. But at their proper heights.

Falier shifted his hold on her waist. "Here, let's get you down."

Alísa placed her hands on his shoulders, like the lift he taught her weeks ago for a dance. It felt good to hold her, to feel her trust as he supported her weight and set her back on the forest floor. He didn't let go, gazing into her eyes looking back up at him. His mouth went dry with the question he needed to ask.

"Alísa, may—"

"It's not my fault! It's not my fault!"

Sesína's frantic voice broke into Falier's mind just before a giant splash broke the silence of the lake. He and Alísa whirled as black scales flashed in the sunlight before disappearing into the water. Graydonn—the first to splash down, apparently—emerged and Alísa lowered her arms, pulling Falier toward the dragons, the moment gone.

"Sesína said you were here," Graydonn said, swimming closer.

Sesína's head poked up. *"I didn't know what was going to happen! I tried to stop Graydonn when I figured it out."*

Blood drained from Falier's face and his hand went to the back of his neck. *"You, uh—you were watching us?"*

While he was sure his face was white as wool, Alísa's gained color.

"*I would have looked away,*" Sesína said, making a gagging sound. "*Obviously.*"

"*I'm missing something,*" Graydonn said, looking between everyone. "*Also obviously...*"

"*Never mind, Graydonn.*" Alísa made her way down to the water line. "*What are you two doing here?*"

Falier hurried to catch up, choosing to ignore the new, horrifying implications of Sesína's Illumination. For now.

Sesína cough-laughed. "*You mean besides ruining your love life?*"

"*That's enough,*" Alísa scolded, though a hint of humor broke through.

"*Ruining...?*" Graydonn's eyes dimmed. "*Did we come at a bad time?*"

Falier pulled at his thoughts, willing himself not to confirm Graydonn's fear. There would be other chances, and it wasn't as though Graydonn had meant to interrupt them.

"*Alísa said she had a new plan for the visits.*" Sesína pulled herself from the water and shook out her wings. "*I could have just stolen it from her mind, but I thought it would be helpful for her to talk it out. Like old times. Before all the other dragons came around.*"

Alísa shook her head. "*You like the other dragons.*"

"*Yeah, but I don't like sharing you with so many.*" Sesína poked Alísa in the rib with her muzzle.

Alísa pushed Sesína's face away. "*You're going to hate my plan, then.*"

Sesína pulled her head back. "*What madness is going on in that mind of yours?*"

Sighing, Alísa jerked her head further up the bank, beckoning them to follow her. "*Namor is right—I can't live in fear of the very people whose trust I'm trying to gain. I need to be in their midst.*"

At the top of the embankment, Alísa took a seat on the stump. Falier sat on the ground in front of her, crossing his legs on the dirt path. Behind him, the dragons, too, lowered to their bellies to hear Alísa's plan.

"*So my thought is, for the next few weeks, I should live in the village.*"

Falier sat up straighter. "*Really?*"

Sesína thrashed her tail, hitting Falier in the back and drawing an "oof" from him. *"That's not a good thing!"*

"Hush." Alísa gave Sesína a look of motherly scolding. *"I don't love it, either, but I can't think of another way. I want them to see me, not just as the Dragon Singer, but as a person who cares about them. And to do that, I need your help, Falier."*

He nodded. *"Anything."*

Alísa rubbed her hands against her skirt. *"I want to work in the Hold. Help with deliveries, cook, entertain—all of it. I know it's a little soon, but are you okay with that? Will your parents approve?"*

Her nervousness made sense now. It was normal for a pursuer and his beloved to spend a few weeks learning each other's family trade. Traditionally, though, it occurred right before a marriage proposal. Still, the thought of Alísa being around his family and them getting to know her more made him smile.

Alísa straightened, her cheeks flushing. *"Approve of my helping. Not anything else. We don't have to rush anything else. I just—"*

Falier cracked a smile. *"I get it. I think I can get them to understand the extenuating circumstances. And you can have your pick of rooms to stay in— there are a couple that are bigger than the one you used last night."*

Alísa pressed her lips together. *"Actually, I'm going to ask Namor and Tenza if I can stay with them. We'll already appear like we're taking things faster than normal. I don't want anyone thinking—other things of us if I stay at the Hold."*

Oh. Falier rubbed the back of his neck, his face warming. *"Yeah. I guess that makes sense."*

"I also want to move the visits into the village square," Alísa said, surprising him. She had been the one to reject that idea before. *"I think getting the dragons in front of the people rather than requiring them to approach us will help. I'd like your input on how to make the visits as unthreatening as possible for them, and for me."*

Alísa cringed and looked down. It appeared she hadn't meant to include that last phrase. For all its benefits, telepathy often bared more than most humans actually wanted to say.

Sesína stood and went to her side, placing a wing on Alísa's shoulder. Falier shifted, preparing comfort her too, but Alísa blew out a shuddering breath and continued aloud.

"I'm sorry. I'm a m—m—mess. B—but that c-c-can't get in the way."

Her eyes glistened, but behind the unshed tears lived a resolve Falier wasn't sure he would have if their positions were reversed. She might be vulnerable, but she certainly wasn't weak. Well-acquainted with pain and practiced in moving despite it. If Falier could shield her from all of that pain, he would, yet this strength which could only show in the midst of pain was exceedingly beautiful.

"Remember what you told me earlier," he said, placing a hand on hers. "You are not alone. We're all here to help, and there are others who will be there who we've already won over. Selene, for one. She actually asked if she could come to the cave tomorrow."

That brought a smile. "She did? That's wonderful."

Falier grinned. "I thought so too." More than anything, he wanted Alísa and his family to get along, and Alísa's happiness at Selene's visit made his heart soar.

Of course, that would only make leaving Me'ran that much harder. Joy turned to a pulling ache in his heart. It couldn't be helped. It was all part of a change in calling. Future heartache shouldn't negate the present good. Music could be found in the mess, and he would cling to its rhythm no matter what.

10

THE HUES OF DRAGONS

Sesína's colors clashed.

After so many visits with the dragons, it shouldn't still bug Selene. Honestly, out of all the dragons, Sesína's personality best suited the clashing colors—a mixture of sweet and feisty. But when the dragoness thrummed as she talked, the emerald of her telepathy strand went to war against the magenta sound-light of her verbalizations.

It wasn't fair. If Selene had to learn two colors for each dragon, the colors should at least have the decency to be complimentary.

"More tea, Miss Selene?"

Selene smiled and held out her clay cup. "Yes, thank you, Marri."

"And you, Sesína?"

Sesína's eyes brightened. She nosed her bucket forward, the dust of the village square puffing up behind it. The movement made her crown of daisies slide down between her eyes.

"Yes, please. This is the best tea I've ever had."

The seven-year-old beamed, pouring ginger tea from her pot into the bucket. One of Marri's friends stood and readjusted the crown, giggling as Sesína poked her side with her muzzle. Sesína's telepathy strand lit up with delight.

"Thank you. I'm afraid I would crush the flowers if I fixed it myself."

Selene stared at the telepathy lights no one else could see. They were odd, to say the least. Telepathy colors always matched one's eyes and came out of their forehead in a tiny strand of light. In conversation, the many threads of the participants would join together in the center of the group like the beginnings of a multi-hued spiderweb.

Across the way, Alísa stood with a small group of adults and Komi.

113

Another spiderweb connected their group together, but Alísa spoke verbally rather than psychically, her white voice-light glowing with an orange halo of tension. Bringing the dragon visits to the square had intimidated her, and tomorrow she would join in making deliveries and gathering goods for the Hold from the shops. The new plan was aggressive for her. Would she be able to keep it up?

"Marri, dear." A new voice caught Selene's attention, a bright circle of lavender. Marri's mother stood in the door of their home, only about fifty feet from the tea party. "It's time to wrap it up. Lunch is ready, and I'm sure the dragons have other things to do today."

Marri's older brother stopped running, letting the kickball get away from him and be picked up by a girl on the other team.

"But Sesína was going to play with me next!"

Sesína arched her neck to look at him, the movement almost regal as she balanced her daisy crown. As she had done with the girls at the tea-party, Sesína added the boy to the conversation so that he could hear her telepathic voice. A new line shot from the center of the telepathy-web to the boy's forehead, turning from Sesína's emerald eye-color to the boy's dark brown.

"I promise, I'll play with you first tomorrow," Sesína said. *"You'll have to teach me the rules, though."*

A satisfied grin formed, and the boy took off again, his mother calling after him that he needed to stop for lunch too. Sesína dipped her head to Marri.

"Here, you take the crown. It will fall off when I fly. Thank you for inviting me to your tea party."

Marri took the flowers with the biggest grin on her face, not even vocalizing her sadness with the other girls as Sesína stood up. Selene followed the dragoness' lead, wiping the dust from her skirts as she did.

"Yes," Selene said, "you were a most gracious host."

Marri's grin didn't change, but Selene couldn't help but think it had everything to do with Sesína and nothing to do with her. As it should be.

Selene fell into step beside Sesína and headed for Alísa's group. The adults, too, began excusing themselves to make their own meals or get back to their shops. Smiles abounded, most of their voice-lights bearing halos of either light-purple contentment or yellow happiness. A few of those leaving came from Falier and Graydonn's group. Harenn, as usual, lay off to the side and merely observed.

A mixture of emotions ran through Selene. Seeing Falier standing tall next to a dragon wasn't uncommon now. Like Sesína's colors, Selene should be used to it, yet she wasn't. Her brother was a slayer—the sweet, servant-hearted boy had dragons' blood on his hands, yet was also a friend of dragons. Pride lived there, but so did fear. Like with Taz, Falier would soon be taken away, albeit with more choice in the matter than Taz. After her beloved had been stolen, Selene wasn't sure she could take another such loss.

Falier caught sight of her. "You ready for this?"

Selene glanced at Twi-Peak. "I think so."

"Are you scared?" Sesína playfully bumped Selene's shoulder with her wing.

Selene smirked, summoning more confidence than she felt. "Should I be?"

"Not at all." Falier gestured to Graydonn behind him. "I've asked Graydonn to carry you, since Komi and Harenn have never had a rider before. I'll take the bumpy ride."

Selene tried not to appear as relieved as she felt. "Ever the gentleman."

"Did you remember a hair-tie?" Alísa came up alongside Falier, already tying her curls back.

Selene fished a strap of green cloth out of her pocket and held it up.

"Good. I learned it the h—" Alísa stopped, her eyes fixing on something behind Selene. She blinked and refocused on Selene's face. "H—hard way."

Selene twisted and saw Yarlan leaning against the side of a house, just watching them. Poor girl—he wasn't going to give her any space.

She gave Alísa a small smile. "Let's go. I'm excited to get up there."

Sesína pushed between Selene and Alísa, blocking Alísa's sight of Yarlan in the process.

Selene walked to Graydonn, reaching back to tie the cloth around her thin blond hair. Hopefully, it would stay. Curly hair held tighter than

Selene's own straight locks.

Graydonn lay on his belly, eyes bright with what Selene now recognized as happiness. An amber strand flew from his head to hers, and she did her best not to flinch at the fast approach.

"Will you need assistance climbing up?"

"I don't think so." Selene stopped at his side, contemplating her next move. Crouched down, Graydonn was shorter than a horse. Of course, there were the spines. They looked sharper than they had before, now that she pictured herself sitting right up against them.

If her little brother could do it...

Selene grabbed two spines and swung up, the tight pants underneath her skirt allowing her to slide into place without compromising modesty. Her skirt caught on a spine and she reached back to situate it around her.

Graydonn shifted. *"Ready for me to stand?"*

Selene wrapped her fingers around the nearest spine. "I think so."

As soon as Graydonn moved, Selene gripped tighter with hands and legs.

"You good?" Falier spoke from Komi's back. No surprise there—Harenn didn't seem the type to stoop to carry a rider.

Selene nodded, forcing herself to settle as Graydonn took a few steps. *Just like a horse. I can do this.*

"Yes, you can," Graydonn encouraged. *"I won't let you fall."*

Selene cringed. He heard her thoughts. So much for being Falier's very capable older sister in the dragon's eyes.

With a trumpet, Sesína bounded into the sky, Alísa grinning as they rose. Harenn followed behind, and Selene watched both dragons spear for Twi-Peak.

"We'll take it slow," Falier said. "Maybe spiraling around rather than going straight up?"

"Sounds reasonable," Graydonn said. *"Are you ready, Selene?"*

Selene looked up the mountain and let out a slow breath. So tall. A thrill of nervous excitement ran through her.

"Yes."

Like a spring, Graydonn's muscles bunched underneath her. *"Hold on!"*

The spring released. Everything in Selene lurched down and back as the dragon launched into the air. The air battered her as he flew past the Hold, banked just at the edge of the rise on which her home sat, and aimed for the mountain.

"Taking off is the hardest part," Graydonn said, his wings pushing them higher and higher. *"It will smooth out soon. Though"* —mirth entered his tone— *"I don't think you're worried about that anymore."*

Selene grinned. Her heart raced with exhilaration as Graydonn flew over the tops of the trees. The mountain, its base a half-hour's walk from the Hold, sped toward them in barely a minute. Graydonn banked in a wide arc, his wing-beats a steady pulse lifting them higher and higher.

"I'm so used to going to the little cave we used to live in," Graydonn said, *"it's strange to head for our new home so far up. Three months near the ground and I forget a lifetime living among the clouds."*

Selene opened her mouth to reply but felt the wind stealing her words. She would have to shout to have any chance of being heard. Instead, she remained silent and looked out over the forest. The miles of trees stretching under the sky stole her breath away. The contours in the land were more obvious up here—forest dipping down in some areas and rising up in others, all clothed in many different shades of green.

"But the little cave is far too small for us now," Graydonn continued. *"Alísa didn't like the big cave when we first came to Twi-Peak, but she seems okay with it now. We offered to let her stay at the lower cave with a few of us at a time, but she wanted to be with the whole clan."*

And now Alísa chose to live in the village. Melancholy for her friend ran through Selene. Hopefully, this new plan of Alísa's would be worth it.

"Would you like me to stop talking?"

Selene shook her head. As if he could see it.

"No!" she shouted, "I don't want to fight the wind!"

As if to emphasize the point, a gust blind-sided them. Graydonn flapped faster, leaning away from the mountain for a moment to correct himself.

"Think your words to me."

"I'm not a telepath!"

"You don't have to be. So long as I've started the connection, you can use it too."

Selene stared at the amber line between Graydonn's head and hers. *Truly? Just think the words and they'll travel the connection?*

"I hear something, but not clearly," Graydonn said. "Your brother pictured an arrow shot from a bow when he was first learning. A little violent for my taste, but it worked."

She squinted. Arrow. Shot through the amber line connecting them. *"How about now?"*

"Perfect! You should be able to do this with any dragon so long as one of them connects first."

Graydonn tightened his bank. The few trees brave enough to cling to the side of the mountain were far below them now. Here where the mountain diverged into its two peaks, only shrubs and patches of purple flowers mottled the rocky crags. Then she saw it—a large hole in the side of the western peak, just above the split.

With a quick word of warning, Graydonn dove, his movements smooth as he took Selene into the darkness. She shivered as they left the light behind and Graydonn's telepathy became her only visual cue. Then the glow of firelight swept over the walls as they entered the interior cavern.

Fifty feet below, a colorful spiderweb of telepathy crossed the floor where the dragons congregated. Flickering firelight revealed shadows of horns, wings, and massive bodies. Fear trembled through her at the sight, and she pushed against it. She wasn't in danger, but soon she would be standing in the midst of creatures most of humanity deemed synonymous.

"You could not be more safe in your own home," Graydonn assured her.

Selene blew out her breath and shifted her grip on Graydonn's spine. She could typically hide such emotions, but telepathy negated much of that ability. Was this how Falier felt when she used her sound-lights to read him?

The constant swirls of orange accompanying Graydonn's wing-strokes became more jagged as he flapped harder to slow their descent.

Anticipating a hard jerk as they landed, Selene braced herself. However, Graydonn set down almost delicately, with barely a hint of a purple thud or bright green scraping of talons against stone. Then came many scrapings as Komi and Falier came in for a landing. Falier laughed as Komi skidded to a stop, the dragoness' bright eyes showing her own mirth.

Selene slid down Graydonn's scales, using his spines to control her descent. Alísa met her on the ground, a wide grin on her face.

"W—welcome! I had them light a fire near the center and had everyone g—g—gather so you can see them. They still aren't quite used to living with someone who c-c-c—can't see in the dark."

From the air, the circle of dragons had looked intimidating. Now their immensity sent a tremor through Selene. Most of them towered over her even at a crouch. Curved talons as long as her forearm scraped against the rock floor, and firelight gleamed on upper canines overlapping jaws.

Alísa reached for her hand with an empathetic smile. "It's okay."

Selene took in a steeling breath. *I know this. These aren't just any dragons. These are Falier's clan. I can do this.*

Selene gave Alísa her hand. The cavern smelled of rock and earth, but as they neared the fire the scent of warm oil overtook it—the scent of dragons. Alísa led them to a space between Koriana and Sesína. At least she already knew the dragons closest to her. Graydonn followed and settled at their backs, hemming Selene in with safety. This would be okay.

"Everyone," Alísa said, her lips not moving, *"this is Selene, Falier's sister."*

Alísa proceeded to name the dragons, pointing to each of them in turn. There were so many new ones, but, helpfully, the feeling of a dragon's name always accompanied their voice. Selene just had to be sure to let each dragon speak to her first until she had them memorized.

Alísa lowered her hand. *"That's everyone except Korin and Saynan. Saynan's on scout duty, watching in case the other dragon clan attacks again. I was hoping Korin would be back to meet you by now, but we can't rush the hunters."*

Selene dipped her head and pushed her words through the

telepathy line. *"It's good to meet you all. Thank you for taking care of my brother."*

Falier twisted to look at her. *"When did you—I've never seen you use telepathy before!"*

"Graydonn taught me how on our flight."

"And you just picked it up." Falier rolled his eyes. *"Typical."*

Selene poked him in the rib, making him twist away. *"I had to catch up. Can't have my little brother outstripping me."*

He grabbed at her hand and poked her back, grinning. *"I can't even have one thing..."*

"I promise, the riding into battle thing is all yours."

Falier's laughter petered out. *"Good."*

He meant it. The violet in his tone spoke of affection—he didn't want her anywhere near the conflict. The feeling matched her own, but after seeing him with the dragons this past week, hearing the excitement in his tone as he told of his faraway adventures with them, witnessing his telepathy grow stronger—Falier came alive here.

So did Alísa. She was always friendly with humankind, but also shy, sometimes almost apologetic for being there. But here, among giants, Alísa stood as an equal.

A gentle rumble came from Koriana. The great dragoness arched her neck, lowering her head to Selene's level.

"I am glad you came to visit us. After weeks of having to be on my best behavior before humans, it is good to see one unafraid to stand on our ground."

Falier scoffed. *"I stand on your ground all of the time."*

"Yes, so you don't count."

Selene shook her head as Falier clutched at his heart in mock pain. *"You have my full support in ignoring him."*

Koriana thrummed, as did a couple other dragons. As the dragoness pulled her head back, firelight glinted off something between her forelegs. Selene squinted and leaned closer to see. They appeared to be giant, lightly-polished gemstones, one sapphire and one a tawny brown.

No, not gemstones. Eggs. Those had to be two of the dragon eggs Alísa had brought back!

"They're beautiful, aren't they?"

Selene looked up to see Alísa, an almost motherly smile on her face as she, too, gazed at the eggs.

"*Yes,*" she replied. "*How long before they hatch?*"

Koriana sniffed and prodded at the eggs, repositioning them. "*Perhaps three weeks.*"

An orange emotion surrounded Koriana's telepathy—tension, fear, or anxiety. "*What's wrong?*"

Alísa's eyes grew sad. "*They're orphans. Dragonets need to bond with a parent so they can be Illuminated as soon as they hatch. Without an Illumination bond to teach them how to live, they'll most likely die within hours of hatching.*"

Koriana gave them another prod. "*We've been taking turns holding them, but it is up to the dragonet to choose—none may force it—and so far, neither has.*"

Selene sat up, kneeling so she could see the eggs better. "*May I touch them?*"

A grumble sounded behind her, and Selene whipped around to find the source. Faern. Brown scales matched his daughter Komi's, yet his brutish look distanced him in Selene's mind from his sweet and curious daughter. Alísa laid a reassuring hand on Selene's arm.

"*I can't let you,*" Koriana said. "*Now that we know dragons can be Illuminated by humans, we'd best avoid you touching them, lest one tries to bond to you.*"

Sesína snorted from the other side of Koriana. "*I turned out just fine.*"

A few thrums echoed around the circle, though some carried more mirth than others. Sesína's eyes darkened, and Alísa placed a soothing hand on her scaly neck.

"*That you did, Sesína,*" Koriana said a little forcefully. "*But best to avoid accidentally forcing Selene into that bond.*"

A soft growl that sounded almost like a purr came from beyond Sesína. "*If you wish to touch an egg, Selene, you may come see mine.*"

Aree. She had scales that matched her mate Saynan's sapphire eyes. Selene turned to face her and saw an opalescent egg nestled in her paws. It glittered like snow in the firelight.

Falier's grin called Selene out of uncertainty. "*Let's go!*"

121

"*Quickly,*" Aree said. "*She's moving now.*"

Staying close to Falier, Selene ventured into the circle of dragons and knelt beside Aree's paws. Long, curved talons made her heart stutter. No danger lurked in Aree's voice, yet for a moment Selene couldn't move. Aree could kill her with a single swipe of her paw, a snap of her jaws. And yet, so could Saynan or Koriana, and she had been near them many times. She had to get past this prey-based fear.

Selene set a hand on the egg. It was warm to the touch, and when she rubbed a thumb over it, she found minuscule holes pocked its surface. The egg shifted, the dragonet pressing against the shell as it twisted inside. A tiny burbling growl raised a light purple aura around the shell.

Contentment.

"*She likes you,*" Aree said.

Selene looked up. "*You don't mean that bond they were talking about?*"

"*No. My dragonet is already bonded to me—there is no fear she would choose another. The others are lost and frightened.*"

Selene stepped back as Falier took a turn petting the egg.

"*But if they're so afraid,*" he said, "*why haven't they bonded to anyone? You've been passing them around for days now.*"

Aree's eyes dimmed. "*Dragonets and hatchlings are unpredictable.*"

Her wings shifted, one scraping along the stone floor to pull something closer to her. Iila. Alísa had mentioned her in the introductions, but Selene hadn't seen her yet.

Falier stood. "*How is she today?*"

"*She has been sleeping off and on to stave off her hunger.*" Aree looked to the cave entrance. "*Saynan was able to grab her something yesterday after flight-training, but she is unfortunately at the bottomless-pit stage of—*"

A high-pitched roar resounded through the cave, sending a flash of bright purple across Selene's vision. She gasped aloud and closed her eyes, pressing her hands to her ears. Falier looped an arm around her shoulders. The echoes of the roar still flickered purple even with her eyes shut, as sound-lights always did. Reflexes sometimes didn't make sense.

"*Do not fear,*" Aree said. "*It's just Korin, returned from the hunt.*"

Selene opened her eyes in time to see a silvery head peek out from under Aree's wing. Cobalt eyes stared up toward the entrance, then turned to her. With a hiss, Iila pulled her head back under Aree's wing.

Falier squeezed Selene's shoulders. *"You all right?"*

Selene looked up, searching for the offending dragon. *"I think so."*

There he was. Scales black as Sesína's blended into the dark ceiling of the cave, but his sapphire eyes showed him circling overhead.

Falier pulled at her. *"Let's get back so Iila feels safe to come out and eat."*

As they went back to Koriana, a purple thud signaled Korin landing behind Aree. A dead stag drooped in his jaws, which he plopped unceremoniously onto the floor.

"Success, finally. This one nearly lost me twice." Korin lowered his head to peek at Iila, his tone turning soft. *"All for you, little one."*

Aree stood, her protective wing dragging awkwardly along the floor as she guided Iila around to the deer. She chomped at the carcass, causing Selene to cringe as bones and tendons popped.

"Take the rest for yourself and Rayna," Aree told Korin, pulling one of the deer's legs free. *"Iila will overstuff herself without an Illumination bond to warn her to stop."*

Rayna snorted. *"He stuffed me yesterday. Give some to Tora and Q'rill—Tora will need the energy if she's to hunt next."*

"I hunt better on an empty stomach," Tora said. *"Makes me meaner."*

Thrums sprang up around the circle in multi-colored flashes. Amidst the spiderweb of telepathy and the bright fire-lit scales of the dragons, the colors shone as multitudinous as the home of the dreki. Overwhelming, yet strangely beautiful.

As Korin removed the rest of the deer from Iila's sight, loud crunching rose. Thankfully, Aree blocked Selene's sight of the hatchling and her meal. The sounds were, however, followed by more snapping and ripping on the opposite side of the circle—Q'rill's meal highly visible. Selene averted her eyes.

"Are you all right, Selene?" Tora. She had noticed. That made Selene cringe even more.

"Yes."

Selene forced her eyes open and looked at Q'rill to prove her answer. One of the largest dragons in the cave, his head would tower over

Selene if she stood next to him, even though he lay on his belly. Add to that the many scars over his neck and side, and Q'rill was one of the most intimidating dragons in the cave. Not someone she wanted to antagonize simply because she was feeling squeamish.

"*You do not need to lie for our sakes.*" Tora nudged her son's neck with her muzzle. "*Q'rill, eat outside the circle and spare Selene the gore.*"

Q'rill lifted his head from his meal. "*She doesn't like it?*"

His voice didn't match his bulk. Though low, it carried an innocence Selene associated with a child. Even the way he cocked his head gave the impression of a curious adolescent, not a battle-hardened warrior.

"It's fine," Selene said. "*I'm a holder, I've worked with raw meat before. Gutted poultry. You just caught me off-guard is all.*"

Q'rill's wings shifted and his eye-lights dimmed. "*I am not attacking you. Why would you need to be on-guard?*"

"*It is a figure of speech, my sky.*" Tora's tone somehow mixed qualities of both a patient mother and one who'd had this conversation many times. "*Selene is saying she was unprepared to see the raw meat. You've seen Singer cook hers. Humans detest blood.*"

An over-simplification, but Selene decided not to risk further confusing the matter through clarification. She studied Q'rill as he looked between his food, his mother, and Selene. He looked as though he was trying to pull together the pieces of one of life's great mysteries. Was this simply due to the difference in their two races, or was there more to it? His mannerisms and the way Tora spoke to him pointed to the latter. She had met humans with delayed mental maturity before—perhaps dragons had an equivalent?

After a few seconds of pondering, Q'rill snapped up one of the legs and dragged the carcass out of sight. Tora's eye-lights brightened as she watched him go.

"*Thank you, son.*"

"*Yes, thank you both,*" Selene said.

Tora blinked slowly, turning her attention to Selene. "*Please excuse the sounds. I know they make humans uncomfortable as well, but Q'rill hasn't eaten in three days. I will not ask him to wait.*"

Selene blinked before she could stop herself. It was hard to master her reactions in a world so foreign and new.

"Three days?"

"It isn't as bad as it sounds," Graydonn supplied. *"How humans eat multiple meals a day when they are so small is incredible to me. Three days is normal for adult dragons not engaged in combat or other rigorous activities. But Q'rill has scouted since his last meal."*

Selene looked to the gap where Q'rill had disappeared. *"Why don't you hunt more often?"*

A few of the dragons looked at each other, eye-ridges raising and talons tapping the ground. They said nothing, and Selene wasn't sure whether it was a touchy subject, or whether it should have been obvious.

"We do hunt often," Faern said, a hum rumbling in his throat. *"It's the fool compromise. We are confined to an area with few clearings and so have to hunt on the ground. Not only does this hinder our movements, it leaves our scent everywhere, so prey run further and further away."*

Koriana's tone was more tempered. *"Korin left at sunrise. Six hours later, he returns. We have been able to gain what we need, but for how much longer I cannot say. Not all dragons only eat every third day. Iila needs a good meal every day now that she's flight-training. Sesína, Graydonn, and Harenn should eat every other day—"*

"Harenn and I can go longer," Graydonn said. *"We just get cranky if we don't."*

"—and Rayna should be eating at least that frequently to help her wing heal."

Selene looked from dragon to dragon as they spoke, trying to comprehend. She stopped at Rayna, noting the long, jagged rip in her wing. A light shame came over her.

"I didn't realize how hard it would be for you to find food. I don't think any of us did."

Alísa looked down. *"That's my fault. I wanted to tell them, but I couldn't get the words out. I was so flustered by Yarlan and the rest of them—I just couldn't do it."*

Silence followed, the dragons neither emoting nor speaking. Finally, Graydonn raised his head.

"The Maker knows. We're supposed to be here, so He will provide. He has

already—we're not starving, and we're making progress with Me'ran."

A pulse of blue came from behind Selene, like a ripple in the air. The lovely color of calm distracted her from the conversation. It shone bright as it first passed her, then dissipated the further away it got. Another came, filling her vision then flowing away in a slow, gentle rhythm that made Selene yawn.

Wait. She sat up straight. It was pretty, but what was it?

She turned around at the same time as Alísa. The pulses originated from Koriana, who nuzzled the eggs between her paws.

"Koriana, are you the one putting me to sleep?" Alísa lifted an eyebrow.

Koriana looked up, the pulses stopping. *"My apologies. The dragonets are restless; I thought to press calm to try and settle them."*

Well. That was new. Selene had never seen empathic powers before. Emotions, sure, but those always accompanied speech. This was different—a force rather than a feeling. Though strange, the new knowledge made her smile. She would always know if someone tried to manipulate her emotions.

Just one more thing to pay attention to...

Koriana nuzzled the eggs once more. *"It doesn't seem to be working. It hasn't for anyone else either, but I thought I would try. It pains me to feel their lonely grief."*

Lonely. Thinking through what she had learned today about bonds, that made sense. These had bonded to their parents, as Aree's dragonet had, but now those parents were gone. Even in the midst of many dragons who cared for them, of course they would be lonely. In some small way, Selene could relate.

Selene shook her head inwardly. It wasn't the same. Her parents were alive, and she considered many in the village friends and loved ones. Unlike her, these dragonets actually had a reason to feel lonely.

She wanted to reach out and caress them, to whisper through their shells that it would be all right and they were safe. She resisted, about to turn away when her vision blurred slightly. She closed her eyes and opened them again. Looked at the ground and the little pebbles making shadows in the firelight, then back at the eggs. The blur persisted, only affecting the eggs. A grayish, greenish mist that looked sickly.

Sorrow?

No. That wouldn't show up unless the babies inside were making noise, or pushing out sadness like Koriana pushed calm. Selene doubted dragons inside the egg knew how to do the latter. Perhaps she saw the sorrow Koriana had tried to combat? But she had never seen someone's emotions apart from their voice before. Why now?

"Hey! Selene." Falier snapped his fingers in front of her, and she started. "Where are you?"

Selene shook her head clear and looked at him.

"I'm here, I just" —she looked back at the eggs, but the mist had disappeared— *"I thought I saw something."*

"You seem frightened," Graydonn said.

"I saw Koriana's empathy pulsing, like I see telepathy strands." Selene smiled to assure him. *"It was strange, but I'm fine."*

Falier shook his head. *"The way your brain works never ceases to amaze me."*

Selene smirked. *"Me too."*

She turned back to the fire, engaging with the dragons as she could and occasionally peeking at the eggs again. Nothing more manifested around them or the others in the space. Instead, she contented herself with the multicolored threads of telepathy shimmering between creatures who were so vastly different from her, yet held such similar souls to her own.

Yes. On that not so far away day when Falier climbed on Graydonn's back and said his final goodbye to Me'ran, he would be okay.

But would she?

11

STORMDANCE

"So you're telling me that if slayers—who have seen firsthand the horrors dragons bring—don't immediately join your side, you'll just kill them?"

Draemen, one of the dairy farmers, plopped a loaf of soft cheese on a sheet of wrapping paper. He squinted at Alísa beneath heavy eyebrows that matched his auburn ponytail.

"Seems a bit extreme."

Alísa stared at the countertop, searching for words. One would think that going about the village and having these conversations for a few days straight would make them easier.

"I would love to give them more time to p-p-ponder and see the t-truth. If there's an option to, I'll t-take it. B—but they actively seek out and k-k-kill dragons. If I told a dragon the t-t-t-t-truth and gave her time to think it over, knowing she'll kill humans in the meantime, aren't those deaths partially on my head?"

"Yes, but that's a dragon. These are humans."

Alísa cast her arm outward, gesturing to Sesína as she kicked a ball across the square, children right on her tail. The dark, overcast sky did nothing to dampen the playmates' moods, squeals of laughter rising.

"There is no d—difference. Both are souls with the c-c-c-capacity for good or evil."

Draemen held up a meaty finger. "I wasn't saying dragons don't have souls capable of good. What I meant is a single dragon can do far more damage in a day than a single slayer. Giving a slayer a day to think something over is far safer than giving the same quarter to a dragon."

Alísa dropped her arm, unsure how to respond. Draemen did have a point, but explaining why she would give a human more time than a dragon was not a conversation she wanted to have with any of her dragons.

Draemen leaned forward on the counter to watch the children and Sesína. "She does seem rather happy with them, doesn't she?"

"Yes. She's amazing with them." Alísa giggled as Serra's youngest dove for the ball, stealing it from Sesína. After two days of speaking to Serra, Alísa had convinced her to let her sons come. As Falier had suggested, having only adolescents around helped ease some fears.

Namor sat on a chair among the small group of people with Komi and Graydonn, absentmindedly rubbing the stump of his missing leg. He had mentioned at dinner yesterday it was going to rain—his stump always ached the evening before a storm.

Further back, in the space between their house and their neighbor's, Tenza moved through her daily routine of sword-patterns hours ahead of schedule. Alísa had seen Kallar lead other slayers through similar movements before, but while their exercises focused on power, Tenza's exercise was almost a dance. Typically, Tenza moved through the patterns in the afternoon while Namor napped, but the coming rain had moved it up.

Alísa turned back to Draemen. "I should g—get over there. Rules of the c-c-c—compromise and all that."

Draemen pushed the cheese toward her. "Until next time."

Alísa placed the paper-wrapped loaf in her bag and pivoted for the dragons and their small gathering of humans. A rain droplet hit Alísa's arm, and the clouds had begun darkening. It would be time for the dragons to go home soon. There went the day.

"There he is!"

A voice in the cobbler shop made Alísa jump. Pressing a hand to her heart, Alísa twisted to see Lethín standing behind the counter. He focused on something past Alísa.

"The man who's going to make Me'ran famous!"

Alísa's heart ached as she followed Lethín's gaze to Falier coming down the path from the Hold. Falier's nod of greeting was stiff, and Alísa recognized a storm behind his eyes even as he smiled pleasantly.

"Morning, Lethín."

"Don't forget us when you find your fame and glory."

"Never." Falier's eyes left Lethín even as he replied, his smile turning genuine as he looked to Alísa. "What did I miss?"

"N—not much, I think. I just finished up myself."

She started to look behind her to see if Lethín listened, but thought better of it. She tapped her temple. At Falier's telepathic connection, Alísa pushed words to him.

"You okay?"

Falier shrugged. *"I don't understand it. But I'll be fine."* Reaching a hand to the small of Alísa's back, Falier guided them toward the dragons. *"Not many people here today."*

Alísa let out a quiet breath. It was indeed a smaller group of humans than normal. Six adults besides Namor—all previous visitors—plus a group of four children playing with Sesína. And, as always, Yarlan watched from the shadows with eyes of stone.

"Probably the threat of rain," Falier added, a hand in the air as though catching raindrops.

"Or the visits are less of a novelty now." Another drop hit her head. *"Maybe everyone who wanted to meet them has already come, and the rest are just staying away."*

"Or it's the rain."

Alísa stopped, turning to face him. *"How will we know when the people are ready to support us before Soren's slayers? More would be on our side now than at the presentation, but I can't imagine that a meeting now would end in our favor. But it's already been two weeks—what more can I do?"*

"Líse." Falier spoke aloud, jarring Alísa out of her telepathic speech. He placed a hand on her shoulder, looking her in the eyes. "It's *only* been two weeks. You can't change the minds of a hundred and fifty people in just two weeks. What we've already accomplished is amazing."

Alísa sighed, looking down. He was right, and there were plenty of reasons not to rush. She had a hatchling and three more on the way up at the cave, all of whom needed time before she headed back into the fray. Not to mention that Rayna's ripped wing had the clan down a warrior.

But every day spent in the safety of Me'ran was another the war raged in the west. Another day her father might be killing innocent dragons, or else might be killed by a dragon. Time pulled at her from both directions.

The patter of rain reached Alísa's ears. A couple parents already called their children to come inside. It was time to send the dragons home. The conversation between Graydonn, Komi, and their visitors lulled as the rain grew, allowing Alísa room to speak.

"I'm sorry to c—c-cut this short, but the dragons should get home b—b—before the rain gets worse."

Sesína's disappointment entered Alísa through their bond, but even she knew Alísa was right. Dragons could fly in the rain if necessary, but the decreased visibility and the possibility of stronger winds made most think twice.

The dragons and humans said their goodbyes and the humans began rushing for cover. Selene held empty delivery baskets over her head. Falier, however, looked up into the rain, joy trickling from him.

"Have any plans for today?"

Alísa shook her head. "Just Hold chores."

"With the rain there won't be much to do." He turned his smile to her. "Want to learn my favorite thing to do when it storms like this?"

Maker above, did she love his grin—its genuineness and the way it crinkled his eyes. She couldn't help but smile back.

"Okay."

"You'll regret it," Selene whispered in mock warning. "At least tell her that your storm ritual is outside before you ask her to agree to it."

"Don't call it that." Falier looked to Alísa, his smile faltering. "Is that okay?"

His plummeting excitement made Alísa rush to affirm. "Yes! You've got me curious now."

Sesína snickered, stretching her wings for flight. *"Yet another of love's downfalls. I'll be in the cave, staying perfectly warm and dry."*

"Me too." Graydonn thrummed. *"Have fun."*

The dragons trotted away, leaping into the sky as the rain grew a little heavier. The downpour would start soon.

Selene sighed in mock long-suffering and reached for Falier's baskets and Alísa's bag. "I'll just make some hot water for tea, then."

Falier grinned as they passed them off. "Thanks!"

"Yeah, yeah. Don't catch a cold."

Falier took Alísa's hand and pulled her into a jog toward the Hold. Selene seemed content to walk, and they soon left her behind. Rain plastered Alísa's hair to her neck and ran down her face like joyful tears. By the time they got to the top of the hill, they were out of breath and laughing. Falier led her around the Hold, through the dancing grounds, and onto one of the forest paths.

Alísa shouted over the growing rain. "Where are we g—going?"

"You'll see."

Excitement quickened Falier's steps and Alísa focused on it, allowing his delight to energize her past the uncomfortable wetness. Weaving with Falier through the trees and brush, she gathered her skirt in her free hand and pulled it out of reach of the grasping brambles. Already the rain began soaking through the fabric and dripping from her scalp down her face.

Falier finally stopped at a clearing barely twenty feet in diameter between the trees. Letting go of her hand, he faced her.

"Now, close your eyes and listen."

Alísa cocked her head. "Why?"

"Trust me."

With a small sigh, she closed her eyes and relaxed, listening for whatever he wanted her to hear. Rain. No birds chirping, no animals scurrying—just rain on the ground, in the leaves, on her head.

"Now what?"

Falier was silent.

"Falier?"

Alísa opened her eyes. There he stood, eyes closed. He looked content, even happy. She must be missing something. She closed her eyes again. The pitter-patter of the rain grew steadily louder, drowning out all thoughts except for how drenched her clothing was.

Falier's voice reached her ears, much closer than she'd expected. "Do you hear the music?"

Alísa tilted her head to meet his eyes, his face a mere foot away now. "I hear noise."

A half-smile graced his face before he pulled away and began searching the ground. "A stick beating a surface is noise, but it becomes music in the hands of one who knows how to use it. I learned a long time ago that Eldra Aeba and Eldra Líla make beautiful music together, and that they welcome students."

Alísa ran through one of Farren's teaching songs to remember the Eldír Falier spoke of. Eldra Aeba, one of the water sisters and steward of the clouds, and Eldra Líla, steward of health and plant-life. Listening to the rain hitting the trees and the larger collections of drops that bent the leaves toward the ground, it made some sense, but she still couldn't understand his full meaning.

Falier bent down, grabbed a couple fallen branches, and hurried back to Alísa. He reached one out to her.

"Learn with me?"

She grabbed the stick but said nothing, watching as he walked to a nearby tree. He began to rap the stick against the trunk. She could barely hear the beat over the crashing of the raindrops against the leaves above them. Closing her eyes again, she listened. Still nothing.

"Try it," he urged.

Alísa walked to the tree next to Falier's and beat time with him. For a percussionist it might be fun, but it certainly wasn't making the rain more musical for her.

Her participation drew a grin from Falier and he began embellishing the beat while Alísa kept time. He looked up to the sky as thunder resounded in the distance and laughed, alive in this moment, hearing something she couldn't. Alísa kept up her beat and focused on him, hoping to hear at least a part of what brought him such joy.

He returned his focus to her, eyes searching. "Do you hear it?"

Alísa wanted to lie to him—say she experienced the same joy—but she shook her head apologetically.

He grinned and held out a hand to indicate the rain. "It's 'The Bard's Daughter.'"

Alísa cocked her head, unfamiliar with the song, and Falier began to sing.

A maiden fair, she danced so free
As bards played in the square,
And when her bright eyes turned to me
My heart she did ensnare.
She called me forth from stock and stand,
"Don't just sit 'round and pine.
My father's band needs one more hand,
Then I may give you mine"

My mother's kiln calls for a potter,
My father's fields, they're ripe with grain,
But I'm in love with the bard's daughter
And can't go home again

Alísa's heart swelled. He surely couldn't hear that song in the storm's cacophony—he was doing this purposefully to aid his pursuit. Yet the choice of song and that he would share it with her in a time and place so obviously special to him brought an unbidden, persistent smile to her face. She passed her stick to Falier and backed far enough away from the tree to dance while he continued singing and drumming, using basic céilí steps in hopes that he would join her.

Alísa danced through the next verse before Falier dropped the sticks and went to her at the chorus, the only music now their voices, the patter of rain, and the rumble of nearing thunder. His hand in hers was warm and his grip strong despite the slickness of the rain. Their water-logged clothing hindered movement, but Alísa barely noticed the discomfort anymore as it slowed the song for the final chorus.

Falier reached for her hand across his body for a spin, the two of them anchoring with their free hands at each other's waist. They spun slowly at first, then Falier grinned mischievously and spun them faster and faster. She fixed her eyes on his as they laughed their way through the last chorus, but dizziness still came. They nearly toppled, but Falier caught himself and pulled her close to keep her upright. Alísa giggled against his shoulder as her head spun.

"You all right?" he said through a laugh.

She pulled away and locked eyes with him. "Yes, you?"

He nodded silently and pushed a strand of hair from her cheek. Dizziness turned to a strange queasiness in her stomach, accompanied by a sudden warmth despite the chill of the rain.

Falier's fingers lingered under her jaw. "May I kiss you?"

Alísa's heart skipped a beat and nerves sent a tingling sensation through her. The thought was wonderful and frightening all at once, but as she stared into Falier's kind eyes and felt the safety of his presence, it was all she wanted.

"Yes."

Falier leaned down. His fingers threaded through her hair and the hand at her waist slipped to the small of her back. His touch was intoxicating, so different from when he held her to comfort her. She matched his pull, hoping he felt the same.

Lightning ran through her as his lips first brushed hers, then planted with a soft firmness. She closed her eyes and savored the warmth of his affection and desire pulsing through her. The kiss was short and sweet, but for those few seconds the world was at peace. There was no war. No mission. No uncomfortably wet clothes. Just them.

They opened their eyes as they pulled apart, and Falier smiled at her. "I love you, Líse."

"I love you, too."

Leaning into him, Alísa rested her head on his shoulder. She breathed past the scent of new rain to the warm, homey one of her pursuer. A part of her wanted to stay there in his arms forever, heart and mind full of his love. But the cold of the rain called to her common sense, nagging until she finally pulled back.

"W—we should get back before we c-c-c-catch a c-cold."

"I've never gotten sick out here." Nevertheless, Falier took her hand and walked them from the clearing.

The trek back to the Hold felt both longer and shorter than the run to the clearing. Alísa's skirts stuck to her legs and she grew colder with every step. But despite the chill, the thought of Falier's kiss warmed her. She glanced at him, then looked back down as his eyes met hers, heat rising into her cheeks.

"Don't tell me you'll never be able to look at me again."

She peeked up at him, noting his cheeky smile. "P-p-probably not without b—blushing."

Falier appeared to think for a moment, his eyes on the canopy. "I'll take it. You're cute when you blush."

Alísa looked down, unable to stop the heat in her cheeks from rising further despite her pleasure.

Falier rubbed the back of his neck. "Sorry. That was an odd thing to say, wasn't it?"

No, just flirtatious. Alísa reached for something similarly so—why did flirting have to feel so awkward?

"Well, if you wanted to make me blush m—more, you succeeded. I m—m—must be adorable n—now."

Falier laughed, the corners of his eyes crinkling. There—that was worth the awkwardness. She leaned into him, bumping his arm with her shoulder as the Hold came back into view. He led her around the back to the kitchen door and opened it to blessed warmth.

Eldra Nahne bless Selene—a steaming kettle smelling of ginger already sat on the countertop, and the fire still roared high. A couple of linen blankets sat beside the kettle.

Alísa stayed by the door while Falier went inside, wringing her hair out before stepping into the Hold. She grabbed the top blanket off the pile and wrapped it around herself. Soon Falier held a steaming cup out to her, which she took gratefully. The warmth of the clay settled wonderfully into her frigid fingers.

Falier grabbed his own blanket and lowered himself to the floor, facing the fire and leaning back against the counter. Alísa took off her boots and joined him, stretching her legs so the fire warmed her feet.

"D—do you do this every time there's a rainstorm, then?"

"Every time I can." Falier blew on his tea. "It's how I became a true percussionist. Lethín taught me a bit when I was little, but I was his first student and—let's just say he's a much better teacher now, if nothing else..."

Alísa gave Falier a sad smile, leaning lightly against him in support. He pushed back against her.

"Once, when I was particularly upset, I ran out into the rain and sat, hoping the rainfall would bless me into a better day. I stayed there for a while, letting the rain drown out my thoughts, until I heard the music. After that, I went out every chance I could to listen and learn. Finding the music hidden in the noise was soothing, and learning to find my own rhythm in the midst of chaos made me a better drummer."

Falier rubbed his cup between his hands. "It taught me that no matter what happens, there's always something good to be found, always a way to move forward. Even if it's cold and hard and sometimes painful. I just have to find it."

Alísa sipped at her tea, the ginger warming her insides. So this wasn't just something he did for fun. This was formative for him, something that affected his very being. And with how flippantly his typically-intuitive sister spoke of it, it seemed that his family didn't even know its significance. That he had invited her...

Awe lowered her voice to a whisper. "Thank you for sharing it with me."

Falier inhaled as though to speak, then let it go with silence. The emotions inside him were a mixture of happiness, worry, and love, all swirling together in their own brew. Alísa took another sip of her tea, longer this time, allowing room for his thoughts.

"I, uh—I think it's one of the reasons I fell in love with you."

Alísa's heart stuttered. This? "W—what do you mean?"

Falier looked at her, and as she met his gaze, she saw an intensity he rarely showed.

"This has gotten me through so much pain in my life. Being told I was weak, dealing with the telepathy migraines, knowing there was something more for my life, but not having any idea how to reach it. There are always storms, but there is also music within them. That's how I see you living too, and I love it about you."

Alísa's lips parted, but no words formed. Her? *She* was living this way? Falier was the optimist, not her. He always found the good in situations, while she got bogged down by her fear, inadequacy, and doubt.

Was he even seeing her correctly? What if this huge thing he loved about her wasn't actually there?

Falier's features softened. "I know that empathic feeling now—Graydonn taught me. Don't doubt, Alísa."

He reached up to the counter, depositing his cup there as he faced Alísa fully. "You learned the truth about dragons, and when your family tried to silence you, you ran after the dragons. You found yourself in the midst of dragons trying to drown out your voice or kill you, and rather than back down you sang them into submission. A few days ago, you found fear and trauma within yourself, and instead of running away, you found a way to safely stretch yourself, while still pursuing your mission."

He cupped her cheek in his hand, still warm from the tea. "You face storms every single day, and every day I see you find what is good and right in the midst of that storm and run after it."

A hot tear streamed down Alísa's cheek. She hadn't even noticed it forming, but two more followed. After all the times she had cried in front of Falier—including a few that, like this, seemed to be for no reason at all—he had every right to roll his eyes, but instead only affection lived there. His voice lowered with tenderness.

"So don't give up when the rain cancels a visit, or when changing hearts seems to be taking too long. Keep chasing the music."

He leaned in and kissed her, his lips light on hers. "Dance with me."

Alísa set her tea down and kissed him back, her heart so full it ached. To be seen like this—seen, understood, and accepted—was all she had ever wanted. She would dance with him forever if he asked it, and she was so very glad their minds were not joined in this moment, for fear that he would see it. As far as propriety went, it was too soon for that declaration.

But having faced both daily life and certain death at his side, having seen each other at their weakest and their strongest, having felt the absolute depth of his love and affection for her, she knew.

So she kissed him again.

INTERLUDE I

Once, travel had been Karn's solace. When the grasses stretching out over rolling hills as far as the eye could see awoke joy, and the chance to tie his sword to a saddle instead of his belt gave a lightness to his heart. When the large tent filled with his few possessions brought more comfort than the tiny canvas spaces he and his men took shelter under when marching on a mountain.

Now, days on the road did little to soothe his heavy heart. Not when his daughter slept in stone caves surrounded by beasts who left her alive only for the power she gave them. Nightmares riddled his sleep, and his waking thoughts filled with everything he could have done differently. If he hadn't rushed into that cave without a plan. If he had fought Alísa's mind-choke harder. If he had watched the night she ran, heard the curtain to her chamber move as she slipped out.

The curtain, embroidered with flowers and birds in Hanah's elegant work, taunted him. Alísa had always wanted to fly, said that joy was sky-blue.

Joy was Alísa.

In the trapped summer heat of his tent, Karn leaned over the map of his territory lying flat on the ground. Once, keeping it pristine had been a priority. Now he kept one of Alísa's graphite pencils wrapped up inside it, using it to mark off each village they passed on the road to Parrin, as well as those further out with his scouts on their way. Each village where Farren and Kallar's song had been spread.

Karn wiped sweat from his forehead and marked off the village his clan had left behind this morning. Just two more days before they reached Parrin, which was central enough in his territory to be used as a base of operations.

This plan was not a slayer's plan. That Kallar had been part of putting it together was near-incomprehensible. Kallar was not a man who set pieces in motion, then sat back to wait—he was a man of action, like Karn himself. They shouldn't be here, in the valleys. They should be climbing the heights, searching cave after cave for a lost girl needing to find her way home.

Yet, Farren had been right when he questioned that method. It took a week to clear a mountain of dragons. It took at least that much time to recover and move on to the next. There were dozens of mountains in his territory, more in Chief Tella's, still more split among the other wayfaring clans. They needed to know where to focus, which meant they needed more eyes and ears open to signs of Alísa's whereabouts.

Maker help me. Alísa needs a patient man, not one with Branni's heart. Not a warrior. Not yet.

The canvas flap of the tent brushed behind him, announcing Hanah's entry. He took in her pristine green dress overlaid with a chiefly red tartan sash across her chest. Her auburn hair draped her shoulders in gentle waves—loose, as it had been the last two months.

And Eldra Branni, continue to give me strength for my wife.

Karn rose and in two steps had her in his arms. Her own were strong as they embraced his ribs, not with desperation, but a returning of comfort. She alone settled his heart. Hanah could have blamed him for his harsh words to their daughter the day she ran, or his inability to rescue her—yet she didn't. He would have felt it empathically, just as strongly as he felt his own self-blame.

"We have visitors."

"Visitors?" Karn pulled back to look at her. That was a rarity.

"Nomads. Normals, by the look of them."

Even rarer. Normals tended to want distance from slayer clans, for fear of a slayer betraying the code and invading their minds.

"They've asked to camp with us tonight." Hanah straightened his tunic with a tug. "Given the last village's news of highwaymen in the area, they're probably looking for the safety of numbers."

Her eyes held her opinion on the matter, almost daring him to disagree. She was right, it would be wrong to turn them away if they sought shelter.

"I'll speak to them."

Passing her, Karn grabbed his sword belt and chief's sash. If it were just his men, he might leave them behind, but appearances were more important before strangers.

He pushed through the door flap into the stagnant summer air. The nomads stood in a cluster at the northern edge of camp—four of them, three men and a woman, all clothed in plain, earthy tones. One of the men sat on his horse, while the others had dismounted. A donkey carried a large, dusty pack and rolled up bed-mats, while another pair dragged a wagon with multiple small doors facing outward, presumably carrying the nomads' wares.

One of the men, wearing a clay-red cloak, sighted Karn and pressed toward him. His strides were purposeful and bold as he passed a few of Karn's slayers with barely a glance. Confident for a man walking into a warrior's camp.

The nomad pressed a fist to his heart in respect. "Chief Karn, I presume?"

Karn returned a nod. "My wife says you're looking to camp with us tonight?"

"If it is agreeable. My brethren and I have long been without company." He dipped his head, tawny blond hair falling past his shoulders. "I am A'varr."

Karn looked past him to the others. "And what is it you do?"

"We create medicines to sell to healers and Holds." A'varr gestured toward the mountains. "There are many places others will not go, not even to find potent remedies. But we, like your slayers, do not fear the wilds, nor what others might deem too dangerous."

The voice of Songweaver Farren came from behind Karn. "You brave the mountains for your wares?"

A'varr blinked, as though surprised Farren had spoken to him. A'varr's reaction was so odd that Karn looked back at Farren as well. The songweaver, too, seemed to be keeping up appearances today. He wore the blue sash of his station as advisor, along with a belt with a long dagger made more for show than anything else. It was how he dressed when first entering a new village or presenting at ceremonies.

Karn turned back to A'varr, who smiled and looked between them. "Sometimes, yes."

The female nomad came up behind A'varr, her eyes a near unearthly green that stood out amidst long, flowing locks of black hair. She nodded at the kitchen tent. "Perhaps you have wounded who would benefit from such remedies in exchange for a hot meal?"

Karn considered the proposal. It had been two weeks since their last battle, all injuries on the mend—yet, if these nomads had any remedies that would keep for a long time, they would certainly prove useful.

"I'm sure we can come to an agreement."

Half an hour later, Karn, his family, and Farren sat in a circle with the newcomers just outside the camp near the nomads' cart, enjoying a meal of rosemary chicken and potatoes. They exchanged news of the area, the tales of dragon attacks and village scandals occasionally accented by Elani telling her thirteen-year-old boys to stop wolfing down their food.

"But the day's cooling down," one of them, Taer, protested. "Kallar promised he'd work with us today!"

Karn raised his eyebrows, looking to Kallar. "You did?"

Kallar shrugged. "L'non asked me to work them on multitasking, now that they've got the hang of basic telepathy and sword skills. Don't know what they're so excited for, though." He sent the boys a smirk. "I intend to work them into the ground."

"Then maybe you *should* get started," Farren said. He rubbed at his temples, apparently nursing a headache.

Elani shook her head at the boys. "You shouldn't be exercising so vigorously just after eating. You will stay and honor our guests."

"There is plenty of time before nightfall," L'non agreed with his wife.

"Night comes more quickly every day," Farren murmured.

Karn regarded his friend. Farren rarely contradicted a parent's word to their children, even in such a small way. The songweaver pulled a hand down his face, blinking blearily.

The female nomad smiled, her voice lowered for Farren's obvious discomfort. "Soon, but not yet, Songweaver."

Farren looked at her, puzzlement on his face. Everything about him seemed off tonight.

In truth, he had been hard at work this past couple of weeks, practicing and performing the Dragon Singer song in addition to his normal duties. It hadn't seemed too much to Karn before, but looking at Farren now—the drooping eyes, the aching head, the barely-touched food—the man was obviously in need of rest.

Hanah leaned forward, reaching her hand across Karn to rest it on Farren's arm. "Perhaps you should get some sleep. You don't look well."

Farren shook his head. "Thank you, my Lady, but I will be fine."

"What of you, Karn?" A'varr spoke rather loudly, considering their whispers. "How goes the war? What news do you carry?"

Karn looked at his plate. These travelers might come across villages he and his men didn't. This was a perfect opportunity to continue spreading the song, yet he hesitated. Each time he told the story, a piece of him died inside, memories of how he had failed his only child coursing through his mind. These nomads had said themselves that they had been without company for a long time—how many villages could they possibly reach that Karn himself couldn't? Was it worth the heartache to tell these strangers?

A'varr's brows pressed together in Karn's silence. "What concerns you, friend?"

Karn ran a hand over his face. Once again, his warrior side did not fully believe in this plan of Kallar's and Farren's. Holding back did no good for Alísa.

With a heavy heart, Karn told the story. The nomads listened intently as he spoke. Farren occasionally added to the conversation, though each time the songweaver spoke he seemed more tired than before. Karn might have to insist Farren take a few days to rest and regain his health.

"That," A'varr said, a note of sympathy in his tone, "is quite the story, Chief Karn. Tragic. You must be desperate to find her, especially if you are telling this tale to complete strangers."

Another of the men nodded. "It cannot help your standing for others to know of this defect in your only child."

Karn tensed, but it was Kallar who spoke first.

"Defect?" He spat out the word as though it were rancid. "This power has been used for our side too. The tragedy is not the power, but that she is stolen."

Kallar's reaction and A'varr's glare at his companion allowed Karn the space to cool his anger. He measured his words and tone carefully. If these nomads could reach even one village, it would help Alísa.

"Yes, Kallar, though I recognize others may think differently. Regardless of how they see me, I seek to spread this story as far as it will go, in hopes that someone might bring news. Farren has crafted a song to inform and soften the hearts of humankind to her plight, and I wonder— do you have anyone in your company able to carry such a song to any villages you visit? Or to any other wanderers you find in your journeying?"

A'varr looked to each of his people. His gaze lingered on the woman the longest, and she straightened under it.

"Yes." A'varr looked back to Karn. "We do. But there are other ways of finding her. Have you no wise men who can divine from the Eldír?"

Farren grimaced, his hand going to his head once more. His face looked paler than normal, too. Karn placed a hand on his arm, partially in comfort and partially in indication.

"Farren has been praying for guidance in where to go or what to do. But the Eldír do not always answer in our timing."

"No, they do not." A'varr held up a finger. "But, in cases of urgency, there are ways to ensure they notice you and give the answers you seek. Your daughter needn't be lost anymore."

At the words, Karn's heart quickened. Answers. Guaranteed answers!

Yet even as his heart leapt for joy, a sense of unease crawled over him. It originated in his hand—the one still on Farren's arm. He regarded the point of contact, confused. He always kept his telepathy tightly bound when not using it, yet now it was loose and pulling emotions from Farren. When had he let go?

"We can help you with this." A'varr gestured to the woman. "Our sister has garnered answers many times."

The woman reached into a pouch on her belt. "Like with our healing potions, all it takes is the right ingredients."

She pulled out a corked vial with a muddy brown concoction inside. Her eyes fixed on Karn. "All that's missing is a drop of blood from the asker, to direct the Eldra to them."

In an instant, the sickly-pale songweaver stood on his feet, pulling his decorative dagger from its scabbard. Hanah gasped and Kallar moved to the edge of his seat. Before Karn could stop him, Farren stood before the woman, his tone sharper than the weapon he held.

"And which of the Eldír bows to man over Maker? Tell me their name!"

"Farren!" Karn stood, grabbing for the dagger. What madness was overtaking him? The songweaver never reacted so intensely.

Something twisted in Karn's stomach as he ran back through the woman's words. As a slayer, his own blood spilled on a regular basis. The thought of adding it to a potion was mildly disturbing, but to save Alísa? He was ready to try just about anything.

"Do you claim to know *all* of the Maker's ways?" The woman stood, stilling the world with her presence. Her tone remained calm, despite Farren's dagger pointing at her throat. "Or the ways of all the Eldír? Do they not give certain wisdom to some and certain wisdom to others, calling us to learn from each other?"

Silence held them for a moment longer. Then, as though waking from a dream, Karn remembered what he was doing. He yanked Farren around to face him, turning the weapon from the woman.

"Farren, what are you doing?"

Confusion crossed Farren's face as he stared back at Karn. Had the songweaver hallucinated, seen a strange vision and now awakened from it? Then Farren's eyes cleared, a new purpose in them as he looked back at the woman.

"You speak truly. Now tell me this—which of the Eldír requires the blood of the Maker's mortal children before giving of His blessings?"

Karn let Farren go, dread filling him. A'varr began to speak again, but Farren cut him off.

"Not one of the Maker's Eldír would dare require such payment." Farren's gaze returned to Karn, certainty filling them. "Only the Nameless and their servants."

An'reik!

Karn's hand went to his sword, but too late. The woman was already moving, reaching into her pouch and throwing another vial on the ground. Words Karn didn't understand poured from her mouth, shaping the dark mist from the vial into three twisting tendrils. They shot out and grabbed Farren, yanking him into the space between Karn and the nomads—the an'reik—and forcing him to his knees. Behind her, one of the other an'reik held a ball of fire in his hands.

Karn heard his family shooting to their feet behind him. Soon Kallar came to his side, sword drawn. L'non ordered his family away.

Fire and ice swirled inside Karn, rage and fear fighting for control. He had let these twice-damned servants of the Nameless into camp, supped with them, and ignored the signs that something was wrong!

"Peace, Karn," A'varr said, gesturing to the swords. "You don't need those."

"Like hellflames!" Karn spat out. A lifetime of fighting beasts twice his size lent strength to his words and stance, but his insides twisted. Dragons he knew how to fight, but these... Could an'reik be wounded psychically? Did their fire burn as hot as a dragon's?

"Tell the witch to let Farren go," he growled, "and I might let you walk out of here alive."

"Your man attacked us first. We did not come for violence." A'varr gave a calming gesture to the an'reik with the fire in his hands, whose flames instantly went out. "We came because you need help. There are stronger ways than you know. They can save your daughter, protect your people, give you power." He tapped his boot against Farren's leg. "Not like this pathetic songweaver who claims to know the Eldír, yet can do nothing against us."

Farren wheezed in a breath. "By Maker's hand, the weak confound the strong—"

The woman bared her teeth and the bindings tightened, choking

Farren into silence.

"You needn't wait." A'varr's eyes were soft with understanding. "You will never need to wait while they are silent again. Let us help you get Alísa out of the dragons' clutches."

At Alísa's name, Karn's world stopped. She was trapped, and every minute the dragons had her was another chance for them to twist her into something that couldn't be saved through any other means than death.

Perhaps he was already too late. Perhaps by waiting he had doomed her.

His mind still open—somehow loosened without his consent—he felt those around him. Fear, confusion, and rage reigned. In the cacophony, his mind reached for Hanah. Hers was the only mind in the space that felt sorrow—such great sorrow. It was almost enough to convince him to give in, if only to see his family whole and feel her joy once more. But just as he thought this, her voice rang in his mind.

"If you give in, Alísa will still be in the clutches of the Nameless even after we've brought her home. Do not yield!"

Her words stoked the fire within, giving him the strength to do what needed to be done. Forming a spear with his mind, he attacked the woman holding Farren. Her eyes glowed with rage as the spear found its mark, and with it a terrible burning screamed through Karn's mind. He reeled, shoving his mental shield into place. It stopped the increase, but pain still burned behind it. Farren spasmed as the dark, grasping mist tightened again.

Kallar shot forward, sword glinting as the fiery an'reik reformed his flames. He rounded Farren, slashing at the witch with a roar. The fourth an'reik parried with his own sword, inhumanly fast, and attacked with a fury that put Kallar on the defensive—a feat Karn rarely saw.

Shaking his head against the pain, Karn joined L'non against the dark servants. As L'non ran for A'varr, Karn ducked under a fireball that drew cries from the rest of his family. He glanced back, but the fire hadn't hit the women or boys, all now running from the danger.

Relieved, Karn turned his focus to the fire an'reik. Just like a dragon. Except he didn't have his shield.

Maker's hand, shield us all.

Karn dodged another blast of fire and ran at the demonic servant. He swung his sword, slashing through armor and bone as the heat of the an'reik bit into him. Darkness swirled through Karn's vision as a dark construct hit him square in the chest, sending him to the ground at the same time as his opponent.

The witch's chanting grew louder, calling the dark constructs to her and her allies. Farren gasped in a breath beside Karn. He seemed to be trying to say something, but his coughing and the blood pounding in Karn's ears made it impossible to understand. Darkness swirled around the combatants, startling even Kallar out of his single-minded fight against the sword-wielding an'reik. He and L'non stumbled back, eyes wide as the dark mists rose.

"Escape—Karn!" Farren coughed. "She's—trying to—escape!"

Not on my watch! Karn yanked Farren's dagger from the ground and threw it at the woman. Terribly balanced and not right in Karn's hand, the dagger flipped and veered off-course, hitting the fiery servant in the arm instead.

The whiz of an arrow came from Karn's left, and the projectile found its mark in A'varr's chest. He stumbled backward, out of the growing darkness. Another arrow hit the swordsman in the back and sent him to the ground. Darkness engulfed the witch and wounded fire-caller, and with a flash of green the two of them disappeared.

Karn swore inwardly. None should have escaped. He stood, the physical and mental burns making him wince, and approached A'varr.

The an'reik's leader knelt on the ground, his breathing shallow against the arrow in his sternum. Blood tinged his lips as he looked up at Karn, a cruel smile replacing the civility that had once been there.

"You—will never—find her in—time. The—Eldír—don't care—unless—we make them."

With his voice came a psychic pull, one Karn hadn't recognized all night until now. As the weakened an'reik fought death, his dark power became clear. A'varr was a slayer, his powers enhanced through giving his soul to the Nameless. That Karn had considered giving his blood without realizing what was truly being asked spoke to A'varr's power.

Praise the Maker for Farren.

Karn shielded his mind against the psychic manipulation and looked A'varr in the eye.

"The dragons sold their souls long ago—they have no choice but evil now. But you—you had every choice, as do I."

Ignoring the heat still searing in his arm, Karn swung his sword, slashing through A'varr's neck and sending his head tumbling to the ground. To his right, Kallar stabbed the downed swordsman through the heart, though the an'reik hadn't moved since the arrow felled him.

As Karn looked over the two bodies and the flames that burned too near his people's tents, he had to fight to keep from retching. Dark powers. Blood magic. Soulless humans. This wasn't his life. This was one of the dark tales of old, from the time when Eldír physically walked A'dem and the Nameless first defied the Maker. Yes, Karn had known an'reik—*sold-souls*—still existed, but this? He was a dragon-slayer, not a slayer of men.

"What should we do with these?"

Kallar's voice brought Karn back from the depths of his mind. The apprentice kicked the body of the dark swordsman, disgust clear on his face. More of Karn's men surrounded them now, including two with bows who had presumably brought down A'varr and the swordsman. Hanah and Elani had returned as well, working to snuff the fires with blankets.

"Karn?"

"Burn them." Karn's own voice sounded far away. "Along with their possessions."

"Kill their animals too." Farren rubbed a hand at his throat. "They may be bewitched, in which case death would be a mercy. Leave no trace of the an'reik—there's no telling what might lurk in their belongings."

"You heard them," L'non said, taking charge. "You two, bring water from the stream and douse the grass fires. You, go to the kitchen tent and bring out the healing potions they gave us. The rest of you, grab shovels and clear a large space for burning the bodies—"

A hand squeezed his shoulder. "Karn?"

Hanah's voice was soft behind him. Karn turned to her, letting her study him and see he was all right.

"You're burned," she said, looking to his sword-arm—the one that had gotten closest to the fire-manipulator. The skin was red and hairless, and a large blister formed just above his wrist, though no flames had actually touched him. Hanah called for Levan to bring a soothing balm, then turned her gaze to the rest of Karn's body to search for other wounds.

"That is the worst of it," Karn assured, reaching his other arm for her. She tucked herself against him, her fear and pride colliding in his senses.

"An'reik in our camp." Farren shook his head. "A slayer's camp! They're rarely so bold."

Karn looked to him. "What does it mean?"

"I don't know. What could they possibly have thought to gain besides death in a camp of warriors?" Farren sighed, looking up into the sky. "I will meditate on this and pray for wisdom."

A'varr's final words came to mind and brought a terrible ache to Karn's heart. "But will we truly get any answers from the silent Eldír?"

Hanah pulled back, concern in her eyes. "Silent, but not absent. How many times have you asked Branni for the strength to defeat your enemies?" She lifted a hand to his cheek. "How many times have I prayed, and you have been brought back safely to me?"

"Yet now, when our daughter needs him, where is he?" Karn looked to Farren. "Where is the Maker?"

Sadness turned Farren's eyes. "The answers of the Maker come when the time is right. Those of the Nameless come quickly, but at terrible cost. Once you give your lifeblood freely to them, they will forever have a hold on you."

Hanah pulled close again. "You did the right thing, my love."

Karn sighed. "I know. You were right. I would give every drop of my blood to save Alísa. But to give my soul would only bring her into the clutches of one worse than even the dragons—one who willingly chose evil. I will not be that man."

He thought of the last time he had seen Alísa. Though she had attacked him, the pain in her eyes and sorrow in her psychic touch spoke to her fight. She had not given in to the bindings of the Nameless, even surrounded by dragons. Now he had to trust that by not giving in to the darkness himself, by choosing the Maker's perfect timing over his own, she would be strong enough to last until that perfect time.

Maker help us both.

12

PERSPECTIVE

The sky made no judgements as one flew through it. It didn't mock, show pity, or hold grudges. It didn't care that humans and dragons were supposed to be enemies, or that this particular pairing blurred the lines between their two races. It didn't even care whether they flew with grace or barely avoided collision with their training partners. As Alísa and Sesína joined minds and claimed it as their domain, the sky was pure joy.

With a trumpet, Alísa and Sesína dove into gravity's hold. They allowed it a glimpse of victory, then defied it with powerful strokes of their wings. The trees reached up for them, wishing they could grab hold and join in the fun, but this joy was reserved for dragons and riders. They pumped their wings and rose, leaving the bright green boughs behind.

A strength song fell from their lips, its quiet lyrics swiftly stolen by the wind. In contrast to the song's softness, they pushed hard at the Singer's power living inside Alísa's mind. It shuddered through the bond like muscles under heavy strain, and threatened to pull their focus from the flight itself.

But it's working!

The thought ran through both of them as the fatigue in their wings lifted. Even as gravity pulled and wind pounded against scales and skin with each wing-beat, the Singer's strength coursed through each draconic muscle.

It feels like we could go on forever!

And that was the feeling they waited for. With barely a shared thought, they stopped singing, stopped pressing power, and simply flew. High above the trees now, they banked and swerved, dodging invisible enemies. Air slipped over scales and caught in clothing and hair. Diving, twisting, stalling, rolling, they moved through the imagined battle like an aerial dance until fatigue reached their muscles once more.

They evened out, gliding as they caught their breath. Thoughts flowed, shared between them so quickly they couldn't tell which words belonged to whom.

The strength song's effects lasted longer than expected.

So maybe dynamics aren't as important as the psychic press of power.

The press is difficult. Louder dynamics help focus the mental exertion.

But they aren't sustainable. A voice can only shout so long.

There's a middle ground somewhere in there.

Between harmful shouting and straining to control.

A quiet trumpet pulled them from their reverie. Awe and curiosity flowed from Saynan as he came alongside them, his feelings especially potent through Alísa's senses. Sesína shook her head as their minds began straining against each other. They would have to let go soon.

Iila clung to the base of Saynan's wings, her own wings stretching wide over his and moving a heartbeat slower. Sesína knew what that was like, learning to fly without an Illumination bond to her trainer. How long would it take Iila to fly on her own?

"*The way you're joined is extraordinary,*" Saynan said, eyes brightening. "*Looking at your astral forms—form, I should say—you shine brighter than I'd expect, even joined.*"

Like the dreki? Sesína and Alísa thought together, each joint inkling tiring them further.

Their tiny minds join to become greater than the sum of their parts.

Maybe that's always how it works when minds are joined completely.

But can you imagine? Being joined to so many at once?

Even our minds are pulling against each other.

Any others would drive us mad.

If two joined minds exhaust us, what would many do?

And, speaking of exhaustion, maybe it's time to stop.

Alísa and Sesína breathed slowly, relaxing their minds to pull apart. Soon Alísa lost Sesína's vision and opened her own eyes. She blinked a few times, the world seeming blurry now after seeing it through a dragon's eyes. No longer could she discern the gaps between Saynan's scales, nor the individual pine needles of the trees below. Yet her fingers flexed and gripped Sesína's spines with a dexterity no dragon possessed, and the sun's rays soaked into her skin and warmed her in a way so different from a dragon's inner fire. Being human was fine.

"I am surprised you decided to undertake this exertion before the others arrive." Saynan thrummed with humor. *"Training with the adults will take all of your skills, and you are already fatigued."*

Alísa gave Sesína a look, though the dragoness couldn't see it. She had made the same argument earlier, but Sesína's eagerness was contagious. They hadn't joined minds to fly like this since their first time on the way back from Rorenth's caves, and this second time was just as exhilarating as the first.

Sesína grumbled in her throat. *"I had to get my time in with Alísa before another dragon takes her."*

Alísa patted Sesína's neck and looked up. Graydonn flew with Harenn and Komi, keeping just behind them as they each flew with a rider on their back. This morning, when Alísa told Falier her goal to give all the dragons experience with a rider, Selene had asked if she could join them. Apparently her flight to the cave nearly a week ago had given her a taste for the sky. Komi carried Selene now, while Falier rode Harenn.

Saynan looked at Twi-Peak. *"I see our clanmates approaching. I'm going to go check on the others and make sure Selene is doing well."*

His teacher tone softened, cushioned by paternal love. *"We're going to ascend now, Iila. I'll turn first, then you can speed your wing-strokes with me."*

With two powerful flaps, Saynan turned completely around and up, spearing for his other students. Alísa followed him and Iila with her eyes. They sped away so quickly she couldn't tell if Iila was responding to his instruction.

"She is," Sesína supplied. *"I wish I could help her like you did for me."*

Alísa smiled sadly. *"She was Illuminated by a dragon. Hopefully, those memories are still alive inside her and she'll be able to use them."*

"Maybe. But are you sure we want her remembering her parents like that? They died because they wouldn't turn to good—"

"We don't know that," Alísa said. *"They could have been killed by my father's clan without ever hearing my call. I don't have the heart to ask Iila how her Illuminated parent died."*

"Even so, they were with Rorenth and aligned with him enough that Iila calls humans vermin. I, for one, am glad I never knew my human-hating father."

A heaviness settled in Alísa's heart. *"Never knowing and forgetting are two different things. I can't imagine ever wanting to forget my parents."*

"Even if they don't turn?"

The shock of betrayal in her father's eyes speared through Alísa, and for a moment, she wavered. Forgetting that moment would let her live with a lighter heart. But before that were years of love. She recalled her father's stories when she was little, and how they laughed as he tried to emulate the dramatic ways of professional storytellers. She remembered her mother's patience in teaching daily skills, and how she would go from quietly mending in one moment to playfully throwing the next torn article over Alísa's head the next.

Her father's cloak around her shoulders in the winter months.

Her mother's embroidery that turned a tent into a home.

Provision.

Warmth.

Love.

Alísa closed her eyes. *"Even if they don't turn."*

Draconic greetings drew Alísa from her melancholy. The rest of the clan neared, scale colors quickly becoming apparent. A flash of blue in the sunlight made Alísa smile—even Aree had come out today, leaving her and Saynan's egg with Rayna in the cave. The only other dragons not present were Faern, who was scouting, and Korin, who nursed a deep gash in his side. After a week of silence from Paili's clan, Galerra had led another attack two days ago. Scouting at the time, Korin had caught the trespassers and called out the rest of the clan, but he was wounded before the others arrived. The dragons had no doubt that he would heal, but it would take time.

Koriana trumpeted at the front of the group and formed a mind-link between herself, Sesína, and Alísa. The connection hummed pleasantly in Alísa's mind as the dragoness reveled in the open sky and sunshine.

One-by-one, dragons joined the link, each mind carrying a distinct signature.

Koriana passed over Sesína and banked hard to circle around, then ascended toward Graydonn. Wing-beats filled the air as the others followed behind her and branched off to circle one another, happiness rumbling in their chests and joy racing through the clan-link as even the more stoic dragons engaged in play.

Excitement pounded through Sesína as she dove into the midst of the clan. She spiraled upward with Tora and Q'rill, then dropped backwards, making Alísa's stomach flip. Righting herself, Sesína swerved between other dragons, moving in and out like a céilí dancer. Saynan and Aree flipped around each other in an intricate pattern, little Iila merely hanging on through the complicated moves. Komi circled the group around the outside, forgoing her normal aerobatics for Selene's sake. Falier whooped as Harenn sped and dove between two other dragons, both obviously unconcerned that Harenn might throw his rider.

Then, at some silent cue, the dragons dispersed. Sesína panted as they all began circling, some dragons across from each other, some on a higher plane than others, but all banking in the same direction.

Saynan spoke to the group. *"Marvelous to have you all here today! Our focus will be on flight-partners, in the form of both wing-dragons and riders. Many thanks to Selene for giving her afternoon to help us train faster."*

Selene waved from Komi's back. *"My pleasure."*

Saynan explained today's training. The dragons without rider experience would take turns carrying a human off to the side. Meanwhile, the unladen dragons would pair up and practice flying with wing-partners, the dragon in the lead performing aerobatics while their partner tried to keep up.

After Saynan assigned partners, Sesína flew to Q'rill. Komi and Harenn followed her, not quite finished with their riders, yet needing to watch the transfer process.

Q'rill flew with his mother in a long, lazy bank, his brown eyes bright as Sesína approached. His mind fluttered with excitement.

"Singer, did you hear? I get to carry you!"

Komi looked to Tora. *"Are you sure he doesn't need to watch someone else do this first?"*

"Yes." Tora's tone was not unkind, but it held a firmness few would dare question. *"He is used to caring for creatures smaller than him."*

That's right. Q'rill was a nurse dragon. With Iila the only hatchling around and her complete avoidance of the 'traitorous' dragons of her former clan, it was easy to forget.

Sesína positioned herself above Q'rill, flapping her wings hard until she matched his gliding speed. Looking down, Alísa noted the adult dragon's girth. Even if Sesína didn't match up exactly, it would be hard to miss him.

Of course, there was the potential of not catching her balance and tumbling off.

That wasn't a helpful thought.

"I'll catch you." Sesína lowered closer, then wobbled at a change in the wind. *"Maybe."*

Alísa rolled her eyes. *"You aren't helpful either."*

"Good," Tora said, ignoring them. *"You're very close. Q'rill, keep gliding and hold your wings steady. Singer, I suggest aiming as close to his back as you can—don't put undo pressure on his wing."*

Swallowing her fear, Alísa pulled her legs up and knelt sideways on Sesína's back. Then, grabbing two spines and sending a psychic warning to Sesína and Q'rill, she swung down. Her feet didn't quite reach him, but as she felt Sesína strain to counterbalance, Alísa dropped. Boots hit leather, and Alísa rushed to grab Q'rill's spines as her legs quaked. He kept his wings steady, stretched taut so the tough hide barely gave under her weight.

Tora's voice smiled. *"Well done, my sky."*

Q'rill gave a quiet trumpet of happiness. Alísa latched onto the emotion, allowing it to run through her and calm her nerves.

"Yes, excellent job, Q'rill. I'm going to move toward your head now."

Having landed in the middle of his back to allow room for failure, Alísa had five spines between her and the spot at his withers where she could comfortably sit. Though the wind pushed against Alísa's progress, Q'rill held his glide as she carefully made her way.

Tension melted away as Alísa settled into the now-familiar rider's position, and a similar feeling of relief floated in from the spectators. She looked at Komi, Harenn, and their riders and smiled.

"And that's how it's done."

Falier patted Harenn's neck. *"Looks easy enough."*

Harenn shook his head from side to side like an animal clearing its fur of water. *"When's it our turn?"*

"You're stuck with him for a while yet," Sesína said, a little too pleased by Harenn's discomfort. She speared past him to join the unladen dragons and their practice. *"Have fun!"*

As Tora, Komi, and Harenn came up alongside him, Q'rill flapped his wings tentatively. Strong muscles shifted beneath his scales as he tried again, harder this time. Alísa rubbed a gentle hand over his neck.

"You doing okay, Q'rill?"

"It feels strange." He twisted his neck as though working out a crick in it. *"Don't touch my neck. I don't like it. Please."*

"I'm sorry." Alísa yanked her hand back and looked down, unsure. *"I'm sitting on your neck. Is this okay?"*

"Yes. That's different."

Q'rill continued twisting his neck, the movement rocking Alísa from side to side. It didn't scare her, having flown in battle, but her response would typically be to tighten her legs against his neck. Was that different too?

Alísa gripped the spine in front of her. *"Q'rill, in a fight, a rider will need to squeeze with their legs. Will that be okay?"*

"That's like a hatchling. That's fine."

Like a hatchling? Alísa looked to Tora for help.

Tora blinked slowly. *"He doesn't like unexpected touches, but he has carried hatchlings for flight-training—he knows the feeling of it and what to expect. You can hang on tightly."*

"Humans riding feels different than hatchlings," Q'rill said. He stopped twisting his neck and began moving his forelegs so that his shoulders shifted underneath Alísa. *"But I am learning. Can we go faster?"*

Alísa nodded, though he wouldn't see it. *"I'm ready when you are."*

Q'rill rumbled in his chest and stopped moving his shoulders, then beat his wings harder to push them forward and up. The wind whisked through Alísa's hair and clothing, raising a smile. He banked into an updraft and spiraled, Tora beside him and the other dragons following behind. Even such simple moves brought a thrill to Alísa's heart. She belonged up here with the dragons.

As Q'rill changed direction, Alísa's skirt caught against a spot with no scales. He flew gently enough for her to twist and free the fabric without fear. A scar stretched in a long swath at the base of his neck, nearly touching the joint of his wing. She had noticed the scars all over his body before, but had never truly looked at them, for fear of being rude. This one looked like the slash of a sword, or perhaps a thrust spear. Looking to Tora, she held similar markings, and in greater number.

How many battles against slayers had they seen? How many of her people had tried to kill these kind souls? How many of her people had they killed in order to stay alive? They trained now in the hopes of carrying slayer warriors in the future, but could that ever come to pass with so much bloodshed between their races?

"*Singer?*" Q'rill's voice entered her mind. "*Why are you sad?*"

Alísa looked up. "*I'm sorry, I was just lost in thought. I'm okay.*"

"*Lost...*" Q'rill paused a moment. "*It is a figure of speech? And you found your way back?*"

Alísa giggled. "*Yes, your voice brought me back.*"

She almost patted his neck again but stopped herself. It was so natural after riding horses all her life, and Sesína also liked the contact. She would need to work to break the habit.

Alísa looked back at the others. "*How are you doing, Harenn and Komi? Getting the hang of flying with riders?*"

Komi sent a mental affirmative. "*The extra weight was unruly at first, but yes.*"

"*I can manage,*" Harenn said. "*Though I fail to see why Graydonn and Sesína like having riders.*"

Falier smirked and gave Alísa an exaggerated look of offense. Alísa smiled and shook her head.

"*How about you, Selene? You doing okay?*"

Selene grinned and spread her arms over Komi's wings. "*Never better!*"

Tora quickened her wing strokes to bring her face into Alísa's view. *"Singer, you have said that this training will prepare us to carry slayers into battle."* Her mind squirmed with discomfort, the most unstable emotion Alísa had ever felt from the dragoness. *"When will this happen, and who are these slayers?"*

Unbidden, Alísa's eyes moved to the clearing where Me'ran sat. Some days it seemed she was making progress, while others made her think she would never win over enough people to convince slayers that her dragons meant no harm.

"I don't know when. As for who, I hope to go from village to village and meet with their slayers. Each village will have two to five slayers bound to them, so we can build trust with a few at a time." Her eyes landed on a puncture scar on Tora's neck. *"I know you have been hurt by many slayers—I won't give your backs to people I don't trust."*

Alísa paused a moment, unsure what to say yet needing to say something. *"I am sorry for what my people have done to you."*

Tora blinked slowly at her. *"Thank you, Singer. Q'rill and I have seen battle, yes, though not many have been able to pierce us with blades. The wounds you see are from an entirely different battle."*

Not slayers? *"Territory fights?"*

"No." Tora faced forward. *"Rorenth was not a kind dragon, and though most of the clan did not follow him in selling their souls, many followed his example of cruelty. Dragons who are different, like my son, were subjected to many tests of strength and I—I was not always able to stop them."*

Heaviness settled in Alísa's heart. The deep hurt emanating from Tora said there was more to the story, but the dragoness said nothing else.

"You two are very brave. I can't imagine what that must have been like."

Harenn's disgust filled their telepathic link. *"An'reik. That any dragon could join with the Nameless is beyond me. It's why my parents had so many border skirmishes with Rorenth's clan—to try to rid the world of such evil."*

Komi growled and Alísa looked back at her. Eyes normally bright with open curiosity now blazed with fire. *"Paili sure has a funny way of showing it, considering she wouldn't help the Singer against him. Even if she didn't join the clan she could have allied herself for one battle! It shouldn't have mattered a different alpha led the charge, or that the alpha was human. All that should have mattered was that he was an'reik and hurt even his own clanmates!"*

Silence took the telepathic link, only inklings of emotions floating through it. Selene was a quiet buzz of interest, taking in a world she knew little about. Q'rill and Falier held a searching quiet, as though they each wanted to say something but didn't know what. Harenn squirmed as though Komi's reprimand were directed at him rather than his mother, and Komi seemed to shrivel as she recognized the effect her words had on the group.

Tora clicked in her throat. *"Many alphas follow only their own interests, or else close themselves off from other points of view. Though I am not sure of carrying slayers as riders, I am glad I now have an alpha who looks beyond her own caves."*

Komi relaxed slightly and sent a mental affirmative. The other dragons followed suit, though Harenn still squirmed with discomfort. Harenn's eyes met Alísa's and he quickly looked away, a twinge of shame rising.

"I've gotten the hang of having a rider," Harenn said, banking away. *"I should give someone else a turn."*

Falier looked back at Alísa, his brow creased in concern for Harenn that mirrored her own. The young dragon had followed through on his promise, fighting for his new clan in the last border skirmish, but he held such unrest within.

"He's right." Cheer rose in Komi's voice, as though she tried to balance out her fellow adolescent. *"Tora, do you want to take Selene now?"*

Tora agreed and Komi went to her, copying Sesína's process. Trepidation whispered through Selene, but she mostly held calm. Alísa watched their progress, ready to command Q'rill to dive and catch Selene should anything go wrong, but her mind lingered on Harenn. She understood the loyalty he still held for his family—the need to defend them and the pain when he knew he could not. Both she and Harenn looked back at the family they had left behind.

The question was, did Harenn look back in hopes of bringing his family forward, as Alísa did for her own family? Or did he look back wishing he could return?

13

BETWEEN TWO WORLDS

When the clan returned to the cave, the majority of them gathered around one of the woodpiles, lighting the fire and settling down after their long day of exercise. Alísa first headed for Falier and Selene, then noticed Harenn stealing away to the darkness of his alcove. The memory of his discomfort pulled her in two directions. Should she go check on him, or leave him alone as he seemed to desire?

A shadow moved in Alísa's periphery, and she turned to see Iila scampering after Harenn, or else away from Falier and Selene. She occasionally walked the cave on her own now, often ending up with Harenn. Alísa had promised her the right to choose whether to stay with the clan or leave when she was old enough to make it on her own, but hopefully her connections to him, Saynan, and Aree were helping her feel more at home here.

With two dragons who needed deeper connections to their new clan, Alísa's choice became clear. Waving off invitations to sit at the fire, she quietly headed for Harenn and Iila.

Iila lowered to her belly at Harenn's side, cobalt eyes bright until they landed on Alísa. Rather than wait for a telepathic connection, Alísa held up her hands in a sign of peace and spoke softly.

"It's only me. The other humans are s—staying at the fire." She looked to Harenn. "D—do you mind if I join you t-two? After all of the action today, I'm ready for a bit of quiet."

The brown glow of Harenn's eyes went out and returned in a slow blink of acceptance. Alísa smiled and picked over the uneven ground, firelight and the glow of dragon eyes lighting her way. She chose to sit beside Harenn on the side opposite Iila, hoping that would help the hatchling feel more comfortable. All three of them faced the fire, still and silent, gentle waves of emotion their only communication.

Alísa hugged her knees to her chest and closed her eyes. How she missed living with the dragons. The hum of their relaxed emotions became a song in her mind, each dragon a different instrument coming together in a harmony that, though sometimes dissonant, soothed her. Harenn's longing and occasional accents of confidence added its own distinct part to the song, while Iila's unrest was a quiet droning beneath everything else. And across the cave, tones of camaraderie won through a hard day of training floated through the dragons' empathy song.

A throb of pain hit Alísa in the side like she had been running for a long time. Korin and his battle wound. She breathed, forcing air in and blowing it back out.

"Are you well, Singer?"

Alísa removed her hand from her side and gave Harenn a soft smile, glad that he was the one to break the silence. *"I feel Korin, but it's better than yesterday. I'm fine."*

Harenn acknowledged her with a light clicking in his throat. As silence took their mind-link again, Alísa wished for Falier's ability to start and keep up a conversation.

"Are you? Well, I mean?"

Harenn tapped a talon on the ground, brightening and dimming his eyes in rapid succession.

"How was flying with Falier today?"

Harenn snorted. *"Odd. I don't like the extra weight when I bank. Will we all have to carry riders?"*

Alísa faced forward, feeling Iila's interest and not wanting her gaze to scare the hatchling. *"That's the hope, yes. Assuming we gain enough slayers to the clan."*

More tapping. *"I had assumed before that Slayer was a special case, due to the mind-kin bond. Unless you expect other bonds to occur? That would be a foolish hope, if so—I cannot imagine any of us bonding with true slayers."*

Alísa hid a smirk. Harenn was never afraid to speak his mind. *"No, I don't expect mind-kin bonds, but the concept Falier and Graydonn employ in battle will work without it—the slayer fighting psychically, while the dragon fights physically. The slayer would just need to use his own telepathy rather than pulling from a bond."*

"Do you expect Branch to ride one day?"

Alísa looked at him. "'Branch'?"

"The old one in the village. The one who always carries an oak branch."

"Ah. That's called a staff."

"It's a branch."

Alísa shook her head. Moving on. *"I don't anticipate Namor riding. I don't think he has any desire to."*

Laughter broke out at the fire, drawing their eyes. Selene mussed Falier's hair, while trying to dodge him poking her in the ribs. That Selene felt safe enough among the dragons to have fun like this warmed Alísa's heart.

If only that could be true for all of Me'ran.

"Slayer and Colors care deeply for each other," Harenn said, *"don't they?"*

"Yes. I've always wanted a sibling—that teasing, but loving relationship."

Harenn's tail twitched. *"Are all human siblings like that?"*

Sadness colored Harenn's tone. He had five older siblings. Was the sadness because he missed them, or because their relationship was much less kind and loving than the holders'? He and Galerra certainly weren't on good terms.

"No. Many, but not all."

Harenn didn't speak, but the hum of his emotions became louder. He needed to say something, but was choosing not to.

"What about dragons?" She glanced at him. *"I've never met dragon siblings."*

"No. Most sibling relationships I've seen are nothing like that. We tend to have bigger gaps in age, and younger siblings steal the parent's Illumination bond when they hatch, which can lead to bitterness."

Alísa nodded slowly. *"May I ask about your siblings?"*

Harenn's talons scraped the stone floor of the cave as he tensed. He remained silent for a moment, then sighed a puff of steam.

"There isn't much to tell. The two eldest, sister and brother, are eight and six summers older than me. They were clan betas by the time I hatched. If I hadn't been told who they were, I would never have guessed we were family.

My brother in particular. He is the clan's aerial combat trainer, and under his watch my wing was ripped badly enough I couldn't fly. He left me behind until Faern—the nearest scout—could take me home, saying I needed to learn the importance of protecting my wings."

Alísa's heart clenched. *"That's awful!"*

"He was reprimanded."

"I should hope so!"

Harenn continued on, as though the story he had just told didn't deserve focus. *"My third sibling is Galerra. She tolerated me, but I think she felt threatened when I was made a scout under Faern instead of her."*

Iila's fear entered Alísa's mind, small but palpable. She didn't like the giant brown dragon, though Alísa had never seen them interact. Was it merely fear of his size and stoic demeanor, or something else?

"My other two siblings aren't with the clan anymore," Harenn said. *"When Mother Illuminated me and replaced her bond, Erris felt listless and decided to find her own way rather than stay with the clan. She invited my youngest brother and me to come along. He went with her."*

"Why didn't you?" Iila asked, surprising Alísa.

Harenn pulled his paws to his chest. *"I was very young, then. I hadn't seen the sickness in my family yet, and it felt like a great betrayal to leave. I promised myself I would never leave like they did."* He thrummed quietly. *"But we know how that turned out."*

Alísa chuckled. *"I'm glad you came."*

Harenn snorted. *"Don't patronize me, Singer. I don't bring much to this clan."*

"Not so. You have fought well and bravely, and I know you will do so again. Your presence in flight-training has kept Sesína growing, and your ability as a hunter has helped keep us alive."

She stared at his bright red scales, wanting to reach out and touch them. But Q'rill didn't like it, and as she thought of it, Harenn didn't seem the type who would find it comforting either.

"Even if you hadn't done those things," she said, *"you came with me. No matter how awful your family was, that was still a sacrifice. I am glad you're here."*

A small thud sounded behind her, Harenn's tail flicking against the ground. He made no further response. She wouldn't ask how he felt about his decision—he was obviously still unsettled by it. But he had answered her questions rather than avoiding them, and that was progress.

Movement at the fire caught Alísa's eyes. Falier waved to her, his voice entering her mind.

"Come join us, Líse? Harenn?"

Alísa looked at Harenn and Iila. *"Would you two like to join the others?"*

Iila's disgust at the thought was palpable, but Harenn began to stand, stretching his legs like a large, red-scaled feline. The hatchling's eyes dimmed as she watched him.

"Come with us, Iila," Harenn said gently, curling his neck around to look at her. *"I'll stay with you. Though, Slayer is not a danger to you. He's kinder than the Singer, if you can believe that."*

Alísa smiled. Iila didn't seem convinced, but Harenn's attempt was touching.

"Besides, look at him." Harenn's tone hardened with sarcasm. *"No weapons, small telepathic ability, a little lanky. You have nothing to fear."*

And there was the real Harenn. Alísa rolled her eyes, yet couldn't help but smile as Iila stood to follow him.

It seemed the moment Selene finally got used to something, another distraction always popped up. After today's dragon riding—an absolute delight—she had realized that the crazy spiderweb of telepathy lines connecting her to the clan didn't seem so odd anymore. It had even been strangely helpful, guiding her eyes to whichever dragon she sought in the wide expanse of the sky.

But now, back in the cave, the gray-green mists around the tawny dragon egg had returned. Komi held it between her paws, seemingly oblivious to the dragonet's sorrow.

Assuming the color was even connected to the emotional halos that accompanied voice-lights.

Selene closed her eyes. *My brain hurts.*

Falier scooted closer to Selene to make room for Alísa. Alísa winced as she sat, probably due to the proximity of Korin's injury, and Falier took her hand. Hopefully, it wasn't too bad—Alísa seemed the type who would suffer in silence.

Did she feel the dragonet's sorrow? Surely if anyone would feel it, it would be Alísa. Yet she, too, seemed to ignore it.

Selene shook her head, looking back at the tawny egg. *Why am I seeing this?* It wasn't a sound-light or telepathy, just a cloud the color of sadness. She blinked several times, but the fog didn't clear away. She looked to the blue egg, held by Rayna. No cloud of any color surrounded it, or anyone else for that matter.

Why Tawny?

"Hey. Selene!" Falier nudged her, his tone the one he always used when she stared into nothing for too long. "You okay?"

Selene blinked. "Yeah. I'm fine. Sorry."

A gurgling chirp surrounded in bright orange confusion pulled Selene's attention back to the egg. The sorrow mists were growing. Even stranger, she could plainly see Tawny through them, yet they shrouded Komi when she nosed at it.

"Something's happening." Komi lifted her head from the mist. *"It's squeaking and rocking, but it's not supposed to hatch yet, right? It's too early!"*

Faces turned to Komi. Selene's heart pounded as the mists grew, starting to spread over Faern. Such great sorrow, and she couldn't do a thing about it.

Faern dipped his head into the mists and sniffed. Surely, he would sense the growing sadness and know what to do.

"Peace, Komi," he assured in his deep voice. *"Dragonets will get agitated on occasion. It is not hatching."*

Selene swallowed. No, it wasn't hatching, but it was in pain.

"Can't you help it?" Selene spoke aloud, unsure she would be understood telepathically with so much going on in her head. She looked to Koriana beside her. "Maybe try pushing calm at it again?"

Another squeak. Koriana lowered her head to Selene's level.

"I'm afraid its sorrow will not pass until it chooses someone."

"But it's growing." Selene pointed, then stopped herself. No one else would see the mists. "Can't you feel it?"

"You can feel something?" Alísa stood and approached Komi.

"Yes. Well, no." Selene shook her head. "I see it. The cloud of sorrow is growing. I can't even see Komi through it anymore. Though I can see the egg…"

She stopped. Crazy. She must sound crazy!

Falier got up on his knees. *"Líse?"*

Alísa shook her head. *"I feel sorrow, but not in great amounts. I felt Sesína's more…"*

Her eyes shot to Selene. *"Is it normal for you to see feelings?"*

Selene shook her head. "I saw it once before with the eggs, but there's nothing coming from Blue, only Tawny."

She swallowed as her throat tightened and her heart sagged. She knew this feeling. It caught her suddenly from time to time, while serving a loud room full of people, or dancing at the céilís. A great loneliness— the feeling that though she was surrounded by people, none of them truly knew her or wanted to. It was a lie, she knew, but that didn't make the feelings go away. Only moments of quiet connection helped.

Laen on her shoulder on the dark side of the Hold.

Chats with Falier while wiping down tables.

Stolen moments with Taz.

"He's all alone," Selene whispered, tears filling her eyes. She shook her head to rid herself of them. "He needs his parent."

Alísa came back and knelt in front of Selene. She took Selene's hand and squeezed it, a gasp slipping out.

"I feel him through you," Alísa whispered. "I didn't even know he was a male until now."

Graydonn and Koriana's heads both came into view, as did Falier. Sesína came around the back, hemming Selene in. The air thickened as they crowded her and sorrow continued filling the space.

"Alísa," Graydonn said, awe filling his tone, *"you don't think—"*

"We should get Selene out of the cave." Koriana's eyes dimmed. *"Before it's too late and she has no choice."*

Alísa shushed them, her eyes grabbing Selene's. "Do you understand what's happening right now?"

Selene blew out a breath, her mind running too fast to fully comprehend. "I think so. If I'm feeling him and you aren't—it's the bond, isn't it?"

Alísa nodded. The dragonet chirped again as it caught Selene's voice. It pleaded for her, fear and hope's colors colliding in the halo of a turquoise voice-light.

"I can have Koriana fly you out of here to try and stop it," Alísa whispered. "I won't lie to you, though—I fear he won't choose another before it's too late. It's not fair for me to ask you to stay, but it's where we are. It will change your life, but I promise you won't be alone."

Selene swallowed and looked to the egg again. She must be crazy to consider this. She didn't belong here with the dragons, not like Alísa and Falier. She belonged in the Hold, serving people—seeing them and helping them along their way.

But, what if she did belong here? She had felt an immediate connection to Koriana the first time they met, seeing the sorrow she hid for the good of the cause. Her holder's duty of attending the visits every day had quickly turned to joy as she participated in tea parties and fascinating conversations about their two races. She had even slid easily into telepathic communication.

The egg rocked again. If nothing else, she understood the dragonet's loneliness. She couldn't leave him to that terrible feeling, and she certainly wouldn't leave him to die, like Alísa feared. It didn't matter how it would change her life—she was his only option.

"Let me go to him."

Alísa smiled, her eyes soft and warm. She stood and looked to Komi—or, where Komi should be. All Selene could see now were the mist and Tawny.

"Komi, give Selene the egg."

"Singer?"

Sesína danced behind Selene, talons skittering on stone. *"After all this time, the dragonet wants a human, just like I did!"*

Faern rose as Selene did. *"Singer, no. You mustn't let this happen!"*

"Yes, don't let her near it!" Harenn said. *"A dragon bound to the Singer is one thing, but another human? It needs a proper parent-bond."*

Sesína growled. *"I turned out just fine, thank you very much."*

"*The dragonet knows who it wants,*" Saynan said, "*who are we to say otherwise? Besides, I have worked with Sesína for weeks now, and she has become a fine and capable dragoness despite the oddities of a human's Illumination.*"

"*Thanks, I think,*" Sesína grumbled.

Koriana looked to each around the fire. "*If any human were to Illuminate a dragon again, Selene is a fine candidate. Yet how much of our wisdom and knowledge are we willing to lose in the next generation of dragons? While Sesína lives well, she will only have her and Alísa's knowledge to pass to her offspring. If we allow more like her, how badly will we hinder our race?*"

"*I agree with Koriana.*" Faern growled, his blazing green eyes on Alísa. "*Alísa-Dragon-Singer, I mean you and Sesína no disrespect, but while I want peace, I also believe that once it has come humans and dragons should separate. We were not made to be together. War will only come again.*"

"*Would the Maker allow Illumination and mind-kin bonds between humans and dragons if we weren't supposed to have them?*" Graydonn looked at Falier, then Selene. "*If He allows it, how can we deny it?*"

Alísa smiled at the young dragon, then set a hand on Selene's shoulder. "*I can't speak to all of your arguments. Yours especially, Koriana, causes me concern. But I do know the dragonets will die without Illumination, and we are running short on time. Their connection has already begun—the dragonet has chosen and so has Selene. Let them go.*"

Selene set her eyes on Tawny and stepped into the sorrowful mists. They began curling back. There was a dichotomy in how they moved, simultaneously fleeing and coaxing her forward.

She knelt before Tawny, still cradled in Komi's paws. Her heart trembled as she reached a hand. There would be no coming back from this. She would be the mother of a dragon. Her parents' first grandchild would have scales. Would she and the hatchling live in the Hold, or in this cave? What would Taz...

She shook her head. Life and death were the stakes here, and she would not let the dragonet die in its loneliness.

Warmth radiated into her palm as she touched the glossy surface of the egg. It moved, more gently this time, as the dragonet inside pressed against her hand.

Selene smiled. "Hi there." She placed a second hand on the shell. "It's okay. I'm here for you."

A burbling chirp answered Selene, the turquoise of it complimentary to the tawny shell.

She lifted Tawny from Komi's hold and pulled him into her lap. "I bet your telepathy color will be bright yellow, just to spite me."

Selene smiled as the smallest halo of light-purple mist rose around the egg. Contentment.

"Did you feel that change?" Alísa spoke to the dragons again, awe and affection flowing through her telepathy. *"For weeks this little one has been lost and afraid, no matter how we tried to help him. And now Selene has rescued him. I do not take your warnings lightly, Faern, Koriana. I don't wish for all dragons to be human-Illuminated any more than I wish all humans would start living in caves alongside dragons—but there is beauty here."*

Selene looked down, oddly embarrassed by Alísa's speech. She stroked the egg, marveling at all the minuscule pocks in the shell. Those must be how the empathy mists got through, since physical barriers could stop psychic powers. All the things she could learn from this precious little one.

Still, she didn't quite understand why she saw empathy mists in the first place. She didn't see them for anyone else, unless there was sound involved. Perhaps she was like Falier—a slayer with weak powers. Or else, one with powers that manifested differently than everyone else's, just like her hearing. Would that have kept the testers from catching her abilities?

"You okay?"

Selene looked at Falier as he sat beside her. She matched his verbal speech as Alísa and the dragons continued with telepathy. "Yes. I think so?"

"You know you have all the support you'll ever need here, right?" Falier looked out at the dragons. "Even those who protest will come around, I'm certain. Especially Koriana—she thinks the world of you."

Selene nodded. "I know. I can't imagine how I'm going to explain this to Mamá and Papá, though."

Come to think of it, where did she stand now? Would she stay in the

Hold when Tawny hatched? That might scare people away, and would almost certainly be a fire hazard. Would her parents insist she stay in the cave? Would the dragons insist? Would they consider her a member of the clan now, like they did Falier? Did they expect her to stay?

"Hey." Falier took her hand from the tawny shell and squeezed. "You're not alone, Selene."

Selene let out a breath and returned the gesture. The dragonet shifted inside the egg, and she set Falier's hand on the shell so he could feel it too.

"I know."

14

MESSENGER

Alísa breathed a sigh of relief as her final delivery of the day came to an end. Serving in the Hold day after day was exhausting. While Falier's energetic, people-oriented personality suited it well, Alísa wondered how the more reserved Selene had been able to do this her entire life. Wake up early to entertain and serve breakfast. Go to homes distributing food. Come back to entertain and serve lunch. Host and arbitrate meetings. Entertain and serve dinner. Host céilís on Friday. And now, thanks to her, attend dragon visits almost every day.

Today's visit had a good turnout, each of the adolescent dragons occupied with their various groups. They all knew the routine now, and most of them enjoyed it. Needing whatever break she could get, yet still needing to be present, Alísa approached Namor. He sat on the bench just outside his house, watching over the visit.

"M—may I join you?"

Namor scooted over, making room for Alísa to sit. She plopped the empty delivery baskets on the ground beside the bench and gathered her heavy bag onto her lap. Nearby, seven children stood in a circle with Sesína playing fivers, a game that required bouncing a leather ball in the air five times before passing it on to the next player, all without letting it touch the ground. Further into the square, two groups formed around the other three dragons. Parsen was the only holder present today—Falier and Selene otherwise occupied by chores. He stood in Graydonn's group, while Tenza stood with Komi and Harenn.

Alísa's bag chirped as she watched Sesína bounce the ball off her snout. Reaching into the bag, she set her hand on the blue dragon egg, spreading her fingers over its surface. She breathed out peace, but it did nothing—in fact, the dragonet let out a gurgle that spoke its frustration.

Namor nodded at the bag. "Any luck?"

Alísa shook her head. After a couple of days for contemplation, the dragons had agreed to let Falier and Alísa try with Blue. It only had perhaps two weeks before it would hatch, and even the dragons who disliked the idea of another human-Illuminated dragon agreed it was better than death. Falier had taken the first turn with it, but to no avail. Alísa and Sesína had no desire to lose their bond, but to save Blue's life, Alísa had to try.

"What do you want from us?" she whispered, rubbing the shell. She kept Blue in the bag and out of sight of the children. She couldn't bear the thought of having to tell them if the dragonet didn't make it.

A quiet trumpet of alarm jerked Alísa to attention. "Graydonn?"

Graydonn's voice entered her mind. *"I sense a human and a horse on the outskirts of my range, on the western path."*

Pushing the bag from her lap, Alísa stood. *"You all know what to do. Go."*

The dragons moved, startling some of the humans. Alísa walked toward them, speaking as loudly as she could. "It's okay. G—G—Graydonn senses someone on the road. The dragons are going to g—g—g" —*breathe, redirect*— "to leave now."

The adolescents loped away, darting between houses into the forest. From his spot in Graydonn's group, Parsen reminded the people not to say anything about the dragons. A foreign sense of peace tickled at Alísa's mind, and she realized with a start that Tenza was using her empathy to calm them, perhaps make them more compliant.

Guilt grabbed Alísa's heart as she added her own calm to Tenza's, pushing hard to make up for the fact that she didn't feel calm herself. The dragons had to remain secret, and children especially weren't known for keeping quiet about things that excited them.

Eldra Branni, forgive me.

Hoofbeats audible now, Alísa looked to the path. A rider on a chestnut horse came into view. The man wore a blue tunic with white stitching over a white shirt and pants. A messenger.

The man glanced about the village as he entered, his gaze lingering on the gathering of people. He didn't slow, however, heading straight for the Hold.

Falier clenched and unclenched his fists as he followed Selene's instructions to wait at the door. *Listen for the hoofbeats, then wait another ten counts.* A more natural response time, she claimed. Though his heart still pounded in nervous anticipation of whoever was coming, he knew she was right.

Graydonn's warning had come with the assurance that the dragons had gotten out of sight in time, and Selene was currently tucking Tawny into a pile of blankets under her bed—he shouldn't feel so anxious. But the last visitors to Me'ran had been Sorenites at the céilí a month ago, before the dragons had been normalized. An unexpected visitor now might cause serious problems if they weren't careful.

Selene came up beside Falier just as he arrived at ten and opened the southern door. She pushed ahead of him, ambling toward the stables. The wait had allowed the rider, a messenger, time to find it and swing off his horse.

"Welcome," Selene said, her tone so normal Falier was glad she had spoken first. She clasped arms with the messenger. "Eldra Tila straighten your way."

The man dipped his head. "Eldra Nahne bless you."

The messenger looked to be in his late twenties, his face angular with pronounced cheekbones, a hook nose, and brows that made his brown eyes look nearly black under their shadow. His hair and beard were pitch black as well, a sharp contrast with all the white in his tack and uniform.

"I don't think I recognize you," Selene said. "Have you been here before?"

"Ah, no. I'm actually very new to the region." He gave a small smile. "My name is Rassím."

"Welcome again, then. I'm Selene. Lunch is still hot inside. I'll get a room ready for you. Allow my brother to take care of your horse."

Falier fought not to glare at his sister as she relegated him to horse duty.

"Actually, I'd prefer to take care of my own animal," Rassím said. "She's a bit particular. And I won't be staying long—my messages are for Soren, though I wanted to stop in and see if you had anything for me. I'll take you up on the lunch, though."

Selene arched an eyebrow, then relaxed into the sweet smile she often used to hide sarcasm.

"Well, at least let me help. You can correct me if I do anything wrong." She led the way to the stable without another word or glance to make sure Rassím followed her.

Rassím gave Falier a questioning look, to which Falier just shrugged. First, she had given him horse duty, then she had taken it herself; half the time Falier couldn't understand a thing his sister did. One thing he did know, though, was strangers shouldn't be left alone right now, hence her escorting him to the stables.

"I'll just make sure food is ready for you, then." Falier nodded at Selene to indicate that Rassím should follow her. Once the man gathered up his horse's reins and did so, Falier went back inside.

"Messenger," Falier announced, knowing his mother occupied the kitchen. "We'll need a lunch in about ten minutes."

"Make that two lunches."

Falier swung around at the voice, seeing Yarlan come in through the western door. Sometimes he hated that each wall held an outside door.

"Peace, Falier," Yarlan grumbled. "I'm not here to cause trouble—I'm as entitled to news of the world as any."

You'll forgive me if I don't believe you. Falier wouldn't say the words aloud—it would do no good to antagonize the man. Hopefully, Namor was on his way too. He could keep his younger counterpart in line.

Falier went into the kitchen, nodded to his mother as she heated corned beef for sandwiches, and grabbed a water bucket and rag. Something to do, to keep his mind off the danger of this situation. Reentering the main room, he set to scrubbing the table nearest the southern door, where the messenger would likely sit.

"Do you hate me, Falier?"

Falier paused at the unexpected question, then scrubbed with more vigor. "I didn't think you cared about that."

"'Care' is a strong word. I don't care what any individual thinks of me. I ask only because I think you waste your energy on me. You missed a spot."

Falier glared at him.

"I think deep down you and I are on the same side," Yarlan said. "Though we both think the other misguided, we both care about the good of Me'ran. Isn't that right?"

Falier dunked the rag with perhaps a little more force than necessary. "What's your point?"

Yarlan shook his head. "I'm just trying to determine if you've lost what has always made you such a good holder. If it came down to Me'ran or the dragons, who would you protect?"

Before Falier could answer, the southern door opened again. To Falier's great relief, Namor, Tenza, and Alísa entered the main room.

Yarlan rapped his fist on the table before turning away. "Think about it."

Alísa approached, skirting Yarlan to come up beside Falier. She touched a finger to her temple, and he connected them telepathically.

"What does he want? You seem agitated."

Falier began scrubbing one of the chairs. *"He says he wants to know the news and isn't going to cause trouble. Now that Namor's here, I think we're okay. What would we do if he said something? Would we have to take the messenger hostage?"*

Alísa shuddered. *"Let's try to avoid that."*

Parsen's booming laugh sounded outside just before the door opened. Selene entered with a smug grin on her face, while Rassím chuckled sheepishly, a slight limp to his step.

"What did we miss?" Falier asked, moving the bucket from the table to a spot against the wall.

"Oh, just that Rassím's horse is indeed 'particular.'" Selene shook her head in amusement. "She was just fine with me in the stall, yet she tried to crush him up against the side as he took off the saddle. He may need to leave her here in exchange for one of ours."

"Not a chance," Rassím said. "She's my father's—I'd never hear the end of it if I told him she was too much trouble for me. Hello." He looked from person to person. "I'm afraid I'm going to disappoint you—I don't have anything particularly exciting to share. Or perhaps you all have something for me?"

The door to the kitchen opened, and Kat stepped through with a platter of sandwiches. "Falier, Selene, help me get drinks?"

Selene smirked at Rassím. "Ale to take the edge off?"

Rassím shook his head. "Just water, please."

"Everyone else?"

Falier counted the water and ale orders and followed Selene into the kitchen, knowing she would have the count as well. As soon as the door shut behind them, he placed a hand on her arm.

"You're being awfully friendly. What happened to my quietly-observant sister?"

"Her loud and boisterous brother lost all sense of calm," she whispered back, grabbing mugs off the shelf. "I've been watching the colors—no indication of malice. So long as Yarlan and the rest keep their mouths shut, we're good."

Falier blew out his breath. Selene's colors were rarely wrong, and now Namor was present to keep Yarlan on tether. Maybe *he* should have some of the ale to take the edge off...

He and Selene brought the mugs out, all six adults having taken their seats at the table Falier had just cleaned. Falier grabbed a sandwich and his own mug and joined Alísa at the next table, Selene coming up with her food and Alísa's water.

"The Southlands, eh?" Parsen said. "That's a ways to come!"

Falier looked at Rassím, interest piqued. "You've been to the Southlands?"

Rassím swallowed his food. "Grew up there."

"What's it like?"

"Beautiful, but of a very different kind than here," Rassím said between bites. "Rocky pillars, hills of sand stretching far as the eye can see, muted green brush with the brightest of flowers, and skies that go on forever."

"What made you come north?" Kat asked.

Rassím's eyes darkened. "My parents' health. The heat wasn't good to them, nor was the turmoil in our village, so we came north. They and my sisters are living in East Russig, where I got my start. The need was greater here, though, and I was ready to see more of the world."

Namor cleared his throat. "Any news from the west?"

"Ah." Rassím lifted his hands in an empty-handed gesture. "Nothing recent, but it's always the same. Another town destroyed by dragons, another second taking the place of a dead chief. Not quite west, but there is a fishing town just east of the Nissen that was destroyed recently—Cherrin. Razed to the ground. No survivors to tell the story."

Alísa's gaze went to her lap, sorrow pouring from her. Was Cherrin the town the dreki brought back news of a month ago? The one Rorenth had destroyed?

"Which actually brings me to the question I've been asking every town since seeing the disaster—and point me toward your slayers if you need to. Have there been any signs around here of dragons?"

Yarlan shifted and his eyes narrowed, but Namor spoke more quickly. "You're looking at Me'ran's slayers; Yarlan and I are it, plus our wives and a widow. I've always said we need more men, as have slayers in other nearby villages, but it never helps. I know Segenn—he wants the fame of having the largest and strongest of the clans, never mind the danger he leaves the unprotected villages in. Obviously, Cherrin is a sign that his way isn't working."

Rassím leaned forward. "You're telling me you've sent messages to the wayfarers asking for help, and they've never responded? They've never sent you anyone?"

"No immediate threat," Namor explained.

"It's amazing how easily a threat can show up when one doesn't prepare for it," Yarlan growled.

"I had no idea." Rassím shook his head. "I've not carried such a message to them before. Rest assured, I'll carry it now. Perhaps they just need to hear it incessantly."

Falier tapped his fingers on his thigh. What was Namor doing? If the wayfarers responded, there would be trouble. Wasn't that what Namor had said they needed to avoid in order to keep Bria's story from repeating?

Rassím downed the last of his water and scooted his chair back from the table. "Thank you for the meal and information. I should check in with the rest of the village, see if they have anything for me."

"I'll accompany you," Parsen said. "Make sure you can find your way and don't miss anyone."

Rassím hesitated only a moment before nodding. "Thank you, that would be a big help, actually. And you" —he pointed at Selene— "don't work any more of your strange sorcery on my horse. I don't want her choosing you as her new rider before I leave today."

Selene smirked. "No promises."

Rassím shook his head, but the messenger's good-natured smile remained as he followed Parsen out the door. The room was silent for a breath as they waited for Rassím to be out of earshot. Kat was the first to break the silence with a sigh of relief.

"Well, that could have gone a lot worse."

Tenza sipped at her ale. "I won't breathe easy until he's out of Me'ran entirely."

Kat's eyes slid from Tenza to Falier, and he watched as they changed from her normal optimism to the fear and sorrow they held all too often now. Tenza was right, but why did she have to say it and make his mother afraid again?

Falier looked to Namor. "Why did you tell him we need more slayers? I thought the point of keeping quiet about the dragons was to avoid that."

"One more messenger taking word to Segenn won't change anything," Namor said, "but it's a bell I must keep ringing. One day, Alísa will leave us and take her dragons with her. When that day comes, Me'ran will still need more slayers. The need will remain until he figures out that I know what I'm talking about."

Namor's voice lowered thoughtfully. "It's strange, though, that Rassím hasn't heard any other village-bound slayers complain about their numbers."

"Perhaps they've given up," Yarlan muttered. "As you said, we've been making noise for years with no ears turned."

"Still, I can't believe no one else has mentioned it to him. That doesn't seem right."

Yarlan scoffed, standing. "There's just no pleasing you, is there? You're angry when people speak and suspicious when they're silent. Maybe instead of seeing dragons where there are none, you should worry about the actual dragons at your front door!"

Alísa flinched as Yarlan stormed out of the Hold without another word. "I'm n—never going to c-c-c—convince him, am I?"

"It seems unlikely, dear girl," Namor said. "We should be grateful he's behaving and leave it there."

Selene faced Namor and Tenza. "Shouldn't somebody follow him to make sure he *keeps* behaving?"

Namor shook his head. "It is enough that your father is with Rassím. If anyone watched Yarlan, he would sense them. Best to stay out of his way and focus instead on the messenger. Despite his outbursts, Yarlan has gone along with all of our plans—following him or doing anything else directly might be the bump in the road that makes the wheel fall off."

15

KNIVES

"Papá, where are you?"

Alísa's heart raced. Giants surrounded her as she tripped through the market, some ignoring her, others beckoning her with promises of safety. Their faces meant nothing to her, so she couldn't trust them. She ran, but she was so much smaller than they. If they gave chase, she would never get away.

She just needed to find him, then she would be safe.

"Papá?"

She clutched at her necklace, her lifeline to him. It was heavier than she remembered. Heavier and rounder. Glancing down, she saw her reflection not in a blue dragon's scale, but an egg. It grew and grew until it was too much for her small body.

Lowering to the ground, Alísa pulled the chain off her neck and let the cracking egg lie in front of her. It shuddered and shook, shrieks piercing through the forming holes.

Her heart raced. She needed her father—he would know what to do. She cried out for him again, but this time no sound came. At least, not from her. The blue dragonet's shrieks became the very words she had tried to say:

"Papá! Where are you?"

As though to emphasize the cry, the shell split down the middle and opened, revealing a child with shoulder-length hair the color of the summer sky. The child was too big to have fit inside the egg, but there it was, uncurling from its fetal position and gazing at the giants, bare back to Alísa.

The child shrank, or, rather, Alísa grew. She grew until she wasn't a lost little girl anymore, but one of the giants. Now the little blue-haired child would only see her as one of the faceless, but she couldn't leave it alone without trying to help.

Alísa touched the child's shoulder. "What's your name?"

It turned around, shining white eyes staring in confusion. Then its face lit up as its gaze fixed on something behind Alísa.

"Papá!"

Alísa turned to see what the child saw, but collapsed to the ground as the weight of the world came crashing in around her.

Mind-choke—one that cut like a knife as it squeezed. Alísa couldn't even find the strength to breathe as its jaws clamped around her. Then she saw them—brown eyes once filled with love now looked on her in disgust through sweat-drenched copper curls.

Papá? She couldn't even find the strength to say his name.

He drew his dagger and pressed it to her throat.

"One word out of you, and you're dead."

The voice wasn't Karn's.

Alísa jerked awake and found she could barely move. A hand pressed hard against her shoulder, weighing her down on the mattress and keeping her from cutting herself on the cool, sharp metal held to her neck. Panic shot through her as the dim morning light revealed cold black eyes staring from above, set in a harsh, angular face, with black hair pulled back in warrior's braids.

Rassím.

Slayer! A slayer who now held her in a mind-choke and pressed a knife to her throat.

"W—what—"

Alísa hissed in a breath as the knife pressed harder. A sharp pain sent a trickle of warmth to her pillow.

"Didn't you hear me, Dragon Witch? One more word, one more sound before Segenn commands, and you're dead. He wants this done a certain way, but he has given me permission to diverge from the path if necessary."

Segenn. The eastern wayfarers' chief!

What could she do? She couldn't call for Sesína—Rassím's mind-choke cut her off from their bond. That was why the choke in the dream had hurt. But the pain hadn't woken her, so Sesína might similarly still be asleep with no idea something was terribly wrong.

Where were Namor and Tenza? Still sleeping in their room? Or with similar assassins at their throats?

Rassím released the pressure on Alísa's shoulder and neck. "Get up, slowly, and do exactly as I say."

Alísa nodded her compliance, swallowing now that the knife was gone. She began lifting the covers off, then remembered Blue curled up in a blanket next to her. If he saw it, he would smash it and kill the dragonet.

She pushed the covers off her, shoving them and the hidden egg to the side as she sat up. Keeping her eyes on Rassím, she stood, fighting not to tremble despite the weakness brought by the mind-choke and the morning chill permeating Ari's old room. Underneath his cloak, two leather straps crossed over his armor in an X, each lined with more knives—throwing knives. Most slayers didn't use those; there were only a few places one could hit to kill a dragon with something so small. Those who used them had to be cool under pressure and have deadly accuracy.

"Outside, witch." Rassím gripped her arm strong enough to bruise. He shoved her through the house, pushing past her cloak as she tried to grab it. There were more important things than modesty right now, but the dignity it robbed her of sparked a wave of anger.

Opening the door, Rassím pushed Alísa outside. The trees still hid the sun, but the day was light enough to see the chaos as slayers in armor and warpaint pulled people from their homes and toward the square. Those gathered stood in a large group in front of the dragon shelter, with perhaps forty slayers encircling them. Only yesterday, villagers and dragons stood there together without fear. Now, though her empathy was quiet in the grip of Rassím's mind-choke, Alísa could see the fear in their eyes, in the tension of their shoulders, in the stiffness of their walk. Even the slayers seemed on-edge, with shifting eyes and hands that fidgeted with their cloaks and weapons.

Rassím wrenched Alísa's arm behind her and pushed her forward. Her bare feet struck dirt damp with dew, and she shivered as a wave of cold ran up her body. Before the growing crowd, two slayers held Namor and Tenza. Namor leaned heavily on Tenza, his staff apparently left behind. Each wore their nightclothes, Namor in a sleeveless shirt and pants that hung to just above the knee, and Tenza in her nightdress, her hair braided behind her. Their shoulders and heads drooped slightly. They were probably being choked as well. The slayers on either side of them had their swords drawn, tips resting lightly against the ground.

Namor's brow furrowed. "Alísa—"

"Quiet, old man," Namor's guard hissed, lifting his sword for emphasis and making Alísa's heart race. "You're lucky we haven't skewered you like the traitor you are."

Alísa looked around cautiously. It was too open here, she wouldn't be able to get away, not unless there was a distraction that would allow her time to bolt between houses before Rassím could throw. But he would just come after her—she couldn't sing and hide at the same time. And they might kill Namor and Tenza in retaliation.

She scanned the crowd, some eyes meeting hers, while others looked away. She didn't know which she wanted more—to see friends who might fight for her, or to see those looking away, who would be in no danger from the slayers.

This can't be Bria all over again—it can't!

Her heart skipped as her eyes landed on Falier and his family being escorted from the Hold. They took in the crowded square with shock. Then Falier saw her. He stumbled to a halt, wide eyes pinned to her. The slayer behind him pushed, prompting him to keep moving to the group of villagers with his family. He looked from Alísa to his family and back, seemingly at a loss.

Alísa shook her head at him, hoping he would understand. He couldn't do anything for her, not right now. She prayed he wouldn't do something stupid, like profess his love in front of the slayers wanting to kill her.

Falier began moving again, walking quickly to get in front of his family. He angled for the front of the crowd, eyes roaming the square, taking everything in. He stopped just behind the front line of villagers, Parsen at his side, Kat and Selene behind them. Falier pinned worried eyes on her, giving the smallest nod. He was there for her, and that frightened her so.

Another group of villagers spilled into the square, all being herded toward the others. A slayer dressed in red—the colors of the chief—was among them, as was Yarlan. Unlike the rest of the villagers, Yarlan was fully dressed, and even had his sword at his side. They had allowed him to dress? Or he had known they were coming.

Anger burned. Of course, Yarlan had known—he was probably who had called for them! Didn't he know what the wayfarers might do to any villagers who had turned to her and the dragons of their own volition?

Together, Yarlan and Chief Segenn approached the front. In addition to his red sash, Segenn wore an earthy cloak and a double line of red warpaint across his darkly-tanned forehead, his black hair pulled back in a tail with a braid on either side. Typically, only a single line of the crowning paint was worn into battle. The double-line was reserved for situations a chief needed his authority acknowledged, perhaps when meeting another clan of slayers or, like now, taking military control over a village.

The guards stood to attention as Segenn stopped in front of Alísa. He looked her up and down with cold detachment, speaking quietly, as though to himself.

"And now the slayers of the east finally prove their worth."

"Segenn!" Meira's voice rose from the crowd. She and her husband Garrick stood at the front with a few of their fellow elders. "What is the meaning of this?"

Segenn ignored her, looking instead to his second-in-command, marked as such by the yellow tartan against black dragon scale armor and a single yellow crown mark. The mark stood out against his dark skin, and his black hair was worn in multiple small braids along his scalp which were gathered into a single tie at the back.

"Has everyone returned, Briek?"

The second—Briek—came forward without even a cursory glance at Alísa. "The whole village is here. We should be quick, before the dragons discover what's happening."

"Did you get her before she woke?" Yarlan asked Rassím. "Before she could alert the dragon bonded to her?"

Rassím grunted an affirmative. "I've never seen anything like it, held in place despite—"

Segenn held up a hand. "Good."

Rassím's grip tensed around Alísa's arm as Segenn interrupted him. Now in the light, she saw he wore the green paint of a scout, a solitary line from above his left eye to his jaw, signifying his low status as opposed to those of higher station, who wore two or three lines.

Looking to each of the guards, Segenn spoke loudly, apparently wanting the villagers to hear him too. "Keep your chokes tight—we don't want a draconic surprise."

The chief turned, his cloak brushing Alísa's leg as he pivoted quickly toward the people, his arms raised as though to embrace an old friend.

"People of Me'ran, your days of living in fear are at an end! No longer will you be captives to the Dragon Witch and her schemes. No longer will threats of tooth and flame hold you—"

A protest rose in Alísa's throat, but Rassím's knife pressed to her neck once more. He hissed out his words, so quiet in contrast to Segenn's speech.

"There's only one way you get through this alive, witch. Stay silent and bow to Segenn's demands."

Demands? He was going to make demands, rather than just kill her outright? A sliver of hope filled Alísa. Whether they were demands she could meet or not, demands meant extra time—perhaps enough to convince Segenn that whatever Yarlan told him was wrong.

"—We of the Maker's gift are here to set you free!"

Segenn paused as though expecting a response, though the one that came likely wasn't what he had wanted. Garrick spoke, louder than Alísa had ever heard the reserved elder speak before.

"You're making a mistake, Chief Segenn. I don't know what Yarlan told you, but we are not captives, and the girl you hold at knife-point has done nothing to deserve it."

Segenn's arms fell to his sides, his face turning solemn. "I see. It is as I feared. Her hold on you is great. It should not surprise me" —he swung around to face Namor— "considering that one of the best of the slayers has also been taken."

187

Namor's eyes narrowed. "This is foolishness, Segenn. Ask any of us—no one has been harmed by Alísa or her dragons."

"Not physically." Yarlan stalked toward him, teeth clenched. "Yet every day you stood by while the beasts entered our minds, corrupted our children! The people were afraid, yet you and the holders did nothing but aid evil's sway over our home!"

Segenn looked back at the people. "Holders?"

A tremble ran through Alísa. *Maker, help us. Don't let them hurt Falier and his family!*

Yarlan grunted. "The witch wormed her way into the boy's heart, but I believe he and his family will be saved when the threat is gone. As for my fellow slayers" —his eyes softened with sadness— "I am not sure."

Segenn's eyes turned to Alísa. In them she found a cold light of triumph, as though she were a new piece of dragon-scale armor to show his might. She forced her chin up, slowly, so Rassím's blade wouldn't cut her again. Slayers respected strength, and she hoped even a sliver showed despite her fear.

"Then let us see." Segenn nodded to Rassím, who lowered his knife. The chief kept his face turned to Alísa, yet spoke loudly enough for the whole village to hear, making her wince as he sent spittle flying.

"When Yarlan's message finally found us, telling of your presence in this village, I knew I had to get here quickly. To save these dear, beloved people from the dragons' grip by any means necessary. Though I am not without mercy."

Though Segenn addressed Alísa, he now looked toward the people, his hands clasped behind his back.

"I know your story, daughter of Karn. The gift you couldn't control. How you were stolen by dragons and forced to sing. Your family's desperate search for hope. Would you be a Bria or an Allara?"

Alísa tried to keep the surprise from her face but surely failed. Namor and Tenza, too, seemed shocked. How did Segenn know this? Did Yarlan tell him who her father was? And Allara? Alísa only learned of Allara from Koriana, she had never heard the name from humans.

"Now I give you a chance to prove yourself loyal to your people. Your mind is cut off from any dragons that might control or punish you—

you are free to show your true colors now. Use your power, free these people from your grip, and, once they are safely within the shelter, call the dragons down one-by-one so we might end them!"

Alísa breathed heavily as Segenn looked at her once more, his eyes boring into hers. She had to speak to him, get him to allow her to sing a memory song so he and his slayers would see the truth. She closed her eyes, trying to settle her heart so that her throat would release.

Eldra Branni, help me. Make Segenn see the truth.

"Chief Segenn, p-p-please hear me. There is m—more going on than you kn—know. I c-c-c-c-can show you, b—but I need to sing it so all will see. I swear, I will not c-c-call the dragons."

The daggers in Segenn's eyes shifted, the respect of a man for his foe turning to contempt. "This? This is the vessel the dragons chose?"

Alísa's insides caved. *Not again. Not again! Great Maker, why?*

"She's telling the truth about not calling the dragons, Chief," Rassím said, apparently feeling it under his choke. "What's more, she doesn't have the aura of—"

Segenn didn't allow him to finish, his voice rising as he looked to Namor and Tenza, then the people. "A fearful girl with a broken tongue, yet you all fell under her spell?" His voice fell quiet. "The dragons must be powerful indeed."

"Segenn," Yarlan said, coming to his side. "I thought I had made it clear. The people aren't entranced. She and the dragons were far more subtle than that, turning them with soft words and promises of safety. Besides Namor and possibly the holders' boy, they were won over by their charms. We just need to clear her influence from the village. Kill the dragons, kill her if you need, and the people will learn their mistake. There's no need—"

"You'd better pray you're wrong, Yarlan." Segenn cast his eyes over the people. The cold calculation which replaced his previously flaunting air made Alísa's skin crawl. "If they chose evil themselves—"

"Then what, Segenn?" Namor growled. "You'll destroy the village, as in Bria's day? Hear the people—look beyond the end of your own nose for once in your life!"

Segenn rounded on Namor, but another voice turned him back to the crowd.

"The dragons aren't evil!" Serra called out, her sons clinging to her. "Not these ones. They've protected us, saved lives. They want peace."

"Quiet, woman!" Segenn erupted. "If Kerrik heard you now—"

"If Kerrik heard you now, he'd fight!" she shouted over him. A few villagers backed away from her, fear filling their eyes. Still others spoke agreement. Rassím and the other guards tensed, one laying a hand on the hilt of his sword.

"Listen to her, Segenn!" Falier's voice was both harsh and pleading. "If you'd just let Alísa show you—"

"Taz, seize the holder!" Segenn barked.

A young slayer with cacao skin looked between his chief and Falier, eyes widening with conflict. Falier apparently took courage from that, stepping to the front.

"—I've seen it all firsthand. If you won't let her sing, then take my memories!"

"Someone shut him up—"

A shout of pain interrupted Segenn's command. One of the guards beside Alísa buckled as Tenza stomped on the instep of his foot, breaking it. Tenza brought her elbow down on the guard's spine, knocking him to the ground. The man holding Namor fell back with a scream, holding his head as Namor broke through his mind-choke. Namor, too, fell as his support left him, but his eyes locked on Rassím. Alísa could almost feel the buzz of astral energy as it shot into her guard and broke his choke.

"Sing!" Namor shouted from the ground. His guard pulled a knife from its sheath, but Namor ignored him. "Show them, now!"

Time slowed, yet Alísa couldn't move as the guard's knife plunged into Namor's chest. Pain and grief bubbled up inside her, and with her scream of anguish Alísa released all the power she could. Slayer and normal alike fell to their knees, many gripping their heads at the astral shockwave.

Alísa's eyes shot to the mountain. *"Sesína, can you hear me?"*

Like clasps on a chest, the Illumination bond locked back into place. Sesína's terror rushed into Alísa as she saw what was happening.

"I need your strength, dear one, not your fear. You will save me, but first I

190

must get the truth into the slayers' heads. Help me hold them in a trance while I do it."

"If you sing for a trance, we can't fly to you!"

Strength faded within Alísa and she sank to her knees. *"Fly here as soon as my song ends. Please, I have to give them a chance."*

Alísa breathed as the remnants of her cry held the people down, feeling Sesína get ahold of her emotions and push strength through the bond as Alísa always did for the dragons. Astral energy restored and multiplying, she sang.

Time stopping.
Normals, slayers, all dropping.
'Round all may these visions wind—
Bind.

Many slayers fought Alísa's grip, their energies prickling and stabbing against her mind-choke. Sesína opened her mind wider, pouring as much strength as she could into Alísa and pushing back against the fighters. But they couldn't keep this up for long, and it would take time for the dragons to get here when the song ended.

Pressing through her grief, Alísa grasped onto visions of discovering the souls of the dragons and the good deeds of her clan, pushing them out alongside her binding lyrics.

Truth stirring.
Dragon souls revealed, spurring
Hope for skin and scale aligned.
Bind.

Hope bringing.
Dragons fight and fall, clinging
To the peace they wish to find.
Bind.

Alísa crawled to Namor, not having the strength to stand. The slayer lay entranced like the rest of the people, his breath not labored, but gurgling with fluids. The knife was in his lung. He wouldn't live much longer. She took his hand in both of hers and squeezed it, hoping somewhere in his trance he knew she was with him, just has he had been for her.

> Truth reaching
> For my brothers' hearts, teaching
> Songs of peace and life to find.
> Bind.

"*Send the clan, Sesína,*" she said, her final note giving out. "*Don't come—*"

"*Like flames I won't come!*"

"*I just took all of your strength. Stay away. I can't lose you too.*"

She gave Namor's hand one more squeeze. "Thank you."

The effects of the song came to an end, the people pulling from her choke. Swords slid from sheaths, murmurs grew into commotion, and Segenn's voice rose above all others.

"Kill the witch! Don't let her strengthen the dragons!"

Alísa's heart sped as slayers rose all around her. She couldn't run—she didn't even have the strength to stand after pouring it all into her song. And it hadn't worked, at least not on the most important person. If the chief had turned, the rest might have followed.

Tenza rose, twisting her guard's sword from his hand as he tried to stand on his broken foot, then kicking him in the side so he fell back to the ground. She turned to face the slayer who had stabbed Namor, who was rising as well, hatred twisting from her once perfectly-guarded mind.

"Hold, D'kin!"

The man who slew Namor halted at Briek's shout. Sweat gathered on the second-in-command's forehead as he turned wide eyes to his chief.

"Segenn, did you see it? This isn't what we thought."

Alísa gasped in a trembling breath. The second! She had reached the second-in-command!

"It's a trick of her power, Briek!" Segenn said. "She can make you see whatever she wants. Fight her!"

"No, what she showed you is true!" Kat called out, many in the crowd echoing their agreement as they rose back to their feet. "These dragons have fought for us. They are our friends."

"D'kin!" Segenn called to the other slayer. "Do it! Break her hold on them, now!"

"Like I'll let you," Tenza snarled, swinging the stolen sword. She stepped over Namor and advanced with furious strikes Alísa would never have expected from a village-bound woman. Namor mouthed her name as she passed, but sound wouldn't come through his laboring breaths.

A shadow moved, and Alísa twisted to see the slayer with the broken foot lunging at her from his knees. She flung herself aside, his dagger slashing across her arm rather than her neck. She scrambled back as he came at her again, murder in his eyes.

Thump! Thump!

The slayer's mouth gaped in shock and pain, and he slumped to the ground. Two knives protruded from his back.

Rassím stood behind him, sorrow in his eyes. "Sorry, friend. Can't let you do that."

"True slayers!" Segenn shouted, wild panic in his voice. "She has turned your brothers—there is no hope here. Set them free!"

For a second of idiotic hope, Alísa believed the villagers safe. But as Yarlan shouted for Segenn to stop and slayers turned with fearful determination in their eyes, cold terror swept over her.

Set their *souls* free. Just like with Bria.

16

WHATEVER I CAN

Falier's blood ran cold as the slayers drew their swords. He turned to his family, his voice hardly recognizable as he screamed at them to run. His mind still fuzzy from Alísa's trance, he tried reaching out to Graydonn again. The mind-kin bond wasn't like Alísa and Sesína's—neither he nor the dragon had ever been able to communicate when one of them was inside the mountain and the other outside.

He was on his own.

Parsen grabbed Kat's hand and pulled her around, angling for the path to the Hold. He stopped immediately as they found a slayer barring the way. The slayer's eyes were wide with the same panic that had filled his chief's voice, and his sword slid from its sheath. Falier's heart pounded wildly as he searched for the slayer's name, but his father found it first.

"Warrin, don't do this." Parsen somehow kept his voice low despite the panic all around him. "You know us, you don't want to—"

"I did know you," Warrin said, his wide eyes hardening with resolve. "Now, death is a mercy."

Falier moved before he knew what he was doing. He rounded his parents, shouting with effort as he formed an arrow with his mind and shot it at the slayer.

Warrin only shook his head like a bug had flown into his ear, but it was enough. His sword-arm faltered. Falier crashed into him, knocking the slayer to the ground. He vaguely heard his mother scream as he wrestled for control, barely saw his father rushing her and Selene past them.

Warrin was bigger than Falier and far stronger. He slammed the pommel of his sword into Falier's ribs, drawing a cry of pain, and rolled them over.

"Warrin, stop!"

Taz's call did no good. Warrin flipped the sword over in his hand, aiming the blade at Falier's heart. Crazed eyes returning, Warrin pulled back to stab him in the chest. "Maker have mercy on both of us."

"No!"

Blood spattered over Falier as a thin, single-edged blade protruded from Warrin's chest. The slayer gasped, looking down at the sword in disbelief before his eyes rolled back into his head and he collapsed. Taz pulled his sword free and pushed Warrin off of Falier.

"Take his sword," Taz ordered, his panicked eyes scanning the frantic mess around them.

Falier did as he said, the broadsword heavy in his long-unpracticed hands. He looked for Alísa and found her still with Namor, Rassím facing away from her with knives drawn, guarding her. In front of them, Yarlan advanced against Segenn, sword in hand.

Yarlan is on our side now?

A woman's scream of pain jolted Falier back to the villagers. Slayers' swords clashed against each other, some defending the villagers, while others sought to kill them. Already multiple people lay on the ground, dead and injured, slayer and villager. Slayers surrounded the crowd except in this one spot, where Taz and Warrin had been the guards.

Falier's arms shook, so he gripped the hilt tighter.

Whatever I can do.

"Taz, they need to get to the Hold. Help me guard the way." Falier didn't wait for Taz to acknowledge, instead shouting for all who could hear. "To the Hold! To the Hold!"

"Right." Taz raised a brow as he took up a defensive position. "Gather them all in one building. That won't be a disaster."

"The dragons will be here soon to defend them. To the Hold!"

There was no way the whole crowd would hear him, but those nearest did. They dove for the path, dodging around slayers locked in combat. One slayer noticed the change and charged for those trying to escape. Taz rushed forward to meet him, pulling a second blade from his back-scabbard and blocking a blow with swords crossed in an X.

In the chaos, it was nearly every villager for themselves. Nearby, Sendi and Marris made for the path to the Hold, the elderly sisters moving more slowly than those around them. One of Segenn's faithful slayers cut down a defending slayer and ran for them.

Fear filled Falier. He was too far away, he wouldn't get to them in time.

"Falier!"

Graydonn! Their telepathic bond locked into place and Falier pulled from the dragon's strength. Rage built the static energy faster than it ever had before, and he shot an astral lightning bolt at the slayer targeting the women.

The psychic attack crashed against the slayer's unshielded mind and the man shrieked an inhuman cry. He fell to the ground behind the women, his sword clanging against the ground.

A cold wave washed over Falier as he pulled back into himself.

Dead. He had felt it at the end of his attack. A man was dead, by his hand.

"But Sendi and Marris are alive," Graydonn growled in his mind. *"Mourn later, do not lose sight of the battle. I am coming!"*

Roars sounded in the sky. The dragons' announcement of their arrival seemed to stop the world, attacking and defending slayers alike looking to the sky in fear. The clan's full mind-link latched into place in Falier's mind as draconic forms came into view.

"Your orders, Singer?" Koriana urged.

Alísa's psychic voice came through, strong with command. *"Protect the villagers. Some of the slayers are on our side, but I can't tell you which except for two."* Images filled Falier's mind, one of Rassím, the other of Briek. *"Only attack a slayer if you see him targeting a civilian. In this battle, sword must meet sword."*

Falier reached out. *"The villagers are heading for the Hold, but we need help protecting them there and on the path."*

Alísa's relief washed over him. *"Graydonn, Komi, Saynan—guard the path. The villagers know you and shouldn't hesitate to run past you. Faern,*

Harenn—keep to the sky and watch over the Hold, in case any slayers slip through. The rest of you, focus on the square."

Sendi and Marris tripped past Falier as the slayers came back to themselves. Falier changed his grip on Warrin's sword, both hands clinging for dear life as some of Segenn's faithful noticed the escape route. They ran from their defending opponents, battle cries rising as they aimed for the people on the path. Falier ran forward to meet one, getting between him and the tanner.

Falier raised his sword to block a blow. The crash of metal rang up his arm and into his heart. As the slayer pressed down against Falier's lesser strength, Falier fired a telepathic arrow, unwilling to unleash the lightning he had used before. Though strengthened by Graydonn's power, it only pinged off a psychic shield.

In a quick motion, the slayer pulled back and kicked Falier in the stomach, sending him to the ground again. Graydonn's fear filled Falier's mind as the slayer raised his sword. Falier rolled, the sword coming down inches from him.

"Get out of here, boy!" Yarlan came into sight, his sword clashing against the slayer who had nearly killed him. "You are no slayer!"

"You're fighting for us?" Falier couldn't stop the words from forming. He stood, his back to Yarlan's to watch for other attackers.

"I fight for Me'ran." His sword slashed across his opponent's chest, sending the slayer to the ground. When Yarlan's eyes met Falier's, they were ice. "None other."

"Falier!" Graydonn came into view, circling once over the path before landing. Pain shot through Falier as the dragon took a psychic blow from a slayer. The dragon shook his head hard, backing up a step. *"Come! Attend to the psychic, while I take the physical."*

Just like with Rorenth. Falier ran as Saynan and Komi landed, forming a shield around Graydonn's mind as he approached. Another blow came to Graydonn, but it bounced off, sending only a fraction of the pain through Falier as it ricocheted. Dropping the cumbersome sword at Graydonn's side, Falier pulled himself onto the dragon's back.

From higher up, Falier could see the true horror of the battle. Bodies on the ground. Villagers clutching at wounds as they ran. A slayer moved to stab an older man struggling on the ground.

Gritting his teeth, Falier dropped Graydonn's shield and sent another lightning bolt flying. The slayer had his shield up, but the lightning overpowered it, sending him reeling. Briek was there a second later, and with a single slash the attacker was down. Briek reached to pull the fallen villager to his feet.

Everything ran together in Falier's mind. Flashes of fire burned in a couple places. Alísa sat on Koriana's back, Sesína nowhere in sight. Exhaustion filled Alísa's voice as she pointed out a struggling villager here, a defending slayer about to be killed there. At some point, dreki arrived and helped guard the path to the Hold. Falier was somewhat aware of mind-spearing a slayer fighting Taz and of Graydonn giving encouraging words to villagers who ran past him.

Then, as suddenly as it started, it was over. Only dragons, dreki, near-fifteen defending slayers, Yarlan, and a few villagers who hadn't made it out yet were left standing.

Falier lowered himself from Graydonn's back, stumbling as he landed. Graydonn lifted a wing to steady him and said something that didn't make it past the ringing in Falier's head. The moans of the injured and the dying were the only things he could hear.

These were his people.

How had this happened?

17

AFTERMATH

The battle ended only minutes after the dragons and dreki arrived. From Koriana's back, Alísa surveyed the battlefield, horror filling the gaps her fading adrenaline left. The remaining slayers gripped their weapons in uncertainty as they looked from the bodies of their former comrades, to the wounded and dead villagers, to the dragons standing over them all. Briek took stock of his remaining men as he wiped sweat from his brow. Rassím knelt beside a dead slayer, pulled a knife from his throat, and whispered a prayer as he closed the man's eyes.

Alísa shivered in her nightdress as she looked over the dead. So many, most of them slayers, though some of the bodies wore nightclothes rather than armor. Villagers who had gone to bed in safety and woke in the middle of a war.

She had caused this. What could she say to those still standing? What was she supposed to do while pain and fear and anger coursed through her like shocks of lightning?

Wincing against the pain in her arm, Alísa lowered herself from Koriana's back to the ground. She took in a ragged breath as she aimed her bare feet away from a spot darkened by blood. The stench of it sent her stomach churning.

A moan from a fallen villager snapped her from her daze. Her eyes shot to those standing.

"B—Briek, p-p-please have your slayers search for wounded. Saynan, t-t-t-take two dragons to the Hold. Bring back anyone you can find versed in healing."

Briek looked anxious, his dark brown eyes flitting to the forest. "Dragon Singer, let me send half of my men back to camp. If any of

Segenn's followers escaped, they may harm or trick those left behind."

That's right, there would be wives and children back at the slayers' camp, some widows and orphans now. Yet another thing she didn't know how to handle.

"Do it. D—dragons, sniff out any survivors, but don't get c-c-close. Mind where you step."

Slayers and dragons moved, each group wary of the other but not moving to attack or defend. Alísa slumped against Koriana's side.

"Well done, Alísa."

"It doesn't feel like it."

The dragoness rumbled in her chest, and Alísa closed her eyes and allowed the feeling to soothe her.

"Alísa!" Tenza's voice made Alísa open her eyes. "Come quickly!"

Namor. Alísa ran to them, the fifty or so paces seeming so very far. Shockingly, Namor still clung to life, the knife in his chest and his breathing ragged. Alísa knelt at his side across from Tenza.

"She's here, Namor," Tenza said, "Ari's here."

Ari? Namor's daughter?

Tenza's eyes held a serious plea, and Alísa settled her mind. If that's what Namor needed in order to let go, she would play the part.

She took Namor's hand and squeezed it, dimly recognizing that Falier stood behind her. "I'm here."

Namor's eyes latched onto Alísa, his hand squeezing tighter than he should have the strength for. His desperation rushed through her, quickening her heartbeat.

"Ari, forgive me! I did better—I did better this time. It was all for you."

Alísa blinked. What did he mean, 'did better'?

"Please forgive me."

Such fear clung to him. That emotion didn't belong in this strong slayer chief, especially not in his death. After all he had done to make her plans reality, it didn't matter what he meant in his last moments. All that mattered was sending him to the Maker's Halls in peace.

"I f—forgive you."

The fear left Namor's eyes, his face slowly relaxing. His grip on

Alísa's hand lightened, and his breathing gentled until it faded into nothing.

He was gone.

Tenza's shoulders trembled. No sound left her mouth and no sorrow poured from her mind, her emotions tightly bound against her. Alísa reached for her, then stopped as someone called Tenza's name. She twisted to see Meira running toward them, Saynan crouching behind her, having just let her off his back.

Meira fell to her knees next to Tenza. "I've got her, Alísa. Go."

Her command was so sure that Alísa didn't hesitate, despite her own grief. Hopefully, Tenza would be able to let her tears flow if she was alone with her friend.

Alísa stood and turned away. She met Falier's eyes as she did and saw a dullness there, like a fog had rolled over him. Then she saw the dark blood splashed over his night shirt. Fear washed over her, fueled by Falier's own panic spiking from within.

"Líse, you're bleeding!" He moved to her left arm, cupping her elbow as he looked.

"S—so are you."

"It's not mine," he dismissed.

The fog in him lifted as his fear took over. Alísa glanced at her arm, then looked away, gasping in a breath that seemed to fill her stomach rather than her lungs. Blood ran from the cut just underneath the short sleeve of her nightdress down to her elbow, one rivulet reaching down her forearm. Her vision blurred and she focused on breathing in through her nose and out through her mouth, willing herself to calm.

This was just a reaction to seeing her own blood. She had seen worse wounds in her life. If it were dangerous, she would have passed out by now.

Falier whipped around, calling to the people in the square. "Medic!"

Panic spiked his voice into a terrible croak that wasn't at all the voice of her pursuer. Alísa shivered and Falier told her to sit, lowering with her. His hands clenched and unclenched on his thighs. He was shaken, more than she had ever seen him before.

"I'm okay, Falier. I j—just need stitches. I'm okay." She wanted to push calm to him, but she was still drained from the song and sorrow. She wasn't strong enough right now to manufacture an emotion she didn't feel.

"Let me, Alísa."

A puff of calm wafted over them as Sesína landed behind her, the dragoness' final wing-strokes sending wisps of Alísa's hair flying up. The empathic calm was so light, Sesína still drained from her psychic exertion, but it was enough to still Falier's hands and loosen Alísa's shoulders. Sesína settled to her belly at Alísa's side, opposite Falier and the wound, panting as she pushed peace toward both humans.

Alísa leaned into Sesína. *"Thank you."*

A man in the square stood from his patient—another man who cradled a bandaged arm—and hurried for their group. Alísa's stomach clenched as he approached, dread overpowering Sesína's calming aura.

Rassím. Was he a medic in addition to being an assassin?

Alísa pushed against the thoughts with logic. Not assassin, scout. And though he had scared her this morning, he had turned to her side. He had saved her life, protected her until the dragons got to the village. She shouldn't be scared of him.

Yet, as the dark eyes that had once held such hatred came closer, fear still reigned.

"I'm sorry, I should have come to you sooner." He was almost to her now. "Let me take a look at that arm."

Sesína stood, a light growl in her throat as she stepped in front of Alísa. *"No."*

Rassím stopped, eyes wide. "I swear, I mean her no harm."

"You already did harm. Back off."

Alísa and Falier watched as the slayer—a man who had surely faced dragons twice Sesína's size—took a step back.

"I know. I know and I want to help, to make up for what I've done."

Sesína snorted. *"You want to help? Go get another medic—one whose knives haven't cut into her!"*

Falier looked between Sesína, Rassím, and Alísa, resolve setting in as he saw the cut on Alísa's neck. He nodded at a woman in the square, one Alísa vaguely recognized.

"Hamma. Switch places with her."

Rassím hesitated, then bowed his head in respect. "I am sorry, Dragon Singer." He emphasized the word 'Singer', as though trying to erase the times he had called her 'Witch.' Then he headed for Hamma, taking with him all the fear Alísa wished she didn't still feel.

"He s—saved my life. I shouldn't feel this w—way."

Falier looked her in the eyes, his own the clearest she had seen today. "Yarlan saved my life, too. Doesn't mean I want him healing me. Hamma will help."

Sesína settled at Alísa's side once more. *"What he said."*

Alísa reached out through the bond, where Falier couldn't hear. *"Thank you. I was going to stay quiet while my heart pounded out of my chest. Once again, you know me better than I know myself."*

Sesína purred, pressing the bridge of her muzzle to Alísa's cheek. *"I am never leaving your side again. I'll sleep outside if I have to, but never more than a few feet from you."*

A flash of disagreement ran through Alísa—if Sesína had been in the village, she would have been killed first. But though Alísa knew Sesína would see the thought, she didn't form it into words, letting the matter be.

Falier took in a long breath, then looked back at the wound. "I think you're right, about just needing a few stitches. I'm sorry I panicked."

Alísa looked him over. "Are you okay?"

He shook his head. "Yeah, I just need to do something. I should go to the Hold when we're done here. My family's going to have their hands full."

Alísa's heart clenched. The holders. "Your family—they're all—?"

"Okay." He gave a smile that didn't reach his eyes. "They got out."

Alísa sighed in relief. "Thank Branni."

Hamma neared, the kindly healer's face devoid of the horror wafting from her. She had visited with Alísa and the dragons a couple of times, and Alísa felt far more peace about letting her see to her wounds.

Alísa placed her clean hand on one of Falier's. "I'm alright, if you want to go up to the Hold." Falier opened his mouth to protest, but Alísa knew he would be better with a task to do, rather than sitting here and waiting with her. "I'll come up as soon as Hamma is finished. G—go, help your people."

Falier sighed, shoulders relaxing slightly. "Okay. Thank you."

He leaned forward as he rose, brushing his lips to her forehead. He turned to Hamma. "Be sure to check her neck too."

Hamma nodded reassuringly. "I'll take care of her."

Falier looked back at Alísa once more, then angled for Graydonn, who stood with Koriana and watched over the movement in the square.

Hamma knelt beside Alísa and went to work, not even flinching under Sesína's scrutinizing gaze. Alísa looked away and gave her attention to the square as well. Some of the bodies she had thought dead now showed signs of life. A few men carried stretchers between them and were bringing more people up to the Hold. Others, men and women alike, covered the dead with sheets, a couple of them skipping over slayers to focus instead on their own dead. Toward the west side, some of Briek's men returned to the square, presumably from their camp. A few women were with them, and Alísa had to look away as two of them flew over the battlefield to collapse beside their men.

Great Maker. What do we do now?

18

CRACKS IN THE MASK

"Are you sure you're ready to go in, Falier?"

Falier patted Graydonn's side, eyes on the Hold door. *"I couldn't do anything before. At least here I can help."*

The dragon clicked in his throat, a sound Falier still didn't quite know how to translate. Arching his neck, Graydonn looked him in the eyes. Falier felt the mind-kin bond shift, like the dragon was peeking around corners and trying to catch glimpses of a story he didn't know. Despite his trust in the dragon, Falier looked away.

"I need this."

After a moment more, Graydonn blinked slowly. *"I will be here."*

A wave of peace washed over Falier from the dragon, and he took it in willingly. He would need steady hands inside. Falier looked over the dancing grounds before turning to the door. Harenn, Faern, Komi, and Saynan all watched from different spots around the grounds, the rest of the dragons still down in the village proper. A couple of young girls sat at Komi's side underneath her wing. A few other people milled around, some pacing and looking anxiously to the Hold doors as though expecting someone to come out with news.

Nahne, give me strength.

Falier went to the door, the feeling of the handle not quite right as he opened it. The main room was loud and full of nervous energy, both feeling similarly odd, like he was dreaming. Healers and holders moved with purpose throughout the space, some tending to people sitting at or lying on top of tables. His mother emerged from one of the rooms on the ground floor, a bag of supplies over her shoulder. She looked out over the main room, her eyes widening as they landed on him.

"Falier!" She rushed to him, eyes on his chest. Or, rather, the blood stain there.

"It's not mine, Ma. I'm okay."

She stopped before him, her hands on his arms in a vise grip. She looked over him as though searching for any sign he was lying.

"Really, I'm okay. Taz saved me, then I worked with Graydonn. No blade touched me."

Her grip released, the creases over her brow smoothing. "Maker be praised."

A cry of pain came from one of the rooms, bringing Falier's purpose back into focus. "What can I do?"

Kat nodded stiffly. "Put on a new shirt, then help make rounds out here. Apply salves, bind wounds, change bandages. When you're done, help Selene in the kitchen. She's boiling water for cleaning wounds now, but we'll all need some calming tea soon. Chamomile, lavender—"

He held up a hand. "Ma, I know which teas are for calming. I'll take care of it—go on."

"Shirt."

"Yes, Ma."

He walked toward his room, pausing as she called after him. "We ran out of beds. Someone's in there, I can't remember who. A man."

Falier entered cautiously, finding Draemen, the dairy farmer, asleep in his bed. The man's hand was tightly bound in a manner that suggested he had lost a finger or two. Falier sent up a prayer of thanks that it wasn't worse, but as his mind went to what could have been, he saw the face of the slayer he had killed.

He shoved it away. He was not a murderer. Warriors who killed to save lives weren't murderers. And he had killed before to save lives. He had killed Rorenth, and his bolts of psychic lightning had probably sent another two or three dragons to their deaths as they plummeted to the ground.

But this one was human, with a face like his own. It was wrong to value that man over the dragons he had killed—all were soul-bearers— yet Falier knew this was the face that would stick with him forever.

Too much thinking, not enough doing.

After throwing on a new shirt, Falier returned to the main room. He paused, surveying the people. He had only a little training in salves and bandaging wounds and sprains. How was this going to work?

Shaking off his nerves, Falier went to the central table, grabbed a jar of ointment and a pile of what looked to be ripped bedsheets, and went to work. It seemed all those with dire wounds—those with lost limbs and those just barely holding onto life—were in the rooms, leaving the lesser injuries here. Some had scraped hands and knees, having fallen in their rush to get away. Some had slashes on their arms or legs, most of them grazing hits and nothing more. The deepest one Falier saw marred the inside of Aresia's forearm. It was in Eldra Níla's hands whether it would heal well enough for her to play her fiddle again.

In the midst of the wounded were fearful children and hysterical spouses. For these, Falier reached out to Graydonn, asking the dragon to flood him with peace in hopes that some might leak from him into the people. That would be the next thing he asked Graydonn to teach him—how to pass on feelings through empathy.

As he moved on to giving out tea, Falier saw many of those in the rooms and heard more stories of those who hadn't made it out. The wife of one of the herbalists had lost a hand to a slayer's sword. The butcher who always had time for a friendly debate had been run through the stomach and lay dying. Another man, a widower who lived with his daughter's family and told the best stories, was still in the square, dead. And there were more.

Somewhere in the midst of things, Alísa made it up to the Hold, just as she said she would. On one pass upstairs, Falier saw her emerge from a room with tears in her eyes, lips pressed together as though the pressure there would keep them from falling.

Had the person died? Who had been in that room?

Alísa pushed a cup of tea into his hands. "He—he won't t-t-take it from me. P-please."

Falier's eyes landed on a wad of spit in her hair. Outrage coursed through him. Alísa wasn't the one who had brought this tragedy, and she didn't have to help with the wounded, yet here she was! He wanted to enter the room and put whoever it was in their place.

But, that wouldn't help her here and now. And, truthfully, it wouldn't help anyone else. Not in this place of darkness.

Falier set the cup down on the railing overlooking the main room and pulled a piece of bedsheet from his pocket. His gaze drew hers to the spit and made her shrink, humiliation spreading across her face.

"Hey," he said, forcing gentleness into his voice. "None of that."

Carefully, holding her hair above the mass so it wouldn't pull, he cleaned the spit away.

She wrapped her arms around her stomach. "Thank you."

He wadded up the sheet and stuffed it back in his pocket. "None of this is your fault, no matter what they say."

She looked away and said nothing. Her hands rubbed up and down her arms as though cold, even though the number of bodies in the Hold had made it stuffy even with every window opened.

"You should take a break."

Alísa let out a small huff. "You first."

Falier couldn't reply to that. He wouldn't take a break until he absolutely had to.

One of the village healers stepped from another room, and Falier gave the cup of tea to him. There was no way he would be able to take it to whoever lay inside, not without spitting in the tea himself, or else throwing it in the man's face. It wasn't her fault, or the dragons'. The fault lay with Yarlan, with Segenn, with the other slayers who would rather kill their fellows than acknowledge that the war wasn't what they thought.

After lunch, Parsen instituted resting shifts for the healers and holders, one of the healers offering up their nearby home for those wanting some sleep. Though his mind whirled and his ribs ached where Warrin had hit him, Falier pressed on, letting everyone else take rest breaks.

By suppertime, the Hold had settled. The main room held only a few of those with lesser wounds, healers and other helpers, and a few who had lost someone and weren't ready to be alone yet—something Falier could understand.

Falier carried two bowls of chicken vegetable soup and a few slices of cornbread to the table where Sendi and Marris sat. Both women were uninjured and had helped in whatever way they could throughout the day. He slid the bowls in front of them, giving his holder mask for the thousandth time, then turned back toward the kitchen.

A hand grabbed his arm, making him flinch before settling the mask back into place. "Yes, Sendi? Did I forget something?"

"No," she said gently. "I just wanted to tell you, thank you."

Falier nodded, though he was fairly certain she had already thanked him for the food.

"No, dear. Really." Sendi took his hand in both of hers, her eyes earnest. "I saw what you did. Even untrained, you defended us. Defended your people with sword and mind. I—I'm sorry for accusing you of abandoning us. Forgive me."

The mask slipped, and Falier struggled to get it back into place. He would not break down here. He would not tell Sendi that he hated himself for killing the slayer, even though it had saved her and Marris. He would not tell her that he could never be a warrior because he couldn't handle what had happened today.

He smiled. "I forgive you, and I'm glad you're both safe."

Pulling away, Falier went back into the kitchen and pushed through the door to the outside. His chest spasmed. His throat ached. He couldn't breathe. Leaning back against the wall, he pressed his fists to his face. He didn't want to break down, he could still be of use inside, but he couldn't hold it back anymore. Faces of the dead rushed through his mind. Flashes of swords and spears. The cloying red of blood.

"Falier."

Graydonn. Falier covered his eyes, like a child who believed an adult couldn't see him if his own eyes were shut. He wanted Graydonn, and he didn't want Graydonn. He wanted Alísa, and he didn't want Alísa. He wanted desperately to be held so he wouldn't fly apart, but for someone to see him like this—broken—was wrong. He was supposed to be a slayer now, supposed to be strong, but strength had abandoned him.

Graydonn came close, the soft pads of his steps and the draconic smell of hot oil and summer wind announcing his presence. A leathery wing tapped Falier's shoulder.

"Is it finally time for you to rest, my friend?"

Falier pulled his hands down his face, smearing unshed tears over his cheeks, and looked at the dragon. Through the bond, he knew Graydonn's meaning. Graydonn had known this was coming, and rather than forcing the issue, he had waited for Falier all day.

Graydonn shifted his wing, pushing behind Falier's shoulder until Falier gave in and let the dragon pull him to his side. Falier looped his arms around Graydonn's neck, holding to him as everything inside continued to tighten. The dragon's presence was soothing, despite the stiff mainstay of Graydonn's wing pressing like a tree branch against Falier's back.

A gentle humor wafted from Graydonn. *"Yes, I know. The Maker did not make dragons for hugging. This is why I called on another."*

Graydonn widened the mind-link to include a third party, making Falier cringe away from the dragon. No one was supposed to see him like this. He recognized the mental signature just before he saw her. Alísa.

He didn't know if that made it better or worse. He wanted her, but he was the comforter in their relationship. He was supposed to be the shoulder to cry on, but all he wanted to do was cry and sob and hate himself. Beyond that, it had been a terrible day for her too—waking up at knife-point, losing Namor, being spat on by those she was trying to help.

Alísa came forward, unshed tears in her eyes. Something about the way she held herself, about the way her mind reached for his, told him that the tears were for him rather than herself. It both helped and hurt.

She touched his cheek. *"As the man I love once said to me, 'You've been carrying everyone else all day. Let me carry you, if only for a little while.'"*

Everything within him cracked. Tears flowed and sobs spasmed in his chest as Alísa pulled in close to him. The pressure of her against his chest ached and soothed, and her hand rubbing circles over his back both calmed him and gave him permission to cry harder.

"They're dead, Líse. So many hurt and I couldn't stop it. And when I could stop it, I—I killed a man. I didn't mean to, but he was—he was going to—"

"I know," she said, squeezing tighter.

Falier flinched as a loud bout of laughter came from the dancing grounds just around the corner. Some distant part of him was glad that others could find ways to be happy in the midst of the horror, yet right now he couldn't find the music. All he could find was the hollow place inside of him he feared everyone else would see.

Graydonn lifted the wing closest to them. *"I will shelter you from others' eyes."*

Alísa pulled Falier under Graydonn's wing, down to the trampled grass where they could sit against the dragon's side. There, she held him much like he had held her after she had faced her father.

"You acted to protect," she said gently. *"It's what a slayer does, what the Maker made us for. A shield for the innocent."*

"But how am I supposed to live with it? How am I supposed to do it again?"

Alísa kept silent for a moment, looking into the darkness. *"You are a protector, Falier. You excel in the domestic ways of protection—encouragement, comfort, service, care—but you have also never backed down in battle."*

She gave a small chuckle. *"I remember when you charged at Sesína, brandishing that branch like a club to save me from her influence. You are courageous, and when the time comes to fight again, I have no doubt you will rise up to protect again."*

She reached for his hand, lacing her fingers through his. *"And it is not weakness to mourn death, even the death of your enemies. Just—in the midst of remembering his face, also remember Sendi and Marris."*

Falier looked down at her. *"How did you—"*

"I told her." Graydonn peeked into the wing-tent, his eyes lighting up the space. *"I probably shouldn't have, but she needed to know what was going on. Her squeezy human hugs are far better than mine."*

A laugh broke through Falier's lips, single and tight, but real. *"Yeah. Thank you both. I—I really don't want to be alone right now."*

Alísa squeezed his hand. *"We're here as long as you need."*

Falier settled down again, his head resting against Alísa's, their backs against Graydonn's warm scales. Tears continued off and on, but the grasping ache inside that he had built up over the course of the day was gone. And though he still feared the faces that would plague his sleep, he finally allowed himself to drift off, knowing someone was there to catch him when he fell.

19

AGAIN

Alísa stretched her neck and rolled her shoulders as she walked the creaking wood floors of the Hold. Her whole body ached from the pain and sorrows of yesterday, not to mention sleeping sitting up against hard dragon scales. She winced as her stretches pulled at her stitches and eased up, pressing her hand to the bandage.

The Hold was far quieter than yesterday—a mixture of good and bad. As Alísa patrolled the building, she found that many had gone back to their own homes, now in a place where they were able to care for their own wounds. She had also discovered two rooms now empty of their dreadfully-wounded occupants. Parsen confirmed both had died in the night. One was the man who had spit in her face, and all she felt was grief. Grief that he had died, and a far more selfish grief that he had died believing she was the cause.

Except, she was the cause.

But she wasn't.

Yet, she was.

Most of the villagers cast the blame on Segenn, cursing his name and citing his arrogance as the cause. If he didn't understand something it couldn't be true, and if someone was more powerful than him, they were a threat.

A few blamed Yarlan, though far more quietly. He had been the one to call Segenn to Me'ran, setting fear alight in the chief's heart. And yet, when Segenn went mad with rage and fear, Yarlan had fought and slain him to protect the village.

And then there were those who turned their gaze away from Alísa, or else fixed it on her with such hardness that she knew they cast the blame on her. If she had never come to Me'ran, had never come back after fighting Rorenth, people would still be alive.

All three lines of thought were true. No matter how many people thanked her for fighting for them, cleansing their wounds, or bringing them breakfast, their lives would have been better if she had never come to them. But now that decision was past and there was nothing to do but keep moving. Namor would have wanted that.

Her bag of supplies chirped, calling her to place a hand inside. Blue wriggled unhappily, growling and gurgling. She had run down to Namor and Tenza's home—*No. Just Tenza's home now*—to grab it this morning. Guilt wracked her for forgetting it in all the craziness. Thankfully, Blue was old enough to create its own heat. Keeping it close was more for bonding purposes now than anything else. Not that it wanted to bond with anyone at all.

Sesína's voice entered Alísa's mind. *"Heads up, there are a few slayers headed your way."*

Sesína, Komi, and Faern were on watch-duty in the square, while Graydonn and Harenn stayed outside the Hold. Alísa didn't expect trouble from the remaining slayers, but she couldn't be too careful at this point.

"A few here too," Sesína continued. *"No trouble, though one gave Faern a mean side-eye. Too bad Faern is too prideful to stoop and give the slayer a piece of his mind."*

Alísa groaned. *"You didn't give him a piece of your mind instead, did you? We want them as allies."*

"I know that." Sesína sent feelings of mock offense, then sobered. *"Rassím is with those headed to the Hold."*

Alísa pulled in a slow breath. Allies. His knife wouldn't turn on her again. He was an ally. *"Thanks for the warning. How are things in the square?"*

A pulse of happiness. *"Komi and I brought the kids to the far side"* — away from the bloodstained ground— *"and are taking turns playing and watching for trouble. Komi's really too big to play fivers, but she wanted to help give the kids a reason to smile. There are a few other slayers staying in the square to take care of their dead, but apart from Side-Eyes they're ignoring us."*

The nickname brought a smile to Alísa's lips—perfect timing as she stepped into the kitchen. Inside, Falier and Kat were hard at work. Smells of cinnamon and vanilla clashed with onion and ginger as they worked on multiple dishes at once. Some form of sweetened gruel and a potato hash, plus a steaming pot of ginger tea.

Falier smiled at her as she walked in, the same smile he had given each time she entered. An attempt at cheer while sorrow and fatigue still pulled at his eyes. Empathically, he seemed in a better place than yesterday, but not by much.

"Who's next?" Kat asked. The holder had dark circles under her eyes and wisps of sandy-blond hair falling from her bun. Had she gotten any sleep last night?

"D—Draemen."

Kat hummed thoughtfully, pointing to the largest pot. "Give him the gruel and some tea."

Alísa winced. "I d—don't think he'll be thrilled by just g—g—gruel."

"The man's lost three fingers—his body needs time to recover."

"You can tell him I would be offended if he didn't want my gruel." Falier lifted a full ladle from the cooking pot and let the contents slop back into the concoction in an attempt at humor. "*Highly* offended."

Alísa smiled and shook her head, then returned to Kat. "Can I take him g—gruel and just a t-t-t-tiny bit of the hash? He's energetic, almost j—jovial."

Kat considered. "All right. A little. And he can't blame *me* if his stomach isn't ready for it."

The easy tease in Kat's voice made Alísa smile. "Deal."

Alísa dished up the food, setting all the dishes onto a tray. Falier opened the door to let her back out into the main room, for which she was grateful. She hadn't been working the Hold enough to balance the tray on one hand like he and his family did. She hurried to Draemen's room, where, as predicted, the portly man groaned at the sight of the large bowl of gruel.

"Prove you can keep food down and lunch will be b—b—better." Alísa pointed to the small plate of hash and winked, trying to channel some form of holder charm. "Kat said you c-c-couldn't handle it, but I snuck you some 'real food', too."

"You're an Eldra."

"Eat it slowly," she said through a laugh. She set the tray on the bedside table. "Don't p-prove Kat right."

"Wouldn't dream of it. Thank you."

Alísa slipped back into the main room just as the slayers entered. Her eyes skimmed over Rassím and another slayer she didn't know, settling on Briek. All of the slayers carried their swords, plus a knife strap for Rassím, but none wore armor. Briek still wore his warrior's braids, hanging loose rather than gathered at the back.

Parsen moved to meet them. The knot gathering in Alísa's stomach pulled toward the slayers as well. She needed them as allies—this was her chance to establish connection, yet the thought made her sick and kept her feet planted.

Briek caught her gaze, his eyes sharp but not unkind. He looked back at Rassím and said something she couldn't hear. Rassím looked from his commander to her and back, his brow creased as he responded. The only word in the exchange Alísa could make out was Briek's firm, "Go."

Alísa hated the fear that trembled through her as Rassím wove through the tables and chairs toward her. Everything about his movement was natural and non-hostile, just as it had been when he came as a messenger, reminding her he was a liar and a spy.

This time, though, he kept his eyes down, as though he feared a look might scare her away. He wasn't wrong, and she loathed it. Her father wouldn't feel this way. Neither would Tella, Toronn, or any other chief she knew.

"Everyone gets scared, Alísa." Sesína's words soothed through her, her presence lending a light calm.

Rassím stopped a respectful distance away, his eyes pinned just above her shoulder. "Briek is calling for a meeting between the slayers and Me'ran's leadership. He requests you be there as well."

Alísa released her breath, realizing with shame that she had been holding it. "Thank you. W—when?"

"Soon. I imagine as soon as the Hold is done serving breakfast."

His eyes landed on the bag at Alísa's hip, and for a second a shot of terror coursed through her. The egg—what if he saw it? But then, he and the rest of the remaining slayers knew the truth now. They wouldn't just smash a dragon's egg if they saw it now, right?

"You're helping with the wounded?"

Alísa relaxed her shoulders. He didn't see the egg—he saw the bandages draping out over the sides.

"Y—yes. As much as I c-c-can."

His eyes met hers. "Do you and the holders need more hands?"

Though a small part of her wanted to shy away, his desire to help calmed a piece of her fear. "P-Parsen would know better than I."

"Ah. Yes. Of course." His eyes lowered again. "Thank you, Dragon Singer."

Rassím was on his way back to Briek before she could answer.

"*That's better,*" Sesína said. "*A healthy fear of an amazing alpha. I might even forgive him someday.*"

Alísa rolled her eyes. "*I don't think he fears me for my alpha-ness. I think he fears you and your wrath if he scares me again.*"

"*Hmm. A healthy fear of a fabulous beta isn't bad. Oh, flame it all!*" Sesína's turn gave Alísa's mind whiplash. "*You distracted me and I dropped the ball on only the second bounce!*"

Alísa picked her way back to the kitchen. "*Go back to your game. I have work to do and a speech to plan.*"

The thought of a speech sent a shudder through her, but if Briek wanted her at this meeting that meant he might actually hear her. The slayers knew her dragons were good, but her song had called for immediate peace, not for dragons and slayers to stand together and fight for the war to end. Now that they had seen the truth and even sort of fought alongside the dragons, perhaps this was the moment her plans finally started coming together.

If it had been up to Alísa, she would have picked anywhere but the dancing grounds for the meeting. It was too painful, a battlefield where she had already lost. Yet the village and even the slayers knew it as a place of meeting, and she had no power to change it.

Kat and Selene gathered the elders, while Falier and Parsen moved chairs outside, Alísa helping carefully due to her stitches. The chairs formed a lopsided circle around the fire pit, allowing room for the nine elders, Falier, and Selene in one half, Briek and three of his slayers in one quarter, and Alísa and her dragons in the last quarter.

Parsen set Alísa's chair out last. The sight of it by itself made her heart twist. Even knowing that Sesína would soon be back from the cave with Koriana and Saynan, her betas ready to back her up, she wasn't sure she was ready for this. She reached for her necklace, pulling it from underneath her shirt to finger the smoothed dragon scale. She had to be strong and speak clearly, like Papá.

Parsen placed a light hand on her shoulder as he passed. He said nothing, but his eyes were full of assurance. Then he looked beyond her.

"Only you can choose when it's time."

His words confused her, but when he didn't look at Alísa again, she realized they weren't for her. She looked back to see Falier standing a few feet away, staring at the circle of chairs as she had been. He glanced at her, looking from her face to the hand at her necklace before speaking.

"Graydonn said you've only asked your betas to stand with you."

She nodded, dropping her hand to her skirt. "I didn't think it wise to bring more, c-c-c-considering it's a m—meeting of the elders."

"Would you consider making an exception for the clan's slayer?" He cringed. "There has to be a better way to say that."

Alísa smiled, relief filling her. "Yes, of course." She stopped, realizing what it would mean for him. "If you're sure. I d—don't think there's any coming back from that in the sight of the elders. N—not all of them like me or the dragons. I'll be okay if you're not ready yet."

A light sadness wafted from him. "There's no coming back from anything now. Everything changed yesterday. I may not be a warrior yet, but I fought for them, and they can't deny it. If some still don't understand that my standing with you is also standing for them, then there was never a chance for me to convince them."

Falier went to Alísa, taking her hand in his. "And I hear that I excel in the—how did you put it—domestic ways of protection?"

Alísa cringed, unimpressed with her own wording from last night.

He chuckled at her reaction. "After the last twenty-four hours, I'm ready to do something I excel at."

The certainty in his statement collided with the wisps of yesterday's pain in the astral plane—a concoction of striving and hope that was wholly Falier. Rising up on her toes, Alísa pressed her lips to his. Falier smiled as he kissed her back, cupping her cheek with his free hand and sending a pleasant chill down her spine.

Crunching footsteps snapped Alísa from her happy daze. She pulled back, heat rushing to her face.

Mirth twinkled in Falier's eyes. "I'm torn. I don't know whether to ask if you're embarrassed to be seen with me, or if you think I excel at kissing."

Alísa ducked her head, sure her blush matched her hair.

Falier squeezed her hand. "Come on. Let's get to our spot."

He looked past her and called out a quick welcome to the first few elders to arrive, then walked Alísa to her chair. She watched as he grabbed a chair from Me'ran's section and carried it back to sit at her side. The elders observed him with curiosity but said nothing.

As more came up the hill, Alísa looked to the mountain, a note of worry in her heart. She wanted the dragons here before the slayers arrived, so the warriors didn't feel like they were being descended upon by the creatures they were trained to fight.

She reached out to Sesína, but quickly realized she didn't need to ask where they were—the joy of flight was in Sesína's mind. Only a few more seconds and three shapes became visible against the gray of the mountain. Then dragon wings sent wind coursing over the dancing grounds.

She set a hand on her lap to calm her skirt, then realized her father's necklace still hung in plain sight. She tucked it away, unwilling that any dragon—save Sesína—know it was there. Maybe settled next to her heart it would somehow grant her Karn's ability as a chief. His strength. His steadiness. His words.

Behind her, Koriana and Saynan settled to their bellies on the grass, their heads high and alert. Sesína trotted up alongside Alísa and sat on her haunches, folding her wings against her back.

"You've got this, dragon-heart."

Alísa smiled gently. *"How is Blue?"*

"Settled with Rayna."

"Good. Thank you." No sense keeping the egg here any longer, especially with slayers around. Besides, she had kept Blue for two days with no success. Time to pass it on again.

Soon Tenza appeared with Meira and Garrick. It was the first time Alísa had seen her since Namor's death. She looked tired, her graying hair undone and dark circles under her eyes, yet she carried herself with the same dignity she always had. Tears gathered in Alísa's eyes as Tenza chose a chair second from the end of the first row, leaving the last chair vacant. A reminder of what was lost.

Then came the slayers, the last to arrive. With long strides, Briek led three other slayers to their designated spot. He wore a red tartan sash, a symbol of his new role as chief over the clan. With him were two men and a woman. The woman walked close to him, her own red sash marking her as Briek's wife. She had the same black braids as her husband and her skin was an even deeper brown than his.

One of the men was new to Alísa. His skin was the lightest of the group, contrasting sharply with his dark brown hair, and he wore the blue cloak of an advisor.

Rassím walked a few paces behind the others. He wore plain browns and greens, his single strap of knives still across his chest. His head angled down, whether in deference or shame Alísa couldn't tell, though when combined with the greens of a scout she recalled the single line of warpaint he had worn.

Rassím has a low position in the clan. Why is he here in this meeting of elders and chiefs?

She had barely a second to ponder before another form behind the slayers brought all thoughts to a halt.

Yarlan. No, no, no—why was he here? Hadn't he done enough? Surely the elders wouldn't let him stay!

Meira stood, fire in her eyes. "This is a meeting of the elders, Yarlan. Go back to the village."

Yarlan didn't break his stride. "I am the chief slayer of Me'ran now. Will you hold counsel without your protector?"

Alísa clenched her skirt in her hands.

"It was your word that brought Segenn here," said a man. "Your word that brought suffering on us!"

"The war would never have come here if Alísa hadn't," a woman declared, sparking murmurings on both sides.

Yarlan lifted his head high as he advanced. "The Dragon Witch acts on behalf of her dragons—they are all she cares about."

Alísa tensed with anger. "Th—that's not t-t-true!"

Yarlan ignored her. "Everything I did was for Me'ran. I called the slayers to protect us from the influence of evil."

Yarlan stopped at the edge of the circle between the slayers and elders, a mixture of anger and sadness in his eyes. "My only regret was not realizing what a fool Segenn was, and I made sure he paid for his treachery by my sword. Rassím can attest to it" —he smirked at Alísa— "as can the witch."

The cool way he said it, assured that even his enemy would have to confirm his claim, tied knots in Alísa's stomach. As eyes landed on her, she forced herself to let go of her skirts.

"It's true. He k-k-killed Segenn."

Yarlan looked back to the elders. "I am Me'ran's protector. I have a right to my place here."

One of the elders Alísa didn't know agreed aloud, causing a couple of others to nod in agreement.

Garrick reached up to touch Meira's arm. "He has a point, love."

Meira didn't sit, defiance in her eyes as she took a step further. Positioning herself between Tenza and Yarlan, Alísa realized. Yarlan matched the heat of her glare.

"Meira." Tenza raised a hand to her friend. "Let him be, if only to speak of his role in everything that happened."

Meira stared Yarlan down a second more, then returned to her seat. The only open chair left was the one next to Tenza. Yarlan moved to grab it, but Tenza leveled her own icy glare.

"My husband may be gone, but his memory is not."

That stopped Yarlan in his tracks. He blinked, hesitating only a moment before his eyes hardened with resolve once more.

"Then let another chair be brought." Yarlan looked to Falier beside Alísa, then to Parsen. "Or are you so short on hands now that I should fetch my own?"

Parsen glowered at him, but Kat stood. She hurried inside and returned, the dancing grounds silent. The slayers stood by their seats, watching the simmering villagers with furrowed brows and wide eyes. Kat set the chair on the side opposite Tenza.

Yarlan nodded his thanks with a satisfied smile, and Kat's hands curled into fists at her sides.

"I move at the call of the elders," she hissed, "and in gratitude that you saved my son's life, but do not think for a second that I want you here."

"Perhaps you'd prefer to join your boy and his monsters, then."

Falier tensed and Koriana and Sesína growled, Koriana louder by far. The slayers flinched, the advisor's hand going to his sword hilt, while Briek's wife fell back a step. Though anger shuddered through Alísa, she held a hand up to the dragonesses for silence.

"React as little as you can manage. We need to not scare the slayers."

Koriana's growl settled to a rumble. *"How else are we to make our thoughts known to one who keeps a shield about his mind? Even the other slayers are shielded."*

"All but the chief," Saynan mused. *"He covers his mate."*

"Dragon Singer." Briek looked from the elders to Alísa, a pinch between his brows. "I did not anticipate your companions. I do not wish to offend, but I have my people to think about. Do I have your word they will not harm us in either the physical or astral planes?"

"You have our word, slayer," Koriana said, reaching out to all in the gathering who were unshielded.

Briek tensed under the words, and Alísa rushed to reassure him. "D—dragons speak by telepathy only, and their w—words do not harm or delve into your p-p-p—p-private thoughts."

"So she says," Yarlan said, looking to Briek. "But don't the slayers say, 'the stronger shapes the weaker?'"

Yarlan spoke to the elders. "It's why we don't communicate in that way, to keep all minds safe from another's influence. It's why I do not allow the dragons into my mind. They have already corrupted a daughter of slayers, pulling her away from our code to speak in this way, and she has taught it to the young holder."

"You speak from fear, Yarlan," Tenza said, her eyes fixed on Briek rather than him. "Namor found her untainted even after she had spent months with the dragons and was deeply bonded to one. Not every saying is true."

Briek raised a hand for silence. "I saw the visions as she sang, and their answers were the only thing about yesterday that made sense. I do not doubt that her dragons are good, I merely wished to know whether the tenuous peace between us yesterday still stands. I accept her and" — he paused as though translating the name from mind to tongue— "Koriana's word."

Relief flooded Alísa. Perhaps Yarlan's presence wouldn't throw everything off after all.

Briek looked to his companions, his words too quiet to hear. The two men nodded as Briek's wife replied, and all four took their seats.

"Let it be known," Briek said, "I have not commanded my men to do the same, yet they have dropped their shields in a gesture of good faith. We will hear the dragons' words."

Saynan and Koriana rumbled gently in their chests, while Sesína pawed the ground.

"One point for us!" Sesína whispered to Alísa, sending an image of Yarlan missing the ball in fivers that made Alísa grin.

"Then you are fools," Yarlan muttered.

Garrick cleared his throat. "Now that we're settled, we need to know whether we are safe. Did more messages go out? Are there other slayers waiting to rise up if Segenn failed?"

"I sent only the one message," Yarlan said. "Segenn was known to me, and his clan the closest to us. With the size of his clan, I thought he would be enough."

Alísa felt a growl in the dragons' minds, though they remained silent. It had been Yarlan's plan to kill them all, perhaps to kill Alísa as well. The only thing holding Koriana back from killing him to protect the clan was Alísa's command. Even Saynan's thoughts held hatred for Yarlan, punctuated by his love for Aree, their egg, and Iila.

Briek sat forward in his chair. "We sent no word to others. We had already received word of the Dragon Singer through her father—"

Alísa's heart skipped a beat. Was her father in the east, then? Or had he sent out scouts to speak to the other slayer clans?

"—but instead of calling for Karn's help, Segenn decided we would be sufficient. It would take too much time for Karn to get here, and our clan is—was—indeed large."

Briek stopped for a moment and breathed. With his shield down, Alísa could feel sorrow spilling from him, yet he kept incredible control over his expression and voice as he continued.

"Now that the whole country knows of Alísa and the Dragon Singers, Segenn wanted to be the one to capture her."

"I'm sorry." Alísa held up a hand. She couldn't wait any longer. "The whole c-c—country knows?"

"Or soon will. Karn's songweaver has surely spread the tale throughout the west by now. The song made it to us two days before Yarlan's message."

Falier glanced at her, his brows lifted in a question Alísa couldn't answer. A song. From Farren. It would be memorable and spread quickly, then. What lies did the world think of her and her dragons?

Briek's advisor spoke up. "We can share it with you another time. It seems this false tale is one you should know."

Alísa nodded her agreement. "I w—would appreciate that."

Briek looked back at Rassím, who straightened and spoke. "The head scout chose me to enter Me'ran. Among other things, I had never been here before and none would recognize me. I dressed as a messenger and entered with the instruction to search for the village-bound slayers. The message from Yarlan said I was to ask if there were any signs of dragons in the area. Yarlan wouldn't be able to answer truthfully, but the question would tell him who I was, then he would take Segenn's response from my saddlebag."

Rassím looked to Selene apologetically. "Hence why I didn't want anyone alone with my horse or touching my saddlebag."

Briek tented his fingers as he took over. "Segenn's message asked Yarlan to get to our camp as soon as possible to plan how to get to her without the dragons nearby. He hoped that separating Alísa from her bond to the dragons would allow her to set everyone else free."

Briek fisted his hands in his lap. "It was never the plan to harm villagers. But when Namor fought so adamantly for the Singer, it shook something loose in Segenn. I saw in his eyes a fear I had never known in him, of something he couldn't understand, control, or solve. It was this fear that turned him against the people, and against those of us who saw the truth in Alísa's song—"

Yarlan huffed. "The only truth in her song was the call to protect the people. Surely not all who fought for us actually believed her?"

Briek hesitated, obviously taken aback by Yarlan's interruption. "No. But it was those of us who did that turned Segenn's fear into madness. Others simply refused to accept the order to kill the villagers. There is a divide among us now."

"But all who are left fought for us?" Parsen asked. "Or did some surrender?"

Briek shook his head. "There were no survivors of Segenn's faithful. None even who escaped—all are accounted for among the living and the dead."

A female elder with anger in her eyes leaned forward. "How many followed Segenn's order to kill us?"

Briek sighed. "I cannot tell you exactly who followed and who fought. I know those I fought and killed, but I saw only what was right in front of me. We survivors could compare notes and compile a list of who stood with us and did not, but what good would that do? It would only provide more opportunities for division."

"Then," Tenza said, "you haven't told the widows which side their husbands took?"

Briek looked to his wife, his eyes softening with sorrow. "I didn't have the heart. Perhaps it is wrong, but for now, to avoid families turning against each other, I am staying quiet on the matter."

"And so instead you let them live with the fear that their husband was one who turned against the villagers?" Tenza's tone was hard. "The truth is painful, but it is far less likely to drive one mad with speculation."

"Perhaps." Briek's gaze shifted as he spoke. His manner seemed to contradict itself frequently, moving from confident to unsure and back. A man used to leadership but not command or ultimate responsibility. Alísa had sometimes wondered how her uncle L'non would respond to leadership if her father were wounded or worse. She could see him in Briek now—a second-in-command forced into chiefdom by tragedy.

"Can you tell us how many remain," Koriana asked, *"and how likely they are to turn on us?"*

Briek looked between the dragons. "Sixteen. I think it is unlikely any would turn on you. Even those who were unconvinced by the song saw dragons fight to protect Me'ran. One even says he would have been killed if it weren't for the flames of one of your kin."

Alísa smiled. "Though I n—never would have wished for such circumstances, it has always been my hope that my c-c-c-clan would f—fight side-by-side with slayers. M—many of them followed me because they share that d—d—d—desire."

She breathed deeply. She needed to keep her throat and tongue loose. Segenn had dismissed her as a broken vessel—she had to prove him wrong.

Briek's advisor leaned in and whispered something to him. His brow raised as he returned to Alísa.

"You say they followed you because they want to fight alongside us? That this was your call to them? What do you mean by this?"

Falier looked at Alísa, an encouraging smile on his face. Alísa breathed again. This was it.

"You've said yourself that my song b—brought t-t-truth. D—dragons are not all evil like the slayers t-teach. Our v—vendetta against them is wrong and m—must end, and there are many dragons who do not agree with b—b—burning villages and stealing livestock. I wish to end the war with a united front of d—d—dragons and slayers who wish for p-p-peace."

"You leave out a crucial fact, witch." Alísa couldn't hold back her wince as Yarlan stood, venom in his gaze. "'Wish for peace.' Once again, she tries to sway with nice words, but the fear on her tongue betrays her."

Alísa fisted her skirt. "It's n—n—n—" *'Not fear.' Come on!*

Yarlan gestured at her, giving Briek a knowing look. "She asks for a fighting force to bring an end to those who don't see her point of view. She will kill slayers who refuse her. Her own people, who have sworn to give their lifeblood to protect humankind!"

"I do n—not simply k-k-k-k-kill those who d—disagree with m—me." Alísa's whole body trembled with tension. "B—but to leave those who would k-k-k-kill the innocent—"

Yarlan stalked forward. "You equate the innocence of a helpless human child to these monsters?"

Falier stood to meet him. "Stop interrupting her! And they aren't monsters—they're soul-bearers!"

Alísa didn't know whether to pull him back or be grateful for his defense. She was losing control, again. What would Papá do? Shout louder than Yarlan? Bark a word that silenced all so he could speak? She had neither within her.

"Speak through telepathy," Sesína suggested. *"I can connect you to all but Yarlan."*

"That won't stop him, and the slayers' ears will prefer spoken word to telepathy. They won't hear me over him."

"Not monsters?" Yarlan looked to Koriana with a gleam in his eyes Alísa had never seen before. "Their eyes and throats glow with hellflames, their teeth and claws rend and tear—"

Alísa's heart raced. What was he doing? Even with his hatred, he had never directly challenged one of the dragons.

"—they've bones outside their skin, and they were denied a true voice by the Maker, just as she was!"

Alísa flinched as Koriana roared behind her. A few of the elders cried out and slayer hands went to swords as the dragoness stood.

"You alone deny our voices, you spawn of the Nameless!" Koriana's tail lashed. *"Perhaps you think it strength, but I see only cowardice."*

Koriana's anger and the fear of the people clashed against each other. Alísa stood, turning her back on Yarlan and reaching out a hand to the dragoness.

"P—peace, K-K-K-Koriana!" Alísa breathed, searching for whatever might assure the people that the dragoness wasn't about to harm Yarlan or anyone else. She turned and grabbed Falier's arm. "You t-t-too. It isn't w—w—w—w—" *Worth it! Spit it out!*

Heat filled Alísa, a mixture of anger, adrenaline, and shame. She stopped trying to speak, accessing the clan-link instead. Some of the villagers and slayers would hear her if they allowed themselves to listen past Koriana's growl, but at least Yarlan wasn't speaking now.

"It isn't worth it to answer those words," she said, acutely aware that the slayers would recognize her shame in the astral plane. *"Peace, please."*

Koriana stopped growling and cut off the villagers and slayers from her communication. *"You would have us put up with this serpent spewing venom?!"*

"You think I want to?" Alísa shot back. *"You think I enjoy him raking my clan and me through the mud? That I've relished allowing such words to spear through me my whole life?"*

Tears threatened at the corners of her eyes. Falier reached a comforting hand to her, but Alísa shook her head.

"No. Don't show more of my weakness to them."

Falier jerked his hand back as though she had slapped it away. The hurt in his expression cleared quickly, though Alísa couldn't be sure if he understood or if it was an act.

"You see?" Yarlan's voice caused them all to turn. The corners of his lips tipped upward as he gestured to the elders. Wide eyes, hands clamped to their chairs, tension and fear throughout the astral plane. "Even those who claim to trust these beasts fear them."

Alísa's heart caved in. Yarlan had known exactly what he was doing when he confronted Koriana.

Parsen gestured to the dragons. "Koriana would never attack us, nor would any others in Alísa's clan. Her outburst is no different than yours, Yarlan."

Yarlan spun on him. "No different? Yet when did you feel the need to escape? When did the slayers' hands go to their hilts? When I spoke my mind, or when the dragons moved?"

A quiet rumble in Koriana's throat came as she lowered back to her belly. *"I am sorry, Singer. I flew right into his trap."*

"But I couldn't silence him." The thought ran through the clan-link without Alísa's consent. It hardly mattered—they all knew it was true.

Briek cleared his throat. "Perhaps we should focus on more immediate issues until cooler heads can prevail."

Alísa took her seat, forcing herself not to slump as her insides caved in. She had failed. Even with some of the villagers vouching for her, all of her work hadn't been enough. She hadn't convinced the one person she needed to—Yarlan—and he was far more adept at swaying a crowd.

Briek continued. "I wish to honor our dead. Since they are currently in the square, I ask that you allow us to hold our ceremony there. We will defer to your timing, as you have your own to mourn."

"You wish to honor them," a man said, "yet you do not know who fought for us and who killed us? How do you plan to do this?"

Briek's brow furrowed as he hesitated. "Some died in madness, others died heroes. I will not dishonor the latter in fear of the former. All lived lives of sacrifice before the tragedy of yesterday. I plan to honor them all for who they were."

Many of the elders stood from their seats in outrage, sending Alísa's heart racing again. Several voices clashed in the air until one man's rose above the others.

"You would honor those who killed our brothers and sisters, and you would do it just outside their homes? I thought you a reasonable man, Briek, but this is the same madness as Segenn's!"

Agreements rang out over the sounds of other elders trying to calm their peers. Only Tenza and Yarlan didn't move. Tenza's countenance was dark—she was likely thinking of the man who had murdered Namor. Yarlan was barely visible behind a few standing elders, his expression blank. His purpose for being here had already been fulfilled.

Briek and his slayers looked shaken, more even than at Koriana's roar. Alísa didn't know what she would have done in Briek's place. His position was impossible, especially with widows and children who needed closure.

"Take your dead from our village," a woman ordered. "Honor them in your own camp or leave them to rot in the forest, but they will not be honored here unless you are certain of their innocence!"

"Have them gone by midday," another said, "so their corpses don't sully our ceremony."

Parsen stepped from the crowd, hands held high in request for silence. Only a few listened, the others still raging. He turned from them and spoke to Briek too quietly for Alísa to hear. Even if she could, what would it matter? She couldn't help this situation, where she didn't know what was right and what was wrong. How could she when she couldn't even fight for her own cause?

"Peace!" Parsen shouted. Most of the elders silenced, the rest following suit as he continued. "Briek has consented—he will take his dead from our village. If that is the last matter here, I suggest we adjourn so we may prepare to honor our dead."

Briek stood, pressing a hand to his heart and giving a curt nod to the elders. He strode from the circle, his people following behind. Only when all were out of sight did the elders relax, though anger still twisted the faces of a few. Many made to leave, grabbing bags from beside their chairs or checking the clasps of their cloaks. None looked at Alísa and the dragons—forgotten in the wake of Briek's request. Ordinarily, it might have made Alísa more comfortable, but now it served only as a reminder that she had failed. This meeting should have been the first step toward slayer allies. Now she was discarded.

Alísa rubbed her hands over her face as hot tears formed. She would not cry here, in the midst of everything.

"You can cry, Alísa," Sesína soothed, opening her wings as though preparing to shield Alísa from view.

"No. Not here." Alísa stood, turning toward the forest.

"Líse?" Falier touched her arm but pulled back as she shivered. *"There will be other chances—"*

"I've had other chances." A sob broke through her wall, and she wrapped her arms around herself. *"I've failed them all! The presentation, the céilí, Segenn, here—"*

Falier shushed her comfortingly. *"We'll make it through this."* He reached again to take her in his arms, but she stepped back.

"No. I need to be alone." Her heart ached all the more as his face

twisted in confusion. She couldn't take that. *"I'm sorry."*

Turning away, she ran into the forest.

20

ENOUGH

Not long ago, Alísa had walked the forest paths every day. Sesína hunted birds and rabbits, while Alísa gathered berries and edible roots, the world at peace. Now, as she ran from the heartache of the dancing grounds with no destination except 'away,' her feet found familiar paths. Past the lake with its softened ground and view of the sky, through trails laid by deer and widened by dragons, and up the slope of the mountain. Following the trickling sound of a creek, Alísa found herself in the cave that had once been home.

She didn't have to wait for her eyes to adjust as she entered the shadows. With the tiny creek to her left, she stepped over the rocky floor as easily as if she had been there this morning. The smell of burnt wood marked her old fire pit, the darkened floor inside a circle of rocks slowly becoming visible. Across the little creek was the dip Koriana had claimed as her bed. Stalactites hung overhead, tips broken to keep the great dragoness from hitting her head on the sharpened rock.

And here, against the wall, Alísa had spread out her blanket and extra set of clothes every night to create something close to a bed. She knelt to touch the patch of smooth rock that had called to her that first exhausted night in the cave. On colder nights, Sesína would stretch her wing over Alísa to provide some form of a blanket. A simpler time.

Tears sprang to Alísa's eyes again, and this time she didn't fight them. She leaned back against her and Sesína's wall and hugged her knees, sobbing into her skirt. What she wouldn't give to go back to that time, when she could pretend she had it within herself to be the Dragon Singer. Before the people knew, before Rorenth's expansion forced her into action, before she learned what it was to be reviled.

Before exposing her weakness.

Her fear.

Her brokenness.

She should have known better. Dragons accepted her, but humankind never had. She could never bring the races together, not as she was. And she had known that. Toronn, Tella, her father—all of them had known she would never lead humankind. If she had listened to them, maybe Namor and the other villagers would still be alive. Maybe—

Footsteps came from the mouth of the cave. Alísa curled her arms more tightly around her legs. It sounded like a human. Perhaps Falier had followed her. She lifted her head just enough that her skirt wouldn't muffle her words.

"P-p-p-please, I s—said I w—w—w—want to be alone."

"So I heard." A rich feminine voice echoed in the cave. "But my orders come from a little higher than you."

Alísa jerked her head up to look at the cave entrance, heart pounding. The light outside revealed a silhouette—tall, feminine, with tightly-curled hair that ended just past her shoulders. The shadow walked with a warrior's swagger, yet had no weapons Alísa could see.

Alísa straightened, swiping the tears from her cheeks. "Who's there?"

The figure stepped into shadow, allowing Alísa's cave-adjusted eyes to see more detail. She was garbed in a sword-maiden's armor—her leather vest, greaves, and bracers dyed dark red with etchings that made them look roughly like dragon-scale armor. The skirt of her bright red dress came down to her calves with two long slits for her legs that revealed tight brown pants underneath.

The woman's skin was deep brown and her curls a fiery orange. She was beautiful, everything about her flawless except for a long scar running from beneath her sleeve to her elbow. But even that carried its own beauty—a proud reminder of a warrior's wound. It all seemed familiar, yet remained just out of reach until the next words from the stranger's lips.

"We meet again, little Singer."

Alísa tensed as memories surfaced. She shot to her feet.

"B—Bria?"

This was a dream. She must have fallen asleep, and now her mind was once again trying to reconcile something within itself, manifesting her darker side as the dead Singer. In the last dream, Bria had told Alísa to abandon the slayers, to end the war by fighting them. Perhaps now that Alísa's actions had led to the death of near thirty slayers, her own mind was taunting her.

Alísa gritted her teeth. "I'm n—n—not you!"

"No, you're not." Bria stopped her advance a few feet away, a sad smile on her face. "You aren't in danger from me, Alísa. And my message is gentler than last time."

I need to wake up. Alísa pinched her arm, then closed her eyes hard and forced them open again. Neither tactic banished Bria.

"Sesína, I need you!"

Alísa's heart pounded. Nothing. It was as if the dragoness didn't exist. What was happening?

Bria shushed soothingly. "Sesína is fine—I'm just not allowing her in. My words are for you alone."

Alísa backed further away. "W—what do you want? Why are you in my d—dreams? Why aren't you acting like a normal d—dream?"

"This isn't a dream." Bria gestured to the stone around them, as though it was proof. "I am not a piece of your mind, nor an imagining. I am Bria—slayer, Singer, soul. Namor told you about my death, did he not?"

Alísa blinked, feeling the blood sink from her face and become heavy in her chest. "The slayers removed your *anam*, k-k-k-killing you. But—you can't be here physically, then. That's impossible. Shouldn't you b—be in the Maker's Halls, rather than on A'dem?"

Bria smiled, a slight twinkle in her nearly-black eyes. "I told you, I have higher orders. The Maker can do whatever He sees fit."

Alísa rubbed her skirt between her fingers. The Maker sent Bria's *anam* to speak to her? Twice?

"Please, sit with me. As I said, I have a message for you, but my story is long."

Alísa eyed her, again looking for weapons or any indication that

233

Bria would attack. If Sesína couldn't enter the dream this time, Alísa would have little defense. Reaching out with her empathy, Alísa tested Bria's emotions. If there had been malice, Alísa would have felt it by now, but something more subtle might be there. Theoretically, emotions flowed from the *anam*, so Alísa should be able to feel something from even this strange visitor.

A strong, warm feeling flowed from Bria, a mixture of compassion and love, but with a dullness to it that spoke of the emotions being held back. Like there was more to them, but Bria was using her own powers to soften the edges.

Cautiously, Alísa lowered herself to the ground. Though the holding back was odd, the emotions themselves held truth. If the emotions were being faked and forced out, the edges would be there.

"You are far stronger in your empathy than I was at your age." Bria gave a knowing smile before turning serious. "You've seen my final battle through Koriana's Illuminated eyes. At the end, the slayers captured me and tried to pull out the dragon inside of me. The process took days. While the body is alive, it clings fiercely to the soul, knowing flesh cannot live without something more inside it. Yet, they are not one and the same, and eventually my body gave in to the pain and let go."

Alísa sucked in a breath. "That sounds awful."

"It was." Bria picked at the edge of one of her skirt slits. "I was a proud woman, and even I begged for death. When it finally came, I watched as the slayers stood over my lifeless body and realized the truth of what they had done. I listened as they wondered what it meant. So odd to hear them speaking of me as dead when I stood among them very much alive. And then I realized, I was still standing on A'dem. Eldra D'tohm hadn't come for my soul."

Bria's eyes took on a faraway look, an after-image of pain and sorrow. "I didn't know what it meant. Was I abandoned? Being punished for something and doomed to walk the land aimlessly forever? Or did Eldra D'tohm simply not come right away as the songweavers teach? So I went back to the battlefield, where some of my clanmates still lay, hoping my friends were still there and waiting to be taken as well."

Bria's brows twitched upward, as though reliving the moment.

"Their souls weren't there, nor was D'tohm. But someone else waited for me—bright and shining in chainmail armor made of pure light. Did you know Eldír can get scars? Branni has many. He's even missing an eye."

Alísa straightened. "B—Branni? Branni was waiting for you?"

"He was my Eldra, once. I abandoned him when I joined the dragons, but he hadn't abandoned me. Told me the Maker wouldn't let him, though he'd wanted to on a couple of occasions." Her eyes laughed. "Can't say I blame him now that I know what a terrible charge I was."

The thought of seeing the Eldra she had prayed to all her life sparked something inside Alísa, shoving aside her caution. "What was he like?"

Bria smirked. "Ever met a mountain bear just woken from hibernation? Take that ferocity, add the blunt honesty of Koriana, and sprinkle a dash of Sesína's over-confidence—though in his case it's certainly called for."

A mixture of warmth and chill ran through Alísa. It was good that the Eldra she called on most was as strong as Bria said, but it also made her feel small. How many stupid things had she asked for the strength to do instead of just doing it and proving herself worthy to be his charge?

Alísa started as Bria's hand came to rest on her shoulder, sending a buzz of warmth over her.

"That's why the Eldír are here, Alísa. Don't think Branni—or the Maker Himself, for that matter—looks down on you when you ask for help. Do you know something Koriana, Sesína, and that mountain bear all have in common? Each has a nurturing side, too. Branni, in all his strength and power, sees his charges not as weaklings, but his cubs."

Alísa nodded, not fully convinced. "So, w—w—why was Branni there instead of D—D'tohm?"

"Branni said he was there to deliver a message—a choice, given by the Maker Himself. I could call for D'tohm and be taken away to the Maker's Halls, or I could remain with Branni for a time and learn to shepherd future Dragon Singers as their Eldra."

Alísa's heart stuttered.

Eldra.

Bria was—?

No, that couldn't be.

Yet as she stared, Bria grew brighter. Each color in her form and clothing deepened, as though every color Alísa had ever seen before were merely an attempt to copy true color. The deep orange of her hair seemed almost ablaze as it haloed her face, and the near-black of her eyes became the truest, darkest brown in the world.

As the colors turned, the hold on Bria's emotions loosened. The deadened edges of her compassion and love sharpened and speared through Alísa. It wasn't like feeling her father's love or sharing in Sesína's joy—the emotions were so pure and true that they burned.

Heart racing, Alísa ducked and shielded her head with her arms.

"Do you believe me now?" Bria's voice echoed.

Alísa shrank further. "Yes. F—f—forgive me."

A light hand touched her head. "Look at me, Alísa."

Though kindness lived in that voice, Alísa trembled. "I c-c-c-c-can't." She winced at the stammer, so blatant in the presence of perfection.

"No." Bria said with a firm gentleness. "I am not the Maker. I do not deserve or demand such reverence. Look at me."

Compelled by the command, Alísa lifted her head slowly. The burning in her mind dulled and vanished as Bria pulled her emotions back under control. Alísa squinted until the brightness died down, but even when she could open her eyes fully, Bria retained such vivid colors that she seemed more real than anything Alísa had ever known.

Bria smiled softly. "There, my cub. You need never shy away from me."

Alísa fought not to tremble as she straightened. "My dream. Th—that was you, t-t-too?"

"Yes."

"W—why the p-p-pretense? Why make me think I was f—f—fighting my own mind?"

"You were. A war raged inside you that night. I merely gave you a visual representation in hope that my greatest failure would not become yours." Bria's hands fisted on her thighs. "You didn't need Eldra Bria at the time. You needed to remember that you had already decided your path would be different than mine."

Something shriveled inside of Alísa. "Then I have failed you. I t-t-t-tried to walk that path, b—but I c-c-can't. I c-c-c-can't do this. I'm not s—s—strong enough."

Alísa sniffed back tears, willing herself not to cry under Bria's gaze. Perhaps this was her best chance at ever getting answers. The Maker never spoke to her, but if anyone else in the universe might know, it would be the Eldra charged with her care.

"W—why did the Maker pick m—me?" She meant to stop there, but as she looked at the Eldra—her Eldra—words flowed. "I'm not like you. N—not like my f—father or any other chief. I have no chiefly p-p-p-p-presence. I speak and immediately lose respect. I c-c-can't even stop p-p-people from interrupting me b—because I get so flustered it j—j—just makes things w—w—w—worse!"

Alísa trembled, effort and hurt weighing her heart. She changed to a whisper so she wouldn't stammer anymore. "If my path is to call both dragons and slayers, then why am I broken and weak—and so afraid? Why, for all that is holy, did it have to be me?"

Bria considered her, squinting in thought. Even there, Alísa could see the warrior within Bria—tactics being weighed before she straightened to speak.

"Do you know why you are afraid, Alísa?"

Alísa thought back to what she and Namor had discovered together in the depths of her mind. "I'm afraid of being seen wrongly by p-people. That they won't g—g—give me a chance because all they can see on the surface is someone w—weak, like my former chief did."

"Yes, but that wasn't my question." Bria tented her fingers. "I didn't ask what you were afraid of. I asked if you knew why you were afraid. Toronn might have introduced it, but you allowed it to grow. Do you know why?"

Alísa shivered under the accusing question. "It w—wasn't just Toronn. It was T-T-T-Tella t-too. And p-people in my father's c-c-clan. And Yarlan."

"I know." Bria's eyes hardened. "And it wasn't right of any of them. But they are not the ones who control your thoughts. They are not the ones choosing to hang on to the wrong things they said about you. They are not the ones who allow those thoughts to drown out all you have accomplished. All of that is you."

A tremor of anger ran through Alísa. Bria was blaming her—the victim?

Bria continued, her voice firm. "The fear holding you down is rooted in your feelings of inadequacy. You cannot accept yourself as the Maker created you, and you fear that others' opinions will prove you right. You will not overcome your fear of them until you accept yourself—strengths and weaknesses alike."

"Y—you don't know what it's like!" Alísa wrapped her arms around herself, her breaths heavy. "To have your own voice b—b—b—betray you every day. To know that n—no matter how hard you t-t-t-try there will always be p-p-p-p-people who see you as inferior!"

"You're right," Bria said, the soft words slamming like a wall against Alísa's anger. "I don't know that pain. I've never had to carry that burden, and even I don't know why the Maker gave it to you. But there is one thing I do know. Look at me, Alísa."

Alísa sucked in a breath. She hadn't meant to look down. Bria's eyes didn't hold the distain of Toronn and Yarlan—why did she always look down?

She forced her eyes back up. Bria's eyes were hard, yet their sharpness was the same as the love that had exploded from her true form. In her eyes was the she-bear defending her cub—hard and deadly, but with claws aimed at something beyond Alísa.

"No matter the reason you were given a difficulty others were not, this truth remains—the Maker knew what He was doing and loves the one He made. You are not a tragedy. You do not need to be 'fixed' to live up to the calling He made you, specifically, for."

Bria's aura of light began to return, gentler this time, but filled with the essence of truth. "And even if you had no calling from Him—even if there was no point for your existence except life itself—His making you declares to the heavens that you are enough. You are enough."

The words hit Alísa like a spear through the heart. Its point sunk into her soul through a hole that was already there, a gash that had been bleeding longer than she could remember. And though pain lived there, the edges of the weapon somehow filled the gaps and stopped the flow of blood that had constantly been draining her life away.

You are enough.

It ran through Alísa like a persistent melody. She gasped in a sob and covered her mouth with a hand. A river of tears flowed down her cheeks as the words echoed in her mind.

They couldn't be true. How could they be true? Spoken from the mouth of an Eldra tasked with a message from the Maker Himself?

You are enough.

"N—no. I'm not."

"Lies. You have to let them go, Alísa. Mortals lie to others and to themselves, but the Maker and His Eldír do not." Bria grabbed Alísa's good arm, pulling Alísa's eyes up again. "You were sung into existence, and the Maker makes no mistakes. You are enough."

Alísa's chest spasmed, her body jerking with sobs. It felt like her soul was trying to breathe through the hole where Bria's words had lodged. She had lived and breathed there for so long. Now she had two choices: Reject the words and suck in air through the wound once more, or somehow, some way, learn how to breathe rightly again.

You are enough.

The tiniest opening of Bria's arms was all Alísa needed. Forgoing all reverence and dignity, she threw herself on the neck of the Eldra and wept. Bria stroked Alísa's hair like a mother would her child. The motion guided Alísa's breaths, soothing the air into her lungs as she clung to Bria and her words.

"You may hear the lies the rest of your life, little cub," Bria whispered, "but only you can allow them to reside in you. I know the dark whispers aren't something you can just turn off after believing them so long, but there is no shame in your difficulties."

Bria loosened her hold, bringing one hand under Alísa's chin so they locked eyes. "Your strength called dragons from under the claws of other alphas—it freed a young man from his doubts and an old man from his ignorance. You will not change every mind, but their choice to stop their ears to the truth is theirs alone. You must make the choice to keep going."

Alísa straightened, swiping at the tears on her cheeks. Her father rose in her mind, how he had rejected her claims of the dragons' goodness twice. How was she supposed to accept that?

Bria gave her a sad smile. "I did not say you should give up on him, but if even he refuses you, that is not your shame. Every Dragon Singer so far allowed something to hinder them. I gave in to anger against the slayers. Allara's pride made her cling to their approval. Do not let shame be what clips your wings, little Singer. Especially not shame over who you are."

Bria stood and reached for Alísa's hand, pulling her up. "You will never know the joy I felt when you told me months ago that you would not walk in my way but in yours. Stoke that flame, let it burn away the lies that tell you there is only one type of leadership, one type of strength. You were not made to be Karn or Tella or Namor or even me. Though you and I may never speak face-to-face on A'dem again, I will sing the Maker's truth over you for as long as you breathe air. You are enough."

Alísa allowed the words to fill her without a fight this time. They were still foreign and stinging, yet as she breathed them in their sharpness began to melt, smoothing over the edges of the hole inside of her. No longer merely stopping the flow of blood, but beginning, very slowly, to bind the wound.

Alísa lifted her eyes to meet Bria's. "Am I supposed to p-pray to you now, rather than Branni? Even though you were once just like me?"

Bria sighed and Alísa flinched, realizing how disrespectful the question sounded.

"I don't like the word 'prayer.' It has worshipful connotations, and neither I nor other Eldír are worthy of worship. Yet, I've found no better word. Yes, when you need strength or courage, I am the one the Maker has assigned to you. I am young and my power is still small, but my strength is enough for my charges, and that is enough for me."

Alísa nodded thoughtfully, so many other questions filling her mind. "Allara—did she b—become an Eldra t-t-too?"

Bria's eyes turned down. "No. That choice was not offered to her. It is rare for a mortal to be offered such a transformation. D'tohm and I and the only humans I know of, and Adne the only dragon."

Dragon? If any Eldra was once a dragon, it would be the steward of fire. "B—but Graydonn says the dragons only p-p-pray to the Maker. Dragons have Eldír, then?"

"All mortals have the same Eldír. Branni, Nahne, any one of us would respond if a dragon called." Bria held up a finger to stifle Alísa's next question. "Think of us as a gift to all mortals. The Maker has given us power to help any who asks, but a gift does not have to be accepted or used. Those who refuse our help and go straight to the Maker may receive His direct aid, but He often prefers to use His servants to enact His will—displaying His strength and truth through vessels weaker than Himself, be they Eldra or mortal."

Alísa's head ached, but she couldn't stop the questions. "Then, are there any other Eldír whose form is a d—dragon?"

"No." A sly smile crossed Bria's face. "There are no Eldír whose true form is human either. I take this shape now only because you know it. Just wait till you see the Maker in His halls—your brain will break."

Alísa shook her head. "I think it's already b—breaking."

Bria grinned, her eyes softening. "I'm proud of you, little cub. Of all Singers, you've come the farthest in the mission. Though sorrows lie along this path, so does joy. Don't give up."

Alísa whispered to herself. "Music in the storm."

Bria smiled knowingly. "That boy of yours has his moments."

Shadows pressed in around Bria, and her colors slowly faded. Panic shot through Alísa. Was she leaving?

"Wait! Don't go. B—Bria! W—what should I do now? How can I reach the slayers?"

Bria's voice became ethereal as her form shimmered. "There are rules no Eldra can break. We give no answers beyond what the Maker allows. My task was to reveal myself and loosen the shackles of the lie entrapping you—I cannot tell you the next step."

She touched Alísa's cheek, giving comfort as her final mists disappeared.

"Use the strength that has been given you, and move."

21

HONOR

The cave was cold in the absence of Bria. Alísa tried to cling to the feeling of Bria's hand on her cheek, or the empathic love that had been flowing around her mere moments ago. But now it was like the Eldra had never been there, just as it had been for Alísa all her life. The only proof she had were the words in her heart that she would never have spoken to herself.

You are enough.

Alísa shivered, the sensation part cold, part awe. The Maker called her that. Enough to meet the calling He had given her. Not as she should be, but as she was. It filled her to overflowing. Yet, where did that leave her? Bria had spoken of her strengths, but hadn't said what they were. What was her next step?

Another shiver. The next step was to get out of this cave.

Alísa squinted as she approached the exit, the summer sun enveloping her. A black form draped over the floor just outside. Sesína. Though she still couldn't feel the bond to the dragoness, she watched Sesína lift her head from between her paws and look into the cave directly at her. Around the dragoness flew several dreki, all fluttering just outside.

Alísa ran to her, the action brightening Sesína's emerald eyes. Sesína stood and pawed at the ground as though holding herself back from running. As soon as Alísa came into the open air, the bond latched back into place. She threw herself on the dragoness' neck and let Sesína's wings enfold her.

"*I really hate being separated from you.*" Sesína growled. "*I don't care that some Eldra wanted to talk to you—anything they have to say they can tell us both.*"

Alísa looked up at her. *"You know? How?"*

Sesína pointed her snout at the dreki. *"Apparently, they have an in. When our bond went silent, I flew to where you disappeared, ready to destroy whoever was cutting you off from me. But when I got here and tried to go into the cave, I hit a wall! Some stupid half-psychic, half-physical light wall!"*

Sesína shook her head as though she had just banged her head against said wall. *"Now, I didn't panic or anything, but—"*

A couple of dreki chittered above them, their negatives flowing through the astral plane.

"Fine. Maybe I got a little—flustered." Sesína snorted at the dreki. *"You can hardly blame me, Laen. Last time it was a slayer holding a knife to her throat! Anyway, I was trying to figure out how to get through the wall when Laen and Ska flew up and told me you were safe. With an Eldra. Who refused to speak to me."* Sesína growled. *"So? What happened? Was it Branni?"*

Alísa ran a hand through her hair. *"Well, how to begin?"*

"Too slow." Sesína touched her snout to Alísa's forehead and the memory of Bria walking into the cave flashed through Alísa's mind. The dragoness yanked her head back.

"No. Way."

Alísa steadied herself with a hand on Sesína's neck. *"Warn me before you do that!"*

"You've been warned." Sesína touched Alísa's head again, memories of Bria's visit spilling from Alísa's mind to Sesína's at triple the speed.

"This is insane! And I missed it!" Memories faded out of Alísa's vision as Sesína gave a mental gasp. *"The dream. I called her a serpent then. Do you think she hates me? That's why she kept me out this time? I don't know if I can live being hated by an Eldra!"*

Alísa rubbed her temples. *"If I recall correctly, she called us a beautiful flame, not just me."*

"Even so." Sesína looked up at the dreki. *"Did you know about Bria?"*

"Singer!" Laen chirped.

Ska and a few others flew to Laen and began swirling around each other in a fluttery dance.

"Return!" "Dreki!" "Branni!" "Eldra!" "Anam!"

Images accompanied the dance, but the few Alísa caught made

about as much sense as the words and their order. Dreki flying around Bria. A zig-zag of stars. A sword in a bloody hand. Darkness with lines of light soaring from Bria's lips.

Alísa slumped against Sesína, dizziness overtaking her. *"Stop. No more. Please."*

With Sesína's help, Alísa lowered to the ground, mental exhaustion taking her. The dreki were sometimes a little too much. Thankfully, this was only about ten of them, rather than the whole clan of sixty. They were splitting up far more frequently than she had once known them to.

The dreki ended their dance, some fluttering to the ground while others landed on Sesína's back and head. Laen took Alísa's shoulder, trilling an apology.

"It's okay," Alísa said. *"Thank you for telling Sesína what was happening."*

Sesína settled to the ground. *"They told me more than that. While we waited for you, I asked them why we've seen so few of them at a time lately. Took a while for me to understand what they were saying, but—"*

Sesína paused, regret passing through the bond. Whatever it was, she was thinking twice about saying it.

"Go on," Alísa said. *"You can't just stop there."*

Steam fell from Sesína's mouth in a sigh. *"There's a divide among them. Chrí and the others' deaths really took a toll. Some, like these here, were inspired and want to continue allying with us. Others, though, are angry. They don't want any more dreki to die and want to keep to themselves."*

Alísa's heart sagged. Even the dreki—creatures so community-focused they literally shared minds—were divided because of her. She pushed against the thoughts, remembering Bria's admonition. The dreki's choice was theirs alone. But the thought of their pain still hurt.

Sesína nuzzled Alísa's cheek. *"I'm sorry. I shouldn't have told you yet."*

"No, it's good to know." Alísa reached up and stroked Laen's neck with a finger. *"You would tell me if you need anything, right?"*

Laen trilled an affirmative.

"Are Rann and the babies okay?"

Laen sent a picture of baby Chrí in flight, her wings tilted in a manner that suggested a very wobbly attempt. In the background, Rís clung to his father's back in continued training.

Alísa smiled. *"Good."*

Dizziness dispelled, Alísa found a light ache of hunger settled in her belly. She looked at the sky, trying to gauge the time.

She straightened. The sun was much further west than she had anticipated. *"It's afternoon already? How long was I in there?"*

"A while." Sesína looked toward the village, the drek on her head flaring his wings out to keep from falling. *"Me'ran's ceremony will probably start soon. Assuming Briek and the slayers were able to move their dead."*

An ache ran through Alísa at the mention of Briek, both for her missed opportunity today and for his unenviable job of walking his clan through this horror. How did one honor a warrior properly when one wasn't sure whether he had died protecting his people or killing them?

Thankfully, that wasn't her question to answer, and there was one warrior she did know how to honor.

"Let's go, then."

Me'ran's graveyard was small. On the southeastern edge of the village, it consisted of perhaps fifty graves marked by stones. Most had names carved into them, and a few included the twisting, knotted symbols of the Maker's peace or of a particular Eldra. Now there were eleven new graves, their stones dark and unbleached by the sun.

Alísa had never fully understood burials. Most of the dead in her father's clan never returned to camp, either burned away by dragon-fire or else cremated where they lay. Carrying the dead back down a mountain wasn't practical with wounded needing assistance, and—to slayers, at least—the body meant nothing without the *anam* within.

How were Briek and his few remaining men handling their near-thirty dead? Deep in the forest in the middle of summer, cremation seemed too dangerous. Would each remaining man be expected to dig three graves? Would the wives help?

Alísa pushed the slayers out of her mind. She needed to be present.

By the time she and Sesína returned, most of the villagers had already gathered. Graydonn and Komi stood on the outside of the gathering, lifting their heads high to watch the proceedings without disturbing the villagers. Alísa and Sesína stood with them.

Parsen, Meira, and another elder stood at the front, presiding over the ceremony. The elder Alísa didn't know began with solemn words about the tragedy, of fear and madness and lives snuffed out too soon. As he spoke, his eyes lifted to the dragons on more than one occasion, his tone sharpening each time.

"Who could have known that the war that plagues our western brothers and sisters could have come upon us so swift and fierce? May the Maker in His mercy grant us peace once more."

Agreement murmured from many in the crowd, a few throwing glances back at the dragons, while others ignored or else were unaware of the elder's accusation. Alísa breathed in the mixture of anger, fear, and grief, and blew it back out. She forced truth through her thoughts—it was true that the war came more swiftly because of her, but it would have come no matter what. Rorenth would still have attacked them, and there would have been no defenders besides Namor and Yarlan. The wayfarers might have stopped a few dragons at the Nissen, but if a horde of dragons had come all at once, they would have made it past.

Had Briek and his people faced many deaths, positioned as they were? Not many dragons crossed the Nissen, but Segenn's territory fell along Rorenth's borders, and Kerrik had thought it too dangerous for weaker telepaths like Falier. Was the honoring of the dead a terrible normalcy to them as it was to Karn's clan, or did they have to work to remember the words to their funeral songs?

Meira stepped forward, continuing the ceremony with words of peace and encouragement. She spoke of the heroism of some of the dead—telling snippets of stories their families had told her. A father who took the blow aimed at his son. A woman who slowed her retreat to assist a man who had fallen. Namor, who had called Segenn out and alerted the other slayers to the chief's madness, and who had freed Alísa to call for draconic aid. The previous speaker glared at Meira for this last bit.

Parsen beckoned Selene, drawing attention from the division of the elders. Her face was solemn and tranquil as she came alongside her father and lifted her flute to her lips.

The notes from the instrument were low and airy, the line of music slow and easy, indicating that the melody she played would soon be sung. Alísa didn't recognize it, and when the people lifted their voices together, she could only hum along. It felt wrong to not sing the words. It was the duty of a chief and their family to honor the dead.

Maker, hear my heart. May what little I can do now still honor them.

A pang ran through her. And the slayers? Who honored them?

Stop. Focus. The villagers. Namor.

The funeral song lasted three verses, all of them different except for the melody. Alísa harmonized with it, switching from a hum to a light 'oo' vowel. Many voices joining in a common purpose brought tears to her eyes, especially at the end as they sang of a day when there would be no more death and souls would reunite in the Maker's Halls.

As the song ended and Parsen called for stories of remembrance, Alísa pondered the implications of the song. Going to the Maker's Halls at death had always been a comforting thought. Seeing Chrí again, Namor, old clanmates—all of that sounded wonderful and good.

But with Briek and his slayers continuously invading her mind, she couldn't help but wonder now—would Segenn be there, too? Or the man who had killed Namor? That seemed so wrong, that Namor and his murderer might both be there.

What of all the hatchlings she had watched be murdered by her clan? When she one day entered the Maker's Halls, would they be there? Would they remember how she had stood by? Would they forgive her because she had risen up to advocate for their kind later in life?

What about her father, who had actually wielded the sword against them? Would he be refused at the door, or welcomed for his service to humankind despite his crimes against dragons?

"Alísa?"

Did one wrong act negate a lifetime of good? How much good did it take to wipe out evil? Perhaps the Maker alone knew the answer to that.

"Alísa!" Sesína arched her neck to look her in the eyes. *"And I thought I had trouble focusing. Where is all of this coming from?"*

"I don't know." Alísa shook her head. *"I'm sorry. I'll focus."*

Stories continued, some bringing laughter and others renewed tears. Most of the dead were people Alísa had never met before or had met only briefly at a céilí or dragon visit. A few spoke for Namor, remembering his story-telling and his life of sacrifice as a wayfarer.

Like Briek and his men and the families left behind.

As the stories came to an end, the holders brought baskets filled with an assortment of flowers. The first elder lifted his hands to the sky.

"May the Maker receive His faithful into His Halls."

The people murmured quiet agreement. Then the families of those killed came forward, taking up flowers and laying them on the graves of their departed. From there, the gathered crowd began to disperse, some taking up their own flowers to set at the graves while others walked home.

Alísa waited as people passed. Glares passed their way, but so did respectful nods and even a few smiles. The division weighed on her heart.

Yarlan stopped as he walked past. Alísa fought not to look at him, keeping her eyes on those still mourning at the graves.

"Admiring your handiwork?"

Alísa stiffened, regretting her lack of control as he smirked.

Sesína bared a fang at the slayer. *"For someone so convinced that we're evil, you sure are pushing it."*

But Yarlan's mind was closed off from Sesína's words. He looked at the bared tooth, then back to Alísa.

"Stop holding her back, girl," he taunted. "Show the people what they really are. I will gladly die to show them."

"You're insane," Alísa whispered. "If they were evil, they—"

"A little louder, witch. Or can't you do it?"

Alísa's heart wavered. She should stop, not give him anything, but Sesína's unheard words called her out. "If they w—were evil, they w—w—wouldn't stop with you. Are you p—putting your p-p-people at risk, or do you t-t-truly b—believe me—"

Yarlan's smirk soured. "Perhaps I push because I want *you* to see the truth as you strain to hold them back. Perhaps I think you worth saving."

Alísa shook her head. "You think I'm nothing."

She reached out to the dragons, the inward focus bringing her racing heart to the forefront of her mind. *"Walk with me. I'm not strong enough to push past him on my own."*

As one, the dragons stood. With Sesína on one side and Graydonn and Komi on the other, Alísa stepped past Yarlan and approached the graves. There were fewer people now, even some of the families had left, making it easy for the dragons to move with her. Alísa wanted to throw up as fear and grief collided within her.

Graydonn touched her back with a wing, a light rumble in his chest. *"You are a dragoness."*

As Alísa's stomach clenched and her heart beat wildly, she couldn't make herself believe it. *"Not yet."*

A few of those remaining walked away as Alísa and the dragons approached, wide-eyed or with thinly-veiled contempt. Others nodded respectfully, making room but not leaving. Alísa went to the holders, giving Falier what she hoped passed as a smile. He returned it, one corner of his lips rising. The silence was loud between them, neither knowing what to say. She had been a mess earlier and talking about it now would be neither private nor polite.

Alísa looked at the basket in Selene's hands. Only a few flowers remained, but the empty baskets on the ground still contained discarded petals. She pointed to one of these.

"May I take the p—petals?"

Selene cocked her head, then nodded. Alísa knelt down and poured petals from all of the baskets into one as the holders watched her. There still weren't many, but it was something. She stood with her basket and took one flower from Selene, whispering her thanks.

She turned away and approached the graves, her throat constricting. Her mind was torn in two, between the guilt for being the cause of the attack and the truth that the slayers had made their own choices. She hadn't been the one holding the sword, nor the one who armed the swordsmen. Still, her guilt went with her as she dropped petals on each of the graves.

The flower she saved for Namor, kneeling with it at his grave. Tenza stood nearby, a black mourning shawl over her shoulders. Alísa clutched the stem of her flower and whispered to Namor.

"Thank you, for everything. We got off on the wrong foot, but we overcame it together. Some days your presence alone gave me strength at the visits. You saw the worst of me when I was overwhelmed, and you encouraged me through it. I think, somehow, you saw the best of me somewhere in there too. I can think of no other reason why you'd—"

Her throat closed with a sob. Sesína's wing brushed her back, soothing her. The pain in Alísa's heart roiled inside of her, spilling through her mind in a sorrowful melody that soon gave way to words.

> Though winds and rains fall, the oak shelters all
> And blesses the world with its song
> Though heat does assail, it welcomes the frail
> Its shadow a comfort so strong
>
> Though strong and severe, the children came near
> To hear the great oak tell his tales
> Though hardened and scarred, it let down its guard
> And welcomed the skinned and the scaled
>
> A great oak has fallen
> A great tree has fallen
> Though nature could not have its way
> A great man has fallen
> A great chief has fallen
> Too soon he was taken away
>
> Though nature had tried to bring him to die
> The oak fell to none of its ways
> But when strangers came with axe and with flame
> The oak took the blows on that day
>
> A great oak has fallen
> A great tree has fallen
> And everyone weeps on this day
> A great man has fallen
> A great chief has fallen
> But we will remember his name

With the end of her song, the sorrow of the young dragons swelled. Whether it was their own or Alísa's flowing into them through her song, grief bubbled up within them and released in low, mournful trumpets. Together, they sounded almost like wolves calling for a lost pack member. Alísa glanced at the people around them, but none appeared frightened. Perhaps they recognized that the dragons' song was in tune with her own.

As the dragons ended their call, Alísa placed her flower with the others adorning Namor's grave. "I hope I can live up to whatever you saw in me. Eldra D'tohm guide you to the Maker's Halls in peace."

Alísa rose and brushed the dirt from her skirt. When she looked up, there was Tenza, tears in her eyes and the slightest of smiles on her lips.

"Thank you." Tenza dipped her head to the dragons. "All of you. You do him great honor."

Honor. Many more deserved it than just those buried here.

Sesína eyed Alísa, wondering at her thoughts before looking to Tenza. *"He and you both saved Alísa's life, as well as many others."*

"He was a great man," Komi said, blinking slowly. *"A mountain of strength."*

"My mother, too, sends her sorrows," Graydonn said, his eyes dimmed. *"She would have been here if she could have done it without hindering others' grief. She knows what it is to lose a mate."*

Tenza nodded quickly, her eyes shining. "Thank you again." With that, she turned away and looked back on Namor's grave.

Alísa walked away, the dragons following. Her mind swam with questions of blame, honor, and grief, the smallest hint of a next step forming.

"What should we do now, Singer?" Komi asked.

Alísa looked around. The village was quiet, almost peaceful. Besides a few mourners still at the grave site, people headed for their own homes, some chimneys already spouting smoke for suppers. One dragon, Korin, lay at the top of the path to the Hold, taking his turn on watch.

"Go home and rest. Tell Korin to go too. Tonight, the slayers mourn, and there is no danger. Only scouts and hunters need be out."

Graydonn stretched his neck toward her. *"Will you come with us?"*

251

"*No,*" Alísa said. "*Tomorrow, probably, but there's something I need to do here tonight.*"

A growl rumbled in Sesína's throat, making the others' eyes dim with concern. Sesína had caught the plan. Alísa waved them on.

"*I need to speak with Sesína alone. Go and rest.*"

Graydonn looked from Alísa to Sesína and back, then thumped his tail on the ground. He and Komi trotted away and bounded into the air. Before their first wing-stroke, Sesína cut off the connection to them and rounded on Alísa.

"*Tell me I didn't see what I thought I saw.*"

"*You probably did.*"

"*Alísa!*" Sesína snorted steam. "*You're just going to walk into the slayers' camp?*"

"*There are men there who gave their lives for Me'ran, who killed their brothers to protect this village. And yet in their time of need, the elders shoved them aside. I will not. As my father's daughter, I cannot.*" Alísa rubbed her arms, pressing lightly at the bandage and letting the pain sink into her. "*I myself cannot.*"

Sesína's anger dimmed, but her anxiety remained. "*Those slayers aren't yet our allies.*"

"*Some of those remaining believed my song.*" Alísa stilled her hands. "*And I believe Briek will not harm me. He is honorable. Even if he refuses me, I will leave in safety.*"

Sesína stamped a foot. "*I'm going with you. They'll think twice before attacking with me at your side.*"

Alísa shook her head. "*I'm not going as the Dragon Singer. Some will see that only as a threat.*" She pulled out her necklace, letting the scale hang on the outside. "*I will go as the daughter of Karn—a chief's daughter coming to honor her dead brothers. They may not be ready to understand a good dragon yet, but this they will.*"

Sesína slumped with a sigh. "*At least let me walk you there. I can fend off any serpents along the way.*"

"*Deal. I need to get something from Ari's room, then we can go.*"

Alísa hurried to Tenza's house, pushing through the main room into the bedchamber she had been occupying. Namor and Tenza's daughter Ari had left a lot behind when she moved out, which was fine by Alísa. Though she was ready to go back to the company of her dragons, it had been nice having furniture and decor for a little while. Especially a real, honest-to-goodness bed.

When Alísa had first started staying there, Tenza had offered up the clothing Ari had left behind. Opening a drawer in the dresser, Alísa rummaged through the articles.

There. Alísa pulled out a red tartan skirt and matching sash, much like the ones she had left behind in her father's tent. The colors of a chief's family. She stripped off her plain brown skirt and put on the red one. Pulling the sash over her head, she situated it across her chest and adjusted the horse-shaped pin at the hip.

Turning to the pile of her things beside the bed, Alísa grabbed her short-sword and strapped it on. Its weight was a comfort. It had been so long since she had worn it, always trying to show the villagers she meant them no harm. But it, like the necklace, was a part of her. Perhaps it was time to stop hiding both. She was a slayer just as much as she had a dragon inside.

But that was too great a decision to make after such a day. She would wear both with pride tonight and figure out the rest another time.

As ready as she could be, Alísa left the chamber, reentering the main room. She stopped abruptly as the door to outside opened ahead of her, Tenza slowly entering and shutting the door. The room was dark, most of the shutters closed against the sun, and Tenza didn't notice her until she had taken two steps inside.

Tenza looked her up and down. "Why did you change?"

Alísa tensed at Tenza's suspicion-filled tone. Surely, she would understand, having been the Lady of a clan once. Yet, Namor's death weighed heavily. Alísa spoke gently and firmly, hoping to find a balance between Tenza's senses of rightness and grief.

"I'm g—going to the slayers' ceremony, to honor those who d—d—died for Me'ran."

Tenza's gaze sharpened. "So you honor my husband, then turn around and honor the man who killed him, while wearing the garb of his daughter?"

Alísa looked down. In her conviction, she hadn't considered that last part.

"I will leave Ari's belongings if you will it." She forced her eyes back up to Tenza's. "B—but I must go. I cannot stand by as Me'ran d—dishonors the men who fought for her. I don't know who d—died well, b—but—"

"Briek is a fool for not giving true closure to his people," Tenza said, ire breaking through her usually tight empathic hold. "They should know who died in honor and who died in disgrace."

"I might agree, but that isn't m—my choice to make. They are hurting, and I want to p-p-prove to them I do c-c-c-care about slayers t-too, n—not just dragons. If I am not able to sort out who d—d—died in dishonor, then I will let the Maker sort it out. If He can hear prayers whispered in the d—depths of my mind, surely He can direct their effects t-t-to the correct souls."

Tenza scrutinized her, the sharpness never leaving her gaze. Then she walked past Alísa.

"Go, then."

Alísa pressed her lips together, sadness for Tenza welling up inside her. She hadn't wanted to hurt her, and now she recognized that a part of her had hoped Tenza would come too. But Tenza made her own choices, and so would she. Not daring to look back, Alísa went to the door and walked back into the summer evening.

When the sounds of shovels scraping into dirt hit Alísa's ears, she knew it was time to walk alone. Finding Briek's camp had been easy due to the trampled path their carts made carrying the dead from Me'ran. She had walked the path easily with Sesína at her side. Now, though she couldn't yet see the camp, her heart raced faster.

Sesína pressed the bridge of her nose to Alísa's cheek, a rumble of dissatisfaction in her throat. *"Are you sure you won't let me come?"*

Alísa placed her hand under Sesína's chin and squeezed. *"I'm sure. Tonight, I am a slayer. You may wait here for me, but don't come any closer."*

"I'll watch the whole time." Sesína closed her eyes and opened the

bond wider, looking through Alísa's eyes. *"Just in case."*

"Thank you."

It took more effort than it should to turn back toward the camp, but Alísa managed it. Slowly, she wound through the forest. The ground was hard beneath her boots, and she couldn't help but wonder how long it took to dig a grave in this environment. They must have been at it all day. A long day of work with only the promise of sorrow at the end, and that after a day of horrors. Those thoughts pushed her forward. Any hope or help she could give them would be worth it.

Soon the edge of the slayers' camp came into view. Tents occupied every space large enough between the trees, and a few horses munched contentedly at shrubbery, their leads tied to low branches. The space was silent—no slayers in sight. Out of respect, she skirted the camp rather than walking through it, following the sounds of digging until she finally saw the slayers.

Men and women alike bent over shovels, some digging new graves, others filling them, the only sounds those of shovels and the occasional grunt of effort. Leather tarps that might have once been tents covered bodies on the ground. Two teenage boys, perhaps fourteen or fifteen years, were among the workers, though no other children were in sight.

One man saw her and stopped digging, confusion dominating his expression. Then he blinked with recognition and straightened.

"Dragon Singer?"

As one, the slayers looked up. Alísa felt herself shrink under their scrutiny. Some faces held confusion. Other expressions darkened, especially the women's. Rassím's eyes widened with shock. Only a few brows were smooth as the people stared. She couldn't see Briek anywhere.

Alísa forced herself straight again. "I w—would speak with Briek."

One of the men scoffed. "He's busy, as you can surely see."

"It's fine."

Relief flooded Alísa as Briek stepped into view from behind a tree. He wiped sweat from his dark brow as he approached her. Exhaustion filled his eyes, posture, and emotions. As he stopped in front of her, Alísa raised her hand to her heart, keeping it open in the sign of respect from one chief to another. Briek looked at her hand, then her face, his eyes unreadable. He didn't return the gesture.

"What can I do for you, Dragon Singer?" His voice was hoarse and guarded. "We are soon to honor our dead."

Alísa breathed. "I am not here as the D—Dragon Singer, but as Alísa, daughter of Karn. If you will p-p-permit, I c-c-c-come to honor the sacrifices of your men."

She looked to the people beyond him, each exhausted by work and sorrow, and her heart went out to them. "If you have a shovel to spare, I would also assist you."

Briek crossed his arms. "Truly? Then you do not share the sentiments of Me'ran and its elders?"

Segenn and the man who killed Namor flashed through Alísa's mind again. It would be best not to lie to Briek. She spoke quietly.

"Some of the dead have brought me great p-p-pain. If I c-c-c-could, perhaps I would find a way to honor only those who died heroes. But this is your c-c-clan, and you are doing your best with what you've been g—given." Alísa looked him in the eyes. "I understand that better than anyone. Our p-p-people's sacrifice should be honored, so here I stand."

Briek scrutinized her, his eyes squinting in a manner she recognized. He wouldn't dig into her mind—not when even speaking telepathically was against the slayers' code—but he was testing her surface thoughts and emotions. She relaxed her mind as much as she could. Let him see who she was and what she meant.

After an eternity of his wary eyes on her, Briek's brow smoothed. He lifted his hand to his chest, palm open against his heart.

"Then I welcome you, Karns-daughter."

Behind Briek, the slayers looked to each other. Some held anger, others hope. Amidst the quiet mutterings, Alísa heard a man speculate that she was merely there to manipulate them, but in Briek she saw belief. She clung to that as he led her through the people. He took a shovel from one of the older men who had been filling a grave and passed it to her.

She took it, steeling herself for the sight of the man within the grave. By Maker's mercy, the dead man's face was already covered. It could be Segenn, or it could be a man who stood between a villager and death. She would never know.

With a nod of respect to Briek and the older slayer, the daughter of Karn went to work.

22

SINGERS & SLAYERS

Alísa could barely move when she woke, every muscle in her body sore. Due to her arm, she had only been able to cover two graves, pushing softened dirt rather than digging into the hard ground, but between that, her long walks, and the overarching sorrow of the day, her body protested anything beyond lying in bed. The slayers' ceremony lasted past dark, the stars bright when Sesína walked her back into Me'ran. Still, Alísa regretted none of it.

Sunlight poured through the open window. Late morning. She had missed her morning work at the Hold. Falier ran through her mind and an ache pulsed through her heart. She had so much to tell him, so much she hadn't been able to yesterday. He was probably still reeling from everything, and she had left him to it. She knew from experience that sometimes the loved ones of a chief were left to fend for themselves. She understood a little more clearly now the choices her father faced.

Alísa pushed up slowly, using only her uninjured arm and protesting abdominals. Gingerly, she stretched her neck, arms, and back, reaching out to Sesína as she did. A light happiness lived on the other side of the bond.

"Good morning, Sesína."

"Morning, sleepy." The dragoness winced inwardly. *"You feel awful."*

Alísa nodded, though Sesína couldn't see. *"I'm surprised you're up."* Dragons tended to sleep more than humans did, taking frequent naps in the cave.

"I had a promise to keep. Some of the kids asked me to play yesterday after the funeral, and I told them we would play this morning instead."

Alísa smiled, then grimaced as she stood. Her legs weren't as bad as her arms, but her back ached as it kept her upright. *"The visits continue, then?"*

Sesína sent an affirmative. *"Saynan is here too. Graydonn's at the Hold."*

"You know that's breaking the rules of the compromise, right?"

"You know what I think of those rules, right? No one is complaining that you aren't here, besides grump-face watching from the shadows."

Yarlan. Alísa shivered. *"Be careful. Namor isn't here to hold him back anymore. You really shouldn't have slept at the porch last night without another dragon here."*

"You're the other dragon. And there's no way in flames I'm leaving you here alone again."

Alísa shook her head. *"I don't count. No teeth, claws, or fire to help you defend. And I sleep far more heavily than you dragons do."*

Dress settled, Alísa touched the chain around her neck. Should she pull it out again? *"Sesína, what do you think? Would showing the dragon scale offend the clan?"*

"You're asking the wrong dragon," Sesína said. *"I see it in the same way you do—a piece of armor won in battle, and a token of your father's love. For all I know, the others might think of it like you might a dragon holding onto the fingernails of a slayer they've killed."*

Alísa grimaced. That was rather gruesome, but it made sense. She left the necklace tucked.

"I'll be out in a moment. I want to see if I can help at the Hold and see Falier. Will you come with me, or stay with the kids?"

"With Yarlan getting bolder, I'm sticking with you like a tree on moss."

Alísa squinted. *"You mean moss on a tree."*

"No, I want to be the tree. You can be the fungus."

"Pretty sure moss isn't a fungus."

"Whatever. The point is, I'm the tree. I'm the one with children climbing on me, after all."

Alísa shook her head, going to the window and peering out. Sure enough, three children, all aged between four and six, hung laughing on Sesína's spines and tail, one of them trying to get into riding position.

Alísa smiled. Sorrows would last for a long time in this community, but there was always room for joy. She thought of Falier and hugged herself. Then she turned to the door and thought of Tenza and her hurt. After their words yesterday, Alísa wasn't sure she was ready to face the grieving widow. But that was the way of a coward. She reached for the door handle.

"I'm going to check on Tenza first."

Sesína sent a wave of peace. *"You've got this."*

With a resolved exhale, Alísa opened the door and walked into the main room. Relief swept over her as she recognized Meira at the table with Tenza, as well as the shutters that had been opened since yesterday. Both women gave tired smiles of welcome, though Tenza's almond-shaped eyes still turned with exhaustion.

"Morning," Alísa said softly, taking comfort from Tenza's smile.

The room smelled of cooling potato and onion hash, and Alísa's stomach rumbled. She had only a small dinner yesterday with Briek and his people, and she had skipped lunch entirely. Leaving her empathy wide open to watch for signs she wasn't welcome, she grabbed the empty plate from her usual spot at the table. After scooping out leftover hash at the dormant fireplace, she sat silently. The food was room-temperature, but her eager stomach didn't care. It took effort not to scarf down the food like her voracious twelve-year-old cousins.

"Meira," Tenza said when Alísa was nearly through, "I would like to speak with Alísa. Would you give us a moment?"

Another shot of nerves ran through Alísa as Meira stood. "I'll be right outside with the dragons."

Alísa took the last bite and folded her hands in her lap as Meira exited. *Maker, give me grace.*

Tenza was quiet for a moment. As usual, no emotions escaped her, leaving Alísa at a loss for how to brace herself.

"How did the slayers receive you last night?"

Alísa took a moment before answering. "Well, for the most part. A few were angry that I w—was intruding, b—but I think others understood. Briek did."

Tenza nodded slowly. "You are stronger than I. My anger was too fierce to do the right thing."

Alísa swallowed as that anger seeped out. "Your anger is justified."

"Yes. But not toward you. I know you loved Namor, and he loved you." Tenza looked up at the ceiling, silent for a moment. "I should also thank you for what you did for him, at the end. He needed that closure."

Namor's last moments flitted through Alísa's mind. The fear that placed Ari's face over Alísa's. "Of c-course. I've never seen him like that before. He wasn't afraid t-t-to d—"

She stopped herself.

"No. Namor was never afraid of death. Only of never gaining forgiveness for the mistakes he—we—made." Tenza eyed her. "You want to ask."

"It's not my place," Alísa whispered, though she craved the knowledge.

"I pulled you into it when I asked you to be the vessel of forgiveness. And before that, without your knowledge, Namor treated you as the vessel of atonement. You are neck deep in this and have a right to know. Ask your questions, before this becomes too hard again."

The way Tenza's voice thickened with her last words sent a prickle behind Alísa's eyes. She blinked to clear it—Tenza didn't need her tears right now, and they might keep her from divulging the answers.

"W—why me? Namor didn't even like me at first. Why was I the v—vessel?"

Tenza looked out the window at the dragons in the square. "Because Ari has dragon empathy, like you."

Alísa's eyes widened. Another one. There was another person with dragon empathy—perhaps even another Dragon Singer—out there!

"Why didn't you mention it before? Where does she live? C—can I meet her?"

Tenza closed her eyes. "I don't know where she is. We never mentioned it because for the last twenty years, Namor blamed himself for Ari running away from home."

Alísa's breath caught. Suddenly the room still full of clothing and decor made sense. Ari had run away, taking only the necessities, just like Alísa had.

"Her dragon empathy developed much like yours," Tenza said. "Unlike your father, though, Namor thought it best that she not attend

261

dragon-killings so as to avoid the pain. Ari hated that he made her stay away, treating her like she couldn't handle it and making the clan think she was squeamish about the war. They had frequent fights about it, but Namor insisted that the clan not learn of the connection, for fear they would think her compromised."

Alísa nodded slowly. She knew what that was like all too well.

"After Namor lost his leg, we left the west and settled in Me'ran, where Ari wouldn't have to worry about her dragon empathy any longer. Ari, however, begged to stay and support the wayfarers in Namor's stead. She was eighteen at the time, ready to live her own life, perhaps start a family with a young man she loved. But knowing she wouldn't be careful about her empathy, Namor and I insisted she come with us. We were finally able to guilt her into coming because Namor needed care and two people would be better than one."

Tenza cleared her throat as it thickened again.

"We lived here quietly for a while, but when the eastern wayfarers came through for supplies, there was her young man. He had followed us east. Ari wanted to go with him, but we refused, unable to stand the thought of her returning to a life that would cause her pain. We made it clear with the man and his chief that we did not bless the potential marriage. That should have kept them apart, but Ari wouldn't have it. Once the wayfarers left and our guard was down, she followed them. The next time the wayfarers came, neither Ari nor her lover were with them, and no one knew where they went. Namor blamed himself. Said he'd been too restrictive, keeping her safe rather than letting her find the purpose she searched for."

Alísa pressed her lips together. The terrible sadness and guilt Namor and Tenza had felt over Ari struck hard. How must her own parents feel? Were they wracked with similar guilt?

Tenza's hand closed around Alísa's, jolting her from her thoughts. The woman's eyes were filled with tears.

"When he looked into your mind and saw what you were, Namor saw his chance to be what he hadn't been for Ari. Guilt plagued him for not being able to go with you the day you left to fight Rorenth. As atonement for that, he insisted we stand with you and the dragons at every visit. And the evening you broke down at the céilí and he helped you through it, he returned with tears of remembrance in his eyes."

Tenza squeezed Alísa's hand, and for a brief moment grief and hope both twisted from her touch. "So don't blame yourself for what happened. It was his gift, the final clasp on the chest of the redemption he so desperately wanted. Besides Ari herself, no one else had the power to grant him that. Thank you."

Tears swam in Alísa's eyes. "Thank you for telling me. I wish I'd known."

"Yes, well, the man was prideful and stubborn." Tenza pulled back, wiping her eye with her thumb. "Men of nobility and valor often are."

Alísa smiled softly. "Yes. They think they've earned the right or something."

"Indeed," Tenza chuckled. The slayer woman regarded Alísa, her guard up once more. "Now, Alísa, you must tell me truly. I held nothing back from you, so you will hold nothing back from me."

Alísa straightened. What was this?

"Segenn mentioned the name Allara alongside Bria and yourself. Is there another Dragon Singer out there named Allara?"

The intensity in Tenza's gaze made Alísa swallow. "There was, yes."

Tenza blinked. "Was."

A chill ran over Alísa, and she rubbed her arms. "Yes. W—why do you want t-t-to know?"

Tenza shook her head. "Allara was my mother's name—"

Alísa's heart skipped a beat, but a quick count silenced her fear. "The Singer Allara died young, about a decade ago."

A deadness took Tenza's eyes. "Ari was named for my mother. Ari is the nickname Namor gave her."

Alísa's heart went cold. First Namor, now...

"Tenza—"

"I had known, deep in my heart, that I would never see her again outside the Maker's Halls," Tenza said softly.

"W—we d—d—don't know that they're the same p-person," Alísa said. "It could be—"

"Tell me about her. Whatever you know."

Alísa swallowed. "I don't think—"

"What did I say about holding back from me?" Tenza's eyes hardened. "What did I tell Briek when he said he wouldn't give the widows closure? Give me closure, Alísa."

Alísa trembled at Tenza's force. She slumped and sighed out a breath.

"I d—don't know much. K-K-K-Koriana told me that Allara learned of her p-powers when she was k-k-kidnapped by dragons. When she learned they expected her t-t-to fight slayers, she sung them to sleep and escaped, killing many of them before going back to her c-clan."

Alísa searched her memory for whatever else Koriana had told her. "Allara's clan feared her p-p-power and t-tried to kill her, but she got away w—with her husband and child. They found a new clan w—willing to let her fight with them. She fought for the slayers for many years, and d—died with honor."

Tenza pulled in a shuddering breath, and sorrow clawed at Alísa's heart.

"You say she had family. Do you know where?"

Alísa shook her head. "I know that the d—dragon who k-k-k-killed her lives in the Prilunes, b—but it's been a decade, and dragons move frequently."

Alísa paused, pondering whether to share more about Paili and her clan. Had Saynan, Faern, or Aree—all from Paili's clan—had anything to do with Allara's death? If Tenza had been mad at her for honoring Namor's killer, how much more her daughter's? Surely if Saynan knew anything about Allara he would have told her by now, even if the others might not.

"That's all I know for sure. I'm s—sorry."

Tenza nodded slowly, her walls going up once more. "I understand. Thank you."

Silence took the room. Alísa fought back her guilt for bringing Tenza more sorrow. She set her hand on Tenza's.

"You know if you ever need anything of me, all you n—need do is ask."

"This *is* what I needed." Tenza's eyes softened, and she placed her other hand on top of Alísa's. "I will be okay."

Alísa didn't fully believe her. The woman had lost her husband and daughter in the span of two days. Still, she doubted Tenza would let her do anything for her.

Tenza glanced at the window and released Alísa's hand. "We should lend our presence to the visit."

'We?' Alísa stared as Tenza rose. "I'll be okay. You don't have to c-c-come out."

"Yes, I do." Tenza reached for the mourning shawl hanging on a peg beside the door. "If I start my day wallowing, I'll never get up."

Alísa pressed her lips together, then spoke carefully. "It's okay to mourn, Tenza."

"I know that." Tenza fixed her with a stare, and Alísa looked down. "I have been and I will continue, but Namor would have continued to stand with you, so now it falls to me. Do not fight me on this—you will not win."

Alísa looked back up at Tenza and the determination in her eyes. Perhaps this was indeed what Tenza needed. She stood.

"Okay. Thank you."

Tenza wrapped the shawl over her shoulders and opened the door, gesturing for Alísa to step outside.

The sunshine instantly warmed Alísa. The square was far emptier than normal—a few people talking with Saynan, plus three children with Sesína. A little girl sat on Sesína's back, grasping to a spine like they were flying. Sesína flapped her wings to aid the illusion, simultaneously sending a gust of wind over two little boys, who flapped their arms like they, too, were flying.

"Faster, Sesína," the girl shouted. "We need to go faster!"

Alísa chuckled, approaching them while Tenza branched off toward Saynan. "Are you chasing someone?"

"No, Miss Alísa," she said matter-of-factly. "He's chasing us."

"Who is?"

"Rorenth. We have to go faster or we'll never beat him!"

Sesína sent apologetic feelings as Alísa fought not to shudder. She had never considered that one day children would play-act moments of her own life, and even if she had, this was too soon. Rorenth's blood-red scales, terrible psychic strength, and flashing jaws ready to consume her were far too frightening to be a game. And yet, how many times had she played similar games based on history songs? How many of those scenes had truly been more horrifying than her young mind could have known?

Alísa let out a quiet breath. "Then you'd better go faster, Sesína."

A new psychic connection entered Alísa's mind. Saynan. *"Singer, the slayer chief is here."*

Alísa twisted. Indeed, Briek was already halfway through the square. He wore plain garb today, no chief's sash or other indication of ranking. His hair was still in the tight scalp-braids and he carried his sword on his hip. He slowed as he neared, wary eyes on Saynan.

Hope flitted through Alísa, but it was dashed just as quickly. Yarlan had seen him first and already headed for him. Options and scenarios ran through Alísa's mind. She could go meet them, but with Yarlan there, she was unlikely to get any meaningful conversation with Briek. She could also just stay here and let Briek see what she and her clan had been up to these past weeks.

The latter seemed a coward's option. Her fear of Yarlan was strong, and it shouldn't be. Koriana would say she should face him. And yet, Alísa knew from experience what the outcome would be—Yarlan would twist whatever she said, and if she allowed her fear of him to claim her, she would lose her words and her voice. It was a battlefield where the odds were sorely against her.

Briek caught her staring, and she lifted a hand in greeting. He returned the gesture, then looked away as Yarlan called for his attention.

Was it cowardly to choose not to put herself in that situation? Her father would face him.

Bria's words flooded Alísa's memory. *I was not made to be my father. There is more than one type of strength.*

Alísa took in a cleansing breath, making herself relax. She would never send her clan to pick fights she knew they couldn't win, not unless there were lives at stake and there was no other option. Perhaps she could apply this principle to herself. There would be times she must speak no matter what, but here, now, was not one of them. She would not hand

Yarlan another victory over her.

"Sesína," the girl on the dragoness' back said. "Don't stop!"

Alísa gave her attention back to Sesína and the children. Sesína had indeed stopped flapping her wings, and the little boys followed suit. Her emerald eyes fixed a curious look on Alísa.

"What's that face for?"

"You would normally make a decision like that with shame written all through it, and I would have to tell you to be brave and dragon-hearted." Sesína's eyes brightened. *"Not this time. Graydonn was right—you are a dragoness."*

The little girl kicked Sesína's sides like a rider would a horse, and Sesína obliged, flapping her wings again with happy contentment flowing through her. Alísa let the feeling fill her and chase away the doubts she already felt about the decision.

"You'll tell me if I retreat when I shouldn't, right?"

Sesína grinned. *"Please. It's me."*

One of the little boys on the ground stopped flapping his arms in the wind. "Are you growling at the bad dragons?"

Sesína closed her lips and looked down at the boy. *"Sorry, no. I was smiling."*

Alísa laughed. "Dragon smiles are different from human smiles, aren't they?"

The boy bared his teeth in an approximation of Sesína's grin, making the other boy laugh.

"It's like I said," Yarlan's voice came.

Alísa tensed and looked in his direction. He walked beside Briek and gestured to Sesína with a scowl.

"Look how they imitate the dragon, and how she just bared her fangs at them. We must put a stop to this!"

"Sorry, Alísa." Sesína drooped her head. *"I gave him that opening. You've told me so many times not to grin."*

Briek looked from Yarlan to Sesína to Alísa, a warrior's caution in his eyes. Alísa swallowed. This is what she had decided, to let Yarlan spew his poison without her there. Perhaps she had made the wrong call. Should she say something now? Briek couldn't know that Sesína's tooth-baring was actually a smile.

Just that. No more.

She breathed in preparation to speak, but the slayer chief placed his hand over his heart before she could.

"Dragon Singer."

Alísa stared at him in shock before returning the gesture. "B—Briek. Good morning."

Yarlan looked just as surprised as she felt, his eyes flitting between them before narrowing into their typical glare.

"I would speak with you when you are able." Briek's gaze wandered to Sesína as she pawed the ground in happiness. He neither scowled nor smiled. "In private. When do you anticipate this visit ending?"

Alísa glanced at the sun's position. "The d—dragons tend to stay until about lunch t-t-time. B—but I am available now. W—where do—"

Yarlan jumped in. "The rules of the compromise require you to stay until the dragons are gone, girl. Even if they didn't, I will not leave my people alone with them."

Briek's expression turned long-suffering. "We can wait until the visit is over, but I do not see what your availability has to do with anything, Yarlan. I said I would speak to her in private."

Yarlan's jaw worked. "With all due respect, Briek, the girl's words are honey-coated hemlock. You would do well to have someone beside you who already knows her ways."

Briek looked Yarlan in the eye. "I may be new to chiefdom, but I am no child. I have heard what you have to say and will give it what consideration it deserves, but I will speak with the Dragon Singer alone."

Sesína's glee blasted through the bond and made Alísa dizzy. *"He told off Yarlan! I love him!"*

Yarlan scowled and clenched his fists when his gaze landed on Alísa and saw her fighting back a smile.

"Then I will pray Branni gives you a warrior's wisdom, Chief Briek." Yarlan threw his hand over his chest.

Briek's lips twitched. "I appreciate that."

Drawing himself taller, Yarlan gave Alísa one last glare and walked away. Breaths came more easily with him gone—even Sesína's delight hadn't fully chased the fear away. Would she ever conquer that fear?

"Is he always so insufferable?"

Alísa tried to spin her answer with humor. "S—sometimes he's worse."

Briek's expression turned thoughtful, and he said nothing, leaving Alísa unsure whether or not she had succeeded.

Sesína came up alongside her, making Briek flinch ever so slightly. *"Tara can't get down."*

Alísa smiled and reached for the girl. "Done flying, then? Did you win?"

Tara pouted as Alísa eased her down to the ground. "Sesína said we did, but it went too fast."

Sesína winked at Alísa, then put her snout in front of Tara. *"Real flight combat goes even faster. You were an excellent rider!"*

Tara beamed and the boys ran up to Sesína, claiming that it was their turn to ride.

"I'm sorry, but we dragons need to go for now. Maybe we can play again tomorrow."

The children groaned their disappointment, while Alísa quirked a brow at the dragoness. *"You have to go? There's still an hour until lunchtime."*

Sesína winked again. *"Yes, but you have a conversation with Briek, and he just sent Yarlan away. There's no way I'm making you wait, whatever it is. I told Saynan."*

Sure enough, as Alísa looked out at the rest of the square, the people were leaving and Saynan was standing up. Briek, too, watched the movement.

"What's going on?"

"The d—dragons are going home. They want us to t-t-t-talk."

"Ah yes." Briek fixed his eyes on Sesína as she trotted to join Saynan. Disbelief ran through his tone. "The dragons who like slayers."

Alísa shook her head. "The d—d—dragons who know that evil and innocence live in b—both races."

Briek did not respond. They watched as the dragons stretched their wings to warm up the muscles. When only humans remained on the ground, Briek gave his attention back to Alísa.

"Is there somewhere we can go?"

Alísa indicated the forest. "Walk with me?"

Briek nodded his assent, and they headed west. He walked quietly beside her, following as she turned off the path to his camp and angled more toward Twi-Peak. Alísa waited for him to speak, gathering from his expression that Briek needed to weigh his words.

"A few of my men think me a fool for coming to you today," he finally said. "They say your coming to us was only a ploy to garner favor. They think I'm walking into your trap."

She scanned the ground. "W—what do you think?"

"I'm not sure." He stepped over a fallen sapling and waited as Alísa lifted her skirt to do the same. "What I do know is that Yarlan's claim that you care only for dragons is not true. In battle, you protected the people. At the meeting of the elders, you were respectful even when others were not. Rassím told me you have been serving and healing alongside the holders."

Briek smirked. "Add to all of this that you have not allowed your dragons to eat Yarlan..."

Alísa chuckled despite herself. "They've never asked."

He laughed too, a low hum of mirth. "Even so, your actions have proven you, Dragon Singer. I think it is only fair I hear what you have to say. You were telling me something about dragons and slayers working together?"

Alísa's heartbeat quickened. A thought knocked at the door to her mind, dancing on the tip of her tongue. She didn't know that Briek or his remaining men could stomach it, but if she finally had her chance, she wouldn't let it pass by.

"The w—war has brought much suffering to our world, to humans and dragons alike. Every day there is more needless d—death of innocents, human and dragon, all b—because each side believes the other incapable of anything but c-c-c-c-cruelty and evil. When I learned that my father's t-t-t-t-teachings weren't t-true, I kn—knew the war had to end."

Her stammer was getting worse as the nerves hit. She could feel it trying to trap her. She desperately wished for Sesína, who could connect her to Briek telepathically. But even if Sesína were here, Briek and his men felt threatened by telepathic speech. Right now, he would only hear her through her voice.

She gestured to the mountain through a gap in the canopy. "My c-c-c-c-clan has p-proven themselves against violent dragons, saving many lives, y—yet when we come to humans and ask for change, we are met only with fear. We need slayers willing t-t-t—to stand by our side and fight to end the war t-t-tearing this world apart. It's the only w—way both races will t-t-take the t-time to listen. We need you and your men."

Calculations ran through Briek's eyes. "We are also needed at the Nissen, to bar the dragons' way east. Though, seeing how many dragons have made it past without our knowledge, I do wonder at Segenn's methods."

"N—Namor has spoken of its deficiencies, and as the d—daughter of a chief, I agree." Alísa paused, weighing her words. "It w—would be better for your men to split up into the villages to bolster their defenses. But even b—better, perhaps, would be to join with me and my dragons for a t-t-time, and bring the war threatening these villages to an end."

Briek breathed a humorless chuckle. "You speak as though it will be easy, ending a centuries-long war."

Alísa looked off into the trees.

"No, it won't be easy." She stopped, and after a couple of steps Briek paused, turning to look back at her. "It t-t-t-takes great courage to f—fight for the innocent on the other side. C—courage in the same vein as defying one's chief to fight for a p-p-p-people he deemed a lost c-cause."

Briek's gaze became distant. "It's a large leap from fighting for humans to fighting for dragons."

"Not when you know them as souls rather than the face of the enemy." Alísa stepped forward, drawing Briek's eyes back to her. In them she saw the smallest flicker of belief. It caught in her heart and ignited hope inside her. "I have found c-c-courageous dragons, Briek, who have fought and d—d—died for humankind. I need courageous humans w—willing to stand with them."

Alísa reached out her hand. "It won't be easy. But it will be right."

Briek looked at her hand, considering. A corner of his lips quirked, and he shook his head.

"I understand now, why Yarlan doesn't let you speak. If he did, you might have won the entirety of the east to your side already." Briek clasped her arm. "I cannot promise all of my clan will follow me, but I'm willing to try."

Alísa's heart soared into the clouds. His statement about winning the east wasn't true—there were plenty of people in Me'ran and elsewhere who would stand against her even without Yarlan as their mouthpiece—but even still, they breathed life into her. She grinned, aware it wasn't very chief-like, but unable to hold it back, especially as Sesína's glee flooded into her.

She had her slayers.

23

THE STABLE

Selene shut the Hold door behind her and leaned against the strong wooden wall. She closed her eyes and let the silence of the outdoors wash over her. Though many of the wounded had moved back home, a few remained, and they and their families were a constant source of sound and light. Outside wasn't truly silent, but the wisps of green wind and the soft yellows and oranges of the birds were a comforting break from the bright lights of anxious, pained, or forcibly-happy human voices.

For a couple of blissful minutes, she let her other, underused senses take over. She ran her fingers over the wood panels and felt their weathered grooves. She pressed the toes of her boots into the soft dirt here at the edge of her mother's garden. She breathed in the warm life of summer and tasted the pollen on the wind. All that was missing was the weight of Tawny's bag over her shoulder and his empathy mists

Her heart held a strange, full ache. A week ago, the tawny egg was only a curiosity. Now, as their bond grew, she found herself thinking of him more and more. But right now—with tensions high and slayers running about—the safest place for Tawny was in the warmth of the Hold's oven. It had felt wrong to put him there the first time, but Koriana had assured her the heat would be perfect, and the light purple mists that had risen as Selene slid him inside confirmed it.

One of the Hold horses nickered in the stable, bringing a new wave of blue sound-light behind her eyelids. She smiled at the greeting.

"All right, I'm coming."

Selene headed for the stable. Grabbing a bucket hanging on the outer wall, she went to the well and set it on the ground. She took the rope for the drawing bucket in her hands and began lowering it. The sun-heated rope prickled against her fingers, and she closed her eyes to soak in the texture and warmth.

Gentle purple footsteps interrupted her focus. Someone else was out here. She forced her shoulders not to slump and opened her eyes, turning to see who it was.

Selene's heart leapt as cacao brown eyes met hers. Taz. Her beloved's smile shown a brilliant white against his dark skin. She fought to temper her own growing smile, careful in this spot so easily visible to others, and turned back to the well.

"Good morning."

"Morning."

The drawing bucket hit the water's resistance and eased in, becoming heavier. As Selene waited the few seconds for the bucket to fill fully, Taz came up alongside her. His arm nearly brushed hers, just close enough to feel his presence without touching.

"Can I help?"

Selene lifted an eyebrow. "Unimpressed with my weak girl arms?"

"Yes." He grinned. "You obviously need someone to rescue you from this terrible task you've never had to do before in your life."

"My hero."

Smiling, Selene handed him the rope. It gave her a moment to look him over. Falier had said Taz hadn't been wounded in the battle against Segenn's faithful, but Selene hadn't seen him since. He seemed well, despite the glow of tension around his voice-light. He pulled against the rope with no sign of injury. His muscular arms held no new scars from training or battle. His hair had changed since she last saw him—curls still cropped short against his scalp, but now with three shaved lines running from each temple down to the nape of his neck.

Taz pulled the drawing bucket from the well and poured the water into the horses' bucket. He made a few exaggeratedly heavy breaths and set the well-bucket back on its hook. Wiping imaginary sweat from his brow, he leaned against the stone.

"There—wouldn't happen—to be—anyone—in the stable—who could help—would there?"

Selene smiled, knowing the true nature of the question. "Alas, I am alone. Don't worry, kind slayer, I can take it from here—"

"No, no." He wheezed and hauled the filled bucket up from the ground. "Far be it from me to leave a maiden in distress."

Letting up his act, Taz carried the bucket through the stable door, Selene following behind him. She stared at the double-sheath on his back, his two blades—shorter and thinner than the typical slayer's broadsword—crossed in an X. Once, the sight brought fear for his safety, the X becoming a target in her mind. Today, her heart shriveled for a different reason.

Taz was a slayer. He had fought for Me'ran alongside the dragons, but Briek had said not all of them were convinced Alísa's dragons were good.

Was Taz convinced? Could she trust him with Tawny?

Taz poured water into each of the horses' pails, very obviously checking the stalls as though he expected someone to be hiding inside. Selene approached him as he set the now-empty bucket on the straw-strewn ground.

"I told you, we're alone."

He gave an easy smile. "Can't be too careful."

Taz reached for her and Selene stepped in, letting him pull her close and kiss her. She leaned into his strength and warmth, lacing her fingers behind his neck. Oh, how she had missed him.

"We've made it this long," Taz breathed, resting his forehead against hers. "I'd hate to be the one who messed it up."

Her thoughts flitted to Tawny. "Me too."

She let him hold her as worry battered her from both sides. The new questions of Tawny's safety and how he would most certainly affect her and Taz's relationship clashed with more aged fears. Fear that he might die in battle. The question of how long they could go on like this—before seeing each other once a year was no longer enough, or his clan arranged for him to marry a nice empath who could produce more slayers, rather than a normal like her.

"You're thinking too much." Taz looked down at her. "And no, before you ask, I'm not reading your mind. I can tell it's racing."

She reached for banter, something comfortable and familiar. "You love me for it. I think so you don't have to."

"Ouch."

One of the horses blew through its lips, making Selene grin. Taz looked back at it and shook his head.

"You sure we can trust these guys not to tell on us?"

"We have an arrangement, don't worry."

Selene pulled him into one of the guest stalls where they could sit and hide if someone came looking for her. Taz pulled his sword-straps from his shoulders and set the sheathed blades on the ground. They settled against a wall on the clean straw, Taz's arm around her shoulders.

Selene picked up a piece of straw and rubbed it between her fingers. How was she going to feel him out on this? Was now even the time? Tawny was safe in the Hold. Couldn't she just enjoy Taz's presence for now?

"I've missed you so much," he said softly. "I wish I could have come see you yesterday, but we were working all day." Bitterness clouded his deep purple tone with a mustard yellow. "You know, because everyone hates us."

"Not so," she soothed. "They're scared and angry."

Taz took up a handful of straw and dropped it. "Are you?"

Selene let out a breath. "Yes. But I'm not angry with you and those who remain. I know you all fought for us." Taz's eyes remained on the straw, and Selene set a gentle hand on his knee. "How are you?"

His eyes unfocused. She knew that fight—he wanted to run from the question. She squeezed his knee, keeping him in the moment.

Taz sighed. "Not good. Seeing you safe and knowing our families are okay helps, but..."

His breath hitched and he gripped another handful of straw, crushing it in his fist. When he spoke again it was barely above a whisper.

"My clan is gone, Selene. Friends, trainers, my chief." He scoffed. "My chief. I knew he had flaws, but I never—not in a thousand years— would have thought he could give the order he did."

Selene pulled her knees to her chest and said nothing. Segenn did have flaws. His utter arrogance was bad enough, but it made him controlling, too. Gathering the biggest clan he could and leaving villages practically defenseless, taking boys to the front lines before they were ready, dictating who his men could and couldn't marry. The step into killing those he disagreed with didn't seem too far a stretch in her mind. Yet, Taz had lived with him and perhaps seen some good she never had.

"How is everyone?" Taz nodded toward the Hold. "Has anyone else..."

Selene shook her head. "Not since the first night. We think everyone's out of danger now."

"Good."

Selene watched as he started playing with the straw again. "You saw your family, then?"

"Had breakfast with them this morning. It took a lot to get away and come here. Bren thinks I'll be able to stay now."

"Can't you?"

Taz shook his head. "There's no one at the border without us. With only sixteen of us left, Briek won't let any of us go, I'm sure of it."

He wiped his hand on his tunic after dropping the last fistful of straw. "Though, one thing that might change is the rules on marriage. I think Briek might be receptive."

Marriage. A week ago, the thought would have filled her with hope that their love could end in anything besides heartbreak. Now, though, anxiety swept in alongside it. She was bound to a dragon now—would soon be Illuminated to him. If Taz thought they would need to live with the wayfarers, that would be a problem. Even if the slayers warmed to the idea of dragons, they probably wouldn't accept one living with them.

But even in Me'ran, it would only work for so long. Maybe a dragon living among the holders would do something good for the people, but Alísa and her clan would leave someday—how would Tawny do without other dragons around?

"There you go thinking again." A corner of Taz's lips quirked upward. "Not having second thoughts, are you?"

His light-hearted tone was haloed in orange. Worry or fear. Selene leaned into him to reassure him.

"I love you, so much," she said. "It's just—everything's a bit more complicated now."

"You're talking about the dragons?"

She nodded.

"Is everyone truly safe?"

"Yes. Everyone's safe." She turned to face him. He needed to believe this, truly believe this, if she was going to be able to tell him about Tawny. "Falier and I know Alísa and the dragons. I've flown with them, been to their cave, and they've never harmed any of us. We trust them."

"You flew with them?" Taz shook his head in bewilderment. "I saw Falier on one's back in the fight."

"Graydonn," Selene supplied. "Their relationship is the most incredible. All of the other dragons are Falier's friends, but he and Graydonn have a special bond. It's made Falier's telepathy so much stronger—"

"Wait. What?" Taz turned his whole body, pulling his arm from behind her. "Falier has telepathy?"

Selene closed her eyes. Hellflames. Everyone in the village knew that now—it wasn't a secret anymore. Except, the wayfarers didn't know yet, not unless they happened to notice Falier using telepathy during the battle.

"Yes."

Taz ran a hand over his head. "But he was tested. When did you find out?"

Selene sighed. "We found out that day. Kerrik said he wasn't strong enough to last long, so he showed Falier how to hide it and left him behind."

Taz's mouth opened and closed. He searched the ceiling before locking eyes with her again. "And you never told me?"

"Kerrik ordered us not to, and what good would it have done? One slip, and he would have been taken away, or punished for hiding it."

Taz gestured to the stall where they hid. "Oh, and I can't keep a secret?"

Selene glared at him, lowering her voice. "It wasn't my secret to tell. I wasn't going to add to Falier's shame by telling his best friend, who got to do the very thing he wanted to do but couldn't."

Taz gave a sigh that was nearly a growl and faced forward again. He studied the ceiling, shaking his head.

"Do you know how hard those first months were? It was never hard to make friends here, but there?" He gripped at the straw again. "I had to fight for every scrap of respect I could get before anyone would even share a laugh with me. If I could have had my best friend with me—"

"Your best friend would have died," Selene finished. "Or that's what we were told. It crushed Falier to stay while you went, but that's how it had to be."

Taz stared up a moment more, then pulled his legs up to his chest, matching Selene's position. "I still wish you would have told me. Even if he stayed here, it might have given us some common ground."

Or driven you apart. Selene didn't say it out loud, not desiring to continue the argument.

"He's doing better. The dragons have been training him. Thanks to their bond, Falier can also harness Graydonn's telepathy."

"See, that sounds like the dragon could be influencing him."

Selene shook her head. "Nothing has changed in Falier's behavior. No warnings hide in his sound-lights. In fact, the only person whose behavior has changed drastically since Alísa and the dragons came to Me'ran is Namor. Was Namor."

Selene took a slow breath. "But even that wasn't odd, considering. The world is changing here." She took his hand and squeezed. This was what he needed to understand. "But I believe it's changing for the better."

Taz looked down at their hands, but his eyes still seemed unfocused, almost dead. She leaned against him, trying to bring him back, make him stay in the conversation.

"I trust you," he whispered, the words warming her. "You and your intuition have always been right. It's just so strange."

"I know. I'm glad you trust me." Selene took a breath and blew it out. "Because I have another secret to tell you. Don't give me that look— it's only been a secret for a week. I want you to know. I *need* you to know, and to listen with an open mind. Can you do that for me?"

Taz looked almost as scared as she felt. It nearly made her stop, tell him 'never mind,' and change the subject. But she couldn't—she couldn't live in the anxiety of not knowing how he would react.

"I also have a special bond with a dragon."

His eyes went wide, and he sat up straight. "Wha—"

"No. Listen. Please."

Taz silenced himself. His fists closed on his thighs, though he seemed more worried than angry.

She told him everything—the orphaned eggs that had refused to bond with the dragons, the empathy mists she had seen twice, how Tawny had cried for her when he heard her voice, and how even the Dragon Singer hadn't felt what Selene had seen.

"And so, to keep him alive, I chose to bond with him."

Taz just stared at her, saying nothing. He didn't move either, except for the deep breaths of air entering and leaving his lungs. It was unnerving how hard he was to read in this moment.

"Please say something."

Taz opened his mouth and closed it again, his teeth clacking together. The corners of his mouth moved upward, though the smile was less one of happiness and more one of shocked disbelief.

"You see empathy mists?"

Selene blinked. That wasn't what he was supposed to take away from her story. "Yes? I don't know. I see telepathy, which apparently isn't normal..."

Taz rubbed his hands down his face, laughter muffling behind them. "Do you know what this means? You might be a slayer? It would actually make sense, if Falier has telepathy—it is genetic. I wonder if your parents each have just enough..." He shook his head. "Anyway, if that's true, then it doesn't matter what Briek or anyone else thinks. No one can tell us we can't be together!"

Selene shook her head, a smile rising. He was avoiding the harder and more important topic of Tawny, yet where he set his focus made it clear that he didn't consider Tawny a deal-breaker.

"I don't know that's what it is," she admitted, "I don't see empathy mists for anyone else, just Tawny. No, actually, that's not true. I saw Koriana pushing out calm once. I don't know, maybe I am a freakish empath who just sees it all in color."

"Hey." Taz raised an eyebrow. "Don't call my lady freakish."

Selene let out a single, breathy chuckle. His lady. The words settled her anxieties and she reached for his hand.

"Even though she's bonded to a baby dragon?"

"Even so." Taz rubbed his thumb over the back of her hand, his brow furrowing in concern. "Selene, I— Do—do you trust me?"

She scoffed. "What kind of question is that?"

"A serious one."

"Of course, I do. Why?"

"I'm not supposed to ask you what I'm about to. It breaks so many rules. But—would you let me look at the memory of when the egg chose you? So I can be sure they weren't tricking you into this?"

Selene's insides recoiled. Speaking telepathically was one thing, but looking at her memories? Did that include her thoughts in the midst of them? It would have to if he was checking to see if she was being influenced.

"I thought you said you trusted my intuition."

"I do," he said hurriedly. "I do, I just— Please." He squeezed her hand. "Please. I love you so much and I just need to be sure. I need to know you're safe."

Everything in his posture, expression, and voice spoke of genuineness. He hated asking her this, but couldn't live with himself if he didn't do it and missed her being harmed. The thought of him seeing everything still frightened her, but so did the idea that he might worry incessantly without it. She didn't know how her life would work with Tawny around, but she did know that she desperately still wanted Taz to be a part of it.

"Okay. Just that memory."

Relief washed over his face. "I swear it."

He kept her hand in his and moved his free hand to her temple. "Relax and keep your eyes open."

"That seems counter-intuitive."

His lips quirked. "Just try."

Taz's eyes hardened with concentration. She flinched as his telepathy light shot to her head, but recovered quickly. The buzz of his telepathic connection was familiar, just like when she spoke with the

281

dragons. Then it sharpened to a high whirring as he delved in. She recoiled, then forced the tension out of her body, relaxing her shoulders and loosening her grip on Taz's hand.

"*I'm sorry,*" he soothed. "*I know that was painful. That should be the worst of it.*"

Images of the last few days flashed through her mind until he came to the right memory. There he slowed, and they watched everything play out just as it had before. Taz marveled at the strings of telepathy and Tawny's cloud of sorrow, and Selene felt his mind flinch as dragon faces came close to her.

"*I used to fear them, too,*" she said, trying to focus on the memory and not the sensation of her mind being stretched out beyond her skull. "*I don't anymore.*"

"*I can see that,*" he said, wonder in his tone.

When the memory ended, Taz pulled his presence back. Selene's breathing came more easily, and she let out a sigh that released her tension. She closed her eyes and let them rest.

"Did you find what you were looking for?"

Taz was silent for a moment. "Yes."

His soft tone made her open her eyes. She stared. A blend of orange and magenta, just barely there, glowed around him, like the cloud of sorrow that had surrounded Tawny. Fear and love. She blinked twice, and it disappeared.

"I found you," he said. Leaning closer, he kissed her lightly. "Just you, in all your self-sacrificial beauty."

"Then—you're okay with this?"

"I don't understand it. I don't even know that I like it." He blew out a breath. "But I know that it was your choice, and you weren't coerced. Not unless the Singer girl has some master plan and used the dragons' varied reactions to manipulate your choice. I think the sound-lights would have alerted you to that, though."

Selene almost snorted. "Alísa's too genuine to be a master manipulator. She's wholly herself."

Taz squinted in thought, eyes on the wall behind Selene. "I guess that answers another question, about her stunt yesterday."

"Stunt?"

"She came to the funeral last night." He leaned back against the wall. "Briek and a few others saw it as an honor, but others were upset, saying she was using our grief to manipulate us."

"She went to you? Alone?"

"Well, one of the scouts sensed a dragon somewhere nearby, but it never came into view. Why? Is that odd?"

"I would have expected her to bring Falier with her, but he was here all night."

Taz hummed. "Falier likes her, I take it?"

Selene couldn't help but grin. "He's fallen so hard. Asked to pursue her after knowing her for a month. Well, knowing her secrets for a month—we had technically met her earlier."

Taz whistled low. "And you're all okay with that?"

"It's hard, thinking that he'll be leaving with her when she heads back west—"

Come to think of it, would Selene go with them now? Tawny was just an egg, would be just a baby, and she didn't have the telepathy that would be helpful when riding a dragon into battle. Questions for a later time.

"—but we like her, and Falier is so much more alive with her and the dragons. It's where he belongs."

"West." Taz gazed out one of the stable windows. "What's her plan?"

"Gather a clan of dragons and slayers, then go try and stop the fighting."

"And you think she can do that?"

"She's already led dragons to fight for humans against their own kind." She took his hand and squeezed it. "If she can do that, maybe she can get through to you stubborn slayers, too."

Taz snorted. "Convincing a few individuals is one thing. Stopping a war is different."

"True. But individuals shape their clans, and clans fight the war." Selene scooted closer to him, straw scraping along the ground with her. "Can you imagine? A world without the war? Where you had a choice where to live, what to do with your life?"

"Who to marry?" Taz smiled, opening his arm to her so she could snuggle up against him. "I would like that. Sneaking around is fun and all, but I don't think we can sneak into marriage." He kissed her forehead, then grinned mischievously. "But I do hear that sneaking off to be alone is more fun after."

"Taz, please. You'll make the horses blush."

He chuckled, his low tone filling Selene with warmth. She closed her eyes and savored his closeness. To never have to separate again. Falier had once bemoaned that Alísa lived up in the mountain and he had to wait on the dragons to get to see her again the next day. He had no idea how good he had it, when she and Taz had maybe one week per year to steal moments like this.

"So." Taz's voice held tension. "A baby dragon. How long until it hatches?"

"Two weeks." She traced one of the flowers on her skirt with a finger. "I'm not scared, but I'm nervous."

He kissed her temple. "You'll be the best dragon ma ever."

Selene swallowed her emotion. "And you're okay with this?"

Taz grasped her hand, stilling it. "No dragon could ever take away my love for you."

"You miss the spirit of my question."

He shrugged and pulled her hand to his lips. "I thought it was a good answer."

Selene gave him a coy smile as he kissed her knuckles. "It was—decent."

A rhythmic pulse of purple filled the upper-right corner of Selene's vision. The sound itself became clear quickly. Footfalls, coming fast up the hill. Not rare, but abnormal enough to pique curiosity, especially after the last few days.

Selene pulled her hand from Taz's and stood, getting up on tiptoes to look out the window. She could just barely see the top of someone's head as they came up.

Alísa? Why was she running?

"What's happening?"

"Alísa's coming." She pivoted and went for the stall door. "I'm going to see what's going on."

"You're just going to leave me, after that fantastic line?"

Selene grinned as she passed him. "If I'm not back in fifteen, come to the Hold. Everyone else will want to see you too, anyway."

Taz gave another half-hearted protest as Selene passed through the stable door. Alísa's footsteps slowed as she crested the hill.

"Falier! Falier!" Alísa saw Selene and angled toward her. "W— where's Falier?"

Alísa's frantic question would have worried Selene if it weren't for the sound-lights shouting her happiness.

"Inside?" Selene thought a second. "Or maybe at the dancing grounds—Graydonn's there. What's going on?"

Alísa beamed at her. "Thank you! I'll t-t-tell you, but—"

"Líse?" Falier ran around the corner of the Hold, Graydonn awkwardly trotting behind him. "What—"

Alísa squealed and leapt at Falier, wrapping her arms around his chest. "He said yes! He said yes!"

Falier's brow furrowed with confusion, but his smile was amused. "I can't keep up with you, Líse. What's going on?"

"B—Briek!" Alísa pulled back, gripping his forearms. "Oh, I have so much to t-t-tell you. Bria and Allara and the s—slayers' funeral—but Briek said yes!"

"Bria—" Falier shook his head. "Yes to what?"

"I t-told him about my hope for d—dragons and slayers c-c-coming together to end the war, and he agreed to try!"

The confusion melted from Falier's face, replaced with elation. "You did it. You did it!"

Laughing, he lifted Alísa and spun her around. The love in his eyes, his voice, his embrace as he set Alísa back down, made Selene smile. But then they kissed, and Selene's older sister mind wouldn't be held back. She counted to five, then smirked and held her hands up.

"All right, all right, no need to traumatize Graydonn, or me."

Graydonn cocked his head. *"I take it that's normally done in private, then?"*

Falier rolled his eyes at Selene. "No, just not in front of prudish sisters." He looked to Alísa, his smile returning. "So, what happened? When did you talk to him?"

"This morning," Alísa said. "He p-pulled me aside, t-t-told Yarlan to leave us alone, and listened. He really listened, and he w—wants to give p-p-partnership a t-try."

"That's fantastic!"

A dragon's trumpet resounded above them. *"Isn't it?"*

Sesína banked over the Hold, coming in for a heavy landing that shook the ground. Sesína shifted from one paw to the other in a happy dance as Alísa ran to her. The girl wrapped her arms around the scaly neck, while Sesína wrapped her wings over the top.

Selene glanced at the stable beyond Sesína. Had Taz been listening? What was he thinking right now?

"So what's next?" Graydonn asked.

Alísa pulled from Sesína's embrace. "Briek is talking to his men today. He said he'll encourage all of them t-t-t-to t-try, but he won't force them. Still, he said there w—was a good chance at least half of them will c-c-come to meet the dragons. I n—need to get to the c-c-cave to let the rest of the clan know. Today, we celebrate!"

"Then what are we waiting for?" Falier grasped one of Graydonn's spines while the dragon's eyes brightened. "Let's get up there!"

Graydonn trumpeted his agreement as Falier pulled himself up. Their excitement was contagious, bringing a smile to Selene's lips. A large part of her tugged toward the mountain, surprisingly strong in the midst of her uncertainty about the future.

Falier looked at her. "You're coming with us, right?"

Selene grinned. "Can I?"

"You and Tawny are family. Clanmates." Graydonn stepped toward her, and Selene noticed that Falier was sitting one spine back from where he normally did. *"I can carry two, especially when one is as light as you. The distance isn't far."*

The declaration of her as a clanmate brought both uncertainty and joy. Selene decided to let joy win in this moment.

"G—go get Tawny," Alísa said. "We'll wait."

Selene turned to the Hold, then stopped. "Just a second. I ran out so quickly, I didn't finish feeding the horses. I'll be fast!"

Without waiting for acknowledgement, Selene ran into the stable and shut the door behind her. Taz waited just behind the door.

"You heard all of that?"

"Yes." Taz whispered back. "Dragons and slayers. I really don't know about this."

Selene went to him, cupping his cheek. "I know it's strange and new. Will you try? For me?"

He gave a weak smile. "For you."

The trepidation in him was worse than what she felt when Graydonn called her a clanmate, but that meant, in this moment, his bravery was greater than hers too. And she loved him for it. She kissed him again—slower, lingering, yet not enough.

"I'm going with them," she whispered.

"I know. Be safe. I'll finish up in here."

"Don't get caught."

"Don't worry," he chuckled, running a hand over his hair. "I'd rather face a dragon than an angry Parsen."

Selene shook her head, blew him a kiss, and slipped outside.

24

TRUE COLORS

The thudding of Alísa's heart danced between excitement and anxiety the morning of the first meeting of dragons and slayers. She hurried through her chores for the Hold and let everyone know what would happen in the square in a few hours. No surprises, not after the last few days.

Word spread rapidly, thanks to the holders and Tenza, bringing with it a mixture of encouraging words and hateful glares. Alísa wished there were a better place for this meeting, but the nearest clearing where the dragons could land and feel safe with sky above them would be over two hours' ride on horseback for the slayers.

When the sun crested the treetops to shine on the square, Alísa reached out to Sesína. The slayers would be here soon.

Falier took her hand, eyes dancing with delight. "You ready?"

"Yes. Thank you for b—being here. Both of you." Alísa leaned around Falier to look at Selene. "How's Tawny this morning? Any signs?"

Selene shook her head. "Nothing unusual. He now understands that oven time means we'll be apart for a while. He squeaked pitifully at me this morning."

"Aw. Poor thing."

"I couldn't very well bring him here. Not this first day, anyway."

Alísa nodded. Iila, Blue, and Saynan and Aree's egg would similarly all stay in the cave today, supervised by Rayna and Korin.

Colorful shapes swirled in the sky above the mountain. Rather than traveling a straight line to the village, Saynan and Koriana led them through aerial patterns. Guided by the clan's mind-link, dragons swooped and dove, banking and twisting around each other in a dance of camaraderie. Alísa had ridden Sesína in that dance a few times now, each time marveling at how close the dragons came to each other without colliding. It was a clan-builder, a show of solidarity, and beautiful even this far away.

"We'll have a time fitting them all in here," Tenza spoke behind her.

Alísa glanced around. Many people had stopped to stare into the sky, while others retreated indoors. A few of the shops had even closed.

At a high-pitched trumpet from Koriana, the dragons ended their dance and turned to the village. In their elation, they sped down the mountainside. Alísa could almost feel the wind whipping around her as Sesína's joy spilled through the bond.

Alísa reached for the clan-link. *Slow down before you get to the village. I know your joy, but you look like you're on the warpath.*

Acknowledgements flowed back to her, raising a gentle smile to her lips. The dragons split off, some banking around the village to come down at a different angle, while others slowed to land. Koriana set feet on the ground first, her landing almost a whisper. Sesína followed behind, talons skidding in the dirt and flinging dust into the air as she slid past Alísa, wings outstretched to slow herself. A few children giggled as they watched her, one running to ask her to play.

Sesína poked the boy's arm with her nose. *Not this morning, sorry. Let's back up so the others can land.*

People backed into shops and alleyways between houses as more dragons landed. Some whispered to each other conspiratorially, others watched with eyes wide with wonder. Dueling emotions rose from them, but the dragons' overpowered them in Alísa's mind. The clan was as ready as they could be. Some still held reservations about working closely with slayers, preferring non-aggression pacts to alliances, but with the help of her betas and the human-dragon bonds within the clan, they were willing to try. If the slayers came with the same mindset, this would work.

Alísa stepped into the midst of the dragons, directing the smaller ones into spaces between houses to make room for the larger ones. She made sure to select the homes of people favorable toward her and the dragons—no sense in further frightening those who still feared them.

"And now your true colors are revealed."

Alísa's heartbeat quickened as she spun to see Yarlan storming closer. Graydonn came out of his alleyway to stand beside her, irritation prickling from him. Across the way, Alísa felt more than heard Sesína growl, while the adult dragons nearest her pinned eyes hot with fire on him. She should have felt safe, but trepidation sped through her.

Yarlan stopped ten feet away, his voice loud for his people. "You break the compromise, and bring warring factions into Me'ran after bringing such sorrow to us!" He spat on the ground at her feet. "Maker judge you for what you have done."

Emotions swirled through Alísa—anger, guilt, fear, sorrow—each grasping at her throat.

But I don't need to respond, she told herself. *I don't need to defend myself—as Briek said, I can let my actions then and now speak for me.*

Alísa lifted her eyes from Yarlan's boots—chiding herself for letting them slide there in the first place—and looked him in the eyes. Her heart trembled at the fury there, so she reached for memories—children playing with Sesína, defending Me'ran in the skies from other dragon clans, Tawny and Selene, Briek. They settled her racing heart and pushed her past the pain. Then she saw Yarlan's wife and sons far behind him, frozen at the sight of the dragons, and her compassion stirred.

"You need a p-p-p-path to the dragon shelter."

Yarlan's fury wavered only a moment, but it was enough to give Alísa confirmation. She turned away from him and reached for the clan-link.

"Everyone, move away from the stone building."

The dragons did as she said, squishing into the eastern end of the square.

Alísa looked at Yarlan over her shoulder. "If you fear d—dragon-fire, Falier and Selene c-c-c-can escort them."

Then she walked into the gathering of dragons—partially to signal to Yarlan that the conversation was over, and partially to calm her own nerves. Did other chiefs and alphas do this? Choose actions that displayed confidence but truly just covered their fears and insecurities?

And there I go comparing myself again.

She glanced between her dragons to see Yarlan leading his family into the shelter, his hand on the hilt of his sword and his eyes everywhere. He hadn't accepted either holder as an escort, though Alísa hadn't expected him to. His wife held the hands of both of their sons, her eyes straight ahead. Alísa had never spoken with Yarlan's family. She didn't even know their names, so careful Yarlan was to keep them away. Did they harbor the same resentment toward Alísa and the dragons?

"Slayers approach," Graydonn said, pointing his muzzle westward.

Alísa checked on Yarlan and his family. Yarlan pushed the door to the dragon shelter shut from the outside. Alísa pressed her lips together. It was too much to wish that he would go in as well. Instead, he marched to the butcher's shop and started a conversation with those inside.

Maker, give me strength while he's here.

Alísa looked to the dragons. *"Thank you—you may go back to your positions."*

The dragons spread back out, forming two groups on the northern and southern sides of the square. They settled to their bellies, every head high and alert.

Tenza, Selene, and Falier approached Alísa to help greet the slayers. Further back, a few people emerged from their homes, apparently curious, while others retreated up the hill toward the Hold, the furthest one could get from the square.

Sesína's voice echoed through the clan's mind-link. *"There they are!"*

Alísa set her eyes on the path to the wayfarers' camp. Briek led his men from the shadows of the forest. They dressed in the same manner her father's clan did when entering a village for the first time—light traveling clothes underneath leather armor, each with their weapons strapped on. The look spoke 'warrior' without threatening a march into battle.

The range of weaponry they carried impressed Alísa. Karn's clan carried mostly broadswords, spears, and the occasional bow and arrow. While some of Briek's men carried a broadsword, many carried different weapons. In addition to Rassím's throwing knives and Taz's twin single-edged swords, three men carried javelins in quivers, and two had crossbows hanging opposite their swords. Many of them also had shields strapped to their backs.

Alísa fought not to place a hand on the hilt of her own sword. As with any meeting of two warrior clans, this was a precaution and a display of strength. Out of the corner of her eye, she saw a couple of shopkeepers leave. Were they afraid a fight would break out? None of the slayers had weapons drawn, nor did any display malice in their gaze or posture.

She counted the slayers. Nine of the remaining sixteen had come, including Briek, and a few looked like they regretted it as soon as their eyes landed on the dragons.

Glancing at Falier and the others with her, Alísa quickened her pace and gave the warmest smile she could manage.

"W—welcome!" She clasped Briek's arm. "Thank you for c-c-coming. All of you."

Briek's gaze flitted to the dragons, then back to her. "Thank you, Dragon Singer."

"Singer!"

Alísa started, twisting at the sound of many tiny wings. Laen, Rann, Ska, and many other dreki flew into the square. Alísa grinned as they twirled around her, catching glimpses of Rís and baby Chrí on Rann and Laen's backs.

"You're here t-too!"

The dreki chittered happy replies as they scattered, fluttering to perches among Alísa's clan. Whispers rose from the slayers, though one carried above the rest.

"Fairy folk? Can we trust them?"

Taz laughed. "These ones, yes. The clan has been friends with Me'ran for years." He elbowed a man next to him. "Told you I'd seen them up close before."

Falier stepped past Alísa, moving in to give Taz a rough embrace. Ska flared his wings as he tried to hold onto Falier's shoulder, making one slayer step back in response.

"It's good to see you here," Falier said.

Alísa smiled to see him next to his childhood friend. Falier had told her stories of them growing up together, and of the pain of separation. She looked to Briek again.

"You told them about t-t-t-telepathy?"

Briek nodded. "They will allow the dragons to speak to them."

"Good. I'll ask the dragons to introduce themselves now."

Briek understood her meaning, turning to tell his men to lower their mental shields. Alísa opened her mind wide as he spoke. The slayers were harder to feel in the presence of dragons, but still she found their trepidation, excitement, and loyalty. Nothing dangerous, though she would keep checking throughout the morning.

Alísa reached out to the clan. *"It's time. This will probably be awkward, but remember, you have more experience with humans than they do with dragons. Do your best. Sesína"* —Alísa looked at Briek— *"connect us, please."*

Sesína's excitement bubbled up as she reached out with her telepathy, bringing Briek and his men into the conversation. Some of the slayers flinched. The buzz of a couple minds disappeared as they instinctively cut themselves off, but they quickly returned.

"Thank you," Alísa said through the mind-link. *"I know this is odd, but you'll get used to it. These are my clan, dragons who have fought to protect humans from other dragons and have befriended many villagers here."*

She gestured to each dragon in turn, introducing them by name. She also introduced Falier, Selene, and Tenza, for those who didn't know them.

When she finished, she looked back to Briek, only to be barked at by the dreki. Laen fluttered from Selene's shoulder to hover in front of Alísa. The emerald drek growled a command.

"Dreki."

"Uh, yes. Sorry."

Alísa gestured to each of the seventeen present dreki, rattling off the names she knew and looking to Laen for support for those she didn't. Selene stifled a laugh as Laen barked her annoyance, while humor rose from some of the dragons. Even a couple of the slayers—Taz especially— seemed amused.

Finally, when Laen was satisfied, she rushed back to Selene's shoulder and chirped happily.

"Clan!" The image that appeared with the word included all those Alísa had introduced—dragons, humans, and dreki.

Alísa blinked. Was Laen saying these dreki considered themselves of her clan now?

Briek chuckled. "That's quite a family you have."

His eyes flitted to the side, then back. Alísa followed his gaze. Yarlan. He had moved, coming out of someone's home, the occupants following with wary eyes on the dragons. Odd. Fewer people remained in the square now.

"*Sesína*," Alísa whispered, "*keep an eye on him.*"

"*You've got it,*" she growled.

Briek began introducing his men. Alísa did her best to commit the names to memory, but knew she would have to lean on Falier and Selene for help. Two weeks as a holder did nothing to help her name-memorization skills. If only human names were like dragons' and dreki's, echoing through the mind whenever they spoke.

"*It's a pleasure to meet all of you,*" Alísa said. "*For the past few weeks, the dragons have been coming to the village to get to know the people. Rather than ask you to try training with souls you don't yet know, I would like to do something similar with you today. Meet each other, ask questions. You'll find we have more in common than we ever thought.*"

"And those things we don't have in common make for fascinating conversation." Falier walked up with Taz, a few more slayers following behind them. "Or comical faux pas."

Graydonn thrummed. "*Indeed.*"

As Falier led Taz to Graydonn and Koriana's group, Alísa motioned for Briek to come with her, heading for Sesína and Saynan. This would be challenging, getting warriors to participate in a meet-and-greet. It probably would have been easier to tell them they would be riding today and just go for it, but she wasn't ready to trust her dragons' backs to them. This plan would give both clans the chance to feel each other out before requiring them to entrust their lives to each other.

Having already planned with Saynan, Alísa tried a conversation-starter. "*I had never seen a white dragon in-person before I met Saynan. Did you know they breathe burning cold instead of fire?*"

Multiple of the men shook their heads, one grunting in mild interest.

"Actually, I did."

The voice made Alísa's heart stutter. Rassím. She forced herself to relax. Since saving her life in the battle, he had done nothing to make her distrust him. She needed to get past the eyes of hatred and the knife at her throat.

"Ice dragons are far more common in the Southlands than here in the north," Rassím said. "Less aggressive than fire dragons as well. Err, in my experience."

He shrank slightly, as though afraid he had offended the dragons. Alísa relaxed a bit more.

"Yes," Saynan said. "My kin tend toward pacifism, even complacency. It is one reason I left them to join a clan of fire dragons. Not to fight humans, mind you, but to be among others I could possibly help." His eyes brightened as he looked to Aree. "Of course, it wasn't completely altruistic. I did have my eye on a beautiful dragoness."

Conversation began to flow, though stunted and awkward at times. As it did, Alísa watched, taking in body-language and tasting emotions. She searched for warning signs as well as connections that might make for a good dragon-rider pairing. Per Alísa's request, Tenza, Selene, and Falier would all do the same. Though she might ask the dragons for their opinions later, there was no sense in doing so ahead of time. They would already be critical, facing men who had likely killed many dragons.

In the background, Alísa and Sesína both noticed multiple families making their way up to the Hold. Within fifteen minutes, the only souls left in the square were slayers, dragons, and dreki. Shops were closed and even Yarlan had disappeared. Relief should have filled Alísa at the realization, but something pinched in her stomach.

Was everyone at the Hold? What was going on?

Laughter bubbled up from Falier and Selene's group. Alísa had to stay present. Her own group was slowly relaxing. After two hours, the trepidation had mostly faded into wariness. The two clans knew they weren't going to attack each other, and that was a good outcome.

When Briek and his men had disappeared on the path back to camp—all but Taz, who stayed with Falier and Selene—Alísa thanked the dragons and dreki.

"You did so well. Briek told me he and his men would take tomorrow to *discuss with the rest of the clan, then they will return the following morning. We'll start some riding training then, but take it slow, as you and they feel comfortable."*

Movement on the path to the Hold drew Alísa's eyes. People were returning, and some of them did not look happy as they looked out over the square still full of dragons. She needed to get up to the Hold and ask Parsen what had happened.

"You're dismissed for the day. Harenn—hunting duty. Komi and Faern—scouting. The rest of you are free. Thank you again."

Tails thumped the ground and acknowledgements ran through the clan-link. The wind of their wings filled the square as they launched—Sesína and Graydonn the only dragons to stay.

"Home?" An image of Twi-Peak flashed through Alísa's mind from Rann as the drek settled on her shoulder. Little Rís whimpered from his back, the sound tickling in Alísa's ear.

Alísa tried to look at Rann, but couldn't quite focus with his face so close to hers. *"Yes, that's our home."* She looked to Laen still on Selene's shoulder, remembering the emerald drek's declaration. *"Do you want to live with us now? Are we your clan?"*

Laen and Rann both trilled. *"Clan!"*

"What happened?" Alísa pressed her lips together, hoping that the question wasn't rude.

Rann sent an image of two trees growing from the same root system, one with lavender growing beside it.

Laen nuzzled Selene's cheek. *"Clan."*

Alísa nodded solemnly. *"All right, then. Sesína, can you still reach Koriana telepathically?"*

Sesína squinted at the mountain and the dragons still on their way. *"Barely."*

"Tell her to expect dreki company. They'll be living with us now."

Sesína pawed the ground, relaying the message as dreki on the rooftops chirped excitedly. Alísa stroked Rann's head with a finger.

"Go on, then." She looked to the people still filing down from the Hold. *"I'll be up in a little bit."*

The flutter of wings filled the air as the dreki rose. They gathered, spinning around each other in happiness before spearing off to follow the dragons.

"*Well,*" Falier said, "*that's new.*"

"*Indeed.*" Alísa pressed the bandage on her arm, watching the dreki disappear in the distance. "*Did you notice the people heading for the Hold?*"

"Yes," Selene said.

Falier looked to the path. "*What do you suppose...*"

"Is anyone else disconcerted by mouths not moving?" Taz looked to Selene and Tenza. "No? Just me?"

"You get used to it," Selene said.

"We should see what's happened," Tenza said, making for the Hold.

Alísa followed, the other humans joining her and the dragons taking up the rear. Falier came up beside her and gestured behind him.

"I'm sure you've already figured it out, but this is Taz."

Alísa looked back at the young man, choosing verbal speech for his comfort. "G—good to meet you. Thank you for c-c-c-coming today."

Taz grinned. "There was no way I was going to just wait to hear how it went. Falier and Selene both vouched for you and the dragons, so something good must be happening here."

Falier looked back at Selene. "When did you vouch for the dragons to him?"

Taz cut in, poking Falier in the arm. "Here's a better question—since when are you a telepath?"

The psychic world distracted Alísa from the answer. They walked the path to the Hold now, discord all around as villagers passed. Anger and fear lived in some, many of them individuals Alísa already knew opposed the dragons. Even those who gave polite smiles to her and the dragons as they passed, though, held tension and strife.

"Taz!" A twelve-year-old boy with dark skin matching Taz's ran from the Hold, his parents walking behind him. "Did you meet them?"

Alísa came to a halt with Falier, Selene, Taz, and the dragons—Tenza continuing on the path. Taz looked back at Sesína and Graydonn, who stood directly behind him, then back to the boy.

"Nope. I have no idea why everyone has been talking about dragons. Haven't seen one since I got here."

The boy gave a long-suffering look. "I mean all of them. Are you going to ride one?"

Alísa smiled. This must be Taz's brother.

"Yarlan's coming," Sesína warned.

Alísa glanced at the slayer coming down the path, then returned to Taz and his brother. He was just another angry face she wasn't going to convince. At least Taz seemed receptive.

"Uh," Taz looked at Alísa and back. "I don't know. If she says so, I guess?"

"Ignoring me now, witch?"

Alísa gasped as Yarlan yanked her around by her hurt arm, fingers crushing around the bandage. He pulled her close enough to see her reflection in his crazed eyes. Hatred spilled from him, more than she had ever felt from him before, as though he had let down his psychic shield just to make sure she felt it.

"You will regret what you've done here!"

Sesína snarled, suddenly beside Alísa. *"I've had enough of you!"*

She grabbed his arm in her jaws and blew scalding air over it. Yarlan let go of Alísa with a shout of pain and reached for his sword with his free hand. Sesína let go too, arching her neck low.

"Try it!"

Alísa fell back two steps, holding her throbbing arm. Falier, Graydonn, and Selene were suddenly there as well, Taz standing in shocked stillness. Alísa's heart raced. Even at his angriest, Yarlan had never touched her before.

"You have torn this village apart," Yarlan snarled. He stepped back with his hand on the hilt of his sword, as though to draw it.

"Yarlan!" Taz's father called from up the path. Multiple people stood with him. "You have lost—do not embarrass yourself further."

"And what does that mean for the rest of us?" another man retorted. "He is not the only one who wants them gone."

"Abide by the word of the elders." Parsen came up from behind, Kat with him. "We have decided in the same manner we do everything. That should be enough for you."

"I can't help but think that you wouldn't say that if your children weren't friends with the dragons," a woman said. "They have brought war and death. The elders are fools for voting as they did!"

Alísa shivered as the villagers' anger added to Sesína's in her mind. She needed to get away, from it and from Yarlan. He hadn't drawn his sword, but his hand on the hilt still concerned her. She grabbed Falier's sleeve, careful not to touch his skin.

"We should keep moving," she whispered.

She saw the light of anger in his eyes as he faced her, but it dimmed as realization took over. The anger assaulting her mind diminished slightly as he raised his shield and blocked his emotions off from her just as Namor had taught him. It didn't do much in this fury-filled situation, but it helped to fill her own thoughts with something other than anger.

"Back away from Yarlan," Alísa told the dragons. *"Slowly."*

Sesína grumbled mentally. *"I'm sick of him always getting away with this!"*

Alísa looked at the angry red burn on Yarlan's arm. *"That is enough. I don't want to antagonize the villagers more than we already have. He hurt me, but he hasn't tried to kill me."*

Graydonn stepped back, but even he wasn't happy. *"And we're just supposed to wait for that to happen?"*

"I—I don't know."

As the dragons backed away, Yarlan's grip on his sword loosened. He looked at Falier, his voice deathly quiet.

"Remember as Me'ran falls apart—you allowed this. And you—" He shoved a finger at Alísa. "You might have won this battle, but the war isn't over yet."

Yarlan pivoted downhill, multiple people turning to follow him as he stalked away. Alísa forced in quiet breaths, cooling her thoughts.

"What was that?"

Taz's voice called Alísa to turn around. His eyes were wide with confusion and outrage, his hand on his brother's shoulder as though to push him to safety at the slightest need.

Parsen's voice rose to answer. "That is the last few weeks coming to a head."

The holder approached the group with sorrow in his tired eyes.

Behind him came Kat, Tenza, and those who had spoken against Yarlan, though most of them simply nodded to Alísa and continued their trek down the hill.

"What happened, Papá?" Selene asked.

"While you worked with the slayers, Yarlan called a village meeting. He motioned that we banish Alísa, the dragons, and any slayer who joined them. Some agreed with him—whether because they think the dragons bring evil, or because they want the war gone from their doorstep. There weren't enough of them to make it happen, though."

Parsen met Alísa's gaze. "You and the dragons are still welcome here, but the events of the last few days have turned people away from you. The village is nearly split down the middle, but you have more elders on your side than not."

Kat came forward. "Including us."

Alísa swallowed, her heart trembling with sorrow. She was doing this, bringing discord to a once-peaceful village and fear to people she cared about.

"I'm sorry."

Kat shook her head, looking to Falier and back. "You're doing what you have to." She brushed her fingers over Alísa's arm. "I wish everyone else saw that."

The motherly affection in Kat's touch and emotions made Alísa's heart ache. They pulled her back to her parents' tent, where she had always been safe.

Kat must have seen something in her expression, because she came closer and wrapped her arms around Alísa. Her hug was stiff, not nearly as warm as Hanah's, but Alísa closed her eyes and let herself imagine the tent—the earthy scent of the leathers, the dim yellow light that filtered through them, and the closeness that spoke of simple safety, before the world changed. Before she changed. The change was good and right, but it was so very hard. And it wasn't likely to get easier any time soon.

25

THE HEART'S CALLING

After another day of holder duties and feeling the strife of Me'ran, flight-training with the adolescents was a much-needed release. Alísa leaned low as Sesína dove after their opponents. Graydonn was fast, his swerves tight and precise, even while considering the needs of his rider. Sesína didn't have the same control, but the Illumination bond allowed Alísa to anticipate the rhythm of her flight and hang on tighter when needed.

Graydonn pulled left, catching an updraft as Sesína speared past him. Sesína shifted her wings to steal her momentum from gravity's pull and climb back into the sky. They chased Graydonn, staying right on his tail. Falier glanced back at them, a wide grin plastered on his face.

"Too wide," Sesína mused. *"Almost as if he—"*

Graydonn tilted his wings upward and flapped, flipping backwards over Sesína.

"Hey, that's my move!"

Alísa ducked, despite the distance between her and Graydonn. *"Any idea how to get away from it, then?"*

Sesína didn't have to answer. Alísa held on as Sesína pulled a sharp right turn, trying to come around behind Graydonn. He didn't pull even, diving past Sesína so she had to scramble to follow.

"Nice evasion, both of you," Saynan's voice entered all minds. *"It will serve you well when fighting larger opponents who cannot—"*

A trumpet echoed over the expanse of the sky, halting Saynan's instruction. Sesína stopped her pursuit, pulling up to slow her flight.

"Was that—"

"Galerra," Harenn warned. *"Our scouts must have missed her!"*

"Shall I call for the others, Singer?" Komi asked.

Saynan's calm voice pressed through the link. *"I can see Galerra—she comes alone, and she bears a truce-boulder."*

Alísa thought back through Koriana's lessons. A dragon from an enemy clan could request an audience by carrying a large stone as they flew. The boulder slowed and weakened the dragon, showing they did not plan to attack, but it was also easily droppable if the request was rejected and the dragon needed to flee.

After two bloody skirmishes between their clans, why would Paili's general come with a truce boulder? Had Galerra finally seen the sickness in her mother? Or did she come to demand Alísa's surrender again?

"Alert the others, Komi, but tell them just to get outside and not to engage. I will hear what Galerra has to say. Everyone, form up."

Acknowledgements ran through the clan link.

"Iila, to me," Saynan commanded. *"Our cave is too far for me to send you alone; you will be safest on my back."*

Iila said nothing and obeyed. Alísa had almost forgotten the hatchling was out here too—she had been flying beside Saynan while the others practiced combat. Alísa scanned the horizon to verify that only one dragon approached. Galerra was almost to them now.

"Sesína, connect me to her."

As soon as the new mental signature buzzed in her mind, Alísa spoke. *"Hail, Galerra! What message do you bring?"*

Galerra growled through the link. *"None for you, Dragon Singer—unless you have finally decided to surrender your foolish quest and join with Paili and Tsamen."*

"You waste your loyalty on alphas who don't deserve it." Alísa tried to send the same growling feeling back. *"I will not ally myself with dragons who reject even slayers who wish for peace."*

Galerra's hostility cooled like a snarl turning to a wicked grin. *"You've joined my updraft, Singer. It seems we both want to separate ourselves from dragons who believe differently than we do about slayer vermin."*

Alísa gritted her teeth as the dragoness twisted words, but Galerra wasn't through.

"Our scouts have seen your adolescents and hatchlings training—don't be shocked, your territory is too large to bar spies. We cannot help but wonder, how

many of you young ones followed this serpent due to your parents' wishes rather than your own? Have you learned to think for yourselves after suffering humankind's follies and backwards ways of life?"

The dragoness' tone softened into something almost sweet. *"Perhaps there is even a young prince who found a life worse than the one from which he came? We will welcome all, even former traitors."*

The world was silent except for the steady flapping of wings and the gentle summer breeze. Alísa let it be. Let Galerra see that her clan would not be moved.

A surge of resolve rushed through the clan-link, and movement caught Alísa's eye.

"Iila?" Worry colored Saynan's tone. *"What are you doing?"*

Swiftly, the hatchling leapt from Saynan's back and began flying on her own again. She did not answer him, did not look back, and began flying with her slow, learner's speed toward Galerra.

Alísa's heartbeat quickened. *"Iila, stop!"*

Sesína moved to intercept the hatchling, but Iila growled and turned to face them.

"You made a promise to me, Singer," she said, blue eyes flashing. *"You said that when I could take care of myself I could leave without repercussions. I can fly on my own now—you have to let me go."*

Alísa tensed. She knew Iila hadn't been happy, had felt her discomfort and raging grief, but she hadn't thought Iila would actually leave.

Saynan's flight slowed, breaking their flight-pattern. *"Singer, did you truly promise such a thing?"*

Alísa pressed her lips together. *"I did."*

Saynan trumpeted, the sound high with worry. He turned to the hatchling. *"Iila, you don't know what you're choosing—come back to me. To Aree. We care about you. Please!"*

"No!" The hatchling made a sound that might have been a roar if she were bigger. *"This isn't my home. It will never be my home!"*

Saynan flew in front of her now, keeping between Iila and Galerra. *"It can be, just give it a little more time."*

"How can it be when my mother's murderer lives here? I hate him, and I

hate the humans—slayers especially—and the Singer has already given up one of the eggs to them. Our kin! How can you stand it? You should be coming with me!"

"The war is not right, Iila, and the Singer is the one who will end it. I know you don't understand, but—"

"If she is your alpha, then you have to listen to her. She promised me."

Iila fixed her eyes on Alísa, expectation glittering in her eyes. Alísa had no way out, and the hatchling knew it. If she took Iila back by force she broke her word, and Iila would look for other opportunities to flee alone. It would be far more dangerous that way, and trust would be broken. It was heartbreaking, feeling Iila's trust so strongly even as she turned away.

Tears welled in Alísa's eyes, and she wasn't sure if they belonged more to her or to Saynan. She looked to Harenn.

"Will she be safe with them?"

Harenn held her gaze. "As safe as she would be with most any other clan."

Iila bolted for Harenn, making Saynan trumpet with surprise. It hurt to hear the steady dragon so uncontrolled. But he had to know what Alísa did—keeping Iila against her will wouldn't work.

"Harenn," Iila said. "You feel as I do. I saw your reaction to Colors and the egg, and I know you hate the thought of carrying slayers tomorrow. Come with me! You heard your sister—if you come back, they'll think you're a hero who broke free of the Singer's influence. They'll be so proud of you, I know it!"

The hatchling spoke freely, keeping her words public rather than forming a private telepathy link. Alísa's heart clenched as Iila's hatred of the clan clashed with her trust that Alísa would keep her word. Didn't she see the awful dichotomy of it?

But Iila didn't see it. What she did see was Harenn—his unhappiness and a chance at redemption with his family. Would he take it? He had to know, like Iila did, that Alísa wouldn't retaliate. She didn't need dragon empathy to understand a desire to reconcile with one's family.

Harenn's eyes dimmed. "I can't go with you."

Multiple dragons perked up from their sorrowful slouches. Alísa hadn't been the only one wondering if Harenn would join her.

"Y—yes you can!" Iila said, her tail flicking and throwing her off-balance. She flapped hard to correct her mistake, hovering before Harenn with dimming eyes.

"*I already made my choice. My heart-calling is here, and there is no redemption for me among my family, no matter what my sister says.*" A growl escaped Harenn's throat as he turned blazing eyes to Galerra. "*Watch out in Berreth's training sessions; he is not as kind as Saynan. Be happy, Iila.*"

The world seemed to still. Iila stared at Harenn open-jawed, her tail drooping toward the ground and her disbelief invading Alísa's senses. Then, without word or sound, Iila flapped hard into a turn and flew toward Galerra. None moved to stop her, not even Saynan, though his whole body turned as he watched her.

Nearly to Galerra, a gust of wind broadsided Iila. Saynan sped forward as the hatchling struggled, but before he made it to her, Iila corrected herself. Saynan stopped as Galerra dropped the truce boulder and dove under the hatchling, taking her onto her back.

"*Learn well, Singer,*" Galerra sneered. Then she turned and flew back toward her territory.

A bleating trumpet broke from Saynan's throat, raw with heartbreak. It coursed through Alísa's mind and body, wrenching her with a sob.

She had failed him, failed Iila, failed Aree. What could she have done better? Could she have changed Iila's mind about humans if she had just tried harder? Spent more time with her instead of in the village? Should she have forced Iila to stay—kept a rotating watch of dragons on her until she saw the light? A hint of reason told her no, but everything else was pain, sorrow, and guilt.

They and the others watched as Galerra and Iila became a speck on the horizon. When Sesína turned to lead the others home, Saynan was the last to leave.

Grief struck Alísa anew as the dragons returned to the cave. Head down and wings drooping, Saynan made for Aree. He had said nothing to Alísa on the return flight, and she almost wished he had screamed at her rather than fly in silent sorrow. At least then she would know what he thought of her final decision; terrible as it was, she could think of no other viable option.

Aree moaned a low, sorrowful trumpet, her wings stretching out as though to follow the cry. Alísa doubled over Sesína's back as sobs wracked her.

The dreki in their corner of the cave leapt into the air in distress, flying toward Alísa.

"Singer?" "Singer?" "Singer?"

"She's fine, but she needs quiet." Sesína punctuated her words with a growl. The dreki took the hint and fluttered back to their place, which after only one night had somehow burst to life with vines and flowers growing from the stone. Even that sight didn't dull the sorrow coursing into Alísa.

"Hang on," Sesína soothed, widening the bond once more and pulling some of the strain away. She lowered to her belly and, after a few calming breaths, Alísa carefully swung off her back and knelt on the floor.

Saynan draped his wing and neck over Aree, the light rumbling in his chest barely audible. Together they lay in silent mourning and comfort, their unhatched dragonet settled between them. The scene raised Alísa's own parents to mind, making guilt coil in her belly. She had put them through this too.

Sesína pressed her muzzle to Alísa's cheek. *"You don't need that right now."*

"But it's true."

Falier came around Sesína, Graydonn behind him, concern in both their eyes. Lowering to his knees, Falier wrapped his arms around Alísa. She sagged against him, careful not to touch any exposed skin so the sorrow wouldn't seep into him.

"I'm sorry," he said.

"Did I do the right thing?"

Falier paused, a flicker of uncertainty rushing through his mind. *"You did the best you could in an impossible situation."*

It helped and it didn't. What helped more was the love pulsing from him, pushing against the tide of sadness.

"For Iila, maybe," she said, holding to him more tightly, *"but for Saynan and Aree?"*

"They're good dragons," Graydonn said, now on his belly too. *"They grieve, but they will understand. Especially now that we know one of us killed Iila's mother. That's why you made the promise to her in the first place, wasn't it? Because you thought it was wrong for her to have to stay with the clan that killed her parents?"*

Alísa's breath shuddered in and out. That was true. It was right for Iila. Why did doing what was right hurt so badly? It seemed there was no end to it—it would be so much easier to just give up.

Harenn. Why hadn't he given up?

Alísa straightened, making Falier start.

"What is it?"

Alísa looked around the cave. *"Where's Harenn?"*

Sesína pointed with her muzzle to Harenn's typical alcove, and Alísa began to stand.

"I need to talk to him."

"Want me to come with you?" Falier said, offering his hand as he stood as well.

Alísa looked at it as sorrow shivered through her again. The offer was more than tempting, but she could make it without the help. He must have sensed her hesitation, because he shook his head slightly.

"I know what I'm offering. When are you going to figure out I like helping you?"

Alísa slumped, pushing away guilt she shouldn't feel. She took his hand, sorrow easing its grip on her heart and allowing her room to breathe. Falier shut his eyes against the influx and blew out a slow breath. He opened his eyes and tried to hide his wince with a smile. Squeezing her hand reassuringly, he walked her toward Harenn.

The young dragon was alone, chin resting on his paws. A much lighter grief wafted from him than Saynan's. Harenn didn't seem to care about much, but he and Iila had been comfortable with each other at the very least.

Harenn jerked to attention. *"Singer?"* He looked between the two humans, his eyes remaining dim. *"What do you need?"*

"I wanted to check on you, and to thank you for staying." She paused, not quite sure how to say what she wanted to say. *"I was glad to hear your words, but also a little surprised. I know this has been hard on you, and I wonder if you would tell me why you didn't go back?"*

Harenn's throat rumbled. *"I told Iila why; you heard me."*

"Yes, but you said it was your heart's calling. I've seen your struggle here. You don't feel like you fit in. You don't believe in my mission with the humans. You hate that tomorrow we'll be training with the slayers. I am so glad you chose to stay, but I don't understand it. I want to understand."

A wry humor wafted from him. *"I want to understand it too, but I can't. All I can tell you is that when you sang for my parents' clan, my heart awoke. You called only for those who believed, and somehow I was one of them. I've been trying to understand it ever since."*

Harenn looked across the cave at Faern. *"When I first began my scout training, we got caught in a downpour of rain. Faern was leading me back to the cave, but at one point the rain became so dense he disappeared. I panicked and began swerving to find him or just find my way out of the rain. He told me to calm down and keep flying based on what I saw before. He said I shouldn't change the course simply because I couldn't see—that was precisely the moment I must choose to stay the course. And so I stay."*

A fresh wave of tears prickled at Alísa's eyes. She had never thought Harenn a particularly wise dragon, but in this moment, he held what she needed.

"May we sit with you, Harenn? Or would you prefer to be alone?"

Harenn hesitated, then rumbled quietly in his chest. *"I would like your company Singer, Slayer."*

Alísa smiled softly and sat beside Harenn as he rested his head back on his paws. They may have lost a clanmate, but here, in shared grief, the bonds of camaraderie grew stronger.

26

TRUTH-BRINGER

Me'ran held a nervous energy as Alísa completed her holder chores. Most shops were open, but a few weren't. Most surprising was the butchers' shop, which two families covered to allow the essential shop to stay open every day. One of the men had been killed in the battle against Segenn, and even still they had opened every day since. Not today.

In addition, two homes had large carts out in front of them, to which the families brought packs and furniture. One already overflowed with possessions and had a donkey tied to it. People were leaving. Because of her.

Just like Iila.

Alísa blew out her breath. Iila had made her choice. Now Me'ran did the same.

Dragons and dreki spilled into the square as Alísa finished her last delivery. The elderly man receiving the basket widened his eyes with awe.

"If Namor could see this," he started. His eyes softened with sympathy, and he placed a hand on Alísa's shoulder. "Good luck today. My wife and I are rooting for you."

A smile made it past Alísa's sorrow. "Thank you."

With a nod, he pulled the basket inside and shut the door. Alísa turned around and faced the square, forcing in a deep breath of warming summer air.

"Here we go."

Graydonn met her first, Falier coming up behind him. The dragon nosed Alísa's arm. *"Briek's coming. You sure we're ready for this?"*

Alísa sighed. *"I'm sure of nothing besides the need to move forward. I'll need you and Falier especially today."*

Graydonn blinked slowly. *"We are here."*

Alísa patted his shoulder, then looked to the rest of the clan. *"Harenn, Faern—I need you two to watch the village today. I don't anticipate problems from anyone besides Yarlan, but I'm sure you can feel the strife in the air. Alert me if there's a problem."*

Faern thumped his tail against the ground. *"Singer."*

"Does this mean we won't be working with riders today?"

The hope in Harenn's voice sparked a bit of sadness in Alísa, but she had anticipated it. It was why she had picked him and Faern for this job. Both dragons were the least likely to be comfortable with a slayer on their back, and she needed today to be full of good experiences.

"You two will not, though I want you to pay attention to the others. Tomorrow will be your turn, and I need you prepared."

Harenn's tail thumped the ground, and he straightened to scan the village with bright eyes.

Satisfied, Alísa walked toward the path to the slayer's camp to meet Briek, Graydonn and Falier following behind. Sesína trotted up to walk beside her.

"Did you notice? Yarlan's house."

Alísa looked, then stared in confusion. The door hung wide open. She hadn't seen him emerge—and wouldn't he have already, to get his family to the shelter? She looked to the shops and alleys, searching the shadows for his familiar form. Nothing.

"I'm going to check it out," Sesína said, veering off-course.

"Careful—if he sees you at his home..."

"Where's she going?" Falier asked, following the dragoness' progress. "Oh. I didn't see them at all yesterday. Do you think—"

"Tracks." Sesína said, sniffing at the marks on the ground. *"Multiple people. They lead to the forest."*

"Is he gone?" Alísa whispered, unable to keep the hope and relief from her voice. That people were leaving because of her was awful, but Yarlan being out of her life would be a ray of sun in the midst of it all.

"I'll ask around later," Falier said, "see if he spoke to anyone. For now—"

310

Falier pointed, drawing Alísa's eyes to Briek and his men entering the village. Looking them over, it was a slightly different group. Eleven slayers approached rather than nine. Two of them were the teenagers she had seen at the burial, and one of the other faces seemed new as well. Perhaps one of the men who had come the first day wasn't coming back. This might be how it worked over the next week, different slayers each day as they decided whether or not they wanted to be a part of what she was doing.

She clasped Briek's arm. "Good morning. I see we have n— newcomers."

Briek introduced the young men, both of whom barely acknowledged her as their wide eyes remained fixed on Sesína and Graydonn. He also introduced a man who appeared to be in his thirties. She had been right about the men swapping out.

Alísa welcomed the new slayers, then addressed Briek. "I would speak with you b—before we t-t-t-try riding. The rest of you c-c-c-can go to the dragons. Falier will introduce the new men."

The slayers didn't move, a few staring blankly at her, while others looked to Briek.

Briek noticed their hesitation. "Go on, then."

The men moved, following Falier and Graydonn. Two of them eyed her as they passed, and Alísa wondered if she had overstepped. Yes, she had told them what to do while their chief was present, but she hadn't thought it particularly commanding. If they didn't like it now, how would they feel as she led them through training, or in battle?

Alísa shook her head. The latter was far off, and they barely knew her at this point. She shouldn't worry too much.

"I was going to say that, but your mind is running too fast." Sesína pushed calm through the bond. *"Settle down."*

Alísa sighed inwardly. *"You're right."*

"You could say that out loud for everyone to hear, you know."

Alísa suppressed a snort. *"I'll let them figure it out for themselves."*

She gave her attention back to Briek, the other slayers all past her now. "I would like your opinion on who should t-t-t-try riding today. I have a c-c-couple dragons not quite ready for it, and I'm sure some of your m—m—men might be in a similar s—situation."

Briek looked past her and Sesína. "I would not put the first-timers on dragonback today, especially the boys. There is one other I am unsure of, but if given the choice he would say yes to save face before the others. Allow me to select the men first, then you can assign them to whichever dragons you wish."

"Very well."

Briek considered a moment. "Though many are ready to try, I cannot imagine any are ready to trust."

Alísa smiled ruefully. "The feeling is mutual. We'll fly in g—groups of three, with Falier or me always one of the three. Your men can watch each other's backs b—b—better with fewer dragons in the sky—same for my dragons. If there are p-p-p-problems, Falier or I will be right there to help. We'll also stay connected to the full clan's mind-link, so those on the ground can get there q—quickly if needed. Is this acceptable?"

Briek's eyes clouded with thoughts. Alísa could almost see him grasping each possibility, then shoving it aside to move on to the next.

"You and I will fly in the first group," he finally said. "And Taz. He has been the most vocal about making this partnership work. If he has a good experience, he won't be silent about it, which may bolster the others."

Alísa smiled. "Done."

Together, they and Sesína walked back. Focusing on the clan-link, Alísa found introductions over and Falier now demonstrating how to mount a dragon. Alísa smiled as he and Graydonn stood at the front to guide the others. If anyone could help the slayers through their fear, it would be the encouraging holder and peaceful dragon.

She stopped at the back of the group, allowing him to finish walking the slayers through not only mounting a small dragon like Graydonn, but also Saynan, complete with an assist from the ice dragon's great muzzle.

"But how do you guide the dragon where you need to go?" A slayer scratched his beard. "Pull on the spine?"

Falier patted Saynan's wither from atop the dragon. "They can make their own decisions flying. The whole clan is versed in aerial combat. When fighting other dragons, you'll want to trust their experience and instincts. I don't think they'll feel you pulling at the spine. Graydonn?"

"Not unless you're hanging off it." Graydonn thrummed, but the men didn't seem amused. His eyes dimmed to normal. *"This is a partnership, and there will be situations where you need to warn or guide us. In those instances, you'll communicate telepathically. For the most part, however, the slayer will focus on fighting psychically while the dragon focuses on the physical."*

"So, no reins or saddle?"

Koriana rumbled in her chest. *"Beasts need such items, not iompróir anam. We will keep you in the air and aimed at the enemy."*

Alísa felt a ripple of surprise from some of the slayers, likely at Koriana's use of the soul-bearer term. Just another part of the mountain they had to climb with these men.

"Alísa and I have talked it through," Briek said, heading to the front. "Not everyone will ride today, as we'll only have two of us in the air at a time. Taz—you and I will go first."

A shock of anxiety ran through the air, but Taz kept his expression calm as he took his place beside Briek. Alísa looked over her dragons. Who should be the first in the air—which ones would bolster the others through their worries?

Her eyes landed on Saynan as Falier slid down his shoulder. She had offered to let him and Aree stay home today, but they had come out anyway, likely eager to have something to focus on besides Iila's absence.

Alísa latched onto the mind-link, feeling the slayers caught up in it as well. *"Saynan, you'll take Briek. Aree, Taz. Sesína and I will join you for this first flight. Falier and Graydonn will take the next pair once we get back."*

The dragons backed away from Saynan and Aree to make room for the slayers. Alísa went to Saynan with Briek, noting that Falier escorted Taz.

Saynan lowered his head to meet Briek. *"Are you ready, friend?"*

Briek hesitated, then firmed his chin. "No, but we have to start somewhere."

Saynan thrummed. *"Well spoken."*

The dragon arched his neck even more, positioning his head as a step for the new chief, as he had done for Falier. Briek moved decisively, stepping onto Saynan's muzzle and reaching up for the dragon's spines. Saynan lifted and Briek caught hold, pulling himself up and into position. Soon Taz, too, sat high on his mount's back. Alísa grinned to see them up there, uncomfortable but willing.

"Good. Slayers, move off to the side. Saynan and Aree don't need much of a running start, but their steps are long."

The men did as she said, moving to stand near Tenza and Selene in front of Tenza's home. Sesína trotted up and turned sideways for Alísa to mount. As Saynan and Aree stood slowly, Alísa fought back a chuckle, comparing the anxious newcomers' heights to her own on Sesína's back.

"I'm going to pretend you didn't just call me short." Sesína stuck out her tongue.

This time, Alísa allowed the laugh. *"Let's show them how it's done."*

With an excited trumpet, Sesína trotted forward. Excitement built in the dragoness with every jarring step, every stretch of her wings. Then, with a coil of muscles, Sesína launched. She banked immediately, circling over the square to find an air-current. Alísa looked down to see the slayers' faces. A few wrinkled with scrutiny, while others loosened with wonder—likely imagining what it was like to fly.

Alísa's revelry jerked to a stop as she looked over the rest of the village. Further north, out of view of the square, another family loaded up a cart. The once peaceful and unified Me'ran was fractured.

"And yet" —Sesína changed her bank to bring Alísa's focus back to the square— *"slayers ride dragons."*

Alísa nodded firmly. That was the music in the mess. She focused on the clan-link as Saynan and Aree rose, finding both terror and exhilaration in Briek and Taz. Just as it should be.

Saynan and Aree climbed swiftly, their great wings catching the updraft. Sesína positioned herself behind the others at Alísa's request, allowing them a clear view of the slayers as the dragons evened out perhaps fifty feet above the tallest trees.

Remembering all the slayers and dragons on the ground could hear them this close to the village, Alísa reached out. *"Briek, Taz—you doing okay?"*

For the first time, Alísa heard Briek's telepathic voice. It was quiet, not like Falier with his smaller power, but with uncertainty.

"*I am. Ascent was difficult, but now that we've evened out I'm better.*"

"*Just in time for us to turn,*" Saynan thrummed.

"*We'll be gentle,*" soothed Aree, the dragoness tilting ever so slightly to circle Me'ran.

"*Difficult how?*" At Briek's hesitation, Alísa added, "*It will help the next riders prepare.*"

"*I felt sick to my stomach as we rose, and the speed was a tad dizzying.*"

Taz's humor filled the link. "*See, I liked the ascent—it tickled.*"

"*Of course, you would like the stomach drop.*" Selene's voice came through, and Alísa could imagine her shaking her head.

Aree glanced back at Taz. "*Would you like to go higher?*"

"*That depends on how it feels to descend.*"

"*Let's wait on that,*" Alísa said. "*We're just getting a general feel today, and I want to finish and get out of the square by lunchtime so we aren't disrupting business too much.*" She tried not to let her dismay over Me'ran's strife get through the link, but was fairly certain she failed. "*Finish the circle, then we'll do some turns. Riders, you'll want to lean into them slightly. Lean the other way or too far, and you'll throw off the dragon's balance.*"

The dragons and riders continued the exercise, Alísa and Sesína giving instruction as needed. By the time they finished, Taz was enthralled by the entire experience. Briek had seemed to enjoy himself as well, a bit of fun peeking through his chiefly veneer.

As Briek had hoped, some of the slayers who had been uncertain now seemed ready to try riding. Briek called Rassím and another man to ride next. Alísa did her best to give friendly eye-contact to Rassím, pushing through the sick feeling in her stomach. The other slayer was perhaps in his mid-twenties and looked excited to be chosen.

After a quick weighing of options, Alísa found her desired pairing. "*Tora, Q'rill—you're up. Tora will take Rassím.*"

As the red dragons came forward, the new slayer's face fell. He threw an affronted look at Alísa. "Surely you have someone who will give me a better ride than the mentally delayed dragon!"

The derision in his tone made Alísa's blood run cold with shock, then boil nearly as hot as Tora's. The mother dragoness growled.

"Keep your venom—"

"Hey!" Rassím spoke at the same time as Tora, his fierce eyes trained not on the dragons, but on his fellow slayer. "You never have known when to keep your mouth shut. All *anam* are worthy of respect, dragon or no. If he is here, then his mother, his chief, and Q'rill himself have all deemed him capable."

Alísa couldn't move, stuck in shock as Rassím, of all people, vehemently defended Q'rill. His eyes were as they once had been when trained on her—cold and deadly. The other slayer's face contorted in flustered indignation, while those not about to ride seemed as surprised as Alísa.

Rassím turned to the dragons. Tora still seethed, while Q'rill cocked his head with an interest that made Alísa wonder if he knew the offense that had been thrown at him. Rassím placed his fist over his heart and dipped his head in respect.

"I apologize for my rude clanmate. Q'rill, I would be honored if you would accept me as your rider today."

The fire in Tora's eyes dimmed slightly, while Q'rill looked to Alísa. His eye-ridges, one marred by talon-scars, raised.

"But, Singer said you would ride mother, and the other man—"

"It's okay, Q'rill," Alísa said. *"Rassím may ride you, if you like."* She turned hard eyes on the other slayer. *"The other man won't be riding today."*

The slayer sputtered. "I— You— Briek said—"

"Alísa's word is law in this matter," Briek said, calling up another man to ride Tora.

The reprimanded slayer narrowed his eyes, looking from Briek to Alísa and back, then returned to the group, muttering to the man he stopped beside. Most of the other slayers just stood in silence, unreadable.

Falier cleared his throat, coming up to the riders. "Right. Okay. Let's get up there."

As Falier helped them through the process, Alísa kept her gaze roaming—watching for warning signs among the slayers and dragons. Tensions were higher now. She should have expected someone to say something idiotic to antagonize the other group. She was proud it wasn't the dragons who had done it.

Soon the riders were mounted. Tora's emotions had cooled significantly. She had already been stuck at the crossroads where the partnership with the slayers was concerned. Hopefully, Rassím had balanced out his fellow slayer in her eyes.

Thoughts pulled at Alísa's mind, calling Sesína's attention. The dragoness rumbled a purr. *"Only if you're truly ready for it. It's okay if you need more time."*

Alísa watched the red dragons circling the village with Graydonn. *"I need to form connections with the slayers sooner rather than later. And I can't continue living with misplaced fear. Stay with me?"*

Sesína nosed her head under Alísa's elbow. *"You've got it."*

The training ended just after noon, the sun beginning to beat hot on the dust of the square. Six of the slayers had ridden, lining up perfectly with the six dragons who were ready this first day. Tomorrow, Alísa would add Harenn and Faern to the mix and hopefully get more dragons in the air at a time.

Alísa dismissed her clan, most taking off for the cave. The slayers, too, began leaving the village, following after Briek.

Heart thudding, Alísa almost swallowed her words, but in a moment of courage called out. "Rassím!"

The slayer turned, startled.

"I w—w—would s—speak to you." She fought not to cringe as her volume and fear combined to halt her words. "If you d—don't mind."

He was already walking back by the time she finished, his fellow slayers raising brows at both of them. Falier, too, noticed and turned concerned eyes to her.

"Do you want me to stay?"

His quiet telepathy warmed her with its gentleness. She threw him a grateful smile.

"Thank you, but I'll be all right. Sesína is staying with me. I'll meet you at the Hold after."

Falier glanced once more at Rassím, then nodded, turning to follow Selene. *"Till after."*

Rassím was nearly to her now. Alísa made eye-contact with him, then took a seat on the bench in front of Tenza's house. Sesína went with her, sitting beside the bench on Alísa's side to give Rassím plenty of room. He hesitated before taking the offered seat, visibly confused.

Alísa swallowed, loosening her throat muscles. Sesína could connect them telepathically, but the slayers weren't comfortable with that yet. It would be better if she used her voice.

"I wanted t-t-to thank you for s—standing up for Q'rill. It w—w—was good of you, and brave to speak for a dragon before your b—brothers."

Rassím nodded slowly. "I wish I could say it was just common decency that led me to do it, but my reasoning is more personal. I have a sister like Q'rill—six years younger than I, yet comes across far younger. You'll never meet a sweeter soul."

Alísa smiled, for the first time not needing to force it around Rassím. "That's Q'rill for us. I d—don't think he even realized the slight. He doesn't expect evil of anyone, even if he should."

"You expected this of us, then?"

Alísa held up warding hands. "N—no, not at all. I meant his old c-c-c—clan. Hearing of his life from T-Tora, most of his scars are from his c-c-c—clanmates. His alpha encouraged it, even. Said he was weak, and it would m—m—make him stronger."

Rassím visibly tensed. "Barbaric."

"Yes." Alísa rubbed a fold of her skirt between her fingers, watching as the village slowly came to life again. "But he is a good fighter. I actually m—m—met him in battle. With T-T-T-Tora nearby to ground him, he knows what to do."

Rassím gave a mirthless chuckle. "As we all must."

Across the way, the family loading their cart started moving again. Parents, a teenage girl, and a little boy who had played kickball with Sesína once.

"I never thought his parents particularly hostile toward us," Sesína whispered.

318

"Me either."

But now there they were, loading up their possessions.

Come to think of it, wherever they went, they would certainly give the reason for why they left. Word would spread soon. There were no other wayfarers in the area—Segenn's territory was large even by western standards—but there were village-bound slayers. Segenn's practice of leaving only one or two slayers per village meant she wouldn't be facing a formidable force anytime soon, but she would have to reach out to them quickly. Hopefully, with Briek and his men at her side to back up her story.

Of course, as Me'ran demonstrated, even the support of slayers wouldn't convince everyone.

"Are you all right, Dragon Singer?"

She pulled herself back to the present. "Alísa, please."

Rassím waited a moment. "Okay. Are you all right, *Alísa*?"

Alísa smiled wryly, remaining silent as she thought. Here with Sesína at her side and common ground found with Rassím, she did want to answer him truthfully. Not *completely* truthfully, as she would with Sesína or Falier, but a glimpse.

"I'm sad," she sighed out, looking out at the villagers. "M—Me'ran used to be so alive and unified. Now there's strife between neighbors, and I know that much of it is b—b—because of me. I did what I had t-to, but it's c-c-c-costing others."

Sadness touched Rassím's eyes. "Yes. Such is the lot for truth-bringers, Dragon Singer or otherwise."

He turned from her gaze, searching the sky. She followed his eyes and watched a few of the dragons twisting through the glorious summer air.

"Five days ago, I would have speared those souls from the sky," Rassím said. "Truth-bringing yields strife, but also life."

"You speak as one who already knows."

"Not in as grand a way you do, but yes." Rassím fidgeted with his chest-strap, making Alísa nervous. Unreasonably so, she knew, but it would be a while before knives didn't raise her heartbeat. "I, uh—I'm what the songweavers call *radharc anam*—a soul-seer."

Alísa looked at Rassím. "Radharc?"

"*Oo!*" Sesína stood quickly and got in front of him, mind racing with the same stories that filled Alísa's. "*Tell me more!*"

Rassím shifted. "It's not as crazy as most lore makes it out to be, like seeing the balance of right and wrong in every person's heart or holding a grand calling from the Maker. At least, not for me. Most people I see look normal—what I *do* see is when someone has been touched by the Eldír or the Nameless. Like you, Alísa. You were touched by light the day of the funeral."

Sesína looked at Alísa and whispered. "*You didn't tell him about Bria, did you?*"

"*No. The only ones who know that are you, Falier, and the dreki.*" Alísa switched back to verbal speech. "That's why you stared at me."

Rassím fingered the blunt end of one of his knives. "I'm typically a better actor, but after everything else..." He cleared his throat. "I had expected the Dragon Singer to be glowing with darkness up until I saw you the morning of—everything."

Sesína snorted. "*How can darkness glow?*"

"It's the only way I can describe it. It's why I was sent as the 'messenger' that day, so if I saw the Dragon Singer I could avoid her until it was time. It shocked me to discover that the terrible Dragon Singer was one of the perfectly normal women I'd met at the Hold. 'Course, I had to firm up and do my job. Perhaps you were worse than touched by the Nameless—perhaps you had given up humankind completely on your own. I couldn't be sure, but everything nagged at me until I heard your song. The truth latched it all into place."

Sesína's tail lashed. "*So, you've seen an'reik before?*"

Rassím's eyes hardened. "Yes. Many. My former village in the Southlands crawled with them."

"Then, you are from the Southlands?" Alísa thought back to the conversation at the Hold and everything Rassím had told them about himself.

"Yes. Most everything I told you was the truth. It's easier to fool fellow slayers when you tell so much truth you don't have time to feel your lies. I am from the Southlands, and we did leave partially for my parents' health. Even more so, however, it was for our safety. A child who could spy an'reik in a town with a contingency of them was a danger to all. Most neighbors preferred not to know when they sold their wares to one who had sold their soul, and there were threats against us because of me."

Alísa shivered. She couldn't fathom living in a village with so many dark ones walking about, holding who knew what power. Legends told of a time when the Eldír rose up armies of humans, dragons, and fairies to fight them—long ago, before the war between humans and dragons. Now the an'reik were only whispered about, rumors occasionally rising of one in some far-away village. Never a village full of them.

"So, you see, people shutting their eyes to the truth is nothing new. This is where hearts are proven, and most hearts don't like being proven."

Alísa sighed, looking back out over Me'ran. "D—does the p-p-p-proving of the truth-bringer themselves ever stop? I feel like I've been p—proved more than my fair share these past months."

Rassím chuckled. "I'm sure you have. And it's worked. Briek saw it. Many of these people have seen it. Your dragons see it. I see it, though I'd wager I don't count now that you know I have a leg up."

"You count." Alísa smiled, looking into eyes that once frightened her so. "Thank you."

Rassím's returned smile held the knowledge that she had forgiven him and they could start over. He dipped his head in respect.

"You're welcome."

27

BLUE

Two dragons slowly circled Me'ran. Their trepidation flowed through Alísa as she and Sesína arced around them. Only a week of training couldn't erase it, especially now that their riders had started training with psychic attack and defense. Alísa pushed peace to the dragons through the mind-link before giving the slayers the order.

"Begin."

She could feel Harenn flinch at the command. Closing her eyes, Alísa watched the war game on the astral plane. The slayer on Komi's back made the first move, throwing a psychic bolt at Harenn. The bolt had little power behind it, but it would still sting if it hit.

Harenn's rider made a shield around the dragon, dark brown like the slayer's eyes. The bolt hit and dissipated against the shield, making relief sweep through Harenn. His rider tore down the shield to create his own attack, just as Alísa had outlined earlier. The riders would volley back and forth, practicing a prescribed pattern of attack and defense while the dragons ran through a pattern of banks, ascents, and descents.

Before Harenn's rider could throw his bolt, however, Komi's rider attacked again, hitting Harenn with a sharp sting that made Alísa gasp. She shook her head against the sensation.

"Hold!"

Sesína growled and darted for Komi, anticipating Alísa's desire. This slayer had broken the pattern yesterday as well.

"Harenn, are you okay?" Alísa asked.

"Fine." Harenn grumbled. *"Just fine."* He likely resented being asked as much as he did being hit out of turn, but Alísa had to ask. She looked to Komi's rider next.

"T'lan, you have to hold to the pattern. If—"

"War has no pattern, Dragon Singer." Though he used Alísa's title, there was no respect in it. He spoke as an elder lecturing a child, as though she had never seen war.

Alísa couldn't hold back a mental growl. "No, but training does until the trainer deems you ready to drop the pattern. This is our second day using psychic blasts and we are most certainly not ready. You have hurt Harenn, just like you hurt Tora. One more break of pattern and you'll find yourself grounded. It will not take long for your brothers to surpass you. Blast, then shield."

Sesína snorted smoke to punctuate Alísa's point, then twisted away to take up their supervisory position once more.

"Shields are a waste of energy," T'lan said. "You told us dragons don't fight psychically while fighting physically—they don't multi-task. If this is as you say" —his tone again betrayed a lack of belief in her experience— "then we will not need to shield our mounts."

Alísa sighed. He wasn't the only one who didn't get it yet. Even now, though he remained quiet, the other rider's similar feelings were strong. She looked back at them.

"Because one day we will face slayers as well. Ready yourselves."

Komi entered the conversation, addressing her rider. "Hit Harenn out of turn again, and I will drop you. Sesína is good at catching people—even so, falling without wings is not an enviable experience."

T'lan was silent at that, his emotions teetering between anger and uncertainty, probably trying to figure out whether Komi would follow through. Alísa didn't give him time to find the answer.

"Again!"

The combatants ran through the pattern. Blast and shield, blast and shield. Tight bank and ascent from the dragons. Blast and shield. Dive. Blast and shield. It flowed like a céilí dance, each move already planned with Alísa occasionally calling out reminders. Finally, she called the end of the pattern.

"Good. Well done, all of you. That's enough for today."

All combatants relaxed, their reactions palpable through the mind-link. It would be a long time before any of them felt comfortable with these exercises, much less a true war game that allowed for improvisation and required trust between partners.

And trust of their commander.

"Want me to smack T'lan when we land?" Sesína whispered.

Alísa smiled and shook her head. *"Komi's threat was enough."*

"I was rather impressed. Think I'm rubbing off on her?"

"Maker forbid."

Sesína looked back and grinned. Her eyes brightened and she nodded toward Twi-Peak. *"I think they're doing all right!"*

Alísa looked in the direction indicated. In the sky between Twi-Peak and Me'ran, Rayna and Korin flew side-by-side. Slow and easy, the mated pair exercised Rayna's wings, her ripped one newly healed. It would be a couple more weeks before she could fly for extended periods and longer before she could carry a rider, but even from this distance Alísa could see her pure joy at being in the sky again.

With two mighty flaps, Sesína slowed to land in the square. Alísa swung down, making eye-contact with Briek amidst a small group of slayers, including his wife—the first women to visit. The rest of the slayers—the teenage boys and those who had already flown today—congregated on the opposite end of Me'ran. Sounds of swords clanging together rose up as they practiced a different form of combat-training.

"You went for a long time with that pair," Briek observed. "Success?"

Alísa pushed her hair back as Harenn and Komi's landings made it fly into her face. "They m—made it through the exercise, and no one fell."

Briek looked past her. "T'lan do what he was supposed to?"

Alísa paused, torn. She shouldn't lie to Briek, but she also didn't want Briek to give T'lan a talk. She didn't need the slayers thinking she ran crying to Briek any time they questioned her.

"He n—needed a reminder, but p-p-p-performed well."

Briek studied her for a moment, as though trying to discern her hidden meaning, then nodded. "Good. Is that all for today?"

"Yes." She looked to the slayers behind him. "Thank you. Feel free t-t-to stay or go. It's a g—gorgeous day."

Briek dipped his head in acknowledgement. Despite his status as chief and the misgivings some of his men had with Alísa's leadership, Briek easily fell into the old patterns of a second-in-command.

"Indeed, it is." Briek's wife took his hand, leading him away to one of the shops. The rest of the slayers in their group followed a different path—most toward their camp, while some headed for the weapons training. Two also nodded at Alísa as they passed.

A commotion of young voices came from behind, and Alísa turned to see Sesína's typical mob of fans approaching with a leather fivers ball.

"Do you mind if I—"

"Go on." Alísa grinned.

Sesína arched low like a wolf pup asking for play. A girl tossed her the ball, which Sesína deftly bounced off her muzzle to begin the game.

Lightness filled Alísa's heart. The conflict was far from settled, but a small sense of peace lingered in the village today. The people so opposed to the dragons and slayers that they wanted to leave Me'ran were gone. Yarlan and his family were among them, though none had seen them leave—at least, none who told Alísa or the holders. Some in the village still didn't like Alísa or her dragons, but their glares and mutterings were now outweighed by Alísa's supporters.

Included among those supporters were some of the nearby village of Soren. As families left Me'ran, Falier and his family had taken Alísa, Briek, and a few of the other slayers to meet with Soren's elders. With Briek's support, they told of the good dragons of Twi-Peak, and a tentative peace was established. A couple Sorenites were even here today, pretending to watch the slayers spar while truly gaping at Graydonn standing nearby.

A glimpse of curly brown hair through the crowd of spectators made Alísa smile. She aimed for Graydonn, careful to stay out of view of those training so she wouldn't be a distraction. Graydonn sensed her and opened a telepathic link, but said nothing. A pulse of worry threaded through his fascination.

"How's he doing?"

Graydonn glanced at her, then back to Falier. *"He's—learning."*

At that moment, Falier lost his footing, stumbling back under the weight of his fifteen-year-old opponent's attack. He tried to correct, but his next sloppy block ended with the sword clanging to the ground.

"Hold," the trainer ordered. He stepped from the spectators near

Alísa to instruct, but Graydonn stretched his wing and blocked Alísa's view.

"*I think Falier's pride would be better served by* not *knowing you saw that.*"

Alísa smiled wryly. She had made the same mistakes as she learned swordplay and could only imagine the embarrassment if someone she loved had seen her. In truth, she could probably use this training too. It had been a long time since she had actually used her short sword.

"*I'll leave him to it, then.*" Alísa patted Graydonn's side. "*Don't worry. Sparring like this is no different from you dragons sparring in the sky. He'll be fine.*"

Graydonn rumbled a half-hearted acknowledgement and Alísa left the spectators just as the trainer gave the order to start the pattern again. Alísa sighed inwardly. Slayers understood that training patterns were how one first learned combat skills. T'lan was just being difficult.

I knew this wasn't going to be easy. Keep moving.

Alísa headed for Koriana, who held Blue between her forepaws within Alísa's bag. All three dragonets were becoming more restless. Eggs would start hatching any day now. Koriana had even told Alísa that one hatching usually triggered others who were nearly ready—the emotions of the experience and the availability of playmates would signal the others that it was time.

But Blue still hadn't chosen anyone. More often than not, the dragonet would growl whenever it switched hands, as though scolding them for not giving it to the correct parent-figure. It frightened Alísa more each day. She had witnessed so many hatchling deaths in her life—she couldn't bear to witness another.

Alísa knelt at Koriana's paws, feeling the dragoness connect telepathically. "*Thank you for keeping it for me while we trained. Any changes?*"

Koriana clicked in her throat. "*We should leave soon. I do not trust these slayers so near the eggs, and this one has become more agitated since they started that awful clashing of weapons.*"

"*Maybe agitation will make it want to latch onto someone.*"

Koriana's eyes dimmed. "*Doubtful.*"

Grasping the straps of her bag, Alísa pulled the thick fabric sides up around Blue and hoisted it onto her shoulder. A gurgling growl bubbled up, undeterred by Alísa's hand pressing to the shell. It didn't want her, that was certain.

Alísa shushed the agitated dragonet. "Let's go for a walk, shall we? That settled my cousins when they were little."

With a smiled goodbye to Koriana, Alísa pushed back into the square. She let her eyes wander over the goings-on. The game of fivers in the middle. Dreki fluttering just out of reach of the humans. The many open shops and a few permanently closed ones. Selene with Taz on the bench outside Tenza's home, Tawny on her lap. Taz's expression spoke both wonder and uncertainty, while his orange drek friend chirped in his ear as though explaining the situation.

Alísa grinned at the thought. The dreki were a welcome addition to the clan, but most were unfamiliar with human conversation. Alísa had found herself in more than one exchange where all she could do was smile and nod as a drek explained through images some concept too abstract for her to understand.

Slayers dispersing from weapons training caught Alísa's eye. She angled in their direction, picking Falier and Graydonn from the crowd. Falier wiped a rag over his face, then tossed it around his neck and let it hang there. His smile when he saw her filled her with warmth.

"Hey Líse. I'd give you a hug, but..." He gestured at his clothes, damp with sweat.

"I appreciate that." She stopped beside him, noting the slayers around them. She knew almost all of their names now, and she watched which ones headed straight home and which ones chose to stay longer.

"How'd the sparring go today?" Falier asked.

"Decently. The slayers are far b—better at attacking than defending, and that wears on the dragons. I could only keep sparring p-p-p-pairs up for a short amount of t-time." She smiled up at Falier. "How'd you do?"

He shrugged. "I only dropped the sword once today. I think they told the kid to go easy on me."

His humor teetered on the edge of good-natured and true self-deprecation. Alísa took his hand and squeezed it.

"I'm proud of you, pushing yourself this way."

"*As am I,*" Graydonn said. "*Though I do wish the practice swords were less sharp.*"

Falier gestured to himself. "No holes yet."

"*Yet being the operative word,*" Graydonn grumbled, head swiveling to watch Rassím and another slayer walk past them. The slayers laughed as they spoke, which did nothing for Graydonn's mood. "*At least our talons are attached and we can easily tell if we're going to hurt someone and pull back in training. How can one tell and be careful with a sword?*"

"It gets easier t—to tell the more you t-t-t-train," Alísa assured.

"Yeah," Falier said, "I'm more worried I'll hurt them than the other way around."

Blue wiggled in the bag, apparently feeling left out. Alísa placed a hand on its shell again. *It's not like paying you any attention helps either.*

Desperation shot up Alísa's arm—terrible and frightening. She yanked her hand away with a gasp, drawing Falier and Graydonn's eyes.

"Líse?"

The dragonet chirped loudly, almost a scream. Alísa's heart thudded. *No. Please not now!*

Falier's smile dropped. "Oh no."

Alísa swung around. "Koriana!"

Her cry turned every head in the square. Alísa ran for the dragoness, passing Rassím and a couple other slayers who had congregated nearby.

"What's wrong?" Rassím asked, watching as she ran past. Alísa didn't stop until she made it to Koriana. The dragonet shrieked again as Koriana sniffed at the bag, rocking violently. Koriana growled a worried note.

"*It's hatching. We have little time.*" Koriana looked to the sky and trumpeted a call for attention. It pulled the dragons in the sky toward them. "*We need to fit all of the dragons in the square.*"

"Uh, Koriana?" Selene called, her bench only about fifty feet away. She clutched at Tawny, who wiggled in her lap with a loud chirp. "Alísa? Is it time?"

Falier looked from Selene to Alísa and back. "I—"

"Go," Alísa said. She wanted to be with Selene, but Blue's situation was more dire. At least Falier being there would mean Selene wasn't alone. Yes, Taz was there, but Falier had more experience with dragons.

In the back of Alísa's mind, she found Sesína ushering the children back to their parents and houses. Good. If the worst happened, no child should be present.

"What's going on?" Rassím came up from behind, followed by a few other slayers. He jumped as the dragonet shrieked in response. "What in flames is in your bag?"

Koriana ignored the question. *"Alísa, put the egg on the ground. Dragons, circle up."*

Heart pounding, Alísa did as she was told, lying the writhing egg on the dirt. *"What are we going to do?"*

"Is that what I think it is?" Rassím said, awe filling his voice. Other slayers pressed close with him, wide-eyed. "I've never seen a—"

"Back off, slayers," Koriana commanded with a growl. Her tone softened as she answered Alísa. *"We need to help it hatch. We'll push courage to it, then when it hatches, we'll try to force it to Illuminate. If we break down all our mental barriers, instinct might take over when it makes eye-contact with one of us."*

Dragons pressed around Alísa in response to Koriana's call. Korin and Rayna had landed, and even the young dragons came near. The only dragon not present was Aree, who had stayed with her egg in the cave rather than bring it near the slayers.

The dragons closed a circle and lowering to their bellies, every glowing eye on the rocking egg. Slayers and normals alike peeked between the massive creatures, their curiosity clashing against the dragons' dread.

This was Blue's last chance. It would probably die here and now. After all their care for it, it had chosen no one.

"You should move back, Alísa," Koriana said. *"If it hatches it will be confused and might lash out. Scales are tougher than flesh."*

With a silent prayer, Alísa backed away, stopping to stand between Sesína and Graydonn. She didn't back all the way out, though—there was a chance she could Illuminate the dragonet as well.

The egg rocked again, shrieking in fear and desperation. Eyes dimmed as the dragons began pressing out courage, trying to give it the strength it needed to hatch and not give up. Then the egg rolled on the ground, circling as the scratches became louder, and Alísa felt a heavy hand on her shoulder.

"What are you doing, letting it writhe alone like that?" Rassím asked, dark eyes fixed on the egg while anger boiled inside of him. It made Alísa's stomach curl in on itself. "It's a child—how can you leave it alone, stuck in its fear?"

Rassím pushed past Alísa before she could stop him, drawing growls from multiple dragons.

"Slayer, get back!" Koriana snapped her jaws in the air. *"This doesn't concern you."*

"Like hellflames it doesn't! Maybe dragons do things differently, but where I come from, we don't leave children to suffer alone."

"That isn't it," came Saynan's calmer voice. *"It hasn't chosen a parent, and it has to or else it will die. We're giving it its best chance to find a parent as soon as it hatches."*

"We know what we're doing." Koriana growled. *"Move!"*

"Maybe if you would just hold her steady, she wouldn't be so flaming afraid and pick a parent!"

"We've tried that," Saynan said, taking a step and breaking formation. *"You don't understand..."*

Saynan's words faded away as Alísa stared at Rassím. The care in his voice was not one she expected, even after he had defended Q'rill. None of the slayers should care enough to fight dragons for a dragonet.

Then, like a key in a lock, it clicked.

Rassím had said 'she.'

"It's you, Rassím!" Alísa ran forward, rounding Saynan's massive legs to get to the slayer. The dragons stopped, heads turning to her. Rassím snapped out of his anger, eyes going wide.

"I'm what?"

"He knows the sex of the dragonet," Sesína said, bounding up beside Alísa. *"The connection has started!"*

Dragon eyes changed all around Alísa—some dimming further,

others brightening. Rassím looked from Sesína to the egg to Alísa, while the dragonet shrieked. Its fear gripped Alísa's heart, but memories of Sesína's hatching pushed it aside. She grabbed Rassím's arm, pulling him down to his knees beside the egg.

"It's you, Rassím. You're the one the d—dragonet has chosen. You wouldn't know her sex otherwise. N—none of us knew until you just t-told us."

Rassím looked between Alísa and the egg, fear and uncertainty flowing. He swallowed. "She will die without this?"

Alísa nodded solemnly.

Rassím stared at her in a daze for a moment longer. Then his eyes cleared and he looked at Blue.

"What must I do?"

Relief swept through Alísa. She took his hand and placed it on the surface of the egg. "Can you feel her fear?"

Rassím shook his head. "The shrieking and writhing tell me she's afraid. I've never felt a dragon's emotions before."

Alísa pressed her hand over top of his. "Try. You know she's an *anam*. If you search for her, you'll find her."

With a breath of resolve, he placed his other hand on the egg, stilling its shaking. His mind opened, and Alísa could better sense his emotions. Awe and doubt mingled together, each pressing forward in a fight to dominate the other.

"I feel it." Rassím laughed in near-disbelief. "I feel her!"

Alísa grinned. "Good. She needs your help to break through her fear." She lifted her hand from Rassím's, giving him control. "Give her p-p-peace so she knows you're there for her, then give her the c-c-c-c-courage she needs to break through."

"You did this before? With Sesína?"

"Yes. I can stay, if you want."

Rassím settled cross-legged and pulled Blue closer. "Please."

Alísa situated herself across from Rassím, Sesína joining her. *"Koriana, we've got Rassím. Stay with Selene and help her through it?"*

Koriana straightened, as though just realizing Tawny was in the process of hatching as well. *"Of course."*

331

Alísa glanced around them. The growing crowd of villagers and slayers stood closer now, having pushed between the stunned dragons. Whispers and murmurs abounded. Some dragons felt only relief, while others sat in reluctant acceptance.

Hatchlings were coming! Soon the cave would be filled with skittering talons and boundless energy—at least until the hatchlings were old enough to know better than to run off into the forest alone or play too rough with human children. Poor Rassím would have to move into the cave like Selene had planned to, only with much less time to prepare.

Blue's cries turned from fear-filled to determined. Rassím kept his eyes on the shell, pushing out courage like Alísa had told him.

"What's going to happen?"

Alísa smiled encouragingly. "When she hatches, the b—bond will form. You'll share memories and she'll learn how t-t-t-to live through you."

Rassím looked at her, eyes wide. "All my memories? I—I've killed dragons."

Alísa swallowed. She hadn't thought of that. Rassím was a true slayer. How would such memories affect a hatchling?

Sesína nosed Alísa's cheek and spoke to Rassím. "Yes, she will see everything and love you anyway. It's not just actions we see—it's belief and conviction and change. She will see that you thought dragons evil and now understand the truth."

"And, what will I see?"

"You'll get her limited memories too. Most importantly, though" — Sesína's eyes brightened with humor— "you'll get her name. I'm so ready to call her something other than Blue!"

"Alísa?" Briek pushed to the front of the crowd, drawing Alísa's eyes. "Rassím? What on A'dem is happening?"

Alísa looked from Briek to the dragons and slayers around him. After two weeks, they were only reluctant allies. Perhaps Rassím and Blue, a most unlikely pairing, were a gift from the Maker.

"It seems our worlds are about to draw even closer together."

A wet crack and victorious chirp silenced the world.

28

CAMARADERIE

The patter of racing paws never failed to put a smile on Alísa's face. A blue ball of energy and scales zipped past her across the dancing grounds, followed by blurs of tawny and white. The latter two branched off to chase Q'rill's tail, but the blue one, Dezra, kept a straight course. She barreled into a kneeling Rassím. The slayer grunted with the impact but managed to stay upright and wrestle her back.

Dezra flapped her wings, clumsy in her excitement, and pushed against him. *"How did you stay up? I was so fast!"*

"Fast is good, but I saw you coming. You've got to be sneaky if you're going to catch me."

Talons scraped, drawing Rassím's attention as the tawny hatchling, Hwinn, slid past him and bolted for Alísa.

"Singer! Singer, catch me!"

Alísa grinned, Hwinn's excitement bouncing through her mind. He slipped and skidded in circles around her, his tail flopping unused behind him.

"Hwinn!" Selene called from the shadow of the Hold. "What did Sesína tell you about your tail helping you make turns?"

"Oh yeah, I have a tail!"

Alísa lunged in Hwinn's distraction, purposefully missing as the hatchling yelped and stumbled over himself as he tried to jump out of the way. She 'fell' to her hands and knees and bopped Hwinn on the nose.

"Got you!"

Hwinn shook his head violently, sapphire eyes brightening. *"But you didn't catch me!"*

With that, he bolted away, first running toward Selene, then getting distracted and charging after Aravi, Saynan and Aree's hatchling. Selene shook her head while Kat stifled a laugh with a hand to her mouth, eyes soft. She had met Hwinn just after he hatched, both he and Dezra needing to eat after their Illumination. A gentle pull of pork from Kat's fingers and a *"thank you, Grandma,"* later, the hatchling had stolen her heart.

Dragons and slayers circled the hatchlings' play area, some conversing, others simply enjoying the hatchlings' antics. Safely outside the circle, Briek led weapons sparring for Falier, the young slayers, and any others who wanted practice. The seven slayer wives mostly stayed together in the shadow of the Hold, though two brave souls sat in the sun near Komi. Dreki interspersed themselves among the clans, many sunning themselves on the backs of dragons, while a couple sat on favorite shoulders. No villagers today, besides Kat and Parsen—the hatchlings weren't careful enough to play with children yet.

"Incoming!"

Sesína's warning flashed in Alísa's mind too late as Dezra bowled into her. Staying on her knees to watch Hwinn had definitely been a mistake. The sky-blue hatchling placed her front paws on Alísa's stomach, carefully keeping her talons off of her, and flared her wings in triumph.

"I got her! I got the Singer! Rassím, did you see me? I was fast and sneaky!"

Alísa laughed. *"You got me. Good job!"*

"Yes, very sneaky. Let her up now." Rassím gave an apologetic look as Dezra backed off her. *"You all right?"*

Alísa smiled reassuringly as she sat up. *"I'm fine. You should have seen some of the bruises Sesína gave me."*

Sesína snorted across the way. *"Sure, throw me to the wolves. I see how it is."*

Dezra pranced in a circle, chanting in a sing-song manner. *"I got the Singer! I got the Singer!"*

"Humans are easy." Aravi hopped up on her back paws, easily using her wings to steady herself. Her white scales glimmered in the sunlight like her father's. *"You two up for a real challenge?"*

Dezra's eyes brightened at the idea, and Hwinn's enthusiastic curiosity blasted out from him. The two of them fell in behind Aravi, all three hatchlings galumphing for Sesína. Aravi jumped, going high while Hwinn and Dezra went low. Sesína played her part, allowing the hatchlings to knock her to the ground and crawl over her. She rolled, careful not to squish the hatchlings a third her size, and pushed them playfully with paws, wings, and muzzle, growling with delight.

Alísa stood and brushed the dust from her dress. Rolling in the dirt wasn't quite the look of an alpha, but she couldn't resist the mixture of joy and excitement pouring from the hatchlings. It brought back wonderful memories of Sesína. The dragoness was nearly four-and-a-half feet tall at the withers now, at the end of a young dragon's growth spurt. She would continue to grow for the rest of her life, but at a far slower pace. Graydonn was two years older than her, but only five inches taller.

"Are you okay, Alísa?" One of the slayers approached, a man in his mid-forties. "Rassím's hatchling hit you pretty hard."

Alísa rubbed her side absently. "Might bruise, but I've had w— worse."

"Again with the wolves!" Sesína whispered through the bond.

Another slayer, this one in his twenties, came up beside the first. "Such energy in those little bodies."

"Reminds me of my children," the first agreed. "When they were much younger, of course."

Alísa smiled. "Where do your children live?"

The slayer listed two villages Alísa didn't know. She hadn't expected to—she knew all the villages in her father's territory, but not much beyond it—but it was a good point of connection nonetheless. Now that the hatchlings were old enough to be out of the cave, it was time to focus on bringing the two clans together for more than just training.

"Tail, Hwinn!" Selene called again.

The hatchlings were now taking turns flaring their wings and jumping over Sesína as she lay on her belly. Hwinn's attempted glide was foiled by his tail catching on Sesína's wing. The hatchling rolled on the other side of Sesína and hopped back up, unfazed. Aravi followed, wings snapping out to carry her over Hwinn. Being Illuminated by a dragon parent gave her an edge over the other two hatchlings. Hwinn and Dezra had learned some in their first two weeks of life outside their eggs, but they still had catching up to do.

"Singer!"

Rís' name and the image of a red dawn flashed through Alísa's mind, just as a light weight pulled at her shoulder. Tiny claws dug into her as Rís slid down her back. The baby drek was twice the size he had been when they first met—perhaps only weighing a pound—but those needles still hurt!

Alísa gritted her teeth against a hiss and reached back to push him back up onto her shoulder. Rís flapped his little wings to propel himself up, catching one in her hair like his mother often had.

Rís nuzzled her cheek, a light melancholy running from his mind to hers. Images flashed—lavenders, cupped hands, fire, purple wing-baubles. His message had something to do with his mother, but besides that Alísa couldn't figure it out.

"She would be proud of you." It was all Alísa could think to say in the wake of such a convoluted message.

Rís trilled softly.

"Is that a baby fairy?" The younger slayer leaned to get a better look.

"Drek," Alísa corrected. "That's w—what they c-c-call themselves. Dreki."

"But they are like fairies of legend?"

Stories stirred in Alísa's memory. There were so many different tales of fairies, some of creatures causing mischief, others of lights guiding people to their destiny, still others of tricksters getting humans lost in the forests never to be seen again. None of those quite fit the dreki as she knew them.

"I'm n—not entirely sure—"

Rís flared his wings and clawed Alísa's shoulder, excitement wafting from him. She fought not to cringe at the pain.

"—but Rís here seems t-t-to think so."

The older slayer frowned. "You let them live in your cave with you, but you don't know what they are? Seems rather foolish to me."

Alísa did her best not to bristle. Empathy told her his statement

336

wasn't meant to be an attack, even if it sounded like it.

"They've p-p-proven themselves to me, much like the d—dragons have—"

A trumpet of alarm sounded in the western sky. Alísa spun to face it. Saynan was scouting today. She couldn't see him yet, but the call was clear.

Galerra was back.

The dancing grounds quieted, even the hatchlings stilling as their Illumination bonds told them something was wrong. Aravi puffed out her wings, mirroring her mother's concern and anger. Hwinn raced to Selene's side, head erect as she crouched to wrap an arm around him. Fear of the unknown shuddered through Dezra—Rassím knew next to nothing about Galerra's attacks.

The older slayer looked at Alísa. "That one of yours?"

Alísa clenched her fists as Saynan trumpeted with more urgency.

No more.

Breathing through the raw hatchling emotions and sending up a prayer for words, Alísa moved.

"Hatchlings, into the Hold. Selene, s—s—stay with them." Alísa looked to the dimming eyes of the young dragons and softened her tone. "The other d—dragons won't get near, but you m—must stay inside until this is over. Do you understand?"

Frightened affirmatives flowed from the hatchlings. Kat stepped from the shadow of the Hold, clapping her hands for attention.

"Come on Dezra, Aravi. Into the cellar—let's go!"

Selene stood from comforting Hwinn and helped her mother shepherd the hatchlings away. Alísa lifted a hand to Rís.

"Dreki littles t-t-too."

Rís gave a tiny growl, but leapt off her shoulder and headed for Selene, his sister already flying to her.

Alísa looked to the others. "Dragons, p-p-p-p-p—" *Breathe. You can do this.*

"You're connected to the dragons," Sesína whispered through the bond. *"Why don't you use—oh. Oh!"*

"—p-prepare to fly. Slayers" —Alísa looked from face to face,

pausing longer on Briek as he and the trainees pushed past the dragons—
"those w—willing to fly, f—follow me."

Alísa went to Sesína, who pawed the ground in a mixture of
excitement and battle-readiness. Climbing onto the dragoness' back,
Alísa looked to the slayers again.

Most stood shocked and unmoving.

"Enemy dragons are c-coming. They've attacked us before and
threatened Me'ran. Let's show them what happens when the races c-c-c-
c-come together!"

"You heard her." Briek went to Koriana. "Any unwilling to fly, get to
the square and watch in case any get past us."

Koriana offered her muzzle, eyes flashing. *"By Maker's wings."*

Three slayers moved quickly, mounting their dragons just a hair
behind Falier.

"Slayers, c-c-c-connect to your dragons—we'll stay in
communication via t-t-telepathy. Launch!"

Sesína burst into the air. As she banked to catch an air-current, Alísa
saw more slayers going to the dragons. By a quick count, there were two
men willing to ride who would have to stay behind. Perhaps one would
ride Saynan next time.

Alísa reached for the clan-link. *"This is a trial by fire. We are not perfect
yet, but I believe we are ready. Dragons, pay attention to your flight-patterns
for your riders' sakes—no flips or hard banks if you can help it. Slayers, this is
an enemy that hasn't attacked any villages. I am not looking to kill them—but
if you must kill to protect yourself or another, you have my leave to do so. I want
a fight they will not forget!"*

"*Dreki?*" Laen's question barked through Alísa's mind.

Aree pulled alongside Sesína, fire in her eyes. *"I see Saynan."*

"Is he all right?"

"Tired, but unwounded. Praise the Maker."

"Dreki!" Laen insisted.

"Praise be," Alísa agreed. *"Dreki, go with Aree to help Saynan. Now, let's
tell Galerra that he isn't alone!"*

Aree growled, the sound shifting into a roar. Sesína joined her,
followed by the others. Grasping the dragons' courage, Alísa gave a battle

cry. Awe flowed from the slayers as her shout pulled the dragons' strength to the surface and gave them increased speed. They hadn't yet seen her give power to the dragons.

Galerra sped to meet them, her dragons keening their own battle cries. They were close enough now to distinguish eye-lights amidst their scales. There were many of them—ten, at least—more than had ever come before.

"Let them come," Sesína snarled.

Alísa shouted again, drawing dragon and slayer voices alike this time. Sesína speared for Galerra, using her superior speed and agility to evade the dragoness' claws. Scales slid beneath Alísa as Sesína slapped Galerra's wing with her tail and dove. Graydonn and Harenn followed behind with Falier and Taz, making use of Galerra's distraction to attack her wing-dragon. Aree split off to attack the dragons chasing Saynan, the cloud of dreki glowing bright and easily keeping up with her.

Wind battered Alísa as Sesína swooped and swerved, but it could not drown out the enemy's trumpets of alarm as they discovered the new slayer combatants. The sounds swelled pride in Alísa's heart—pride for her dragons and dreki, for the slayers who took the risk to ride, and even a little for herself. She shaped the emotion within her and channeled it into a new strength song.

> The air within our lungs, the fire in our hearts,
> And if our strength should fade, my song shall be the spark.
> May courage never fail, may hope command the skies—
> The wind beneath our wings. Together we will rise.

Galerra roared in outrage and her clan's behavior shifted. Some command had been given through their clan-link. Combatants broke apart, Galerra's dragons swirling away and turning their eyes on Alísa.

Alarm spiked through Sesína. *"Evading!"*

Enemy dragons converged. Alísa switched her song to one of binding, selecting the closest dragon as her target. Sesína dodged and swerved, diving lower every chance she got so dragons couldn't attack from below. A dragon dove past them and flicked its tail up. Sesína veered away but caught the edge of a tail-spine in her side. Alísa cried out for her, using the pain to further her binding as the enemy dragon's mind squirmed and speared against her. She was far better at strengthening dragons than mind-choking them.

Graydonn whisked past them, slamming into an attacking dragon, while Harenn and Komi followed behind. Briek's mind reached for the same dragon Alísa attempted to choke, closing the gaps and sending the dragon careening into the treetops. Another dragon fell away from Sesína, then another, both mind-speared by slayers.

Finally, Galerra trumpeted again, and her dragons broke off, each one turning west to follow their commander.

"Connect me to Galerra," Alísa ordered.

Sesína, though utterly exhausted, growled with pleasure and turned her muzzle west. The buzz of connection brought with it rage and a hint of shame.

"Tell your alphas I will no longer tolerate these petty attacks. The next incursion into our territory will be met with deadly force. And if Paili wants to meet me in war, tell her to come herself!"

Galerra's mind burned against Alísa, but Sesína broke off the connection before the general could spew her venom. Galerra didn't fight to regain the connection, instead leading her dragons in the direction of the Serpent's Fangs—four sister mountains formerly in Rorenth's territory, where Tsamen and Paili had apparently moved their clan.

Sesína trumpeted, fatigued yet joyous. Other dragons joined her, then came cheers from the slayers and barks from the dreki. Joy, fatigue, and pride flowed through the clan-link, along with something else. Faint, but certainly there, this emotion flowed from drek, dragon, and slayer alike. It extended out from itself and pulled the others in, creating a shared space for all of them.

The first strands of camaraderie had arrived!

INTERLUDE II

Karn stood over the map beside N'lan, the slayer chief of Parrin. Red, yellow, blue, and black tiles spread out before them, touching villages, mountains, and a few empty areas as well. N'lan ran a hand over his chestnut hair as Karn placed a new yellow tile at the Serpent's Fangs, then a blue one at the village of L'rang.

"We're running out of options," N'lan said. "Every day a new report comes in of another confirmed dragon clan, but no word of a Dragon Singer with them. Perhaps she's lying low now. If that's the case, you're better off storming mountains than waiting here."

Karn shook his head. "There were signs of dragon-on-dragon conflict when I saw her last. Either the dragons who have her were the clan already in the mountain or, more likely, they were a separate clan using her to claim more territory. If my instincts are correct, they will still be on the move. Chief Tella and her wayfarers are watching that mountain in case they come back. It's only a matter of time before they show themselves again."

"Time we may not have." N'lan pointed deeply-tanned fingers at two black tiles sitting within twenty miles of each other, each one between villages. "If reports are to be believed, the Nameless are creating more an'reik in this area. Have you considered they may be using the dragons and Alísa to do it? Perhaps we should concentrate our efforts here."

Karn caught himself rubbing his fingers over the burn scar on his sword-arm. He forced his hand down and his voice steady. An'reik were not his concern in this moment.

"No. We stick to the plan until there is a confirmed report of a

Dragon Singer. Village-bound slayers will be enough to keep a few an'reik at bay. Besides, the tales of Bria never speak of her creating an'reik. The people she turned fought with fists and weapons, not demonic power."

Karn scanned the map, then pointed at a village southwest of L'rang. "We'll send the next party here—"

The door opened behind Karn, and he turned to see Hanah standing in the frame, out of breath. In the lamp-light, her auburn hair looked almost red, making her look so much like Alísa it hurt.

"Messenger, Karn. From Tella."

Karn didn't waste a second, charging for the door as Hanah led the way. N'lan followed directly behind. Down the stairs of N'lan's home, through the outside door, and into the cobblestone street, where members of the clan already gathered. Hanah strode with purpose, the crowd parting for her out of sheer necessity.

The messenger stood just outside the Hold as a young woman took his horse to the stable. Though he wore the traditional white and blue signaling his peaceful mission, the jagged talon-scar on his left arm marked him as a slayer rather than a professional messenger. Kallar, Farren, and L'non already stood nearby, each backing up a step at their Lady's approach.

"What news?" Hanah asked, ending her brisk pace before the man.

The messenger clasped his fist to his heart with a respect many slayers didn't show the Lady of a different clan.

"Segenn has fallen. A survivor speaks of a Dragon Singer."

Segenn? In the forests? Karn caught Kallar's look of regret, which quickly turned to frustration. They had ruled out the eastern forests as an option—most dragons wouldn't stay there, with too few mountains and places clear enough to hunt. They had come all this way when they should have gone in the opposite direction!

"Fallen?" N'lan came up, disbelief in his eyes. "What do you mean, fallen?

"Segenn received word of the Dragon Singer much further into the forests and moved against her, hoping to catch her and her dragons off-guard. The village of Me'ran was already under her control, and by her power alone she turned half of them to her side and used them to kill their brothers. The dragons weren't even there for most of it."

No. It couldn't be.

Karn staggered back a step. He had seen Alísa only a little over a month ago. After two months among the dragons, she still had kept them from attacking him in the cave that day. Could one more month make that much of a difference? To twist his kind, good, meek Alísa into this?

There must be a second Dragon Singer. It was the only thing that made sense. Alísa couldn't have done this. She couldn't be so turned by the dragons, so changed beyond recognition.

Yet the fierceness in her eyes as she insisted the dragon she released was good misted through his mind. She could fight when she wanted to.

But destroy a clan of slayers?

"What is her name?"

The slayer paused. "Excuse me?"

"The Dragon Singer. What is her name? Did the survivor describe her?"

Incredulity flashed across the slayer's face. "How can you even ask that? You were the one who alerted us all in the first—"

Karn didn't know what he was doing until it was done. He clenched the man's tunic in his fists, holding him off the ground and inches from his face.

"You forget your place! You will answer me! Did the survivor describe the Dragon Singer or give her name?"

The messenger breathed heavily, obviously working to suppress the urge to fight. "The survivor is a slayer bound to Me'ran. He witnessed everything—it's your flaming daughter."

Karn's jaw tightened, as did his grip. "You—"

"Karn." A hand pressed on Karn's shoulder. "Release him."

Hanah. He hadn't realized the world tinting red around him until her voice broke through it. He breathed, forcing his anger down before setting the slayer back on his feet.

"Rest with the holders," Karn told him simply. "We leave tomorrow."

The man glowered at him, but Karn no longer cared. He turned away, walking back through the gathered crowd, hardly seeing them as he passed.

"Karn," N'lan said, "shouldn't we—"

"If you can spare any men, tell them we leave at daybreak."

N'lan said something else, but Karn didn't hear it. He might have heard Hanah respond, but as he tromped further and further from the crowd, the world in both sight and sound became fuzzy.

Alísa. It was Alísa.

He was too late.

Holy Maker, why?! Karn's boots pounded into the dirt, punctuating his anger. *I did as I was supposed to! I denied the darkness in faith that You would protect her, that You would bring me to her before it was too late!*

What could he do now? If she had truly bewitched a village for the dragons and become powerful enough to turn a slayer clan against itself—what hope remained for her? For either of them? His heart would give out before he could do what needed to be done. He couldn't save the world if it meant sacrificing his precious daughter.

Karn threw back the curtain to his tent and turned not into his own chamber, but Alísa's. Her few possessions lay in a pile in the center of the space, ready for her return. Her large pack with what clothing she left behind. Her rolled up bed-mat. The mountain-bear furs that had kept her warm at night. He knelt to pick up the fur and hold it to his face, letting it soak up the tears as sobs shuddered through him.

It was no use. No matter how hard he prayed or tried to believe there was some other explanation, he couldn't shake it. Alísa was gone. The dragons had taken her, changed her, warped her into something that would kill her own people and perpetuate the horror that had been wrought on her.

And he would have to kill her to stop her and free her soul.

A hand lighted on his head, Hanah pulling him into her embrace. Her arms were strong. He should be holding her, yet he couldn't find the strength to resist. Pressing his ear to her heartbeat, he wept for their daughter.

"All is not lost, my love." A hot tear fell into his hair as Hanah stroked it. "Love is stronger than any dragon, the Maker and Branni stronger than the Nameless. You've told me time and again you would save her—"

Hanah's voice broke, and she swallowed. "I believed you, and until you remember, I will hold enough faith for both of us. You will bring her home."

Karn breathed, trying to regain the ability to speak, but it wouldn't come. He didn't deserve such deep belief from Hanah, not after he had already failed Alísa twice—once making her run away and once when her captors stood right in front of him.

Branni and Maker above all, help me save Alísa.

29

PEACE

Alísa watched the astral plane as Sesína made a long, lazy bank around the combatants. Explosions of brown, blue, and green erupted from multiple slayers on dragonback, while the dragons swooped around each other attempting tail-slaps, talon-less bats of a paw, and other ways to 'wound' each other. With Koriana on a scouting venture with Briek, and Sesína with Alísa watching the fight, that left ten dragons for this war-game.

Five hits to a dragon—psychic or physical—knocked the dragon and their rider out of the game. The slayers were now allowed to decide for themselves when to attack psychically and when to defend. Some adopted the strategy of only shielding, but most of the warriors needed more action and attempted blasting other dragons without accidentally hitting one of their own teammates.

Amazingly, Falier was the most adept slayer in the skies. None of the other pairs had the mind-kin bond that allowed him to anticipate his mount's moves and share psychic strength. That also made him and Graydonn a tempting target.

Pent-up energy rippled through Sesína. *"I hate being a leader. Leaders have to watch too much. We need practice too!"*

Alísa nodded, watching as a red dragon nearly spun his rider off. *"Connect me to Harenn."* Once connected, she growled. *"Harenn! One more roll like that and I'm saying Taz fell off and you're out."*

The dragon sent back a grumble. *"You'd rather we die? Tora almost had us!"*

"And the last two times?"

That shut him up. At least he was trying. He had accepted a rider

346

every day without complaint, much to everyone's surprise. Whether the riders accepted Harenn, however, was another question. Though Taz didn't necessarily enjoy it, he put up with Harenn's aggressive flying best. Two other slayers found riding Harenn a challenge worth tackling, but they tended to try and control him rather than work with him.

A tinge of jealousy filled Alísa each time she watched the dragons and slayers train. The men could attack psychically far more easily than she could. All they had to do was think it, gather their strength, and blast it forward. She had to weave words together, and when her attacks hit, pain shocked back to her through her dragon empathy. It worked better for her to either push strength to her dragons and allow them to press the attack, or to weave a long-lasting shield.

Saynan swooped in right behind Graydonn and opened his mouth as though to breathe ice over Graydonn's tail.

"Point for Saynan against Graydonn," Alísa said, in case Graydonn didn't sense it. That made four hits against Graydonn—only one more before he and Falier were out of the game.

Alísa patted Sesína's neck. *"What do you say we help them?"*

"Cheating?" Sesína looked back, her eyes brightening. *"I didn't know you had it in you!"*

Ideas formed in Alísa's mind. *"Less cheating, more a surprise change in the game. After all, we need practice too."*

Sesína grinned and looked to the group, trumpeting for attention.

"Your battle is interrupted," Alísa said to both teams. *"The Dragon Singer appears and calls a dragon out from each team. She sings strength into them, resetting their wound counts. The rest of you are outraged and form a tentative alliance against us. You can still attack the opposite team, but you might be better served focusing on us first. Graydonn, Komi—you're with me. Go!"*

With another trumpet, Sesína swooped into the fray. Graydonn, Falier, Komi, and T'lan connected to them in a new team-link, and Alísa sang her strength song, channeling her power through it. Her dragons surged with new energy, rushing through the tangle of the other teams and landing blows while they gathered themselves.

Saynan roared a command, and the dragons converged on Sesína—

just as Galerra had commanded her dragons to do weeks ago. A solid plan, especially with their eight pairings against her three. Graydonn and Komi rushed to Sesína, their riders shouting battle cries as they sent psychic blasts flying at the other dragons. Alísa's stomach hit her throat as Sesína rolled from one tail-slap and straight into another dragon's paw. A psychic blast hit them in absence of a psychic shield. Alísa switched to a shielding song—the strength song would last Graydonn and Komi a few minutes before she'd have to sing it again.

Her team kept track of hits through the link. They were quickly overwhelmed, but seemed to enjoy the challenge—intense concentration merged with camaraderie and joy, mingling in a playful competitiveness.

Sesína took her third hit from Faern's rider just before giving Faern his final hit. Graydonn trumpeted a warning and Sesína back-flipped over Harenn, who growled a protest at her aerobatics after Alísa had scolded him for the same.

Komi now had three hits, Graydonn four. Falier switched to solely shielding Graydonn rather than attacking other players, leaving the attacks to Graydonn. Saynan was right behind him, about to pretend to breathe ice again, but Komi swooped in and slapped his wing with her tail, giving Saynan his fifth and final hit. Sesína's trumpet of congratulations turned into a bleat as Tora slapped her tail with a paw. Four hits.

A trumpet of resignation came from Graydonn as he received his fifth hit. He dove below the fray, taking himself and Falier out of the game. Komi gave Harenn a tail-slap, while T'lan sent a psychic bolt at the same time, taking Harenn out.

Psychic bolts hit Alísa's shield from three different slayers at once, all approaching fast on their mounts. Sesína wove past the first, but their teamwork was solid, and a tail-slap caught on the tip of her wing. Five hits. Sesína trumpeted in mock pain and dropped from the sky, her dramatics covering her true sadness at being out of the game.

Alísa patted her neck as Sesína evened out over Me'ran. *"I stacked the odds against us. We'll get them next time."*

"Yeah." Sesína looked back, a glimmer in her emerald eyes. *"It was*

fun, though."

Soon Komi fell from the fray and joined Sesína and Graydonn circling below with the other 'dead' dragons. *"Who got you, Graydonn? I didn't see."*

"Q'rill."

Komi thrummed. *"You should know we had a bet going. For the rest of today and tomorrow, we all have to call Q'rill and Rassím by the titles of 'champion'."*

Confusion ran through Falier. *"For taking Graydonn down?"*

Komi sent an affirmative. *"You work together too smoothly—the rest of us need to catch up with you."*

Good humor flowed from T'lan. *"I told Komi we should turn traitor when you got your fourth hit—take you out and claim the title—but she's too honorable."*

Sesína cough-laughed. *"So you're saying we need to keep you two together so she keeps you honest?"*

T'lan winked at her. *"Probably wise."*

Alísa followed a feeling of pride through the team-link to Falier. She smiled—it was a rare feeling from him. He was still pretty terrible with a sword and knew it. Being targeted by the slayers because of his prowess would hopefully counteract some of his frustration.

She pushed her own pride to him. He would learn to use the sword, Alísa had no doubt, but he was born to be a dragon-rider.

Trumpets of victory sounded above as Tora and Q'rill knocked the last dragon of the opposite team from the sky. Komi trumpeted congratulations back to her former teammates.

"Well done, everyone," Alísa said as soon as Sesína reformed the full clan-link. *"That's it for today. You're dismissed until the céilí—see you all there."*

Twilight was Alísa's favorite time of day in the summer. The slowly cooling air, the shadows casting across the ground in melancholy shapes, the world relaxing from the business of day into the calm of night. The music of the céilí seemed so much more colorful when the world was draped in shadow.

Alísa advanced past her partner—a Sorenite—and retreated back on his opposite side. She currently faced the Hold, where people gathered to talk through the song, a few absently clapping to the beat. The Sorenite reached for her hand and spun her twice before sending her to the left toward her next partner.

The dancers had almost made it all the way around the circle this song, each pairing only getting a few steps together before they moved on. Alísa far preferred dances where she could get a feel for her partner as the song progressed, but she smiled as she danced among the people. Me'ranians, Sorenites, and slayers alike danced in this circle, finding a harmony that didn't always exist in real-life, but had become more common as time passed.

Alísa stepped around her new partner, adding a spin so she could sneak a peek at the dreki dancing around the fire. Their jewel-like wing-baubles glittered in the firelight, adding a sense of wonder, and a few young children spun and jumped underneath them, giggling at the fairy-like creatures. Beyond the dancers, dragons lounged at the edge of the forest, their eye-lights both eerie and comforting. A few people stood among them, chatting amiably as they watched the older children play tag with the hatchlings.

Alísa smiled—her world was at peace.

The music slowed through the last few steps of the dance, allowing more room for her slayer partner to embellish the lady's moves with spins or lifts. New to céilí dancing, he only spun her once, but she beamed at him as though he had just led with all the talent of one of the holders. He was here, and one of the few slayers actually joining the dance. They bowed to each other, then turned to the musicians to applaud them.

Selene and Taz sat on one of the musicians' benches, closer together than Alísa thought their instruments should allow. Both the wood flute and the low fife required a little bit of elbow room. Alísa grinned as Taz tried to say something and Selene interrupted him with a kiss. It had been a week since she and Taz had gone to her parents and told them how they had been in love for years. Apparently, Parsen and Kat had already figured it out and took little convincing to support Taz's pursuit.

Briek, too, gave his blessing, once again proving how different he was from Segenn. Alísa had met a few chiefs who required their slayers to marry other slayers because it would produce stronger progeny. All she could think of was brood mares when they spoke of it—it made her sick.

A hand took hers and pulled her from her thoughts into a spin. She caught glimpses of Falier as he spun her swiftly, ending in a cuddle position with his arms around her waist and her back against his chest. She leaned into him, savoring his warmth and affection.

"I know I asked you to dance the last one and am technically supposed to ask someone else to dance before I come back to you." He kissed her temple. "But since that was a partner-trading dance, I'm going to say I've already danced with someone else and can definitely claim you again."

"Claim me?" Alísa looked back. "D—don't I get a say in the matter?"

"I don't feel you pulling away."

She leaned against him. "I'm just t-tired. And lazy. I g—guess I'll dance with you again."

A new song began to play, but without any announcement or a caller coming to the front. Selene's flute sang a long, quiet note into the night, Taz's low-fife coming underneath with a bass note that reminded Alísa of her father's bedtime stories when she was little.

Her breath caught in her throat as images rose. The world was not at peace—it never would be while they were apart and he was living for lies.

Concern flowed from Falier. "You okay, Líse?"

Alísa swallowed and nodded. "J—just remembering. They p-p-p—play well together."

Falier seemed unconvinced by the change in topic, but rather than press, he pulled her around to face him. "It seems we've hit the last lullaby before the people go home. Dance with me anyway?"

Alísa smiled softly. As Falier tightened his hold around her waist, she laced her fingers behind his neck. His skin against her fingers brought his emotions closer—concern, affection, melancholy, and desire. They settled in her heart and mingled with her own emotions, and she hoped

351

he sensed hers as well as she did his. They swayed to the music and Alísa wondered that anything could feel so simultaneously strong and gentle as Falier's arms.

"Have I told you that you're amazing?" he murmured.

"A few times," she whispered back. "Why now?"

"This. All of this. Slayers, normals, dragons, and dreki. None of this would have happened without you." Falier kissed her forehead. "You see people so deeply, and with all of their differences bring them into community."

Alísa chuckled. "You make me sound like a holder."

"Hey, I'm a holder with slayer powers. Maybe you're a slayer with holder powers."

Alísa hummed, tilting her head up to kiss him. "Maybe."

"*Singer!*" The heavy buzz of Koriana's telepathy shocked Alísa to attention. "*Slayer-Falier, good. Briek and I must speak with you.*"

Alísa loosened her hold on Falier and twisted to look into the sky. Koriana's form passed between Alísa and the stars, barely illuminated by the firelight.

"*What's wrong?*"

"*Slayers gather at the Nissen River!*"

30

A DESPERATE PLAN

The dancing grounds were quiet and shadowed, the céilí's bonfire beginning to burn down. With most of the people gone home, the shadows cast by those remaining somehow seemed darker.

Alísa, Briek, and their lieutenants gathered around the fire, joined by a few villagers. Certain elders had been carefully selected and quietly asked to stay after the festivities. The people would learn of the threat soon—Alísa wouldn't keep that from them—but their panic would do no good as they figured out what to do.

Once the dragons pulled all the humans and Laen into the mind-link, Alísa looked to Koriana.

"Please tell us exactly what you saw."

Koriana tapped her tail on the ground. *"Multiple slayer clans across the Nissen to the south—"*

Chief Tella's territory. The thought shuddered through Alísa.

"—one group camping a mile from the bank. It was big enough to be two clans, but there was no divide between camps, so I am not sure. Another group was further west and barely visible until I got closer to the river. That second group traveled in a line approaching the first."

"And you're sure they aren't simply a group of travelers?" Tenza asked. "A moving family, or a band of bards?"

"I cannot be sure without flying directly above to see their weapons, but I have seen many travelers in my time as a scout. This appeared as a wayfaring slayer clan."

"Which is worrisome," Briek said aloud. Though he would speak telepathically during training, he always seemed more comfortable verbally. "There is no reason for a wayfaring clan to leave their territory unguarded. None except a threat too big for one clan, which rarely happens outside the Prilune mountain territories. If this second group is indeed a slayer clan, they march to face a threat equal to a clan of fifty or more dragons. With Alísa's tale of defeating the great red beast and his clan, I can think of only one other such threat: Dragon Singer."

"We must not have moved fast enough in telling the surrounding villages about us—or else, someone called for them anyway." Alísa rubbed chilled hands over her skirts. *"Chief Tella is proud, but I don't think she's too proud to refuse to call for aid."*

Briek's brow raised. "You know Tella?"

Alísa swallowed back her emotions. *"I met her once. My father took me to honor her father's death and acknowledge her chiefdom."*

A look of understanding crossed Briek's face.

"Is there a way to get a message to her?" Parsen asked. "Tell her the truth of what happened and that there is no danger?"

"Yes, Briek," Kat said, her hands fisting her apron, "can't you send some of your men?"

"I can," he said. "But I doubt they would be heard. The clans are gathering for war. They likely believe the narrative Segenn did—that the Singer has overtaken our minds. They're as likely to kill my men on sight as to hear them—perhaps more."

"How do we get through to them, then?" Kat asked.

"We can't just let them come," Saynan agreed, *"else we have a far greater tragedy on our hands."*

Briek looked at Alísa. "Our best bet is Alísa singing to them like she did us, but we can't expect them all to listen and turn. There will be a battle."

Koriana thrashed her tail. *"And how do you propose we get Alísa close enough to sing without them killing her on sight?"*

Darrin—Briek's second—stroked his shaven chin. "Maybe if Sesína flies her high enough to be out of range of spears and arrows? If the rest of us are there, we can block psychic attacks until she has them under control."

Alísa shook her head, placing a hand on Sesína's wither. *"I could barely hold down Segenn's clan, and I only did it by draining Sesína's energy completely. She can't be flying me."*

"What if we help you hold them down?" Briek said. "We won't be able to hold all of them, but we might be able to choke enough of them that you and Sesína can get the rest."

"It will be a struggle to get to the point where we could hold them," Saynan said, *"and, in the meantime, they will have their weapons. If we're focusing on psychically holding them down, some of us will be cut down in the process."*

Saynan looked to Alísa, a strange peace wafting from him. *"It is a sacrifice we will make if you choose it, Singer. We must protect the hatchlings and civilians here, and we must face the slayers eventually."*

Laen barked an agreement. *"Protect!"*

Alísa's heart caved in on itself as everyone looked at her. Such a sacrifice was too great. She doubted she could sing for peace as her clanmates were cut down all around her. Especially by her father's clan. That group traveling from further west was him—the more she considered it, the more she knew it was so.

"Thank you, Saynan," she forced herself to say, *"but I will not settle there just yet. What other plans can we find?"*

"What of a less war-like approach?" Graydonn said. *"Perhaps we simply show up at the western edge of the Nissen, ask to parley and show them a group of dragons and slayers united? Wouldn't that give them pause?"*

"It might," Briek said. "They might also see the dragons and panic. They think you held villagers under your sway and might think the same of us if we approach side-by-side."

"We cannot win with all of these lies the slayers believe!" Graydonn lashed his tail in frustration. *"Anything we do, they will twist into something nefarious, even the most good and peaceful of actions!"*

Falier placed a hand on Graydonn's neck, and the dragon slowly relaxed as they exchanged words in confidence. The picture was like the first time the two of them met, the typically calm and peaceful dragon's hidden anger rising to the surface. Only this time, instead of trembling behind Alísa, Falier stepped up to douse the flame. He had come so far since that day, now even leading Briek's slayers by example as they watched him interact with the dragons as friends and fellow soul-bearers.

And now they all would die—one of Alísa's families at the hands of the other. Her handful of dragons and slayers could not win against two, possibly three, full clans of slayers honed and hardened by life in the war-torn hill country. Even her strengthening songs wouldn't be enough.

There had to be a way to even the odds—to turn some of the coming slayers to her side before a battle. If she could find a way to talk to them before they armed themselves for war, her clan might stand a chance.

But how? Segenn hadn't given her a chance to speak, keeping Rassím's knife on her at all times. He had expected her to be like Bria— at least, the Bria the slayers remembered—fully against the slayers, ready to trick or else destroy them. Slayers and dragons alike compared her to her predecessor. Eldra Bria forgive her, she hated it so!

How could she prove she came not for war, but for peace? How could she prove her sincerity?

A chill passed through her, bold and terrifying.

Surrender.

Sesína clipped Alísa off from the rest of the group, reacting before the idea fully formed. *"No."*

"Not the clan. Just me."

"Absolutely not!"

"A woman under the control of dragons would never do it. Bria would never have given herself up."

"There's good reason for that!" Sesína's tail thrashed, drawing the attention of a few in the circle. *"Didn't you hear what Briek said would happen if he sent some of his slayers? How much more would they kill the Dragon Singer herself?"*

Sesína's fear left an acrid taste on Alísa's tongue. She reached for Sesína's snout, but the dragoness pulled back.

"Papá is there," Alísa said, trying to soothe her. *"He won't let them kill me. If I can get to him first, I'll be safe."*

Sesína snorted steam. *"And if you don't?"*

Alísa sighed. *"Remember Bria's last battle? These odds are worse. If we face them head-on without turning at least some of their ears to the truth, I'm dead anyway. At least this gives us a chance."*

She reached out again and stroked Sesína's muzzle, accepting the dragoness' fear and sorrow as it lanced through her. Now everyone stared at them. She blew out a trembling breath.

"Connect me to them again, dear one. I'll need everyone's help to plan this right."

Begrudgingly, Sesína connected the two of them back into the group. The telepathy lines were eerily silent as Alísa turned around to face them.

"Graydonn was right—we need a peaceful approach first if we're going to win this. Show the slayers the truth and pray some turn to join us." Alísa braced herself for the barrage. *"I'm going to surrender myself."*

Emotions hit her, all different from each other and mixing terribly. Graydonn slumped as though he regretted asking about peaceful options now. Kat clenched her apron tighter, looking between Alísa and Falier. Falier's stare held both resignation and anger. Koriana's eyes flared with fire.

"Absolutely not!"

"They'll kill you." Briek shook his head. "My men are more likely to be safe with them than you are."

"Especially with Tella," Darrin agreed. "She's ruthless."

"Singer, I must say I agree with the slayers," Saynan said, his eyes dimming. *"You going in by yourself is folly."*

"It's idiotic," Koriana snapped. *"Whether they kill or capture you, where will our clan be without your song when the time comes to fight? And believe me, no matter what happens with this 'plan' of yours, there will be a time to fight. Without you, we are crippled beyond our ability to beat them."*

Alísa shook her head. *"Koriana, you know we cannot win this fight. You showed me Bria's final battle. Her clan faced a similar slayer army and had more dragons than we do, and she lost. We cannot win against two full western clans. The only hope we have is to lower their numbers before the fight, and the only chance we have of gaining their ears is if I go to them unarmed and without an army of dragons and turned slayers behind me."*

Koriana huffed her anger and frustration, her eyes dimming from battle-ready to pain-stricken.

"Líse," Falier said, touching her arm, *"Briek said they'd kill his men before they had a chance to talk. What makes you think you will be given any quarter?"*

"*Papá is there.*" Alísa firmed her chin. "*His clan is the one Koriana saw approaching, I'm sure of it. If I can get to him first, he'll keep them from killing me. Once we're together, I can convince him.*"

Unbidden, her father's eyes of betrayal flashed through her mind's eye. He hadn't listened then. He had never listened to her when it came to dragons.

Alísa pushed the thought away. This time would be different.

Briek folded his arms. "And if you can't?"

Alísa shook her head. "*If we wait here, we lose and civilians die. If we attack, we will probably die and the clans will have been given no chance to hear the truth. If we go under a white flag, the clans will only see an army of dragons and we will die. If I go alone, they may kill me, leaving you to decide whether to fight and die or flee to fight another day. But if they don't kill me, some slayers will turn and come to our aid when we fight the rest.*"

She looked from human to dragon to drek. "*This is our only real chance.*"

The world went silent but for the buzzing of telepathic connection. Fear and anger churned like a lake in the middle of a storm, rushing over and through Alísa until slowly it gave way to acceptance.

Sesína lowered to her belly, chin on the ground in defeat. "*I hate your logic.*"

Alísa sighed. "*Me too.*"

"While you're out risking your life on your own," Briek said, pain in his eyes, "what are the rest of us supposed to do?"

"*I don't want to approach with an army. Strong scouts might sense slayers or dragons on the other side of the river and be less inclined to believe I come in peace. But, as Koriana said, a fight is likely unavoidable.*"

"*I believe I said 'completely' unavoidable,*" Koriana grumbled.

"*Is there a way to get the clans there without alerting the others?*"

Briek cleared his throat and looked up at Koriana. "There is. But the dragons won't like it."

Koriana narrowed her eyes. "*Try me.*"

"If we hold you dragons in gentle mind-chokes—"

Even Saynan snorted at that, swirling frost descending from his nostrils, while Koriana growled beside him.

"Hear me out." Briek held up pacifying hands. "We land a couple miles east of the river. Then we surround each dragon's mind in a light choke—a shield, if you will. The gathered slayers will be watching for dragons, not men, and the shields will keep you from being noticed. It's not fool-proof, but it might buy time before we're found out."

Briek paused, looking Koriana in the eye. "Can you and your people trust us to do this and not fight us?"

Koriana grumbled in her throat, but the fire in Koriana's eyes dimmed. *"We will do what we must. Still, I doubt enough of their slayers will turn for us to win when it comes time to fight."*

"We have allied slayers in the area." Graydonn clicked in his throat. *"Village-bound men of Soren and other villages who at the very least tolerate us. If they know slayers are coming with violent intentions, perhaps they will rise up. We can gather any who are willing to fight while Alísa goes to her father."*

"And when do we fly in to rescue you, Singer?" Koriana arched her neck to look Alísa in the eye. *"We cannot simply leave you with them until they all see reason—the longer you are among them, the more likely you will be harmed."*

Alísa's heart rebelled against the dragoness' statement. She wanted to save them all; if she had enough time, surely she could do it!

Koriana caught the thought. *"Alísa, there comes a time in everyone's life where a choice must be made. You are going to give them that choice, as you have always fought to do, but you have to know and allow that some will choose not to change. This is war. The stakes grow higher by the day, and the time given to choose grows shorter."*

"I have to agree with Koriana," Briek said. "While it is true that more time may convince more people, it is also true that the war will still rage on in the background. The longer you give to those who have already chosen to fight and die, the less time you give to the civilians who never chose it and whose only chances lie in our bringing the war to an end."

Alísa swallowed as tears filled her eyes. The clan's hatchlings rose in Alísa's mind, followed by all those she had been forced to watch be slaughtered at slayer ceremonies. She shook the tears away. Though it hurt like flames to admit, Koriana and Briek were right.

"Give me two days with my father," she said. *"That should be enough to*

convince him of the truth and gain an audience with the rest of the clan. Those gathering will wait on the opposite side of the Nissen with Sesína, who will keep an eye on me through our Illumination bond and warn you if things take a turn for the worst."

"One problem," Falier said. "Even if the slayers don't sense her presence, they're sure to see your bond. As soon as they look to the astral plane, they'll see it and choke it off. You won't be able to communicate."

Alísa looked down, heart sinking as her safety-net unraveled into a pile of string. "You're right. I won't be able to tell anyone what's happening."

"You won't." Falier patted Graydonn's wither. "But I will. I'm going with you."

All eyes were on him now, his parents looking especially confused. Alísa cocked her head. "What are you talking about?"

"Mind-kin. Our bond isn't a constant connection like Illumination—if Graydonn and I aren't speaking to each other, no one will see our bond in the astral plane. We can be separate until we need to call for each other and, assuming we're within range, can send a quick message and break off before anyone sees it. I'm not sure how far a mind-kin bond will reach, but we can test that before we go into the camp."

"Sesína," Alísa whispered, eying the wonderful, beautiful, incredibly-stupid man beside her, "help me speak with Falier alone." Once Sesína cut them off from everyone else, Alísa spoke again.

"You know what you're volunteering to do? The others don't think I'll make it through this. Even Sesína fears for my life."

Falier's eyes softened. "I think you're right and you going to them is the best plan we've got. I also know that whether or not the mind-kin bond would be helpful, I would never let you go in there alone. I'm just glad I can be of more use than simple moral support."

Even as a part of her shrunk back from Falier putting himself in danger, the other part settled in relief, knowing she wouldn't be alone. Her heart trembled as Chrí, Sareth, and Namor all rose in her mind's eye, and she breathed to steady herself. As with the others, including the many still living alongside her, she couldn't strip that choice from Falier.

But Holy Maker and Eldír Nahne, Branni, and Bria—don't let him be next.

31

GOODBYES

Surely I'm forgetting something important.

Falier stared at the nearly half-full pack sitting on his bed, then looked about his room once again. Was this really all he needed? A change of clothes, a water canteen, a little dried meat and fruit, and a wool blanket? Alísa had said to pack light. They didn't need non-essentials as prisoners of war.

He breathed to steady himself. Prisoner of war. That's what he volunteered for last night. To be completely out of his element, held captive by warriors, and unable to serve Alísa in any way besides calling for reinforcements—and that only at the absolute right time.

No pressure.

Falier paused at the door handle. Even if things went well and he came back, this would be one of the final times he would be in this room, this building, this village. If Karn and Tella accepted Alísa and the dragons, the next logical step would be to stay in the west, where the war raged hottest. Hopefully, in all his striving, he had somehow done right by Me'ran.

Blowing out a breath, Falier opened the door. His family waited right where he had left them after breakfast—sitting at the table closest to the kitchen. They stood quickly, his parents coming forward while Selene held herself and Hwinn back. His father's face was stoic, while his mother screwed hers up to hold back tears.

What could he say to them? He wanted to tell them he would be okay, yet he knew better than to speak of what he didn't know. As his mother drew near, her breaking heart evident, he said the only thing he could.

"I have to go. I can't let slayers come hurt us again, and I won't let Alísa face them alone."

Kat nodded, the motion full of tension. She opened her mouth as though to speak, but no sound escaped her throat. Falier opened his arms to her, and his mother fell into them. Her hold was iron, like she might never let go. A small part of him wanted that—the part that still felt like a child lost in a new world.

But she did pull back, abruptly, as though someone else had ripped her away. Wiping her eyes with her sleeves, she turned away from him. Would she ever forgive him for this?

His father drew close and placed a hand on Falier's shoulder. Falier's eyes didn't leave his mother until his father squeezed lightly.

"You were made for this, my son. Gifted by the Maker, trained in service by Eldra Nahne, blessed in battle by Eldra Branni. We are so proud of you."

Falier couldn't help but glance at his mother again. She kept her face turned away. His father squeezed again.

"Both of us. Trust me."

Falier breathed back tears, then embraced his father. "Love you, Pa."

"I love you too." His voice was heavy with unshed tears. "May the Maker protect you, His hands a shield about you."

Falier breathed in the prayer, echoing it back to his family in his heart with a pulse of new meaning. Alísa had said before that slayers were made to be a shield for others. Everything he would face would be for this purpose—to shield Me'ran from the coming storm. Perhaps it was sacrilegious, equating himself with the Maker's hands in this moment, but the thought gave him strength.

With one last squeeze, Falier pulled away from his father and went to Selene and Hwinn. At some silent direction, Hwinn broke from Selene's side and rushed to Falier.

"Are you ready, Uncle Falier? You have all your things?" Hwinn got up on his hind legs and sniffed at Falier's bag, wings wobbling to help him keep his balance. *"Where's your drum? What if they like music?"*

Falier squatted down to him, unable to hold back the chuckle that always came when the dragon called him 'uncle.' *"I don't think the bodhrán will be necessary this time. I'll come back for it."*

"And then I get to go too, right?"

Falier looked up at Selene. That was a question he couldn't answer. She approached them, addressing Hwinn but keeping her eyes on Falier.

"Yes, darling. We'll follow Alísa and Uncle Falier."

Standing, Falier accepted his sister's embrace. *"You've decided, then?"*

"Hwinn needs to be with dragons, and I want to be with you."

Falier pulled back and quirked a smile. *"And it definitely has nothing to do with Taz coming too, right?"*

Selene shrugged. *"I was trying to be sweet and sisterly."*

"Sisterly is good, but I see right through sweet."

Selene gave a sad smile. *"Yeah, I guess that's your area, not mine."*

Falier took in the melancholy that broke through her banter. He didn't sense that Selene didn't want him to go—Hwinn would also be more subdued if that were the case—but fear lingered in her.

"I'll be careful."

She shook her head. *"If you were being careful, you wouldn't be going. Be wise."*

"Promise. Love you, sis." He looked down at Hwinn. *"Take care of her while I'm gone."*

The hatchling flared his wings, blue eyes brightening. *"Promise!"*

Falier grinned, raising eyebrows at Selene. *"Looks like I'm leaving you in good hands, err, wings."*

Selene's lips quirked and she nodded at someone behind him. *"Go on, then. Save the world or something."*

Falier followed her eyes to Alísa standing at one of the doors. She'd pulled back her hair from her face in a mass of springy curls, ready for riding. She wore her brown cloak with a black blouse and red tartan skirt underneath, and the sapphire dragon scale pendant she typically hid lay on top of her blouse. She looked every bit a chief's daughter—a slayer precariously balanced between her own people and another.

He went to her, adjusting his pack over his shoulder as he walked. His parents stood off to the side, his father whispering something to his mother. She still wouldn't look at Falier, and it sank heavily in his heart.

MICHELLE M. BRUHN

Alísa's own melancholy was palpable as she looked over his family, and he knew she was thinking of the day she left her own, not knowing if she would see them again.

He stopped in front of her. "Ready?"

"Almost." Alísa took his hand. "There's something you n—need to see."

As Alísa grabbed the handle to the door, Falier realized they were at the southern door, not the northern one leading to the dragons' typical landing site. He barely had time to feel confused as Alísa pulled him outside.

Falier pulled in a breath as a crowd of villagers filled his vision. The expectation on their faces gave way to both smiles and tears as a few claps turned to applause. Falier swallowed back tears as the support of those he loved filled his heart to overflowing. He wasn't going to cry. He wasn't going to cry, but oh the aching joy of this moment!

He looked down at Alísa. *"How? We just found out last night—no one knows."*

"I used my new holder skills and went door-to-door. They know you're going with me to protect them. Even some who don't like the dragons are here, solely for you." She squeezed his hand and let go. *"Go on."*

Taking in a steeling breath, Falier turned back to his people. As the applause died down, he walked into their midst. Sendi caught his arm and gave him a hug, followed closely by Marris. More hugs and shoulder slaps followed, accompanied by well-wishes and promised prayers. Some people were missing—the absence of Lethín was particularly glaring in the wake of his sister, Aresia's, encouragement—but those who had come warmed his heart.

These were people he had spent his life serving, people he would gladly risk his life for, no matter how frightening. He didn't need their appreciation—he would have moved forward without it—yet it was the greatest gift they could ever give him.

And the second greatest? That some of them went straight to Alísa to encourage her after speaking to him. Alísa looked embarrassed by the attention—shoulders hunched and chin tucked even as she smiled—but it obviously bolstered her spirits as well.

Once everyone had their chance to say goodbye and wish them luck, Alísa took his hand and led him around the Hold to the dancing grounds, where Graydonn and Sesína waited. She seemed to grow taller as they retreated from the crowd that had brought him such joy. They were so different from each other in that way, and the knowledge made what she had done for him even more beautiful.

As soon as they were out of view of villagers, Falier pulled Alísa to a stop. She looked back at him, curious.

"*Thank you,*" he said, pushing love and gratitude through their mind-link. "*I didn't know how much I needed that. You did.*"

Alísa ducked her head in happy embarrassment. "*I was a little scared I'd be wrong. I know I would be far more comfortable just sneaking out without a word. Fewer chances for tears. But I guessed correctly?*"

Falier wrapped an arm around her waist and pulled her tight against him, planting a firm kiss on her lips. He savored the feeling of her tension melting away as she gave in to him, of her hand grasping his sleeve and pulling him closer, of her lips caressing his.

He pressed his forehead to hers as they ended the kiss. "*Does that answer your question?*"

She hummed a gentle affirmative, still clinging to his shirt. "*I'm glad.*"

Maker above, she was beautiful. He kissed her once more and, reluctantly, let her go. They were already leaving later than they had intended.

They split off to meet their dragon companions as Graydonn and Sesína came forward. Alísa giggled behind him, and he turned just in time to see her shove Sesína playfully. The dragoness must have said something snarky, probably about the kiss.

Graydonn watched Falier as he mounted, one eye-ridge raised. "*I still don't understand the kissing thing. I see nothing romantic about smashing muzzles together.*"

Falier shrugged, settling between two spines. "*I don't know that I can explain it to you.*"

"*It's a long flight to the Nissen. Perhaps we can discuss the differences between human and dragon courting rituals.*"

"Uh..." Falier slipped into vocalizing.

"You're embarrassed? Maybe Alísa can help—her ability to explain human-ness to dragons has always impressed me." Graydonn looked at the females, then swung back to Falier. *"That makes you more embarrassed?"*

"Wait!"

Falier nearly jumped out of his skin at his mother's voice, and he turned to see her running toward him and Graydonn.

"Ma?"

She stopped beside Graydonn, breathing heavily. Tear stains still marred her cheeks, though her eyes were clear now. She placed a hand on Falier's leg.

"I'm sorry, I know you have to go, but I—I couldn't. I was trying to—to—" Tears welled in her eyes, and she shook her head at herself. "And there I go again. I just wanted you to remember me without tears—"

She turned away to wipe her eyes and returned with a sniffle. "I *am* proud of you, Falier. I'm sorry I al—almost let you go without—"

Falier slid off Graydonn's back and wrapped her up in his arms, his heart aching and healing at the same time. She wasn't mad at him for leaving—she was trying to be strong for him and failing in her own eyes. He let go of his hold on his psychic powers, allowing himself to soak in her love even amidst her fear. That was all he needed.

"I love you, Ma."

"I love you, too," she whispered, squeezing him tightly, then letting him go.

Falier backed away one step, then another, placing a hand on Graydonn's warm scales. His mother watched him, then traced from his hand to Graydonn's face. She blew out a breath and approached the dragon.

"Take care of him." She glanced at Falier, then back. "Of each other."

Graydonn blinked slowly and bowed his head in a very human manner. *"Always."*

She nodded firmly, then began backing away. "Go on, then."

Falier studied her a moment more. She had wanted him to remember her as strong in this parting, and he would do just that. There she stood, sorrows and fears trying to bind her, and love allowing her to break free of their hold. The epitome of strength.

Without another word, he pulled himself onto Graydonn's back. He glanced at Alísa, who wiped away a tear with her sleeve. At a silent command, Sesína launched into the sky.

Falier patted Graydonn's neck. *"Let's go."*

"By Maker's wings."

The dragon launched into the sunlit morning, circling as he found the air currents that would carry them to the clouds. Falier looked down one last time. His father came up beside his mother and now watched the rising dragons, his hands on her shoulders. In the doorway, Selene leaned against the post and shielded her eyes against the sun, while Hwinn flapped his tiny wings as though to follow.

The sorrow finally found its way into Falier's eyes, and he faced front, allowing the wind to tear it away. Maker willing, he would come back, and then he would allow the tears to fall in joy. Until then, he would follow his calling, his passion, his love, westward.

32

SURRENDER

The Nissen River ran quietly beneath Alísa's gaze, a stoic guardian between her and the task ahead. She wished it were louder so it might drown out all the thoughts rushing through her—memories of a clan that had never listened to her before. The eyes of disapproval from her elders. The carefully-hidden taunts from the younger. L'non's disappointment. Kallar's soured protectiveness. Her father's betrayed eyes.

Sesína nudged Alísa's cheek with her snout. *"These thoughts are making it very hard for me to let you go."*

Alísa stroked the scaleless muzzle, staring at the grove across the river keeping the slayer camps from sight. *"I'll make it. This is just like flying into Tsamen and Paili's cave. Papá is Tsamen, who might be convinced if I can get to him first. Tella—I hope she isn't like Paili, but I'll avoid her as though she is."*

"That isn't comforting," Sesína snorted. *"That meeting didn't go as we'd planned either."*

"Does anything go as planned for us?"

"There he is," came Falier's voice from behind. They turned to see Graydonn emerging from the trees. His excursion revealed that the mind-kin bond stretched about four miles—little more than a tenth what the Illumination bond could do, but it would be enough to reach the slayers' camp.

Alísa tried to keep her voice steady, forcing herself to speak aloud as she would have to for the next couple of days. "We have w—what we need, then. There's nothing more t-t-to delay us."

"Only if you're ready," Falier said. "They aren't crossing the river to war yet—we have time."

Time for my resolve to die, maybe. Alísa rubbed her arms. "If there are m—more c-clans coming it would be best to get in before them."

Graydonn's eyes dimmed as he approached, deep care pouring from him. *"I never thought when you came to Mother and me that I would one day take you back. But it cannot be helped. Be brave, Alísa."*

The dragon touched her forehead with his snout and Alísa placed a hand under his chin—the embrace they had established what seemed so long ago. They were older now, wise and weary despite the short time they had known each other. What she wouldn't give to be back in the first cave with just him, Sesína, and Koriana, training for the future, but living in peace.

But such a wish was selfish, and it denied the good that had come too. More good would come—she just had to fight for it. And live to see it.

Alísa looked to her companions. "We'll have to be quick, in c-c-case there are scouts on the other side."

"One last thing," Graydonn said, his eyes shifting away. *"I need to block a part of your memory."*

Alísa blinked and stepped back. "W—what?"

Falier nodded solemnly. "Graydonn and I realized a flaw in the plan a few minutes ago. If we're going to have your father read your mind to see the truth, he'll see our plans too."

"He would notice instantly if we blocked the whole plan from him," Graydonn continued, *"and he'd probably dig until he found it, so that isn't the answer. But there's one critical item we can block without them realizing: the mind-kin bond."*

Falier took Alísa's hand. "Knowing an attack is coming is one thing—they'll guess that anyway, and it might even help them make their choices faster. But if they see that Graydonn and I can talk, they'll mind-choke me, taking away our ability to get you out if something goes awry. We can't let that happen."

"So," Graydonn said, *"we block out your knowledge of the distance at which the mind-kin bond works. Falier will act as though we can only communicate within a mile of each other, which shouldn't worry the slayers since they would be able to sense a dragon within that range."*

Alísa's heart thudded. She fully trusted Graydonn and Falier, but tampering with her mind? Sesína, too, recoiled at the thought, but she said nothing. She knew it was necessary too.

"I will only block those few moments we've talked about the distance," Graydonn said. *"When Falier convinced you to let him come with you, what we did just now to test the distance, and this conversation. You'll still know that the bond exists, but when Falier says it only works within a mile, you'll believe him. He will act as though he just came to support you."*

Alísa rubbed sweaty hands in her skirts. "All right."

Graydonn approached her with slow steps and pressed his snout against her forehead. *"The memories won't be gone, just blocked. If we don't have to use the bond—which would remind you of it on your own—I promise to unblock you at the end of all of this."*

Alísa closed her eyes. "I trust you. D—do it."

Sesína launched across the Nissen, the power in her limbs making Alísa marvel. To think of the little black hatchling in her lap who didn't know what her own wings and tail were, and then to feel the way she navigated the winds rushing over top of the river, made Alísa's heart swell with pride. Graydonn and Falier followed as they crossed low over the water. It took only ten wingbeats before they landed in soft green turf on the other side. Alísa slid off quickly, coming around to Sesína's front to plant a kiss on her muzzle.

"Go now, dear one. We'll find my father and it will be okay."

Sesína nudged her cheek in return. *"Be wise and bold, dragon-heart."*

With that, Sesína leapt into the air, Graydonn at her tail. Falier took Alísa's hand as the dragons crossed the watery span and loped into the cover of the trees. Alísa squeezed hard. Despite her fear of him being hurt, the comfort and assurance he gave would help her through this.

"We're ready." Graydonn's tone held sorrow. *"I wish I could say I will be gentle, but the point is to sever the Illumination bond. Instead, I will be quick. You have Alísa, Falier?"*

A jolt of anxiety ran through Alísa, one she couldn't be sure whether it belonged to her, to Sesína, or both of them.

"Hold on a second," Falier replied, turning his attention to Alísa. *"Do you want to sit down?"*

Remembering the pain when Namor severed the bond, Alísa nodded. Falier walked her to a tree and sat at its base. Pulling her to his side, he leaned them back against the trunk. She settled her head on his shoulder, allowing him to hold her as he told Graydonn they were ready. Alísa reached out to Sesína, sending what comfort she could and finding something already there. Graydonn lay right beside her, a paw over hers as platonic love flowed from him.

Alísa's heart ached for him. He didn't want this job. But no one else could do it, and so he would.

"Brace yourself. Three, two, one..."

Pressure filled Alísa's head as the Illumination bond stopped up. She pressed into Falier, and he tightened his arms around her, whispering something as the pressure grew. It pressed against her ears, then into her throat, until finally—

SNAP.

Pain shot through her head and echoed throughout her body before silencing into nothing. Numbness washed over Alísa as her mind floated in a void. Sesína was gone.

"It's okay, Líse," Falier said, his voice far away. "Graydonn's got Sesína, and I've got you. It'll be okay."

Alísa breathed in his words, forcing herself to think logically. Sesína was fine, safe on the other side of the Nissen. They had been separated before and survived. It would be okay.

Slowly, her senses went back to normal. She felt the gentle breeze chilled by the river, heard the birds in the trees, smelled Falier's warmth. She snuggled closer, grounding herself in his strength. His stubble scratched against her forehead as he kissed it, and he let out a small huff of a laugh.

"What?"

"I just realized what I forgot. I didn't shave this morning, and I didn't pack a blade. Not that they'd let me keep one anyway."

"I like it."

Falier shifted to look down at her. "Really?"

She hummed an affirmative, rubbing the fabric of her skirt between her fingers. "Is Sesína okay?"

Falier didn't answer for a moment, looking into the distance. "Yes. Graydonn says she went into a daze like you did, but she's coming out of it. He'll take care of her."

Alísa drew in a long breath, focusing on the sensation of it filling her body before she released it. Sesína would be fine. If only the mind-kin bond could reach across the distance so Falier could keep an eye on Sesína while they were in the slayer camp. But that couldn't be helped, and they needed to move soon. Judging by what they had seen of the camps from the sky, they would have to skirt Tella's camp before they would reach Karn's. And they would have to do it without being spotted by her scouts.

"We'd b—better get moving now." Alísa sat up straight, and Falier watched her closely. "I'm feeling better. The p-p-pain is gone, and though my mind still feels like it's drifting in a void, we need to get out of here."

Falier helped her up, keeping hold of her hand as she turned northwest and entered the grove between them and the slayer camps. Birds called around them. Squirrels chased and chittered at each other. Browning leaves twisted in the air as they fell to the grassy floor. So long as nature moved around them, they should be safe from scouts.

Falier rubbed his face and a buzz of connection filled Alísa's mind. It soothed her in Sesína's absence. *"Ma always makes Pa shave. I didn't think to ask what you liked."*

"You don't have to not shave just because I like it. I've never asked what you like either."

"Well, for the record, I like it when you wear blue. Brings out your eyes. That necklace works really well." He reached to poke the dragon scale at her chest, then pulled back with a shock of awkwardness that turned his neck red. *"Sorry. Just, you've hidden it so long."*

Alísa fought back a giggle. His embarrassment was adorable. *"Thank you. I thought it might help to display it today."*

Releasing her empathy, Alísa checked their surroundings again. A snake slithered out of their way and Alísa shuddered as she remembered its eight-foot cousin Sesína had fought. No wings on this one, though, and its patterning showed its harmlessness. Nothing out of the ordinary.

"*Are you thinking a full beard? Or more like a week's worth trimmed?*"

Alísa snickered. "*You're stuck on this facial hair thing. You don't have to do it.*"

"*I've never seriously thought about it. Every once in a while, sure, but holders are traditionally clean-shaven.*"

"*Yes. No beards in the soup, please.*"

"*But I'm a slayer now, or something like one. If my lady likes beards there's no harm in trying, right? So—full or trimmed?*"

"*How should I know? I've never seen you with either.*"

Falier hummed. "*Maybe I should just let it go until you tell me to stop.*"

"*Or you want to stop.*"

"*I think I'm willing to do whatever makes you more likely to kiss me.*"

Alísa covered her face with a hand as laughter bubbled up. Sesína would be coughing up a storm if she were here right now. And that thought ached. She settled, lowering her hands to her sides again.

Falier sighed, taking her hand. "*I was hoping to distract you.*"

"*You did.*" She stretched up on her toes to kiss his prickly cheek. "*Thank you.*"

They continued in silence, Alísa watching for movement. They would come to the western edge of the grove soon, hopefully far enough north to skirt around to Karn's camp.

Finally, the end of the grove came in sight. Beyond it rose the four mountain peaks that made up the Serpent's Fangs. It and the village at its southern foot—L'rang, Kallar's home village—marked the south-eastern corner of her father's wayfaring territory. In-between the mountains and the grove, lightly hidden by brush, the tops of sun-bleached leather tents were just visible. And further north, the second camp she assumed to be her father's.

Anxiety rippled through Alísa. Apparently, her estimation of how far north to travel had been off. They should go back to avoid detection, then go further north.

Alísa backed up, pulling Falier with her. He followed without a sound, leaving the world in complete quiet except for the heavy beating of Alísa's heart in her ears.

Wait. Quiet? The camp wasn't so close that birds and animals would silence themselves. If scouts found them here—

"Falier, cut the tether. Don't let them see we're slayers!"

Falier's eyes widened. He did as she said, scanning the forest. Alísa forced herself to breathe. If scouts found them, they wouldn't necessarily know who they were. She would just have to figure out how to get to her father.

"I thought Tella gave orders to all you village folk."

The voice made Alísa's heart stop. They had been spotted!

A blond man stepped from the trees. His hair was braided tightly against his scalp on one side while the other flew free, and he bore green warpaint running from his forehead down past his cheekbones in the manner of a scout.

"You aren't to be anywhere near the camps." The scout looked to Falier. "There could be an attack at any moment. Now get out of here!"

Alísa fought not to breathe a sigh of relief. He would let them go— he thought they were just normal lovers out for a stroll.

Falier fell into the part, taking Alísa's hand again. "I'm sorry. I didn't realize how far we'd come."

"Palin!" Another voice came from just behind the first, loud and angry. A man with similar warpaint and a bushy brown ponytail walked from behind a tree, a bow in hand. "Check the astral plane before beckoning strangers! They were speaking telepathically, and the boy isn't a slayer of North Russig or Kiln."

The second scout pulled an arrow from his quiver and nocked it, pointing the weapon at Falier. "You've got five seconds, boy. Why are you here?"

Falier let go of Alísa's hand, holding both palms out in surrender as Alísa did the same.

"We followed Karn from his territory to join him," Falier said. "We've just gotten a little turned around looking for his camp. You wouldn't be able to help us?"

Palin squinted at him as more footsteps came from multiple directions. "Then why claim you had come too far?"

Alísa took a step to draw their attention from Falier. "P-p-please, just t-t-t-take us to K-Karn. He'll know who we are."

"Alísa?"

The familiar voice stopped her breath. She turned slowly as a man with bright green eyes, black braids, and tanned skin with a long talon scar on his right arm approached. Drennar, her father's head scout.

"You escaped?"

"The witch herself!" The archer aimed his bow at her, but Drennar ran forward, getting between them.

"You kill her without Karn's say and nothing will keep you from death's door. We take her to him, alive."

"And risk her calling the dragons to our women and children?" The archer snarled. "Move aside."

"Wait." Palin's eyes hardened. "I don't think Tella would be pleased if we killed her without orders. Why don't we mind-choke her? That'll stop any spell she tries."

Another scout came into view, one Alísa didn't recognize. "Yes, take her to Tella."

A heavy wave of weakness came over her. Mind-choke. She fell to her knees, Falier dropping to catch her.

"She is Karn's daughter," Drennar argued, his voice faint behind the mind-choke. "It's his right—"

"Yet there are three of us, Karns-man," the archer said, "and only one of you. Call your chief if you will, but she goes to Tella."

Alísa's heart raced, and though she could barely lift her head under the choke, she turned desperate eyes to Drennar. He avoided eye-contact, speaking only to the slayers.

"If Tella kills her before Karn sees his daughter, there will be no stopping his wrath."

"You'd best be quick, then," the archer said, lowering his weapon.

Drennar took off at a run, and Alísa silently thanked the Maker. *Bless him with speed, Branni. And Bria, give me strength.*

The archer spoke to Falier. "You, carry her. No sudden moves, and one hum out of you" —he glared at Alísa— "and I don't care what either chief does to me. You'll not bring your dragons down on my family."

"That's not why she's here," Falier said. "We've come in peace to see—"

"One of us can take her just as easily," the third scout snarled. "We don't need you, traitor. Take her or die now."

Falier's breath shook before he mastered himself. He placed Alísa's bag on her lap, then lifted her up with an arm around her back and one under her legs. Fighting the mind-choke, Alísa tried to wrap her arms around his neck, but at her movement the choke tightened. Her head lolled back, and Falier adjusted his grip until she rested against his shoulder.

Black rimmed Alísa's vision under the slayer's tight hold. If she stopped fighting the choke, she would surely fall asleep. Shadows passed over and around her. Boots tromped over twigs and fallen leaves. Soon voices rose up all around her, neither recognizable nor distinguishable.

A loud voice pressed around her. The words were indecipherable, though at their presence the mind-choke began to ease. Slowly, the world came back into view—an unimpeded sky, wayfarers' tents all around, and slayers young and old surrounding her.

"Put her down, traitor." The loud voice, now clearly a woman, spoke. "Let her kneel."

Falier's breaths were heavy and he complied slowly, making sure Alísa could hold herself upright before kneeling beside her. He tried to put on a brave face, but his fear still showed. They were in trouble.

The woman, Chief Tella, stood tall amidst her slayers, her head inches above some of her men. She could probably stand eye-to-eye with Falier. Her sandy blond hair was pulled back in long rows of braids, some with thin streaks of red fabric woven within. A red tartan sash crossed her dark brown fur-lined tunic, along with the strap for a quiver of javelins. Her eyes were shaded with kohl, and she bore the chief's crown of red warpaint across her forehead. Even if the mind-choke fully lifted, Alísa was sure she would feel this chief's presence clouding around her.

This was what she had compared herself to, not so long ago. Fierceness, presence, command—all good qualities in a warrior chief, and all far removed from Alísa. She could only hope that her own, different strength would be enough to get through the walls surrounding Tella and her clan.

"What were you doing skulking around my camp, Dragon Witch?" Tella came closer, making it harder for Alísa to look her in the eye under the mind-choke. "After what you did to Segenn, I wouldn't have thought you so stupid as to come near without draconic aid. Did you come to summon the dragons in the Fangs? Or does your army lurk nearby?"

Alísa licked her dry lips. "I've c-c-come to bring a chance for p-p-p-p-peace. There is no army near, and the d—dragons in the Fangs are n—not my allies."

Tella smirked, stalking in front of Alísa. "I would have thought living among dragons would tame your fearful tongue, Karns-daughter. But then, I suppose even dragons fear me."

"You should not underestimate her, Chief Tella."

Alísa froze, her heart shuddering. She knew that voice. Swallowing against the fear in her throat, she looked past Tella to where the crowd of slayers parted. Yarlan stepped into view.

"Her stammering tongue is likely punishment for the words she has chosen to speak. They have already deceived many—do not listen to her lies."

Falier visibly tensed beside Alísa. "The one full of lies stands beside you, great chief. I was there in Me'ran. I saw dragons with nothing to gain defend us against dragons and slayers alike."

Yarlan huffed. "Nothing to gain besides the souls of the people, you mean. In fact—Chief Tella, you should have the boy choked as well. You cannot see it, but he is bonded to a dragon just like the witch. He can call the dragons at any time."

Falier's eyes widened. "The bond only works within a mile! Graydonn is much further away—"

Tella looked pointedly at one of her men, and Falier's frantic protest rasped to a stop. The panic in his voice squeezed at Alísa's heart. He had never been choked before. As Falier hunched beside her, Alísa directed her own fear into prayers. Everything was spiraling out of control—she needed to gain it back.

"Chief T-T-T-Tella, please. I c-c-came to surrender myself to you and my f—father, rather than risk outright w—war. P-p-please, allow me to m—make my case."

Yarlan crossed his arms. "We'll be here a while."

Alísa swallowed as his comment drew chuckles from some of the slayers. While some of the villagers in Me'ran looked down on her for her stammer, they tended to do so in ways far more subtle and quiet. She had forgotten how bad her verbal stops made her look before warriors. With Briek and his men she had been able to prove her capability via telepathic speech, bringing them to a place of respect even when she did use her voice.

Here, she had no such help.

Tella, despite her earlier derision, remained stoic. "Speak."

Alísa fought not to show relief. "W—would you c-c-call for Karn?"

"I do not need a man blinded by love to help me decide. Speak."

Alísa breathed a steadying breath. Drennar said he would get her father—where were they?

"G—great Tella, the war is not what we think—"

"Here we go." Yarlan rolled his eyes.

"The d—dragons are not soulless c-c-c-creatures steeped in evil, but beings w—with the ability to ch—choose good or evil. Some—"

"Even if that were true" —Yarlan came up alongside Tella— "that only makes their atrocities that much worse—wouldn't you say?"

Tella didn't respond, but her expression showed that Yarlan had her ear. Alísa swallowed against the tightness in her throat.

"Some of the dragons only want p-p-p-peace. They will even fight their own k-k-k-k-kind to protect innocent humans. As Falier said, w—w—we have seen this firsthand."

Tella huffed. "Funny how in centuries of war you are the first to tell such a tale. If some dragons are so benevolent as you say, where have they been?"

Alísa opened her mouth to speak, but Tella raised her voice.

"Where are the stories of travelers rescued from highwaymen by these good dragons? Of an'reik burned in their fires? Of villages protected by tooth and talon rather than sword?"

Tella paced before her warriors, as though giving a rousing speech before they charged into battle. "Have they been cowering in their caves this whole time, while only their warped brethren courageously fight the slayers? Is goodness weak while evil stands tall? No. Goodness stands and fights, while evil makes excuses to masquerade as light."

Many of Tella's men agreed verbally, ranging from grunts of approval to resounding cheers. A look of pride settled in Tella's kohl-rimmed eyes before she returned her hardened gaze to Alísa.

"The question is, have the dragons tricked you, or are you wearing the mask yourself? Either way, after what you did to Segenn, I doubt there is any hope for you."

It was all Alísa could do to return Tella's gaze. By the chief's logic, anything could be excused as a lie or a trick—every experience would amount to nothing in the wake of Tella's righteous fury.

Tella faced Falier. "And what of you? Are you so bound by her spells that you, too, are a lost cause?"

Falier appeared to regain some strength despite the mind-choke, straightening to look Tella in the eyes. "I'm not under any spell, great chief. I know these dragons, and I believe in Alísa's message of peace between the races."

Tella spat on the ground between them. "To make peace with the Nameless is to turn one's back on the Maker. If your soul is so lost, perhaps it would be a mercy to kill you here and now."

Alísa's heart raced as multiple slayers gripped their weapons a little tighter. "We don't follow the Nameless! Nor d—do my dragons. They c-c-c-call on the M—Maker, as I do. We—"

In one swift motion, Tella had Alísa by the throat. Alísa gasped and gripped the chief's arm, her knees in the air, her toes searching for purchase underneath her so she could breathe. Falier gave a strangled cry and reached for her, but another slayer held him down. Yarlan grinned wickedly.

"No one, not even Karn's daughter, blasphemes in my camp," Tella snarled, lifting her higher. "By the Maker and all that is holy, if you even think His name or those of His Eldír again, I'll—"

"Tella!" A booming voice shook the air and a sword slid from its sheath behind Alísa. "Put. Her. Down."

Papá!

33

FAMILY

The wrath in Tella's eyes died, her face smoothing into nonchalance. "Karn. Good of you to join us."

She released Alísa, letting her fall back to her knees with a jarring thud. Alísa caught herself with a hand on the ground, the other protecting her throat as coughs shuddered through her.

"It seems she's picked up a nasty habit living among the dragons," Tella said. "The Maker doesn't take kindly to blasphemy, and neither do I."

Karn's voice was like dark clouds just before the first flash of lightning. "Then save your strength for the dragons, not their victim!"

His dark leather boots came to rest beside Alísa, blood-red dragon scales covering his shins. Alísa glanced up at him as she straightened, but his hard eyes focused on the other chief. L'non stood behind the slayer holding Falier down, hand on the hilt of his sword.

"You!" Kallar's voice erupted behind Alísa, full of the lightning Karn held back. "Release her. I'll keep her from calling the dragons."

At Tella's nod, her clansman released the mind-choke, which Kallar replaced smoothly. His choke was gentler than the other slayer's, seasoned with his possessive protection. Desperation tinged his voice as it entered her mind.

"You came back. Tell me this isn't a trick of the dragons. Tell me you chose this—that you broke their hold and came home."

So strange. He had spoken to her mind-to-mind like this only a few months ago and she had felt scandalized, even violated, by it. Now that she knew the difference between delving into memories and simple telepathic speech, his mind-voice no longer bothered her.

"There was no hold to break, Kallar. You'll see, assuming Tella lets me go."

A hint of threat entered his voice. *"Oh, she'll let you go."*

"You know Bria's end as well as I do." Tella's voice still rang with authority, but more quietly in respect for a fellow chief. "Our ancestors weren't able to save her from the dragons' hold, and no Dragon Singer on their side can be allowed to live."

"She's my daughter, my responsibility. I will decide what must be done!" His hand came to rest on Alísa's head, his voice turning sorrowful. "And, whatever it is, I will be the one to carry it out."

The defeat in his last declaration shuddered through her. He really thought it was possible he would have to kill her.

"Then what do you propose we do?" Tella frowned.

"Give us time to see if we can help her. I'll take her back to my camp, let her be with family. If we can break the dragons' hold, all will be well."

"Can her father truly be trusted to make the right call?" Yarlan glared at Alísa. "The witch has tricked many people, how much more those who love her?"

"You're afraid of him." Kallar's protectiveness surged. *"What did he do?"*

Alísa didn't respond, but Kallar surely felt the pain of memory and tremors of inadequacy. Why was it still there? She had come so far as she worked with Briek and his men, not to mention the dragons. Would she never be rid of it?

"Hold your tongue, slayer!" Karn snapped at Yarlan. "Who do you think you are?"

"Yarlan is the witness," Tella said. "The one who told us of Alísa's whereabouts. He talks too much, but his point is valid. You may take her, but two of my men will go with you to ensure your people don't let their guard down. If they hear so much as a hum, they will not hesitate to end the threat."

Karn took a breath, tempering himself. "Understood."

"And what of the boy?" Tella gestured at Falier. "What shall we do with him?"

"He is nothing to me. Keep him."

"No." Alísa leaned against her father so he would look down. His fiery curls were unbraided, speaking to his haste, and his brown eyes were weary, holding a deep sorrow she knew she had caused.

"Papá, Falier and his f—family have c-c-cared for me—fed and sheltered me. W—we invoke the right of hospitality."

Suspicion prickled around her mind, all from Kallar. She fought to hold her feelings back. If Kallar saw that Falier was her pursuer, there would be a whole new problem on their hands—one that needed to be resolved, but not right now.

Karn looked from Alísa to Falier, then sighed. Unless her family disowned her or Falier did something to forfeit his right, Karn's honor was now bound in treating Falier the way his family had treated her.

"Give me the boy too, Tella."

"Good, don't slough your unwanted prisoners off to me. He's bonded to a dragon—keep him choked." Tella turned her back on them. "Palin, Shochar, stay with them."

Her slayers came forward and the rest of those gathered began to disperse. Karn stared at the guards for a moment, then turned his eyes to L'non.

"You've got the boy?"

L'non nodded once and Falier winced, presumably as the mind-choke changed. She wouldn't think that her uncle's choke would pain him, though.

Karn offered Alísa his hand, pulling her attention. She wobbled as she stood, and her father took her by the arms to stabilize her. His grip was desperately tight, as though he needed to make sure she was truly here and not just an apparition. Conflict flickered in his eyes, stuck somewhere between the hardness of a chief and the softness of a father.

"I'm okay, Papá," she whispered.

"Karn," Tella said, calling both their gazes. Yarlan still stood proudly beside her. "We would speak to you, out of earshot of the witch."

Karn's jaw tightened, but he kept his expression stoic. "L'non, Kallar, take them to my tent, and stay with them."

"Of course," L'non said.

A moment of hesitation, then Karn released her and followed Tella. With a steadying breath, Alísa bent to grab her bag from the ground, meeting Falier's gaze as she came upright. He tried to hide his worry behind a smile, but she knew his eyes. If only she could go to him, embrace him, and let their fear and relief mingle together in comfort. But now was not the time. L'non took hold of Falier's arm and pulled him away, walking toward Karn's camp further west.

Kallar came alongside Alísa and guided her with a hand at the small of her back. The sensation prickled, and she took quick steps to get away from it.

"Well, at least I know one thing hasn't changed about you." Kallar's irritation sparked, the only thing Alísa could feel under his choke. *"I'm here to help you. I'm the greatest ally you have right now."*

Alísa tried hard not to focus on Falier—her true ally—by choosing a different, more emotionally-charged topic to mask her thoughts. *"Does Papá really think he'll have to kill me?"*

"We all know it might come to that." Kallar never had been one to mince words, though his tone was soft with sadness. *"Seeing you now, I have hope it won't. Still, if the dragons do have you, we'll do whatever we have to in order to save humankind, and to save you."*

Kallar looked at her, his unblinking azure eyes intense. *"And I will save you, my Lísa. No matter what it takes."*

He pulled away from their mind-link, hardening his power in the mind-choke, where Alísa could neither respond nor feel his emotions. The remnants of his last statement left her short of breath. Love, duty, and sorrow mingled, each equal to the other in strength. He did truly care for her, in his own way. The feeling made her long for Falier's arms, where the care was deeper and richer. The arms of one who actually wanted to understand her.

Palin and Shochar walked at the rear of their group, letting Kallar and L'non walk them freely through Tella's camp. It was eerily quiet here. The people were restless. Kallar stayed vigilant, as though he expected someone to attack them at any moment. Adults spoke in hushed tones as they passed, while young teens were herded into their tents. They felt threatened by her, and it made her heart hurt.

They crossed a small expanse with no tents or carts before moving into her father's camp, where the faces became familiar. Momentary joy would shine on them, only to be replaced by fear, concern, or revulsion. Alísa forced herself to breathe and walk tall. She was the hope of peace, not the threat of destruction. They didn't understand yet, but they would.

"Alísa!" Two young voices came from her left, and she turned to see her twelve-year-old cousins running for her. They didn't stop, didn't shrink back, and it filled her heart with joy.

"Levan! Taer!" She quickened her steps, strength surging through her at the sight of them.

"Stop!" L'non barked, sending a jolt to her heart that froze her. He ran to stand between her and the boys. "She isn't well. Go to your mother."

"But—"

"Now."

Tears filled Alísa's eyes as the boys plodded away, dejected. She had never seen L'non so forceful. For it to come because of her 'condition' cut her to the core.

L'non turned to her, sorrow in his eyes. "I can't let them see you like this. Not until you're whole."

"I'm not broken, Uncle," she whispered.

His eyes hardened and he didn't respond. Alísa looked to Falier, whose eyes filled with sympathy. What she wouldn't give to run into his arms without fear of repercussions, but even now she felt Kallar's eyes on them. She got back in line and followed L'non's leading once more.

The group continued their march until they finally reached her family's tent. Again, Alísa's heart leapt for joy as she caught sight of her mother and Trísse talking just outside the canvas door. Her mother's back was to her, but Trísse immediately locked eyes with Alísa. Her hair was pulled back in two thick braids that joined at the nape of her neck, and she wore a dark green dress with a tight leather swordswoman's vest. Her short-sword's handle peeked over her shoulder in the attached back-scabbard. Most of the women in camp wore similar battle-garments.

Disbelief covered Trísse's face, causing Hanah to turn around. Her mother's face became pale as death, stark against the hand she raised to her lips. Then Hanah ran, the men wisely stepping aside as the Lady of the clan threw her arms around Alísa. Fear and sorrow melted away in her mother's embrace, giving way to tears of relief.

"Mamá."

"Oh, my precious girl!" Hanah squeezed harder. "It's true—you're here!"

"Yes, Mamá." Alísa closed her eyes as tears wet her mother's shoulder. "I'm here."

Hanah pulled back, looking Alísa up and down as though ensuring every piece of her was there. "Are you all right?"

"Yes."

"That remains to be seen, Hanah." L'non came up from behind. "Karn is with Tella, but will be back soon. Then we can assess the problem."

Hanah glanced at L'non, then back to Alísa, her expression clouded with worry.

"Come inside, then." Her eyes landed on Tella's guards and hardened. "What are they doing in my camp?"

"They're part of the agreement," L'non said. "They're to stay nearby as Tella's eyes and ears."

Hanah shook her head as the guards pressed closer. "My tent is for family only. You may stay outside."

"I beg your pardon, Lady Hanah," Palin said, "but that is not the agreement. We are to stay in earshot of the Dragon Wi—"

"Watch your tongue, Tellas-man." Hanah's eyes became daggers. "This is my camp and my daughter, not Tella's. You will stay outside. If your chief has a problem with this, she may come see me."

Turning her back on them, Hanah gave her attention to Falier next. Falier straightened and threw his fist over his heart in respect.

"And who is this?"

"A friend, Mamá," Alísa said. "Falier has been at my side for m— much of my journey. He's here as my support and witness. W—would you bring him under your t-tent as well?"

Falier gave a nervous smile as Hanah stared at him a moment longer. What a way to meet her family.

Hanah nodded. "Keep an eye on him, L'non."

She grabbed Alísa's hand and pulled her toward the tent entrance.

"Wait a moment. Trísse?" Alísa looked for her friend, but she was nowhere in sight. She had probably wanted to give the family space—public displays of affection weren't her thing—but after months of separation? Perhaps she was angry.

Of course she was angry. Alísa hadn't even said goodbye before leaving, then had shown up in the middle of a battle in the presence of dragons. Alísa was the enemy now.

Pressing on, Alísa followed her mother into the tent. The sight brought tears to her eyes. The chest of traveling clothes and weapons by the door, the embroidered symbols in the leather walls, the low table where she and her family knelt for meals.

Home. But, somehow, not home anymore.

Hanah closed the flap behind the others, blocking out the glaring sunlight and two unwanted guardsmen. She grabbed Alísa's hands and pulled her close again, enfolding her in arms of fierce love.

"How did you escape?" Hanah whispered, stroking Alísa's hair.

"I didn't have to," Alísa whispered back. "It's not what you think. But I want to wait for Papá."

Hanah pulled back slowly, her eyes searching Alísa's as though the answers were there.

"Just who did you say this was, again?"

Alísa cringed, turning to see Kallar eyeing Falier. The slayer's chin tilted up to compensate for the inch of height difference. Falier stared right back, his expression a distinct, *So this is him, huh?* His words were far more polite.

"Falier, son of Parsen. Holder, slayer, and Alísa's friend and confidant."

Alísa fought back a sigh of relief. Falier remembered this wasn't the time or place to make enemies due to his pursuit. It would come out soon, but at that point there would be much bigger topics to handle, like ending the march on the east.

"Holder?" Kallar's face bunched with disgust as he turned to Alísa. "You hate holders. What are you doing with him?"

Alísa felt her face go red as Kallar's declaration drew stunned confusion from Falier. "Falier and his family w—were very k-k-kind to me."

Falier's brow rose. "There were holders who weren't?"

Alísa shrugged, hoping to end the conversation. Kallar wasn't done, though.

"So, what, he helped you escape?" Kallar looked Falier up and down. "I doubt he could do much with his weakling powers."

"Kallar, please!" Hanah scolded. "If he's here with Alísa, there's obviously a good reason for it."

"He was with her before," L'non said, drawing all eyes. He studied Falier. "Yes, I'm sure of it. He was on the green dragon's back. He helped Alísa escape us that day."

Kallar's eyes widened, then narrowed to slits. "You!"

He charged forward, grabbing Falier's shirt before anyone else could move. "I could have saved her that day, but you stopped me! How? I should have broken through your choke like the thinnest layer of frost!"

Falier threw his arms up between Kallar's and pushed out, breaking Kallar's hold on him. Fire lit both of their eyes as they stared each other down.

Alísa shoved between them. "S—s—stop it!"

As though waking from a dream, Falier's eyes cleared. He backed up a step, palms out in peace, the tension in his shoulders releasing. Kallar, on the other hand, turned his fire to Alísa.

"Was he under the dragons' control then, or yours? His powers amplified by you? Is that how you destroyed Segenn's wayfarers, too?"

"You know nothing," she growled back. "Everyone, from Falier t-t-to Segenn himself, acted of their own accord!"

"What is going on in here?" Shochar burst through the tent flap, a hand on the hilt of his sword.

Hanah whirled on him. "None of your concern. Get out."

"It is our concern," he growled as Palin followed. "Tella—"

"Sent you to make sure she doesn't sing." L'non held a quiet authority that balanced out the rest of the tent. "That is all. You will leave now."

"How do we know a raised voice doesn't have the same effect?" Palin's hateful glare found Alísa. "If she calls the dragons—"

"She's still in a choke—her voice means nothing if she's choked." Kallar stepped between them, his jaw clenched against his fury. "You think we'll allow her to call them? Just sit back and watch it happen? You are redundant here, Tellas-men—go back to your mistress!"

"That is enough!" Karn's voice preceded his entry, stern and commanding. Tella's guards seemed to shrink as he walked in, like wolves before an alpha. "Get out. If you enter my tent again, Alísa and the boy won't be my only prisoners. I will treat you with far less compassion than I do these who have been bent against their will. Move."

Karn stayed directly in front of the tent flap, forcing Palin and Shochar to slink past him to exit. Those left in the tent didn't relax even after the guards left, Alísa barely able to breathe in her father's presence.

His eyes moved to Kallar, his voice quieting. "You know better than to antagonize them."

Kallar's eyes shifted away. "I won't let them threaten her. As you said, if anything must be done, we should be the ones to carry it out. Not Tella, her slayers, or anyone else."

Karn's eyes lighted on Alísa, showing more affection than he had allowed before Tella and her men. Behind them was a weariness Alísa had never seen there before, not even after a week away in battle. Now that she could study his features, she saw his first gray hairs at his temples and even a few sprinkled through his beard. Had she done that to him?

He went to her, cutting the distance with long strides before wrapping her in a fierce hug. She pressed into him, burying her face in his shoulder. His earthy scent spoke of home and safety, and she wished she could be rid of Kallar's choke and fully feel her father's love pouring over her.

"I feared the next time I saw you would be on the battlefield," he whispered, "or else in the Maker's Halls. Instead, you found your way back to me."

He pulled back, holding her elbows so that her arms rested atop his. He studied her face, the eyes she had feared facing again still full of love for her.

"Alísa," he spoke as if his voice could harm her, "Tella has many concerns about you, most fueled by that new advisor of hers."

Alísa swallowed. Yarlan was Tella's advisor now? That didn't bode well.

Karn noticed her tension and squeezed her elbows. "That man hates you more than many slayers hate dragons. But where he saw manipulation of the villagers, I can easily see you trying to find help from humankind even under the dragons' noses. Neither he nor Tella understand that a Dragon Singer might remain on the side of her people. But it has happened before."

He glanced at Kallar, then back to Alísa. His voice became stronger, not with anger. but hope.

"Tell me it has happened again. Tell me you used your power to get away from the dragons who held you hostage, and that you ran home to those who love you and can protect you."

Alísa squeezed his forearms, silently thanking the Maker, Branni, Bria, any who would listen, that they were now on the needed path. Fear clutched at her heart as she remembered all the times she had tried to tell him this truth and had failed. She pushed it aside. He was here, he was asking, and this time she would give him proof he could not refute.

"The only way I c-c-can explain it so you'll understand is for you t-t-to see it for yourself. Look in my m—memories and see what has happened these last few months. Share it with everyone here, if you c-c-c-can. You all need to see this."

Karn's brow creased. "Alísa, no. The mind is sacred—I can't just delve into your memories and share them with everyone. It's a violation, against the slayers' code."

"I know, Papá, b—but this is the only way. If I t-t-t-tell you what happened, you won't believe it." Hurt filled his eyes, but it was true. "I want you to see it and know I'm not hiding anything. I g—g—give you permission. P—p-please."

Karn searched the ceiling of the tent as if the answers were hidden somewhere in the hide. He seemed to deflate before looking back to her. "If this is the way to get answers—to save your life, my Lísa—I will do it."

Alísa smiled and gave him a peck on the cheek. She pulled him to kneel on the ground, the rest following suit. They sat in a circle, Karn on her left and Kallar taking her right hand. Alísa didn't pull away. He needed to see it too. Hanah took Karn's hand and L'non took Kallar's, Falier completing the circle across from Alísa. His twilight eyes were calm and sure, reminding her this was exactly where she needed to be.

"Release the chokes." Karn eyed Falier. "We'll all be connected, so we'll be able to sense the boy if he tries talking to his keeper."

Falier looked immensely relieved. "I won't reach out to my friend, sir."

Alísa's lips twitched as he emphasized 'friend' over 'keeper'. She couldn't even imagine Graydonn as the overbearing master her father thought he was.

The world opened before Alísa as Kallar released the choke. It felt like she had been held underwater for hours, her mind burning like lungs starved for air, and now she had finally surfaced. She breathed deeply of the emotions in the tent—her parents' mixtures of love and fear, Falier's relief, L'non's lightly-droning calm, and Kallar's anger, muted by his perpetually-tight hold.

"Everyone close your eyes and relax your minds," Karn said. "If you fight this, you won't see Alísa's memories, and you'll make it harder for the others too. Lísa" —he faced her, holding Hanah's hand behind him— "you keep your eyes open. Let me see inside them, and don't pull back when the pain comes. I will be as gentle as I can, but this will be difficult and will take a long time."

Alísa breathed low and let it out, locking eyes with him. She would give up every memory and thought she had if it would save him.

"I'm ready."

Karn took his own steeling breath, then his eyes hardened in concentration and a force pressed against her mind, like a very large needle seeking to break through the surface. She fought to keep her eyes open against the pain and breathed. She had to stay relaxed.

Alísa inhaled sharply as the needle broke through. Pressure moved from the outside of her mind to the inside, crowding her thoughts and pressing them outward. Her eyes unfocused and the world around her faded out into a vast hilly country under the cover of night. Stars dotted all around her, not just in the sky, but floating around her like whispering fireflies. Here her father knelt beside her in the dark, staring and searching amidst the floating memories, tensed with vigilance.

"*What are you looking for?*" she asked, her words stark against the shimmers of past conversations.

"*Signs of the enemy. Tainted memories, a guardian.*"

"*There's no one here but me, Papá. You or the others would have felt it if Sesína were still present.*"

"*Sesína?*" His astral eyes narrowed. "*So there was a dragon here.*"

"*You'll soon see that if anyone was 'tainted' by our relationship, it was her.*" She took his hand and led him through the field of stars, approaching a memory ripe with fear and confusion—the start of it all. "*You'll want this one first.*"

Karn nodded solemnly and reached out, touching the memory with a finger. "*The day you crossed the line and released a dragon. How did it get you to do it? How did the creature get such a hold on you that—*"

"*There was no hold on me. Show the others, then watch and see.*"

Karn expended a great deal of psychic energy, pressing the images and sounds out into the minds of those in the room. Then the scene progressed to where Graydonn had broken through Kallar's mind-choke to plead for her help.

"*You lied to me,*" Karn said. "*I asked you for the dragon's exact words, but you hid from me that it called you 'Singer'.*"

"*I had no idea what it meant.*"

He was silent for a moment. "*I suspected, you know. Your empathy for them was a clue too great to ignore, but if anyone found out what you were*" — fear and sadness flooded from him— "*they would have put you on the frontlines and used you. I only meant to protect you from that fate, but in so doing I condemned you to something worse. Forgive me.*"

"*You condemned me only to the truth. Wait and see.*"

The other events of the day sped by, pausing so Karn could examine Graydonn's words and check for malicious intent. The anger of everyone in the room—except Kallar—rose as they together saw the apprentice slap her.

"*I already apologized for that,*" Kallar said, surprisingly with a hint of shame. "*Can we move on?*"

Alísa locked onto the emotions of the room as they sped through the next few months. Fear and anger dominated the beginning of her journey, between Farren letting her go and the dragons who either wanted to kill her or make her their Dragon Singer. Any memory with Sesína and their Illumination inspired a mixture of revulsion and wonder. Every speech she made and battle she faced brought pride.

The moment Paili declared she had killed the Singer Allara and now would similarly kill Alísa, Kallar's rage sent a wave of red coursing through the view. Even the anger that came when he saw Alísa accept Falier's pursuit seemed dull in comparison.

Then came the trials at Me'ran—the heartache as the people she and her clan had risked their lives for abandoned her, the struggle against Yarlan, defending against Paili's dragons. Segenn and his clan came to Me'ran and the scenes slowed at Karn's bidding. His anxiety spiked as he watched every movement, heard every word, and watched how she handled it.

When Briek led the turned slayers in defending the villagers from Segenn and his faithful, a wash of both horror and relief flooded over Alísa, more visceral than anything else she had felt from him throughout this process.

Was he seeing his own future here? Would he be Briek, or Segenn?

Finally, they came to yesterday and this morning and her plan was laid bare before them. They knew everything now. Which villages supported her, how many dragons and slayers were in her clan, Sesína and Graydonn resting across the river, and Alísa's belief that this was the only way to get Karn and the others to trust her.

Karn pulled back, breathing heavily with the exertion, and Alísa's vision cleared to the physical world once more. The tent was dark now— twilight outside—and she could hear her companions shifting as they looked around them. It had been early afternoon when they had started. The mind-share must have taken six, maybe seven, hours!

Now, in the darkness, confusion reigned. Confusion, a little pride from Falier, and boiling frustration in Kallar.

"So you chose them." Kallar's hand jerked away. "You chose the dragons over your family, your people!"

No one else spoke.

"I f—fight for what's right," Alísa said. "For both humans and dragons."

"Is it right to turn against your kin? So what if a few dragons have hearts? They're still monsters!"

"Kallar!" Karn whispered harshly, snapping out of his daze. "Tella's men are still outside. Do you want them to hear and take her away?"

The apprentice lowered his voice, though it still held all the forcefulness. "We should have told her, Karn, helped her make sense of it before she went with them. I warned you. But oh no, 'Maybe if we stay quiet, she'll never find out.' Now look what your 'protection' has done! We had a chance to guide her to be the next Allara, but now all she's done is sully my mother's name!"

Alísa blinked. Had he just said—

"M—mother?"

Kallar looked back to her. "Yes. She was cursed the same as you. The same as Bria. But she didn't let that turn her—she was strong enough to resist the dragons' pull. She gave her life at the side of her clan, calling dragons from their caves and singing them out of the sky until the end."

The flame in his eyes dimmed. "I'd hoped to change the ending of that story with you. I would have stayed at your side in the battles, keeping all evil from you, while you served your people with your songs. But now I see you clearly. You would stab me in the back to protect your precious dragons!"

L'non put a heavy hand on Kallar's shoulder. "Settle down."

"That's not true," Alísa whisper-shouted back. "I k-k-killed dragons who wouldn't repent of their violence! I t—"

"And now you plan to lead your army against us if we don't see things your way?"

"W—what do you want me t-t-t-to do? Continue letting you k-kill those who don't deserve it? Letting you k-k-kill children? You saw everything—you know that's what it is!"

Even in the dark, Alísa could see Kallar shaking, his breaths quick and tight. With a shout, he threw a fist against the ground, making Alísa fall back into her father. The sound echoed through Alísa's ears and mind as Kallar's mind raced unguarded, his walls cracking and setting free the

393

cacophony of emotions battling within him—rage, frustration, confusion, sorrow, and an unbridled need for vengeance. It all coursed over Alísa, making her tremble in its wake.

Kallar stood, his footfalls heavy as he went to the tent-flap.

"Kallar," Karn said, turning after him, "where are you—"

"Have to clear my head." His voice was low and dangerous, and Alísa half-expected him to punch one of Tella's guards as he left. Instead, the apprentice merely stomped away, taking the dizzying swirl of emotion with him.

Alísa looked to each of those remaining, straining to see their expressions. They looked lost, unsettled. Her mother clenched her skirt in her hands.

"Karn," her mother said, her tone shaky, "is what we saw true?"

Karn's hand in Alísa's squeezed hard, as if he thought she would be lost again if he let go. Or, perhaps, that he would be. His emotions were guarded, only wisps of confusion and anger making it through.

"I had expected there would be lies in your mind," he whispered. "I had expected to break through them one-by-one and show you where the deceit lay. But this—if this is a lie, it was spun by the Nameless themselves, for no mortal could craft such things in such detail."

"It's the truth."

"Then the world will crumble in its telling," he said, still deathly soft. "The men will stumble by it, some never to rise again, and those who do rise will not know how to move forward. How can we protect humanity if we can no longer tell who is our enemy?"

He shook his head, the walls around his mind firming. "Even the mind can lie if it thinks it's telling the truth, and there are too many discrepancies between your story and what slayers have known to be true for generations."

She was losing him! "No, Papá—"

"I need to think on this." His statement was firm and final. "No matter the answer, it is too late to do anything about it, and you are tired."

His voice gentled with the last phrase, his hand caressing Alísa's cheek and wiping at the trail of tears.

"Sleep in safety tonight, Lísa. L'non and I will keep watch against dragons and slayers alike. We'll speak more in the morning."

A chasm opened in Alísa's heart, threatening to swallow her whole. He was supposed to understand now, like Namor had. Why, for all that was holy, could Namor see it when her own father could not?

"Hanah, bring the bedding out here," Karn said. "We'll all stay in the main chamber tonight. L'non, if you need to get anything—"

"I'll make do with whatever you have. Do you want me to choke the boy again?"

"No," Karn said. "His bond only works within a mile—we'll watch both of them, just in case, but we should save our strength. Alísa, you will sleep beside your mother near the chamber curtains. You" —he looked across the circle with a sigh— "Falier. You will sleep against the other wall."

"Yes, sir."

Falier's tone was sure, but Alísa could feel the weariness of the day over him like a thick, dark cloud. She stood and took a step toward him, only to feel a heavy hand on her shoulder.

"Alísa," came her father's uncertain tone.

"You saw everything," she said firmly. "Who he is to me and w— what he's done. Let me g—go to him."

Karn looked to Falier and back to Alísa, then lowered his hand. "If Kallar comes back and finds you in his arms, his wrath will be fierce. Keep that in mind."

Alísa ran the final few steps and fell to her knees beside Falier. He pulled her into a tight embrace. The buzz of his psychic touch filled her mind, though neither said anything, content to feel each other's presence. Their fear, anger, and sorrow mingled together, first squeezing harder around Alísa's heart, then relaxing as comfort spread over them. Comfort couldn't dispel the terrible clouds, but it did give them room to breathe.

"Líse. I was so scared for you. When Tella had you by the throat—"

"I'm okay." Alísa buried her face in his neck. *"Are you? Did they hurt you when they choked you?"*

Falier shook his head, kissing her hair. *"I'm fine. It was probably for the best—I don't know if I would have been able to stop myself from calling Graydonn when she..."*

395

Something tickled at the back of Alísa's mind as Falier trailed off. *"Call him? But he can't hear you from here. Or—no. He can. That's why you're here."*

Falier cringed. *"First chance I get, and I blow the secret. But I guess now that the mind-share is over you can know without danger. Just, don't let them back into your head, or else they'll see it and keep me choked."*

Alísa nodded slowly. Visions of memories flashed before her eyes, like remembering a dream. *"Can you keep from calling them? If they had come before, we'd all likely be dead right now."*

"I know. I will, just—try not to brush so closely with death again."

Alísa looked at the tent-flap, thinking of the guards beyond. Of Kallar, and the rest of the clan she would soon face, assuming her father let her speak to them.

"I'll try."

34

BREAKING

Alísa woke in dim morning light, the leather hide of the tent transforming sunlight to a warm orange-yellow that brought memories of sweeter times. Her mother stirred beside her, gently pulling her hand from Alísa's. She hadn't been ready to let go of her by the time the family had settled for sleep.

Her father, too, had stayed close after taking the first watch of the night. Alísa had woken for a few seconds as he laid down behind her. Sleeping here, in her family's tent between her parents, their love and care wafting over her, should have felt like the safest place in the world.

Instead, it felt almost like a cage.

Hanah noticed Alísa's open eyes and smiled. She pushed a strand of hair from Alísa's face.

"Sleep if you can. You've been through so much."

Alísa shook her head, beginning to sit up. "I'm fine, Mamá. I had good sleep."

It was a partial lie. Sleep had been plagued with dreams, of battle and clanmates both current and former. She barely remembered the details, but her heart sagged with their weight.

Hanah gave a sad smile, then stood and went into her and Karn's chamber, presumably to change into new clothes for the day.

A strange wave of happiness hit Alísa as she realized that her own clothes—those she had left behind when she ran—would probably be here too. She could wear one of her old favorite outfits. Something blue, perhaps? No. A chiefly red would be better as she addressed the clan.

She sat up and stretched, then noticed the azure gaze across the space. A wave of nerves coursed through her as she faced Kallar kneeling at the tent's entrance.

"You came back," she whispered, hoping to not wake anyone.

"I took third watch," Kallar said simply.

Alísa looked around the rest of the tent, first to her sleeping father, then to L'non and Falier. Falier rested his head on his forearm, his chest slowly expanding and deflating under the plain woolen blanket.

"Don't worry," Kallar said, bitterness lacing his tone, "I didn't kill your precious holder boy. Not yet, anyway."

Alísa looked back at him, her empathy stretching to all corners of the space. No real danger lived in his statement, but then, Kallar always guarded his emotions except in outbursts of anger.

She stood, heading to her old chamber.

"What are you doing?"

Alísa looked back at Kallar. "I'm going to change." His gaze turned suspicious, and Alísa sighed. "I'm n—not going t-t-to run. I know it isn't safe for me out there."

Kallar stared a moment longer, then his scrutiny passed. "Be quick."

Without hesitation, Alísa slipped through the flap of hide that led to her chamber, her fingers brushing one of the birds her mother had embroidered. Her travel bag bulged with her meager possessions—a heavy blanket, a pair of shoes, a blue cloak, and three sets of clothing. Digging through, she selected the red tartan tunic dress. Its short sleeves left her cold in the morning air, so she fastened her blue cloak over the top, the color matching one of the strands of the tartan.

When she left the chamber, Hanah was speaking with Kallar at the door to the tent. Her mother saw her and reiterated. "I'm going to organize the breakfast crew. I'll be back soon." With that, Hanah slipped out the entrance.

Nervousness and excitement rippled through Alísa. Breakfast. The clan typically ate the meal gathered in the center of camp, either all together or in many smaller groups. It was too much to hope that L'non might let her eat with Levan and Taer, but maybe she would see Trísse again, or Farren.

Alísa's skin prickled as she realized Kallar was staring at her again with those hard, unblinking eyes. Almost looking through her to something else behind her.

Like what she had seen as Namor helped her walk through her emotions.

The thought took her aback. Her old chief Toronn's gaze had always been eerily unblinking and hard too. Did Kallar really see her the way Toronn had—a disappointment, an inconvenience, a waste of breath? Or did she merely see similarities in their gazes? She had felt his care for her yesterday, and, despite it being unwelcome, it had been real. Her own feelings for him were complicated—she had never loved him, barely even liked him, but she did want to save him.

Namor and Tenza flashed through her mind's eye. Had he caught the relation as Karn sifted through her memories last night?

Alísa set her jaw and went to him, drawing a raised brow from Kallar. Four feet from him, she lowered to her knees. Where to begin?

"Allara was your mother?"

"Don't want to talk about it."

Ire ran through her as he shut her down. She shouldn't be surprised—he had always closed himself off from her. It was one of the reasons she had always known she couldn't trust him.

Try again. "Did you know what she was?"

A blank stare, like she was the biggest idiot in the world.

"D—did you know what I was all this time?"

That made him blink. He sighed deep in his throat. "Yes."

Alísa nodded as memories surfaced. "That was what you wanted t-t-t-to tell me. What Papá told you never to reveal."

Kallar squinted. "How do you know about that?"

"I overheard the t-t-two of you t-talking the morning after Azron."

Kallar's shoulders slumped very slightly. "Your father is the greatest slayer I've ever known—strong and wise—but he is a fool when it comes to you. He should have told you. Trained you. Then maybe you wouldn't have turned out this way."

Alísa wanted to tell him that she 'turned out' exactly as she should have, but knew it would only start an argument neither of them could win. She grabbed onto something else.

"You never listen when you d—don't agree with something. So w—

why didn't you t-tell me?"

Kallar's gaze lowered, giving Alísa reprieve from its burning.

"My mother kept her powers a secret from all but the clan that betrayed her and the slayers of L'rang. Karn's logic was one I'd heard all my life, so I didn't fight it like I should have. I've regretted that since the day you ran."

Alísa shook her head, looking up at the leather roof. "All I ever wanted was t—t-to know why I felt dragon emotions, why I was alone. I d—didn't want to be alone."

Kallar snorted. "Could have fooled me."

Alísa clenched her fists. "Maybe I wouldn't have felt that way if you had said something."

Kallar glared at her, his eyes cold, hard jewels again. "What, so I'm to blame for all of this? For you hating me?"

"I don't hate you."

He ignored her comment, his voice raising. "As if everything between us could have been fixed by that one thing? As if you weren't so closed off and stubborn and completely unreasonable?"

"Me? *I'm* the c-c-c-closed off and stubborn one?"

Bodies stirred behind Alísa, and she winced. Kallar had no idea how to keep quiet when he was mad, and she had followed him.

"You're the one who never tried," he said, quieter now. "You can't tell me that my telling you what you were would have changed that."

Alísa swallowed. "No. I'm just saying maybe we could have been friends."

She stood, breaking eye-contact. Why had she even tried? He would never hear her. He saw only what he wanted to see, just like Toronn.

"You okay, Líse?" Falier's quiet voice entered her mind.

Alísa kept her expression still. *"I'm fine. Just trying to reason with a stone wall."*

Turning away, she saw her father and uncle sitting up. Karn gave her an exasperated look, like he always did when she and Kallar argued. She looked away. Falier's presence was no longer in her mind, or else she would have begun talking to him. It was probably just as well—who knew how often Kallar was checking the astral plane?

The tent stayed silent for a little while, but for her father's instructions on getting ready for the day. He went into his chamber to change into fresh clothing, coming back out quickly so that Kallar and L'non could go to their tents and do the same. As soon as Kallar left the tent, Alísa went to Falier. He cast a sidelong glance at Karn before connecting to her psychically.

"No luck with Kallar, then?"

"None. I thought it was going well at one point, but then he completely shut down again." She pressed her lips together. *"I have no love for him, but I don't want him dead. I had hoped a night of sleeping and thinking would help him see the truth."* She looked at her father. *"I think his only hope is if Papá does. He might follow him."*

"I'm sorry. This isn't turning out at all like you wanted."

Not at all. She was supposed to have spoken with Karn's clan yesterday after he read her mind, then with Tella's today. Illumination shared a whole life in a few hours—she had thought sharing a mere three-and-a-half months would be faster. Sharing a couple months with Namor hadn't taken nearly so long—but then, Namor hadn't stopped and delved into certain scenes like her father had.

"What's the plan?"

Alísa pursed her lips. *"Hopefully, we'll breakfast with the clan and convince Papá to let me speak to them. Then, with the force of his clan behind me, we'll go to Tella and her clan. That is, assuming Papá decides I—"*

The connection cut off suddenly, making Alísa gasp. It felt like a knife had severed the link. Falier winced, and they both looked at Karn. His brows angled in anger.

"Not being held in mind-chokes is a privilege. I will rescind it if you speak telepathically again. And you" —Karn looked at Falier, eyes blazing— "should respect my daughter's privacy. Stay out of her head."

"I'm sorry, Papá." Alísa took a step closer to Falier, drawing her father's gaze. "But Falier does respect me and my p-p-p-privacy. We were just t-t-talking. It w—won't happen again."

"If he truly respects you, then he should have no need of secrets from me."

Falier ducked his head. "Yes, sir."

Soon L'non and Kallar returned, L'non addressing Karn as soon as he entered. "The camp is restless. They want to know what's being done about Alísa."

Alísa perked up. "Let me t-t-talk to them."

"No," Karn said, "not yet. I still don't know what to make of all this. You will not see them until I do."

When it came time for breakfast, Hanah, L'non, and Kallar all brought back two plates each, not allowing Alísa or Falier to leave the tent. Throughout the morning, Alísa's family interrogated them, asking about moments and information everyone had already seen the night before. The dragons' claims to follow the Maker rather than the Nameless. The reason Tsamen's dragons followed Alísa. The reason Rorenth's dragons followed Alísa. What made Alísa run away in the first place? What made Falier trust her and the dragons? What was the dragons' end goal? The questions kept coming, all accompanied by scrutiny with no indication she was getting through to any of them.

As the noon hour neared and the sounds of the kitchen tent stirred again, Alísa looked to her father. "Papá, p-p-please, I have to speak with the c-clan—"

"No."

"But we're running out of t-time! If you c-c-can't make up your mind, then let them d—decide for themselves."

Karn sighed and shook his head. "I have made up my mind. I'm sorry, but I cannot let you do it. Not now."

Blood drained from Alísa's face, her fingers going cold. No. He couldn't say no! He couldn't refuse the truth—if he did, she and her clan were bound to save lives by killing him!

"B—but you know! You saw! How c-c-c-c-can that be a lie? You said it yourself—no mortal c-c-could have woven such a lie. Do you really think I've been t-t-t-touched by the Nameless?"

"No," Karn said. "I know everything I saw through your eyes was true."

Alísa's heart ran cold. "W—what? But—but why? How—"

Karn placed a hand on her cheek, infinite sadness in his eyes. "I believe you, but there is so much you don't see, and the fact that there are good dragons in the world does not mean this war can end. Out of two clans of thirty or more dragons each, you called out ten. And though you claim that at least those from the Prilunes were proved by your song, two of them are those who most despise allying with slayers."

Alísa's mind flitted to Faern and Harenn. She had no argument against her father there.

"You've had to force them to take riders," he continued, "and the younger one still fights against it. And you think that you can make all dragons live at peace with us?"

He said it so gently, but the last statement seemed a slap in the face. Tears prickled behind her eyes as her hopes and plans crumbled to dust.

"Alísa, I will not let you throw your life away for something that will not work."

Alísa hunched with grief, pulling her face from her father's hand and clenching her skirts. She bit back the tears as her arms trembled under the weight of his statements.

'So much you don't see.'

'You think you can?'

'Throw your life away.'

Like a terrible wave it washed over her—he believed her, but he didn't believe *in* her. Even after everything he had seen her do in her memories, he didn't think her capable of bringing peace. She would never be enough in his eyes, and it doused her flames to mere embers.

"You're wrong." Falier's voice sounded so far away. "It can work. It has worked. I've seen it with my own eyes—humans and dragons who didn't get along working together regardless."

Alísa lifted her head in fear as Kallar snarled at him. "This isn't your place, holder."

Falier ignored Kallar. "There will always be humans and dragons who refuse—Faern and Harenn still made the choice to move, and Alísa was the catalyst. She led us, but every human and dragon you saw made a choice. You can too."

Falier met Alísa's eyes, pure belief shining in them. *"If Sesína were here right now, what would she call you?"*

Dragon-heart. Alísa pursed her lips. *Don't give up, dragon-heart.*

"You're right, P-P-P-Papá, I haven't been able to convince everyone, not among dragons or slayers. B—but I can't stop trying just because of that, or b—b—because some need more guidance than others. You, a chief, should know that. Don't leave your c-c-clan in the dark, k-killing and being killed in ignorance. Let me tell them, and let them decide for themselves."

"You will tell them," Karn assured, "but not yet. If you do anything now, Tella will kill you."

"Not if you stand up to her."

Karn's eyes hardened. "Her clan is nearly twice our size. Would you have me sacrifice the women and children—your mother, aunt, and cousins—simply so you can inform people of *some* dragons' innocence?"

"Then let me speak to T-T-Tella too. If I don't, many good men and dragons will be lost t-t-tomorrow! No matter what happens to me, my c-clan will not let you march on the east to k-k-k-kill civilians like Segenn."

"There will be no reason for us to march if we have the Dragon Singer." Karn leaned forward, placing a hand over hers. "I know you fear for your friends. When your dragons come, I'll let you send a message through Sesína telling them to flee and leave you behind. *That* is how we'll save lives. When the dust settles, we'll see if we can figure how not to kill good dragons. We'll stop using hatchlings for training, at the very least. But peace between both races on a large scale will never work, and I will not see you die for it."

There it was again. "Papá—"

"I will not argue it anymore. That is final." He squeezed her hand, his tone softening again. "I won't tell Tella about the coming attack. Your friends aren't looking to kill women and children, they're looking for warriors, so only a very few of her clan will be in danger. If Tella doesn't expect an attack, she won't be able to kill many of your friends before you can send them away. This is the only way, Alísa."

Alísa pulled her hand away, crossing her arms over her abdomen and refusing to look at him. There was indeed another way, a plan forming in her mind, but to accomplish it, she needed to be defeated in his eyes. She covered her mouth with a hand and allowed the tears she had previously refused.

Oh, Papá. How can you be so close and yet so far away? Making a way for my clan to live, yet refusing their purpose. My purpose.

L'non brought up something about Tella's clan and letting them know anyway, but Alísa barely listened, watching for the opportunity to signal Falier. It came quickly, as Kallar took up L'non's argument and looked away from her. She pushed a strand of hair back, making eye-contact with Falier and letting her fingers linger a little too long at her temple. Falier's face didn't change as he connected to her.

"If he's going to let you connect to Sesína to tell them to retreat, there's a chance she could find you and take you up to lead the charge. With your song, we still might succeed."

"Falier." She paused only a moment, knowing the difficulty of what she was about to ask. *"I have to tell my father's clan, to give them an opportunity to turn and give our clan a better chance in the battle. They're gathered for lunch now. If I can get out there, I can tell them all. But I need a distraction to slip out the back."*

Falier's eyes and lips twitched before mastering himself once more. *"If you go out there and do anything unsanctioned, Tella's guards will kill you."*

"And if I don't, everyone will die. I can't rely on Papá to do this—it's up to me now. If I play this right, I might even get the chance to take the truth to Tella as well."

"Líse—"

"Please, Falier. I can't let them die without giving them a chance to choose, and I will not lie down like my father wants. But I need your help."

Falier's emotions squirmed, moving between fear, pride, and love. He wanted to protect her, not send her to what could be her death. It was a terrible thing to ask of him, but it was all they had left. Finally, Falier sighed, his shoulders slumping and his face displaying the conflict he felt.

"Make it obvious I'm communicating telepathically. I'll give you your distraction."

Alísa pressed her lips together, fighting back tears. *"Thank you."*

He gave her a small, sad smile. *"I love you."*

"I love you."

"Hey!" Right on cue, Kallar took the bait. "Stay out of her head!"

"What did I tell you two?" Karn looked between Alísa and Falier.

"Don't make us keep you in mind-chokes."

Falier smirked, his eyes fixed on Alísa in a way she had never seen before, reminiscent of Kallar's possessiveness. His eyes slid to the jealous apprentice beside him.

"I don't particularly care to air our sweet nothings to other ears. I was trying not to rub it in your face that Alísa chose me over you, but if you insist—"

Alísa's heart clenched as Kallar rammed a fist into Falier's gut. All eyes turned from her, L'non and Karn both moving as Kallar aimed a second punch at Falier's face.

"Go!"

Falier's command jarred Alísa from her stupor, and she crawled to the rear edge of the tent. By the time she lifted the leather and slipped out, Falier was fighting back and her father and uncle were trying to grab hold to break them up. There wasn't much time before they realized she was gone. She ran for the center of camp.

Small groups of people came into view as she rounded her uncle's large tent, totaling a little over thirty people, all recognizable and eating in relative silence. A head framed with blond hair lifted up to see her, Aunt Elani's eyes widening in shock as she recognized Alísa over the heads of her two young boys. Alísa and Elani had never quite seen eye-to-eye, so as Elani's lips parted to say or, more likely, shout something, Alísa forced her first notes.

> Here's a tale you think you know:
> A daughter's broken mind,
> How dragons sought to bring her low,
> And how her soul aligned.
>
> But through the shards of brokenness,
> Can the light shine through?
> Don't close your ears to dissonance.
> Attend and hear the truth.

Alísa focused her powers, twisting her empathy together into strands of telepathy that coursed over and through all within earshot. Some merely listened, not having the presence of mind to fight her, but others struggled, squirming under her psychic hold. She had to be fast, while she still had strength to give.

Maker, let them hear me. Bria, give me strength and words.

A dragon voice calls to the maid,
This slayer he calls friend.
To Maker's wings he calls for aid.
The weakest he defends.

Can evil work in noble deeds?
Or darkness graciously?
Will Nameless spawn e'er fight and bleed
For frail humanity?

Alísa's strength waned as people fought to break from the trance. She fell to her knees, straining to give as much of her energy as she could.

Multiple new signatures pressed in against her, hard and unrelenting in their struggle. One burned with an all too familiar hatred.

She turned to see Yarlan approaching, accompanied by another man she assumed was one of Tella's guards. Alísa pressed against them but couldn't match them, not while she fought to keep the images flowing to her father's clan. Behind them came her father, L'non, and Kallar—they, too, fighting against her.

Tella's guard drew a sword, only a few yards from her, his walk halting, but advancing nonetheless. She couldn't stop. Her story wasn't over—she had to wrap it up before he got to her and hope the truth she brought would live even after he cut her down.

A shot of hot, excited energy coursed over Alísa, filling the recesses of her aching mind. *"I almost didn't believe Falier when he told us what you're doing. You are insane, dragon-heart!"*

Joy spread through Alísa as Sesína's energy redoubled her own. She pressed again at Yarlan and the other advancing Tellas-men, stopping them in their tracks.

"*This might be worse than when you jumped from Koriana's back in the middle of a battle.*"

Alísa smiled and turned her last verse around so she could focus enough to speak to Sesína. "*And you're here to catch me again?*"

"*Always.*"

Sesína's strength coursed into Alísa and focused on keeping the advancing guards and family-members in check, while Alísa pressed her freed-up energies back over the people.

Time and again, the dragons prove
Their souls are all their own.
Now armed with truth, the daughter moves,
But will she stand alone?

Oh brothers, through her broken parts,
Can you see the light?
The choices made, the searching hearts,
In skin and scales alike?

Now armed with truth, the daughter moves,
But will she stand alone?

As Alísa held onto her final note, Sesína's anxiety coursed over her. "*The clan is ready—we're coming to get you out of there.*"

"No," Alísa said. "*Papá is here, and I can feel his desire to protect me. If he succeeds, I'll be able to talk to Tella. If he doesn't, I'll be dead before you can get here. Be ready, but hold your positions.*"

A growl coursed through the bond. "*If you die, I'll fly to the Maker's Halls and give you a thrashing you'll never forget.*"

"*I believe you. By Maker's wings.*"

"*By Maker's wings.*"

Alísa faced Yarlan and Tella's guard and ended her song. As her resistance ended, they pushed forward, the guard stumbling to his hands and knees, while Yarlan ran at her full force, pulling his sword back. Alísa ducked and rolled from the swiping blade, feeling the rush of air as his sword cut over her head. Sounds clashed all around her—the growl of her attacker, her father's shout, and the distant rumble of thunder.

Karn and Kallar pushed past the fallen guard, but they weren't close enough as Yarlan moved to stab Alísa through. His hatred had finally been given its way.

A blur of motion, a clang of metal on metal, and Drennar stood in front of Alísa, blocking Yarlan's attack.

"You will not harm the chief's daughter!"

Karn and Kallar made it to Drennar's side, L'non stopping to hold down the fallen guard. Kallar growled at Yarlan through gritted teeth.

"Stand back or I'll run you through!"

Karn turned wide eyes on Alísa, his mind clamping down hard around hers and sending a jolt of pain through her as Sesína was once again ripped from her. Alísa pitched forward, and Karn fell to his knees to catch her.

"What have you done?" he whispered. "Didn't I tell you this wouldn't end well?"

"I had to tell them the truth," Alísa whispered back, "no matter what you say. Take me to Tella. She must hear me too, before it's too late."

Karn's eyes hardened. "That's not your decision."

She forced herself upright, trying to stand. "Yes, it is."

"She's forfeited her life," Tella's guard spat from the ground. "She put your clan under her spell and called to a dragon nearby—surely the 'great Karn' heard the roar."

Roar? Alísa's mind raced back to the thunder she had heard in the cloudless sky. Had it actually been Koriana, or one of the others? *Sesína, keep the clan back!*

"We have our orders, Karn," Yarlan said, staring down Drennar and Kallar. "You can't afford to oppose Tella. Or is your clan siding with the witch?"

"What I saw wasn't what I expected." One of Karn's slayers stepped up. "She doesn't seem possessed at all."

"Is it true, Karn?" another clansman asked.

Behind him, a few others of her father's clan stood, some with hands on their sword hilts. Others watched wide-eyed from the ground, staring at her or searching the sky, unsure what to do. Another sword slid from its sheath and Alísa whirled to see Trísse coming up beside her.

"And here I thought you hated being the center of attention," Trísse said, hard eyes fixed on Tella's guards.

Alísa's heart warmed as Karn's people moved around her, one after another, but even so, she had to speak to Tella and her people.

"P-P-Papá, I will go willingly. I must—"

"Dragons!"

Alísa's heart stopped as multiple shouts came up, some from this camp and some from Tella's. She searched the eastern skies for dragons flying over the river. *No, Sesína! Not you!*

"There!" A man pointed southwest. "From the Fangs!"

Alísa's blood ran cold. Paili and Tsamen were in the Fangs. Alísa squinted at the sky to see many tiny dots growing. Had they felt the power in her song from that far away? Or was the roar the others heard a warning from one of their scouts? Galerra had warned her never to cross the Nissen, and now she stood in the midst of their greatest enemies!

An alarm horn sounded in Tella's camp, and Yarlan growled. "You see—the witch has called them here to destroy us, just as I've always known she would. Kill her now, before she can—"

"No!" Alísa said, panic rising. "Those aren't my d—dragons! I didn't c-c-c-c—"

"Her song didn't call for dragons," a slayer said, echoed by a couple others.

Fear wafted from Karn, the only emotion she could feel under his choke as he began his mental calculations. He looked up suddenly.

"Senarr! Varek!" Two clansmen came to attention. "Gag and guard her—keep her under a mind-choke. We'll prove to Tella she isn't behind this."

"No! Papá, let me—"

His mind-choke tightened even as his sorrow flowed. He held her up, speaking gently.

"I know you didn't call these, but if you do anything in this battle, Tella will blame you for the dragons' strength. I will not lose you again."

He nodded to someone behind Alísa, and a strip of cloth pulled at her mouth from behind, slipping between her lips and pulling harshly against her cheeks.

"You're making a mistake, Karn!" Falier's voice rose up. Her father and the others must have forgotten him as they came after her. "Let her prove herself—"

Karn glared at him. "Him too, Varek. And choke them both!"

Senarr pulled Alísa's hands behind her, binding them with rope, while taking over the mind-choke. Karn turned away, shouting his orders.

"You two, go back to your chief. Men, to the frontlines! Hanah, Elani, get the women into the grove and make sure those who can wield weapons are armed. Move!"

Karn and the clan dispersed, boots pounding the ground, swords sliding from sheaths, and shouts of both fear and courage going up amidst the camp. Now what? It seemed some of the clan believed her, would perhaps have even fought for her, but now they were being torn away by the attacking dragons.

The specks in the sky grew into shapes she could recognize—thirty-strong, with eyes aglow in rage and brewing fire. The two clans of slayers might win together against Paili and her clan, but death would take many, and Alísa could do nothing to stop it.

Paili was close now, her giant ruby-scaled body at the front as her clan spread out to attack the slayer camps on multiple fronts. The fire growing in the alpha female's belly and throat was evident even from Alísa's position as Paili dove for the men on the frontline.

A familiar roar shook the eastern sky, and Alísa watched in pride and horror as Koriana charged onto the scene and collided with Paili, knocking the red's flames away from the slayers on the ground. More of Alísa's clan followed in her wake, slayers at the base of each neck. Her clanmates slammed into dragons aiming flames at camps still full of women, children, and unarmed slayers.

But Karn and Tella's warriors took aim at every creature in the air.

411

35

OTHER EYES

Harenn banked over the northern edge of the slayer camps, not slowing, for fear he would be caught by a psychic blast. Taz's legs clamped around the base of his neck, and Harenn rumbled in his throat to fight the sensation of choking. The dumb slayer should be used to flying by now—they had practiced plenty.

It could be worse—he could have T'lan's meaty legs. Poor Komi.

They cleared the last of the trees and Harenn went low, flying fast over the larger of the two camps. He scanned the faces as he went by, searching for any sign of Alísa-Dragon-Singer.

Nothing.

"We should get higher," Taz urged. *"Out of range of spears and arrows."*

"They can't get us at this speed. We need to find the Singer."

"They can hit you. I've seen it happen. Look, I want to find them as much as you do, but Koriana assigned that task to Graydonn and Sesína. It's our job to keep the other dragons at bay until we know whether she turned the slayers. Now let's move!"

Taz kicked his heels against Harenn's shoulders, drawing a growl.

"How many times do I have to tell you I'm not a horse?"

Taz's tone turned infuriatingly light. *"At least three more."*

Harenn banked again, catching a glimpse of fleeing women. Some had red hair like Alísa-Dragon-Singer, but she wouldn't flee like these women. She would be running toward the battle if able to do so.

"Harenn!" Koriana's voice echoed loudly in his mind. *"Get away from the slayers, now!"*

The great dragoness' order shuddered through his heart and mind. Koriana wielded her position well—everything within him pulled to honor her word because his alpha had designated her as a beta. He was a good member of this clan. Useful. He would do as he should.

Sending an affirmative, Harenn shot upward, nervous energy coursing through his wings as he climbed into the battle. His eyes darted about, searching for a clanmate to support.

Saynan. The warrior ice dragon didn't need help from anyone, but having a wing-dragon would allow him to focus better on the fight before him.

Harenn dodged a blue dragon—a hunter in his father's clan—then skimmed past the tail of a green one—a scout only a year older than him. Taz shot a psychic arrow at the scout, drawing a trumpet that clamped around Harenn in tight jaws of sympathy. That dragon hadn't been a friend, more of a rival, but they had still known each other, trained and eaten together.

Harenn released a roar of frustration and anger. He had come prepared to fight slayers, not to face his old clan. After the Singer had unleashed the riders on them, he had hoped to never see them again. He had been foolish.

"Left, Harenn!"

At Taz's urgency, Harenn veered, narrowly avoiding the barbed tail-slap of a dragon twice his size. Taz sent a psychic arrow at the dragon—another of the hunters. Much as Harenn hated having a rider, he could admit this team-up was helpful at times.

"Thanks."

The slayer's surprise hit Harenn like icy rain. *"You're welcome."*

Harenn banked to follow Saynan, keeping his gaze on the white dragon's tail and following him in his twists and turns. Saynan acknowledged his presence with a quick mental affirmative, accepting Harenn as his wing-dragon. Saynan's rider hunched low over his neck, holding tight as he scanned for foes. They were high enough that the slayers on the ground could only tickle his mind with their attacks, which allowed the riders to attack rather than focus on defense.

A familiar trumpet sent lightning through Harenn's mind—small and female. He scanned the sky until he spotted a silver dragoness, a hatchling. *Iila.*

"*Slayer*," Harenn said, swinging his snout in her direction. "*Don't aim for the little one. I won't fight her.*"

Saynan trumpeted in alarm. He had seen her too. The ice dragon accessed the full clan's mind-link, his voice low and commanding as Koriana's had been. "*Iila is here. If she goes after you or your rider, do what you must, but if you attack her first, know that I will ground you!*"

Harenn shuddered at the thought of frozen wings unable to get airborne.

Koriana growled at her fellow beta. "*Stick to the mission, Saynan. Iila made her own choice. You may not be able to save her.*"

Saynan spat ice at another dragon, the spray flying further and faster than Harenn had ever seen. It caught a warrior dragoness on the wing, seizing her flight. Her fall attracted three of Tsamen's dragons, one of whom went to catch her, while the other two went for Saynan.

Harenn roared a battle cry. "*Slayer, this is your chance to prove yourself!*"

"*You just pay attention to the physical realm. And, by the way, it's Taz.*"

Harenn snorted smoke. "*Hang on!*"

Forcing back his anxiety, Harenn dove to intercept. He went straight for the wings, locking his eyes on them and not daring to look in the dragon's face. The dragon saw him and twisted out of the way.

It felt like flames coursed through his wings as Harenn beat back wind and gravity to follow his opponent, reversing his course with a twist that nearly turned him upside-down. Taz shouted a word Harenn didn't recognize, his legs clamping harder as he fought the change in momentum.

"*Harenn, I swear, one more of those and I will tell Alisa when this is over!*"

A thrum formed deep in Harenn's belly. "*I might just have to drop you, then.*"

Taz clamped tighter in response, a sliver of fear pulsing from him.

Harenn shook his head to loosen the choking grip. "*That was a joke.*"

"*Could have fooled me.*"

"*Just lean into the turns,*" Harenn growled. "*I've never let any of you fall. I don't plan to start now.*"

Harenn snapped at the tail of his opponent, blue scales reflecting the sunlight into his eyes. The dragon zipped left and right, trying to throw him off. Taz shot a psychic spear, making the blue dragon trumpet with pain. Harenn dove as it slowed, planning to come up underneath and slash at its belly.

"Harenn!"

The booming voice of Berreth, his brother and former trainer, squeezed Harenn's stomach. His wing-beats faltered and his opponent whisked away.

"What was that?"

Harenn shook Taz's incredulity from his thoughts, scanning the sky—left, right, above, below, behind.

There. Below and to the left. The gray scales that were nearly black, the vivid green eyes that locked on him as though he was still a hatchling.

"Traitorous serpent!" Berreth snapped his jaws in the air and rose in pursuit. *"Following the Singer to potential glory is one thing—carrying her vermin on your back is another!"*

Harenn shuddered, fighting back the fears of his youth. He had only been a hatchling when Berreth had left him to die—he was stronger now. He knew his giftings, he just had to put them to use.

"Harenn, are you okay?"

Taz's concern was more embarrassing than touching. Harenn flew in a tight circle, watching as Berreth and his muscled girth fought against gravity.

"What are you doing?"

"Any shot you get at that gray brute, take it."

Harenn dove, spiraling full-speed toward Berreth. His brother's eyes locked on him as his talons spread. Berreth flapped harder to the left, adjusting for Harenn's spiral to catch him as he sped past.

As soon as Berreth committed to the change, Harenn flared his wings to stop the spiral. He came down Berreth's back and sliced at his tail. At the same time, Taz attacked, the psychic and physical wounds yanking a trumpet from Berreth's throat.

Harenn flared his wings, catching an updraft and coming back around. *"Again, slayer!"*

"How many times do I have to remind you it's Taz?"

415

"At least three more."

Harenn circled in close to his brother, and Taz shot another psychic arrow. Berreth swiped his talons as Harenn came close, snapping his jaws at Harenn's wing and missing by a mere foot. Harenn darted to the other side, hoping to scrape his talons across the back of Berreth's wing.

"Nice try, hatchling."

Breath flew from Harenn's lungs as he caught a wing-slap, Berreth having twisted his massive girth to chase after him. Harenn scrambled to get between Taz and gravity and keep him on, the slayer clinging to him. Harenn dodged another wing-slap with quick beats of his own wings.

"You've gotten faster," Berreth admitted, his eyes brightening. *"But try dodging this!"*

"Left!"

Harenn understood too late, roaring with pain and rage as another dragon slammed into his side. The blue dragon drove him downward, flattening his wing against him. Not broken, but surely bruised and currently useless. Berreth dove after them, his eye-lights changing from mockery to fire. Taz pulled a dagger and stabbed the blue dragon in the leg, not seeing the flames above him.

"Slayer, jump!"

Flames leapt from Berreth's mouth, falling over Harenn's face just as Taz jumped from his back.

Harenn accessed the clan-link, *"Someone, catch him!"*

He blinked through the pain of the flames over his eyes, watching as Berreth descended toward him. The blue dislodged, getting out of the way of the beta dragon, only to get slapped aside by the tail of a massive brown dragon.

Faern!

The brown snapped his jaws at the descending Berreth, aiming for the throat. Berreth pulled his head back and tried to course-correct, but Faern latched onto his chest and wing with his talons. The slayer on his back screamed a battle cry and drove his sword through Berreth's wing as the beta tried to beat Faern back.

"I've got Taz!" Komi's voice filled Harenn's mind. The ferocity of battle hardened the edges of her voice, replacing her typically carefree

tone. She and T'lan rose into view. *"Let's get to the outskirts and get him remounted."*

Harenn beat his wings back from the tumbling giants above him, his bruised wing protesting as he turned south. Komi came up alongside him, Taz dangling from her front paws. Her vigilant green eyes searched for enemies as they flew away from the battle. The other dragons stayed far away from the grappling Faern and Berreth.

Once far from the others, Komi positioned herself above Harenn as they were taught. Taz's legs clamped even tighter than before as he settled back into position.

"Thank you, Komi," Taz said, courage wrapping around the quaking fear in his mind. *"And you, Harenn. Unless that was your attempt to get rid of me?"*

Harenn thrummed, despite himself. *"I'll have to try harder next time."*

"Let's not."

A roar of rage stopped Harenn's heart. He knew that roar intimately. The proximity of it pulled at his mind, threatening to open up the Illumination bond he had never wanted to feel again.

Paili.

"Father!" Komi cried, darting back toward the fray.

Harenn turned to follow her, then nearly choked as he saw his mother descending on Faern and Berreth. Fear trembled through him, smoke slipping from his jaws unbidden. Komi didn't slow, spearing forward even as Paili dug her talons into Faern's back. Taz shot a psychic arrow at her, but it did nothing to stop her from clamping her jaws around Faern's rider.

"No!" Taz shouted. "Oh, great Maker, no."

Faern's rider didn't even have the chance to scream, dead as he fell the dwindling distance from Paili's maw to the ground.

Faern didn't let go as Paili ripped at him, jaws at the base of Berreth's head. Three pairs of wings tried to keep them all aloft as they tumbled, but Faern and Berreth had already fallen quite a distance since Harenn had left them.

"Harenn! We have to get back in there!"

Taz's mental voice was piercing, shrill enough to break Harenn from his anxiety-fueled stupor. Harenn dove after Komi, but he knew they wouldn't be fast enough. The tumbling dragons were too close to the ground now.

With a jerk of his head, Faern snapped Berreth's neck, the terrifying eye-lights of Harenn's former trainer shocking out. The mass of three dragons fell faster with one only dead weight now. With a terrible crack, they landed on the ground in a heap, Berreth's body at the bottom, and Faern stuck between him and Paili.

Paili stumbled away from Faern, one of her wings flopping limply at her side. Slayers with their swords and spears surrounded them, Paili roaring a pain-filled battle cry and lunging at them with tooth and talon.

Behind her, Faern didn't stir. Two slayers made it past Paili, spears aimed at him. Then Komi shrieked a cry that rocked both the physical and astral planes as her Illumination bond was ripped away in her father's death.

PAIN!

Trísse stumbled as it ripped across the astral plane and echoed in her mind. Strong. Biting. Like her heart being ripped out through her throat. She had felt this pain before.

Loss.

> *Fear.*

>> *Loneliness.*

It prickled at the back of her mind, then ascended, filling all the dark spaces. Rising grief to the surface.

No! No grief. Not here. Not now. Why did it have to hit at the worst of times? The women here, hiding in the grove, needed her strong. Father would have wanted her strong!

Keep it down. Deal with it later.

PAIN!

Hatred twisting.

> Biting.

>> Thrashing.

Trísse pitched forward, stomach heaving, mouth gasping for air as a presence jarred her body and soul. *"Who are you? What do you want with me?"*

"Father!"

The voice echoed, stirring images foreign and familiar. Lessons in swordplay and flight. Long talks and wordless contentment. Protection and provision. A slayer and a dragon.

Dragon.

A large, brown dragon with eyes like grassy hills in the springtime.

This wasn't Father.

But it was.

But it wasn't.

Trísse grabbed her head as her mind expanded. It felt sticky and swollen like infection in a wound.

"Snap out of it!" came a new voice. Male and human and terrified. *"You're going to get us killed!"*

Flashes of vision whirled past. Wings. Flames. Sky. Grass. Blood. Like a dream of falling and knowing you could never wake.

"He's gone." The first voice returned. Grief. Though rage reigned in it, Grief was the voice's name. *"He's gone, and he's never coming back."*

PAIN!

Trísse hurled the contents of her stomach, vaguely aware of someone holding her hair back.

"Where is the Singer?" Grief asked. *"Why didn't she help us?"*

Alísa? *"What do you know of her?"*

"She could have stopped this. Now the world will burn! The world will burn and I'll be left alone forever!"

Trísse wiped away the sweat and bile with her sleeve. She knew something of this. Alísa had left her too. And in Trísse's hour of need, when her father's body was left behind in a burning heap on the mountain, Alísa hadn't been there.

Instead, she had been with the voice.

Dragon.

One of the ones in the vision. The song. It had to be. But, Trísse couldn't feel dragon emotions. She never had before.

"Who are you?"

Trísse couldn't tell if she had asked it, or if Grief had, or if both had asked at the same time.

Another vision. Tooth and talon. Blood and scales. A man's scream.

"*I can't stop it,*" Grief said. "*I can't see. Father!*"

The shriek flared Trísse's own grief to life again, spiraling through her like smoke caught in the kitchen tent, seeking the vent but unable to find it. Terrible, asphyxiating sorrow.

Father.

A dragon.

A slayer.

"*Father is dead.*" Her voice and Grief's mingled together like the blood of their clanmates on the battlefield. "*And your kind killed him.*"

PAIN!

Trísse breathed, thinking through her father's lessons. When others' feelings were trapped inside, what did she have to do?

Breathe.

Find what portion was hers.

Breathe.

Where was the separation?

Breathe.

Was there a separation?

"*Who are you?*"

"*Where is the Singer?*" Grief cried. "*Can she stop this? Can you stop this? Where is the Singer?*"

Singer.

Dragon inside a slayer.

Her kind killed him.

Her kind.

My kind.

Your kind.

Our kind.

Komi.

36

RELEASE

Alísa screamed against her gag as Faern and his rider fell, her insides twisting as Komi's scream only moments later confirmed Faern's death. Senarr's hold on her mind slipped as her muffled voice crashed against his choke. The slayer grunted with effort as he wrangled her back, the mottled shadows of the glade casting over his damp brow.

Varek drew a dagger from his belt and held it to Falier's throat. "I won't kill you, Alísa, but I doubt the chief will fault me for killing him. Stop fighting us, now."

Alísa slumped, showing her compliance. *Faern, Komi, I'm so sorry. I should have been out there with you.*

Varek pulled the knife away, leaving Falier breathing heavily. He looked so ragged in this moment, gagged and tied, the beginnings of a black eye from Kallar. Falier leaned lightly into her, pressing his shoulder to hers. She returned the gesture, gleaning whatever comfort she could from his touch. She had done this to him.

No. None of that guilt—not for Falier and not for Faern. If she allowed it, she wouldn't be able to get back up. Both had chosen to be here, and she couldn't allow unmerited guilt to hold her down.

A roar sent Senarr and Varek's hands to their swords and made Alísa tense. Not one of her dragons. A copper dragon dove at Karn's camp, its rattling inhale preceding a torrent of fire. A shudder ran through Alísa at the destruction, and she thanked the Maker camp was emptied of people. Her mother had led Trísse and the others far into the grove, out of sight and scent of the attacking dragons.

"Do we attack?" Senarr asked, his fury rippling around her mind. "We can choke it if we're fast enough."

"And let them go?" Varek jerked his head at Alísa and Falier. "Camp can be replaced. The men who will die if she escapes cannot."

Another draconic cry, this one long and guttural, almost like a slayer's battle cry. A flash of black flew after the copper dragon, trailed by green. Both Alísa and Falier straightened as their closest friends dive-bombed the attacking dragon. Sesína zipped underneath the copper and slapped the underside of its wing with her spiked tail. Graydonn cut around, anticipating the dragon's turn away from the pain, and slashed at the dragon's neck with his talons. Scales kept the blow from cutting deep enough to kill, but the copper dragon trumpeted in pain as it fled.

They were so close! But would they be a match for Senarr and Varek? They would have to land to get to them, and the trees would make maneuvering difficult at best.

Alísa leaned back against the tree. No, calling for Sesína and Graydonn right now would only call them to their deaths.

Senarr looked back at her. "That little black one. That was yours?"

Alísa nodded, forming her thoughts into loud words and praying he would hear her as he held her mind in the choke. *"My dragons will not attack camp. They know I'm here and that there are slayers here who now understand. Do you understand?"*

Senarr's eyes first widened, then narrowed. "Doesn't matter." Varek looked at him funnily, but Senarr paid it no heed. "Chief told me to guard and protect you. I can't let you go even if I wanted to."

"And do you want to?" Varek crossed his arms. "Did she get in your head with that story?"

Caution swept over Senarr's face. "I don't know. But it would account for the dragons attacking other dragons out there, rather than merely focusing on us."

"Dragon clans fight each other all the time."

"But in the presence of slayers? I've never seen it."

"And I suppose you've seen dragons in every situation under the sun? You know exactly how they think?"

Senarr held up his hands in peace. "I didn't say I fully believed it, just that I can't help but wonder. And I'm not going to set her free on a hunch. I'll not risk my wife on questions I don't know the answers to."

Varek's brow smoothed. "Good. You had me worried."

A shadow moved behind Varek, and with a loud thump he crumpled to the ground. Trísse stood in his place, lowering her sword from hitting the pommel on Varek's head. She bent her knees into a ready-stance.

"Trísse! What do you think you're doing?"

The young woman's dark eyes were hard, her olive skin perfectly at-home among the shadows of the trees. "Stopping more bloodshed."

Alísa wanted to shout for joy, her heart filling with it. Trísse was here, and fighting for her!

Trísse lunged, swiping at Senarr's chest. The slayer reacted swiftly, drawing his sword to block just in time.

"Stop this nonsense!" Senarr raised his sword to parry another slash, then advanced. "I know she's your friend, but setting her free will only make matters—"

Senarr drew in a sharp breath as Falier turned hard eyes on him. The choke over Alísa's mind wavered, a light pain ricocheting through her as Falier mind-speared Senarr. Trísse took advantage of the distraction and swung at his blade, twisting to wrench the sword from his grasp. Another hit from Falier and the mind-choke snapped away from Alísa. Senarr fell to his knees and Trísse hit his temple with the hilt of her sword, knocking him out.

Sesína's voice filled Alísa's mind. *"Are you hurt? What just happened?"*

Trísse knelt in front of Alísa. "Hurry up and turn around. They need you out there."

Alísa did as she was told, wishing the gag was already gone. *"I'm okay, what about—"*

Pain lanced through Alísa as the clan's mind-link became accessible, her dragons' every injury rushing through her at once. An arrow through Sesína's wing and one in Graydonn's hind leg. Rayna's newly-healed wing burning from over-exertion. Talons across Korin's muzzle. Bites and slices in Koriana, Tora, and Saynan's legs. A deep bruise in Harenn's wing. The worst of it belonged to Komi—slashes across her side and a rip through her wing, all dulled by her grief and rage.

Trísse pulled back from Alísa's bonds with a hiss of pain as a part of it transferred through their skin-contact. "Damn your dragon empathy, Alísa! How are you still conscious?"

Alísa shook her head, unable to do anything more until Trísse got the gag off her. Trísse moved to that job, leaving Alísa's pain-charged wrists. Alísa stretched her jaw and cheeks as the fabric came loose, wincing with her dragons' pain. They needed her strength. Grasping onto the pain-filled clan-link with all she had, Alísa poured out her strength song, accompanied by multiple trumpets of joy and anticipated triumph from her dragons.

> Dearest dragons, don't give in
> To pain and fear that pull you down.
> My song will stir your strength within.
> Shake loose the shackles and break out.

From her kneeling position behind Falier, Trísse looked up at Alísa with wide eyes. A shock of realization coursed through Alísa—Trísse felt the song too. She shouldn't, though. Only those the song connected to should feel its power.

But she couldn't ponder that just yet. She had to finish the verse and give the dragons enough strength to last them a bit without her song.

> For I, dear dragons, was held too—
> Fear once made me easy prey.
> So hear these words I sing for you;
> May my song help you find your strength!

Alísa breathed as her dragons' pain eased. It would return if she didn't keep sending doses of power, but they would be okay for a moment. She looked to Trísse.

"W—why?"

"You're welcome."

Alísa gave her a look she hoped communicated the severity of the situation. Trísse sighed.

"I think I believed you before, but it didn't occur to me what I should do until Komi appeared in my mind."

Falier whipped around, pulling off his gag. "Komi?"

"I don't know how it happened. One minute I was standing guard beside the women, the next a voice entered my mind, trying to fill and share the space. I tried to fight it, but the grief—"

Trísse looked down suddenly, breathed out a long breath, and looked up again. Alísa knew that move—it was what Trísse did when she felt things she didn't want to deal with right then.

"The grief called to my own. It was like when Farren tunes his lute and two of the strings make notes so close to each other that they warble and pound in your ear. That's what the voice did to me until I accepted it and the pounding stopped as the notes finally became one."

A grin split Falier's face. "Mind-kin. It has to be."

"B—but how? They've never met—"

An insistent trumpet sounded in the camp, and Alísa twisted to see Sesína and Graydonn standing just outside the trees, looking in at them.

"Come on!" Sesína said. *"You can figure that out later—we need you out here!"*

Alísa stood. "We have to go."

Falier and Trísse followed suit, the latter looking lost. "I don't think I can do much more—it's taking all of my empathy to keep Komi calm enough to think. Fighting Senarr was too distracting—if it had taken longer..."

"Then k-keep helping her. She's hurt bad enough as it is. K-k-k-keep her sane and get her to leave if the p-pain becomes too much."

Trísse set her jaw, nodding first to Alísa, then to Falier. "Branni strengthen your hands."

"And yours."

Alísa and Falier charged out of the tree-cover, Alísa throwing her cloak from her shoulders. They leapt onto their dragon companion's and launched into the sky. Alísa ran a hand over Sesína's neck as they ascended, drawing a clicking purr from the dragoness' throat.

"I missed you, dear one. Now, what's happening?"

"Koriana and Saynan are in command. They have most of the clan

fighting dragons only, high up out of the reach of spears and arrows."

Alísa winced as she remembered the arrow in Sesína's wing. She should have removed it before they took off.

"I'll be fine as long as you sing again."

Without another thought, Alísa launched back into her strength-song, feeling her dragons' fatigue melting away again. Her voice knew the melody and lyrics intimately, allowing her to listen as Sesína made her report.

"At the southern edge of the grove, there's a group of eastern slayers working to shield us from psychic attacks. It's hard for them—they can't tell which dragon is which unless they're flying low enough that a rider is visible, so really they're just trying to keep all dragons in the air. Tora and Q'rill are watching out for them, in case Karn or Tella figure out what's happening. The dreki are on the other side of the river with Selene and the hatchlings."

"Hatchlings?" Alísa's heart dropped. *"What are they doing here?"*

"We needed all the dragons we could get. Aree is a strong fighter, and Rassím an excellent rider. Me'ran is too far away for the Illumination bonds, but the opposite side of the river isn't. As I said, the dreki are there to protect them."

"Singer," came Koriana's voice. *"What is the word on the slayers? Should we engage?"*

Alísa ran through numbers and fears and convictions. *"No. Keep doing what you're doing. Some of the slayers turned, but the attack came so suddenly I have little idea who. I need to stop this fight. I'm going to find the chiefs and alphas and ask them to parley. Everyone, try to avoid killing blows, but do not endanger yourselves."*

"Paili's still on the ground, where Faern fell."

Koriana's words brought a shock of raging grief from Komi. Its lightning seized Alísa's mind, then dulled as another mind rose up in the clan-link. It brought order to Komi's chaos with a gentle firmness.

Trísse. Great Maker, how had that happened?

"I have eyes on Tsamen," Saynan said, bringing Alísa back to the present. *"Southern edge of the battle."*

Alísa gripped Sesína tightly and set her eyes south. *"Let's go!"*

37

ALLARA'S BANE

Kallar ducked under his shield, interlocking it against Tern and Merrik's on either side of him. Blazing heat roared against the shields, directed over their heads and to the sides. It caught in the grasses to their right, but they didn't dare move until the rush of wings sailed past them.

Kallar pivoted to watch the green beast who had just attacked them. "Choke it!"

Tern and Merrik shot psychic spears in tandem with Kallar. Kallar's hit first, drawing a pained trumpet from the monster. It must have sent its own spear at the same time, because pain seared into Kallar's mind like burning coals.

Gritting his teeth, Kallar pulled back and let his partners begin the choke. This was the third time this battle he had been hit by a dragon's psychic attack. Dragons typically relied on physical strength and fire. Psychic attacks weren't rare, but three in the space of only half-an-hour—and all focused on him—was an anomaly.

Kallar shot the dragon again, this time spreading his power over its mind instead of ramming into it. His power added to his men's and sealed the gaps, locking the mind-choke around the dragon. Glowing brown eyes dimmed as the choke completed and it fell twisting from the sky. Kallar pressed against Tern and Merrik's power, keeping the choke sealed until the dragon cracked against the ground.

PAIN!

Instinctively, Kallar pulled his power back to himself and formed a shield around his mind. He searched the sky—where was it coming from?!

"Kallar, what are you doing?" Tern, olive skin just as sweat-soaked as Kallar's, kept his eyes fixed on the dragon. Merrik grunted with effort beside him.

Kallar growled at himself and sent his power back out, reinforcing the choke. He shook out his sword-arm as the psychic pain settled there. Pressing through it, Kallar passed Tern and Merrik, running for the downed dragon. Its right wing was broken at the mainstay, just before its wing-fingers. It shuddered, likely fighting the mind-choke.

Stupid creature—a break like that would keep it grounded and likely bring it more suffering before death.

Then again, Kallar wouldn't just lie down and let death come either.

He shook his head to rid himself of the thoughts. It was just a monster looking to continue preying, just like the dragon that had taken his mother. It was not like him.

Setting his eyes on the dragon's soft underbelly, Kallar drew his sword back and plunged it into its heart.

Lightning ripped through him, and this time he couldn't hold back a cry. Pain coursed over his mind and wound its way down into his chest. Lungs contracted, blood pounded, knees buckled. He ripped his mind from the choke and wrapped his power around himself. The pain echoed over and over, but ceased growing.

Someone was targeting him. One of the twice-damned dragons? Or maybe one of Alísa's traitorous slayers?

"Kallar, flames!"

Kallar didn't hesitate at Merrik's call, dropping against the dead dragon's belly and pulling his bronze shield up over him. The fire hit the shield square-on, forcing it back against him. Blistering heat burned his arms as flames splashed around the shield. He involuntarily remembered the terrible pain when his whole left arm had caught fire in a cave-storming.

He gritted his teeth. That had been the worst pain he had ever felt—far worse than these flaming psychic attacks. If he could pull through that pain, use it to create psychic spears, and make it to the other side alive, he could certainly make it through whatever this thrice-damned psychic attack was.

Kallar pushed up the moment the flames died, twisting to mind-blast the dragon who had just tried to kill him. Another rush of wings sounded behind him, and dread sunk his heart. He hadn't checked to make sure there wasn't a second dragon following the first. There wasn't time to turn and block with his shield, only time to duck and hope the dragon missed.

He dropped, but the dragon merely passed over him. A gray one, scales like storm clouds, with a rider on its back.

Koriana.

Kallar cursed himself for remembering. He shouldn't remember. It didn't matter. It was a dragon, and that was the end of it. It shouldn't matter which of them he took out.

Should it?

No.

Besides, with how high most of them flew, he couldn't tell which dragons had riders until they were right on top of him. By then it would be too late.

Just like this had been too late.

Koriana could have killed him.

Stop using its name!

Kallar pulled his sword from the dead dragon, the wound squelching as he did. The oily stink of the brute mixed with the tang of blood. Tern and Merrik were on him now.

"You good?" Tern asked.

Kallar grunted an affirmative and searched the skies for the closest dragon. He would choke it out of the sky, remember his training and why he fought. Who cared if a few dragons had hearts? They were still going to kill his people at Alísa's command if they didn't 'listen to her.' They were still the enemy. She—she was the enemy.

Loud roars echoed just south of them, and all three slayers turned to see the commotion.

Kallar squinted. "What in hellflames?"

Three dragons fell from the sky, grappling. They were fighting each other, blood spraying into the sky as a red one gouged holes in the back of a brown. The brown had a death-grip around another dragon's neck, and with a forceful twist of its head it killed its fellow.

"Come on!" Kallar ran for the mass of falling dragons, knowing Tern and Merrik were with him. The beasts wouldn't break their fall fast enough—he would make sure they didn't make it back into the skies if they survived the crash.

The ground quaked when the dragons landed, nearly toppling Kallar. He slowed for a couple of steps before regaining his balance and charging, sword and shield high. So far, only the red dragon moved, standing ten feet tall at the withers, left wing limp at its side. The red scales evoked frightening memories Alísa had so *helpfully* brought back to the surface. He shoved them aside. He wasn't that eight-year-old without weapon or power anymore. This dragon would fall by his strength.

A Tellas-man circled around to make sure the brown dragon was dead, while another approached the red at the same time as Kallar. A loud shriek pierced the cacophony of battle, making Kallar wince. He glanced up but didn't see any other dragons diving for them. He refocused on the monster before him.

The red dragon roared a challenge, fire stoking in its belly and lighting its maw.

"Choke it!" Kallar ordered.

Tern and Merrik didn't hesitate, blasting the red dragon as Kallar did the same. As soon as his power hit the dragon, pain flared up his shield-arm. This time, he didn't pull back, pushing himself through the pain. The dragon's mind squirmed under their attack, biting and clawing at them, adding to Kallar's suffering. They had to make this quick!

Kallar sealed the choke against Tern's power and shifted to seal the other side. Then the dragon charged, blasting flames at him and his men. Kallar dodged in a roll, coming up at one end of the fire. Tern's power disappeared from the choke, the towering flames cutting off his sight-line to the beast.

Damn it! Kallar pulled his own power back into a shield.

The Tellas-man rounded the other side of the fire, and Kallar took his cue from him. Merrik fell in behind him, Tern still finding his way around the wall of flames. Kallar and Merrik had the more dangerous end, with flames, teeth, and talons all directly in front of them.

The dragon snapped at him, and Kallar slashed its lip with his sword. It coiled back to strike again, and he rolled, coming up beside the hurt wing. Merrik came from behind, ducking underneath the dragon's chest to slash at its legs.

A rattling inhalation warned Kallar, and he dodged as the dragon breathed fire underneath itself. His heart seized as Merrik screamed, engulfed in flames, and was silenced by a stamp of the dragon's foot.

Another shout of pain came from behind the dragon—the Tellasman, slapped away by the dragon's tail. He fell back several yards and lay there, dead or unconscious Kallar did not know.

Tern ran up behind him, launching a javelin at the dragon's chest. It pierced the tough skin by the withers, drawing a shriek of pain. The dragon charged, snapping at Tern as he drew his sword.

Kallar shouted a battle cry. He would not lose Tern too! He ran for the wing dragging limply on the ground, two of its fingers twisted at awkward angles. Kallar raised his sword and hacked at it. The dragon whirled away from Tern, talons extended to swipe at him. Kallar jumped back, sending a psychic spear into the dragon's mind.

PAIN!

Kallar staggered, then shouted at the dragon again. *That's right, look at me!*

The dragon breathed fire, and Kallar dodged toward the injured wing, slashing at the leather as he ran. To his shock, the beast moved the wing, pulling it up and out of the way of his sword. It happened so fast, he barely saw the tail hiding underneath it. With a force that would break a man, the dragon swung. Kallar jerked his shield up.

Bronze bent.

Bone snapped.

Feet left the ground.

The world went black.

Hazy sunlight glazed over Kallar, streaming in from his bedroom window and warming his aching body. He lay in a bed that part of him knew he hadn't slept in since he was fifteen. His now-adult body sank into a mattress far softer than his bed-mat. His head and shield-arm throbbed, and in the hall beyond his closed door, a voice rose. It called to his heart, and a part of him filled with joy and wonder even as his mind told him she was dead. Mamá was dead.

The door opened, and there she was. Thick black hair cascading in waves it only ever had just after unbraiding it. Slanted brown eyes typically hard that softened only for family. Blue dragon-scale armor that wrapped around her slender arms and disappeared under a bronze breastplate.

Kallar tried to sit up, to show her the man he had become, who choked dragons from the sky before their flames could take another mother from her children. But he couldn't. His body felt like stone, heavy and immovable.

Allara sat on the bed at his side. A roar echoed somewhere nearby, but Allara's gaze didn't leave him. Her slender fingers reached out and pushed a strand of hair from his sweaty brow. Love and compassion zinged through her touch, painful in their sharpness. He had never felt it that strongly from anyone before.

"It's a heavy burden you now carry," she said, her tone quiet. "If only you knew it sooner, you might bear it more easily."

Burden? What did she mean?

"The burden of knowledge," she said, as though reading his thoughts, "that dragons are *iompróir anam*. You can't unsee it, can you? Their names, the choices they make for good and evil, their emotions that mirror our own. It's a terrible burden to bear, fighting an enemy as personal as you are. It's easier when they are soulless."

Another roar, closer this time. His shield-arm throbbed.

Allara's gaze intensified. "There isn't much time, but you have to understand this. The pain you've been feeling throughout this battle is because of this knowledge—"

So Alísa awoke dragon empathy in me?

This time, Allara truly seemed to read his thoughts. "Almost. Any slayer who knows the dragons are souls may gain the ability to sense dragon emotions—many of Alísa's men can now—but they won't feel the terrible pain I knew as a Dragon Singer. The terrible pain *you* now know."

Her words knocked the air out of him. The psychic attacker. It wasn't a dragon, wasn't one of Alísa's slayers—it was him. He was—

"Yes. You are a Singer, like me."

It was him. His own mind betraying him on the battlefield, sending him shocks of pain over and over again, every time he let down his shield to harm a dragon!

Allara's compassion swelled again, sharper than any emotion he had ever felt. He wanted to pull his telepathy into a shield and retreat from it, but he couldn't move his powers any more than he could his body.

"Listen to me, my cub. You need to get up now—you need to leave the battlefield before the pain kills you."

Kallar grit his teeth, trying to rise and failing again. "If Alísa can do it—"

"Alísa has dealt with this for four years, and she has not made it her mission to kill dragons."

Smells of earth, smoke, and blood filled Kallar's nostrils, all scents that didn't belong here in this hazy room. A roar echoed again, and this time Allara's gaze moved to the window, hardening.

"You have to wake up, Kallar."

Everything within him recoiled at the order. He would rather stay. His world was breaking. If he felt pain whenever he fought dragons now, how long could he last? And if Karn fell to Alísa's wishes and stopped fighting against the dragons, the thing Kallar had devoted his life to? What would be his place if he went back? His mother was here. He could stay here, in whatever afterlife she had found.

The sky out the window darkened. Cracks formed over the walls as the world shook. And outside a new voice rose.

Alísa.

"This place isn't real," Allara said as his own mind told him the same. Grass tickled his face now, and the roars and Alísa's voice grew louder. "You couldn't stay here, nor should you."

As the room shook again and the glass of the window broke, a blur shifted over Allara's features—dancing lights that played tricks with his mind. The tiny glimpses he caught revealed darkening skin and fiery curls. And her voice, too, shifted into something ethereal and coated with love.

"You have a life to live, my cub. I pray you'll find your way."

Kallar's shield-arm jerked with pain as his mind recoiled. This wasn't his mother.

"Move, Kallar," Not-Allara said, fear suddenly in her voice. "Move!"

Kallar opened his eyes, his face in the dirt and grass. A rattling breath sounded to his left. Driven by instinct, he rolled to the right. His sword was gone, but the shield was still strapped to him, bent in on itself. His shield-arm shot lightning through him as he curled beneath the bronze. Flames shot above him, the edges of the blast licking his shield.

He pushed up as the fire passed, sending searing pain through his left arm. It bent in the shield's straps in a way it wasn't meant to. Using only his sword arm, he pushed himself to his knees.

Before him, the red dragon snapped at the air, now much further away than it had been. It had flung him back nearly thirty feet. A black streak zipped around it, flying in erratic circles while a figure with red curls clung to its back.

"*Finally, you wake up,*" came a voice he recognized from Alísa's memories. Sesína's—no, *the dragon's* tone was full of disgust. "*Move it, Kallar! Paili's going to blow!*"

Paili? The name was familiar.

No—no names! It was a dragon, just like any other.

As though that would change what his mind already knew.

Anam.

"*Go, Kallar!*" Alísa's voice came through. "*You're hurt—get out of here!*"

Run. His mother—no, that trickster Bria told him to do the same. With his shield-arm broken, his sword lost, and the promise of psychic pain to come, perhaps that was best.

But, he never ran.

"*You've proved me right, standing with the slayers this day!*" A deep female voice—the red dragon—roared through the puny black dragon's mind. "*If I hadn't had a scout watching—*"

"Paili," Alísa interrupted, desperation tinging her words, *"it's not what you think! I was with them to try to get them to stop, and they were listening! Many of them—I would have convinced more, but you attacked before I could!"*

"You think I care?!" The red swiped at the black. *"The slayers destroyed my family, and hundreds of others. I'll not see you put more of them on the backs of dragonkind!"*

The black dragon dove at the red's unhurt wing, ripping at its scaly back before pushing off to avoid snapping jaws. The red's tail sliced through the air, making the black yelp as it barely cleared the flying appendage. Another bout of flames shot above their heads, making Alísa's dragon duck down, right into the backhanded swing of the red's paw.

Pain pounded through Kallar as the black dragon and Alísa crashed to the ground, Alísa flying further than the dragon and avoiding being crushed by the black scaly mass.

Heart pounding, Kallar stumbled toward Alísa. He had to get to her, every thought in his head screamed to save her from the dragons and drowned out the pain in his own body. She dry-coughed, likely from the wind being knocked out of her.

"What blessing from the Maker," the red dragon said, jaws opening to reveal more flames as it locked eyes on Alísa. *"The chance to destroy two Singers in a lifetime is an opportunity I relish!"*

The world stopped.

That was why he knew the name Paili—she was in Alísa's memories. His blood boiled as he looked at the red dragon, first with the eyes of an eight-year-old boy as it descended with flames upon his mother, then with the eyes of a slayer who was no longer powerless.

A Dragon Singer, am I?

Kallar roared, focusing all his psychic energy into the sound, directing every drop of power he had into a blow he intended to rip a hole through Paili's mind. The dragoness turned her blazing orange eyes on him, fortifying her mind against his. She latched on with iron talons, and he pushed harder, wrestling against the pain pouring into him.

"K-Kallar, p-p-pull back!"

He didn't heed Alísa's call. He would die before he backed off this monster who had stolen his mother, his childhood, his family's happiness! If Alísa hoped he would let this spawn of the Nameless free, she was badly mistaken!

His knees buckled as pain seared his mind, but he didn't slow, sending blow after psychic blow into Paili's mind and each time heaping more pain on himself. It pounded through his mind and aggravated his broken arm.

"Help me choke her!"

Alísa's order woke Kallar from his raging stupor. He yanked himself back from Paili's mind, slipping from her grappling hold with his sudden change in direction. The dragoness hadn't moved physically since his attack began, focusing all of her energy on the psychic realm. Now she stalked forward, eyes alight with brewing flames.

"BIND!" Alísa sang, weaving the word around long, raspy notes.

Kallar followed her lead, his "bind" more shout than song. The growing fire stopped in Paili's throat as they poured their psychic energy over Paili's mind. Alísa's mind latched onto his, and he nearly yanked away as a draconic nature rippled through it. Sesína was helping her—the little dragoness was apparently all right. He pushed the thought from his mind and held on, stretching over Paili's mind as Alísa spread in the opposite direction. Spikes jabbed into him as Paili wrestled against the choke, her fury rising as Alísa's sorrow swelled.

With another call of "bind," Alísa's power slammed into Kallar's, completing the hold over the dragon. Paili seized, toppling over onto her damaged wing. Alísa winced as the pain crashed against both of them, but Kallar held firm, grasping at Alísa's end of the choke like a drowning man to a rope.

"Don't you let go, Alísa! Don't balk on me now!"

Kallar rose and marched toward the dragon. Pain called him to slow as his useless arm hung with the weight of his shield, but he was a slayer. Slayers didn't stop because they were in pain or dying. He was the son of Allara, whose songs had brought about the slaying of more dragons than any in Karn's clan could ever boast. He would not stop.

A few more feet and he found his sword. It felt strangely heavy in his hands, but one look at his target roared strength to life in him once more.

"*And so I prove you a liar with my dying breath,*" Paili told Alísa, all psychic fight gone. "*You and your dragons are traitors. You've even turned Harenn against me.*"

Alísa's mind quivered, but she didn't let go, didn't stop weaving her binding song even as she responded in her sorrow.

"*I never lied to you, Paili—you just refused to see. I can't let your blind hatred destroy my family, be they dragons or slayers.*"

Kallar gripped his sword tightly, approaching the dragon's heart. Every step seemed heavier. The vengeance he had pursued since his mother's death would come to a close today. Whether it would make him whole or empty him completely, he couldn't say—and right now, he didn't much care.

"This is for my mother."

With a shout, Kallar turned his mind-choke into another spear, plunging it into Paili's mind as his sword twisted into her heart. Pain screamed in his mind, echoed by a loud, terrible cry from Alísa. The pain sent him to his knees and blackened the world. When sight reappeared, Kallar's knuckles were white on his sword hilt, and the monster was finally—*finally*—dead.

Kallar pulled his sword from the dragon's body and stumbled back around it to see Alísa. Sesína was at her side, nudging her up. Alísa's gaze landed on Kallar and soon her voice entered his mind, borne by Sesína. Her sorrow and loneliness ran together.

"*You were like me, all this time, and you still let me think I was alone?*"

Perhaps at another time he could have forgiven the ignorant accusation, but his arm throbbed, and his mind was ragged, and his heart felt like it was draining out like the heart of the dragon behind him.

"*You* were *alone, until your memories forced the curse awake in me.*" Kallar opened his mind and let his pain flow to her. "*You did this to me!*"

Shock and hurt zapped through their connection before Sesína snapped it shut. Good. Let her know she made a mistake.

Why did he feel so dirty?

A shout drew Kallar's attention. Tern was running toward Sesína, sword in hand. Words poured from Alísa's lips—something about a shield—and she leapt onto the dragoness' back. Growling, Sesína launched them into the air, leaving Kallar behind to stare after them.

38

PAIN

Harenn swerved and swooped lower, Galerra and Azri on his tail and their fierce anger coursing over him in waves. Alísa's last strength-song was waning, her focus somewhere else entirely, though he didn't know where. He couldn't pay any attention to it—not if he wanted to survive his sisters.

"Traitor!" Galerra snarled in his mind. *"I gave you the chance to return, and now you dare follow your serpent Singer into our territory with a slayer on your back?"*

A bolt of psychic energy flew from Taz to Galerra, making her falter in flight and giving Harenn more space to flee. All his clanmates were too distracted with their own battles to come to their aid, but so long as he kept flying and Taz kept batting back his pursuers, they would make it. Alísa had a plan—she would make it stop soon.

Galerra roared in frustration. *"When I catch you, that slayer will die first!"*

Harenn paid her no heed. Galerra had always been a talker. He was far more worried about Azri's silence. Her prowess in battle and status as the first-Illuminated had earned her the title of beta early in life.

"They're both still there, Slayer?"

"The bigger one is coming up on the right. I guess that means you'll—"

Harenn twisted, diving to the left and using gravity to gain more speed. Taz gripped hard, pulling at the spine in front of him while leaning into the turn. The correct lean made Harenn thrum deep in his throat as he leveled out.

"You're finally catching on. They still on us?"

"Yes, further back now. Think we can lose them?"

"*No,*" Harenn said, "*but we might be able to find a wing-dragon to help. See any of ours?*"

Taz fell silent for a moment. "*The only one I can tell is ours at this distance is Saynan—unless your old clan has another ice dragon? Up and to the right.*"

"*Good. We'll head there. Tell me as soon as Azri and Galerra are level with us. I don't want to ascend right into their talons.*"

"*The gray one is level and closing fast.*" Another shot of psychic energy. "*Red is leveling—now!*"

Harenn beat his wings, sharp heat coursing through them. They had been at this too long without Alísa's power, but his sisters would also be fatigued. He just had to work harder than they did, as he always had.

"*Left!*" Taz yelled.

Harenn dodged the talons of a green dragon as it dove at him, careful to twist far enough to keep Taz safe too. The green fell past him, hopefully getting in the way of one or both of his pursuers. Saynan was close now, spraying ice over the top of a gray dragon's wings. Thankfully, the gray was too small to be his father, Tsamen. He was the one dragon Harenn didn't think he could force himself to fight.

"*Harenn, I lost one of your sisters! I can't see—*"

Harenn shrieked as talons dug into his sides, latching in and pushing deeper as Azri continued her ascent. His wings pinned to his sides with the change in momentum, and with an audible snap, Azri crunched the mainstay of his wing in her jaws. Harenn clawed desperately at her long legs, unable to reach her chest or belly. His movements seemed only jerking bursts of pain as he struggled to break free.

With a battle cry, Taz shot psychic arrows into Azri one after another. Azri quivered with pain, letting go with one leg. She swiped at Taz, and the slayer pulled his leg up higher on Harenn's side. A second swipe caught him, ripping through soft flesh and drawing a scream from his lips. Still, he hung on, attacking her psychically, taking his pain and fashioning it into weapons that would spear deeper into her.

"*Harenn!*" Alísa's cry came through the clan's mind-link and immediately he felt her song begin to filter through him. With a surge of strength through the pain, he struck Azri's free leg before she could hit Taz again, crushing the bones of her lower leg-joint in his jaws and drawing a trumpet of pain from the beta dragon.

"*What now, serpent?*" Galerra roared from above. A second later, talons dug into his wings.

"*Jump, Taz!*" Harenn cried, the image of Faern's rider in his mother's jaws flashing through his mind.

"*Like hellflames!*"

Metal scraped as Taz pulled his sword from its sheath. He hadn't dared let go of Harenn's spine with either hand before, but now his desperation was great. Jaws snapped behind Harenn and a blade sliced through the air as the slayer fought for his life. Their lives.

Harenn focused on Azri, but even with Alísa's song his vision blurred in and out, red fog at the edges. He snapped at her, missing her head by a few feet, and pulling back to avoid being crushed by her jaws. They were losing altitude, Azri pulling him down as Galerra pushed. Did they know this was how Faern died—was that why?

A roar came from below, high and more like a shriek, but with no pain attached. Azri's grip in his sides loosened as something slammed into her chest. Silver scales flashed as Iila slashed at Azri's neck. The beta let go of Harenn with a trumpet of pain, blood spraying from the wound. Azri batted at the smaller dragon, sending Iila tumbling through the air. Harenn couldn't tell if she was injured or not, and his vision blurred as he bled. Only Galerra's hold in his wings held him up now, and every time she dodged Taz's blade, the leather ripped.

Saynan roared above him and slammed into Galerra, and with a final rip his wings were free. Harenn tried to keep them spread, tried to slow his fall in hopes that Taz might still make it out alive, but his broken wing flapped up in the descent, turning him sideways. Taz gripped tightly, and a grim thrum passed through Harenn. And he had complained about the discomfort of the slayer's legs around his neck before?

"*Harenn, I've got you!*" Iila. The hatchling pushed up on his belly on the side with the broken wing and open gashes. Harenn roared in pain, but she didn't waver, keeping his descent under control.

"Good job, Iila," Saynan said, coming underneath. A loud crack came from the ground below. Azri with her possibly mortal neck-wound? Galerra with frozen wings? He probably should feel sorrow at their loss. He didn't hate or fear them quite like he had Berreth. Perhaps he would mourn them later.

Or perhaps never. His eyes drooped, and he only vaguely sensed the change when Saynan took Iila's place beneath him, the white dragon's scales turning very dark, then disappearing with the rest of the world.

Harenn's pain was excruciating, but so long as Alísa felt it, it meant he still lived. Her songs fell out-of-tune as her clanmates' pain echoed through the clan-link. In dealing with the minor wounds of Galerra's intermittent attacks, Alísa had become better at accepting her dragons' pain and letting it pass through her, but this—these were no minor wounds.

The war stood before her in all its frightful ugliness. Faern was gone. Komi's mind was still a fire just barely under control. Tora and Q'rill guarded the eastern village-bound slayers who had been discovered moments ago by Tella. Saynan and Iila were taking Harenn to the ground, where they would be in grave danger. Fire spread over the field in burning patches. Smoldering slayers and slashed dragons littered the ground.

And she had thought she could stop it?

Alísa shook her head, gripping Sesína's spine as the dragoness dodged another dragon's tail. She couldn't give up. The plan to find Tsamen had been derailed by Paili's rampage against her father's clan—against Kallar. Now that the hate-crazed alpha was gone, perhaps Tsamen would listen to reason. Or perhaps he would be enraged.

But Harenn lay dying, and there might be others of Tsamen's children in the fray. Not to mention the rest of his clan, who fared the worst of all three sides in this battle. He might stop to save them. But first she would have to get his attention, and ending the strength song would hurt her clan right now, like it had Harenn.

Harenn. Alísa scanned the field, finding him and Saynan at the southern end, a few hundred yards away from the slayers. That would work.

Alísa reached out to the clan. *"We need to regroup, get you all together so you can protect each other. Get to Tora and Q'rill and the slayers they guard."*

Alísa began her song again, pouring her remaining strength into it as her dragons converged. Tora and Q'rill's scales were like rubies in the sunlight, growing steadily larger as Sesína descended.

Three pairs of slayers were locked in combat in front of the dragons, the rest of Karn and Tella's people blocked off by a line of fire. Alísa shout-sang a mind-choke, binding one of Karn's slayers before he could slash his sword across an easterner's chest. Sesína landed behind another and swiped his legs with her tail, earning her a searing psychic bolt. Alísa gritted her teeth against it, changing back to her strength song as Falier mind-speared the third attacker. The defenders knocked out their downed attackers quickly.

Above their heads, Alísa's dragons twisted and veered toward them. *"Graydonn, Komi, and Sesína, sweep over the line of fire and make sure no slayers cross it. Add to the flames if you have to. The rest of you dragons, take on as many riders as you can and head to Saynan and Harenn. Riders, shield your dragon—the rest of you slayers, mind-spear any dragon who comes near."*

Sesína leapt back into the air to help Graydonn and Komi as the clan worked. The adult dragons could each take three or four riders for a short amount of time. Komi, wounded and stricken as she was, shouldn't take on more, but she and T'lan worked well with Graydonn, Falier, and Sesína to keep the attacking slayers back.

The last of the slayers loaded onto Tora's back, and the dragoness launched after Q'rill. Alísa breathed out through her mouth, doing her best to release her tension. Her clan wouldn't need her strength song for a little bit, but her father and Tella's slayers would notice the congregation of her dragons soon. This had to be quick.

"Komi, go with them. Graydonn and Koriana, you're with us."

Sesína beat her wings hard against the air, rising to get out of reach of archers and launched spears. Alísa sent an image of her father to the dragons, Falier, and Briek. *"Find him."*

A shock of fear and revulsion coursed through her, all from

Graydonn. Alísa twisted to look at him, sending concern. *"What happened?"*

Falier answered instead, his tone strong but with an aftertaste of sorrow. *"Don't worry about it. We'll do our part so you can do yours."*

Alísa stared at him, but Falier shook his head. He wasn't going to elaborate.

"There!" Sesína said, a trumpet escaping in her excitement as she pointed with her muzzle. Sure enough, there was Karn. Two other slayers stood beside him and three more stood far closer than she would have liked.

Alísa sent instructions, then set her eyes on Karn. *"Go!"*

Sesína dove, Graydonn and Koriana right behind her. The dragons leveled off at fifty feet above the ground, their riders scanning for threats. Sesína pressed lower, her nose pointed straight at Karn. L'non shouted in surprise and narrowed his eyes, focusing for a mind-choke. Karn reached for his shoulder, but before his hand landed L'non fell forward, caught in Falier's mind-choke. The younger slayer at their side fell to Briek's attack immediately after, leaving Karn the only one standing.

Every bone in Alísa's body rattled as Sesína landed in front of Karn. The stench of blood and smoldering flesh assaulted Alísa's senses as she reached for her father's hand.

"P-Papá, if the bloodshed is ever going t-t-to stop it's here and now. C-c-come with me."

Karn shook his head. "Alísa, I've seen what you're doing for us and have told my men not to target the dragons with riders. But the other dragons must be stopped."

Alísa looked to the trio of slayers beyond him, their fists tight around their weapons as they slunk forward. Despite her father's apparent order, they wouldn't tolerate Sesína's presence much more. Especially with Koriana and Graydonn circling overhead.

"Tsamen and his clan are not evil. They're only attacking b— because they thought I was going to help you k-k-k-k-kill their c-clan. I need you to trust me. Please."

"They attacked our camp—"

He wasn't there yet. She would have to force the matter. *"Do it."*

"With pleasure."

"—what kind of chief would I be if I don't protect—"

Sesína twisted deftly, swiping her tail and taking Karn's legs out from under him, then bounding for him. The other slayers shouted and ran forward, swords and spears in-hand, but the extra slayers on Koriana's back speared their mental shields, slowing them down. Sesína launched, her talons squealing against Karn's breastplate as she lifted him into the air. Her wing and leg muscles all protested the act, aching through Alísa as they pushed higher.

Karn shouted beneath them, but the wind stole his words.

"I'm trying to tell him that telepathy is needed when flying," Sesína grumbled, "but he's got a shield around his mind."

Alísa sighed. "Yes. It's important on the battlefield, and he's not used to speaking with it. I doubt it's even occurred to him as a possibility yet. How long can you hang on?"

"Not very. He's stopped struggling now, so that helps, but I've never carried two people before. He's heavy."

Graydonn and Koriana lined up at Sesína's wings, they and their riders scanning the skies for threats. Alísa joined them in searching the skies, looking for one dragon in particular.

There! A massive gray dragon swooped over the field below them, his attention fully on the slayers now that her dragons were out of the way. Focusing on him, Alísa breathed deeply and sang.

> Great Tsamen, hear this Singer's call,
> Let your dragon heart perceive.
> My song may strengthen, calm, enthrall,
> But dragons it cannot deceive.
>
> I did not stand among the clans
> To rally against dragonkind.
> For peace I came to take a stand,
> A peace you and your mate declined.

At Alísa's song, Tsamen's dragons turned burning eyes on them. A black dragon roared and sped for them, but Alísa's slayers choked it quickly. Another took its place, but before it could get close, Tsamen let out a long roar. The attacking dragon veered away, apparently ordered by its alpha. Tsamen rose from the field of slayers, other dragons following his example and making lazy circles in the sky. Good—he heard her!

> Now dragons rage and fight and die,
> And yours have paid an awful cost.
> Their blood now stains both field and sky,
> And Harenn's life is nearly lost.
>
> How many more must die this day?
> Or would you stop and hear my plea?
> A slayer chief comes to parley.
> Call off your clan and follow me.

Tsamen circled opposite Sesína and her wing-dragons. As her song ended, Tsamen's mind latched onto hers, clawing at the power fading away with her voice. Alísa winced at the suddenness of the move, but she forced herself not to shrink back from him. He was an alpha, his mind hot with command and confidence, but as they regarded each other, Alísa found a seed of sadness within him. She reached for it, letting it pour into her. He had lost much in this battle.

"*You cannot win this, Tsamen,*" she said. "*Please trust me—I was made to bring peace between our races. It's why I came to you months ago, why I was with the slayers today, and why I ask you all to parley now.*"

Tsamen waited before responding, his presence an odd prickle against her mind, as though he were searching without digging deep into memory.

"*I fear I am a fool, little Singer, to listen to you now. Let me see my son, and I will come with you and see if indeed you can talk slayers into truce.*"

Alísa squinted up at him. "*Only you. The rest of your clan must wait a distance away. My clan will not harm you. I will sing this promise if I must.*"

"*It is enough.*"

446

"Good." Alísa accessed the clan's mind-link. *"Tsamen is coming to see Harenn. Let him pass. And be ready, the slayer clans will head in your direction soon. We're coming with my father. Maker help us."*

39

UNITED

Alísa gripped Sesína's spine as they made an awkward landing. Sesína flapped her wings hard as her back legs touched the turf, keeping herself upright until Karn got his feet under him. Karn pulled from her grip as soon as he touched the ground and pivoted, taking in the surrounding dragons.

The ground seemed to wobble as Alísa slid off Sesína's back. She nearly toppled into her father in her haste to get to him, clasping his scale-clad arm to remain upright. Karn jerked in surprise, his whole body tense as he looked between the two gatherings of dragons—Tsamen's clan a couple hundred yards south, and Alísa's right in front of him.

"What have you done?" His voice was low and tight, his eyes battle-hardened. "Why have you brought me here?"

"T-t-to p-parley," she breathed out. She hadn't realized how much the constant changing of her songs had taken out of her, nor how far back it had pushed the pain. Now closer to the dragons and without a song to focus on, the weight of it all crashed onto her.

The Illumination bond opened wide, Sesína groaning as she took on as much of the pain as she could. *"I'm sorry I didn't do this sooner—I had to focus on keeping us airborne."*

"I know, dear one. No apology is necessary."

Alísa took one hand from her father's arm and loosened her grip with the other, trying to convey confidence. Meanwhile, her innards clenched and twisted so hard she wanted to retch.

Koriana and Graydonn landed behind Sesína, Graydonn furthest back, while Falier rubbed a soothing hand over his neck. It was then Alísa realized part of her terrible queasiness belonged to Graydonn, and with only a thought more she remembered—her father and uncle had killed Graydonn's father, and Karn had been the one to hold the spear.

If their places were reversed—if Graydonn's father had killed hers and now stood in front of her—would she show the same mercy to the dragon? Would she give as many chances to him as she gave her father? What about justice for Graydonn and Koriana? The questions shuddered through her violently.

Her clan gathered on a rise, slayers interspersed among the dragons, some of the riders staying mounted. On higher ground as they were, the slayer clans would have to run uphill and then about fifty yards to get to them, allowing a little extra time should an attack occur.

Hopefully, this parley would keep that from happening.

Within the gathering of dragons, Tsamen lay on his belly next to Harenn. The young dragon lay on his side, lungs heaving. At this distance, Alísa couldn't tell the difference between red scales and bloody wounds. Saynan stood over them, his sapphire eyes hard and watchful. Taz sat at the white dragon's side while another slayer cleaned a nasty slash on his calf, his eyes moving between Harenn and Tsamen. Iila lay against the wounded adolescent's neck and nosed his head.

With Sesína's help, Alísa reached out to Saynan. *"How is he?"*

His eyes dimmed. *"Not good. Iila used her fire to stop the bleeding, but the wounds are deep. If he lasts the night, he may have a chance, but moving him will most likely kill him."*

Alísa nodded as the dragon's unspoken meaning came over her. There was no retreat for Harenn—his only chance was if she won this fight.

In the northern field, slayers began gathering together—likely rallied by Tella. If only they had been able to grab her as well—but Tella would have fought much harder than Karn, and it was all Alísa could do to bring these two leaders together while getting her clan to safety.

"It won't be 'safety' for long, dragon-heart," Sesína said, nosing at Alísa's arm. *"We need to hurry."*

Alísa took in a slow breath, exhaling through her mouth. It did nothing to stem the anxiety.

"Tsamen," she called, "I'm afraid t-t-t-time isn't on our side, and we c-can't move further from the slayers without k-k-killing Harenn."

Her father tensed and reached for his sword as the great gray dragon rose. Alísa grabbed his hand as it touched the hilt, stopping him from drawing it. He sucked in a breath, wide eyes going to Alísa as her pain rushed through the skin-contact. He left his hand on his weapon as she pulled away. She couldn't blame him. Even if he understood that her dragons wouldn't attack without her command, Tsamen and his clan were a different case entirely.

"I won't let him hurt you," she whispered.

Karn glanced at her. "I'm the one who should be saying that."

Alísa shook her head. "Stay beside Sesína."

Tsamen stopped south of them, his back to his clan and his burning eyes on Alísa and Karn. Alísa strode forward, gritting her teeth against the pain trying to pull her to her knees.

"*You must let me take Harenn, Singer,*" Tsamen said, his voice a commanding quiet. "*The slayers approach, and I will not leave him to them.*"

Ire rose at the insinuation that she would leave Harenn behind. "*Neither will I. To my dying breath, I will not leave any of mine to them. But you speak as though there's no hope.*"

Tsamen growled. "*The slayers won't hear you. How could they, when the one you have selected won't even lower his shield to communicate?*"

Alísa twisted toward her father. His hand remained on his sword, though to his credit he hadn't drawn it.

"Lower your shield, Papá. We w—won't let them harm you here in p-p-parley." *Please, don't make me speak verbally this whole time.*

"*Your father?*" Tsamen's eyes brightened eerily. "*So this is why you think you can force a peace. Clear the smoke from your eyes, Singer! You may have found some slayers willing to accept your point of view, but you will never remove the bloodlust staining their minds.*"

"Bloodlust?"

Alísa jumped as her father's voice rose behind her. Apparently, he had done as she asked.

"You, a dragon, speak of bloodlust when it is your kind that rampage through villages, burning and devouring every human in sight?"

Tsamen sliced his tail through the air. "*Watch your words, vermin.*"

Only those who follow the Nameless dare eat iompróir anam.*"

"Then you have burned villages," Karn said with finality.

"Enough," Alísa growled, lifting a warding hand to both of them. *"We're here to talk, and name-calling and blame-casting will do no good."*

She looked to Tsamen, not pausing to give either leader a moment to take control. *"Your attack was unfounded, Tsamen. As I said before, I am not siding with the slayers against dragons. I came because the slayers gathered to go to war against the eastern villages. I came because I believed my father would listen to me."*

She turned hard eyes on her father. *"And you. You have seen now that I was not stolen by dragons, nor twisted to some dark will. In case you haven't noticed, these dragons answer to me, not the other way around. Every life taken at my command was that of someone who would harm civilians. I have judged dragons and humans alike in this regard."*

Tsamen snapped his jaws in the air, making Alísa's heart skip a beat. *"You prove yourself false here. You have given the hatchling-murderer Karn far more chance than you have given dragons. I will consider your call for peace when the talons of justice are through with him."*

At the alpha's words, his fifteen-some dragons roared their approval. Eyes and throats brightened with brewing fire, and Tsamen took a step closer.

Alísa, too, stepped forward, anger rising. She bared her teeth at Tsamen, feeling the presence of her dragons forming up behind her.

"You will not touch him! He is under my protection, just as you are from him in this parley."

"Then look behind you, Singer. Is your 'protection' sufficient for this?"

Behind Alísa, shouts rose from Tella and the slayers. Blood rushed from her face, tingling in her arms and legs amidst the pain echoing from her mind. The slayers were far too close. She was out of time. Neither group would hear her, her words drowned out by lifetimes of hatred. There were only two choices now—flee and fight another day, or stand and hope that some might see the light before the end.

A single sob crashed through her, then she lifted her head and sang the words her clan and allied slayers knew well.

Until fire meets fire, and sword meets sword,
Until man gives life for dragon,
And dragon gives life for man.
Woe to the ones who will not stand!

At Alísa's call, her dragons prepared for battle, forming up so that Alísa, Sesína, and Karn stood safely tucked between Koriana and Tora. Talons dug into earth, wings lifted, and eyes locked onto Tsamen and his dragons.

Briek slid from Koriana's back and drew his sword, leading others to do the same. "I'll see it done."

Together, he and the easterners formed a line behind the dragons, each man ready to face Tella and her slayers. Only Falier remained with the dragons, with no weapon besides his and Graydonn's telepathy.

Alísa's heart pounded. This was the final test of her clan, to stand for each other as the rest of the world came against them. Between both lines of her warriors lay Harenn, Taz, and Iila. The sight of the hatchling raised thoughts of those beyond the river.

"Aree, Rassím—you should go to your girls."

Conflict rose in both of them—the need to stand with their clan clashing against the need to provide for their hatchlings. It was true, Alísa needed them, but the closer the band of slayers got, the more she realized they couldn't win this fight. Dezra and Aravi were old enough they might survive if the Illumination bond was torn from them in death, but they would become as Iila had—aimless and unsure how to live.

Alísa looked to Aree. *"Tell the dreki to come take your place. Aravi needs you."*

Aree thumped her tail on the ground. *"Aravi is relaying the message. Come, Rassím."*

Reluctantly, a hint of shame rising, Rassím pulled back from the line of his brothers and ran to mount Aree.

"Those are the ones with hatchlings?"

Alísa looked back at her father. "I've ordered them t-to leave. I w— won't let you harm their little ones."

A pained grunt drew her eyes from her father. Taz winced as he rose

452

from beside Harenn, his leg wrapped in strips torn from a tunic. Alísa hurried to him, protesting, but he raised a hand to stop her.

"I know I can't do much in my condition, but I can still choke slayers who get too close to Harenn." He drew his sword. "They won't take him without a fight."

Iila growled, rising. *"For once—and only once—I will agree with a slayer."*

Alísa pressed her lips together. Iila was so young, but Tsamen and Paili obviously thought her capable, and the determination flowing from her made it clear she wouldn't obey if Alísa sent her away.

"Thank you. Both of you."

Harenn's pain still pulsed with Alísa's every heartbeat. She knelt and placed a hand on his cheek. His eyes were closed, his pain-filled breaths snorting with every heave of his chest.

"You did well, my friend," she whispered.

Karn's shadow fell over them, making Taz stiffen and Iila deepen her growl. Even as Harenn's pain streaked through Alísa, her clan's courage became the rock beneath her feet. She stood and faced her father.

Karn looked from the two groups of slayers preparing for battle, to the two groups of dragons growling on his other side, and back to her.

"This is the world you wish to create?"

There was no incredulity or condescension in his tone, but she knew it all the same. Dozens dead lay beyond them, with many more deaths coming swiftly. Division. Chaos. But somehow, in the midst of it all, she saw the beauty he wouldn't—the unity of her clan and the bravery flowing through their veins as they fought to end the fighting.

Alísa lifted her eyes to meet Karn's. "It is a f—far better world than the one you c-c-claim must be."

Swift footfalls approached from the north, approximately forty slayers left between Tella's clan and Karn's. L'non ran beside Tella at the head of the mob, already partway up the hill.

"For Karn!" L'non shouted, and many of the other slayers took up the cry. They thought she had taken her father to kill him.

Oh, Uncle, how wrong you are.

Karn ran forward, sprinting for her line of slayers, his hand on his sword. A shot of fear coursed over Alísa. An attack from behind, and she would be too late.

"Briek!"

But Karn didn't attack. Leading with his shoulder, he bowled a slayer aside. Then, past the line of easterners, thirty paces from Tella and L'non, Karn drew his sword and held it high.

"HALT!" His voice boomed, clashing against the war-cry and the trembling ache in Alísa's heart.

L'non froze, Tella only taking a few more steps before stopping herself. Behind them, the rest of the men came to a stop, some faces still contorted in rage, others wide-eyed with shock or perhaps fear.

"Tella," Karn said, lowering his sword. "Good of you to finally join the parley."

Alísa's breath left her in a silent, astonished laugh.

He sees it.

Tella's eyes narrowed. "Parley? You parley with these creatures?"

"And with Alísa, who has proven she can keep them under control."

Tsamen growled at that, prompting Alísa to face him. *"I know. I'm sorry—he's just trying to pacify her. Please, let it pass for now. I'll make them see you rightly, great alpha."*

The growl turned to a grumble. *"We'll see."*

Karn eyed Tsamen and Alísa, then faced his men again. "L'non, men, stand down."

"Fools!" Yarlan pushed his way to the front, stopping beside Tella. "Did we not say yesterday that love would blind him?"

Heart in her throat, Alísa made her way past Briek's men and partway to the chiefs. No matter how Yarlan's voice awoke anxiety or how much empathic pain she held, a chief could not hide behind her warriors.

L'non looked from Karn to the dragons to Alísa, then slowly sheathed his sword and walked up the hill to Karn's side.

"If Alísa called a parley, we can trust her to keep it. We found nothing to the contrary in her mind yesterday or today. Kallar will verify that as well." He looked to Karn. "Forgive me. I feared the worst."

"We often do." Karn clasped his brother's arm and reached his other hand to Tella. "Let's hear what she has to say."

Tella crossed her arms. "I heard her arguments yesterday. What point is there in hearing such blasphemy again?"

"B—because now the t-t-t-truth stands before you." Alísa took a step closer to Tella, avoiding Yarlan's hateful gaze. "See with your own eyes. D—decide—"

"Yes." Yarlan stalked forward to meet her. "Allow her to spill her lies while her cursed dragons catch their breath and form new plans. If nothing else, the witch is good at stalling."

He stood just beneath Alísa now, his eyes level with hers on the hill. Praying none could see the trembling in her heart, Alísa forced herself to meet his gaze. She could not back down—*would* not back down. Not here, on a battlefield soaked with the blood of so many men and dragons. It had stopped for a moment—she had made it stop. She couldn't allow it to start again simply because of her insecurities, not when so many depended on her.

Yarlan's smirk was predatory, filled with the assurance that he would win again. But as Alísa held her eyes high, she caught something she hadn't before. The fuel for the hateful fire in his eyes. Briek's words she had once discarded returned to her. *'I understand now why Yarlan doesn't let you speak.'*

Yarlan was afraid of her.

Something shifted within Alísa. The spear of truth stopping up the wound in her heart softened around the edges again, yet blood did not flow. And when she breathed, she breathed rightly.

Yarlan's eyes narrowed. "What are you smiling about?"

Alísa breathed again, feeling the air enter her body. Even alongside the dragons' pain coursing through her, it felt like freedom.

"I see you."

Yarlan blinked. The crease between his eyebrows told her he didn't understand her words, but he didn't need to.

"Tella." Alísa looked over Yarlan's shoulder to the chief. "I know mere words mean nothing t-t-t-to you, s—so let my actions speak for me." She stepped to the side so Tella could see her fully. "I came to you without an army. I surrendered m—m—my mind t-to my father without the protection of my b—b—bonded dragon. And when another dragon c-c-c-clan attacked your c-camps, my dragons forced their flames away from your vulnerable."

She took another step toward Tella, praying that her tremors of pain would not be seen as fear. Yarlan's gaze followed her, but she forced herself to focus on Tella. Yarlan was no longer the important one here.

"P—p-please. Your ears are all I ask."

Tella looked to Karn and L'non, then back to Alísa. Her expression was almost bored.

"Fine, Karns-daughter. I will hear you."

Alísa let out a quiet breath, smiling again. As Tella moved toward Karn and L'non, Alísa turned to join them.

Metal scraped behind her. "Ignoring me again?"

Yarlan clamped his hand around her arm and yanked her back. Heart pounding as she caught sight of a dagger aimed at her chest, Alísa reached for the only weapon she had.

PAIN!

Grasping the dragon empathy pulsing through her, she surged every ounce of it into their skin-contact. The pain she had spent years facing and acclimating to overwhelmed the psychic shield Yarlan always held. The dagger fell from his grasp and his knees buckled as he screamed his agony.

Alísa jerked away and stumbled back, clutching at her arm. It felt like it was on fire, all of the clan's pain concentrated there. Multiple people called her name, Sesína the loudest as her fear and fury echoed.

"I'm okay," Alísa told her. *"Don't come. Seeing you break ranks will agitate the slayers. Yarlan's attempt was bad enough—I need to keep them calm."*

Sesína's roar of frustration was more telepathic than verbal, which told Alísa she would obey.

Falier and Karn both ran for her, but Tella arrived first. She passed Alísa and grabbed the front of Yarlan's shirt, yanking him to his feet and downhill from her so she could look down on him. Her eyes blazed.

"You would dishonor your chief, breaking the parley I just agreed to?"

Yarlan's brow still bunched in pain. "You—you don't know her like I do. She is crafty, turning people to her with pretty words. She will—"

"Do you think me a child? Do I need protection from a man softened by village life, whose boots are sated by dust rather than mountain stone?" Tella looked past him. "Shochar!"

Karn made it to Alísa and placed a hand on her cheek.

"Are you—" He jerked back, wincing. He didn't finish his question, his eyes showing he knew the answer.

"Líse!" Falier slid to a stop on the incline. He very purposefully reached for her shoulder, where her dress covered her skin. "Did he—"

Alísa shook her head, watching as Shochar came up and wrenched Yarlan's arm behind him.

"Take him," Tella ordered. "I'll deal with him later."

Yarlan's voice took a tone of panic. "Look at Segenn's men—she can't be allowed to turn more to her side! You're making a mistake!"

Tella watched impassively as Shochar took Yarlan to the back of the ranks, then faced Alísa and Karn. "Forgive my clan's dishonoring of the parley. We will hear what the Dragon Singer has to say."

Alísa dipped her head. "Thank you, T-Tella. C-c-c-c-come, w—we must include Tsamen and his d—dragons."

Tella gave Karn a pointed look, as though to accuse him of not thinking that through. Karn merely set his jaw and nodded Alísa onward.

40

TRUTH

The pain of the dragons' wounds had spread evenly through Alísa's body again by the time she and the chiefs made it to the top of the hill. She couldn't decide which was worse—the throbbing ache over her whole body, or the burning flame in only one section.

Sesína met her just beyond Briek's men, eyes dim and movements subdued. *"I should have been there. He could have—"*

"But he didn't." Alísa lifted a hand to Sesína's snout, unafraid to touch her since she already held a part of the pain.

Sesína nuzzled her hand. *"I'm really proud of you."*

Alísa smiled, then noticed Laen on Sesína's back. *"When did they—"*

"Right after you left to speak to Tella. I've never seen them move so quickly and silently—they were like wind. Really creepy wind."

"Singer."

Alísa nodded respectfully to Laen, noting the other dreki sprinkled on the backs of dragons. *"Thank you all for coming. Keep watch for me."*

Laen chirped an affirmative and Alísa turned back to the chiefs. L'non had accompanied Karn, and Tella had a man with her as well. He wore a red sash across his chest that matched the tartan of Tella's tunic, marking him as Tella's husband. Beyond them, Briek and his men still faced the slayer clans, a line of defense against them. To Alísa's other side, Tsamen stood near Harenn. Behind him, Koriana, Saynan, and the others faced Tsamen's dragons, every eye-light bright and alert.

Falier took Alísa's hand, squeezing hard as some of her pain siphoned through the contact. "I won't be much help standing among the slayers if this comes to blows, but I can give you whatever strength I have. You've got this. Show them."

Alísa squeezed his hand, breathing easier as her pain split into thirds. She was exhausted, but her father's words on her behalf, her clan surrounding her, and the presence of her dearest friends, bolstered her.

The chiefs, seconds, and alpha dragon all fixed their eyes on Alísa. She let out an anxiety-filled breath and imagined its replacement as the cool dark green of peace. Again, letting it relax her throat and tongue. With her third breath, she sent up a prayer to the Maker, Bria, and any other Eldír who might listen that she wouldn't get too tongue-tied as she raised her voice loud enough for all to hear.

"I grew up knowing dragons as t-t-terrible, violent beasts who all followed the Dark One and his N—Nameless. I watched as villages b—b—burned and warriors went to battle, never to return. Evil, the slayers t-told me. Soulless, or else broken beyond repair. And when my mind opened to the dragons, feeling their p-p-p-pain and suffering at c-countless ceremonies, I knew I too was t-t-touched by evil. B—broken."

"But one day, I learned that everything I knew was wrong. D—dragons had souls that could choose to live for good, evil, or anything in-between, j—just like mine. I learned my m—mind was not broken when I saw through their eyes. And what I saw t-t-t-terrified me—the good, p-passionate defenders of humankind I grew up among were, to the dragons, evil. Monsters. Heartless beyond recovery."

Alísa looked between the groups. "So, who was right? Was I brainwashed by the slayers, or p-p-possessed by the dragons, to see both races in these lights? Or are these merely the lies each k-k-kind t-tells itself to bear the true terror of this war?"

Alísa held Tella's gaze. "Dragons are not followers of the Nameless any more than humans are. Both races have their an'reik, but many c-c-c-call on the Maker. Let me show you and everyone else. My song will not harm or hypnotize, only show you m—moments of my life. My mind will be open. Yours will be safe."

Tella's jaw tightened and her eyes searched something invisible in the space between them. Then she looked back at her husband.

"If I go mad, do not hesitate."

He nodded. "I will keep watch."

That apparently was enough for Tella, who returned her hardened gaze to Alísa. "Go on."

Murmurings rose up from the slayer clans, surprise first among their tones. Would they all follow Karn and Tella's commands, or would they block her out? Yarlan certainly would.

Alísa reached through her clan's mind-link. *"Briek, men—you keep watch too. I do not trust them all to listen—some may try to attack the dragons while my song holds them captive."*

Her slayers' affirmatives ran to her just before their minds cut off from the clan-link, their shields up against her images that might distract them. She was as prepared as she could be.

Memory swirled at the forefront of Alísa's mind—all the times she had witnessed dragons fighting for humans or the other way around, and all the times they connected in Illumination, mind-kinship, or simply friendship. This was what they needed to see.

With a tired, grit-coated inhale, Alísa sang:

Joy sings in the sky
A song I recognize
Son's and daughter's eyes
Open up to find
Their voice is not so different from my own

Tiny voices plead
In shells of lonely grief
Hearts tune to their beat
And eyes open to see
Illuminated, heard and loved and known

Like calls out to like,
A hope to walk beside
A friend who can confide,
Purposes aligned
Scaled or skinned, their kin won't fight alone

Bondless, others stand,
Giving all they have
Turning from their past
To guard each other's back
Oh, will you hear these former hearts of stone
These voices not so different from your own

Alísa stumbled as her song ended, a wave of fatigue crashing over her. She fell against Sesína, the dragoness' stance firm and steady. Falier shifted his hold on her, pulling her upright and draping her arm over his shoulder. He grasped Alísa's wrist, continuing to pull away her pain. Alísa leaned heavily on him, shaking with the strain to stand.

"No one can say you held anything back today," Falier said, his love pouring into her. *"Whatever happens, I am so proud of you and happy to be at your side."*

Alísa pressed into him in silent thanks. Slayers, dragons, and dreki all blinked or shook their heads as the last of her song's images faded from their minds' eyes. Some of Karn's and Tella's men stood closer to her line of slayers than before, swords drawn, but Briek had kept them at bay. Confusion, awe, fear, betrayal, calm, and anger intermingled in the space.

Then, with a rumble deep in his gut, Tsamen lowered to his belly. Behind him, many of his dragons followed, and those who did not were soon growled into submission by the others. None would stand while the alpha lowered himself in respect.

"What is it you wish of us, Singer? As you once said, may dragons be the first to answer your call."

A thump brought Alísa's eyes back to the slayers, where her father pressed his hand over his heart, his eyes fixed on her. Then he turned to his men.

"Look well, slayers. Even if the images you saw were mere conjurings, you see the truth laid out before your physical eyes. A line of dragons and a line of slayers, guarding each other's backs and ready to fight for each other to their last breaths. If nothing else proves Alísa's words and memories, this does."

Karn unbuckled his sword-belt and dropped the weapon at his feet. "The next death will not be by our hands. Stand down."

Mutters and murmurs rose up from the slayers, some immediately following their chief's example, others moving more slowly. Right in the center was Kallar, moving with eyes that for once seemed unfocused, almost dead to the world. Where was he now?

Tella's men didn't move, their eyes fixed on their chief, waiting for the word. Tella shook her head, glancing at Karn.

"You lay down your weapon as though the dragons lay down their teeth and talons. A foolish and unnecessary gesture." She lifted her hand to her heart, nodding once at Alísa before giving her order. "Stand down, men. We will not attack unless attacked first."

Thank the Maker. Alísa breathed out a quiet sigh. She looked to Tsamen again, speaking aloud for the many slayers who wouldn't have heard the dragon's previous question.

"Tsamen, you asked w—what I wish of you and your c-c-clan. I seek peace and alliance. Vow to leave the human villages in your t-t-territory alone. If I hear otherwise, w—we will c-come against you. Alternately, if slayers c-c-come against you, c-call and we will be there. I do not ask that you send d—dragons to join me on the frontlines, but if any desire it, you must allow safe p-p-passage without retribution."

Alísa nearly stopped, then added. "I also require a mountain in Rorenth's former t-t-territory, so I might have a base c-close enough to hold up my end in this alliance. I will hide in the east no longer. Is this acceptable?"

Tsamen blinked his agreement, a rumble in his chest. *"It is. I ask only one thing, Singer. Give me the slayer who killed Paili."*

Kallar. Lightning shot through Alísa. Tsamen still wanted his justice, despite her call to grace as both sides stood down. If that was what it would take...

Alísa set her jaw and pulled away from Falier, approaching the alpha with pain in her marrow. Let him see what he truly demanded.

"I killed your mate. I k-k-killed P-Paili."

Sharp intakes of breath sounded behind her. Koriana stepped between her and Tsamen, growling with her wings spread.

"You will not have her."

"I do not want her," Tsamen growled. "She lies—I saw the slayer in her mind."

"I may not have w—wielded the sword," Alísa said, pushing past Koriana, "b—but I held her d—d—d—down as she threatened me, Sesína, and others, all while refusing to heed my warnings."

Alísa dropped to her knees, unable to stay standing any longer. "Set me aflame if you w—wish, but remember that at the same moment, your children nearly k-k-killed Harenn, their b—brother, your son. In this battle, blood covers us all. So t-t-t-t-take me, or let it go."

Tsamen stared at her, his eyes dimming in and out with fire, sorrow, and everything in-between. He lowered his head to the ground, resting his chin on his paws. "Singer."

Alísa breathed a sigh of relief and reached out with telepathy, her voice aching. "Go. There may be survivors on the field. Find them and take your dragons home. I will secure the same promises from the slayers and give them the same warnings."

She grabbed onto her clan's mind-link. "Tora, Q'rill, Korin, take your riders and accompany them to search for survivors of any clan. Saynan, put out all the fires you can. Rayna, bring Rassím back—we need a medic. Komi, find Trísse and bring her here with medical supplies as well. Tell her of Taz's injury specifically. She'll know what to bring and can help. Falier, tell Tella and Karn that any they want to send back to help search for survivors may go, but that I still must speak with them."

She heard Falier's voice as though it was much further away. She was so tired. As Tsamen and his dragons did as they were told, Koriana lowered to her belly at Alísa's side, shading her with a wing. She touched her scaleless muzzle to Alísa's arm.

"That such a little body can hold so much..." Koriana rumbled as some of the pain seeped into her. "Don't you ever offer yourself up like that again. Don't you know it would have started the fighting all over?"

Alísa leaned into the dragoness and her motherly protection. "Yes, and Tsamen couldn't risk that. Hopefully, my point got across besides."

A trotting stride came up from behind, and soon Sesína's chin rested on Alísa's shoulder. "They're doing as you said, all of them. Even

Yarlan is stalking off defeated. You did it, dragon-heart!"

Then came Falier, with Karn and Tella close behind. At the sight of her, Falier fell to his knees and reached for her head, pressing his forehead to hers and letting out a shuddering breath. Her pain seeped into him, while his love, fear, and a light anger took its place.

"I know you knew what you were doing, but don't you ever do that again."

"You know you're the second one to tell me that?"

"Sesína got to you first, huh?"

Sesína rumbled in her belly. *"No, I told her to offer herself up as many times as she could throughout her life. We're keeping a tally, trying to outstrip all the heroes of old."*

"What's wrong with her?" came Tella's voice.

Falier tensed, anger rising, but Alísa shook her head. *"She doesn't know. Let me see them."*

He sighed and pulled away, taking her hand and kneeling beside her. Koriana, too, pulled away, which allowed some of the pain back in. That was fine—it would be un-chiefly for Alísa to address Tella and Karn with the great dragoness' nose against her arm. Not that it was very chiefly for her pursuer to be holding her hand either.

Tella knelt beside Karn in front of Alísa, her posture perfect, while Karn leaned forward with concern. Both their eyes flicked to Koriana on occasion, and Tella kept her hand near the dagger opposite her sword. Alísa couldn't expect anything different yet. Taking in a shuddering breath, she addressed the chiefs.

"I w—would offer you both the same alliance I offered Tsamen. Vow to march on no mountains. If dragon c-c-clans are violent, send word and let me approach them first. If we require your assistance t-t-t-to stop them, we will ask it of you. If any of your slayers w—wish to join us, let them come without retribution. Finally, I would ask for help in spreading the word about my c-c-clan, my mission, and the t-t-truth about the dragons."

Tella crossed her arms. "It already takes too long for me to respond to violent dragon clans without having to wait for a message to get to you. The distances are too great. I will not wait longer while my charges fall by dragon-fire."

"I hate to admit it," Sesína whispered, *"but black-eyed slayer lady has a point."*

Alísa's lips quirked before she could stop it. She hurried to cover it up. "I understand. An amendment, then. You will attack only c-c-clans of v—verified violence against humans, and you will not smash eggs or t-t-take hatchlings for t-t-training. You will still c—call for us, and we will clean up your mess."

That last statement sent a wave of surprise over Tella's face. She recomposed quickly. "This is acceptable."

"For me as well," Karn said. Concern still covered his face, but he kept his voice even as he spoke. "If that is all, Alísa, I would speak with you alone."

Anxiety washed over Alísa, partially for whatever conversation might come, and partially for the pain that would come as Falier let go. Sesína would still help, though it would redouble the pain for her as well.

"I'll be okay, dragon-heart. We'll rest soon. You need to speak with him."

Alísa let out her anxious breath. Sesína was right.

"Okay."

Tella stood, removing herself from the group first. Sesína, Koriana, and Falier left far more gingerly, Falier with unnecessary feelings of guilt twisting through him as he let go. Alísa fought to keep her breathing steady as her head pounded. She breathed through it—it wouldn't be long before she would have help again.

Karn swallowed, guilt and sorrow rippling from him as he looked into her eyes. He reached out his hand.

"Let me feel it."

Alísa studied his face—the extra worry lines that hadn't been there only months ago, a smattering of gray at his temples, and eyes that told her no matter what grief she had already brought on him, he needed this.

Gently, she pressed her palm into his, relief swelling through her as the pain lessened. The weight on her heart and lungs lifted, allowing her breaths to lighten. Karn tensed at the contact, muscles in his arms and face contracting. He gripped her hand tightly, a signal that she shouldn't pull away. She didn't attempt it, not until tears overflowed onto his cheeks. When she pulled back, he tightened his grip once more.

"F—forgive me, my Lísa," he said, stuttering with either pain or sorrow. "It seems I was wrong all these years. You have become a great chief, all on your own."

A sob rolled through Alísa. She had expected him to say he was wrong about the dragons, or to apologize for never taking on the pain before, neither of which needed any apology. She hadn't needed him to take on the pain, and as far as the dragons went, he was merely in the same spot as the rest of slayer-kind.

But this...

She squeezed his hand. "I forgive you."

41

CONSTELLATIONS

A dragon's muzzle was a pointy thing. Especially at three o'clock in the morning. Falier pushed at Graydonn's snout, missing entirely and hitting only air the first two tries.

"I'm awake."

"Good, because I'm not," Graydonn replied slowly. *"You can take the watch yourself, then."*

Graydonn lifted his wing and all the warmth that had stayed locked underneath whisked away into the starry night sky. Falier sat up and shivered, reaching for his discarded cloak.

"Warn a guy next time," Falier said only semi-facetiously.

Above them, Koriana loomed, her eyes dim with exhaustion. *"I hope I can trust you two to stay awake?"*

Graydonn stood and stretched his forelegs with a wide yawn. *"Of course, Mother. We've got the easy watch."*

"Doesn't feel easy at the moment," Falier said, allowing a small smirk at his mind-kin. But it was true—the last watch of the night was far easier than second watch, which required two interrupted sleeps. He and Graydonn would simply have to stay awake until the others started waking up. Then there would be more people to talk to, breakfast to make, plenty to keep them busy.

"Are you ready to transfer the mind-choke?" Koriana looked to Sesína and Alísa sleeping on the other side of the campfire. *"It needs to be smooth—no cracks, or else Alísa will wake up with the sudden pain."*

Falier stood, gathering his cloak around him, and walked a little closer to Sesína. The dragoness slept with neck and tail curved around her, creating a circle of warmth for Alísa to rest in much like Graydonn had done for him. Sesína's wing draped over Alísa but didn't fully cover her, allowing Alísa's head to stay visible to whichever dragon was on watch and responsible for keeping as much of the clan's pain away from her as they could.

Falier sighed lightly. She would still feel pain in her sleep from Sesína and whichever dragon shielded her. Alísa hadn't wanted the slayers on watch to choke her, willing to put up with a little more pain to avoid Briek or his men having that access. If only Falier were a little stronger, a little steadier with his powers, he could do it and keep her from Graydonn's pain. But at this point, the dragon would have to do.

Alísa twitched in her sleep, her brow furrowing and unfurrowing a couple times before she settled.

"Well done," Koriana said. "I'll leave it to the two of you now. Even if the rest of the clan is up, don't wake me until the Singer has a task for me, else I will bite you."

There was just enough threat in Koriana's voice to make Falier flinch. Maybe giving the toughest watch to the temperamental dragoness wasn't the best of choices. Then again, who was he to question Alísa's choices on that front? Even with Koriana, Saynan, and Briek's help, she'd had a lot to oversee before she could finally rest.

After her father left to deal with his clan, she had brought order to camp, setting men and dragons about tasks. The dead—Faern, his rider, and two village-bound men—had been gathered just down the hill from them, their bodies awaiting tomorrow morning's honoring. Rayna and Korin had been sent hunting so the dragons could eat and replenish their strength. The wayfarers had gathered their supplies and set up tents to share with the village-bound men. Tora and Q'rill had been sent across the river to help keep the hatchlings corralled—they would join the clan here only after Alísa was confident there would be no attack by disgruntled slayers.

While the healthy had gone about their tasks, the wounded dragons flamed each others' wounds. Taz had gotten the worst of the wounds among the slayers. They would have to watch those gashes closely, lest infection set in and he lose the leg. Another rider's back was badly scalded from flames just missing him, one of the village-bound men had a concussion, and multiple others had cuts requiring stitches.

All in all, Alísa had done incredibly after the battle, despite the dragons' pain and emotions inflicting her. She was cut of different cloth than anyone else he had met, somehow able to keep moving through it all. Perhaps the dragon inside her that brought her the pain also gave her the strength to bear it.

Falier yawned and took a seat on the ground close to the fire, reaching his hands out to the warmth. Graydonn came up behind him and laid on his belly, allowing Falier to lean back into the heat of his inner fire. Crickets chirped beyond camp, all hiding somewhere in the endless grasses.

The hill country Alísa loved so much was indeed beautiful, but in the dark with only a sliver of moonlight it seemed like he was lost in it. Falier focused on the camp instead—tents full of slayers, dragons and dreki interspersed amongst them. Who would have thought that the boy Kerrik held back would end up here?

He reached out to Graydonn. *"Do you ever get the feeling that the world is too big for you?"*

"Big, yes. Too big?" Graydonn shifted, his muzzle pointing to the sky. *"Sometimes. Father once told me it had to be big to fit so many lives, stories, and wonders into it. He showed me the stars and said even in the vastness there was room for individual stories to be immortalized. It somehow both helped and made me feel even smaller."*

Falier chuckled. *"I was about to say the same thing."*

Graydonn thrummed. *"What's your favorite constellation?"*

Falier shook his head. *"I don't know them—I know some names, but not patterns. Selene, Taz, and I would make up our own when we were younger."*

Graydonn made a clicking sound low in his throat. *"Father and I would spend hours watching them when Mother was on the night scouting rotation. If you close your eyes, I can show you."*

Falier chuckled. *"I think closing my eyes isn't something I'm supposed to do on watch-duty."*

Graydonn thrummed. *"I suppose not. But you have a companion. I'll keep my eyes and mind open."*

Falier shrugged and closed his eyes. Graydonn's mind had been on his father all day—perhaps he needed this.

A jumble of stars with four especially bright ones appeared in his mind, directed there by Graydonn. *"This is Belinor's Ship, which led the first fire dragons to Arran. See the hull of the ship?"* At Falier's nod, another group of stars appeared. *"This is the Warrior's River, from which the mountains grew. I never thought it looked like a river, but apparently that's what it is."*

Falier laughed. *"All right."*

"This one looks more like a river to me, but it's called Bria's Song." A few especially bright stars zig-zagged over a field of dimmer ones.

"Bria's Song? I bet that's a constellation known only to the dragons. I wonder if humans call it something else?"

Graydonn's wings shifted. *"I don't know. I wonder what it takes to get a constellation recognized. Can we just pick something that hasn't been named, call it Alísa's Song, and get everyone else in the world to agree?"*

Falier grinned at that idea. *"Is there a group of stars you know doesn't have a name?"*

The images from Graydonn faded away. *"It's hard for me to see patterns I haven't before, like you did with Selene and Taz. Father occasionally would make up his own, but I just remember what he showed me."* Melancholy came over Graydonn. *"I wish I were better at it."*

Falier watched the dragon for a moment, waiting to see if he would say more. He didn't.

"I'm sure he would be proud of you."

"I hope so. I know he would be proud we found and helped Alísa, but..." Graydonn lowered his head to the ground, eye ridges shifting. *"His killer was right in front of me. I could have avenged him. But he's also Alísa's father, and the chief of a clan we need as allies. I couldn't do that to her, and I know Father wouldn't have approved of it. So why do I feel this way?"*

Falier leaned back against him and looked up at the sky, searching as though the right words hid amidst the lights. *"It's all a mess, war and peace, who lives and who dies. I'm sorry you have to go through this. You were very brave, facing him and not giving in to the hatred you feel."*

Graydonn clicked in his throat. *"Father always preached against hatred, teaching the hatchlings that humans didn't have to be the enemy. Got him in trouble with the alphas a few times, but that didn't stop him. I think he would like you."*

"Why?"

"A kind human who accepts dragons and gives all he has to fight for peace? I can't imagine why."

Falier gave a rueful chuckle. *"'All I have.' I guess that's true, no matter how little it is."*

Graydonn growled, turning amber eyes on Falier. Even though he knew the dragon would never hurt him, Falier found himself bracing his hands on the ground.

"What?"

"You need to stop."

"Stop what?"

"Belittling yourself. No one here does it, not even the slayers. Alísa certainly doesn't. Stop lying to yourself."

"You didn't see it," Falier said. *"Alísa was in constant danger the last two days, and I couldn't do a thing about it. I want to keep her safe, but I'm learning more and more that I can't."*

"And you think she judges you for it? Did she ask you to come in order to keep her safe?"

"She didn't ask me—I forced myself on this mission."

"Yes, for two reasons, as I recall. Because the mind-kin bond would be more helpful than Illumination—which was true—and because you didn't want her to be alone. It brought her immense relief when you said you'd go with her."

Falier let out a breath, slowly recognizing truth in Graydonn's words. 'Immense' was surely an overstatement to make him feel better, but—

He tensed as an image flooded his mind's eye—Alísa at the dancing grounds, surrounded by dragons and humans as they made their plans for facing the westerners, and a wave of soothing balm crashing through the astral plane.

"That," Graydonn said, *"is the exact memory—the feeling her emotions gave off as you said you would go with her, even if only for moral support. You gave her that and more. If you want to keep training in swordplay and telepathy so you are a better warrior, that is beneficial, but it has never been necessary for your role in our clan. You support, inspire, and comfort. That is enough for me,*

enough for the slayers we helped learn to ride, and enough for your beloved and alpha."

Graydonn slapped Falier on the back of the head with his wing, a light mirth threading through his severity. "*And I will keep bashing that into your head until you believe it.*"

Falier smirked, rubbing his head. "*Careful, my skull's not as thick as a dragon's.*"

"*Could have fooled me,*" Graydonn thrummed. They were silent for a moment as Graydonn looked back up at the sky. "*You helped me too, you know. Even when I knew I couldn't avenge my father, standing near that—that man brought back all the fear of that day. You choosing to stay with me while Alísa had the rest in hand was truly a help to me. Thank you, my friend.*"

"*You're welcome.*" Falier smiled, looking up to find Belinor's Ship again, then pointing to the right of it. "*What's that one?*"

Graydonn squinted, then lowered his head close to Falier's to better see where he pointed. "*That's Razinth, the sea serpent. He tried to take down Belinor's ship—it took twenty dragons and many sailor's harpoons to bring it down.*"

"*Wow.*" Falier pointed again, this time to the brightest star in the sky. "*And that one?*"

"*That star is the tip of H'kara's muzzle, always pointing north.*"

"*What did H'kara do?*"

"*What did—*" Graydonn's eye-ridges raised. "*She is the mother of all dragons.*"

"*Oh.*"

"*How do you not know that?*"

Falier smirked. "*It's not like I had many dragons around to teach me legend and lore growing up.*" He pointed again, this time at two bright stars close together. "*What about that?*"

"*Hellipsekinnimoth.*"

"*Now you're just making stuff up.*"

"*How dare you!*" Graydonn's eyes brightened as he thrummed. "*Hellipsekinnimoth was the greatest of all dragons. He ate the second moon.*"

"*There is no second moon.*"

"*Not anymore. I told you, Hellipsekinnimoth ate it.*" Graydonn poked

Falier in the side with his muzzle. *"You should pay more attention if you're going to ask these questions."*

Falier shoved him away with a laugh. *"And you should make up more believable names."*

"Don't blame me, dragons are born with their names. Blame Hellipsekinnimoth."

Falier shook his head. *"So those two bright ones don't have a name?"*

Graydonn snorted lightly. *"Not that I'm aware of."*

"Good. Now we just have to construe a way to call it Alísa's Song."

"Well, if two stars can be a dragon eating the second moon, it could surely be a song. Or maybe the twin stars should be named Alísa and Sesína, the first human and dragon to Illuminate."

"I don't know, Sesína's already got a big enough head. Does she really need a star named for her?"

"Her head isn't that big," Graydonn said. *"She just talks like it. I think Alísa would prefer having Sesína up there with her, to take some of the attention away from her."*

Falier leaned back against Graydonn. *"Yeah, you're probably right."*

Graydonn rumbled thoughtfully. *"Do you think we'll be remembered in lore? The first dragon-human mind-kinship? Do you think about how we're living history?"*

"There are days I stop and wonder at it all. Other days, like today, it's just a blur of blood, sweat, and tears."

Graydonn clicked in his throat. *"Then wonder now. Tents interspersed between sleeping dragons. A new mind-kin bond formed under the oddest circumstances. Two human-Illuminated hatchlings just across the river. This moment, thrumming about the stars. History we can smell, taste, hear, and touch. Maker be praised."*

Falier smiled, looking up at the stars again as his scaly best friend's warmth battled the night air. *"Maker be praised."*

42

PYRES

Morning sunlight glimmered over scales and armor as Alísa's people gathered around their dead. Slayers and dragons alternated, allowing the dragons to fully encircle Faern in the traditional way of honoring a dragon warrior. After speaking with Koriana about the arrangements, Briek and Alísa had agreed the dragons' ceremonial cremation would be sufficient to honor the men as well. Between the living and the dead, the dragons had dug a four-foot wide circle, a precaution to keep the fire from spreading over the grasses.

At the top of the rise, Saynan officiated the proceedings, Aravi and Iila at his side and a sleeping Harenn just beyond them. Harenn breathed raggedly and moaned in his sleep, but he was alive. How well he would recover, none could answer, but Saynan was sure he would live. It seemed wrong to honor Faern, Harenn's former trainer, without Harenn's wakeful presence, but none knew when he would awaken. With the honoring of Karn and Tella's fallen warriors coming at the noon meal, Alísa had decided to hold her ceremony now.

Every breath took conscious effort as Alísa fought to stand unwavering among her clan. Last night had been worse. The dragons' fast healing had helped overnight, but the deeper wounds still pounded in her mind and rippled out over her body. Korin's slashed muzzle burned in her cheek, multiple leg-wounds made her walk with a limp, and Komi and Harenn's punctured sides made deep breaths difficult.

As yesterday, Falier refused to leave her side, standing beside her and Sesína and soaking up a third of her pain without complaint. His eye was swollen and purple, and a portion of that pain also settled within Alísa. All the other wounds she felt were taken in battle—this one was taken specifically for her. She pushed up on tip-toes to plant a gentle kiss on Falier's scruffy cheek just as Saynan began to speak.

"It is legend among dragonkind that the mountains grew from the blood of the warriors of old, and that the blood of today's warriors ensures they will never fall. So too with these, for dragon and man alike gave their lives yesterday to build a new mountain, a home where all may come to live without fear. The blood of a warrior is their gift to the living. Though we mourn their absence, may we never mourn their honorable sacrifice. Each of these stands before their Maker unashamed, ready to rest in His Halls or fly in His unimpeded Skies."

Alísa smiled at the dragon's addition of the humans' wording of the afterlife. What was it truly like there? Were there halls to live in, a sky to fly in, or something wholly other, like Bria said the Maker Himself was?

But now it was her turn to sing, not a time for contemplating the eternal. As she sang her all-too familiar lamentation, her thoughts drifted to others who had given their lives in this war for peace. Sareth. Chrí and the other dreki. Namor.

After her final note, humans and dreki fell back as instructed. The dragons in the circle lifted their wings as though preparing to fly, and their throats and chests rattled as they breathed deep into their bellies. A few slayers flinched at the sound, knowing it as one of impending death.

Alísa squinted as fire leapt from the dragons' jaws and coalesced over the fallen warriors. Her hair whipped around her as the dragons beat their wings toward the center, fanning the flames hotter and higher. The flesh of the fallen burned quickly, even Faern's massive body turning to ash before Alísa's eyes. Her hand became slick with sweat in Falier's. She backed up, Falier following her lead in retreating from the heat.

Once behind the dragons and their pumping wings, Alísa watched the pillar of fire. Awe filled her. She had seen many warriors honored in cremation, but never a dragon's ceremony. Together, their fire burned hot enough to destroy even scales. A twinge of guilt hit Alísa as she thought of Sareth. He should have been honored this way too.

I'm sorry, Sareth, for leaving your body like I did. May your anam *be rested and joy-filled in the Maker's Skies.*

Other slayers, too, stepped back to watch, as did Dezra and Hwinn, following the lead of their human parents. All remained in reverent silence until the dragons' fires ran dry and their wings stilled. The pillar of fire dissipated into the sky, leaving behind a blackened patch of earth and a small pile of white ashes soon to be scattered by the wind.

Tears ran silently down Alísa's cheeks. Falier pulled her close, pressing a kiss into her hair as she leaned into him. She breathed out a shaky breath. How many more friends and allies would she have to mourn before this was over? Was there even a possibility it would end before she, too, entered the Maker's Halls?

An hour later, Alísa, Falier, and Briek stood with Karn and Tella's clans, keeping to the outside with Sesína. The slayers gave them a wide berth, many of the men being sure to stand between the dragon and their families. A few showed hostility in their eyes, but Alísa and her party sensed no immediate danger.

Trísse stood with her mother, brothers, and younger sister, the latter of whom clung to Trísse's hand for all she was worth. At twelve years old, she was just developing her gift of empathy and likely had a difficult time with all the new sensations coming from the mourners.

Alísa breathed the sorrow in and back out, the action coming more easily here than with the dragons. Despite wishing for the company of her dragon clan, standing apart from them and their pain for a while provided much-needed relief.

The slayers had cleared the grasses from a large section of ground just outside their camps. Here, dry wood gathered from the grove near camp undergirded the bodies of thirteen men, six from Karn's clan and seven from Tella's. Both numbers were terribly high for clans with as much experience as theirs. The chaos of yesterday's battle had taken its toll. Some of the bodies were already charred beyond recognition, but as Karn spoke his peoples' names before the clans, Alísa knew each one. The months of separation and memories of their dismissal of her did nothing to dim the pain as their family members looked on with tears.

"We commit their souls to the Maker," Tella said, eyes lifted to the sky, "these warriors who have made the world a safer place for humanity."

Karn nodded solemnly. "May we now honor their bravery by emulating it as we step into a new world."

Three men from each clan came forward with torches—L'non, Drennar, and Kallar for Karn's. Each wore full armor, except for Kallar's left arm, which was wrapped and in a sling. The deadness she had seen in his eyes yesterday was still there. It was almost frightening when she could only remember ever seeing hard focus.

The warriors lit the wood pile, the flames rapidly spreading over the oil-drenched bodies. The chiefs stepped away with them and Farren took their place at the front. He looked the same as ever—tall, confident yet humble, graying brown hair pulled back in a long ponytail, and a lute in his hands. Falier squeezed Alísa's hand as the songweaver sang his lament—the same one she always used. She had never wanted to weave her own, not having the presence of mind to create a new song in those sad moments, nor wishing to dwell on the sorrow outside them.

At the end of his song, Farren's gaze landed on Alísa, sorrow and joy mingling in his eyes.

"Stay," he mouthed to her, to which she nodded acknowledgement. She hadn't seen him while a prisoner of her father. Though today wasn't the day to catch up, she desperately needed a reunion with him, no matter how brief.

Many of the people dispersed, most toward the kitchen tent, where a meal had already been prepared. It was custom among warriors to share a meal after honoring the dead, a symbol of their intention to live the life their fallen brothers had died to give them. This time, Alísa would not go with them. Common sense and the heightened tension around her told Alísa her presence at the meal would hurt more than help. She had honored the men, and that was what mattered to her.

A few people lingered to watch the fire—mostly family members and clan leadership, though Kallar had disappeared already. To those who stayed, Farren whispered encouragement, going from family to family as he always did.

Falier put an arm around Alísa. "He's the one who taught you songweaving?"

Alísa hummed an affirmative. "I spent a lot of t-t-time with him growing up. It helped to pass the t-t-time when Papá was away, and I didn't have any friends my age."

"What about Trísse?"

"She came later. Even then, she liked to b—be alone on occasion."

"He ever teach you any instruments?"

Alísa shrugged. "I can find my way around a lute and do basic drumming patterns."

"No kidding." He looked down at her. "You never mentioned that. You could have taken a turn at the céilís."

She smirked and shook her head. "That's exactly why I d—d—didn't say anything. I far prefer singing. I'll leave the d—drumming to you."

"You can sing and drum at the same time."

"Maybe *you* can. I never got the hang of musical multi-tasking."

"She's far too modest," Farren said, approaching with open arms. "We were getting there."

Alísa grinned, pulling away from Falier and running the few steps into Farren's embrace.

"I missed you, dear one," he whispered, squeezing before pulling back and looking her in the eyes. "I prayed for you every day, though it seems many of my prayers faced the wrong direction."

"W—what do you mean?"

Farren's smiled wearily. "I had been so sure it was the Maker's will for you to leave, but when I found out you were taken by the dragons, I knew I must have been mistaken. How could something so terrible have been the Maker's will for you? Truly, though, it seems I heard Him correctly that night. His plan merely looked different from anything I could have imagined. One day, you must weave the story for me."

Alísa pressed her lips together as tears filled her eyes. "I would be happy to."

Farren wiped a tear from her cheek, then looked past her. His smile wavered as his eyes landed on Sesína, but he recovered quickly.

"This is one of your good dragons, then?"

"Yes." Alísa turned to face the dragoness. "This is Sesína. You'll hear her v—voice in your head. D—don't be alarmed, she isn't reading your mind."

"Yes, I am vaguely aware. It is good to meet you, Sesína."

"And you, Songweaver Farren." Sesína gave a friendly cock of her head. *"I've always hoped to hear your music in person. Your training helped make her an amazing Dragon Singer."*

Farren relaxed slightly at her words. "I'm glad to hear it."

"This is Briek, chief over my slayer allies." Alísa gestured to him, and Farren nodded in respect. "And this is Falier, my p-p-pursuer and a dear friend besides."

"Pursuer?" Farren squinted, looking between them. Alísa immediately regretted her wording, having put Falier in an awkward position. She had spoken to Farren before about her dissatisfaction with her expected marriage to Kallar, but perhaps now wasn't the time to tell him she had found someone better for her.

But the furrows in Farren's brow smoothed and the songweaver reached to clasp Falier's arm. "You couldn't have chosen better, young man."

Falier visibly relaxed. "I know. Good to meet you."

"Alísa!"

Alísa's heart leapt, and she spun around to see her cousins running for her. She rushed to meet them, wrapping an arm around each of them even as Aunt Elani scolded them for running so close to a dragon. Alísa rubbed a hand in Taer's already-messy curls, laughing as he playfully slapped her hand away.

"I missed you boys so much!"

"We missed you too," Levan said.

"I'm so glad you didn't go crazy like everyone said," Taer added.

L'non gave Alísa an apologetic look. "Taer, that isn't something you say to somebody."

"But I am glad. What was I supposed to say?"

Alísa allowed herself to laugh. "It's all right, Uncle. I understand."

Elani's worried gaze fixed behind Alísa. "Is it safe?"

"P-p-perfectly. Sesína won't hurt them, nor will the others."

"I'll trounce you in fivers, though," Sesína said, trotting over. *"I'm kind of an expert now."*

Elani cringed with unease as Sesína sat on her haunches in front of her and L'non. The dragoness' mind filled with thoughts of mischief, feeding off memories of Alísa and Elani's strained relationship.

"Don't do anything to alienate them," Alísa whispered. *"We want good relationships, even if it would be fun to bug her."*

"Who says I can't do both?" Sesína looked at the adults and spoke rapidly. *"Hi there. I'm Sesína, master of ball games and tea connoisseur. Kids love me. The only harm I ever caused one was when I may have accidentally hit the ball too hard into one's stomach and he fell down. He didn't cry and we're still friends. Can I meet your sons?"*

L'non blinked, Elani just stared, and Alísa couldn't hold back her laughter.

"She also holds my m—memories of them and loves them like I d— do. She's safe."

L'non looked between her and Sesína, then nodded slowly. "Okay, but no playing today."

Sesína's eyes brightened, and she whipped around to see Levan and Taer. The boys left Alísa's side, Levan more cautiously while Taer's wariness was only evident in the psychic realm.

"Alísa," L'non said, "your father asks to hold an audience with you and your lieutenants today. In a couple hours, if possible."

Anxiety gathered in Alísa's stomach at the strangeness of a formal request. "Okay. W—where will we meet?"

"He asks we meet nearer to your camp to avoid panic. Many here are still uneasy."

Alísa smiled to herself. That he was coming to her showed he truly did trust her dragons wouldn't attack him.

"Of c-course. In that case, we'll t-t-take our leave now and he can c-come whenever he's ready. What does he wish to discuss?"

"The alliance. I can't say anything beyond that."

That vagueness did nothing to stem her anxiety. "Thank you, Uncle. I'll see you soon."

43

ALLIANCE

Alísa regretted not asking to meet near her father's camp. Sitting near the dragons she had more emotional support, but the pain had also returned. She and her lieutenants waited at the bottom of the rise near the blackened cremation circle, Laen sitting on her shoulder and very purposefully not touching her skin. The distance from the rest of the clan dulled the pain enough that she could hold it with only Sesína's help. Though Falier stood with her, she did not hold his hand. He deserved a break after holding her pain so many times over the last day. Knowing he would object strongly to this reasoning, though, she instead told him that hand-holding wasn't appropriate for a meeting such as this.

The human specks on the field grew steadily larger, now obviously more people than Alísa expected. It wasn't a problem—her group was large as well—but she wondered who her father would bring besides L'non, Kallar, and possibly Hanah.

Drennar. The head scout made some sense.

And Farren?

Alísa stood, Laen spreading her wings to steady herself as she did. She shaded her eyes against the afternoon sun. Yes, that was Farren. What a songweaver had to do with this, she wasn't sure. Perhaps he was here as a witness, expected to weave a tale for future generations. The thought made her both excited and nervous.

Briek and Falier followed her lead, standing while the dragons lay behind them at Alísa's request. Koriana and Saynan retained the advantage of height even on their bellies, so it didn't rock their dragon sensibilities too hard. Sesína hated it, her head only coming to Alísa's shoulder, but the humans would sit soon.

Once Karn and his people were within thirty feet, Alísa pressed her hand to her thudding heart in respect. "W—welcome."

Karn returned the gesture, his men and Hanah following. Alísa introduced her lieutenants, and, though she already knew his men, Karn responded in kind for the benefit of her company.

"I see you've honored your fallen warriors." Karn looked at the cremation circle past her. "I would have come, had I known."

Alísa allowed a smile, gladdened both by the truth in his words and by the fact that he had not known. She and Briek would have understood the gesture and been honored by it, but dragons did not think in the same way. Some might have understood the honor Karn bestowed by attending, but others would not. Better for all that he had not come.

"Thank you," she said. "P-p-p-please, sit. We're all allies here."

Alísa sat first and watched her father and his people's reactions. Her parents knelt on the ground with dignity and no hesitation, though Alísa sensed Hanah's ill-ease. L'non and Drennar both watched the dragons warily as they knelt, L'non with a little more confidence than Drennar. Farren sat cross-legged, curiosity in his gaze. Kallar sat beside the songweaver, eyes still dead to the world. Despite Alísa's dislike for his typical intense stares, she might prefer that to this. Where was he?

Alísa fixed her eyes on her father. "What is it you wish to speak of?"

She almost called him 'Papá' at the end, but stopped herself. They met now as chiefs—equals. If she called him anything it should be Karn, but that was too strange.

"Next steps," he said. "I want to know where you plan to go from here."

Alísa nodded slowly, unsure why he needed a meeting with witnesses to ask her this. "As I told Tsamen yesterday, I p-p-plan to stay in the west. The m—mountain I asked him for is the same one where you confronted me a c-couple months ago. We can't move there yet—I have a dragon too injured to move. Once he is healed, though, we will t-t-t-take the mountain as our new home."

Alísa gestured to Briek. "We'll also be taking some of the slayers b—back east. The village-bound have families t-t-t-to get back t-to, and a couple wayfarers have expressed the d—d—desire to bind themselves to

Me'ran."

"I see. And once your clan is settled, what will you do?"

Why did she feel like this was a test? Some way for him to once again point out how her plans wouldn't work?

Alísa briefly looked to her clanmates. "I haven't c-consulted with my lieutenants on specifics yet, but I p-p-plan to visit caves and villages to convince them to stop fighting and c-c-create a network of allies." She braced herself for the holes her father was about to poke into her statements. "It will be difficult getting slayers to listen if I fly in on d—dragonback, but hopefully my riders and our alliance with you and T-T-Tella will help."

"You keep using that word—'alliance.'" Karn tented his fingers. "What you worked out between Tella, myself, and the dragon clan was more peace treaty than alliance."

Alísa sighed inwardly. *That* was the hole he was going to poke? "Okay, but hearing of p-p-peace—"

"But I want more than a peace treaty. I'm coming to you with an offer of alliance."

Alísa felt her jaw loosen and hurried to shut it again. "I—You are?"

"It's as your" —he looked at Falier, grasping for a word— "lieutenant said yesterday. I told you that peace would never work on a large scale, and he said it was a matter of choice. Individuals deciding to make it work, no matter their reservations. You showed us the truth yesterday, and now we all must choose. I choose to support you and your efforts. Forgive me for taking so long."

No. She would not cry. She would not allow the sobs aching in her chest to release, or her voice to squeak, or her hand to fly up to her mouth.

Alísa swallowed, forcing her hand back down to her lap. "H—h—how will it work?"

Damn it—she squeaked at the end. Some alpha chief she must seem.

Karn's eyes softened. "I can provide you the support you need to enter villages without fear. We can coordinate travel times, and while you and your dragons fly to speak with other dragon clans, my clan will travel from village to village on foot as usual. You meet us at the villages, and we tell your story. If either race gives us trouble, we come to each other's aid. We'll start in my territory where my influence is greatest, and work from there."

Alísa nodded, mastering her emotions. "And T-Tella's clan?"

Karn smiled weakly. "I spoke with Tella, and she has declined. She will hold to the peace treaty, but nothing more. Though, I did ask that she take on any of my men who wish to stay out of our plans. There will be some, I guarantee it. Even without knowing of this alliance, a few deserted last night. Some have deserted her as well, including your tormentor from Me'ran."

So Yarlan was gone again. Though she had finally faced him and won, she hoped he and his blind hatred were out of her life for good. Maker knew there would be plenty of others like him she would face in the future.

"And w—what does your c-c-clan get out of this?"

"Truer safety for the villages in our charge, and beyond that..." He looked up at the towering figures of Koriana and Saynan. "I have never wished to harm the innocent, but now I know there is blood on my hands only the Maker Himself can wash away. Until such a day comes, I and many of my men will want the opportunity to correct the mistakes we have made."

A chill passed through Alísa as she thought again of her father's crimes. He seemed truly repentant, but though she was the alpha of this clan, it was not her blood covering his hands.

"I must speak with my lieutenants for a moment," she said. "Would you wait?"

Karn dipped his head. "Of course."

Alísa turned around, looking from clanmate to clanmate. *"Well? I think his plan sounds solid, but I know I am biased toward him. What do you think?"*

"I have a bias like you," Sesina said, *"but for what it's worth, I agree with you. His plan seems like our best shot."*

Laen sent an affirmative, though her trill was more growly than usual. *"Watch."*

"I concur," Saynan said. *"I do not want these slayers anywhere near*

Aravi or other vulnerable dragons, but an alliance does not require such proximity. This will also allow for more slayers, which you've been pushing for as long as I've known you."

"They can do more for you than my men and I," Briek said. "The people you approach will know Karn. Seeing men they know were once fully against the dragons will be more powerful than seeing strange slayers riding dragons."

Falier nodded slowly, but said nothing, looking to Koriana.

Alísa blew out a breath. Karn had killed Koriana's mate. That the dragoness had held herself back twice now with him directly in front of her seemed a miracle. *"And you?"*

Koriana growled low, making Alísa flinch. *"If I told you I want him dead, Singer, would you give him to me? Or would you tell me to 'let it go,' as you told Tsamen?"*

Alísa shivered. *"Neither. Tsamen needed to wake up to the cycle he wanted to perpetuate. You know already, and you know that I cannot give you the chief of a clan that has repented and with whom we've made peace. But we do not have to work with him. You never have to see him again—I would grant you that, even if it meant I, too, would never see him again."*

The great dragoness lowered her head to meet Alísa's eyes. *"Tell me truly, Singer—have you ever asked Tora, Rayna, or Korin if they killed innocents in their time with Rorenth?"*

Alísa blinked at the sudden change in topic. *"No. Nor have I asked the others, technically. My song to Tsamen's clan did not call for those who had never shed blood."*

"Why not?"

Alísa searched the air. *"I called to those who would choose to fight for peace. If they had killed before, their joining meant they were choosing not to kill innocents again."*

The intensity of Koriana's gaze seemed to pierce Alísa's heart. *"And what about Rorenth? What if he had repented?"*

"Rorenth was—" She couldn't say it. *"He was bound to the Nameless. He wouldn't have repented."*

"But if he weren't an'reik?" Alísa flinched at Koriana's use of the word. *"If one like Rorenth had killed those humans all on their own, then turned and vowed to do so no more, would you have accepted them?"*

Alísa's heart quaked at the thought, the gleaming teeth and blood-red scales that haunted her nightmares coming to the surface. It was difficult to separate what part of him was lost in the hold of the Nameless and what part of him was just a dragon. She saw the dreki's images from the slaughter Koriana had alluded to—fire raining from the skies to snuff the lives of normals who had no chance against him.

She closed her eyes. How could she forgive that?

Laen purred in her mind and directed her back to one of the images. Then it took on a horrible clarity—emerald and ebony scales descending in Rorenth's wake, eyes alight not with happiness, but with fire meant to destroy.

Rayna and Korin.

Hope-filled Rayna, who cared for the eggs and Iila whenever duty took the rest of the clan into the skies, and who risked her life to fight with a rider yesterday despite her wing being only just healed. And Korin, who never failed to give up a portion of his meal to one of the younger dragons, and who now sat on the rise thrumming and trading barbs with Briek's men.

"Yes," Alísa said, opening her eyes. She reached up to pat Laen in thanks. Maybe it wouldn't have been true before, but certainly now. "I would."

Koriana blinked slowly, her inner eyelid sliding open a second behind the outer. "Then I will accept your father's repentance. I will not interact with him beyond what alliance calls for, but I will not allow my grief to hinder our work."

"Thank you." Alísa reached out and touched Koriana's muzzle before the great dragoness pulled herself up straight once again.

Alísa stood and turned around, Briek and Falier following after her once more. "We accept your offer of alliance."

Rising to his feet, Karn took Alísa's proffered arm, clasping it in a show of camaraderie. He flinched as her pain flashed through him, but he held more firmly for it. Everything within Alísa wanted to hug him, and though maybe she shouldn't, she gave in to the urge and wrapped her free arm around him.

"Thank you, Papá," she whispered.

With a small chuckle, Karn returned the embrace. "For future reference, this is not how meetings between chiefs typically conclude."

Alísa laughed, giving one last squeeze before pulling away. Next came her mother, then L'non and Farren, each one's love and pride filling her and nearly crowding out the pain. Drennar and Kallar both stood to acknowledge her, but neither moved for more, as expected.

"We should get back to the clan," Karn said, straightening his tunic. "We're still in mourning, as I'm sure you are, but I couldn't wait to speak with you about this."

Alísa nodded rapidly. "I'll see you soon."

With that, Karn faced north and led his people away. Kallar, however, did not follow. His previously dead eyes had regained a little of their intensity, enough to make Alísa wonder if she had been wrong about preferring normal Kallar.

"I need to talk to you." He eyed the others. "Alone."

Sesína bristled. *"I don't like that. Whatever he has to say, he can say it with me here too."*

"Líse?" Falier took a step closer.

Alísa stared at Kallar, pressing past the dragons' pain and ignoring Falier and Sesína's desire to protect her. Anger and confusion wafted from Kallar, but neither in the amounts she would have expected. It was like the emotions sat at the edge of a deep chasm. Perhaps at one time the chasm had held his bottomless well of anger, but now it held only emptiness.

Alísa shivered, rubbing a hand over her arm. "It's okay. Let me t-t-talk to him."

"You're sure?" Falier asked.

"Yes." She gave him a small smile. "I'll be fine."

Sesína nudged her arm. *"I'll be watching."* Then she reached a wing for Falier, pulling him along with her as she ascended the hill after the others.

"K-Kallar," Alísa said. "You've seemed lost since we k-killed Paili." A spark flashed in his eyes, then died again. "W—what's wrong?"

"Why didn't you give me up?"

"G—give you up?"

"That alpha dragon. He—It asked for me, didn't it? For killing its mate. Why didn't you give me up? Or better yet, why did you save me from that first monster?"

"You were hurt, I c-c-couldn't—"

"Yes, you could have." His voice gained strength. "One blast of fire was all it would have taken, and there were plenty of others fighting around us you could have saved. So why did you save *me*?"

"Why are you mad at me for it?"

Kallar grabbed his head and growled. "Do you know what you've done to me? I had a mission, a plan, a calling, and you—in one day, you took it all away!"

Alísa backed off a step as Kallar rubbed a hand over his face and breathed. There was the anger she had expected, yet the hatred that came with it wasn't fully focused on her.

"I had worked myself out to be the hero, you know," Kallar said. "I was going to find you and free you, either purging the dragons from your head, or killing you if they were in too deep. A mercy killing, because I was the only one strong enough to do it."

His eyes fixed on her, hard and clear again. "And then you come back in your right mind, with images and memories I can't refute no matter how hard I try. And then instead of choosing the dragons, you save my life, give me revenge on my mother's killer, and prevent her—*its* mate from killing me."

Alísa shook her head. "I don't understand. Why are you angry at me?"

"Because! The thing I've devoted my life to is gone. My chief and master is all in on your mission now. And if I leave to do what I do best, storming caves with Tella or another clan, I'll have your flaming memories in my head making me question everything. Not to mention all the blood that's already on my hands. You should have just let me die!"

He turned away, and Alísa shuddered as his pain and loathing echoed through her. For once in their relationship, his intensity triggered pity rather than fear. He had never broken in front of her. What should she do with it? He didn't trust her, so talking him through it would do no good. She didn't even know if she could talk through something so raw.

"I couldn't. I m—may not love you, Kallar" —his shoulders tensed, but she pressed on— "but I've never wished harm on you. P-Papá loves you like a son, and the m—m—men respect you. You..."

Alísa paused. She had once argued the opposite, but it had truly been to spare herself marriage to him. Now that she was the alpha of her own clan and Kallar still the heir to Karn's, there would be no marriage looming if she finally admitted it.

"You are good for the c-c-c-clan." She smiled, possibilities rising. "I know it's new and frightening t-t-t-territory, b—but as you walk through it, the men will follow."

Kallar glanced at her. "So that's why you saved me? So I would turn the men to your side?"

His voice was dangerously quiet—the silence before the attack. She shouldn't have run that far ahead. Alísa hurried to correct herself.

"N—no. I just mean that everyone else is having to figure this out t-t-too—you wouldn't be alone. If you'd just try—"

"Look, I don't care, okay?" He whirled on her. "I'm not your father, blinded by affection for you, or a nice guy like your flaming holder boy! I may never storm a cave again, but I will not stoop so low as to make friends with those monsters!"

A fire lit inside Alísa. She had tried to be gentle, but who was she kidding? Kallar never responded to gentle. He didn't want her encouragement? Fine.

Alísa grabbed his good arm and pulled. "Come with me."

He pulled against her. "What in hellflames do you—"

She gripped harder. "You want to know why you're so m—miserable? C-c-come with me."

Alísa pulled at him again. He didn't break her hold, but he held back just enough that she had to half-drag him up the hill. The dragons' pain grew heavier with each step, and Kallar hissed in a breath. His emotions shut off from her as he raised his shield around his mind.

"Damned dragon empathy."

"Awful, isn't it?" She shot a withering look at him. "So convenient that you can b—b—block it out."

Kallar glared right back. Without a word, he dropped his shield, his every muscle tensing as he did. They crested the hill into view of the dragons.

"If this is a trick to get me to feel sorry for your monsters, you'll be greatly disappointed."

"Enough!" Alísa growled, stumbling as she stopped them in front of Harenn. The dragon's eyes were open, though his head lay on the ground in weakness. Alísa hated that this would be the first he saw of her after being so terribly wounded.

"I will not stand by and let you slander them when you know the t-t-t-t-truth! Open your eyes. These are the faces of souls—our brothers and sisters. This is the face of b—bravery against all odds. Look into his eyes and see your reflection."

She threw Kallar's hand from hers and stepped away, watching as he stared at the wounded dragon. His heaving breaths nearly matched Harenn's for a moment as fear overtook his anger. Then his mind cut off from her, from everyone. With a final glare at Alísa, he marched back down the hill, never looking back.

44

CLAN

Alísa pulled at the blades of grass, letting them slide through her fingers. The sounds of camp were dulled here at the bottom of the hill, more so as a gentle breeze ran over her. It cooled the sun on her skin and Sesína's scales. If she closed her eyes and just breathed, she could almost forget the remnants of pain flickering through her and her strange empty sorrow over Kallar's refusal.

Sesína nosed her arm. *"You won, dragon-heart. You have peace with Tsamen and Tella, and your father is your ally. Don't let someone you never particularly liked ruin it."*

"I know." Alísa leaned forward, bringing her knees to her chest and resting her head atop them. *"I just don't understand. He's like me."*

Sesína growled. *"He's like his mother."*

Alísa shuddered. *"I hope not, for all our sakes. Don't tell anyone about this yet. He's still with my father, so there's time for him to come around. If Koriana or some of the others found out who he is..."*

A grumble ran through Sesína's throat, but then Tenza surfaced in her thoughts. She sighed steam, the feeling of it uncomfortably hot on Alísa's sun-warmed skin. *"Yeah. Okay."*

A gust of wind burst over them, yanking at Alísa's ponytail and fluttering in Sesína's wings. An exclamation of surprise made Alísa look up to see Trísse nearly losing her balance as the winds wrestled with her pack and the bed-mat rolled under her arm.

Alísa grinned and pushed to her feet. "T-Trísse! You're back!"

"I'm trying, anyway."

Alísa ran to her and took the bed-mat. "I wasn't sure you would. Mind-k-k-kin don't have to stay together. Not like Illumination."

Trísse shook her head. "You're going to have to teach me your terms sometime."

Alísa smiled apologetically and gestured to the pack. "H—how's your family t-taking this?"

Trísse shook her head. "Honestly, not great. It's a lot of change in a short amount of time. After Papá—well, Ma's taking it hard."

The sorrow that wafted at the mention of Trísse's father sent Alísa's heart into her stomach. "Your father?"

Trísse stared at Alísa for a long moment. Then she looked down, blowing out a pent-up breath.

"Papá was killed almost two months ago," she said, the words twisting in Alísa's heart. "It was the same day Chief found you with the dragons."

"Oh, Trísse." Alísa reached for her, but stopped herself. It would only transfer the dragons' pain to Trísse, and Trísse had never been the hugging type.

"I thought it was you." Unshed tears glimmered in Trísse's eyes. "That's why I left when they brought you to camp, instead of staying to see you. I thought it was your dragons who killed him. Between your song for the clan and Komi, I know what really happened now. I'm sorry I doubted you."

Alísa pressed her lips together. "I would have thought the same thing. I'm so sorry."

Trísse swallowed, shaking away the tears without a single one falling. "I think that's why this mind-kin bond formed. I understood Komi's grief the most."

Alísa nodded silently, though there had to be more to it. Other dragons in her clan had felt deep emotions near humans before, and none of their minds had latched onto a human because of it, nor even to another dragon. It may have been a factor in forming the bond, but not the whole story.

"What about T—T-Tern?"

Trísse bit her cheek, thinking before speaking. "We had a fight. A bad one. There's no coming back from it."

"Trísse—I'm sorry."

Trísse didn't acknowledge, moving straight into the facts. "He left with a few others last night. He tried to get me to come with him, said that he needed me safe from the dragons. I told him I believed you, told him about Komi, but he got mad. I got mad too." She cleared her throat. "There were other problems, before this. It's better this way."

The ache coming off her spoke differently. Trísse would know Alísa sensed that, but after all that had happened in their months of separation, Alísa wasn't sure how far she should push.

"H—how do you feel about all of this?"

Trísse gave a weak smile. "Doesn't matter what I feel. I'm part of your clan now."

"Of c-c-course it matters how you feel."

"What I *know* is I can be of more help here. Komi needs someone close to her and, strangely, I'm it. I've never felt so at ease with someone so quickly in my life. And—believe it or not—I missed you."

Trísse pulled Alísa into a hug, too fast for Alísa to warn her about the pain. Trísse tensed at it, then relaxed, holding the embrace a few seconds before letting go.

"Don't get used to that."

Alísa chuckled. "Wouldn't dream of it."

She turned to walk beside Trísse, heading back toward the rise where the rest of the clan congregated. Sesína stood now, pawing the ground excitedly.

"Welcome to the clan, Trísse!"

Trísse looked the dragon up and down. "Thanks."

"I suppose now that it's official, there's a few things about the clan you should know. First off, I'm a beta, so you'll want to stay on my good side. Fortunately for you, I already like you thanks to Alísa's memories—you just need to keep it that way."

Trísse shot a bemused smile at Alísa. "She's your second?"

Alísa tilted her head. "Dragon c-c-clans have multiple seconds. Koriana organizes my scouts and hunters, Saynan oversees t-t-training, and Sesína is—learning."

Sesína coughed, an approximation of a human's scoff. *"I'm more than that. The alpha is my rider, and I'm an expert in dragon-human relations."*

Alísa smiled. "That you are."

"*Thank you. Now.*" Sesína looked back to Trísse. "*One more important thing you should know right away. We require all clanmates below the rank of beta to call Alísa 'oh great alpha.' None of this familiarity stuff.*"

Alísa put a hand over her eyes. "*Why would you—*"

"I knew her before you existed, hatchling." Trísse smirked, crossing her arms. "I can call her whatever I want."

"*Are you going to take that, Alísa?*"

"I'm demoting you."

Sesína lowered to her belly, practically slithering to Alísa's side. "*But—but oh great alpha, I'm only looking out for your best interests!*"

"Is Sesína groveling?" Falier's voice came from up the hill. "That's not something you see every day."

"*I've been demoted!*" Sesína whined in mock pain.

"*About time,*" Graydonn thrummed, coming up alongside Falier.

"*If I weren't so distraught, I would fly up there and smack you right now!*"

"Better run, Graydonn." Falier laughed as he looked to Alísa. "Supper's ready, Líse—I was just coming to let you know."

Alísa gestured up the hill, looking to Trísse. "Hungry?"

Trísse eyed the camp. "Do any of them know how to cook? Like, really cook?"

Alísa followed Sesína as the dragon climbed the hill. "Falier does, as d—does his sister."

Trísse's eyebrows raised as she kept pace. "A slayer who can cook well. That's a rarity."

"He's a holder, actually. And a slayer."

"Wait." Trísse stopped, a teasing grin spreading. "Did my eyes deceive me, then? You two were holding hands. Don't tell me you like a holder!" At Alísa's bashful smile, Trísse laughed. "And here I thought the dragons were a big change for you. Kallar give him the shiner?"

Alísa's stomach knotted. "Yes."

"How did you keep him from killing your boy?"

"There w—were other things g—g—going on."

"*You two coming or not?*" Sesína asked, feeling Alísa's discomfort at the direction of the conversation. She was already at the top of the hill.

"The stew smells divine."

Alísa sent a small smile up the hill and hurried to catch up, Trísse right behind her. The pain-level rose as they crested the hill, but along with it came the warm pulling of camaraderie. Alísa breathed it in, searching specifically for that feeling.

Sesína went to one of the three campfires, choosing the one where Harenn lay sleeping. Most of the other young dragons were there as well. Taz, too, sat at this fire, his bandaged leg outstretched and his orange drek friend on his shoulder. Just beyond Graydonn lay half the remains of a deer, which Sesína began to claw at for the portion she would cook for herself.

Falier approached Alísa and Trísse with two bowls of stew in hand. "Thank Nahne, Ma thought to send a cauldron and other supplies. Not much food left after this, but I figured tonight was a night to celebrate."

Alísa smiled, taking a bowl. "Definitely."

Trísse took the second bowl, absentmindedly stirring as she watched the giants around her with a wary curiosity. Dragons brightened their eyes as they acknowledged Alísa's presence before returning to crunching their meals.

Alísa placed a hand on Trísse's shoulder. "C-come on, let's sit."

While Falier jogged back to the cooking fire, Alísa led Trísse to the spot next to Komi. The rush of paws through tall grass sounded behind them.

"New friend! New friend!" Hwinn whisked past them, talons ripping at the turf as he tried to slow too late.

Dezra learned from his mistake, coming up a little more slowly and sitting on her haunches in front of Alísa and Trísse. *"You're Komi's mind-kin?"*

Hwinn hopped up next to her. *"Are you going to be her new rider, instead of T'lan? Uncle Falier rides Graydonn because they're mind-kin. Have you met them? He's making the food with Selene, but they say we can't eat it. Vegetables hurt dragon stomachs. But Sesína says ginger is okay, at least in tea. Do you like tea? Selene won't let me try it yet."*

Trísse held up a hand. Pointing first to Dezra, then to Hwinn, she said. "Yes, I don't know, briefly, and yes."

"Impressive." Selene walked up, carrying two bowls of stew on each arm. "I can barely keep up with him. You'll do fine here."

"That's what I told her yesterday." Taz waved to Trísse, reaching for one of Selene's bowls with the other hand. "We didn't scare you off last night?"

"Last night, no." Trísse watched Dezra and Hwinn running circles around each other. "We'll see about today."

Komi thrummed. It was a quiet thing, yet it was more the cause of Alísa's smile than Trísse's sarcasm or the hatchlings' boundless energy.

"Dezra, Hwinn." Rassím walked up with two plates, each containing a large, steaming hunk of venison. "Leave the poor girl alone and come eat."

The hatchlings raced to him, leaving Trísse with a half-amused, half-relieved expression.

"Is it like this all the time here?"

Graydonn thrummed lightly. *Only when they're awake. Thank the Maker they're beginning to sleep more often now.*

"*You're* thankful?" Rassím looked up from giving the hatchlings their meals. "Imagine what I feel."

"I d—don't have to," Alísa said, taking her seat. "Sesína was a handful."

Sesína trotted up, plopping her cooked meat on the ground next to Alísa. *"Was?"*

"Okay, still are."

"Thank you. Couldn't bear to think I'd lost my touch."

Alísa chuckled and looked back at Trísse. She still stood staring at the hatchlings, seemingly deep in thought. Shaking her head, Trísse came back to the present and lowered herself beside Alísa. Guilt wafted from her as she stared at her stew.

"You okay?" Alísa whispered.

Trísse bit her cheek, then whispered back. "You were right the whole time. Why didn't I see it?"

Alísa looked at the hatchlings, then returned to Trísse. "We were lied to all our lives, as were our parents."

"But you saw through it."

"I don't know why." Alísa pressed her shoulder to Trísse's. "That's the past. We all know the truth now, and we're going to keep setting things right. I'm glad you're here."

The corner of Trísse's mouth twitched upward and she turned to her stew. Her guilt remained and likely would for some time. Honestly, Alísa still held guilt for the hatchlings that had been killed in front of her. Knowing what she had told Trísse and actually believing it were sometimes two different things. It was a battle many of her clanmates would likely fight their entire lives.

The conversation over supper ranged from quiet musings to boisterous laughter. The other gatherings within camp appeared similar, all fighting to find the balance between grief for lost clanmates and the joy of life made possible through sacrifice.

Conversations lasted into twilight, when Alísa finally felt that Trísse would be okay without her for a while. Quietly, she stood and walked from the fire. She passed by each group, acknowledging individuals who caught her eye, but continuing on until she made it to the outskirts of camp. Though she loved her clan and their varied emotions were primarily pleasant, they were still a crowd.

At the edge of their hill, she lowered herself to the ground. The grass was tinged brown and beginning to gain the prickliness of late summer. The sun had disappeared behind the mountains, painting their rocks in blue shadows and the sky in oranges and pinks. Alísa breathed in the breeze and enjoyed its fingers in her hair. Her hill country. After four months that felt like four years, she had returned.

Across the valley, tiny fires marked the gathering places of her father's clan. On a night like this, clear and beautiful, she would have picked a spot at Farren's campfire and listened to him weave a heroic ballade or pluck contemplatively at his lute while others conversed. Would she ever get to do that again?

Footfalls crunched in the grass behind her. She glanced back at Falier, who waved tentatively, unsure whether he was welcome. She smiled, letting her eyes linger on him just long enough for him to understand that he was, then turned back to the valley.

Silently, Falier sat next to her, knees pulled to his chest and arms resting atop them. For the first time today, he allowed his exhaustion to show. Even the black eye hadn't seemed to quell his positive energy until now. His guard was down.

He followed her gaze and stared at Karn's camp. White smoke rose up from one of the campfires as someone threw a bucketful of water to douse it.

A light hum of telepathy formed between them. *"What are you thinking about?"*

Alísa pulled her fingers through the grass. *"The night I ran away, with no idea where this was going. The little things I miss, and what I've gained."*

She looked back at her clan. *"If you had told me then that all of this was going to come of it, I never would have believed."*

Falier's eyes twinkled through the fatigue. *"I couldn't have told you then. We lived in two different worlds."*

"Exactly. Sometimes I look at them, at all of us, and I wonder if it's all a dream. Worlds colliding and somehow not breaking. Or" —she looked down at the grass, remembering Namor and Faern— *"not completely."*

Falier placed a hand on hers and squeezed, his sorrow mingling with hers. A bout of laughter called his eyes to one of the fires behind them, and he smiled again. *"No, not completely."*

His continued attention drew Alísa's gaze to the clan—dragons, humans, and dreki mingling as one. She exhaled slowly, releasing her empathy and allowing the crowd—*her* crowd—back in. Storm clouds loomed, both sorrow for what was lost and the fearful promise of more battles to come. Yet in their midst, Alísa's senses danced. The world softened as the fading light turned the hardness of scales and steel to something gentler. The winds of the hill country whisked through camp, bringing with it scents of warm food, wood smoke, and freedom. Laughter and thrums rose up from the campfires, emphasized by the occasional bark of a drek. Camaraderie thrived here, music Alísa would never let anything drown out.

EPILOGUE

Wayfaring. Yarlan had forgotten how much he hated it. The constant moving, the uncertainty of each new camp site, the blasted flexibility of a tent's "walls." He yanked the rope as he tied the sun-bleached leathers into a tight roll. This was never the life he wanted, nor one he wanted to give Essie and their boys.

They could have tried going back to Me'ran rather than convincing other dissatisfied slayers to leave with him in search of another clan. With the Dragon Witch here in the west now, it was possible Me'ran would be safe. But he would forever know in the back of his mind that heresy was spreading in the west and he could have been fighting it. His conviction would become poison, slowly killing him from the inside.

And so, here he was. A week into desertion with perpetual winds, little shade to be found, and the ever-present smells of horse.

Yarlan stood and surveyed camp. His was the last tent down besides the supply tent, and everywhere slayers and their wives busied themselves. Essie helped pack up the items within the supply tent. Two men loaded tents and packs onto the cart. A woman shoveled dirt over the remains of the breakfast fire. A few people loaded saddlebags with their paltry possessions.

As with the rest of the week, tension filled the air—little conversation, weapons on every hip, uncertainty in every eye. They headed south toward the Prilune Mountain Range, but none knew which clan would take them or what would happen next. Terrible questions were whispered around the watchfires. Would they find themselves fighting their former clans in the near future? How far would Alísa's lies spread? And, with such a turn in the war, could humanity even win?

"Papá! Papá!" Palin's excitement broke the tense quiet of camp, calling many eyes to him. Yarlan's children were the only ones in camp, the next youngest a nineteen-year-old warrior. The eight-year-old ran to Yarlan, cradling something in his hands. His five-year-old brother L'sar followed after, eyes wide with excitement.

A smile tugged at Yarlan's lips. Despite everything, his family was whole. He bent to see what new treasure his sons had found.

"Papá, I caught a snake!"

Yarlan tensed and pulled back, then relaxed as the coloration and lack of wings revealed the snake's harmlessness. He cleared his throat.

"Impressive."

"I helped." L'sar patted Palin's arm repeatedly, begging his brother's acknowledgement.

Palin shook his head. "You watched."

"No! I— I— I was over there." L'sar pointed to the horses. "And then the horses, I was feeding them, and then I dropped the grass because the snake was running away, and I chased it."

"You scared it." Palin looked at the snake as it tasted the air. "Can we keep it, Papá?"

"Somehow I doubt your mother will appreciate that."

Movement on the horizon caught Yarlan's eye as the boys discussed the find. Shielding his eyes from the morning sun—*it's bright far too early here*—he counted five travelers on horseback and a couple of pack mules cresting a hill just north of camp. Perhaps they were on their way to L'rang, the town now two days behind the slayers. As Yarlan caught sight of the travelers, two at the front began trotting toward camp.

A few other slayers noticed the approaching riders at the same time as Yarlan, and by unspoken agreement they moved to meet the strangers at the edge of camp. Essie came up alongside him, her brown hair pulled behind her in a braid—necessary for the wind-blasted country in which they now lived.

"Who do you suppose?" Essie asked in a hushed tone.

Yarlan shook his head in response. He could see no distinguishing marks on the riders' clothing or tack, they had no merchant's cart, and only one of those approaching carried a sword.

"You should go back with the boys."

Essie gave him a long-suffering look. "I put up with that when there were dragons around, but I don't need protection from strangers."

Yarlan gave her an apologetic half-smile. The urge to send her away had become engrained thanks to the dragons invading Me'ran—that had been the only way to ensure her and the boys' unguarded minds were not harmed by the dragons' telepathy. But these were men, not dragons, and though Essie wasn't a warrior, she wasn't a child either.

The two riders neared—a man bearing the sword and a woman. The swordsman was unremarkable—pale-skinned, dark-haired, and plain-clothed. The woman, too, wore plain earthy garments, but underneath her crown of dark braids shown bright green eyes that seemed to see through the physical world to something beyond.

The woman raised a hand in greeting. "Morning, good slayers."

"Morning," Yarlan said. "What brings you to our camp?"

The woman swung down from her horse, her companion following suit. "We have important information that will turn the tide of the war against the dragons."

A Karns-man, Harrík, crossed his arms. "Truly?"

"Truly." The man came up to stand just behind the green-eyed woman. "We were carrying it to L'rang and their slayers, but wayfarers such as yourselves are better equipped for it, standing on the front lines."

The woman nodded agreement. "We would speak to your chief."

"We have no chief," Harrík said, bitterness lacing his tone.

"No chief?" The man looked over their garb and weapons. "You aren't slayers, then?"

"We are." Harrík said. "But we're in search of a new clan. Our former clans have been—tainted."

That was a generous way of putting it. Yarlan humphed and Essie put a hand on his arm, likely warning him to be polite.

The woman cocked her head with interest. "Tainted?"

"Corrupted," Yarlan said. A better term, more accurate to the state of those who had bowed to the dragons. "You've heard of the Dragon Singer?"

"The song of Karn's clan?" The man looked to his companion and back, a flame of anger in his eyes. "Don't tell me—"

"She turned them." Yarlan spat into the grass. Essie whispered his name, likely in admonishment, but he continued nonetheless. "After wreaking havoc in my home village in the east, she's come here. Karn and Tella have both allied themselves with the dragons. We alone escaped their hold."

Surprise flashed through both of the strangers. The woman quickly recomposed herself, but the man's hands clenched at his sides.

"If only we had known sooner," the swordsman said. "Even if Karn rejected our aid, Tella might have—"

Essie gripped Yarlan's elbow, pulling his attention from the man's diatribe. His irritation died as soon as he saw her pained expression.

"Ess?"

"Send them away." Her eyes darted to the strangers and back. "Something isn't right."

"You sense something?" Yarlan studied his wife, unsure. Essie was an empath, but she wasn't particularly strong. If she felt something, he should too. He opened his mind wider, but found nothing.

Essie shook her head and backed up a step, looking to their children on the other end of camp. "I can't explain it. Please, make them leave."

"Hush, my friend." The strange woman's voice rose and caught Yarlan's attention. She placed a hand on her companion's shoulder, silencing his rage against the dragons and their witch. "What's done is done. We must move forward."

Her piercing green eyes landed on Yarlan. "If what you say is true, then you need our aid now more than we thought."

Grass rustled behind him, and he looked briefly to see Essie pressing through the gathering slayers to get back to their boys. Good. If trouble came, there were horses right there for them to get away, but he felt more concerned about Essie than about the strangers. He sensed no danger from them, and any aid was welcome at this hopeless stage of the war.

"And what can normals offer us?" Harrík crossed his arms, his expression a cross between amusement and annoyance.

The woman smiled a little. "What if I told you there were more ways to fight than you know? That there are fires hot enough to melt scales, methods of pushing beyond human limits of strength, and protection for even a normal's mind? Would this be aid enough?"

"I would say your tale reeks of fantasy."

"Or lore." One of the wives said, quiet with suspicion. "It sounds like the false powers the Nameless granted in days of old."

"I assure you," the woman replied with an easy laugh, "there's nothing false about such powers."

A glint of recognition flashed over Harrík's face, and his hand shot to his sword. "You! You were one of the an'reik who attacked Karn!"

An'reik? Yarlan fell back a step and mirrored Harrík's defensive action as others did the same. The strange man moved to draw his own sword, but the woman grabbed his hand, stopping him.

"Your chief attacked us." Her eyes locked on Harrík's and her tone remained steady. "We merely defended ourselves. We are enemies of the dragons, not of you, good slayer."

A Tellas-man drew his weapon, teeth gritted. "You lie! Dragons serve the Nameless, just as the an'reik do! Why would you fight your allies?"

The woman stood unflinching as another slayer drew his sword, her hand still keeping her companion from aggression. That hand kept Yarlan from drawing his own sword, curiosity filling him. He had faced the Dragon Witch and her lies for months—how would this pawn of the Nameless, one who freely claimed their power rather than hiding behind scales, differ? With his brothers-in-arms beside him and his wife and children far behind, he kept a hand on the hilt but made no other move.

The woman's gaze fell on the Tellas-man who had spoken, and an almost sad smile formed.

"That, my friend, is the great lie of the centuries. The Nameless are villains in lore" —she nodded to the woman who had mentioned that before— "but have you ever seen them commit the atrocities dragons do?"

"The legends say—"

"And who keeps the legends?" This time the swordsman spoke, his voice tempered. "Is it not the songweavers and oracles, who claim wisdom from the Maker and His Eldír? It is a simple matter for revered individuals to spread lies."

The woman pulled her hand from his arm, apparently assured that he wouldn't attack now, and took up the reins of the conversation again.

"The Nameless turned against the Maker, this is true, but because they wanted to help humanity in ways He wouldn't allow. They wished to grant power, to give us a way to subdue the dragons and fae-kind, to provide methods to combat the evils of the world, perhaps in time even the chance to stand on equal ground with the Eldír. So the Maker declared them the enemy. A war was fought and the victors spun the tales, going so far as to equate dragons—who burn villages and devour children—with the Nameless, solidifying their lies with a picture too visceral to refute. Until now."

Harrík raised a brow. "Now?"

"Now we know of the Dragon Singer. One who seeks to ally humanity with dragonkind—an abomination! When Karn's song reached us, we knew it was time to rise up out of isolation. The Nameless Ones offer power to those who would fight the Dragon Singer—power to equal and surpass hers."

Her blazing green eyes softened with something akin to compassion, if that were even possible for an an'reik. "It will mean fighting those she has turned—your former brothers and sisters—but you are ones who have already shown the strength to stand for humanity. Stand with us."

The world went silent, but the astral plane trembled around Yarlan as the slayers considered her words. Emotions wavered, oscillating between fear, anger, hope, and even agreement. The moment's eerie familiarity made his stomach turn, the faces of Me'ran rising to the surface of his mind. He would not remain quiet as another witch tried to claim the loyalty of his people.

Yarlan looked back at his wife, concentrating his powers into a line of communication. *"Ess—an'reik! Get out of here, I'll find you when it's safe!"*

She jumped as his words entered her mind, the sensation jarring. Then, with a glance at him, she grabbed the hand of their youngest and said something Yarlan couldn't hear. Trusting her with the rest, Yarlan drew his sword and pointed it at the witch.

"The Dragon Singer lies and so do you! I wouldn't bow when she tried to take Me'ran and I will not bow here!"

"Stay your hand." Harrík gripped Yarlan's arm. "I would hear more."

Yarlan growled and twisted away. "Would you turn so easily from the truth we've known from infancy? The truth that has served us well?"

"Has it indeed served you well?" The witch gave Yarlan a sympathetic look, then turned to the others. "You say some of you are of Tella's clan? Who is more zealous for the Maker than she? Yet now she has bowed to humanity's enemy. Clinging to the Eldír didn't protect her or give her the power to defeat her foes. Branni has failed her—he has failed you. We will not."

Her eyes landed back on Yarlan as slayers murmured around him. The confidence there made his blood boil. He had failed once, but as soon as he knew he had someone on his side to stop the swordsman, he would do to this witch what he had failed to do to Alísa.

Branni's strength, he prayed for himself and his fellow slayers. But arguments rose around him, borne of the fear and discontent of the last week.

"Dragons are the ones who have hurt us. When have the Nameless or their an'reik?"

"Can we fight alongside them without giving up our own souls?"

"What if she's right? The Maker didn't protect Tella."

"If they truly offer the power to defeat our enemies, why shouldn't we join forces?"

Yarlan gritted his teeth. "Blasphemy!"

Unable to wait any longer, he pulled his sword back and pushed through the others, ready to stab the witch through and end the confusion of his brothers. The woman reached for something at her belt and he prepared to parry a dagger or short sword. Instead, she threw something at the ground.

Black mist exploded in Yarlan's vision, and he swung his sword and hit nothing. *Damn it—she must have retreated in the smoke.*

Another sword—perhaps two—slid from their sheaths behind him, more slayers joining in the charge. Yarlan pressed his attack, but something wrapped around his legs, sending him to the ground face-first. The mist cleared, revealing the boots of the witch mere feet away. Yarlan struggled to rise, but felt more rope constraining him, slithering up his body by some dark power. The black mist had solidified around him, ending in a gag across his mouth.

The witch chanted something and Yarlan heard a slayer hit the ground. He twisted to see what was happening, catching sight of a man and a woman struggling against dark bonds similar to his own.

The witch switched back to an intelligible language. "See again, your people have attacked first. We do not wish to fight you, but neither will we let you slay us again."

Many of the slayers stood in shock, some with weapons drawn, but none moving. The two strangers stepped past Yarlan, approaching the cowards who hadn't dared to move.

"I understand this is new and frightening," the witch said. She laid a hand on a slayer's arm briefly and began looking each of them in the eyes. "But you know you need help to defeat the Dragon Singer and her growing army. Open your minds and see I do not lie. Already other slayers have joined our cause. Some have accepted the power of the Nameless, and others have remained as they are—the choice is yours. Come with us—they camp just a few miles away. Speak with them and know that what I say is true."

Among the crowd, Harrík looked down at Yarlan and the other two on the ground, then back up at the witch. "What about them?"

Again the play at compassion rose in her eyes as she followed his gaze. "I will let them go when it is safe to do so. They have already rejected the Singer, and we need as many slayers out there willing to face her as we can get."

That seemed to settle the matter for Harrík. His eyes lifted and he spoke encouraging words to the others. Yarlan pulled and raged against his bindings as his people went to their horses and carts and began to follow the swordsman.

The youngest of the warriors—Tern, one of Karn's men—slowed as he rode past. His brow creased in uncertainty, eyes flitting from the bound woman of Karn's clan to Harrík and back.

The witch came up and patted Tern's leg. "Go on. I will make one last plea for their aid then let them go."

That didn't seem to settle the boy's fears, but he fixed his eyes on Harrík and kept riding. Soon the horses and carts disappeared over the next hill, following after the an'reik who had stayed watching this whole time. Praise the Maker, Essie and the boys were not among them. She must have gotten them out. Why hadn't he listened to her sooner?

"Now," the witch said, looking at Yarlan, "for that last plea."

She moved one of her hands in a rising motion and the bonds constricted around Yarlan and lifted him from the ground. With a word from her, the dark mists pushed his body until he knelt on the ground. He growled and nearly gagged on the grittiness of the portion stretched across his mouth. Then she turned and did the same to the other two slayers left behind, the mists placing them in a line a few feet apart from each other.

The witch approached the Karns-woman and laid a hand on her head. Yarlan's breath trembled as the witch's pupils dilated beyond her unearthly irises, turning her eyes fully black. The Karns-woman struggled and groaned through her gag, then fell limp against the bindings as the witch drew back.

"And still you hold on" —the witch shook her head— "despite how the Eldír have abandoned you."

In one swift motion, she drew a dagger from her belt and plunged it into the heart of the slayer woman. The dark mists around her scattered, letting her fall to the ground, dead.

The bound Tellas-man breathed heavily beside Yarlan, fear and rage twisting from him. His eyes narrowed in concentration and Yarlan felt his powers gather in the astral plane and release in a bolt. The witch grimaced, but the Tellas-man screamed, the gag doing little to silence his agony.

Yarlan clenched his fists. She had said something about psychic protection against the dragons. Had the slayer's attack rebounded against him?

The witch laid her hand on the man's head, her eyes turning black again. He struggled, twisting and grunting, then suddenly stopped and looked up at the witch. She grinned as the bindings around him dissolved, not into the air as they had for the Karns-woman, but into his skin.

Now it was Yarlan's turn to breathe heavily. What was that?

The witch placed a hand on the Tellas-man's shoulder. "Rise. Follow your brothers. And if any asks, tell them of this cowardly woman who refused us and left unharmed."

The man looked down at the dead woman, face impassive. Then he stood and marched toward the hill where the others had disappeared. Yarlan ground his teeth against the gag. *Traitor!*

Then the witch stood before him with a coquettish grin. "Don't worry—I haven't forgotten you."

Her hand pressed against his head and pain knifed into his skull. He gathered his thoughts and pulled at his telepathy. His power rushed toward the bolt of pain from both sides, ready to cut through the attack and form a barrier against another. But when his power slashed in from both sides, it merely hit the attack and shuddered. It was like his telepathy was a wooden practice sword against his foe.

Amidst the pain, another sensation appeared—a serpent brushing against his mind, coiling around and searching for a way inside. He pressed his telepathy again to no avail. He could do nothing against whatever dark power this was.

Branni—help me! Give me strength!

With a hiss, the darkness pulled away. The serpent left and even the remaining pain seemed to dim. Yarlan pulled air into his lungs, having forgotten to breathe. What had happened? He hadn't done anything.

Branni?

The witch straightened, frowning. "You too. I did so hope we could force your hand like your brother." She tilted her head back at the Tellas-man. "With your memories at our fingertips, you would have been a great asset against the Dragon Singer. But, since you're shielded..."

With the remnants of pain still coating his mind, Yarlan hardly felt the witch's dagger sink into his chest. All he felt was an impact and his body barely following the command to breathe.

The witch grinned. "Can't have you fighting us."

"You can—drop the act. I know you and the—Singer are allies." Maker above, it hurt to talk. His voice wheezed with each word. But if he was going to die, he would do so with pride. "I rejected one—witch's lies. Why—would I—bow—to yours?"

The witch chuckled. "Oh dear, this is delicious. My lies were plentiful, yes, but that wasn't one of them. I'm afraid you were so very wrong about little Alísa. She and her dragons attempt the Maker's work."

Lies. Why was she still lying? He was dying—the dark bindings the only thing keeping him upright now. What point was there in lying? Shuddering against the pain, he opened his mind wide to take in as much information as he could.

She hummed, fingering the hilt sticking from his chest and sending shocks of lightning through him. "Yes. You and your family—who I'm sure we'll find before long—would have been safer with them. At least, for a time."

Not lies. Not even a hint of deception in her tone or the waves of astral energy coming off of her. But that—that couldn't be true.

"Oh," she said, "and thank you for the information you did give—last we heard she still hid in the forests. Now we know to up our timetable. Helpful little slayer."

Helpful. He had—

Alísa wasn't—

What had he done?

The witch leaned in, a knowing smile on her lips as she whispered. "Know that. Despair. And die."

She pulled the dagger from his heart, pausing to wipe the blood on his sleeve before sauntering away. The dark mists dispelled, and Yarlan fell to the ground. Blood coated his tongue and his body convulsed with coughs that wouldn't come.

Essie.

Their boys.

He had failed them.

He had failed the Maker, fighting tooth and nail against—

Yarlan's mind fogged as the ground soaked up his lifeblood. His

509

eyes closed.

Oh, great Maker, forgive me.

ACKNOWLEDGMENTS

First off, I want to thank you, dear reader, for coming on this journey with Alísa and me. Writing a sequel is tricky business, and the process for *Stormdance* was especially, well, stormy. There were many days I found myself having to relearn the same lessons Alísa and Falier were learning. I hope this story encouraged you even half as much as it encouraged me.

Thank you to my fantastic team of beta-readers—Bethea, Claire, Ericka, Isaac, Kaitlyn, Kayla, Liz, Maegan, and Serianna. Your feedback was invaluable, and I loved fangirling alongside you as I read your comments (or fanguying, in Isaac's case).

To Katie Phillips—thank you for taking my character arcs and prose to the next level and for your continued friendship and encouragement.

Thank you to Kaitlyn for sharing in my sorrows and triumphs one email at a time. Who knew that *Deathnote* could lead to such a fantastic friendship?

To my Street Team—Andi, Claire, Clare, Denica, Emily H., Emily S., Isaac, Kaitlyn, Katie, Kelly, Liz, Maegan, Mairi, Margaret, Marie, Rachel G., Rachel J., Rae, Sasha, and Serianna—you all rock! Thank you for your help in an amazing book launch!

Thank you to Bethea and Serianna, for being the bestest friends and allowing me to pick your brain about fixing plot holes and avoiding too-cheesy moments. Your verbal-processing is just what I need to figure out my own brain.

To my parents—thank you for your support and for never once telling me art was invalid or that I needed a back-up plan. This musician and author could not ask for better parents.

Pidge and Meeko, thank you for being such good boys—for purring when I need it, lying on my arms while I try to type, and letting me take your pictures beside books all of the time. Best. Marketers. Ever!

Finally, to Yahweh Shalom—the LORD my Peace. You have calmed certain storms in my life and walked me through others in their fullness. Thank You for always bringing me through. May the truth shine amidst the fiction and bring glory to You.

ABOUT THE AUTHOR

Michelle M. Bruhn is a YA fantasy author whose stories focus on outcasts, hard questions, and hope. She is passionate about seeing through others' eyes and helping others to do the same, especially through characters with diverse life experiences. She finds joy in understanding others, knows far too much about personality theories, and binge-watches TED Talks on a regular basis. She spends the rest of her free time making and listening to music, walking, reading, and snuggling with her cats.

www.michellembruhn.com
Facebook & Instagram: @michellembruhn
Facebook Reader Group: Readers and Songweavers
Email Newsletter: www.michellembruhn.com/follow

Find out where Alísa's connection to the dragons all started in *Mindsong*, available for free at www.michellembruhn.com/follow

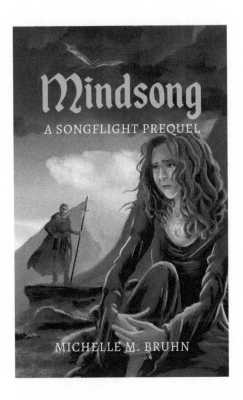

Alísa has finally started developing her psychic power of empathy, growing in her psychic strength as every slayer must. But when the excitement of the clan's ceremonies is drowned out by foreign sorrow, rage, and fear, Alísa and her father discover there is more to her developing empathy than they'd initially thought—a mystery that may one day condemn her in the eyes of the clan.